C000247117

MANDEVILLE

broadview editions
series editor: Martin R. Boyne

Contents

Acknowledgements • 7
Abbreviations • 9
Introduction • 11
William Godwin: A Brief Chronology • 47
A Note on the Text • 51
Historical Timeline for *Mandeville* • 53

Mandeville: A Tale of the Seventeenth Century in England • 57
    Volume I • 57
    Volume II • 189
    Volume III • 311

Appendix A: Godwin, "Fragment of a Romance" (1833) • 449

Appendix B: From Godwin, "Of History and Romance"
(1797) • 461

Appendix C: Contemporary Reviews • 469
  1. From P.B. Shelley, Letter to Godwin (7 December
     1817) • 469
  2. From P.B. Shelley, Letter to *The Examiner* (28 December
     1817) • 469
  3. From *Champion* (1817) • 471
  4. From [John Gibson Lockhart,] *Blackwood's Edinburgh
     Magazine* (December 1817) • 472
  5. From an Anonymous Response to Lockhart, *Blackwood's
     Edinburgh Magazine* (January 1818) • 475
  6. From *The British Review and London Critical Journal*
     (1818) • 477
  7. From [James Mackintosh,] *The Edinburgh Magazine, and
     Literary Miscellany* (1818) • 478
  8. From Jean Cohen, Preface to French Translation of *Mandeville*
     (1818) • 479

Appendix D: Historical Background: The Commonwealth,
Cromwell, the English Revolution, and the Restoration • 481
  1. From Godwin, *History of the Commonwealth of England*
     (1824–28) • 481
  2. From John Thelwall, *The Tribune* (3 June 1795) • 482
  3. From Godwin, *History of the Commonwealth of England*
     (1824–28) • 485
  4. From Gilbert Burnet, *History of His Own Time* (1724) • 489

Appendix E: Religion and the Politics of Church
Government • 491
  1. From John Milton, *Of Prelatical Episcopacy* (1641) • 491
  2. From John Milton, *The Reason of Church Government*
     (1642) • 491

3. From Godwin, *History of the Commonwealth of England*
   (1824–28) • 492
4. From Samuel Rutherford, *Lex Rex* (1644) • 493
5. From William Everard, Gerrard Winstanley, et al., *The True
   Levellers' Standard Advanced* (1649) • 493
6. From *Encyclopedia Londinensis* (1810) • 494
7. From Samuel R. Gardiner, *History of the Civil War*
   (1889) • 495
8. From David Hume, "Of the Parties of Great Britain"
   (1741) • 496

Appendix F: Ireland • 499
1. From Laurence Echard, *The History of England* (1720) • 499
2. From Godwin, *History of the Commonwealth of England*
   (1824–28) • 501
3. From Godwin, *History of the Commonwealth of England*
   (1824–28) • 503
4. From "Act for the Settlement of Ireland" (1652) • 503
5. From Godwin, "To the People of Ireland" (1786) • 504
6. From Godwin, "Ireland" (25 December 1821) • 505

Appendix G: On Extreme Phenomena: Cultural, Physical, and
Psychic • 507
1. On War • 507
   a. From Carl von Clausewitz, *On War* (1832) • 507
2. On Wounds • 508
   a. From *The Complete Dictionary of the Arts and Sciences ...*
      (1764) • 508
   b. From *The Works of John Hunter* (1835) • 509
3. On Madness, Dissidence, and Trauma • 510
   a. From Godwin, "Of the Rebelliousness of Man"
      (1831) • 510
   b. From Philippe Pinel, *A Treatise on Insanity* (1801) • 513
   c. From John Ferriar, *An Essay Towards a Theory of Apparitions*
      (1813) • 514
4. The Literature of Power • 516
   a. From Thomas De Quincey, *Letters to a Young Man*
      (1823) • 516
5. The Power of the Negative • 518
   a. From G.W.F. Hegel, *The Philosophy of Nature* (1830) • 518
   b. From F.W.J. Schelling, *Ages of the World* (1815) • 520
   c. From F.W.J. Schelling, *Philosophical Investigations into
      the Essence of Human Freedom* (1809) • 522

Select Bibliography • 523

Acknowledgements

This edition has been undertaken with help from the Canada Research Chairs Programme, and from the Academic Development Fund small grants programme at the University of Western Ontario. David O'Shaughnessy and Mark Philp were kind enough to let me look at their digital edition of Godwin's *Diary* before it was published online, and Nicholas Halmi offered his hospitality, both intellectual and personal, while I looked at material in the Abinger Collection at the Bodleian Library, Oxford. Dr. Jeffrey King provided me with invaluable help as a research assistant for this edition. Had it not been for Jeff's fortuitously mentioning at a NASSR conference in Vancouver that a paperback edition of *Mandeville* was badly needed, Don LePan, to whom particular thanks are also due, would probably not have encouraged Broadview to take on the project. Gordon Barentsen meticulously checked the accuracy of the text and provided final logistical help, and Denis Johnston has been a patient and indulgent copy editor. I thank Julie Carlson for urging me to undertake this edition, despite my fondness for abstruser researches into German metaphysics. Finally, Pamela Clemit has also been extremely generous in responding to my questions and speculations about the text's publishing history.

I would like to thank the Bodleian Library for permission to use selections from Godwin's essay "Of History and Romance" for Appendix B, and for giving me access to other unpublished materials in the Abinger collection. I would also like to thank Oxford University Press for permission to reprint selections from A.V. Miller's translation of Hegel's *Philosophy of Nature*, and the State University of New York Press for permission to use selections from Jason Wirth's translation of Schelling's *Ages of the World*, both in Appendix G. My introduction draws on my recent article, "Between General and Individual History: Godwin's Seventeenth-Century Texts," *Nineteenth-Century Prose* 41.2/3 (2014): 11–60. Permission to use this material is gratefully acknowledged.

William Godwin. "Of History and Romance." MS. Abinger c. 86, fols. 23-28; from *Caleb Williams*, Penguin, 1987 and 2005. Reprinted with the permission of The Bodleian Libraries, University of Oxford.

G.W.F. Hegel. *The Philosophy of Nature*, translated by A.V. Miller. Oxford: Clarendon Press, 1970. Reprinted with the permission of Oxford University Press.

F.W.J. Schelling. Excerpts from *The Ages of the World*, translated by Jason M. Wirth. State University of New York Press, 2011.

Abbreviations

Full publication data for each title is given in the Select Bibliography, p. 523.

CNM   Godwin, *Collected Novels and Memoirs*

CW   Godwin, *Caleb Williams*

DBF   "Publishing Papers" for *Mandeville*. In *British Fiction, 1800–1829: A Database of Production, Circulation, and Reception*. http://www.british-fiction.cf.ac.uk/

HCE   Godwin, *History of the Commonwealth of England from Its Commencement to the Restoration of Charles the Second*

HR   Godwin, "Of History and Romance" (see Appendix B, pp. 461–68)

PJ   Godwin, *Enquiry Concerning Political Justice and Its Influence on Morals and Happiness*

PPW   Godwin, *Political and Philosophical Writings of William Godwin*

Introduction

> I am not contented to observe such a man on the public stage, I would follow him into his closet.
>
> —Godwin, "Of History and Romance"[1]

> Just as the old injustice is not changed by a lavish display of light, air, and hygiene, but is in fact concealed by [this] gleaming transparency ... the inner health of our time has been secured by blocking flight into illness without in the slightest altering its aetiology. The dark closets have been abolished as a troublesome waste of space, and incorporated in the bathroom.
>
> —Adorno, *Minima Moralia*[2]

Beginning ...

By the early nineteenth century the reputation of William Godwin, the once famous author of *An Enquiry Concerning Political Justice* (1793/1798), had endured a period of decline and Godwin was struggling to earn a living. At the end of 1817 he published his fourth major novel, *Mandeville*, which he saw as being on a par with his greatest success to date, *Caleb Williams* (1794). *Mandeville* followed a long hiatus that we see in the careers of other writers after the 1790s: William Blake (1757–1827), Samuel Taylor Coleridge (1772–1834), and in Germany the philosopher Friedrich Schelling (1775–1854), for whom delay and inhibition (*Hemmung*) were a central concern from 1809–15. In all these cases, a certain depression followed an idealism whose basis was always unsettled. Idealism remains "the soul of philosophy," Schelling says, but realism must now be "its body."[3] This depression is hysterically sublimated by Blake in the "major" prophecies and ascetically cordoned off by Coleridge in a "minor" poetry. Godwin too chooses the skew of the minor, writing "a minor history" of Milton's nephews in 1815 rather than one of Milton himself, and then this novel on the interregnum between the exe-

---

1 See below, Appendix B, p. 464.
2 Theodor Adorno, *Minima Moralia: Reflections on a Damaged Life* (1951), trans. E.F.N. Jephcott (London: Verso, 2005), 58; hereafter cited parenthetically in the text.
3 Schelling, *Philosophical Investigations into the Essence of Human Freedom*, trans. Priscilla Hayden-Roy, in *Philosophy of German Idealism*, ed. Ernst Behler (New York: Continuum, 1987), 244.

cution of Charles I and the Restoration from which the major figure, Oliver Cromwell, is absent.[1] But for Godwin, the retreat into the minor becomes not just the personal malaise of the misanthropes who fascinate him, but a deeply ethical and paradoxically public gesture, given the transference between the personal and the political on which much of his fiction is based. This transference confesses the stalling of the romantically enlightened project of political justice by personal traumas, yet insists on the profound importance of pathology to history.

In his 1797 essay "Of History and Romance" (*HR*) Godwin wrote that he would rather follow a man "into his closet" than observe him on "the public stage." His "Tale of the Seventeenth Century in England," as he subtitles it in preference to the less public "Domestic Story,"[2] is a historical novel about Charles Mandeville, who never enters history, because he never leaves the closet of his psychic history: his "eternal war" (p. 210) on the unimpeachably "good" Clifford, who unbearably even becomes engaged to Mandeville's sister. As a "private chronicle,"[3] the description Mary Shelley uses to put pressure on official history, Godwin's novel is a missed encounter with a history that exists on its fringes as an absent cause readable only through its symptoms. The novel is set in the Civil War period that saw the beheading of Charles I (r. 1625–49), the "English Revolution," and the Protectorate of Oliver Cromwell (1653–58), but it is book-ended by two

1 See Tilottama Rajan, "Uncertain Futures: History and Genealogy in William Godwin's *The Lives of Edward and John Philips, Nephews and Pupils of Milton*," *Milton Quarterly* 32.3 (1998): 75–86. I adapt the term "minor history" from Gilles Deleuze and Felix Guattari. For them "minor literature" is not literature written in a minor language but arises from a minor position within a major language, and thus has a "high coefficient of deterritorialization" (*Kafka: Toward a Minor Literature*, trans. Dana Polan [Minneapolis: U of Minnesota P, 1986], 16–20); hereafter cited parenthetically in the text.

2 Godwin's publisher Constable wanted him to remove the words "in England." Godwin agreed to substitute the more innocuous "domestic story" for purposes of an advertisement (letter of 7 October 1816 in *DBF*), but later insisted on the restoration of the original subtitle on the title page (16 April 1817, in Constable). Unless otherwise noted, all references to the correspondence between Godwin and Constable are by the date of letters reproduced in Thomas Constable, *Archibald Constable and His Literary Correspondents*, 3 vols. (Edinburgh: Edmonston and Douglas, 1873), vol. 2, 77–95.

3 Mary Shelley, *Valperga: Or, The Life and Adventures of Castruccio Prince of Lucca* (1823), ed. Tilottama Rajan (Peterborough, ON: Broadview, 1998), 439.

uprisings ex-centric to its setting "in England." The first is the Irish (or Ulster) Rebellion of 1641, in which the infant Mandeville's parents perish in the massacre of Protestant settlers. Charles, the sole survivor, is saved by his Catholic nurse, only to be taken from her by the severe Hilkiah Bradford, chaplain of the garrison, who then becomes his tutor in the forlorn castle of Charles's uncle Audley. Hilkiah then dies and the boy is sent to school at the venerable Winchester College. The second uprising is the rag-tag assault that Mandeville himself leads on the marriage coach bearing his sister Henrietta and his former classmate Clifford, who has recently inherited a fortune by converting to Catholicism. Clifford escapes unharmed, but Mandeville is severely disfigured. The novel ends with Mandeville traumatically yet triumphantly contemplating his face in a mirror, on the eve of a Restoration whose domestic version he has refused in dis-figuring the reconciliation figured in the marriage of Henrietta and Clifford. For this marriage of a Presbyterian brought up (by adoption) as an Anglican, to an Episcopalian turned Catholic, is the very symbol of the settlements and expediencies at the heart of the Restoration.

Yet *Mandeville* is not only *about* blockage; it is also the product of Godwin's own holding back from writing a radical version of the genre of the historical novel, which Sir Walter Scott (1771–1832) was installing as a form of nation-building. Though Scott is sensitive to the losses of history, they cannot hold up a narrative of British modernity that moves past the inevitable failure of the Jacobite rebellion in which the Highland Scots tried to reclaim their independence: a failure that only reconfirmed the union of England and Scotland in Great Britain. The marriage that concludes *Waverley* (1814) is the token of this settling for things as they are. So what form would a radical version of the historical novel take, given that Godwin questions what he calls "institution," which does not simply consist in public institutions but "insinuate[s] itself" even into the arts and our "personal dispositions" and "most secret retirements" (*PJ* 1.4–6)? Years before Scott's novels, which Godwin read while the idea of *Mandeville* was forming,[1] Godwin had attempted a radical history in *St. Leon*

---

1 According to his *Diary,* between 1815 and 1816 Godwin read Scott's recently published *Waverley, Guy Mannering* (1815), and *The Antiquary* (1816). In addition to the texts to which he refers in the Preface, he also re-read work by the Jacobin novelists Robert Bage (1728–1801) and Thomas Holcroft (1745–1809), and read Byron's Oriental Tales (1813–14), Coleridge's *Christabel* (1816), and Caroline Lamb's *Glenarvon* (1816), which makes Byron the leader of the 1798 Irish Uprising.

(1799): one that also subscribes to a discourse of improvement, though in a quixotically ironic and hypothetical mode that posits without instituting. *St. Leon*, a virtual narrative about a gambler and alchemist, leaves behind the ties of nation and family after the death of St. Leon's wife and thus questions the very institution of the novel as a form of socialization, as the hero migrates from life to life in different countries. For much of the novel St. Leon, who by sheer chance acquires the philosopher's stone, uses his wealth for purely selfish purposes. However, in the last segment Godwin experiments with an enlightened radicalism, as his protagonist arrives in Hungary and tries to rebuild its war-ravaged economy. In the end he fails miserably, both in his New Deal economic experiment and in dealing emotionally and intellectually with Bethlem Gabor, a character whose pure hatred foreshadows that of *Mandeville*'s Hilkiah. But St. Leon is a paper-character who is not really affected by his many setbacks, and given that he has the elixir of life, we can imagine the spirit of hope he retains surviving into a further life.

In the two decades between *St. Leon* and *Mandeville*, Godwin produced only one novel, *Fleetwood* (1805), a domestic story about a misanthropic bachelor, who in the course of his wanderings meets a close friend of Jean-Jacques Rousseau called Macneil. Macneil and his family drown at sea, having made Fleetwood the guardian of their one surviving daughter, Mary. A profound ennui and perverse patriarchal privilege draw Fleetwood to marry his young and melancholically wounded ward (at the suggestion of her late father), and then to turn against her in a misogynistic jealousy that abjects both the institution of the family and Fleetwood's own warped resistance to it. Godwin's withdrawal from literature for the next twelve years is the autobiography of a stalled relationship to the resistances of radicalism. For *Fleetwood* contains curious, displaced autographs of figures from Godwin's intellectual and personal life: the eponymous hero, who bears the name of Cromwell's son-in-law; his wife, who has the almost generic name of both Godwin's wife and daughter; the unconventional marriage of Mary's parents, which ends in a will-to-death when they abruptly emigrate to Italy and drown; and Fleetwood's Iago-like betrayer Gifford, the name of the editor of the *Anti-Jacobin Review*. These traces involve a puzzling distortion of the private and public by each other, as the failure of progressive politics is displaced into a series of domestic pathologies. They are Godwin's confession of a prematurity in the project of political justice, but also in its critique, which must then be set aside for many years, its mistakes and energies alike unreadable.

Fleetwood, subtitled "The New Man of Feeling," in distinction to Henry Mackenzie's more benignly sentimental *The Man of Feeling* (1771), seems to share little with *Mandeville* except for a misanthropic protagonist. Fleetwood's feelings are aimless, whereas Mandeville is possessed of and by a powerful passion. As Godwin's son-in-law Percy Shelley (1792–1822) writes, the novel's interest is of an "irresistible and overwhelming kind"; even "Caleb Williams never shakes the deepest soul like Mandeville" (Appendix C1, p. 469). But while working on *Fleetwood*, Godwin read several works of late-seventeenth-century history, some of which (by Gilbert Burnet [1643–1715] and Edward Clarendon [1609–74]) he used for *Mandeville*. Godwin had complained that from the moment "the grand contest excited" in the Stuart period was "quieted" by the Glorious Revolution of 1688, the history of England became a history of "negotiations and tricks" rather than "of genuine independent man" (Appendix B, p. 465). In retrospect we can see *Fleetwood*, which is set in the eighteenth century, as domesticating the restlessness of the negative that surfaces in the Civil War period within the private sphere of a sensibility uneasy with itself. We can also see why Godwin resisted calling its predecessor in the historical series a "domestic story."

Yet Godwin clearly had difficulty in beginning this predecessor that would be the key work in his aetiology of a "damaged society" (Adorno 52). In approaching his publisher Archibald Constable for an advance contract for *Mandeville* (18 December 1815), he mentions that "seven years ago" he had had an idea that would furnish a "foundation for a superstructure of fiction" that he sketched out over a week, and "three or four years ago" he set out to compose this work, but wrote only four pages before being distracted by having to earn his living by writing children's books. He did not receive the contract until 24 April 1816 and began writing only at the end of May. The correspondence with Constable shows Godwin apologizing for the slow pace of his work, the last instalment of which he sent in on 22 October 1817, several months after the novel had been announced. In these days before the use of speed presses, Constable resorted to asking Godwin not just for individual volumes but for parts of volumes that he could send to the printer so as to have the whole ready more quickly. Nevertheless, with the printer being in Edinburgh and not London, Godwin was loath to part with the manuscript, individual parts and sentences of which he revised again and again.

Godwin published "Fragment of a Romance" (Appendix A), which he mentions in the letter to Constable, only in 1833, 24 years later. The fragment ends in a traumatic massacre of the Spaniards by the Moors, similar to the one which opens *Mandeville*, and after which the narrator is like "a man, the bones of whose limbs have been broken," such that "in the seat of each fracture there remains an unseen knot or protuberance" (Appendix A, p. 455). Godwin's references to the fragment in the partial draft of the Preface (25 November 1816)[1] and the Preface itself (18 October 1817) give it a particular place in the emotional genesis of a novel whose personal importance he continues to mark by publishing its germ so many years later. But the fragment itself formulaically prolongs the childhood idyll that precedes its catastrophe; it is mechanically binary in its opposition of Christians and infidels, and artificially distanced in time and place from the history of Godwin's own country. The fragment skirts the trauma that Godwin knows is there, but does not probe its heart of darkness, hence his difficulty in beginning what he knew he had to do. The "superstructure" to which Godwin refers, and into which he might have wanted to absorb this trauma, is for a series of tales in which, drawing on the legend of the seven sleepers of Ephesus, he would create a hero with the faculty of falling asleep and waking up again in a different century. The trope best describes *St. Leon*, but the seven sleepers are not just a figure for the continuations and second chances that we see in that novel. They are also a figure for repression, which Godwin uses in a political context in 1795 to describe those who fall asleep, then awaken and expect nothing to be changed.[2]

And clearly much had changed between the 1790s, whose spirit Godwin still held on to in *St. Leon*, and 1817. The policies of the conservative government of William Pitt (1759–1806) and its successors had closed down dissent. These policies included the Treason Trials of 1794, in which prominent members of the radical London Corresponding Society were arrested, as well as a series of so-called "Gagging Acts," which extended from the

1 Bodleian Library, Abinger Collection, c. 29, fols. 70–71.
2 "They are like the seven sleepers, that we read of in the Roman history, who, after having slumbered for three hundred years, knew not that a month had elapsed, and expected to see their old contemporaries" (*Considerations on Lord Grenville's and Mr. Pitt's Bills ...*, PPW, 2.155). See also below, p. 61, note 3 <Preface to vol. 1>.

1790s to 1819 and severely curtailed freedom of association and speech and freedom of the press. On the other side of the Channel, reforms in divorce and race laws during the French Revolution (1789) had been turned back by Napoleon (1769–1821). Though Napoleon's imperial ambitions were defeated at the Battle of Waterloo (1815), this was a further stage in the establishment of Britain's role in imperial history, as Godwin was aware in writing on Ireland and India. There was a momentary resurgence of the spirit of the 1790s in 1815–16,[1] a motivation in Godwin's writing of *Mandeville*. But in general, the radicalism of the 1790s was quietened by the Regency period:[2] a development repeated in current criticism's tendency to reorient Romanticism around the novels of Jane Austen (1775–1817), Scott, and the Regency rather than the revolutionary period. For as Anthony Jarrells says, while the Glorious Revolution of 1688 produced no major literature of its own, it became a refuge to which those terrified of the outbreak of the French Revolution in 1789 could return, thus resulting in the depoliticized category of "literature" as a way of resisting and containing "the dangerous effects of print."[3]

But indeed, the institution of literary criticism that shaped this "literature" (or rather *belles lettres*) goes back before the nineteenth century to the eighteenth century's reaction against the period of *Mandeville*. This period, the seventeenth century, with its explosion of print comparable only to the 1790s, has been described as both "'an information revolution' and 'the central trauma of English history.'" As Lee Morrissey points out, taking notions of publicness and democracy back to the time of the English Revolution thus yields a far more open, violent, and contentious notion of the public sphere from the model of liberal consensus and communicative rationality that Jürgen Habermas derives from the eighteenth century.[4] The print culture of the

---

1   B.J. Tysdahl, *William Godwin as Novelist* (London: Athlone P, 1981), 131. Hence the further series of Gagging Acts in 1817 and 1819.

2   The period 1811–20, when George III was deemed unfit to rule, and his son, the Prince of Wales, served as Prince Regent.

3   Anthony Jarrells, *Britain's Bloodless Revolutions: 1688 and the Romantic Reform of Literature* (Houndmills: Palgrave Macmillan, 2005), 7–14, 17–19.

4   Lee Morrissey, *The Constitution of Literature: Literacy, Democracy, and Early English Literary Criticism* (Stanford, CA: Stanford UP, 2008), 9, 25, 28–29, and more generally 1–53.

1640s, which is only one of the resonances between the interregnum and Godwin's period, is thematized in miniature in the episode at Winchester College, in which Mandeville is falsely accused of secretly owning a book of anti-monarchist cartoons. In a gross parody of the Eucharist, he is sentenced to eat the book: a political scar that dogs him for the rest of his career. Opening up the public sphere to the dissensus it quiets down, Godwin's novel, as we shall see, also pushes against the sense of "taste" so valued by the "literary criticism" that the eighteenth century invented to control meaning and ensure the social stability threatened in the years before the Restoration. Godwin had "gone too far," according to one biographer.[1]

Godwin's Negative Dialectic: *Mandeville* and *History of the Commonwealth*

In the dominant narrative of British history as the consolidation of this stability, the key event was the Glorious Revolution, which finally disposed of the Stuarts[2] and the divine right of kings, instituting secularization and enlightenment through the Hanoverian succession which consolidated constitutional monarchy.[3] Furth-

---

1 Peter H. Marshall, *William Godwin* (New Haven, CT: Yale UP, 1984), 340.

2 The Stuarts reigned from 1603 until the execution of Charles I in 1649, and then from 1660–1714. However, it was only the first four Stuart monarchs (James I, Charles I and II, and James II) whose Catholic allegiances supported a belief in absolute monarchy (see "Political and Religious Background" below). In 1679, during the reign of Charles II, the first Earl of Shaftesbury (who figures in *Mandeville*), introduced a bill to exclude Charles's brother James from the succession, but the bill was defeated in the House of Lords in 1681. This period is known as the Exclusion Crisis. With the birth of James II's son in 1688, which would have meant another Catholic heir, matters came to a head and William of Orange, who was only fourth in the line of succession but was backed by English Parliamentarians, invaded England, ruling jointly with his wife Mary from 1689. Although she was James's daughter, Mary was a Protestant like her husband. William, who survived his wife (d. 1694) and ruled till his death in 1702, when he was succeeded by her sister Anne, also a Protestant, who reigned until 1714.

3 Since neither William nor Anne had surviving children, in 1701 he introduced an Act of Settlement that excluded Catholics from the succession and placed it in the hands of Sophia, dowager Electress of Hanover, a granddaughter of James I. After her death in 1714, her son, Georg Ludwig, became Anne's successor as George I.

er moments in this nationalist progress are the union of Scotland and England as Great Britain in 1707, the absorption of Ireland into the United Kingdom in 1800, and the British victory at Waterloo in 1815, just before Godwin began planning *Mandeville*. Yet Waterloo was no simple defeat of Napoleon, in whom the Romantics saw progress and empire complexly mixed. It was also part of the nexus that led Godwin's contemporary Carl von Clausewitz (1780–1831) to theorize what would become the discipline of military history and the beginning of modern conceptions of warfare (Appendix G1a). Thus, in returning to the seventeenth century after the "peace" of Waterloo, Godwin tacitly takes aim at several agendas: the dominant narrative of British history followed by Scott and David Hume (1711–76); its complicity with a new global order that is still with us today; and finally, Edmund Burke's view in his *Reflections on the Revolution in France* (1790) that the British had avoided the excesses of the French Revolution, which conveniently forgets Britain's bloody past and the beheading of its own king, Charles I, in 1649.

On the other hand, even as Godwin tacitly critiques Burke, he does not subscribe to the equally progressive history imagined on the radical side by his friend John Thelwall (1764–1834) in the 1790s (Appendix D2). According to Thelwall's utopian scenario, which never came to pass, the English Revolution failed because it was promoted by a small body of men in a pre-modern age of superstition and fanaticism. But the French Revolution would succeed because of a much more widely based "enlightenment" and democracy. For Godwin, as for Thelwall, the "Bloodless Revolution" of 1688 was nothing to be proud of, but in Godwin's more negative dialectic neither the traumas nor the potential of the English Revolution could so easily be put in the past. Hence his sense that despite their undemocratic rule, the "grand contest excited under the Stuarts," rather than the "insipid" age that followed it, is the place where we must still look for a "history of genuine, independent man" (Appendix B, p. 465), even if it is marred by fanaticism. Or as Hegel puts it, "periods of happiness ... when antithesis is in abeyance" are "blank pages" in history.[1]

Against Scott, who narrates the merger and acquisition of Scotland by England as part of modernity, Godwin therefore returns to a period before the Restoration, and to Ireland as the traumatic infancy both of Mandeville and of British history itself.

---

1   G.W.F. Hegel, *The Philosophy of History*, trans. J. Sibree (New York: Dover, 1956), 26.

He then draws this earlier era back into his own time through the resonance between the Irish Rebellion of 1641 and the Irish Uprising of 1798, which preceded Ireland's incomplete absorption into the United Kingdom. However ambivalently, Scott affirms the narrative of stabilization at the end of *Waverley*. For the marriage of the eponymous hero, who has been rejected by the passionate Flora, to the more rational Rose Bradwardine, thematizes Scotland's transition from Highland to Lowland culture and anchors the Revolution and Settlement of 1688–89 in domestic harmony. By contrast, the brutal ending of *Mandeville* reminds us of the violence and unresolved problems underlying all acts of union, settlement, or restoration, be they personal or public. It reminds us, moreover, that the way forward lies through rather than around these problems.

In the next decade Godwin would write a massive four-volume *History of the Commonwealth* (*HCE*; 1824–28), a more temperate complement to his novel about the interregnum. *HCE* is a realistic return to the internally vexed project of political justice, but is in its own way a history that does not foreclose progress. In *HR* Godwin had valorized an individual history focused on transformative (or in the case of *Mandeville*, traumatic) particulars over a "general" history that studies mankind "in a mass." Discerning "the causes that operate universally upon masses of men" (Appendix B, pp. 461–62), general history is dry in its details and given to generalizing patterns that ignore singularity and contingency. But in the many twists and turns that the essay takes, Godwin goes on to replace the binary of individual and general history with one between ancient and modern history, and then one between "romance" and history. He proclaims the writer of romance the true historian (p. 467), only to perform an about-face at the end of the essay, by equivocally giving back the advantage to the historian (no longer distinguished as individual or general). For now it is the romance-writer who indulges in broad simplifications, while the historian, with his eye for detail, opens a space for the "single grain of sand," the contingencies, that can potentially alter the entire "motion" of the earth and over time "diversif[y] its events" (p. 468).

What emerges from the productively unsatisfying nature of the many optics on history generated by the essay is a certain value that Godwin does after all see in "history." For one could well describe his corpus, including his novels and children's books, as a universal history in bits and pieces and in different media that constitute entrances and side-entrances into history. Indeed the essay's opening binary is also troubled by a text such as Godwin's life of Milton's nephews, which consists of two individual histories in general form (since they are not written in the first person, as the novels are), or perhaps two general histories in individual form. Thus by the end of *HR*, read in conjunction with the larger corpus, it is clear that we need to go back to the beginning and reconsider not just history but also "general" history. For in practice, a good deal of Godwin's work after 1798 *is* general history with some admixture of unique particulars that stop it from being a totalizing history. It is helpful, then, to think of two different forms of general history. One is history as a "universal science," which Godwin associates with the Enlightenment historians Hume and William Robertson (Appendix B, p. 463), and which he critiques at the beginning of *HR*. The other is described by Michel Foucault, who actually conducts his critique of a "total" history that "draws all phenomena around a single centre" by way of what he calls "general history," which occupies "the space of a dispersion." Total history is a universal science that insists on unities such as periods or centuries.[1] But general history is "gray, meticulous, and patiently documentary"; it "operates on a field of entangled and confused parchments, on documents that have been scratched over and recopied many times."[2] It is this history that Godwin evokes at the end of *HR*.

Returning to *HCE*, this text is everything that Godwin criticizes in general history: it is a "labyrinth of particulars" (Appendix B, p. 462) in which the reader gets lost, and it is full of "dry and minute particulars" (*HCE* 1.x). Yet it is also the kind of general history whose details harbour the grain of sand that allows us to reflect on how things might have evolved otherwise. *HCE* is the major prose work of Godwin's later life, standing in relation to *Mandeville* as *Political Justice* does to *Caleb Williams*. It covers much the same period as the novel, and also stops at the Restoration, as the point where the "visionary attempt to estab-

---

1 Michel Foucault, *The Archaeology of Knowledge and the Discourse on Language*, trans. A.M. Sheridan-Smith (New York: Pantheon, 1972), 4, 9–10.

2 This is Foucault's account of genealogy in his slightly earlier "Nietzsche, Genealogy, History" (*Language, Counter-Memory, Practice: Selected Essays and Interviews*, trans. Donald F. Bouchard and Sherry Simon [Ithaca: Cornell UP, 1977], 139); hereafter cited parenthetically. The terms have much in common, but as Foucault later practices "genealogy," it becomes a more diachronic term, where "general history" is more a field of simultaneities.

lish a republic in England" (Appendix D3, p. 486) comes to an end, becoming totally extinct after the Glorious or Bloodless Revolution (Appendix D1, p. 481). But the individual and general history could not be more different. *HCE* is as dispassionate as *Mandeville* is paranoid and traumatic, and focuses on the republican side, where the novel includes only Royalists. *HCE* contains no grand narrative of either the justice or the failure of the republican cause, and in that sense does the work of the historian whose very empiricism, in its inconclusiveness, keeps a place for contingency at the end of *HR*.

In other words, *HCE* is not what Nietzsche calls a "monumental history" that "generalize[s things] into compatibility."[1] Although it contains individuals (such as John Pym, John Hampden, Edward Coke, Sir Henry Vane, and Robert Devereux, 3rd Earl of Essex), there are so many of them that, except for Cromwell, they fail to stand out; their histories are introduced, interrupted, and resumed across a period of two decades, in which Godwin largely moves from 1641 to 1659, but also loops back and forth between different years, as if scratching over and recopying a document several times. Within the tangle of particulars that makes up its volumes, one man stands out: Cromwell, subject of the fourth volume. Interestingly Godwin speaks of Cromwell in the language of *HR*, when he writes that "the fertility of his conceptions ... was incapable of being exhausted," and that "we seek in romance, for characters" like him, only to find "a real personage, whose exploits do not fall short of all that the wildest imagination had ever the audacity to feign" (Appendix D3, p. 486). Yet the fourth volume is no romance but a balanced historical assessment. Earlier Godwin says, of Cromwell's crowning of himself as Lord Protector, that he "broke this party in pieces ... he drove the firmest and most enlightened among them by main force from the helm of the state" (*HCE* 3.562). But in the fourth volume, shifting partly to the individual, he presents Cromwell as having compromised his principles, but also as having shown concern for the poor, reformed the law, protected the universities, and many other progressive accomplishments. On that basis he concludes that if Cromwell "had lived ten years longer" his "purposes and ideas ... would not have been antiquated and annihilated almost as soon as they were deprived of his energies to maintain them" (Appendix D3, p. 488). In the

---

1 Friedrich Nietzsche, *The Use and Abuse of History*, trans. Adrian Collins (Indianapolis: Bobbs-Merrill, 1949), 15.

web of historical complexities within which Godwin discusses Cromwell, romance, then, provides no more than a horizon within which we can continue to reimagine the visionary attempt to establish a republic in England.

Why did Godwin put so much effort into this grey and meticulous history, for which he worked with new state papers not available to Hume (*HCE* 1.ix)? Or what is the interface between this text and his much more powerful if claustrophobic novel? One answer is that he wished to consider the seventeenth century in England within a larger field of political complexity than the novel afforded. Here it is important to emphasize that *HCE* is not about a lost republican moment that can only be an object of nostalgia. As Godwin says at the outset, England "was not sufficiently ripe for a republican government" that might never be appropriate (Appendix D1, p. 482). *HCE* therefore conveys the republican moment into the larger field of the English Revolution, and is the positive (if unfulfilled) side of an unfinished project of deconstruction that is both contested and pushed forward by the trauma of *Mandeville*. The battle of King and Parliament, the Long Parliament, the Commonwealth, and even the Protectorate itself are all among the "expedients" (Appendix D2, p. 484) or "experiments" (Appendix D3, p. 488) produced by this seminal period in British history.[1] Indeed, as Rowland Weston points out, *HCE* "downplays the *revolutionary* nature of the republicans' activity, insisting that, in exceeding his prerogative, the King had created a revolutionary situation that the republicans then inherited and attempted to manage according to their more evolved political lights."[2] Consequently, unlike Godwin's children's histories of Greece and Rome, *HCE* does not end but begins with the republican moment, so as to think with and beyond it. In this sense, though from a different side of the political spectrum, it does not rule out the rational dialectic that Lukács sees as characterizing the historicism of Scott as a "middle way between extremes," though it stops short of anything quite as clear as a dialectic.[3]

---

1 For brief descriptions of these events, see Historical Timeline for *Mandeville*, pp. 53–56.

2 Rowland Weston, "William Godwin and the Puritan Legacy," *Nineteenth-Century Prose* 39.1–2 (2012): 430.

3 Georg Lukács, *The Historical Novel*, trans. Hannah and Stanley Mitchell (Harmondsworth: Penguin, 1976), 32. For further discussion of *HR* and *HCE*, see Tilottama Rajan, "Between General and Individual History: Godwin's Seventeenth-Century Texts," *Nineteenth-Century Prose* 41.2/3 (Spring/Fall 2014): 119–23, 125–32.

A second answer is that *HCE* stands as a sign of the importance of history to Godwin, something often missed by reviewers and commentators. Thus one contemporary sees him as great "only in depicting the emotions of a single being" and suggests that he should not have tied *Mandeville* "to a particular epoch in English history," especially one dominated by "fanaticism" and "pedantical affectations."[1] But Mandeville is not simply a Byronic hero—a type invented by Godwin, but not removed from a social context as in Byron. He is also, to adapt Foucault, a body that is "the inscribed surface of events ... totally imprinted by history and the process of history's destruction of the body" ("Nietzsche" 148). Thus on the one hand, in the novel history is pushed into the background, its events becoming mere props for Mandeville's psychic history. The execution of the King and death of Cromwell are mentioned only in passing, the Restoration not at all. So if by history we mean perspective, a sense of background and foreground, *HCE* reintroduces this wider history. It opens *Mandeville* in a different window, so that the individual can be lifted into the general, and the possibility of waking up in a different time raised by the seven sleepers trope can be held open. And indeed, the trace of this longer history does enter the novel. For throughout the narrative a later voice is underlaid in Mandeville's: one that comments on women's exclusion from education, expresses doubts about the faith placed in kings, makes favourable comments on Cromwell, and analyses religio-political history (pp. 153–54, 192). In minor literature everything is charged with a "political immediacy," such that "a whole other story is vibrating" in what we read (Deleuze and Guattari 16–20), and *HCE* reminds us of the stakes of this other story.

Yet on the other hand, the very skew by which history is thrown out of focus by being pushed into the background provides the novel with its unique psychological curvature, and calls in question the possibility of straightforward historical representation. For as Hans Kellner says, history can be grasped only by getting the story crooked: "To see the text straight is to see *through* it—that is, not to see it at all except as a device to facilitate knowledge of reality."[2] Thus, through the usurpation of public by private history Godwin also opens *HCE* in another

---

1   Abinger Collection, c.31, fols. 36–41. The anonymous review consists of what seem to be galley proofs but it is not known where it was printed.

2   Kellner, *Language and Historical Representation: Getting the Story Crooked* (Madison: U of Wisconsin P, 1989), 4.

window, forcing us to rethink the stalled potential of the English Revolution in the "closet" of Mandeville's passions, which as I will suggest, are themselves overdetermined by the religio-political environment of the time. This negative dialectic (in Adorno's well-known term) in which history cannot proceed till we have given due weight to what deviates from and impedes its progress, is what communicates to the novel a certain urgency. For *HCE* is a dispassionate text: the "grand contest" that is the motivating horizon of Godwin's passion for the seventeenth century is lost in its labyrinth of details and historical agents, whereas in the novel it is concentrated and mobilized, though pathologically distorted, through the eternal war between Mandeville and Clifford.

This negative dialectic is also something with which Godwin's contemporary Schelling was struggling in his *Freedom* essay and other work from 1809 to 1815: work important to Marxist Idealists such as Ernst Bloch (1885–1977) and Slavoj Žižek (b. 1949).[1] In his *Ages of the World* (1815), Schelling complains that "humans show a natural predilection for the affirmative," for what is "outpouring and goes forth from itself," like the sisterly love Mandeville attributes to Henrietta. But they cannot understand what "closes itself off" (Appendix G5b, p. 521), as when Mandeville says, "I dug a ... deep foss, and threw up an intrenchment, to cut me off from creatures wearing the human form" (p. 171). Schelling's work is an attempt to grasp this resistance and negativity as the very condition of possibility for freedom. As such, it provides a more philosophically intensive analysis of what Godwin calls the principle of "rebelliousness," the sense of "not being at home" (Appendix G3a, p. 511), which is the core of German definitions of the Romantic as opposed to the Classical (by Friedrich Schiller, G.W.F. Hegel, and the Schlegels). And indeed, though critically, Godwin *was* likened to the Germans by reviewers (Appendix C4, p. 474; Appendix C5, p. 476). Clifford, who is always cheerful, is the epitome of someone who is at home, breathing "his native air ... in a castle which is his in full propriety" (Appendix G3a, p. 511). But from *Caleb Williams* onwards, Godwin was fascinated by what he called the "*fomes peccati*" or "black drop of blood in the heart of every man" (Appendix G3a, p. 511).

In his middle work Schelling also wants to understand the role that evil and disease play in the body, and by extension the body

---

1   See Jürgen Habermas, "Ernst Bloch: A Marxist Schelling," *Philosophical-Political Profiles*, trans. Frederick G. Lawrence (Cambridge, MA: MIT P, 1985), 53–79; Slavoj Žižek, *The Indivisible Remainder: An Essay in Schelling and Related Matters* (London: Verso, 1996).

politic. In the cluster of concepts in which he links "evil" to disease, but makes dis-ease with things as they are the ground of freedom, Schelling uses the analogy of a sick body to explore the part's withdrawal from the whole. Hegel, for whom the body also stands in for the psyche, similarly discusses illness as an "irritability" in which a part of the body withdraws into itself, becoming "the negative of itself" (Appendix G5a, p. 518), in an "active maintenance of self."[1] But strikingly, Schelling describes disease as a capacity and not just a disability: "The individual member, such as the eye, is only possible in the whole of the organism" but "has a life for itself, indeed a kind of freedom, which it makes evident through the sickness of which it is capable" (Appendix G5c, p. 522). This language of disease is also throughout *Mandeville*, passing through its pathologization as madness when Mandeville is locked up at Cowley, and culminating in the wound he bears with him for the rest of his life. This is not to say that Mandeville's condition is desirable: it is, as Schelling says, "only a phantasm of life ... a hovering between being and non-being."[2] At the same time, disease and evil are words for what makes us uncomfortable, leading Blake to pose the question of whether what we call evil might not actually be "the active springing from Energy."[3] In Schelling's genealogy of morals then, disease, which is called evil, is the skew of truth. Put differently, pathology and psychopathology, as the part's sequestering of itself in an obstinate selfhood, are errors, but errors are tropes, twistings, or metaphors for what can, for the present, only be made known as "the negative of itself."

"Perverse Identification"

At the core of the novel is the "causeless *aversion*" by which Mandeville is possessed (Appendix C4, p. 474), and for which he finds an inadequate objective correlative in Clifford. For Clifford seems totally benign, and even intervenes to spare Mandeville from eating the book in the cartoon episode, though as Mandeville observes, he always performs his generosity in public (p. 211). Yet Clifford is certainly not petty or nasty, in the manner of

---

1 G.W.F. Hegel, *Philosophy of Nature*, trans. A.V. Miller (Oxford: Clarendon, 1970), 359.

2 Schelling, *Freedom*, 244.

3 *The Marriage of Heaven and Hell*, in *The Complete Poetry and Prose of William Blake*, ed. David V. Erdman (rev. ed., Berkeley and Los Angeles: U of California P, 1982), Plate 2.

unworthier antagonists such as Mallison, Mandeville's former classmate who conspires with his uncle, the lawyer Holloway, to worm his way into Audley's confidence, keep Mandeville under surveillance as unbalanced, and steal his legacy. Mandeville's "absolute war" on Clifford (Appendix G1a, p. 508)—"I must kill him; or he must kill me" (p. 187)—has led most commentators to dismiss him as "mad" or to play on his name, Man-D(evil),[1] a reading more appropriate to a medieval morality play than to a complex psychological novel. More convincingly, Gary Handwerk reads the repetition-compulsions and obsessiveness of Godwin's heroes as evidence of the traumas that stall "liberalism," but he sees an unbridgeable gulf between the "enlightened aspirations" of *PJ* and an essentially "Romantic historical sensibility."[2] I suggest, however, a more dialectical relationship between Godwin's radicalism (rather than liberalism) and a sense of trauma that is deeply revolutionary as well as pessimistic.

For Clifford is no more than an alibi for the radical deconstruction of a damaged society that Godwin conducts through Mandeville. Clifford is always cheerful and gracious. But as Adorno argues, in terms curiously apposite to *Mandeville*, if a "psycho-analysis" of our culture were possible, it would "show the sickness proper to the time to consist precisely in normality. The libidinal achievements demanded of an individual behaving as healthy in body and mind, are ... performed only at the cost of the profoundest mutilation.... No science has yet explored the inferno in which were forged the deformations that later emerge to daylight as cheerfulness, openness, sociability, successful adaptation to the inevitable." Mandeville is the symptom of this mutilation by "characteristics ... laid down at even earlier stages of childhood development than are neuroses" (Adorno 58–59). Through him we are forced to know what the "good" abjects or excludes, the supreme condescension even of its attempts to be "understanding," and the violence of the good as a form of normalization.

To perform this deconstruction, or unsettling of the system of social and psychic institutions that undergirds our culture, Godwin in all his novels sets up what I have called the *fantasy* of

---

1 William St. Clair, *The Godwins and the Shelleys: A Biography of a Family* (Baltimore: Johns Hopkins UP, 1989), 440.
2 Handwerk, "History, Trauma, and the Limits of the Liberal Imagination," in *Romanticism, History, and the Possibilities of Genre: Reforming Literature 1789–1837*, ed. Tilottama Rajan and Julia Wright (Cambridge: Cambridge UP, 1998), 70, 80–81.

a "perverse identification" with characters who ought to disturb us from a conventionally moral standpoint.[1] Discussing how this identification is produced, Freud argues that its "precondition ... is that the spectator should himself be a neurotic ... who can derive pleasure" from the "recognition of a repressed impulse." But as Freud concedes, if we see ourselves as normal, this recognition "will meet only with aversion." Given that normality is profoundly repressed and neurosis is closer to the truth, Freud's question is how an author can shake up an initial repression in a "normal" spectator. For if the character seems too removed from normality, the transference cannot operate: as Freud says, we will "send for the doctor" and pronounce the character "inadmissible to the stage." To "induce the same illness" in the spectator as in the character, the repression must first "be set up." It is for this reason that Godwin builds a powerful case for Mandeville's escalating paranoia, so that we are not faced, as Freud says, "with a fully established neurosis," but are "made to follow the development of the illness along with the sufferer."[2]

Leaving aside the Irish massacre in which Mandeville is not a personal target, there is the cartoon episode at school, and then the Royalist Penruddock insurgency against Cromwell, in which Clifford is given the secretaryship, partly because of his Episcopalian vs. Mandeville's Presbyterian family origins (see "Political and Religious Background," below, p. 33). Then when Mandeville returns to Oxford there is the invective heaped on him by his friend Lisle as a result of the false rumours of disloyalty to the King that dog his life after the cartoon episode, and finally there is Holloway's scheme. It would be hard not to sympathize with Mandeville given that in all his novels Godwin makes the hero of his "tale his own historian" (in *CW* 448). But the word "historian" is worth noting since, as we have suggested, Godwin's own voice is often underlaid in Mandeville's. In other words, the narrative is not so much told as *received* in the first person, such that we may not literally identify with Mandeville but have a responsibility to hear him.

To be sure, Mandeville's attitude to Henrietta and Clifford is unreasonable, nor is he someone we would want to befriend in "real life." But in this period when thinkers such as Coleridge

---

1 Rajan, *Romantic Narrative: Shelley, Hays, Godwin, Wollstonecraft* (Baltimore: Johns Hopkins UP, 2010), 89, 136–38.

2 Sigmund Freud, "Psychopathic Characters on the Stage," in *Complete Psychological Works*, ed. James Strachey, 24 vols. (London: Hogarth, 1953–74), 7.308–10.

and Immanuel Kant (1724–1804) were beginning to see the aesthetic in terms of a suspension of conventional judgment, Godwin makes literature the space of the "absolute secret," giving it "the *right to say everything.*" The phrase is from Derrida, who specifically ties "literature" to "a certain non-censure," opposing it to the *belles-lettres*[1] that the English instituted as literature in the eighteenth century. From this perspective, paranoia is not just a pathology but has an "emphatically analytic quality," in Thomas Pfau's words, as "an urgent, counterfactual narrative bent on stripping the real of its deceptive symbolic veneer."[2]

Adorno's analysis of a damaged society is part of his larger critique of the complacency of "enlightenment" in the wake of events in our own time. Thus it is no accident that Henrietta, who tries to woo Mandeville back to health and is the spokesperson for normality, is very much an Enlightenment figure. Sent to England as a baby to spare her the violence in Ireland, she is brought up by her mother's friends, the Willises, and watched over by the Montagus, an aristocratic family which did not actually live at Beaulieu until the eighteenth century (p. 147, note 2). She quotes the Earl of Shaftesbury's *Characteristics* (1711), written by a descendant of the Shaftesbury who actually appears in the novel: an anachronism Godwin highlights (p. 310). If Mandeville impossibly idealizes her this is because somewhere he must preserve an object of love, if only as the possibility that *he* could be other than what he is by being capable of love. But as the psychoanalyst André Green points out, idealization is a form of disconnection. Its conventionalism marks an inability to integrate the good object into the ego, an uneasy instinct that the "good" cannot be integrated because there is something missing in it that prevents it from being posited except as fantasy.[3] Hence Mandeville concedes that Henrietta's "Arcadian" existence, marked "only by the succession of the seasons," is a "fiction of the visionary poets" (p. 240).

But Henrietta is actually drawn with a fair amount of sociological specificity. She and the Montagus are the product of the "structural transformation of the public sphere" that Habermas traces to Britain in the eighteenth century. Habermas draws on

1 Jacques Derrida, *On the Name*, trans. Thomas Dutoit (Stanford, CA: Stanford UP, 1995), 27–28.

2 Pfau, *Romantic Moods: Paranoia, Trauma, and Melancholy, 1790–1840* (Baltimore: Johns Hopkins UP, 2005), 79.

3 Green, *The Work of the Negative*, trans. Andrew Weller (London: Free Association Books, 1999), 45, 71, 261.

Hannah Arendt's account of the modern (as opposed to ancient) public sphere as having arisen when the transference of the domestic (or *oikos*) into the public (or *polis*) leads to the "rise of the 'social.'" Insofar as the public is made of "privatized individuals coming together to form a public," in Arendt's more direct critique, the social effaces the historical. But insofar as the private exists only in public, there is also no such thing as the truly private. People have their feelings in public, as the private is "deprivatized" and exists for the purposes of the social. Even the "intimate sphere" is caught up in the "ambivalence of the family as an agent of society" and the "reproduction of capital," as Henrietta cannot marry Clifford till he inherits a fortune. In effectively adopting Henrietta, the Montagus oversee this "patriarchally structured conjugal family type,"[1] although in benevolent and liberal rather than repressively conservative ways. Yet the darker side of this liberalism emerges in the episode in which Mandeville is locked up in a "receptacle for lunatics" in Cowley (p. 405). Because Henrietta and Mrs. Willis take lodgings nearby, we may identify Cowley with one of the "humane" facilities for the mentally ill being set up in Godwin's time, and described by Samuel Tuke in his *Description of the Retreat near York* (1813) and by Philippe Pinel (Appendix G3b). But if we do so, Mandeville's account of "the cords" and the "blows" he endures at the hands of his keepers (p. 234) reminds us of how much is covered over by the humane psychiatry that we too may wish to practise in reading the novel as part of a regime of moral management. For in this period before the Age of Reason, madhouses were places of confinement and not cure, as indeed they continued to be in the nineteenth century. And from this perspective Henrietta's arguments can only be "like the song of the Sirens" (p. 240).

Political and Religious Background

Mandeville is set in the only period in English history that was not a monarchy. Often therefore associated with anarchy, the interregnum gave Godwin (who had doubts about the concept of anarchism with which he is sometimes associated) a thought-environment in which he could hew to the root meaning of the

---

1 Jürgen Habermas, *The Structural Transformation of the Public Sphere: An Inquiry into a Category of Bourgeois Society*, trans. Thomas Berger (Cambridge, MA: MIT P, 1996), 19, 51, 55, 151–59; Hannah Arendt, *The Human Condition*, 2nd ed. (Chicago: U of Chicago P, 1998), 36–49.

word *an-arkhe* as a going before beginning, rule, or institution.[1] It was a time of religious sectarianism, indeed fanaticism, captured in the way Godwin fills *Mandeville* with references to the Bible and religious groups: Waldensians, Albigensians, Quakers, Levellers, Latitudinarians, Fifth Monarchists, and others. But the importance of religion in this period before the rise of the social, and thus of a certain passion, also signals that history was still a "grand contest" rather than a game of "negotiations and tricks" (Appendix B, p. 465). Moreover, in a world that was not yet secular, church government was the site at which political structures were being renegotiated. The very proliferation of religious groups was thus a form of political and social invention: "Every month produced a new scheme or form of government" and "every man did that which was right in his own eyes."[2]

Since Henry VIII Anglicanism had been the established religion of England, and the contamination of church and state by each other had been an ongoing issue. With the accession of the Stuarts, England and Scotland moved closer to absolute monarchy, as Charles I asserted the divine right of kings and suspended Parliament in 1629. In broad terms we can distinguish three forms of church government at the time with different political implications: Episcopacy, Presbyterianism, and Congregationalism. The first of these placed bishops firmly under the authority of the Archbishop, analogically guaranteeing the authority of the King. At the other extreme, Congregationalists, a family of Protestant denominations deriving from the theologian Robert Browne (c. 1550–1633), believed that each congregation had the right to run its own affairs. Thus, according to Godwin's contemporary Charles Buck in his *Theological Dictionary* (1802), Congregationalism "reject[ed] all church government."[3] Congregationalists of many stripes, both fanatical and democratic, emigrated to America after the Restoration and played an important

---

1   Though critical of it, Godwin does concede that "Anarchy awakens thought, and diffuses energy and enterprise through the community" (*PJ* 2.369). On *anarche* as an epistemology in *PJ* see Jared McGeough, "'So Variable and Inconstant a System': Rereading the Anarchism of Godwin's *Political Justice*," *Studies in Romanticism* 52 (2013): 278, 282–86.

2   *Encyclopedia Londinensis, or, an Universal Dictionary of Arts, Sciences and Literature, etc.* ..., 6 vols. (London: J Adlard, 1810), 1.514.

3   Buck, *A Theological Dictionary, Containing Definitions of all Religious Terms* ... (1802; rpt. Philadelphia: Joseph Woodward, 1826), 112; hereafter cited parenthetically within the text.

role in gaining independence from Britain. The Presbyterians were somewhere in-between, devolving authority to elders or presbyters, but not to individual congregations. Initially supportive of Parliament because of their oligarchic church structure, the Presbyterians eventually became alarmed at the ensuing anarchy and realigned behind the King.

However, the religious and political maps cannot be neatly synchronized. The Congregationalists are generally correlated with the political group known as Independents, from which Cromwell emerged. But not all Independents were Republicans; by the nineteenth century Buck considers them supporters of limited monarchy, and while Cromwell used them to check the power of the Presbyterians, towards the end of the century they became allied with the latter, so that Buck sees scarcely any difference between them except that the Presbyterians were less Calvinist than the Independents (258–60). Intersecting these shifting divisions of political parties that had more or less important religious connections was a clearer distinction in self-fashioning between the groups dismissively dubbed "Cavaliers," who supported the King, and Roundheads, so called because they wore their hair close-cropped and not in ringlets. Though the Roundheads were on the side of Parliament, many actually supported constitutional monarchy, and it was only in 1649, when hostility to the King was at its height, that republican Roundheads pushed for the complete abolition of monarchy and establishment of a Commonwealth. The terms Roundhead and Puritan overlap: some Puritans, though not all, wore their hair close-cropped. The word "Puritan" is also a broad term, denoting a "superior purity and simplicity [in] modes of worship," but not necessarily a doctrinal deviation from the Church of England; nevertheless, in the Tudor-Stuart period Puritans were Non-conformists (Buck 505–06), and dominated the parliamentary opposition to King Charles. During the Civil War period the Puritans forged an alliance with the Scottish Presbyterians, but it is not clear that Presbyterians (in England for instance) were always Puritans. Hilkiah seems a Puritan; Shaftesbury is clearly not.

Finally, the parliamentary side also included the "Levellers," a group of Independents who emphasized equality, religious tolerance, and extended suffrage (to every male head of a household), and who were instrumental in setting up the New Model Army[1]

---

1 The New Model Army was created by the Parliamentarians in 1645. It was new in that it was a full-time and professional army,

that initially facilitated Cromwell's rise to power. The Levellers broke with Cromwell when he, in turn, began to assume absolute power, and thereafter their star fell. But when they were still influential, since functioning within Parliament tended to moderate radical ideas, it was far from true that they wanted to bring all men down to the same common level. That role was played by the Diggers, ecologically-minded agrarian socialists who called themselves the "true Levellers," and whose religiousness was the motivating force behind a radical democracy (Appendix E5, p. 493) that resurfaced in the group known in the 1960s as San Francisco Diggers. Among the many religious groups not represented in Parliament, while the Diggers were social radicals, others such as the Fifth Monarchists were apocalyptic, theological radicals. Altogether, religion, politics, and morality combined and decombined in ways that were confusing, yet whose unsettled nature offered new revolutionary possibilities.

Charles Mandeville's place in this religio-political web is complex, and it registers the stresses and contradictions of a history from which he is shut out. Indeed, given the novel's emphasis on wounding, his body is a kind of archive: "the inscribed surface of events ... totally imprinted by history and the process of history's destruction of the body" (Foucault, "Nietzsche" 148). Though Mandeville seems a staunch Royalist, he becomes one when only a child at Winchester College, and for the most arbitrary reason: namely the discovery of the book of anti-monarchist cartoons in the room he shares with Waller, a puny boy he has befriended because of his own perverse, almost self-loathing sympathy with outsiders. In this episode, which mirrors the pamphlet wars of the 1790s, Mandeville takes the rap for Waller, and thereafter must prove his loyalty to the King again and again. But Mandeville actually comes from an unaligned Presbyterian family (p. 200), and the affiliation is significant. Unlike the religious Presbyterians in Scotland, the parliamentary Presbyterians in England followed what Godwin calls "a middle and temperate course" and, as Mandeville proudly notes, were "the original stirrers of the war between king and parliament" (pp. 156–57). As indicated, their structures of church government initially led them to question the King's promotion of

---

whose members could not serve in Parliament, and were liable for service anywhere in the country (rather than being tied to a single area or garrison). Though disbanded after the Restoration, it is the forerunner of the modern army.

absolute monarchy and refusal to call Parliament for eleven years. However, they then became alarmed at the mixture of radical democracy and proliferating religious sub-sects they had helped to unleash, and regrouped behind the King: a switch evident in the career of Waller's father. And indeed, Mandeville himself draws attention to the way the resulting suspicion of the Presbyterians would influence his fate (pp. 158, 203).

One could well see the Presbyterians' moderate inclinations as making them precursors of the constitutional monarchy that came in after the second Stuart dynasty failed, when James II (r. 1685–88) was replaced by William and Mary in the "Revolution" of 1688. Or one could see their wavering as expedient, as may be the case with the Earl of Shaftesbury, who provides Mandeville with his first, tainted recommendation in public life. But it is significant that Godwin and others saw the Presbyterians as progressive (Appendix E3), allowing for a genealogy that connects them to the later Dissenters of whom he himself was one. Thus Buck describes the English Presbyterians as "a body of Dissenters who have not any attachment to the Scotch mode of church government" any more than to episcopacy, and who have the most in common with the Independents (469). The fact that Mandeville is a Royalist but a Presbyterian thus becomes immensely significant. On the one hand, Godwin made a deliberate decision to focalize the events of the period through a Royalist, and to include no Republicans in the narrative. This one-sidedness gives the novel its psychic shape, which Godwin creates by reading against the grain of his own commitments, twisting history into the heart of its resistances, and registering the trauma that led someone like Burke—whom he deeply respected—to turn against his own progressive sympathies and defend tradition in his attack on the French Revolution. On the other hand, the very differences shut down by this foreclosure of the other side, are internalized on the Royalist side through the difference of the Presbyterians from the Episcopalians. Yet it is not that Mandeville's family origin is a "position" in any positive sense. Politically speaking, Mandeville is a *tabula rasa*; indeed the political positions of the novel's characters are almost all inherited and unscrutinized. Thus Oxford, which Mandeville briefly attends, was a university staunchly loyal to the King when the Anglican Archbishop William Laud was its Chancellor but was then caught up in the contentions of the period after the executions of Laud in 1645 and Charles in 1649. But except for Lisle's repudiation of Mandeville when he hears about the cartoon episode, one would scarcely have any sense of how intensely these contentions raged at Oxford, let alone of their intellectual content or the implication of the Presbyterians in them.[1] Mandeville's Presbyterianism, which is not really "his," therefore does no more than place him in an uneasy relationship to the oppressive Royalism of the other characters, creating a space for what has not yet been worked out, what has not yet come to consciousness.

For Godwin also could not embody opposition to things as they are in a republicanism that was not yet available for the future, having missed its place in the present. It is not simply, as Thelwall argues (Appendix D2), that the uneducated nature of the masses limited republican enlightenment to the select few, thus allowing resistance to take the form of fanaticism and giving Cromwell a chance to seize power. Republicanism was itself flawed: the Civil War period and Protectorate saw the inception or continuation of colonialism in both Ireland and Barbados, and arguably Parliament contributed more to the oppression of the Irish than a King who was half the time on the run from his adversaries. In *HCE* the "virtuous" men who "made the visionary attempt to establish a republic in England" (Appendix D3, p. 486) thus disappear from the stage early, like the idealized poet Clare in *Caleb Williams*, or they are lost in a tangle of historical details. Instead, on the one hand, the spirit that originally animated them is sheltered for future thought by being withheld from the narrative, just as Godwin had done with Milton, in writing a life of his nephews instead. And on the other hand, in the negative dialectic that forms his sense of history, Godwin conveys or rather (dis)figures his opposition to things as they are in the "damaged life" of someone from the other side.

Mandeville's relation to Ireland is equally important to the skew of history. Godwin had been interested in Ireland since 1786, a concern that continued into the 1820s, when in the population debate with Thomas Malthus he addressed the miserable treatment of the Irish by Britain as an international problem that could again reopen the "peace" achieved by Britain's victory at Waterloo. A pirated edition of *Political Justice* was published in Dublin, and in 1800, shortly before the Act of Union that made Britain the United Kingdom, Godwin visited Ireland at the invitation of the Irish patriot and barrister John Philpot Curran (1750–1817). *Mandeville* is dedicated to Curran, and in eulogiz-

---

1 See G.C. Broderick, *A History of the University of Oxford* (London: Longmans, Green, 1900), 138–50.

ing Curran in 1817, Godwin describes him as one of the last of the "fellow-labourers" in "the cause of general liberty."[1] On the face of it Mandeville, unlike Godwin, should have no sympathy with Ireland, the scene of his parents' violent death. Yet one of the novel's most striking passages curiously repeats an image Godwin had earlier used of the relationship of Ireland and England. Mandeville writes of the "inter-destructiveness" that binds him and Clifford as conjoined twins:

> Mezentius, the famous tyrant of antiquity, tied a living body to a dead one, and caused the one to take in, and gradually become a partner of, the putrescence of the other. I have read of twin children, whose bodies were so united in their birth, that they could never after be separated, while one carried with him, wherever he went, an intolerable load, and of whom, when one died, it involved the necessary destruction of the other. (p. 230)

In his 1786 letter "To the People of Ireland," urging them not to be seduced on economic grounds into a union with England, Godwin had used a similar image, writing that there are

> few objects more calamitous or more unnatural, than the union of two countries circumstanced as I have described. It is like that refined piece of cruelty, scarcely to be named by the tongue ... of tying a living body [Ireland] to a dead one [England], and causing them to putrify and perish together. (Appendix F5, p. 505)

In the repetition of this image, counter-intuitive as it might seem, Mandeville is subtextually aligned with Ireland as a victim of oppression. Moreover, the last sentence of the novel, where he speaks of himself as a negro on whom Clifford has "set a brand with a red hot iron," stunningly inverts what would have been the child's position as the son of a family aligned with "tyrannical planters" (p. 448), albeit not in the West Indies but in Ireland, 150 years before debates on the abolition of slavery were raging in Godwin's own England. In the circumstances it is not unreasonable to see in the struggle of Mandeville and Clifford a displaced version of the "grand contest" that animated the Stuart

---

1   Godwin, *Uncollected Writings* (1785–1822), ed. Jack W. Marken and Burton R. Pollin (Gainesville, FL: Scholars' Facsimiles, 1968), 463.

period: namely the struggle of Parliament and King, or of the anonymous against those born to the royal manner and "brought up in reverential ideas of kingship" (p. 173), like Clifford. Hence the fact that Mandeville describes the scenes of "flight, and pursuit, and anguish, and murder" after the massacre as "visionary scenes" that remain more exhilarating than his "monotonous" and "eventless" life in his uncle's house (pp. 109–10). And hence the drive that he draws from these half-memories of his infancy in Ireland, the place of his psychic birth as a subject of injustice, even if this subject is what Jacques Lacan calls a *corps morcelé*, a body in bits and pieces,[1] like the body politic of Britain itself.

Misanthropy, Melancholy, and Fanaticism

Apart from Henrietta and Clifford, two other characters provide the coordinates for the emotional landscape within which we are asked to reflect on this damaged society. One is Mandeville's uncle, Audley. After his father, the brutish Commodore Mandeville, separates him from his beloved Amelia, Audley gathers himself around the "one event" that is for him "the only reality," and forms a wounded, narcissistic self around this "sadness" which "had become a part of himself" (p. 106). Audley's misanthropy is part of a cultural trauma inscribed as heredity in Mandeville's personal and cultural being. But his radical passivity too easily forgoes the anarchic deconstructiveness that we find in Mandeville's paranoia, which, to cite Pfau again, is its own form of discernment, stripping the real of its symbolic veneer.[2] For while "hatred" is Mandeville's "ruling passion," Audley is the soul of gentleness: with his passing it feels to Mandeville as if "an abstract principle, one of the capital articles of my creed, was destined to die" (pp. 305, 308). Audley's "melancholy" (p. 106) is better described as depression—a less aestheticizing term that was not used in diagnosis until the late nineteenth century. His "apathy and neutrality" (p. 236) result in a complete lack of affect and inability to concentrate himself emotionally. Thus Audley, who in his death stands beyond his nephew as "a celestial spirit" (p. 304), is also less than him, "unequal to contention," "sinking,

---

1 Lacan, "The Mirror Stage as Formative of the I Function as Revealed in Psychoanalytic Experience," *Ecrits*, trans. Bruce Fink (New York: Norton, 2006), 78.

2 Pfau, *Romantic Moods*, 79.

as without power of resistance, under any thing that presented itself in the form of hostility" (p. 87).

At the other extreme is Mandeville's hysterically anti-Catholic tutor Hilkiah. While Hilkiah does not seem personally invested in the political issues that preoccupied the parliamentary Puritans or the theological radicals, he conveys a voyeuristic excitement at living in the midst "of the confusions of a civil war" (p. 126), and a perverse identification with the revolutionaries and assassins he denounces. Indeed, as he rants against Popish plots or on behalf of Protestant martyrs, the differences between Catholic and Protestant are confused and fused in a sadomasochistic fascination with violence and the position of the outsider. As a symptom of his culture and a thoroughly dislikeable person, Hilkiah nevertheless injects a dark urgency into the novel's first volume. His clothing and severity identify him as a Puritan or Calvinist (p. 110), but his interest in "cabalistical divinity" and obsession with the number 666 make him far from orthodox (p. 119). As such, Hilkiah is a channel for a "third culture" that was partly oral and sub-literate but also associated with a new explosion of fugitive print forms and a diversification of religious subsects. For as Christopher Hill argues, the English Revolution was not limited to the conflict of King and Parliament, but was the scene of a "popular heretical culture, which rejected the ideas both of court and established church, and of orthodox Puritanism." This third culture, whose views were "often expressed crudely, jumbled up with magical and prophetical ideas," was strongly anti-clerical and emphasized the Bible as "interpreted by individual conscience."[1] It encompasses a range of fundamentalist, apocalyptic and also radically democratic sects.

These sects are largely absent from *HCE*, as is the broader environment of religious fanaticism that begins in the novel with the Irish massacre. But their suppression after the Restoration is one reason why Godwin describes British history after the Stuarts as insipid. And moreover, not all of these sects were bigoted. Some espoused religious toleration, and others, such as the Diggers (see above, p. 33), who called themselves "True Levellers" in distinction from the parliamentary Levellers, argued for radical democracy. In other words, many of Godwin's ideas of political justice are part of a genealogy linking his own form of rational dissent to the religious dissenters of the seventeenth

---

1   Christopher Hill, *Milton and the English Revolution* (London: Faber and Faber, 1979), 69–79.

century. These include his communistic ideas on property and his emphasis on "the right of private judgment" (*PJ* 1.170), according to which the individual must consult his own conscience rather than institutionalized public opinion.

What makes *Mandeville* a return to the 1790s is this minor history that resonates in the novel through Hilkiah. For Hilkiah is both the animus and the animating principle that separates Mandeville's non-conformity from Audley's. His prophetic passion and anger are his legacy to Mandeville. But his incoherence as a character—at once disciplinarian and anarchic—suggests the unfinished, unprocessed nature of what minor history transmits to the future. And his virulent anti-Catholicism indicates how this legacy comes forth warped and convoluted by everything that has not yet been set right in the culture's various attempts at the expediencies and restorations that repress underlying contradictions. Not that Mandeville is attached to his preceptor in any positive way; indeed, he feels a "rooted aversion of heart" from "this good man" who is always associated with "painful sensations" (pp. 129, 141). But Hilkiah's influence works itself "deeply into the substance" of the boy's character (p. 123), in the misanthropy that structures his psyche as the negative of itself. At the same time, Mandeville also says that he "retained the principle of rebellion [against Hilkiah] entire, shut up in the chamber of my thoughts" (p. 129). Though he speaks Hilkiah's language and quotes the Bible, he has no real stake in the religious contentions of the period, apart from the arbitrary "circumstance" (*PJ* 1.26) of having been tutored by Hilkiah. This perhaps is why Mandeville lives on into the Restoration, though anonymously, as the figure for "something not yet made good that pushes its essence forward"[1] in the trauma of the seventeenth century.

... Ending

Godwin's novels are notable for not conforming to the conventional sense of an ending. *Fleetwood* ends dissatisfyingly, while *St. Leon* does not really end, since its hero may still be alive as we read. For its part, although the climactic trial scene of *Caleb Williams* thematizes the function of plot as the bringing of matters to a decision or judgment, Godwin subverts this reading for plot by turning around three days later and writing a new ending for the novel: the text thus allows us to imagine two conclusions, or more. But *Mandeville* terminates in a particularly abrupt and

1 Habermas, "Ernst Bloch," 70.

shocking way: although he may be 52 when he tells his story (p. 228, note 4), the novel ends much earlier with the title character contemplating his disfigured face in a mirror when he is just short of 21. Did Godwin intend the novel to end where it does?

It is often assumed that he did not, and indeed an anonymous author "completed" a Gothic and parodic fourth volume, which is bound with *Mandeville* in the British Library copy.[1] One argument for a presumed fourth volume is Godwin's offhand comment that the novel required six (not four) volumes. Godwin also drafted an Advertisement to a second edition for which he hoped (15 December 1817), in which he says that he planned to end the novel with the Titus Oates conspiracy in 1678,[2] but whether he will ever do so "depends on a variety of circumstances."[3] However, this is more a fantasy for keeping the novel in the public eye than a firm intention, and in the letter asking Constable for a contract, as well as in all correspondence with

---

1   *Mandeville; Or, the Last Words of a Maniac! A Tale of the Seventeenth Century in England. By Himself* (London: Effingham Wilson, 1818). Don Locke (*A Fantasy of Reason: The Life and Thought of William Godwin* [London: Routledge and Kegan Paul, 1980], 277) conjectures that the anonymous author is S.J. Arnold, based on Godwin's comment to Crabb Robinson that *Mandeville* would be finished by Arnold, "who it seems, talked of finishing *Caleb Williams*" (Edith J. Morley, ed., *Henry Crabb Robinson on Books and Their Writers*, 3 vols. [London: Dent, 1938], 1.215). But this comment cannot be taken as fact, still less as an indication of Godwin's intentions. Given that he never saw *Caleb Williams* as needing to be completed, it may well be sarcastic.

2   Titus Oates (1649–1705) was one of the fabricators of an alleged "Popish plot" to kill Charles II that led to the persecution and execution of several Catholics. The point of beginning with the Irish massacre and ending with the Oates conspiracy would presumably have been to show that the Restoration did not resolve Britain's murderous religious factionalism.

3   Morley, *Henry Crabb Robinson*, 1.215; Abinger Collection, c.30, fol. 128. But Godwin's claim in the Advertisement that he "gave the volumes as they stood" because his bookseller came to "my house" and asked for them is a bit disingenuous. Godwin had sent Constable the "last leaf of Mandeville" on 16 October and saw the novel as finished. Promises of further instalments are a common trope in the period, designed to maintain interest, and Godwin was anxious on that score as he saw Constable promoting Scott and minimizing his work (2 December 1817). Moreover, it was around this time that Constable's partner Robert Cadell (1788–1849), who was running out of copies of the novel, was toying with the "ruse" of saying a second edition was in the works (letter of 20 December in *DBF*).

him, Godwin speaks only of a three-volume work. Indeed the three-volume structure is modelled on the three-act structure of a play: the shift from the quotation about Moses in the wilderness from Exodus that provides the epigraph to the first two volumes, to an extract from Shakespeare's more militaristic *Henry V* as an epigraph to Volume 3, signals a structure in which this last volume is appropriately designed as a crisis and climax.

A second argument for a further volume is provided by Mandeville's occasional references to writing from a wiser perspective (pp. 191, 220). But these references are in Volume 2, and in a period prior to the invention of the speed press, authors often handed over long works to the printer in parts. Godwin's correspondence with Constable is full of negotiations on this matter and concerns about the printer being in Edinburgh. So we should not be surprised if there are inconsistencies and holdovers, in effect genuflections to taste, from an earlier stage of conception. At some point Godwin may have thought of the novel as a confession, a form that his novels are often seen as taking. As Foucault argues, during the Reformation and Counter-Reformation confession assumed a new importance as a technique of domination in which, by renouncing past behaviours and "telling all," the subject was normalized, analogically procuring the normalization of his readers.[1] But there is little evidence in the text of this mandatory maturity. More typical is Mandeville's insistence that it is "the torment of the reflex act of the soul, eating into itself, that furnished the spark that lighted up my flame" (p. 195).

I therefore suggest a different hypothesis: that Godwin meant the novel to end with Volume 3, but hit on the scene of Mandeville contemplating his face in a mirror as the most effective finale only at the very end. Godwin wrote to Constable on 19 September 1817, saying that it was hard to imagine being closer to finishing a novel without having done so, but promising the third instalment of Volume 3 in a week (*DBF*). According to his *Diary*, where he documents his daily progress, he finished *Mandeville* on 1 October and started revising this last instalment, but then he interrupted his revisions from 6–8 October to write six more pages, before going back to his revisions. He interrupted the revisions for two days to write a memorial to Curran, who had just died, and to whom he dedicated the novel. He then finished revising on the 17th, wrote the Preface on that day and the next,

---

1   Michel Foucault, "Technologies of the Self," *Ethics, Subjectivity and Truth*, trans. Robert Hurley et al. (New York: New P, 1997), 43.

and sent Constable the remaining pages on the 18th, after which the novel was published on 1 December. Godwin's finishing the novel, only to write another six pages, suggests something very much like what happened with *Caleb Williams*. In other words, it seems possible that he initially ended the novel with the penultimate chapter, whose last paragraph begins "Aye, my story is arrived at a festival" (p. 441), but then added what is now the final chapter, which amounts to roughly six pages in manuscript.[1] It would be hard to overestimate the difference between these two "endings."

Chapter XVI focuses on Henrietta's "betrayal." Had the novel ended here, it would indeed have concluded with the kind of hysterical rant that provoked the anonymous fourth volume subtitled "last words of a maniac!" It would be no more than a domestic story, not much better than *Miserrimus*, an admiring imitation dedicated to Godwin.[2] The further chapter adds two things: the assault on the marriage coach which replaces the Oates conspiracy, and the shift of focus from Henrietta's betrayal to Mandeville himself, whose tone is now tightly controlled and not histrionic. Unlike the previous chapter, which brings Mandeville's psychic disintegration to a head, the final paragraph of this further chapter is the mirror-stage of Mandeville's birth as a subject. Yet this is a subject who survives as what Agamben calls "bare life,"[3] one who has exchanged his position as the son of parents allied with the planters in Ireland for that of a negro slave

---

1 I base this on the ratio between printed pages and the two pages in manuscript that Godwin describes the Preface as occupying.

2 Frederick Reynolds, *"Miserrimus." On a Gravestone in Worcester Cathedral is this emphatic inscription Miserrimus; with neither name nor date, comment nor text* (London: Thomas Hookham, 1833). The novel reduces *Mandeville* to a version of the triangle of Mandeville-Clifford-Henrietta, as Miserrimus is ruined by fatal passion and kills the brother of the woman he loves. The novel echoes Godwin's image of a living body tied to a dead one (63) and has a similar scene in which the protagonist contemplates his wound in a mirror (57–59).

3 The phrase is from Giorgio Agamben, *Homo Sacer: Sovereign Power and Bare Life*, trans. Daniel Heller Roazen (Stanford, CA: Stanford UP 1998), 1–2, 7, 11. Bare life is the remainder that can neither be included nor excluded after the transference of the domestic into the social described by Arendt, which leaves no place for the private person within the *polis* except as that which must be abjected. "Homo sacer" is the name that Agamben gives to this abandoned life of "one who can be killed but not sacrificed" (114).

in a later plantation, and whose very facelessness is the face of anonymous history:

> I had received a deep and perilous gash, the broad brand of which I shall not fail to carry with me to my grave.... My wound is of that sort, which in the French civil wars got the name of *une balafre*. I have pleased myself, in the fury and bitterness of my soul, with tracing the whole force of that word. It is *cicatrix luculenta*, a glazed or shining scar, like the effect of a streak of varnish upon a picture. *Balafré* I find explained by Girolamo Vittori, by the Italian word *smorfiato*; and this again—I mean the noun *smorfia*—is decided by "the resolute" John Florio to signify ... "a mocking or push with one's mouth." The explanation of these lexicographers is happily suited to my case, and the mark I for ever carry about with me. The reader may recollect the descriptions I have occasionally been obliged to give, of the beauty of my person and countenance....When I first looked in my glass, and saw my face, once more stripped of its tedious dressings, I thought I never saw anything so monstrous....The sword of my enemy had given a perpetual grimace, a sort of preternat- ural and unvarying distorted smile, or deadly grin, to my countenance.... Even as certain tyrannical planters in the West Indies have set a brand with a red hot iron upon the negroes they have purchased, to denote that they are irreme- diably a property, so Clifford had set his mark upon me, as a token that I was his for ever. (p. 448)

To be sure the identity Mandeville claims here is defiantly trau- matic, stubbornly attached to the marks and imprints of his sub- jection. Yet there is something triumphant in this (self-)discipline, which comes from the fact that master and slave, Clifford and Mandeville, are finally equals. Now Clifford is indeed tied to Mandeville, as the dead body of England is tied to a living body. Or perhaps not a living body but a body that lives on, in Derrida's particular sense of living on (*sur-vivre*) as "non-closure," a "posi- tion of disturbance," and "the endurance of that which cannot exist."[1] Because Clifford has hurt Mandeville, he is at last guilty; he will never again be "good." The figure that is Clifford has been ruined, disfigured.

---

1   Sarah Guyer, "The Rhetoric of Survival and the Possibility of Romanti- cism," *Studies in Romanticism* 46.2 (2007): 251–52.

Readers have always had difficulty with this ending. One reviewer criticized it for its "*surgically* technical" language and pedantry, dismissing the novel itself for its "elaborate," metaphoric style (Appendix C5, p. 477). But this is to miss the bitterly ironic and shifting tone of the passage: just as Mandeville's Biblical language figures a passion that has found no name, so too the pedantry of this passage is the very cicatrix of which it speaks, a tightening and drying of the skin over a wound. If metaphor, as Ortega y Gasset says, "substitutes one thing for another—from an urge not so much to get at the first as to get rid of the second,"[1] the cicatrix as the scar of this euphemism, this turning away, is the laying bare of the substitutions that inform even the barest facts and the wounds they cover over—a laying bare that is in turn its own form of covering.

The tone of this passage is therefore elusive, at once disturbing, perverse, and exhilarating. We cannot simply dismiss Mandeville as disturbed because we find the scene disturbing. The passage must be turned back on itself, read again and again, not just for Mandeville's resistances but for our own resistances to what does not agree with traditional criteria of "beauty" that lead us to turn away from an ending that is too hard to face. For in it Godwin holds the mirror up to the making of figures and the evasions of reading that make literature conform to taste instead of being the place of the absolute secret. He presents Mandeville reading his face when the "tedious dressings" have been removed to reveal the unvarnished truth behind the symbolic veneer. But even that truth can be grasped only tropologically and rigidly through the commentaries of lexicographers—tropologically or figuratively, because the passage functions as a series of substitutions, turning from French to Latin to Italian, as if to emphasize something that remains withheld, a dark energy that has yet to be deciphered.

But despite this absolute negativity and sense of incompletion, since the novel had begun with an uprising, its return to a moment of rebellion—introverted into Mandeville's private uprising—also brings the plot full circle, giving it a bitterly formal completeness. For Godwin literally follows Mandeville into his closet, so as to bring the concealed psychic violence of history into the open. Throughout the novel, Mandeville has seen himself in terms of disease and wounds (for example, pp. 209, 231, 317,

---

1 José Ortega y Gasset, *The Dehumanization of Art and Other Writings on Art and Culture* (New York: Doubleday, 1956), 31.

346, 365). But they are "secret wound[s]" (p. 331). Whether they are described as psychic or as physical, or as "cancer[s]" that fester within (p. 192), in the terminology of a period increasingly interested in wounds they are not yet strictly "wounds" (Appendix G2a, p. 509). In this final scene, however, the "gaping" wound that has existed all along (p. 251) is made external, allowing Mandeville finally to speak as a survivor of war, so that Godwin can remove the tedious bandages from the myth of Restoration for which the concluding "festival" is only one figure. For given the way Godwin's voice is underlaid in that of his protagonist in the final paragraph, Mandeville in this further ending is not just a private person but the "tablet" of an ongoing cultural memory (p. 210) that continues to be imprinted with the traumas of a damaged history. As important, the concluding reference to slavery also brings the novel full circle into Godwin's present. Returning to the plantations in Ireland with which the novel began, the last sentence links them to the racism and imperialism of Godwin's own time in a circle of political injustice that includes Mandeville's personal wounds. And it reminds us that this circle implicates right and left, the policies of kings from Charles I to George IV, but also the republican Cromwell's transplantation of his rebellious Irish subjects as slaves to the West Indies (*HCE* 4.172–73). The narrative, as we have seen, ends when Mandeville is just short of the age of maturity, even though he actually lives on into the Restoration. And this is because Godwin cannot see his way to the more conventional story of historical maturation in which Britain, unlike France, had its revolution and regicide in a period before the Enlightenment. It is because the violent period before the Glorious Revolution remains, even now, in the moment of our reading, an open wound like the "deep and perilous gash" across Mandeville's face.

William Godwin: A Brief Chronology

1756   Born, 3 March, 7th of 13 children, to Anne Hull and Dissenting minister John Godwin, a strict Calvinist.

1767   Sent to board for three years as the sole pupil of Samuel Newton, a follower of Sandemanianism, an extreme Calvinist sect.

1773–78   Attends Hoxton Academy, a Dissenting Academy in London; becomes a minister at Ware in Hertfordshire.

1779–82   Problems with and doubts about his profession; begins to read freethinking and Enlightenment philosophers such as Rousseau and d'Holbach.

1783   Forced to give up the ministry; moves to London; tries unsuccessfully to start his own school and writes *Account of the Seminary*; decides to make a living as writer; publishes *Life of Chatham*, *Defence of the Rockingham Party* (his first political pamphlet, in defence of Whig politician Charles James Fox), *Herald of Literature* (reviews of fictitious books "about to appear").

1783–84   Anonymously publishes three novels: *Imogen*, *Damon and Delia*, *Italian Letters*.

1785–86   Editor of new Whig journal, *Political Herald and Review*.

1789   Storming of Bastille; French Revolution.

1790   Publishes *The English Peerage* anonymously; writes, but does not publish, *St. Dunstan, A Tragedy*.

1791   Meets Mary Wollstonecraft; they do not get on.

1792   Wollstonecraft's *A Vindication of the Rights of Woman*.

1793   Execution of Louis XVI of France; Reign of Terror begins; 1st edition of *An Enquiry Concerning Political Justice*, widely influential; comes to know many politicians as well as literati, both men and women.

1794   First major novel, *Things as They Are; or, The Adventures of Caleb Williams*; multiple arrests of reformers, including Thomas Hardy (founder of London Corresponding Society), John Thelwall, Thomas Holcroft, and John Horne Tooke; anonymously publishes *Cursory Strictures*, arguing from the constitution against the prosecutions for treason.

1795   Prime Minister William Pitt tries to cripple the radical movement by introducing the two so-called

"Gagging Acts": the Treasonable and Seditious Practices Act and the Seditious Meetings Act; in response, Godwin publishes *Considerations on Lord Grenville's and Mr. Pitt's Bills*.

1796   Second revised edition of *Political Justice*; meets Wollstonecraft again.

1797   Publishes *The Enquirer, Reflections on Education, Manners and Literature*; marries Wollstonecraft, who dies following childbirth; Godwin left to look after daughter Mary and Fanny Imlay, Wollstonecraft's daughter by the American adventurer Gilbert Imlay; adopts Fanny.

1798   *Memoirs* of Wollstonecraft; edits her *Posthumous Works*; 3rd revised edition of *Political Justice*; becomes increasing target of anti-Jacobin abuse.

1799   Second major novel, *St. Leon: A Tale of the Sixteenth Century*.

1800   *Antonio*, a tragedy, is performed, unsuccessful; visits Ireland at invitation of John Philpot Curran; beginnings of cataplexy, a disease of the nervous system.

1801   *Thoughts occasioned by the Perusal of Dr. Parr's Spital Sermon*; writes *Abbas, King of Persia*; after unsuccessfully proposing to Harriet Lee (1798) and Maria Reveley (1799), marries Mary Jane Clairmont, who brings her son Charles and daughter Jane (Claire) into Godwin's home. Though Godwin presents Mary Jane as a widow, both children were born out of wedlock, probably to different fathers.

1803   William Godwin, Jr. born; *Life of Chaucer*; increasing financial troubles.

1805   *Fleetwood; or, The New Man of Feeling*; opens bookshop with Mary Jane to earn a living; writes children's books under pseudonyms Edward Baldwin and Theophilus Marcliffe; *Fables Ancient and Modern* (Baldwin); *The Looking Glass: A True History of the Early Years of an Artist* (Marcliffe).

1806   *Life of Lady Jane Grey* (Marcliffe), *History of England* and *The Pantheon* (Baldwin); Charles James Fox dies.

1807   Godwin's play *Faulkener* is performed; moves family of five children to larger premises at Skinner Street, an up-and-coming neighbourhood which never becomes gentrified; starts Juvenile Library.

1808	As legal title of No. 41 Skinner Street unclear, Godwin stops paying rent.
1809	*Essay on Sepulchres*; *History of Rome* (Baldwin); *Mylius' School Dictionary ... to which is prefixed a New Guide to the English Tongue* (Baldwin).
1810	*Outlines of English Grammar* (Baldwin).
1812	Meets Percy Shelley and his wife Harriet.
1814	Daughter Mary elopes with Shelley and takes Claire Clairmont with them to the Continent.
1815	*Lives of Edward and John Philips, Nephews and Pupils of Milton*; *Letters of Verax*, arguing against war with France; Battle of Waterloo.
1816	Travels to Edinburgh and meets Walter Scott; Fanny (Imlay) Godwin commits suicide in Swansea.
1817	The Treason Act, 1817; *Mandeville: A Tale of the Seventeenth Century*.
1818	*Letter of Advice to a Young American*.
1819	Suffers stroke. Following the Peterloo Massacre, when a cavalry charge brutally suppressed a massive protest in Manchester, "Six Acts" introduced to curtail freedom of association, freedom of the press, and freedom of speech.
1820	Response to Malthus, *Of Population*.
1821	Publishes letters on Ireland, population.
1822	*History of Greece* (Baldwin); evicted from Skinner Street.
1823	Increasing ill health as cataplexy worsens; following Shelley's death, Mary Shelley returns to England with son Percy Florence (Godwin's only descendant).
1824–28	*History of the Commonwealth of England*.
1825	Declares bankruptcy, sells Juvenile Library; national financial crisis which brings down banks and publishing houses.
1830	*Cloudesley: a novel*.
1831	*Thoughts on Man*; Mary Shelley writes memoir of Godwin.
1832	William Jr. dies of cholera.
1833	*Deloraine*, Godwin's last novel.
1834	*Lives of the Necromancers*.
1835	*Genius of Christianity Unveiled*, a critique of Christianity; withheld by Mary Shelley and published in 1873. Publishes son's novel *The Orphans of Unwalden, or the Soul's Transfusion*, with a memoir.

1836   Dies, 7 April, with Mary Jane and Mary Shelley at
        his side; Mary Shelley begins biography of Godwin
        but gives it up to produce official edition of Shelley's
        poems.
1841   Mary Jane Clairmont dies.
1851   Mary Shelley dies.

A Note on the Text

The text is based on the first and only authorized edition of the novel (Edinburgh and London: Constable and Co., and Longman, Hurst, Rees and Brown). The novel was not reprinted until its inclusion in 1992 as volume 5 of Godwin's *Collected Novels and Memoirs* (*CNM*), though two pirated editions were published in 1818 in Philadelphia (M. Thomas; printed by J. Maxwell) and New York (W.B. Gilley), and there was also a contemporary French translation (see Appendix C8, p. 479). The manuscript of the novel was sold after Godwin's death in 1836 to Dawson Turner, an antiquarian and botanist who bought several other Godwin manuscripts. It was again sold in 1859 and cannot now be traced.

The American editions differ from the original in some important respects. Both are in two and not three volumes. The New York edition ends its first volume with Chapter IX of the original edition's second volume, while the Philadelphia edition ends its first volume with Chapter VII. While the original has an epigraph from *Exodus* on the title pages of the first two volumes, and one from Shakespeare's *Henry V* on the title page of the third volume, both American editions include only the first epigraph, thus destroying the three-act dramatic structure of the original, in which there is a turn from melancholia and exile to action at the beginning of the final volume. They also omit Godwin's important note on Shaftesbury at the end of the original second volume.

I have retained the original spellings and punctuation in both *Mandeville* and the Appendices, correcting only obvious errors. *Mandeville* is an extraordinarily learned text, and the title character frequently quotes from the Bible, Milton, and other writers. There are numerous citations of Shakespeare, particularly *Hamlet*, *Macbeth*, and *Othello*, which is also an important intertext for Godwin's third novel, *Fleetwood*. This learning, and indeed pedantry, are a vital part of the character of Charles Mandeville, who uses literary and religious quotation as a form of psychological armour and as a way of marking himself as a special individual. While I provide references for long quotations, I have annotated brief quotations from Shakespeare and the Bible only when they are significant. For a thorough tracing of the allusions the reader can consult Pamela Clemit's invaluable edition of the novel in the *CNM*.

Three thousand copies of *Mandeville* were printed, and the novel, according to Constable's partner, Robert Cadell, was attended with "prominent success," such that Cadell, who had been cautious about a second edition in early December 1817, leaned toward it by mid-December, based on what seemed to be the "rapid sale" of the 3,000. A few days later, unable to find copies to ship to Ireland, he was speculating on a second edition of 1,500–2,000, and despite the risks that sales might have peaked, he concluded: "We cannot do any I think but print a new Edition instantly." But by the end of the month he had backed off in response to discouragement from Constable himself.[1] Nevertheless, Johann Hüttner, a German correspondent in London who reported on recent works to Goethe, is typical in not having a taste for the novel, yet conceding that of the new novels "none had extended its reputation beyond the lending libraries as much as this one."[2] Though many have been keen to pronounce *Mandeville* a failure, the facts are more complex, and 3,000 was actually not a small print run at the time.[3]

1 *DBF*, letters from Cadell to Constable (4, 15, 20, and 26 December 1817).
2 Christian Deuling, "Mediating Literature: The German Foreign Correspondent Johann Christian Hüttner (1766–1847) in London," in *Informal Romanticism*, ed. James Vigus (Trier: Wissenschaftlicher Verlag, 2012), 45–46.
3 *Mandeville* was seen as being in competition with Walter Scott's contemporaneous *Rob Roy* (*DBF*, letter from Cadell to Constable, 20 December 20 1817). But though Godwin was far from being as successful as Scott, the above figures were actually good: 500–750 was a typical run, even for a novel. See the Introduction by Michael F. Suarez and articles by James Raven and Katherine Sutherland, in *The Book in Britain: Vol. 5, 1695–1830*, ed. Michael F. Suarez and Michael L. Turner (Cambridge: Cambridge UP, 2009), 30, 92, 680.

Historical Timeline for Mandeville

1594–1603   Nine Years' War or Tyrone's Rebellion in Ireland;
             Hugh O'Neill fights against English rule in Ireland.
1599   Birth of Oliver Cromwell.
1603–25   Reign of James I, King of England and Ireland
             (King of Scotland, as James VI, from 1567); called
             himself King of Great Britain.
1618–48   Thirty Years' War: war encompassing most of
             Europe, initially religious and then political,
             involving France and Habsburg powers.
1625   Accession of Charles I and his marriage to
             Catholic Henrietta Maria of France.
1625–26   Attempted impeachments of James Villiers, Duke
             of Buckingham (James's favourite and then
             Charles's Chief Minister); to prevent this, Charles
             dissolves Parliament in 1625 and 1626.
1627–28   Charles sends expedition to help French
             Huguenots; dissolves Parliament (1628); Bucking-
             ham assassinated (1628).
1628   Charles assembles new parliament (1628–29)
             which includes Cromwell as MP for Huntingdon.
1629–40   "Eleven Years' Tyranny" during which Charles
             does not recall Parliament.
1633–39   Thomas Wentworth (later Earl of Strafford), Lord
             Deputy of Ireland, raises taxes from Irish Catholic
             gentry, promising religious concessions.
1638–59   **Events of *Mandeville*.**
1640   *Short* Parliament (3 weeks); Charles recalls Parlia-
             ment briefly to raise money to quell Scottish
             rebellion; Strafford recalled to England; sent to
             quell rebellion in Scotland.
1641   Strafford executed by Bill of Attainder; Ulster
             Rebellion: Irish fear resurgence of Protestant
             power after execution of Strafford.
1641–42   John Milton's five anti-prelatical tracts, arguing
             against the episcopal form of church government
             (Milton later served as Cromwell's Secretary for
             Foreign Tongues, 1649–59).
1640–45   Charles's close advisor Archbishop Laud tries to
             impose episcopacy in Scotland (1640); Laud

imprisoned in 1641, tried and executed by Bill of Attainder in 1645.

1640–53   *Long* Parliament (known as Rump Parliament after 1648); Cromwell MP for Cambridge (1640–42); Charles at odds with increasingly powerful parliament; Charles suspected of sympathy for Catholic Irish.

1642–46   First English Civil War: conflicts and machinations between Roundheads (Parliamentarians) and Cavaliers (Royalists).

1645   Parliamentary Puritans introduce professional army known as the New Model Army, which was disbanded at the Restoration.

1647   Levellers' manifesto, "Agreement of the People" (extended version issued May 1649); failed Putney Debates between Levellers (John Lilburne, Richard Overton, William Walwyn) and Cromwell and Henry Ireton, which aimed at new constitution. Levellers influential in New Model Army.

1648–49   Second English Civil War.

1648   Charles I negotiates secret treaty with Scots, promising religious concessions; they promise to help restore him to throne; Scottish invasion of England; Parliament divided on Charles's rule. Execution of Royalists Sir Charles Lucas and Sir George Lisle (28 August); Pride's Purge, in which members wanting to negotiate with King were prevented from sitting for parliament by New Model Army (December), thus reducing Long Parliament to "Rump Parliament" of 80; Charles imprisoned in Hurst and then Windsor Castles.

1649–53   "Commonwealth" period.

1649–51   Third Civil War: conflict between parliamentarians and supporters of Charles II; conflict of England with Ireland and Scotland; 30% of Irish population killed or exiled during this period.

1649   Charles tried for treason by Rump Parliament, executed (30 January); Scottish Covenanter Parliament proclaims Charles II as King of Great Britain, but will not let him enter Scotland unless he proclaims Presbyterianism throughout Britain and Ireland (6 February); Council of State appointed (14 February), rules along with Rump Parliament; Parliament abolishes monarchy and House of Lords (March); arrest of

Leveller leaders for sedition (28 March); Diggers' or "True Levellers'" Manifesto published by Gerrard Winstanley and others (20 April); England declared a "Commonwealth or free state" (19 May); act outlawing unlicensed publications (20 September); Cromwell becomes Governor of Ireland; Massacre of Drogheda (September); Cromwell brutally suppresses Irish Royalists during his Irish campaign (1649–50).

1650   Cromwell appointed Commander-in-Chief of New Model Army; Charles II lands in Scotland, and becomes King of Scotland; in response to this threat, Cromwell leaves Ireland and returns to England; Charles concludes Treaty of Breda, securing alliance with Scottish Covenanters; Parliament passes Blasphemy Act to suppress radical religious sects (9 August); Cromwell defeats Covenanters at Battle of Dunbar (3 September).

1651   Charles II crowned at Scone in Scotland (1 January), Commonwealth recognizes him only as King of Scots; Charles and Scots invade England (5 August); final defeat by Parliamentarians at battle of Worcester (3 September).

1652   Fleetwood, Cromwell's son-in-law, appointed Governor of Ireland; Act for the Settlement of Ireland (12 August): mass confiscations of property and executions.

1653   Cromwell dissolves Rump Parliament (20 April); Nominated Assembly known as Barebones Parliament assembles (24 July), consists of 140 members, including only five and six for Scotland and Ireland respectively (who were English soldiers serving there); Cromwell becomes Lord Protector (16 December).

1655   Penruddock Uprising by Royalists.

1658   Death of Cromwell at age 59 (3 September); replaced by his son Richard.

1659   Richard Cromwell deposed by military junta; Commonwealth briefly restored.

1660   Restoration of Charles II (b. 1630).

1667   Milton, *Paradise Lost* (rev. ed. 1674).

1678   John Bunyan, *The Pilgrim's Progress*.

1685   Death of Charles II, succeeded by his brother James II.

1688   Glorious Revolution: James II deposed and replaced by his son-in-law William of Orange, beginning

	England's parliamentary monarchy. William establishes Convention Parliament.
1689	Bill of Rights, presented by the Convention Parliament, invites William and Mary to become joint sovereigns of England.
1701	Act of Settlement settles the royal succession on the Electress Sophia of Hanover and her successors.
1707	Union of England and Scotland (creation of Great Britain).
1715	Jacobite Rebellion ("The Fifteen"), to restore James II to British monarchy.
1719	Jacobite Rebellion ("The Nineteen").
1745	Jacobite Rebellion ("The Forty Five").
1756	Birth of William Godwin.
1760	George III comes to the throne; King till 1820.
1776	American Revolution begins.
1783	William Pitt the Younger becomes Prime Minister.
1789	French Revolution begins.
1790	Edmund Burke, *Reflections on the Revolution in France*.
1792	Reformer Thomas Hardy founds London Corresponding Society; Thomas Paine, *Rights of Man*; Mary Wollstonecraft, *Vindication of the Rights of Woman*.
1793	Godwin, *Enquiry concerning Political Justice* (1st ed.).
1793–94	Execution of Louis XVI of France: Reign of Terror.
1794–95	Treason Trials and Gagging Acts (see Godwin Chronology, p. 47): Pitt attempts to cripple English radical movement.
1798	Irish Uprising, led by barrister and revolutionary Wolfe Tone (1763–98); 3rd edition of *Political Justice*; Napoleon invades Egypt; Joseph Johnson, radical publisher, imprisoned for "seditious libel."
1800	Union of Great Britain and Ireland (to form United Kingdom).
1804–15	Napoleon's reign as emperor.
1806	Battle of Jena, University of Jena destroyed.
1807	Napoleon invades Germany.
1811–20	Regency period: Prince Regent, later George IV, rules in place of "mad" King George III.
1814	Walter Scott, *Waverley*.
1815	Battle of Waterloo, final defeat of Napoleon.
1816	Caroline Lamb's *Glenarvon*, a *roman à clef* in which Byron is the leader of the 1798 Irish Uprising.
1817	*Mandeville*.

MANDEVILLE.

A TALE

OF THE SEVENTEENTH CENTURY

IN

ENGLAND.

BY WILLIAM GODWIN.

———

And the waters of that fountain were bitter: and they said, Let the name of it be called Marah.

Exodus, Cap. xv.

———

IN THREE VOLUMES.

———

VOL. I.

EDINBURGH:

PRINTED FOR ARCHIBALD CONSTABLE AND CO.
AND LONGMAN, HURST, REES, ORME, AND BROWN,
LONDON.

———

1817.

[DEDICATION]

To the memory of the sincerest friend I ever
had, the late John Philpot Curran, (who a few
days since quitted this mortal stage) I affectionately inscribe these volumes.

[William Godwin,] October 25, 1817.

C. Baldwann

PREFACE[1]

Approaching, as I now very rapidly do, to the period when I must bid the world an everlasting farewel, I am not unwilling to make up my accounts with it, as far as relates to this lighter species of composition. On this occasion, I am contented to talk, to that small portion of the world whose eye is ever likely to light upon these prefatory pages, with the communicativeness of an intimate friend.

Eight years ago I began a novel.[2] The thought I adopted as the germ of my work, was taken from the story of the Seven Sleepers in the records of the first centuries of Christianity,[3] or rather from the Sleeping Beauty in the Wood, in Perrault's Tales of *Ma Mere L'Oie*.[4] I supposed a hero who should have this faculty, or this infirmity, of falling asleep unexpectedly, and should sleep twenty, thirty, or a hundred years at a time, at the pleasure of myself, his creator. I knew that such a canvas would naturally admit a vast variety of figures, actions, and surprises.

When my respectable friend, the publisher of the present work,[5] found means to put in activity the suspended faculty of fiction within me, I resolved to return to the tale which, eight years before, I had laid aside. But the nearer I looked at it, the more I was frightened at the task. Such a work must be made up of a variety of successive tales, having for their main point of connection, the impression which the events brought forward should produce on my sleeping-waking principal personage. I should therefore have had at least a dozen times to set myself to the task of invention, as it were, *de novo*.[6] I judged it more prudent, par-

---

1 Godwin wrote the Preface after completing the novel (*Diary*, 17–18 October 1817), but had drafted twelve lines of it earlier (*Diary*, 26 November 1816).

2 See Appendix A, p. 449.

3 The seven sleepers of Ephesus, later canonized, were third-century Christians who slept in a cave in Turkey to escape the persecutions of the Emperor Decius. According to legend, they woke up two centuries later in the reign of Emperor Theodosius and restored his faith. Mary Shelley also refers to this legend, a figure for getting a second chance, in her *Mathilda* (1819; 188). But see Introduction, p. 16, for Godwin's use of the legend as also a figure for repression.

4 Charles Perrault (1628–1703), whose collection of fairy tales including "Bluebeard" and the "Sleeping Beauty in the Wood" was translated into English as *Mother Goose Tales* (1729).

5 The Scottish publisher Archibald Constable (1774–1827); see Introduction, p. 15.

6 Anew.

ticularly regarding certain disadvantages under which I found myself, to choose a story that should be more strictly one, and should so have a greater degree of momentum, tending to carry me forward, after the first impulse given, by one incessant motion, from the commencement to the conclusion. Such was my motive for rejecting my former subject, and adopting that which is here treated.

Every author, at least for the last two thousand years, takes his hint from some suggestion afforded by an author that has gone before him, as Sterne has very humorously observed;[1] and I do not pretend to be an exception to this rule. The impression, that first led me to look with an eye of favour upon the subject here treated, was derived from a story-book, called Wieland, written by a person, certainly of distinguished genius, who I believe was born and died in the province of Pennsylvania in the United States of North America, and who calls himself C.B. Brown.[2] This impression was further improved from some hints in De Montfort, a tragedy, by Joanna Baillie.[3] Having signed these bills against me, I hold myself for the present occasion discharged from all claims of my literary creditors, except such as are purely transient and incidental.

To proceed in the same style of confession and unreserve. I am not aware that, in my capacity as an author, I owe any considerable thanks to the kindness of my contemporaries; yet I part from them without the slightest tinge of ill-humour. If ever they have received my productions with welcome, it has been because the same public impression, or the same tone of moral feeling, had been previously generated in the minds of a considerable portion of my species, and in my own. When I have written merely from a private sentiment, and thought to try whether, as Marmontel says, they valued me for myself,[4] (which I did in the Essay on Sepulchres, and the Lives of the Nephews of Milton)[5] my recep-

---

1 [Godwin's note:] Tristram Shandy, Vol. I. chap. xxi. Edition 1775.

2 *Wieland; or, The Transformation: An American Tale* (1798). The American writer Charles Brockden Brown (1771–1810) is thought to have been influenced by Godwin's *Caleb Williams* (1794).

3 Joanna Baillie (1762–1851) wrote *De Monfort* (1798), one of several plays on the "Stronger Passions of the Mind." Godwin's reference to "literary creditors" ironically alludes to the fact that he was perpetually in debt.

4 "Alcibiades, or the Self," by Jean-François Marmontel (1723–99), is a story about a hero who wants to be loved only for himself.

5 During the period when his "powers of fiction" were "suspended" (1805–17) Godwin turned to historical non-fiction. Both the *Essay on*

tion has been such, as might be well calculated to cure me, if I had been constitutionally liable to the intoxications of vanity. Yet I have never truckled to the world. I have never published any thing with the slightest purpose to take advantage of the caprice of the day, to approach the public on its weak side, or to pamper its frailties. What I have produced, was written merely in obedience to that spirit, unshackled and independent, whatever were its other qualities, that commanded me to take up my pen.

There are two or three things, which I still meditate to perform in my character of an author. But whether life, and health, and leisure will be granted me sufficient for the execution of what I design, is among the secrets of "time not yet in existence." In either event I feel myself altogether satisfied and resigned.

Sepulchres: or, A Proposal for erecting some memorial of the Illustrious Dead, in all ages on the spot where their remains have been interred (1809), and the *Lives of Edward and John Philips, Nephews and Pupils of Milton* (1815) are experiments in minor or anonymous history. On the *Lives*, see Introduction, pp. 11–13.

CHAPTER I

I was born in the year 1638. The place of my birth was the borough of Charlemont,[1] in the north of Ireland. My great uncle passed over to that country in the train of the Earl of Essex, in his famous and unfortunate expedition thither undertaken forty years before.[2] The military reputation of my great-uncle was considerable, and he died full of years and of honour, under the pacific administration of Sir Arthur Chichester.[3] My father, who, as well as my great-uncle, was a younger brother, was bred to the same profession, was sent over to Ireland for the advantage of being under his uncle's eye, and was at this time an officer in the garrison of Charlemont under William Lord Caulfield, a brave officer, now grown old in the service of his sovereign.[4]

Ireland was a country that had been for ages in a state of disturbance and violence. No people were ever more proud of their ancestry and their independence than the Irish, or more wedded to their old habits of living;—and the policy of the English administration had not been such as to wean them in any degree

---

1 A town in Armagh, one of the counties of Ulster.

2 Robert Devereux, 2nd Earl of Essex (1567–1601) and favourite of Elizabeth I, was briefly Lord Lieutenant of Ireland in 1599. He was sent to suppress the rebellion of Hugh O'Neill, Earl of Tyrone, but signed a truce with him and went back to England, where he was executed after an abortive coup against the government. His son, the 3rd Earl of Essex, opposed Charles I and receives limited praise from Godwin in *HCE* (1.17, 34–35).

3 Arthur Chichester (1563–1625), brought to Ireland by Essex, was Lord Deputy of Ireland from 1605 to 1616, after the end of the Nine Years' War (1594–1603), also known as Tyrone's Rebellion. He oversaw widespread persecution of the Irish Catholics, whom he saw as a major threat to the crown. "Pacific" denotes a regime of pacification.

4 Sir William Caulfeild, or Caulfield (1587–1640), 2nd Baron Charlemont and governor of Fort Charlemont. The Barons and Viscounts Charlemont were the greatest landowners in County Armagh from the time of Elizabeth I. After the death of the 3rd Baron Toby, who replaced his father as governor upon the latter's death and who was shot in 1642 on the orders of Phelim O'Neile, and after the death of the 4th Baron Robert (1622–42?) from an overdose of opium, the third son William (1624–71) became 5th Baron. Godwin seems to confuse the two William Caulfeilds in suggesting that the William Caulfeild "now grown old in the service of his sovereign" at the time Mandeville writes his memoirs is the same William Caulfeild under whom Mandeville's father served.

from the partialities to which they were prone. The latter years of
Elizabeth however had conduced much to the enfeebling of their
military strength; and the pacific system of James seemed, for a
long time, to be no where attended with so much success as in
this island.[1] His system in Ireland, was that of colonization,[2] of
placing large bodies of civilized strangers in every great station
through the country, and undertaking, by a variety of means, to
reclaim the wild Irish from what might almost be called their
savage state. The government of his lieutenants and deputies was
not exactly that of benignity;—it was characterized by many forfeitures, and by a vexatious inquiry, in every direction successively, into the titles by which the Irish chieftains held their
estates; but it was so equally tempered with severity and firmness,
as to produce the spectacle, scarcely before known, of a profound
peace in the island for almost forty years.

It was towards the close of this period that Thomas Lord Strafford was appointed, by Charles I, to the office of Lord-Lieutenant.[3] In his government there was a greater proportion of
sternness than in that of his predecessors; his character was in the
highest degree arrogant and imperious, but there was a steadiness
in his measures, and his proceedings were stamped with the features of intellect and ability,—so as to appear well calculated to

---

1 Elizabeth I (1533–1603) reigned from 1558 until her death. James VI of
   Scotland and I of England (1566–1625), son of her rival Mary, Queen
   of Scots, was King of Scots from 1567, and King of England and
   Ireland from 1603 (although England and Scotland remained individual
   sovereign states until the Act of Union in 1707). "Pacific" means "paci-
   fying"; James was often called the "Pacific King."
2 "Plantation," literally and metaphorically, was a civilizing project involving the planting of English virtues in Irish soil. It could consist in a slow
   "Anglicization" or a more drastic "colonization" that involved the
   uprooting of the existing culture and seizure of land. Thus, while the
   early modern use of the term "colony" to denote a group of settlers or
   emigrants is sometimes taken to be less imperialist than our understanding of the term, the line between this practice and a more centralized
   colonialism is difficult to draw even in this period. Of the period before
   the events of the novel, Godwin says that James I had "sen[t] over
   numerous colonies from Great Britain, with the alleged purpose of
   reclaiming the wild inhabitants, and improving the neglected soil, so as
   to render that country a valuable appendage to the empire" (*HCE*
   1.216).
3 Charles I (1600–49) reigned from 1625 until his beheading in 1649.
   Thomas Wentworth, 1st Earl of Strafford (1593–1641), was his Chief
   Minister and Lord Deputy of Ireland from 1633 to 1639.

impress a people like the Irish with awe and respect. They hated him, but you could scarcely see that they hated him. They did not, even to their own thoughts, fully analyze and confess their passions; they felt towards him the sensations inspired by a sort of superior nature,—the core of their thoughts was dread and aversion; but their gestures were paralyzed; the expression of these sentiments died away upon their tongue; the public language that followed him was that of approbation and honour. Ireland was substantially less tranquillized than under Sir Arthur Chichester, and the other predecessors of their present austere ruler; but it exhibited every external indication of tranquillity and submission.

Strafford was finally withdrawn from the government of Ireland in the beginning of the year 1640. His absence was intended to be short; but the growing convulsions of his native country detained him, and he never returned. This produced a very new state of things in the country where he had presided. His successors were not of a character to impress either respect or terror upon the people they governed, and the Irish began to reflect in an independent spirit upon their condition. An unexpected view of things opened upon their thoughts. They had contemplated the ascendancy of the English government as a detested thing; but, at the same time, as an evil that it was as much in vain to struggle against, as the laws of nature, or the convulsions of the elements. The other subjects of this government had, for some time, been under different impressions. The people of North Britain, offended with the injudicious and narrow-minded efforts that had been employed to impose upon them episcopacy and a liturgy, had risen in open resistance against the tyranny, and had quelled the oppressor.[1] The English, who had long despised the naked and unvarnished despotism that had been attempted over them, were now ripe for the combined and

---

1 James I used the terms "north" and "south" Britain for Scotland and England respectively. The reference here is to the Bishops' Wars (1639–40), which revolved around the contention between the Presbyterian system of governance (without bishops) favoured by the Scottish people, and Charles I's desire to impose on Scotland an Episcopalian system of church government (with bishops). Godwin discusses the political implications of the two systems of church government in *HCE*, 1.41–49 (see Appendix E3, p. 492). Charles's desire to introduce an Anglican-type liturgy can be read with Godwin's comment that "mere form" in religion is conducive to a mentality that "retain[s] things sluggishly in their present posture" (*HCE* 1.50).

irresistible assertion of their rights. The Long Parliament assembled towards the close of 1640;[1] and they began their operations with an open attack on the confidential ministers of Charles I. Strafford in particular was the object of their unrelenting prosecution, and he was put to death by the sentence of the highest court of judicature, in the spring of the following year.[2]

All this was greatly encouraging to the Irish. The period was favourable; and if they neglected to improve it, they would

---

1   From 1629 to 1640, Charles I exercised Personal Rule and did not call parliament. In April 1640 he recalled it to raise money to quell a rebellion in Scotland, but dissolved the Short Parliament after three weeks. He again called it in November 1640 for financial reasons, and the Long Parliament then sat from 1640 to 1653.

2   Strafford was recalled from Ireland in 1640. Caught in the struggle between Charles and Parliament, he was impeached by the House of Commons, and 26 of the 40 articles against him concerned his Irish administration. The case was complicated because, technically, high treason could only be against the King and not the people; the Parliamentarians therefore argued that to act against the people and divide the King from his people was treason. In his eighteen-day "trial" by Parliament Strafford conducted his defence with eloquence (*HCE* 1.88–89). Fearful that the impeachment might fail, the Parliamentarians passed a Bill of Attainder (21 April 1641) which pronounced Strafford guilty and circumvented the need for a public trial. Charles tried to save him, but was compelled to sign his death warrant, and Strafford was executed on 12 May 1641. In *HCE* (1.86–96), where he discusses Strafford at length, Godwin sees him as inheriting the spirit of "liberty" from his family, only to become "the most dangerous man to the liberties of England then present," as he ingratiated himself into Charles's favour. While allowing that Strafford was technically innocent of treason, if treason is defined as being against the King and not the people, Godwin sees his execution as a national imperative. For Godwin the Bill raises complex ethical issues of law vs. justice; indeed Godwin's republican heroes were not unanimous in voting for it. But while allowing that law restrains the community "from exercising their natural liberty of being the judge and the chastiser of their own wrongs," he argues that there are "extraordinary" cases in which law must be suspended for a higher and future good. Indeed, even though Strafford was never given a legal trial, Godwin speaks of the parliamentary proceeding as if it were a trial with the possibility of acquittal (1.88–90). The more moderate account of Strafford in the novel may be the result of an overlaying of Mandeville's voice on Godwin's; yet the intertwining of the two voices is evident in the description of the Long Parliament of John Selden (1584–1654), John Hampden (1595–1643), and John Pym (1584–1643)—Godwin's republican heroes in *HCE*—as "the highest court of judicature."

deserve to be slaves.[1] They had both example and opportunity to animate their efforts. What they had suffered before, they now ventured to shape into thoughts; and what they thought, they dared to speak. Their murmurs were audible; and the stream of the population was agitated, like ocean before a storm.

The discontents of Ireland were first published through the constitutional medium, her parliament. This assembly sent over her commissioners, to assist the English legislature with additional charges against Strafford. They called loudly for the redress of some of the most oppressive grievances that had been imposed by the stern lord-lieutenant. They demanded the establishment of certain *graces*,[2] which had long been promised by the crown, and the object of which was to quiet the litigious and technical inquiries at law, that had too frequently been set on foot to disturb the Irish landed proprietors in their possessions. Thus far all was well; and the puritan and the papist had gone hand in hand in the assertion of general right.

But there was another and a deeper discontent at work in this unhappy country. The majority of its population was Catholic, and all the religious emoluments of Ireland were reserved for the Protestants. The country had struggled for ages for her independence; it was a war of the oppressor against the oppressed; of civilized man, or man claiming to be such, against man almost in a state of barbarism; and, incidentally only, for nearly a century past, of the two great denominations of the Christian religion against each other. The party, or rather the great mass of the population of the country, who were in opposition to the government, felt that they were the ancient proprietors of the soil. Irish manners and Irish sentiments, every thing that was local in

---

1 The word, picked up in the novel's last sentence, is not entirely metaphoric. Irish *slavery* (as distinct from serfdom) existed before African slavery. Under James I, Charles I, and Cromwell, thousands of Irish were sent to the West Indies as slaves. In *HCE* Godwin refers to England "buy[ing] and sell[ing]" the Irish (1.231). He also refers to (English) prisoners taken after Penruddock's insurrection in 1655 (see p. 197, note 1) being shipped to the West Indies as "slaves," though their slavery was limited to five years, unlike that of the negroes on the sugar plantations (4.172–73). "Galley" and "penal" slavery are not quite the same thing as the "chattel" slavery instituted on the basis of race, but in the case of the Irish they come perilously close.

2 The "Graces" or "Matters of Grace and Bounty to Ireland" were legal and governmental concessions made to the Irish in return for their cooperation.

human society, was with them; the party that, in a great majority of cases, lorded it over them, they regarded as aliens. And when we add to this general view of the case, the recollection that must necessarily accompany it, of all the individual circumstances, and all the bitter aggravations that attended each act of oppression, we may easily conceive what must have been the state of the Irish mind. But all this would have been a matter of infinitely less magnitude than it actually was, had it not been inextricably bound up with considerations of religion. The artifices, or rather the mistakes and bigotry of the priesthood, infused a venom into the hostility existing on either side, that all together gave "note of a fearful preparation."[1] These things I can state impartially now; but it is through a course of incredible mischief and suffering only that I have learned this impartiality.

The calamities that overwhelmed Ireland towards the close of the year 1641, might in part have been foreseen by a skilful observer, but not by such men as then sat at the helm of her government. There is no instance perhaps in the records of mankind, of such profound supineness and security upon the eve of so terrible a storm. I am not, however, writing a piece of national history; and therefore I shall only say, that the conspirators had finally chosen the 23d of October, as the day on which their insurrection should break out through a very extensive line of country.[2]

The principal leader of the conspirators in the province of Ulster, was Sir Phelim O'Neile.[3] He was of a licentious and brutal temper, oppressed with debts, stirred up with the ambition

---

1 From Shakespeare's *Henry V*, 4.Chorus.14, "Give dreadful note of preparation," on the impending battle between the English and French. Along with *Hamlet, Macbeth*, and *Othello, Henry V* is one of the Shakespeare plays most frequently evoked in this text.

2 The episode is known as the Ulster Rebellion, a name also sometimes given to the Irish Uprising of 1798. The uprising, which continued over ten years, was spearheaded by Catholic gentry rather than by the utterly dispossessed.

3 Sir Phelim O'Neile (c. 1604–53) was one of the leaders of the Ulster Rebellion. Later captured by the Parliament forces in 1653, he was offered a pardon if he would confess that his commission in instigating the rebellion came from Charles I, but he refused and was executed. The negative portrayal of O'Neile here expresses Mandeville's point of view as the son of Presbyterian settlers. Godwin's account of O'Neile in *HCE*, and particularly of Charles I's role in the Ulster Rebellion (and thus the underlying contradictions in the political scene of the Civil War period), is far more nuanced.

of standing at the head of his name and figuring as the O'Neiles his predecessors had done, and unscrupulous as to the means by which his purposes were to be achieved. The first exploit marked out for him, was the gaining possession of Charlemont. The most obvious step towards that end that suggested itself to his thoughts, was to invite himself to sup in the castle, with Lord Caulfield[1] and the principal officers of the garrison, on the night of the 22d of October. This nobleman, who was accustomed to live with his Irish neighbours on terms of unsuspecting confidence, cheerfully accepted the proposal. No symptom of hostility had shown itself; every thing was as in a state of the most perfect peace and security. Sir Phelim came, attended with a numerous train of followers; but this occasioned no surprise; it was the custom of the times. His manner was frank, companionable and courteous. Lord Caulfield was particularly desirous to do honour to his guest. The rugged chieftain was gifted with a considerable vein of convivial humour; and the officers of the garrison exerted themselves to catch his tone, and be as easy, mirthful, unrestrained and confiding, as he apparently was. The wine circulated; a general face of festivity prevailed; the song, the jest, the tale, was occasionally interspersed; every thing bespoke the fair and friendly meaning both of the entertainer and his guests. Lord Caulfield expressed himself as conceiving a happy omen, from this sociable meeting of the ancient Irish and the English settlers; and Sir Phelim echoed his sentiment, and devoutly prayed that no future misunderstanding might ever occur to disturb so edifying a harmony.

The entertainment had at length advanced to that point, that the good humour of those who feasted was not unproductive of some obstreperous symptoms of hilarity; yet a noise was suddenly heard from without, that fixed the attention of all, and overpowered for a moment the mirth that went round the board. It was the sound of a scuffle; but that speedily subsided, and was succeeded by the sound of many feet as in military movement. The eyes of those at the table were turned on each other. The visages of Sir Phelim and his friends were evidently firm and unruffled; not so the governor and his English officers. The apartment where they sat had doors at the two opposite ends; these doors suddenly flew open; and a file of Irish, appropriately armed,

---

1 Toby Caulfeild, 3rd Baron Charlemont (1621–42), succeeded his father as Governor of Charlemont and was shot on the orders of O'Neile. Toby's younger brother William, the 5th Baron, was instrumental in O'Neile's apprehension and execution; see above, p. 65, note 4.

entered at each. Lord Caulfield rose to expostulate; but Sir Phelim suddenly stopped him, with the air of a man who feels that he has the game in his own hands.

"Lord governor," said he, "and as many of the officers of the garrison as I see here, I have come among you in frolic and merriment, but the purpose of my visit is serious. You are my prisoners. It is in vain to resist; your men are already secured; you shall have no reason to complain of your treatment; we mean you no harm. But to-morrow all Ireland rises in the assertion of her rights. Our plan is entire and unbroken; Dublin is ours; every fort and garrison in Ulster, Leinster, Munster, and Connaught,[1] is ours. We meditate no injury; not a drop of blood shall be shed, if it is in our power to avoid it. But we will have our rights. We will not be trampled upon as we have been by a handful of foreigners; we will not submit to have our estates torn from us, because we or our ancestors have meritoriously drawn our swords in the sacred cause of our country; we will not allow our inability to produce certain deeds and musty parchments, to be set up against immemorial possession to oust us of our lands; we are resolved that the holy Catholic faith, to which every man of Ireland is a sincere adherent, shall no longer go naked, like a dishonoured wanderer, but shall be clothed again in all her pristine magnificence and splendour. I repeat, we bear you no hostility; we mean you no harm; but this castle of Charlemont we claim for us and our cause; and you must be contented for the present to remain my prisoners."

Lord Caulfield felt the indignation of a soldier at the language addressed to him. He reminded Sir Phelim that he had himself nothing to complain of, that could in any degree excuse his revolt from his sovereign. His family had experienced no severity from the government, nor been deprived of any of their possessions. He had been bred a Protestant, and must first be a recreant[2] to the religion in which he had been instructed, before he could be a traitor to his king. The governor added, with emphasis and fervour, that no cause could be honourable that was served by such means. "You came under my roof as a friend; I exerted myself to receive you, as became your rank and your former life. You have abused my hospitality; you have treacherously used the

---

1 The four provinces of Ireland, to the north, east, south, and west respectively; a rhetorical way of referring to the whole island.
2 Apostate; abandoner of one's religious faith.

language of kindness, and the professions of good faith. Fairly you could never have overpowered me and the brave men that stand beside me. I received a trust from my royal master; wrest it from me by the open means of a soldier, and welcome! But you have taken advantage of my weakness, or rather of my sincere and honourable mind, which, incapable of deception in itself, knew not to suspect it in another. You have made me," and a tear burst into the old man's eyes[1] as he spoke, "a worthless servant to my king. You have disarmed me by a paltry device, and prevented me from that which it was my duty to do, discharging faithfully the trust reposed in me, and either conquering his foes by my own valour and that of those under my command, or dying with the sword in my hand, and being overcome after I had exerted every energy of an officer and a man in vain."

It was a singular concurrence of circumstances that enabled Sir Phelim and his fellow-conspirators to commence their revolt in so formidable a manner. Lord Strafford had raised an army of eight thousand Irish, principally Catholics, to assist his master in subduing the Scottish revolt. Charles however, from the joint imbecility of himself and his counsellors, Strafford excepted, after having marched his forces to the borders of Scotland, yielded the whole question to his rebellious subjects, and subscribed to all the conditions they thought proper to impose upon him, without drawing a sword. Thus his Irish levies were rendered useless. They were consequently disbanded; and that no ill effects might result from their being turned loose on the public, it was agreed with the Spanish minister, that they should immediately be re-enlisted for the service of his master. Sir Phelim and his fellow-conspirators were among the most active for the execution of this measure. But the companies being enrolled, various pretences were raised to baffle the embarkation of these troops for the Spanish service. It unfortunately happened, that both the English and Irish parliament forbade the transport of these troops; and merchants were even obliged to give security, that they would not lend their vessels for this purpose. Thus formidable bodies of men were left at large under the most dangerous leaders; and those who commanded them, were in some sort invited to med-

---

1   Toby Caulfeild was not an old man at the time, being only 19. Godwin
     may be confusing the father (who was dead by now) with the son. This
     conflation of various Caulfeilds gives the impression of greater stability
     in the English administration of Ireland than is warranted.

itate for themselves the destination upon which they should be employed.[1]

Lord Caulfield and his garrison, officers and soldiers, of which my father was one, were marched under a sufficient guard to Kinnard, in the neighbouring county of Tirone,[2] the principal seat of the insurgent into whose hands they had fallen. Here they were at first treated, as Sir Phelim had promised they should be, with as much courtesy and humanity as circumstances would admit.

But a war of this sort is never carried on with those decorums, and that spirit of forbearance and accommodation towards an enemy, which is sometimes practised between civilized and polished nations. The plan originally laid down by the insurgents was to seize all forts and garrisons, to retain the gentry as hostages in their hands, the better to secure a degree of moderation on the part of government, and to shed as little blood as possible. But they resolved to possess the land of their ancestors, and not to suffer any settlers from the superior island to remain in their borders. This immediately led to much cruelty. The British[3] had made for themselves comfortable and pleasant habitations, abounding with corn, cattle, and every other accommodation, that an industrious people could draw out of a picturesque country and a fertile soil. They had lived among their Irish neighbours with every appearance of good fellowship; and the demonstrations of love and affection on either part had been mutual.[4] Hostilities between them had ceased, for almost as long a time as the memory of any one living could reach; and nothing could exceed the quietness and security with which the new settlers

---

1 In *HCE* Godwin also describes the political destabilization (and opening) created by "placing arms in the hands of so numerous a body of Catholics." There he is clearer that Charles did not want to disband a force that could be useful to him in his struggle with Parliament. Parliament, for its part, forbade the embarkation of the forces because it did not want them re-employed by Spain, through whose agency they could still be a threat to England and Protestantism (1.218–22).

2 Tyrone, a county in Ulster, now in Northern Ireland.

3 "British" here means the English in an expansionist mode. Although Britain did not constitutionally exist until the 1707 Act of Union, James I called himself King of Great Britain and Ireland.

4 There are clearly inconsistencies between the description of colonization earlier in the chapter and the more benign account of settlement here, which allow us to see through Mandeville's unthinking acceptance of the British point of view.

enjoyed their possessions. It may easily be imagined with what feelings they received the mandate, that they must dwell there no longer. The success of the Irish in Ulster however was such, that nothing could resist their pleasure. The whole province, together with the counties of Longford in Leinster, and Leitrim in Connaught, with the exception of a very few strong places, fell into the power of the rebels. All this was achieved in the short space of a week; and, at the same time, O'Neile saw himself at the head of thirty thousand men. If any of the British repaired to a spot where they conceived they should be able to defend themselves, they were, for the most part, tempted to give up the undertaking, by the offer, on the part of their assailants, of assurance for their lives, and whatever they could take away with them, with free passage and a safe conduct to any place to which they might think proper to retire.

CHAPTER II

All this was calamitous enough; but the evil did not end here. Their enemies were, for the most part, men of barbarous habits, miserably accoutered,[1] and unaccustomed to obedience. It would need the most exact discipline to keep in order bodies of men, circumstanced as the Irish were on the present occasion. The British were of course disarmed, and ignominiously led away in herds, as totally disqualified and unworthy to live any longer intermingled with the people by whom they were now conveyed into banishment. The Catholic priests, who had been the principal instigators of the insurrection, sedulously[2] taught their hearers, that a Protestant was a sort of being whose neighbourhood was pestilential to the true votaries of the cross, and that, wherever he dwelt, he brought down the displeasure and curse of the Almighty upon the country in which he was harboured. Hatred and contempt are powerful inciters to cruelty. The British, circumstanced as they were, were hated as heretics, and despised, because they were in the power of their enemies, and could make no retaliation to any contumely[3] that might be heaped upon them. Insult went first, and plunder speedily followed. The Irish took from the fugitives the valuables they were

---

1 Outfitted.
2 Diligently.
3 Insult, contempt.

carrying away with them; they next stripped them of their clothes. The season was now become inclement and severe. The unhappy wretches, who were suffering every species of privation and inconvenience, could not always help, in the bitterness of their hearts, reproaching their conductors with perfidy, who had first disarmed them on the faith of the most solemn engagements, and now took advantage of their helpless condition to rob them of all that remained to them. The Irish, in the topics of heresy, and the assured damnation of their victims in another world, found copious matter for recrimination. From words they proceeded to blows. The vigorous and the infirm, men, women and children of the English, were mingled together in this calamitous march. The rebels had, of course, no consideration for the infirmity or inability of those they conducted, but goaded them along like beasts.[1]

In every thing that is most horrible and revolting to an ingenuous mind, such is the constitution of human nature, it is often the first step only that is difficult. A child, a woman, a sick or infirm old man among the fugitives, became incapable of proceeding any further: the cavalcade could not stop for this; and they were left to perish with hunger and cold by the side of the highway. Such an event must either melt the most untutored heart to pity, or the emotion that spontaneously arises, must be subdued by an antagonist sentiment of careless barbarity and sanguinary[2] scorn. Hard words were mutually given and returned between the persecutor and the victim. The debate which began in words, did not always end so. The skein, or Irish dagger, was an ever-ready instrument; and an uneducated and hot-blooded kern[3] found no difficulty in consummating his invectives and his rage with a mortal wound. The first drop of blood that was shed seemed to be the signal for every kind of barbarity. Murder, when it had once unfurled its standard, did not satiate its impulse with one, but with hundreds of victims. Boys of seven and eight years

---

1 The Ulster Rebellion was a traumatic moment in Protestant history and the way it was constructed, and despite his sympathy for the Irish in *HCE*, Godwin's account of it there is similarly affecting. He claims that 40,000 people "and by some computations five times that number, are said to have perished in this undistinguishing massacre" (1.239). Laurence Echard (c. 1670–1730), one of Godwin's sources, puts the figure at 40,000–50,000 (*History of England*, 513; see Appendix F1).

2 Causing bloodshed.

3 A lightly armed foot-soldier.

of age, children at the breast, women far advanced in their pregnancy, seemed often to be made the preferred objects of destruction. He that has once dipped his hands in blood, appears to have
no more obvious way of stifling the whispers of remorse, than by
wading deeper and more deep in pitiless cruelty. Presently the
dagger was found too slow and powerless an instrument, to
gratify the barbarity that wantoned round. Drowning was a com-
modious means for wholesale destruction, and was resorted to on
multiplied occasions. The most tragical scene of these inflictions
was the bridge of Portnedown, in the county of Armagh. The
bridge was first broken down in the middle by the rebels, and the
fugitives were then driven upon it from one end and the other.
With pikes and swords they were forced over into the water, and
as many as attempted to save their lives by swimming were
knocked on the head with poles, or shot at from the banks. One
hundred and eighty persons perished thus in one day; and these
executions were frequently repeated.[1] An extraordinary consequence followed upon this. The apparitions of several of the
persons thus murdered, were shortly after seen nightly on the
surface of the river in which they perished. The shapes of men
and women suddenly bolted out of the water, showing themselves
naked waist-high, and upright in the stream. This vision continued for many days; the spirits uttered horrible and terrifying
cries, and imprecated revenge on their murderers; so that many
of those persons who had not shrunk from the destruction of the
Protestants while alive, could not endure the presence and the
voice of their ghosts after death. All who lived near the scene fled
from the fatal spot with affright, and took shelter in the neighbouring towns, from the hearing of sounds which it was not in
mortal hardihood to endure and live.[2]

Such were the tales that were daily, and sometimes hourly,
brought to my father and his comrades in their confinement at
Kinnard; and it was soon manifest that this war, which began

---

1 Godwin uses almost the same words in *HCE* (1.239).
2 [Godwin's note:] These facts are attested by many witnesses on oath;
   and Dr Ferriar, in an Essay on the Theory of Apparitions, has endeavoured to account for them, from natural causes. [The reference is to˙
   John Ferriar, M.D., *An Essay Towards a Theory of Apparitions* (London:
   Cadell and Davies, 1813), who describes this particular episode in traumatic historiography at length (124–31; Appendix G3c of this edition).
   Godwin draws on Ferriar's account of the visions allegedly seen by Irish
   rebels at Portnedown Bridge in the aftermath of the massacre.]

with professions of clemency, was rapidly degenerating into a scene of cruelty and massacre, such as has rarely occurred in the annals of the world. The first excesses commenced among the rudest of the people, and were perpetrated by boors, unacquainted with almost the slightest tincture of civilization. Yet, once begun, it would have been difficult to stay their progress, especially in a case like this, where the affair was strictly a rising of the population to give law to the land. But, difficult or easy, the experiment never was tried.[1] O'Neile, and most of the other heads of the conspiracy, were as bigoted, as hardened, and as brutal, as the lowest of their followers. Sir Phelim himself was totally without that firmness and serenity of spirit, which, in souls of a happier temper, preserves them from being too much elevated by prosperity, or cast down by adverse events. When he looked on the number of his forces, and the extent of territory that lay unresisting before him, his heart dilated with pride, and he believed that he had only to show himself in his strength on this side or on that, and all would yield before him. On the other hand, he was too impatient and arrogant, to be able to encounter with equanimity anything that thwarted him. Amidst all the great and mighty victories of which he boasted, he did not fail to experience some reverses. These rendered him frantic, in proportion to the unmeasured joy that showed itself in him on other occasions. He was repulsed before the castle of Augher; and he immediately ordered the Protestants of three adjacent parishes to be massacred.

But the most considerable check he experienced at this time was at Lisnegarvy (now called Lisburne). He could not endure that, while he had gained possession of the whole open country of Ulster, a few principal places still had the audacity to defy his arms. Of these Carrickfergus was the chief; and, to reach this place with effect, it appeared necessary first to take in the intermediate garrison of Lisnegarvy. For this expedition he drew out four thousand of the choicest troops from the myriads that followed his standard. The attack was sustained and repelled with steadiness and vigour. But in this affair the British proved the superior. The repeated assaults of the besiegers only served to swell the heaps of their slain; and the English boasted, that the number of the enemy killed on this occasion, trebled the amount of their whole garrison.

---

1 The attempt to do political justice to the Irish here suggests that Godwin rather than Mandeville is speaking.

The disappointment sustained by O'Neile in this attempt drew out all the savageness of his nature. His ferocious spirit seemed to search, how he could most signalize his vengeance, and leave the most memorable record of what a man, possessed of unlimited power, and cursed with the utmost depravity of will, could do. Among the rest, he recollected Lord Caulfield. This nobleman was the first victim that had fallen into his savage grasp. He had been drawn within the sphere of his power, by the modesty of Sir Phelim's carriage, and the ostentatious exhibition he had made of the gestures of peace and good faith. He was the first man that had received the pledge of Sir Phelim's honour, that he should suffer no injury. Lady Caulfield and his children, together with the wives and families of several of the officers of the garrison of Charlemont, had been made prisoners at the same time, and were all confined within the same walls. The house was the house of Sir Phelim, which had been assigned them for their protection. The master of this house gave orders, that they should all, without distinction of sex or age, be put to the sword. There was not a man of O'Neile's staff, that lifted his voice to remonstrate against so diabolical an outrage. The satellites of this monster were too faithful in their obedience, and too much sympathized with the spirit of their master, not to execute his mandate to the minutest letter. My father and mother were numbered among the corses of this bloody day.

I was a little more than three years of age, at the time when this tragedy was acted. I do not remember the scene distinctly in all its parts; but there are detached circumstances that belong to it, that will live in my memory as long as my pulses continue to beat. My father, Lord Caulfield, and the other officers, would doubtless have met their fate with firmness, if they alone had been concerned in the catastrophe. The scene would have resembled what we read of the sack of Rome by the Gauls, when the fathers of the senate sat each man in his ivory chair in the porch of his own house, and, without changing the position of feature or limb, expected their fate, while, to the barbarians that traversed the city, they appeared rather divinities than men. The prisoners of Kinnard had, for many days, looked forward to their death. The successive accounts of barbarities that reached them, were like the distant thunder, and taught them to anticipate the moment when the storm would fall with accumulated violence on their own heads.

But within the narrow bounds of their imprisonment they were not alone. The ruthless chieftain into whose hands they had fallen, had hurried along every creature he had found of the better class in the castle of Charlemont, and hemmed them round in this devoted spot. Who could behold with unaltered eye the entrance of the barbarians, that already in their purpose devoted the women and children shut up in Kinnard, as victims to expiate the destructive bravery of their countrymen in the defence of Lisnegarvy? The prisoners were unarmed, not unresisting. They seized every weapon of offence that chance threw in their way, and determined to procrastinate their destiny, or to sell their lives at a high rate. Several of the savages fell in the first assault. Their reception taught them caution; they retired to somewhat a greater distance, and fired vollies into the midst of us. Every shot told. I cannot go on with the narrative. Dying groans, and piercing shrieks, and the fierce and tremendous cry of insult and triumph on the part of our invaders, made up the horrible concert. They pursued the unhappy wretches they were sent to destroy, to garrets, and along the roofs of the building. They ceased not, till the funereal and agonizing cries which had lately tormented the air, gave place to a still more funereal and awe-creating silence. Murder had done his work, and there no longer remained a victim to destroy.

From the general massacre of the English within the walls of Sir Phelim's residence this day, I was the only one that escaped. My preservation was owing to the fidelity and courage of an Irish woman-servant, to whose charge I had been committed. Her mistress and family she could not save; but me she caught up in her arms with a resolution that nothing could subdue. "What have you there?" said one of the murderers; "that child is an English child." "By the Virgin," replied the woman, "it is my own flesh and blood; would you go for to confound this dear little jewel, as true a Catholic as ever was born'd, with the carcases of heretics?" "Let the child speak," answered the ruffian, "he is old enough; who do you belong to?" "To me! to me!" shrieked the woman, in an agony of terror. "Speak!" repeated the assassin, and lifted over me the instrument of death. I hid my face in my nurse's bosom. I did not comprehend the meaning of the question, but I felt that the faithful creature who embraced me was my protector. "To Judy," said I; "Judy is my mammy." "Begone," said the murderer sternly, drawing back his skein, "and mix no more with this dunghil of Protestant dogs."

Judith carried me away, with the intention of retiring with me to her native village, and bringing me up as her own child. On any other occasion this might easily have been done, but not now. The insurgents, who had begun, as I have said, with vows of moderation, and a resolution to avoid as much as possible the imbruing their hands in blood, having once overstepped this limit, and dipped their hands in one murder after another, felt that there was no retreat; and avowed their determination not to leave one Briton, man, woman or child, alive in the districts where their power was supreme. Judith was questioned about me again and again, in different places through which she passed; and all her self-command, fervour, and quick turns of ingenuity, were scarcely sufficient to preserve me from the hostile sword. Convinced but too fully of the imminent dangers that hung over my life, she turned her steps in the direction of Dublin.

At length, at the town of Kells,[1] it was her fortune to fall in with the reverend Hilkiah Bradford, who had for several preceding years been chaplain to the garrison in which I was born. He immediately knew her. He suspected the meaning of her expedition, and felt that he had some recollection of my own features. Judith shewed the sincerest transports of joy in meeting him, and thought that all her troubles would now be at an end. She was however mistaken in her calculations. Hilkiah,[2] who was a man of the utmost integrity and purity of heart, willingly took me under his protection, but insisted on an immediate and irrevocable separation between me and my faithful preserver. The reverend clergyman was imbued with all the prejudices, that belong to the most strait-laced of the members of his sacred profession. His continual theme was that the church of Rome was no other than the spiritual Babylon, prophesied of in the book of Revelations; and the text of scripture on which he was ever most prone to descant, was, "Come out of her, my people, that ye be not partakers of her sins, and that ye receive not of her plagues."[3] He was fully convinced that a Papist was more especially an object of the hatred of the almighty creator, than either a Heathen or a Mahometan. And, if such were the sentiments familiar to his youth, and in which he had been too fatally confirmed by the conspiracy of the Gunpowder Treason,[4] and the diabolical crime

---

1 A town about 65 kilometres north-west of Dublin.
2 An Old Testament name, meaning "God is my portion."
3 Revelation 18:4.
4 The Gunpowder Plot or Jesuit Treason (1605) was a failed plot by Roman Catholics to blow up the House of Lords while James I was present, as a prelude to a hoped-for popular revolt in the Midlands during which James's young daughter was to be installed as (*continued*)

of the infatuated Ravaillac,[1] it may easily be supposed how much strength this opinion gained in him, by the dreadful scenes with which he was at this moment surrounded.

Fearful was the contention between Judith and the reverend Hilkiah, as to the destiny to which I was now to be consigned. The exertions of this uninstructed matron were not less strenuous, than those of the woman whose the living child really was, when she pleaded before Solomon.[2] She, who had shielded me again and again from the daggers, already dropping with gore, of her savage countrymen, thought foul scorn to be baffled by an unarmed heretical priest. She had congratulated herself on her success, when she had escaped from the lines of the rebel Irish, into a town that was at this moment filled with English, fugitives and others. But she found herself further from the purpose of her affectionate heart here than before. My life, indeed, was now in safety. In that thought she truly rejoiced. But was it to be endured that she, who had nursed and fed me from her own breast from the hour of my birth, and who had just brought me hither unhurt through a thousand hair-breadth escapes, should now be thrust out from me with contumely, as one whose touch henceforth would be contamination and pestilence to me? She raved; she intreated. "And was not it myself that saved him? And has not he owed his life to me times without number? And am not I ten times his mother? Jewel, dear, you have no mother; you have no father; suddenly, fearfully, they have been taken from you; there is nobody now in all the world that can do for you but Judy. Mr Bradford, you cannot be so cruel; you are a priest, though you are not a Roman; I have always thought you a good man. Who shall take care of the poor helpless wretch, if I am put away from him, who am his natural fosterer? You do not mean to be the death of him! Kill me, cut me to pieces, but do not ye, do not ye, be so

---

Catholic head of state. It was in response to James's failure to improve the position of Catholics, as he had promised; its leader was Robert Catesby, aided by Guy Fawkes.

1   François Ravaillac (1578–1610), a Catholic schoolmaster and religious fanatic who assassinated the French King Henry IV in 1610 because of his connections with Protestants.

2   Biblical king of Israel noted for his wisdom. In 1 Kings 3:16–28, two women come before him, claiming to be the mother of the same infant. Solomon suggests that they should cut the child in two, and when one of the women says that she would rather give up her child than see it killed, he awards custody to her.

barbarous as to put me away from him, and leave me alive. My child! my child! my child!"

It will easily be imagined, that I was moved to the utmost degree with the agonies of my nurse, and that I joined my anguish, my tears, my cries, my intreaties, to hers. But this was a portentous moment, in which all human emotions, except within a certain definite limit, were utterly extinguished. Bigotry was lord paramount on every side, and strode along triumphant, unhearing, and cased in triple adamant, over the ruins of every feeling of the heart. Had the contention been only between Judith, and the reverend divine who claimed to take me under his protection, without doubt her more energetic spirit, and her more muscular limbs would have borne off the prize. But, in the street of Kells, she was wholly surrounded with British,—with creatures who had just, through every degree of hardship and misery, escaped with life, who had each one left behind a husband, a wife, or a child, the prey of this bloody pursuit, and to whom it was agony to see among them for a moment a being of the race of their destroyers. The more clamorous the unhappy woman showed herself, the more importunately she forced her intreaties and her shrieks upon their hearing, by so much the more inexorably were they resolved to expel her. Was a woman of this accursed, savage, Irish, Popish brood, to be supposed to have any feelings, or any feelings entitled to the sympathy and favour of a Protestant heart? They repelled her with every degree of contumely; and, when at length she sunk senseless under the protracted contest, they flung her out of the town, like some loathsome load of contamination, too pestilent for wholesome British senses to endure.

From Kells, my victorious protector bore me away in triumph to Dublin, and thence, with the least possible delay, procured a passage on board a frail and crazy bark for England. The general opinion then was, that the insurgents would in a few days get possession of the metropolis, which they would not fail to make a scene of greater horror and devastation than any that had preceded, and that not one native of Great Britain would be left alive in the island; at least such was the firm persuasion of those, who had passed through the scene of all these horrors, and who felt their escape, and their continuing to exist, as an incredible miracle. All who could provide themselves with a passage, though at never so excessive rates, were eager to quit the devoted coast. And, to heighten the calamity, there was a succession of violent winds and impetuous storms, such as had never before been known. Our poor fleet of barks was slenderly victualled, and loaded with passengers. But no danger, and no distress, could induce them to make land again, preferring, as they did, all the hostility of the elements, to the bare chance of falling into the hands of the infuriated enemy. We were in perpetual danger of perishing at sea, and much the greater part of the vessels that left Dublin at the same time, were actually cast away. Our passage was not accomplished under three months; a great number of the persons on board had expired with hunger; and those who reached the British coast alive were so much enfeebled with the extremities they had endured, as scarcely to be able to drag their bodies on shore.

CHAPTER III

Mr Bradford, on his arrival, immediately hastened to London, and from thence wrote to my uncle, my father's elder brother, who in consequence of the late calamity was become my natural guardian, to ask his directions how he was to dispose of me. The answer he received expressed my uncle's wish that I should be brought to him without delay, and added a request that my preserver would have the goodness to accompany me. These directions were no sooner known, than they were carried into execution; and, at the end of the second day from our leaving London, we reached in safety the place of our destination, which lay immediately on the verge of the sea, on the shores of the English channel.

I resided constantly under the roof of this uncle for the next following eight or nine years of my life; and it is therefore necessary that I should here describe the most remarkable features of this residence. I did not immediately see and feel these particulars, in such a manner as to have enabled me to describe them, if I had been early removed from the observation of them; but they insensibly incorporated themselves as it were with the substance of my mind; and my character, such as it was afterwards displayed, owed much of its peculiarity to the impressions I here received.

The dwelling-place of my uncle was an old and spacious mansion, the foundation of which was a rock, against which the waves of the sea for ever beat, and by their incessant and ineffectual rage were worked into a foam, that widely spread itself in every direction. The sound of the dashing waters was eternal, and seemed calculated to inspire sobriety, and almost gloom, into the soul of every one who dwelt within the reach of its influence. The situation of this dwelling, on that side of the island which is most accessible to an enemy, had induced its original architect to construct it in such a manner, as might best enable it to resist an invader, though its fortifications had since fallen into decay. It was a small part of the edifice only that was inhabited in my time. Several magnificent galleries, and a number of spacious apartments, were wholly neglected, and suffered to remain in a woful state of dilapidation. Indeed it was one wing only that was now tenanted, and that imperfectly; the centre and the other wing had long been resigned to the owls and the bitterns.[1] The door which formed the main entrance of the building was never opened; and the master and all that belonged to him were accustomed to pass by an obscure postern[2] only. The courtyard exhibited a striking scene of desolation. The scythe and the spade were never admitted to violate its savage character. It was overgrown with tall and rank grass of a peculiar species, intermingled with elder trees, nettles, and briars.

The dwelling which I have thus described was surrounded on three sides by the sea; it was only by the north-west that I could reach what I may call my native country. The whole situation was eminently insalubrious.[3] Though the rock on which our habitation was placed was, for the most part, of a perpendicular acclivity,[4] yet we had to the west a long bank of sand, and in different directions various portions of bog and marshy ground, sending up an endless succession of vapours, I had almost said steams, whose effect holds unmitigated war with healthful animal life. The tide also threw up vast quantities of sargassos[5] and weeds, the corruption of which was supposed to contribute eminently to the same effect. For a great part of the year we were further involved in thick fogs and mists, to such a degree as often to render the use of candles necessary even at noonday.

The open country, which, as I have said, lay to the north-west of us, consisted for the most part of an immense extent of barren heath, the surface of which was broken and unequal, and was scarcely intersected with here and there the track of a rough,

---

1 A bird from the heron family, found in marshy areas.
2 A secondary door or gate in a city or castle wall.
3 Unhealthy.
4 Ascending slope.
5 A large seaweed with a rough sticky texture.

sandy, and incommodious road. Its only variety was produced by long stripes of grass of an unequal breadth, mingled with the sand of the soil, and occasionally adorned with the plant called heath, and with fern. A tree was hardly to be found for miles. Such was the character of the firm ground, which of course a wanderer like myself, avoiding as carefully as might be a deviation into quaggy and treacherous paths, selected for his rambles. The hut of the labourer was rarely to be found; the chief sign of animal life was a few scattered flocks of sheep, with each of them its shepherd's boy and his dog; and the nearest market-town was at a distance of seventeen miles. Over this heath, as I grew a little older, I delighted to extend my peregrinations; and though the atmosphere was for the greater part of the year thick, hazy and depressing, yet the desolateness of the scene, the wideness of its extent, and even the monotonous uniformity of its character, favourable to meditation and endless reverie, did not fail to be the source to me of many cherished and darling sensations.

My uncle was the eldest son and lineal representative of the opulent family of the Mandevilles, and could boast that he was proprietor of four or five splendid and delicious mansions in different counties of England. It will naturally be asked therefore, how he came to chuse the most uninviting of them all, and to live in it in so obscure and unlordly a style? The answer is simple: because so to live suited the frame of his mind.

Audley Mandeville, my uncle, had from the hour of his birth been the object of his father's persecution. There was an opposition of tempers between them, that seemed to render harmony for any length of time impossible. My grandfather was a naval adventurer, and had twice sailed with Sir Francis Drake round the world.[1] His countenance and figure bore strongly the marks of the hardships he had endured. His manners had all the rudeness which is supposed characteristic of a sailor. He was not without some proficiency in the line of his profession; but in all other matters he was as ignorant as a Hottentot;[2] and every kind of knowledge and refinement with which he was unacquainted, he thought himself entitled to hold in utter contempt. It will

---

1 Sir Francis Drake (c. 1540–96), navigator and politician of the Elizabethan era and second in command of the English fleet against the Spanish Armada in 1588. Drake made one, not two, trips around the world in 1577–80.
2 The derogatory name given by Europeans to the native people of southwestern Africa.

scarcely be regarded as an exception to this character, that he considered rank and fortune with the utmost partiality, and set no small value on those advantages, in this respect, with which he was himself endowed. He had particularly the highest notions of the prerogatives annexed to the paternal character, and the obedience he was entitled to exact from his offspring. He had a Herculean frame, and a robust constitution; and in this article, as well as the rest, he seemed to regard his own endowments as the standard of human excellence.

Audley, his eldest born, was precisely such a son as would be most unwelcome to such a father. He came into the world in the seventh month of his mother's pregnancy. It was with the greatest difficulty, and by dint of the most unremitted tenderness and attentions on her part, that he could be reared to man's estate. He was deformed in his person. He was, as the poet expresses it,

A puny insect, trembling at a breeze.[1]

He was scarcely equal to the most ordinary corporal exertions; and the temper of his mind corresponded to the frame of his body, tender as a flower, deeply susceptible of every unkindness and whatever thwarted his views and propensities, unequal to contention, and sinking, as without power of resistance, under any thing that presented itself in the form of hostility.

Yet this delicate creature was not slenderly furnished with intellectual endowments. Unqualified as he was for every species of hardihood, his happiness was placed in sedentary pursuits. He was an elegant scholar, and displayed the most lively and refined taste as to all those objects which address themselves to that faculty. He was, in particular, a most admirable musician.

All these qualities, which, to a person capable of appreciating them, would have rendered him an object of love and esteem, were lost, and worse than lost, upon my grandfather. He was not satisfied to regard them with negligence and contempt; they became to him every day more and more the objects of inextinguishable abhorrence. The consequence of all this was, that, after a trial of some years, my grandfather and my uncle seldom met. The son shrunk with unconquerable terror from the presence of his father; and the father exerted himself to forget that he had such a son, and was inexpressibly mortified at any thing that brought back the fact to his recollection. Meanwhile, the educa-

---

1 Alexander Pope (1688–1744) in his "Epistle to Burlington" (108).

tion of Audley Mandeville was entirely domestic; he was supposed not to have strength to contend with the difficulties of a public seminary. He was therefore in some sort a prisoner in the paternal mansion; he took no exercise without being previously informed that his father was from home; and he had continually present to his thoughts the depressing conviction (for in that way it certainly operated upon him) that he was the object of his father's detestation.

The consolations he possessed to support him under these melancholy circumstances were few. His mother was his principal comfort, and her he regarded with sentiments scarcely short of adoration. His mother had also a niece, who was become an inmate in the house. This young lady was the progeny of my grandmother's sister, who had married unhappily, against the consent of all her family, and whose husband had turned out a profligate, and had deserted her. The young lady I have mentioned was the only offspring of this marriage, and was now completely an orphan.

Amelia Montfort had, in the result of these accidents, been made the equal and almost constant companion of her more high-born cousin. They had a similarity of tastes, and their studies were in many respects the same. Like Audley, she had a keen relish for music, and had studied under the same masters. They often therefore joined their respective performances, either with the voice or the instrument. My uncle had a voice so singularly melodious, as to have gained him the appellation of the little nightingale. Though deformed in his person, his eyes were remarkably beautiful; and his countenance had an expression of sweetness, modesty and diffidence, that seemed irresistible. While Amelia laboured with her needle, the tediousness of her employment was often relieved to her, as Audley read aloud some favourite author, while she plied the sempstress' toil. She was not permitted the advantage of masters for language; but this privation was made up to her, particularly in Italian, by the instructions of Audley. As he had scarcely any other companion, the society of Amelia was singularly dear to him. Yet much of his time was spent in sequestered solitude. His literary diligence was often too severe and unremitted to allow of an associate; but this separation and study only made the conversation of his confidential and constant friend the more precious to him, when his hours of study were at an end.

It was scarcely to be imagined, that two young persons of different sexes, whose tastes were in many respects the same, should be so constantly together, without their being impressed with a mutual passion. To Audley Amelia was all the world, as for weeks together he often saw no other human creature, except his mother, his instructors, and the servants. His mother however died, before he was of an age when vigilance on this subject is usually resorted to. Commodore Mandeville, now a widower, substituted in the place of his wife, as superintendent of his household, a maiden sister of his own, Mrs Dorothy Mandeville, a person of a very notable character, who, as soon as the duties of her function were performed, always found relaxation and refreshment in books. Her library however was not numerous, being entirely confined to two subjects,—books of devotion, and books of genealogy and heraldry. Between her active and her sedentary occupations her time was fully engrossed; and she was a person of so much importance in her own eyes, that there was scarcely any other living being that she could think entitled to much place in her thoughts. Audley and Amelia therefore, now growing towards man's and woman's estate, went on in the same train to which they had been accustomed while children, or rather with a greater degree of attachment and effusion of soul than ever, without awakening the smallest suspicion in the elevated mind of Mrs Dorothy.

Audley Mandeville however had not contented himself with expressing the partiality he felt, in general terms. Even from his boyish days he had been accustomed to talk to Amelia of love and marriage; and she listened to the tale with no less delight, than that which he felt in giving it utterance. This was the sacred secret of their privacy; they never alluded to it in words, but when all witnesses were far removed from their discourse; and they found in the joys they anticipated, and the plan of secluded and noiseless life they purposed for the future, a topic of conversation that could never be exhausted. Audley fervently protested, that, knowing no other life than this, being, by the infirmity of his constitution, shut out from more active and boisterous scenes, and having learned, from the inhumanity of his father, to detest the sentiments and manners of his species in general, he would never yield to mutability and alteration, would never give ear to any other scheme of existence than that which his heart told him was the only one worthy of his adoption, and would either live for his Amelia, or cease to live at all.

The first person who was induced to remark the nature of the communication going on between Audley and Amelia was a servant-maid; and, as this female was of a fretful and malignant temper, to which nothing was so distressing as to see other persons delighted and happy, she did not fail officiously to communicate her observations to Mrs Dorothy. The old lady was astonished; she never could have believed it. It never could have come into her head, that the blood of the Mandevilles could degrade itself by an ill-assorted wedlock.[1] She had indeed allowed herself to doubt, whether her brother, the commodore, had conducted himself with his usual propriety, in matching with the mother of Audley. But, that Audley himself should fix his choice on a degraded branch of his mother's family, a girl without a shilling, and whose father, if he had met with his deserts, would have paid the forfeit of his life to the injured laws of his country, she would as soon have thought of the lord of the forest engendering with a serpent, or the eagle with the wren.

After some deliberation however, and having satisfied herself by mute observations that the suggestion was something more than the groundless garrulity of a chamber-maid, she hastened to impart all she knew to the ear of the commodore. The commodore was still more astonished than his sister. His son indeed was the object of his aversion, and he never liked to be reminded of his existence. He regarded him with ineffable contempt, as concentring in his person and habits every thing that the naval hero most emphatically despised. The tale however of Mrs Dorothy, placed poor Audley in a new light in his eyes. He now for the first time confessed to himself, that the eldest son of an ancient and opulent family stood for something. He would have been glad to regard this child of his wrath as a mere zero; but that he should marry at all, and still more that he should join himself in wedlock to the lowest ignominy and disgrace, for such he regarded the match that was suggested, was indeed a shock he was little able to sustain.

Presently however he recovered himself. "No, no," he exclaimed, "it cannot be. I see how it is. The knave has been playing his waggish tricks with the girl. They have been making a scholar of him; and if scholarship is good for nothing else, it will teach him not to throw himself away like a natural.[2] But this must not be. It is too bad, in one's own house, and among one's own kin. We must send the girl away. If the fool will be sowing his wild oats,

---

1 The couple are ill-matched in terms of rank. For marriage between first cousins, see below, p. 99, note 2.

2 Simpleton.

he must contrive to do it as his betters did before him, and in a way not to make a noise in the world."

In answer to this harangue, Mrs Dorothy produced to the commodore a copy of verses in Audley's hand-writing, in which Amelia stood for the object of his devotion, and all the sentiments were expressive of the happiness of a wedded life, however frugal, rustic and obscure, where love spread the board, and a union of hearts sweetened the cup. The commodore, not without difficulty and hesitation, construed the scroll; Mrs Dorothy's annotations were of considerable service; the studies of the naval hero had not laid among the votaries of the Muse. At length however he began to apprehend something, and inclined to the opinion, that all might not be lies, even though the tale was told in verse.

Fury succeeded to scepticism and investigation. He sent to summon this ill omened son to his presence. This was an incident that scarcely occurred once in a number of years, and it threw poor Audley into a fit of trembling. There was nothing servile and cringing in the temper of the youth; and his tremors did not flow from any infirmity of his intellectual nature, but from the delicacy of his frame, his total want of experience in the tempests of the world, and the terror which always seized him, when he heard his father's name, and still more when he was placed within the sound of his voice.

"Well, Sir," said the commodore, "here is a pretty story I have heard. Do you know that paper?" throwing down the copy of verses which Mrs Dorothy had introduced to his notice. Audley took them up, and seated himself with the paper in his hand, that he might ruminate on the scene in which he was engaged, and listen with the more convenience to whatever his father should think proper to deliver.

"You are a hopeful youth to think of marrying! Why, are you arrived at these years, and understand nothing of such matters yet? Do not you know, that the marriage of the heir is the most considerable event that can happen in a family like ours? Have you never heard, that the king is always consulted upon it, and that, if you were left without a father, he would be your guardian, and could give you in marriage to whomever he pleased, without your having the smallest voice in the matter?[1] The power that

---

1 At the time, the heir to an estate, if an orphan, would become a ward of the King, who would have control of the person's property until he reached the age of majority (a practice obviously subject to abuse).

would be vested in him, if you were an orphan, while I live, is fully in me. Do you think, because I take but little notice of you, and judge it a misfortune to my race that I should have such a son, that I will allow you to run your own course, and be the ruin of our house to the latest posterity?

"I know however how to act in such a case. I shall instantly send away the minx, where you shall never hear of her again as long as you live. I am indeed quite competent to act in the affair; and it is only a mark of my condescension, that I trouble myself to say a word to you about the matter. But I wish, once for all, that you should be thoroughly informed of the nature of the case. As you have once gone wrong, it is fitting you should be put upon your guard, that there may be no danger of your committing such an error a second time. And therefore I now expect, that you will profess your entire contrition for the offence of which you have been guilty, and sign a paper, declaring that you will never think of this Amelia, and that you will never take the remotest step upon the sacred subject of marriage, without having previously obtained my full sanction and concurrence. It is out of my fatherly kindness, that I have taken the pains thus largely to explain the subject to you. I am not used thus to take my child, over whom I hold an absolute and uncontrollable power, into a participation of my counsels; and, I trust, in the present instance I shall see the visible effects of all this condescension and consideration I have had for you."

Audley Mandeville, as I have already said, was one of the most timid and uncontending of human creatures, and of all persons existing on the face of the earth, stood the most in awe of his father. You would have thought, that a harangue of this oriental[1] and unsparing sort, would have sunk him into earth, or shivered his delicate frame into a thousand atoms. It proved otherwise. What cannot the powers of almighty love effect? He shook off his infirmities, and appeared altogether another creature from what he had been from his birth up to the present moment.

"Sir," said he, "do not think to awe me by the severity of your tones, or the sternness of your aspect. What have you ever done for me? When have you ever exerted the smallest care in my behalf? You have deserted me from the hour of my birth, as the bird of the wilderness deserts her eggs,[2] leaving them to be hatched as they may. When I was a child, did you ever hold me in

---

1 I.e., despotic.
2 The ostrich.

your arms? Did I ever experience from you one caress, or so much as a smile? Have not your voice and your presence always been to me a source of unmingled terror? Did you ever wish me to live? Did you ever love me for a moment? I have a conception of the character of a father; and had it been my lot to have been blessed in such a relation, I think I could even have adored the being, who was the source to me of unspeakable sensations. But I am the outcast of the world, cut off from every friend. I have been a prisoner under the paternal roof, and have more dreaded to approach you, than the vilest slave to the most cruel eastern tyrant. Thus blighted and forlorn, what could I do? I have found a friend, a friend that is more than all the world to me. I have but one consolation: there is but one tie by which I hold to the present scene of existence. But that consolation has now for years made up to me the loss of every thing else. My cousin is to me a spring of inconceivable delights. When I am fatigued, she cherishes me; when I am sick, she is my nurse; when I am overwhelmed with all the griefs that my state and constitution cast upon me, her smiles are the only thing that make existence supportable. She calms my impatience; she drives away my inward distress by the sweetness of her countenance; her power over me is without a limit, I cannot part with her. She is the pole-star by which I steer through the voyage of life; and if you put out her light, my days and nights to come will be purposeless, and wrapped in everlasting darkness. You have done me no good; you have scarcely at any time troubled yourself with anything that concerns me; in this, which is every thing to my poor desolate heart, I conjure you let me alone. I will not be awed; I will not be cajoled; nothing shall turn me aside from the part I have chosen for myself. I know not why I speak this; not with the hope to move your inflexible spirit; but I speak it to lighten my heart. All my paths shall be direct; and the few words I shall utter—few certainly shall I ever address to a father—shall at least be unstained with duplicity and falsehood."

In these artless strains did this poor inexperienced youth pour out his sentiments to his flinty-hearted father. The commodore was inexpressibly astonished at all that he heard. He had not doubted that his son, every thing that he had ever yet known of him being made up of a shrinking and sensitive diffidence, would have felt annihilated, and incapable of uttering a word, before the anger of his father. The commodore had cruelly wasted his great guns upon him, at the same time that he believed, that the smallest intimation of his pleasure would have deprived Audley of all

power of resistance, and that, where he condescended to interfere, the whole question was settled in a moment.

CHAPTER IV

Meanwhile, though the commodore was absolute and dictatorial
in his temper, he was not at the same time without his wiles. The
enemy that he could not conquer by force, he was not indisposed
to take in by stratagem. A view had just opened upon him, that
he had not in the smallest degree anticipated; and he drew in his
fierceness. He had the prudence to stop in his career, and allow
himself time to revise his measures. He muttered words of resentment and menace; but what he said was confused and incoherent; and he abruptly ordered the youth from his presence.

All that had passed thus far, had proceeded without impediment or reflection. The commodore no sooner heard the unwelcome information from his sister, than he acted upon it. It was
most congenial to his temper to use decisive measures; and,
where he thought he could settle a business at once, he did not
relish the subjecting himself to protracted trouble. But, before his
interview with his son was over, he recollected an appointment
that had been made with a distant relation of his late wife, who
had undertaken to conduct Audley to London, and initiate him
in those scenes of populous and busy life, which were so remarkably contrasted with any thing the youth had yet witnessed. From
the scene which had just passed, and the unexpected resoluteness
Audley had displayed, the commodore began to think, that whatever steps might be taken for the summary removal of Amelia, it
might be more prudent to take in his son's absence. Every thing
now passed in quiet for several days, the commodore's fury
seemed to have evaporated itself in threats; and Audley, unskilled
in the treachery of the world, suffered himself to be lulled into the
same security, as before this explanation had taken place. He
thought of his father only at rare intervals; but Amelia was always
before him; he was in her presence as often as he pleased; he
dreamed of her every night, and in these few days he had
advanced whole years in love. The affection that reigned in his
bosom, contracted in some nameless way new sweetness, from
being now looked upon as a thing forbidden; at the same time
that he had so little meditation and calculation for the future, that
he lived with his whole soul in the present time, and was contented. To say all in a word, Audley was constitutionally a

dreamer; and his day-dreams, as always happens in this disease, moulded themselves in correspondence to the propensity of his mind.

At length the cousin arrived with whom his journey was to be taken. The course of Audley's life had been uniform; and this had infused into him a sort of *vis inertiae*,[1] a disposition opposite to that of "such as are given to change." When he thought of London as a vision only, the thought was by no means without its attractions; but when the time came that was to turn it into reality, he shrunk instinctively away, and wished the engagement had never been contracted. He could scarcely remember the time when he had slept out of his own bed; the sort of prison-life he led under his father's roof, made him but so much the more completely master of the arrangement of his time; all the little machinery of his studies was about him; but, most of all, he must leave Amelia behind him; and he felt that the whole world would be a blank to him, where she was not present. Amelia however was zealous to press him to the expedition; she declaimed earnestly, but sweetly, against the supineness and indolence that she saw was growing upon him; she told him, that now was the age at which he ought to store his mind with observations, and make trial of that activity which talents like his required from their possessor. What could not the exhortations of Amelia achieve? He set out on his journey with a heavy and foreboding heart; and when the time of leave-taking came, he seemed to have a melancholy presentiment that he was parting from the idol of his soul for ever.

The stage was now free for the machinations of the old commodore and his sister Dorothy. They had cabaled and counselled together, previously to the departure of Audley; if that can be called counsel, where the veteran seaman laid down the law never to be contradicted, and his obsequious minister applied all the energy and activity of which she was mistress, to carry his mandates into execution. The wing of Mandeville House in which Audley and the ladies resided, was the very mansion of tranquillity; not so that portion of the building which was occupied by the master. He had for his chosen companions two of his sea-mates that had been disabled in the service,—one that had lost an arm, and another that, from a fracture of the knee-pan,[2] was not able to support himself without a crutch; and their midnight orgies

---

1 Power of inertia, or passive resistance.
2 Kneecap.

were occasionally turbulent and clamorous. Dorothy and the commodore had agreed, considering the dangerous turn of mind that Audley betrayed, that the only way of putting to rest the question of Amelia, and freeing themselves from all further trouble on the subject, was to marry her; the two gentlemen that dwelt at Mandeville House, both bachelors, presented themselves most conveniently for the purpose; and it was canvassed with all due formality, whether the cripple, or he that was maimed of an arm only, was most eligible for the purpose. The lot at length fell upon Thomson, the cripple; he was completely a man in every dimension; when he sat, or when he stood, there was nothing to object to in his figure; it was only when he moved, that he was deficient. Beside that, he was ten years younger than his companion, having only reached the thirtieth year of his age.

Amelia was in reality far from being that paragon of perfection, which the imagination of her fond lover had painted her. She had a considerable talent for music; she had a soft and flexible temper; lent an accommodating ear to every thing that was said to her, and was not without the power of comprehending to a certain extent the notions of her favourite Audley. She was daily in his society; and perpetual opportunity had increased her capacity of following the peculiar train of his ideas. Add to which, she had an ingenuousness of countenance, which, paradoxical as it may sound, deluded the spectator; it made him give her credit for more than actually passed in her mind. All together, she was not in all probability the woman that would have fixed Audley's choice, if he had lived in the world, where a number of other candidates would have continually passed before his eyes. But what could be expected? They sang together; they read together; he was her zealous and affectionate preceptor;[1] and love rendered her three times a more improving and promising pupil to him, than she would have been under any other master. In his life he had never seen another female of his own age, with whom he had held even one hour's familiar communication. And it was the characteristic of Audley's mind, that whatever impression was once strongly fixed upon it, was indelible. No time could efface it; no illusions, no machinations, however artful, had power over it; his soul remained for ever faithful to its first predilection; and though shattered, so to express myself, into a thousand pieces, the image was but multiplied by the violence it received.

---

1 Teacher and mentor.

The business was now, as we have said, to marry Amelia; and Lieutenant Thomson was fixed upon for the husband. The commodore opened the plan in the first place to his young friend. The two divisions of the family lived in a state of so great separation, that Thomson had scarcely seen Amelia; but he had seen her. The commodore inquired of him, in the first place, how he stood inclined to marriage, and, next, what he thought of the niece of his patron?—to both these questions the answer was encouraging. Amelia was not destitute of the advantages of youth and beauty; and Thomson considered it as no small benefit, to become in some sort a member of the Mandeville family. The commodore spoke of settling him in a comfortable independence, and talked of bestowing one thousand pounds upon his niece as her portion in marriage. These were considerations that by no means operated to induce the lieutenant to slight the proposal.

"But I must be frank with you, Jack," continued the commodore. "I am your friend; I hope you know that. I will not therefore deceive you; I will tell you the whole truth. This girl has been brought up in my house; she was the niece of my poor wife that is gone; she was the orphan child of a worthless father, and we could do no less; she has been brought up with my son Audley. You know my son Audley; I believe you have seen him; a poor unfortunate being, deformed, and that never had a day's health. He has lived shut up in a band-box;[1] knows no more of the world than a child. He never spoke to a woman in his life but this girl and his own mother; yet this poor wretch has taken it in his head, forsooth, that he must have a wife. Amy, to do her justice, is a likely girl; he has seen her every day, and thinks himself in love with her. The girl very naturally would have no objection to marry the heir of the Mandeville estate; and so, if we do not mind and look about us, they think to make a match of it.

"I need not tell you, my dear Thomson, that that must not be. The girl is a likely and a good girl; but she is no match for a son of mine. Nor indeed is it my wish that this poor creature should marry at all. He has not the wit to govern himself; he must always be in leading strings;[2] and is there any sense in placing such an object at the head of a great family? His children, I dare swear, would be all such poor helpless creatures as himself. But his

1 A small box of cardboard or thin wood for holding articles of clothing (originally neck-bands).
2 Strings or straps which support a child learning to walk.

brother Henry [my father], whom I have just put into the army, is as likely a young fellow as you shall see on a summer's day. The king himself [James I.], who is an admirer of fine young men, I assure you, took a great deal of notice of him, when he was introduced at court on his appointment: and it is him I look to for the continuance of the Mandeville family.

"And now I have laid open my heart to you, Jack. You have made the circumnavigation of the globe, and are not a poor ignoramus like this hopeful heir of mine; but (I say it without flattery) must know something of the world. You know that such things as this boy and girl have taken into their heads must not be; but that we, who are older and wiser, must take care and see every thing right. Now then, Thomson, what I ask of you is an act of friendship; and as I have been always kind and faithful to you, I hope you will not deny me; and I assure you, you shall be never the worse for it in the end. It is natural, as I said, that the girl should like to marry the heir, and be at the head of Mandeville estate. But she is a good girl in the main, and will make a good wife. She shall be set right in this freak[1] of hers; I will take care of that. What say you?"

Lieutenant Thomson was a good-hearted, generous young man, and regarded the being serviceable to his friend as the first of human virtues. He had no objection to marriage; he liked the person of Amelia; and he was not displeased with what the commodore had dropped about an establishment and a portion. Thus far his motives were selfish; but it was not a small recommendation of the plan in his eyes, that, in pursuing it, he was to confer an essential benefit on his patron. He entered thoroughly into the ideas that had been stated to him; he was convinced that the heir of a great family ought not to be thrown away upon an unequal marriage; and he saw all that had yet passed between the young people, as an idle and unauthorized fancy, which it became their elders warily to counteract. He answered therefore, that, provided Miss Amelia could be thoroughly cured of this foolish notion of hers, and could approve of him for a husband, it would give him the greatest pleasure to adopt the commodore's proposal.

The negociation having been thus far successfully conducted, the harder task remained, of reconciling the mind of Amelia to the project. This part of the business was devolved upon Mrs Dorothy. The influence of the commodore was reserved, like that of the descent of a god by the Greek tragedians, as a last resource,

---

1 A thing or occurrence that is irregular; an aberration.

to be used only in an embarrassment that nothing but the descent of a god could solve.[1] Mrs Dorothy could reason with her niece; and Amelia would feel herself free, with a person of her own sex, to express her objections. If the commodore had spoken, what he said would of course have been received in silence; and that consent is most to be relied on, and by consequence is most acceptable to the party by whom consent is desired, which is given in words.

Mrs Dorothy took the young lady roundly to task. She first communicated to her all the observations she had made. Amelia blushed abundantly. She had flattered herself, that whatever had passed between her and Audley, as it had constantly passed in the sacredness of privacy, had been a secret to all but themselves. Maiden modesty always feels the discovery that a partial sentiment has been nourished towards a person of the other sex, with a sensation like guilt.

Mrs Dorothy proceeded to enlarge on the unsuitableness and enormity of such a match. She could not have believed that Amelia, who had been admitted under the roof of Mandeville House out of charity, could have been guilty of so ungrateful and treacherous a return, as that of seducing the heir. It could only be ignorance, that caused her for a moment to harbour the idea of such a union. The laws of England,[2] and of the whole civilized world, rendered the thing impossible. A crowned head might as well be expected to be joined in wedlock to a shepherdess, a thing that did well enough in a romance, but was not to be found anywhere else. She told her niece the story of the Earl and Countess of Hertford, who lay in separate imprisonment for nine years, in consequence of having contracted an unauthorized marriage, till

---

1 Mandeville alludes to the Latin term *deus ex machina*.

2 Mrs Dorothy may be converting custom into law, or simply threatening Amelia. Cousin-marriage was a grey area in morality, and in the Victorian period it came to be thought of as biologically unsound (although Queen Victoria and Prince Albert were cousins). However, while marrying a dead wife's sister was against church law until 1907, cousin-marriage was not against either canon or civil law. It could be frowned on, but was also used as a means of keeping property within the family. From an emotional point of view, cousin-marriage kept a young person within the safety of the first or birth family, as opposed to the second or conjugal family. Indeed marrying or loving on the basis of affinity rather than difference explains the fascination of some Romantic writers with sibling incest, which more obviously violates the incest taboo and was forbidden.

at length the death of the lady finally restored the Earl to his liberty;[1] to which she added many other anecdotes, which plentifully occur in the instructive annals of Queen Elizabeth. She added, that the commodore had resolved to apply to the government of his country for an interdiction against so disgraceful an act; but that he had kindly allowed her first to try the strength of expostulation with Amelia, before he had recourse to so terrible an expedient. The consequence of the idea being persisted in, and, still more, if the rites of the church were resorted to, to sanction a thing in its own nature so abominable, would be the utter ruin of Audley. He would undoubtedly be committed for life to a solitary imprisonment, and cut off from every shilling of his inheritance, by a decree of the court of Star-Chamber.[2] Mrs Dorothy here overwhelmed her poor unprotected hearer with an account, altogether unknown before, of the delinquencies of her father, which, as the ancient maiden set them forth, subjected him to the penalty of an ignominious public execution, and cut off his posterity from the possibility of ever becoming mixed with the better orders of society.

This eloquent harangue was finally wound up with an appeal to every generous feeling in the heart of Amelia. The fate of her beloved Audley was placed completely at her disposal. The young man, like all persons brought up with the notion of becoming heirs to a great estate, was headstrong and obstinate, inaccessible to the sober suggestions of reason, and obstinately bent to run on destruction. It was in the power of Amelia only to save him. By marrying another she would preserve him for ever from the possibility of fatal mischief; while he himself, seeing that there was no hope for him in the pursuit of this destructive scheme, would soon be restored to quiet and self-possession, and would finally, by the innocence of his mind, and the eminent talents with which

---

1   Edward Seymour, Earl of Hertford (1539–1621) secretly married Lady Catherine Grey (1540–68), sister of Lady Jane Grey, in 1560 without the royal consent required for persons of royal blood. They were imprisoned in the Tower, where she died; he was released in 1571 and contracted another secret marriage.

2   The Star Chamber was an English court of law that sat at the royal palace of Westminster and was supposed to ensure the fair enforcement of laws against those so prominent that no ordinary court would convict them. It met in secret with no indictments, rights of appeal, juries or witnesses. By the time of Charles I it had become synonymous with the abuse of power by the King and his circle, particularly Archbishop Laud, and was abolished by the Long Parliament in 1641.

he was endowed, become a comfort to himself, and an ornament to his family and his country.

The discourse of Mrs Dorothy drowned the fair face of Amelia in tears. A thousand varying emotions contended in her bosom as it proceeded. She saw all the fond hopes with which the sweet music of Audley's voice had inspired her, withered for ever by the pestilential breath of her aunt. The first impulse of her soul however was a generous one. She would never, no never, be a cause of calamity to her cousin. For herself, it did not signify what became of her. She had never thought herself of much importance in the world; and now, that it was discovered to her that she was at best only a dishonoured branch of a respectable family, her depression was complete. She had never flattered herself to be more than the ivy that might be supported by the nobler stem of her illustrious lover; but that she should injure him, and wither the honours that were so truly his, she could die a thousand deaths rather than endure the idea. She was now altogether worthless and nothing; and let her be sacrificed.

The situation of this generous girl was truly a pitiable one. By the unfeeling contrivances of the commodore and his sister, she was attacked in this point, that was every thing to her, with her only protector at a distance. They did with her what they pleased. They made her believe what they pleased. What chance had she, in a contest with these grey-headed conspirators? The very pith of all they insisted on was, that whatever measure it was necessary for them to pursue, must be taken without exciting the smallest suspicion in the mind of her beloved admirer.

It was so arranged, that the moment Mrs Dorothy had exhausted the whole artillery of her eloquence upon her niece, the commodore entered the room where they were sitting. This completed the defeat of Amelia. She might have expostulated with her aunt; she might have ventured upon a few timid questions and objections. But the presence and the voice of the commodore struck her dumb. She threw herself at his feet. "Oh, sir," said she, "dispose of me as you please. I grieve for my offence; I intreat you to pardon any confusion and mischief I may have occasioned in your family. I would not for the world be a cause of injury to your son."

The commodore, finding her in this tractable and humble frame of spirit, endeavoured to soothe her. His soothings were like the softened roarings of a bear murmuring her maternal regard to her cubs. This was a style of address to which his rugged nature was altogether unsuited; he could afford little more than some inarticulate indications of what he meant; and it was incumbent on Amelia, to take the will for the deed.

Whatever remained to be done was speedily effected. Short courtship suited best, with such a marriage as was now in hand. The poor lieutenant, was little versed in the temper and manners of the frailer sex; and all that was coldness, and a certain unconquerable horror at the sacrifice Amelia was making, he unsuspectingly set down to maiden coyness and reserve. She was of a nature so gentle and so mild, that she could not deport herself disdainfully to any one. Add to which, Thomson was not of a romantic temper. He knew, that the wedlock he was contracting was not a match of love. He took to wife a beautiful and amiable young woman, with a handsome portion, and, by so doing, conferred an essential benefit on his patron; and he saw no reason to be discontented with his lot. As to Amelia, the painful duty (for duty she esteemed it) in which she was engaging, she wished to have over as soon as possible. When it was done, and could not be recalled, she hoped she should feel more resigned to her fate. But all the interval was nameless repinings, and horror, and anguish,—a state of mind too terrible long to be endured.

Audley in the mean time had been led away to London. For a few days he was amused with the journey, and the multifarious objects which the metropolis presented to his observation. He saw the king, and the Duke of Buckingham,[1] and Prince Charles. It was at the time that the two latter were just returned from Spain; they were at the height of their short-lived popularity; and the nation overflowed with gratitude to them, for *not* having brought over the infanta to be their future queen. Audley received a letter from Amelia, full of tenderness and love; and he was delighted. One of the conditions arranged by the old people with his mistress, when they terrified her from her loyalty and her vows, was, that she should receive no more letters from her lover. She admitted that this was best; she knew she could not read the ardent effusions of his unsuspecting soul, in her present state of mind, and live. She even made it her own request, that she might not so much as know when a letter from him was brought. She prescribed to herself for the present the impossible task, of forgetting that he existed. Ah, how little was her acquaintance with the subtlety of love, and how much did she overrate the firmness and resolution of which she was capable!

---

1   George Villiers, 1st Duke of Buckingham (1592–1628), a favourite of King James I and then of Charles.

For Audley, he lived a few days upon her first letter; but it was not long, before he began to pine for another and another. No second letter ever came to his hand. He wrote under a still increasing anxiety and perturbation of mind. What he wrote contained so ingenuous and unaffected a picture of a beating and a bleeding heart, that even the persons who had conspired the death of all his hopes on this side the grave, began to be moved. The commodore ordered the man of business who was his agent in London, to wait upon his son, and acquaint him with the marriage that had taken place. Audley listened to the man; but he did not understand him. It was as if the fellow had used words, wholly unconnected with the possibility of a meaning. In all the vocabulary of poor Audley, there was no phrase that could express the marriage of Amelia with another.

There was a sensible portion of time in which the mind of the young man remained in this state of stupefaction, and he really could not understand what his visitor came to announce to him. The posture which succeeded, was that of unbelief, a firm rejection, as of an impudent invention that was sought for some reason or other to be imposed upon him. In sentiment, he relied upon the fidelity of Amelia, as upon the pillars of creation. In reasoning, he knew how possible it was that one should lie; that his father or another should seek to deceive him in this point; but that the tale should be true—was impossible.

He ordered without a moment's pause the quickest mode of conveyance to be provided for him, and he set out for the Mandeville estate. During the journey, his mind was in the greatest agitation. He adhered most constantly and inflexibly to his first conclusions; but from the region of the brain, where thought succeeds thought with such trackless swiftness, he could not wholly shut out ideas of an opposite kind. He reached Mandeville House, fevered, and burnt up with a thousand emotions. He thought only of his cousin; he inquired for no one else. There is something in the supernatural tone of an anxious mind, that awes even the most brutish. The servants dared not speak to him, or answer his questions; they could only tell him that Miss Montfort was not there. He hastened to her apartment; all was silent and deserted, and spoke death to his spirit. Nothing appeared, as it used to appear. Her bed looked as if it had not lately been occupied; her books and her desk were gone; he saw only the virginals (harpsichord) with which she had been accustomed to soothe his cares. He called for his father; but the habitual temperature of both was reversed; the commodore had seen him unseen as he passed along the gallery, had marked the wildness of his eye, and the vehe-mence of his gestures, and had not the courage to approach him.

The fatigue of mind and body which Audley had undergone, was a thing to which he was altogether unused; he sunk under it, was no longer able to support himself, and was quietly conducted to his bed. In the night he was seized with a strong fever; in the morning he became delirious. He called incessantly for Amelia. Shortly after, in fancy he beheld her before him; he then saw her torn away by ruffians; he heard her screams; his own screams were agonizing, and pierced to the soul; it was by force only that he could be confined to his bed. When the first violence of his delirium subsided, he expostulated with his attendants with an inconceivable flow of eloquence; he intreated them to attempt to deceive him no longer; it was ineffectual and impotent; he knew that Amelia would never give him up; nothing could diminish this confidence in him. "Then, oh, bless me with the truth! let my ear hear words responsive to those that repose in my heart! bring her to my presence; let my eyes once more be made happy with the light of her countenance; let my hand once more be pressed in the hand of Amelia! I will give up my family; I will renounce all claims to my inheritance; I will maintain her with the labours of my hands; I will dwell with her in the wilds of America; and no one that has known me, shall ever again be annoyed with the mention of my name."

The commodore was inexpressibly astonished with the incredulity of his son, and thought it became him to put an end to it. For this purpose he caused a letter to be written by Amelia herself, announcing the event. Its contents were as follow:

"Audley, I am married. It is for your sake I have done this. Nothing but the consideration of your welfare, could have pre-vailed with me. If I had not complied, your ruin would have been inevitable. I have removed the only obstacle that could turn you aside from that career of honour and virtue, for which nature designed you. Do not be angry with me. The act by which I have sealed our separation, was not the act of infidelity or indifference. Forgive it! But, above all, be happy, my l——! Be happy!"

This letter was speedily conveyed to the young man's hands; and it effected in him an entire revolution. He gazed upon it earnestly. He studied it intently, as if his whole soul were riveted upon its contents. In the hand-writing he could not be mistaken. His knowledge of it was as intimate, as his acquaintance with the features and voice of the writer. It was that evidence, which alone could convince him of the reality of his calamity.

All his agitation was now past. No more of violence, or raving, or impatience, was ever again discovered in Audley. The tears at first rolled in streams down his cheeks; but not a muscle of his face was moved. He remained the statue of despair. No smile from that day ever lighted his countenance; no accident ever raised up his head, or prompted him to look upon the heavens, or with a direct view to behold the sun or the stars. Narrow as had been the scene of his education, in this one event he had lost every thing. The society of Amelia, the being for ever united to her, was the only boon in the globe of the living world that he had ever desired. And now all things were the same to him,—except that he had a preference for looking on desolation. All within him was a blank; and he was best pleased, or rather least chagrined, when all without was a blank too. There never perhaps was an example of a human being so completely destroyed at once. He was the shadow of a man only.

I know not whether the commodore himself did not sometimes almost repent the work of his hands. One thing however is certain, that, much as he disliked this son before, he was now exceedingly anxious to alter the succession of the estate, and fix the inheritance upon my father, Audley's younger brother. My father however always steadily opposed the project. Whether, in spite of this opposition, it would have been effected if the commodore had lived, I cannot determine. An accident however, the consequence of inebriety, cut him off, shortly after the events of which I am speaking. Another chance happened in no long time following, which completed the tragedy. Amelia died in childbed of her first child, and the infant did not survive her. Thus every thing was wound up with Audley at once. He was left uncontroled, the master of himself and of an ample fortune, with no other disadvantage, than that he totally wanted the spirit to enjoy the one, or to use the other. This was the state of mind in my unfortunate kinsman, which solves the riddle that occurred, and shows why, being the lineal representative of an opulent family, and proprietor of four or five splendid and delicious mansions in different counties of England, he was induced to choose the most uninviting of them all, and to live in it in so obscure and unlordly a style.

My uncle had felt much regard for my father,—as much as was compatible with the peculiar turn his mind had taken; which was to dwell for ever on one event, to consider that in relation to himself as the only reality, and scarcely to bestow so much regard on every thing that existed in the world beside, as an ordinary

human creature would bestow upon the shadows of a magic lan-
thorn. Years rolled over the head of this unfortunate man in vain.
While he was young, the amiable object of his early love was all
that interested him on earth; and, as he grew older, habit produced upon him the same effect, which had at first been the child
of passion. He loved his sadness, for it had become a part of
himself. All his motions had for so long a time been languid, that,
if he had been excited in any instance to make them otherwise,
he would scarcely have recognized his own identity. He found a
nameless pleasure in the appendages and forms of melancholy, so
great, that he would as soon have consented to cut off his right
hand, as to part with them. In reality he rather vegetated than
lived; and he had persisted so long in this passive mode of existence, that there was not nerve and spring enough left in him, to
enable him to sustain any other.

My uncle felt a marked kindness for me for my father's sake.
Though fortune was of no value to this victim of sorrow, yet he
could not help being conscious that his brother's conduct had
been peculiarly honourable, when he refused to concur in the
commodore's plan for disinheriting his eldest son, and rather
chose to expose himself to his severest displeasure, than aid in the
injuring a person so near to himself, so inoffensive in his
manners, and who had in himself no powers of defence against
the meditated wrong. My uncle therefore received me with kindness, and immediately appointed for me and Mr Bradford, who
was prevailed on to become my tutor, an apartment in his house.
Beside the individuals of the family I have already named, I had
also a sister; but she for the present resided with her mother's
relations.

CHAPTER V

I was too young in years when I entered my uncle's mansion, to
have a clear notion of what were the first impressions I received
there. I remember only the silence, the monotony, and the gloom,
that pervaded it. My uncle had his apartments; and I and my tutor
had ours. It was a general rule through the house, that no one was
to intrude himself on the master uncalled for. If by any rare accident I came within sight of him unexpectedly, I was instructed to
hide myself, to steal away with cautious steps, and to do nothing
that might excite observation. My education was grave and sad;
but if the restlessness of boyish years chanced at any time to awake

me to a gayer tone, the sight of my uncle checked my buoyant spirits at once, my countenance fell, and my thoughts became solemn. No emotion however of aversion or dislike ever accompanied this. A harsh word never fell from his lips; an angry tone never escaped him. The only expression of displeasure of which he seemed capable, was some gesture showing that he suffered and was distressed, but always without any token of resentment, or word of reproof. I thought therefore of my uncle with awe, never with fear. I saw in him a mysterious being exciting my wonder, and in whom I was ever most unwilling to occasion displeasure; but at the same time a being incapable of inflicting the smallest mischief. It is strange, but from my own experience I can aver it to be true, that this silent, inoffensive, and mournful carriage, rendered it a thousand times more impossible for me ever to forget the attention that was due to him, than the fiercest tones and the most passionate demeanour could have established in my mind.

Still my uncle was not so altogether dead to all that passed around him, but that he considered himself as my natural guardian, and held it his duty that at certain intervals I should be summoned to his presence. These intervals gradually settled themselves into a distance of one month from each other. On the first Sunday in every month I looked to visit his apartment. I was conducted thither by my tutor, and generally received from him before we set out, an admonition as to the behaviour it would be proper for me to observe. Our visit seldom lasted more than two minutes, and was always attended with a small donation, which to my youthful mind associated it with ideas of pleasure. My reverend preceptor, who knew his cue, constantly said something, without being asked, upon the topic of my proficiency. The good man however, who displayed surprising powers of copiousness and amplification on all other occasions, seemed at these times like one rigidly formed in the discipline of Lycurgus.[1] My uncle I am sure would have expired on the spot under one of the ordinary homilies of Hilkiah. Commonly, when approached, my uncle held out his hand to receive me. Sometimes he would withdraw the hand already held out, as if the touch of hand to hand had something too much of life in it for him to be able to endure, and would take hold of my coat. I have known him lay his hand

---

1 Legendary lawgiver who established the military reformation of Sparta in the eighth century BCE. Whether or not he existed, he is the symbolic founder of this Greek city-state which was known for its discipline and austerity.

upon my head; but for him to kiss me, or seat me on his knee, was impossible. That would have been utterly in contradiction with the unenterprising apathy that constituted his existence.

I was my uncle's only visitor, and my visits were uniformly such as I have described. He would no doubt have preferred receiving me alone, had he not feared, that the thoughtlessness of my years might sometimes make me overstep the limits of quietism[1] which he found necessary, and that the restraint of my tutor's presence might be requisite. Beside, that in receiving us together, he considered himself as discharging two duties, extending towards me the notice of a parent, and giving encouragement to my preceptor in the exercise of his functions. But it is not to be conceived to what a degree my uncle found these visits exhausting to his spirits. He continued indeed inflexible in the resolution to go through this painful duty; but he was sometimes obliged to defer the visit for several days, before he could summon up energy and firmness enough to receive us.

The precautions of my uncle against the turbulent and boisterous spirits he anticipated in a boy, were scarcely necessary in my instance. I never was a boy. It will easily be supposed from the description I have given of the house and its neighbourhood, that I did not meet with many occasions to excite my hilarity. The entire household, as always happens to a certain degree in the mansion of an opulent country-gentleman, were moulded after the fashion of their master. You might have thought yourself in the monastery of La Trappe,[2] or the withdrawing-room prepared to receive those who had visited the cave of Trophonius.[3] To an

---

1 A set of Christian beliefs that arose in the 1670s and 1680s and elevated passivity and contemplation over virtuous action.

2 Abbey in Normandy where the Cistercian order was reestablished in 1664. The order had existed since the Middle Ages, suffered greatly under Henry VIII's dissolution of the monasteries (and again during the French Revolution), and in 1664 was thoroughly reformed as the Order of the Reformed Cistercians of the Strict Observance, known for maintaining a general (though not total) atmosphere of silence.

3 Proverbial phrase for looking gloomy or melancholy. According to one version in Greek mythology, when Trophonius and his brother Agamedes built the treasury for Hyrieus, King of Boetia, they did so in such a way that they could rob the treasury at will. When Agamedes was caught in a trap set by the King, Trophonius cut off his brother's head and hid it so that he himself would not be implicated. He was then swallowed up by the earth. Later he became associated with an oracle in a cave at Lebadia, where his ghost in the form of a serpent would address suppliants who always returned looking unusually gloomy.

observer of a satirical and biting vein, which was not my case, it would have appeared a ludicrous spectacle to see how every one, from the steward down to the scullion, seemed to ape the manners of the master. They had all and severally a solemn countenance, and a slow and measured step. When you spoke to them, they seemed to hesitate whether they should answer you; and if the final decision was in your favour, the answer was framed by the most concise and sententious model. Mr Bradford formed the only exception to this rule. He was of importance enough in his own eyes, to make it unbecoming that he should shrink into the mere imitator of another. Except in the presence of his patron, as I have already stated, he had therefore a great deal to say for himself. It will presently be seen, how far his discourses are to be considered as discordant with the general tone of this silent mansion.

The sort of intercourse in which I thus lived with my fellow-beings, formed me early to a habit of reverie. I delighted to wander; but I was not delighted with objects of cheerfulness. It will already have been seen, that I was not often intruded on with impressions of this sort. I loved a hazy day, better than a sunshiny one. My organs of vision, or the march of my spirits, gave me an aversion to whatever was dazzling and gaudy. I loved to listen to the paltering of the rain, the roaring of the waves, and the pelting of the storm. There was I know not what in the sight of a bare and sullen heath, that afforded me a much more cherished pleasure, than I could ever find in the view of the most exuberant fertility, or the richest and most vivid parterre.[1] Perhaps all this proves me to be a monster, not formed with the feelings of human nature, and unworthy to live. I cannot help it. The purpose of these pages is, to be made the record of truth.

One thing is particularly worthy of observation in this place. It is strange, young as I was, how the scenes which immediately preceded my quitting the shores of Ireland, lived in my mind. I thought of them by day; I dreamed of them by night. No doubt, the silence which for the most part pervaded my present residence, contributed to this. All was monotonous, and composed, and eventless here; all that I remembered there, had been tumultuous, and tragic, and distracting, and wild. I saw in my dreams—but indeed my days, particularly that part of them which was passed in wandering alone upon the heath, were occupied to a great degree in visionary scenes—I saw, I say, in my dreams,

---

1 A level space in a garden, occupied by ornamental flower-beds.

whether by night or by day, a perpetual succession of flight, and pursuit, and anguish, and murder. I saw the agonising and deploring countenances of Protestants, and the brutal and infuriated features of the triumphant Papist. I recollected distinctly the expiring bodies I had beheld along the road-side in my flight, some perishing with hunger and cold, and some writhing under the mortal wounds and tortures that had been inflicted by their pursuers. All this of course came mixed up, to my recollection, with incidents that I had never seen, but which had not failed to be circumstantially related to me. It would indeed have been difficult for me to have made a separation of the two; what I had heard, had been so fully detailed to me, and had made such an impression upon my juvenile fancy, that it stood out not less distinctly pictured to my thoughts, than if I had actually seen it. This was all the world to me. I had hardly a notion of any more than two species of creatures on the earth,—the persecutor and his victim, the Papist and the Protestant; and they were to my thoughts like two great classes of animal nature, the one, the law of whose being it was to devour, while it was the unfortunate destiny of the other to be mangled and torn to pieces by him.

It is now necessary that I should introduce my reader to a more intimate acquaintance with the reverend Hilkiah Bradford, the instructor of my youth. His figure was tall and emaciated; his complexion was of a yellowish brown, without the least tincture of vermillion, and was furrowed with the cares of study, and the still more earnest cares of devotion; his clothes were of the cut that was worn about forty years before; and his head was always decorated with a small velvet skull-cap, which set close to the shape, and beyond which the hair, though itself kept short, protruded above, below, and all around.[1] His gait was saintly and solemn. He conformed himself not at all to the celebrated maxim of Plato, of "sacrificing to the Graces."[2] He went on directly to the great end of his calling, his duty to his Heavenly Father, without ever condescending to think how his manner might

---

1 Hilkiah's skull-cap suggests that he may be a Puritan of the "separatist" variety. However, since Godwin concentrates in him both the bigotry and potential of a religious sectarianism that was highly complex, it would be a mistake to tie him too narrowly to one denomination. See Introduction, pp. 38–39.

2 In his *Lives and Opinions of Eminent Philosophers* the Greek biographer Diogenes Laertius (c. third century CE) quotes the renowned philosopher Plato (427–347 BCE) as exhorting his pupil Xenocrates to "sacrifice to the Graces" (4.6).

impress, favourably or unfavourably, his fellow-mortals, mere "earth and worms." He was, as I find it expressed by an eminent historian,[1] speaking of an individual who seems to have had a striking resemblance to my tutor, "a person cynical and hirsute, shiftless in the world, yet absolutely free from covetousness, and I dare say from pride." Like that person also, he seemed to have a peculiar vocation for, and delight in, the instruction of youth. In this occupation, he laid aside that bluntness that accompanied him upon other occasions; and if he was not critically persuasive, yet there was something so unequivocally zealous and affectionate in his manner, as answered all the purposes of persuasion.

He was familiarly conversant with the Greek and Latin languages, and with poetry; yet he did not disdain to commence with me in the first rudiments of infant learning, and gradually and gently led me on, from the knowledge of the alphabet, and the union of two letters in a syllable, to an acquaintance with many of the sweetest and the sublimest monuments of ancient lore. In these respects I found myself most fortunate under his guidance;—yet I must own that he did not receive exactly the same sensations from Ovid and Virgil that I did.[2] He had a clear apprehension of their grammatical construction; but he was not electrified, as I often was, with their beauties. The parts in which he most seemed to delight, were those, in which these poets bore the most resemblance to certain passages of sacred writ; so that, as Mr Bradford persuaded himself to believe, they must have had some undiscovered access to the fountains of inspired wisdom. He found the Mosaic account of the creation in the commencement of the Metamorphoses, and the universal deluge in Deucalion's flood. But, above all, he was struck with the profoundest admiration in reading the Pollio of Virgil; he saw in it clearly a translation

---

1 [Godwin's note:] Wood, Athenae Oxonienses, Vol. II. Col. 671.
[Anthony Wood (1632–95) was the author of *Athenae Oxonienses: An Exact History of all the Writers and Bishops who have had their Education in the Most Antient and Famous University of Oxford* (1691–92; rev. and enlarged 1721). Mandeville refers here to Wood's description of Ezrael Tonge (1621–80), a virulent anti-Jesuit later associated with Titus Oates in the fabrication of the "Popish Plot" in 1678. The association of Hilkiah with Tonge is anachronistic, and marks the persistence of religious fanaticism even after the Restoration, into the Enlightenment period.]

2 Ovid: Publius Ovidius Naso (43 BCE–17 CE), author of *The Metamorphoses*; Virgil: Publius Vergilius Maro (70–19 BCE), best known as the author of the Roman epic *The Aeneid*.

of the inspired raptures of the prophet Isaiah foretelling the coming of the Messiah;[1] and he exclaimed, as he went on, with a delight, a thousand times repeated, and never to be controled, "Almost thou persuadest me that thou art a Christian!"[2]

The gloominess of my character might have made me an unpleasing or unpromising pupil to many instructors, but not so to the reverend Hilkiah. In the premature gravity of my features he read a vocation to the crown of martyrdom, if such should be the fortune of the Protestant church in our time as to demand of its faithful adherents the sealing their sincerity with their blood: and, as my tutor regarded light laughter, and merriment, and the frolics of youth, as indications of the sons of Belial[3] and heirs of destruction, he hailed with proportionable delight my inflexible seriousness as the token of a happier destination. Nor did I fail to entertain a regard for my preceptor, fully correspondent to that by which he was animated towards me. I saw the singleness and simplicity of his heart; I felt his entire innocence of those tricks, and that hollow and hypocritical personation of an assumed part, which, with young persons of any discernment, so early introduces an opposition of interests, and a trial of skill between the master and scholar, which shall prove himself the most successful deceiver. My preceptor never treated me like a child; he considered me as a joint candidate with himself for the approbation of the Almighty in a future state; and this habit of thinking is calculated, probably beyond any other (when sincerely cultivated), to level all distinctions between the rich and the poor, the young

---

1 Hilkiah sees classical texts as having value only insofar as they contain shadowy types of Christian truth. Thus Deucalion foreshadows Noah. In the Greek legend, Zeus sends a flood to destroy humankind because of its wickedness. Deucalion is warned of the impending disaster by his father Prometheus, and takes refuge along with his wife in a huge chest that comes to rest atop Mount Parnassus at the end of the flood, after which the earth is repopulated. Similarly, because Virgil's fourth *Eclogue* (addressed to the consul Gaius Asinius Pollio) celebrates the birth of a child, it was thought by Christian commentators to prefigure Christ's birth.

2 Adapted from Acts 26:28. Hilkiah often cites scripture, and indeed never quotes anything else. These quotations will not be identified except when the reference is important.

3 One of the four crown princes of Hell, whose name means "worthless" in Hebrew. Milton describes him more favourably than the other fallen angels, as being "For dignity compos'd and high exploit," though "all was false and hollow" (*Paradise Lost* 2.11–12).

and the old, and to introduce a practical equality among the individuals of the human race.

This just and upright man had all his passions subdued under the control of his understanding: there was but one subject, that, whenever it occurred, inflamed his blood, and made his eye sparkle with primitive and apostolic fury; and that was, the corruption of evangelical truth, and the grand apostacy[1] foretold to us in the Scriptures. In a word, the spring and main movement of his religious zeal lay in this proposition, "that the Pope is Antichrist."[2] I was well prepared to be a ready hearer of this doctrine: for, had not my father and my mother fallen untimely victims under the daggers of Irish Catholics? He was, if I may so express myself, the more like one possessed in speaking on this topic, for he claimed to be collaterally descended[3] from John Bradford,[4] the famous martyr in the reign of Queen Mary—a man who, in the flower of his life, defied all the torments of fire for the sake of Jesus, and who scorned to purchase the clemency of his persecutors, by an engagement in the smallest degree to remit his exertions to convert his fellow-creatures from the errors of Popery.

Mr Bradford took care, that I should be early initiated in the main topics of controversy between the church of England and the church of Rome. Idolatry—this was the first and favourite subject of charge against the professors of Popery. The first of the ten commandments, the basis of all Christian morality and duty, was that "God alone should be worshipped." The second, which the adherents of Antichrist found it necessary to blot out of the catalogue, was, that we should "make to ourselves no graven image, or the likeness of any thing in heaven above or earth beneath, to bow down to it, and worship it." But the Papists, in defiance of these prohibitions, had saints for every day in the calendar, and addressed their prayers to all the host of heaven,

---

1 Abandonment of religious faith.
2 The antagonist of Christ who deceptively resembles him (1 John 2:22, 4:3; 2 John 7). Protestant Reformers such as Martin Luther (1483–1546) and John Knox (c. 1514–72) identified the Papacy with the Antichrist.
3 A collateral descendant is any relative descended from the brother or sister of an ancestor (for example, a niece or grand-nephew).
4 Protestant martyr (c. 1510–55) who was burned at the stake during the reign of Queen Mary I (1516–58). She took England back to the Roman Catholic faith when she became Queen in 1553, and began a campaign of persecution against Protestants.

beseeching their interposition with the Almighty, and vainly imagining that they would be more near to hear, or more inclined to favour, than the omnipresent and all-merciful Creator. Add to this, their crucifixes, and their images and pictures of God and his saints, which they employed as incitements to devotion, in express defiance of the revealed will of the Most High. Yet is there no sin, against which the denunciations of God's word are more frequent and terrible, than the sin of idolatry? In the Bible we are forbidden to "call any man master on earth"; yet the Pope has been erected into the infallible head of the church. In the Bible we are told, "If any man shall add to the words of his revealed will, God shall add to him the plagues that are written in the book; and if any man shall take away from them, God shall take away his part out of the book of life"; and we are specially warned, that we adhere to the communications we have "received from Christ Jesus, and beware lest any man spoil us after the traditions of men." Yet the Papists have both added to and taken from the written word of God, and have expressly placed their vain traditions upon a level with the inspired writings themselves. It is clear therefore, that "God has given them up to a reprobate mind, and abandoned them to a strong delusion that they should believe a lie; that they may perish with the children of this world, and not be made partakers with the heirs of light":—in fine, that every one who died unreclaimed from the errors of Popery, would be the object of God's wrath and condemnation in a future world.

Mr Bradford was particularly shocked with the unbounded usurpations and arbitrary power of the church of Rome. He found in her the "beast with seven heads and ten horns, and upon his horns ten crowns, and upon his heads the name of Blasphemy."[1] Under another figure she was typified by the "woman, arrayed in purple and scarlet colour, that sat upon this beast, drunk with the blood of the saints and the martyrs, and having a golden cup in her hand, from which she made all nations, and all the kings of the earth, drunk with the wine of her fornications."[2]

---

1 Revelation 13:1, referring to the Beast of Revelation which comes out of the abyss, calls on men to worship it and persecutes true Christians, until it is defeated by Christ in the Battle of Armageddon and thrown into the lake of fire.
2 Referring to the Whore of Babylon, another allegorical figure of evil, in Revelation 17:4–6.

"How unlike was all this," exclaimed my preceptor, "to the simplicity of the divine author of our religion, who declared that his kingdom was 'not of this world,' and who, while on earth, had not 'where to lay his head!' The Popes on the other hand claimed, that 'whatsoever they bound on earth should be bound in heaven, and whatsoever they loosed on earth should be loosed in heaven.' They usurped the power of giving away crowns, and setting up and deposing kings, and in the height of their intoxication set their foot upon the neck of emperors. There was no end to their pride, their pomp, and their temporal magnificence. They claimed the whole wealth of the world as theirs. They, 'as God, seated themselves in the temple of God, showing themselves that they were God.'"[1]

My preceptor was further revolted at the sanguinary character of the church of Rome. She put the dagger into the hands of her votaries, and caused them to commit innumerable massacres. Assassination was one of her favourite means for achieving her purposes. He loved to expatiate upon the examples of Balthasar Gerard, Clement,[2] and Ravaillac, beside others with whose stories he was accurately furnished. The Gunpowder Plot, if it had been completed as it had been designed, would have exceeded all these in horror. The cruelties of the Inquisition furnished also a copious field of declamation to Mr Bradford.[3] To these he added the wholesale extermination of the unresisting

---

1 In this paragraph Hilkiah alludes to a number of books from the New Testament in addition to Revelation, including Romans, Matthew, Luke, John, Thessalonians.

2 Balthasar Gérard (c. 1557–84) was the assassin of William I of Orange (1533–84), leader of the Dutch movement for independence from (Catholic) Spain. He was gruesomely executed for his crime. Jacques Clément (1567–89) was a Dominican friar who assassinated Henry III (King of France from 1574 to 1589) during the French Wars of Religion (1562–98). Henry had flirted with Protestantism as a child (the only reason for Hilkiah to see his assassination as a horror), though he was later leader of the Royal army against the Protestant Huguenots.
Although all the plotters named by Hilkiah *are* Catholic, he is fascinated by a violence that he repeats in his violent hatred of them.

3 The "Inquisition" seems to be used generically here (as in many Gothic novels) to denote a papally ordained political power that acted against heretics and was notorious for its secret procedures and torture.
Although the Spanish Inquisition (instituted in 1478) is the best known Inquisition, there were others, including the first Inquisition in twelfth-century France, directed against the Albigensians.

Albigenses and Waldenses.[1] The idea of burning a man alive for his opinions, was the most infernal, that cruelty had ever devised. No bigotry perhaps could persuade its adherent, that a man attached even to death to the religious opinions he had formed, was a criminal, in the same sense as a murderer, or a robber, a man who broke through all the restraints of morality, or violated all the securities of society, that he might indulge in depravity and excesses. The unfortunate victim of the law against heretics, was usually a man of exemplary moral habits, and who sacrificed every baser and sensual inticement to the dictates of his conscience. He was therefore, if erroneous, rather an object of pity, than of ferocious vengeance. Mr Bradford usually wound up his argument on this particular head, with the favourite maxim of the most liberal at the time of which I am speaking,—that all sects and every denomination of creed were entitled to toleration, except the Papist, who obstinately refused, when in power, to grant toleration to those that differed from him, and who therefore deserved that the "measure which he dispensed, should be rigorously measured to him again."

But if Mr Bradford regarded the whole church of Rome with horror, and all her members as obnoxious to the pains of eternal damnation, the Popish priesthood,

> eremits and friers,
> White, black, and grey, with all their trumpery,[2]

were particularly the objects of his aversion. He considered the craft of Popery as calculated with infernal subtlety, to enslave the minds, and subjugate the understandings of all its lay-adherents. The celibacy of her clergy[3] had the immediate effect of creating a vast body of men, dispersed in all kingdoms, provinces, parishes of the Christian world, with few considerations to bind them to

---

1 The Albigensians (also called Cathars or Manicheans) were heretics who believed not in one all-encompassing God but in two equal principles of good and evil. By contrast the Waldensians or Vaudois, persecuted from the twelfth century onwards and nearly annihilated in the seventeenth century, were an early Reformist group within the Catholic church, which rejected graven images and were concerned with social justice. Originally associated with Peter Waldo, who died in the early thirteenth century, the group still exists today and is included in the Alliance of Reformed Churches of the Presbyterian order.

2 *Paradise Lost*, 3.474–75.

3 There is no indication that Hilkiah himself is not also celibate.

their particular country or neighbourhood, and who therefore to an astonishing degree formed part of the wheels and pins of the vast mechanism, by which the conclave of Rome undertook to control the civilized world. By means of her dignitaries, she did not fail to superintend the education of all persons of royal or elevated birth, and to have some of her clergy admitted to political offices, and possessing the secrets of all cabinets. Auricular confession,[1] and the sacrament of absolution, was a stupendous device for subjecting the consciences of all, men, women and children, to her despotic authority. The doctrine of indulgences,[2] dispensations, and pardons for sin, to be issued from the Papal chamber, strongly inforced this, and brought vast sums of money into the disposal of the Visible Head of the church. The first encouraging men to sin by the hopes of forgiveness, and then granting them absolution, was a nice game, by which the power of the clergy over their illiterate followers was increased to an incalculable degree. The doctrine of purgatory, and of masses for the dead, was another admirable machine, for raising to the utmost height the power of the church. Every man who was anxious for his state in the future world, could not fail to feel strongly excited, to appropriate a part of his possessions for the delivery of his soul; and every child or heir to an estate would be influenced by the same motive, whether out of affection to his predecessor, or from ostentation, that he might appear to have that grace of piety and natural affection, to which he was really a stranger. The vast armies of monks, nuns and friars, with their mitred abbeys and convents of all sorts, were another great reinforcement to the church of Rome, and, by forming a part of the national manners of the different countries in which they were established, seemed to afford a security to the church, that could never be overturned. Neither did my preceptor fail to be furnished with a copious collection of the frauds of the clergy, by which they seemed arrogantly to insult the understandings of mankind, from the holy house of Loretto,[3] and the transforma-

---

1 Private confession to a priest in a confessional box or booth.

2 Indulgences permit the full or partial remission of punishment due for sins that have been committed and forgiven through the process of absolution. While the original idea was that such indulgences drew on the Treasury of Merit accumulated by Christ's sacrifice and the penance of various saints, their actual sale was a point of contention when Martin Luther initiated the Reformation.

3 According to legend, the Virgin Mary's house in Nazareth was brought through the air by angels to Loreto in Italy.

tion of the bread and wine in the sacrament into the body and blood of Christ, to the relics of the saints, and the milk of the virgin exhibited in a thousand churches. Thus insolently were the best energies of our nature trampled on by a set of hardened impostors; and the flock of Christ (for such they ought to have been found) cajoled and terrified out of the use of their own eyes and their own judgments, at the same time that, by the mortal sin of idolatry, they were made to consign themselves over to eternal damnation.

Mr Bradford was singularly delighted with those tremendous stories which are to be found in the history of the Reformation of Religion in Scotland, particularly relating to the eminent confessors, Patrick Hamilton, and George Wishart.[1] Hamilton, a young man of noble birth and extraordinary talents, was betrayed to the stake by Alexander Campbell, prior of the Dominicans, who, under the cloak of friendship and a desire to be better instructed, extorted from him a full confession of his sentiments, and then accused him before Chancellor Beaton, primate of Scotland. Far from relenting at the tragic catastrophe thus treacherously occasioned, Campbell was present at the execution, and still insulted Hamilton at the stake; when the martyr, seized with a prophetic afflatus,[2] turned towards his tormentor, reproached him with his faithlessness and his hypocritical professions of favour to the principles of the Reform, and then, with a solemn and awestrik-

---

1 John Knox's *The History of the Reformation of Religion within the Realm of Scotland* (1587) includes the stories of the two Scottish martyrs. Hamilton (1504–28) was the great-grandson of James II of Scotland and travelled to Europe, where he came into contact with the ideas of Martin Luther and Desiderius Erasmus. He attracted the wrath of Archbishop James Beaton (c. 1473–1539), but Beaton could not proceed against him because of his high connections, except by allowing him to preach openly, so that he would then convict himself. Hamilton's death helped to spread the Reformation in Scotland and his only book, *Loci Communes*, can be found in John Foxe's *Actes and Monuments*. In 1546 Archbishop David Beaton (c. 1494–1546), nephew of the first Beaton and the last Scottish cardinal before the Reformation, had Wishart (c. 1513–46) tried and burned as a heretic, perhaps to distract attention from criticisms of him for policies that had led to two invasions by England. Knox was a disciple of Wishart, who helped spread the teachings of John Calvin and Huldrych Zwingli in Scotland. Wishart's death led to the second Beaton's assassination, which was a turning-point in the triumph of Protestantism in Scotland.
2 Divine creative impulse or inspiration.

ing accent, cited him to answer this within forty days, before the judgment-seat of Christ. The consequences were memorable. Campbell is related to have been immediately seized with a supernatural horror, which he was by no means able to shake off, to have declined shortly into an incurable frenzy, and presently after to have died, to the terror of every beholder.

The concluding scene of the life of Wishart is not less impressive. He was condemned to be burned alive by the sentence of Cardinal Beaton, nephew and successor to him who had tried Hamilton; and the cardinal had the inhumanity to cause a gallery to be prepared in his castle of St Andrews, with tapestry, silk hangings, and cushions of velvet, that he might gratify himself with beholding the execution. But, while a priest appointed for that purpose exhorted Wishart, now surrounded with flames, to repent of his heresies, and ask pardon of the Almighty, the victim imperiously commanded him to be silent, adding, "This fire occasions trouble to my body indeed, but it has in no wise broken my spirit; but he who now looks down so proudly upon me from yonder place, (pointing to the cardinal), within a few days shall be as ignominiously thrown down from it, as he now proudly reposes himself there."[1] All which was punctually fulfilled. A courtier, to whom the cardinal had refused a boon which he earnestly solicited, in revenge assassinated the prelate in his bed-chamber, and threw his dead body into the streets, from the very balcony which he had shortly before occupied at the execution of this holy martyr.

My preceptor was profoundly addicted to cabalistical divinity,[2] and especially to that branch of this science which he deemed applicable to the church of Rome. He was particularly gravelled[3] with that triumphant argument of the Catholics, built upon the concluding promise of our Saviour to his church, "Lo, I am with you always, even to the end of the world," and the insulting tone with which her votaries demanded of the Protes-

---

1 Adapted from Knox's *Reformation*.
2 The Kabbalah is an esoteric school of thought which developed within Judaism but has also been taken up by Christian and New Age mystics. It tries to explain the relationship between an unchanging and mysterious element and the finite universe. Some less educated Puritans turned to it as a quick means of access to the secrets of heaven and earth, but Hilkiah's fascination with a broader "cabalistcal divinity" is another indication that he cannot be neatly fitted into the categories of Puritan, Presbyterian, and so on.
3 Perplexed.

tant, what becomes of this promise, if, as you say, the visible church of Christ for more than a thousand years has been universally plunged in damnable error, so as to deserve to have applied to her the description of "Babylon the Great, the mother of harlots and abominations of the earth?"[1] Against this attack Mr Bradford had no other resource, than an attempt to trace in ecclesiastical history, the "two witnesses clothed in sackcloth, that were to prophecy one thousand two hundred and sixty days"; and to show that, in the intervals of greatest darkness and most universal apostacy, God "had yet reserved to himself seven thousand men, who had not bowed the knee to the image of Baal."[2] But the study to which the reverend Hilkiah most indefatigably applied himself, was the "number of the beast, which is the number of a man; and his number is six hundred and sixty-six."[3] This he had turned in a thousand ways; he had tried it in arithmetic; he had essayed it in anagram; every way it afforded him conclusions, that seemed to point at the latitude of Rome. Still my preceptor had a secret misgiving, that he had not arrived at the right solution. We were at one time not without some apprehension, that, by the severity of this inquiry, his wits would have been unsettled, and that he would have been rendered a qualified candidate for the cells of Bedlam.[4]

A book that my preceptor particularly recommended to my attention, was Fox's Acts and Monuments of the Church;[5] nor

---

1 Matthew 28:20 and Revelation 17:5.
2 Adapted from Revelation 11:3 and Romans 11:4. Baal: one of the seven princes of Hell, considered Satan's main assistant during the English Puritan period.
3 Revelation 13:18.
4 Bedlam, implying uproar and confusion, was a hospital for the insane, whose methods at the time were far from humane. The name is a corruption of the Hospital of St. Mary of Bethlehem in London.
5 John Foxe's *Actes and Monuments of these Latter and Perillous Days, Touching Matters of the Church* (1563) was commonly known as the *Book of Martyrs*. The second edition (1570) was expanded to 2300 pages and had 160 woodcuts, and the book continued to be updated after Foxe's death in 1587 with the addition of new material, for instance on the Gunpowder plot (1605). It was further updated in 1641. While Foxe began with the early Church martyrs and saw himself as a historian, the last of the *Actes'* five books dealt with the persecution of Protestants under Queen Mary I and was influential in exciting anti-Catholic feeling.

did I need much persuasion to a study, to which my temper inclined me, and which occasions that sort of tingling and horror, that is particularly inviting to young persons of a serious disposition. In this tremendous volume the engravings eminently help to inforce the dead letter of the text. The representation of all imaginable cruelties, racks, pincers and red-hot irons, cruel mockings and scourgings, flaying alive, with every other tormenting method of destruction, combined with my deep conviction that the beings thus treated, were God's peculiar favourites, the ornaments of the earth, the boast and miracle of our mortal nature, men "of whom the world was not worthy," produced a strange confusion and horror in my modes of thinking, that kept me awake whole nights, that drove the colour from my cheeks, and made me wander like a meagre, unlaid ghost, to the wonder and alarm of the peaceable and well-disposed inhabitants of my uncle's house.

CHAPTER VI

In advancing thus far, I have, for the sake of presenting in one view ideas of a particular kind, outrun the course of my narrative, and must now return to bring up some smaller anecdotes of my early years, which, by this method of arranging my materials, have been put somewhat out of their place. Amidst the dreary uniformity of my uncle's residence, every arrival of a stranger was hailed, like a festival day in a school-boy's almanack. It promised some novelty: it was solemnly announced; and with no less effect, than when the pedant, from his eminence apart, "and in his own dimension like himself,"[1] makes proclamation of a holiday. Though I was of a gloomy and saturnine cast, it is not to be understood that my heart did not beat, and my blood did not tingle, like those of my fellow-creatures. There was this difference between me and my uncle, though in the gravity of our dispositions we considerably resembled each other. To judge from appearances at least, he desired no novelty, or none of an extrinsic sort, and shrunk from all disturbance. He was used up as to the views and prospects of life, and cherished hope in his bosom no longer. Not such was the condition of my existence. I hoped for, and I dreamed of, pleasures yet untasted. I was no friend to light laughter and merriment; but my heart was susceptible of

---

1 Adapted from *Paradise Lost*, 1.793–95.

attention and curiosity; and the novelties that presented themselves to my senses I was well disposed to investigate. The world to me was yet in its nonage,[1]—had all the freshness and vigour of youth; I had much to see, much to learn, much to make trial of, and much to taste. I felt like one for whom adventures and great events are reserved, and, as we find it expressed in the common story-books, who is "to go out, and seek his fortune." When the arrival of a stranger was announced, I felt again and again a sort of prophetic anticipation, This may be to me the eventful moment, big with a thousand causes of admiration.

Many a stranger arrived at our postern, who, to the nicety of a critic in language, would have been a stranger no longer. But it was not so to me. The very butcher who came once a week to bring us provisions, did not, even by the unvaried regularity of his approaches, altogether divest himself of the grace of novelty. The chimney-sweeper was another of those rare phenomena, who, by the repulsiveness of his sable hue, and the cry by which he proclaimed that he had reached his unenvied height, communicated some sensation to my childish organs. But the visitor dearest to my youthful curiosity, was the pedlar. Pedestrian as he was, the pack which he bore on his shoulders, displayed, when unfolded, a multiplicity of temptations to expence that was truly astonishing. Besides gloves, and stockings, and handkerchiefs, and ribbands, and linens, and stuffs, for the men and the maidens, I generally found among his treasures some toys, or implements of childish industry, upon which I did not fail to set an immeasurable value. The vender himself was ordinarily a Jew, and was in my eyes the greatest curiosity in his whole collection. I watched his physiognomy with sly and sensitive vigilance. I asked him questions about himself, his travels, his language, and his countrymen, and not only gained information that furnished to me a copious field for fancy and rumination, but found also considerable entertainment in his jargon, and the uncouth accent and articulation with which he delivered his answers.

I have already done full justice to the virtues of my preceptor; I have shown my esteem for him, and the ascendancy he possessed over my mind. In matters of opinion that was complete. I was convinced of his integrity; I admired his intellectual powers; I was lost in astonishment at the greatness of his attainments. I was conscious of the limited sphere of my own knowledge; I distrusted my judgment; I looked up to him as an oracle. Such is the

---

1 Period of immaturity.

natural indolence of the majority of human minds; we love to have some one at hand, upon whose decision, in questions of truth and falsehood, of good and erroneous taste, of prudence or the contrary, we can rely, and thus save ourselves from the fatigue of investigation, and, as we fondly hope, from the dangers of being misled and erroneous.

Most men, after this ample confession, will be surprised when I add, that I scarcely loved Hilkiah. I am ashamed of the perverseness of my own heart when I speak it; but it is the truth. Hilkiah was my instructor, with powers much more ample than those of an ordinary instructor. I had no parent; and my uncle, who stood to me in the room of one, was of too passive and retired a character, to be appealed to, or to be expected to interfere as an umpire between us. I felt the extraordinary powers with which my tutor was invested, at the same time that I felt he had not those claims over me, which the mysterious ties of nature instinctively impart, or by prejudice and long established custom impose on the unformed mind. Hilkiah too was aware of the full extent of his trust, and was well disposed to avail himself of its prerogatives. Add to which, there is something in the sacerdotal[1] character, that scarcely fails to inspire into him in whom it is vested, a magisterial tone, and a disposition, such as I have already described in Mr Bradford, amply to unrol the volume of his lessons, and to accompany his instructions with a full statement of the causes and considerations by which they are inforced.

All this was insupportably galling to me. When my instructor dwelt upon those conceptions which had no special application to myself, and which seemed to me branches of the great code of immutable truth, I was patient, submissive and docile; but when this elaborate style was applied to things that thwarted my inclination, or was made the vehicle of pointed reproof upon my character or actions, I was by no means equally tame. The extremely unfavourable impression which was thus made upon me, was perhaps partly owing to the solitary nature of my education. I did not find myself one of a tribe, whose feelings were common with each other, and who might have afforded me the example of a cheerful or a careless submission; I dwelt in a monarchy, of which I was the single subject. I was not indeed a tumultuous and refractory pupil; I did not give much trouble to my preceptor; but on that very account these things revolved incessantly in my mind, and worked themselves more deeply into the substance of my character.

---

1 Priestly.

The part of my narrative in which I am now engaged, would perhaps to many men appear tedious and frivolous. It was not frivolous to me; and the history of my maturer years would be very imperfectly understood, without the explanations I am here endeavouring to give.

One of the subjects on which Mr Bradford thought proper to lecture me, was my pride and self-conceit. In my own opinion, I had no pride but what was becoming, and no esteem for myself greater than that in which I was amply justified. But my preceptor thought otherwise. He explained to me with great emphasis, that humility was the cardinal virtue of a Christian, without which it was impossible to enter into the kingdom of God. It was the distinguishing feature of evangelical religion, that its professors owed, and confessed they owed every thing, to the mere mercy and unmerited favour of their creator. He required nothing at our hands but the explicit and unequivocal acknowledgment of his sovereign grace; and unless we emptied our hearts of all merit and presumption, and confessed that in ourselves we were entirely abominable and worthless, we could form no expectation of his favour.—I found this doctrine hard to flesh and blood.

Hilkiah went on to insist, that the most ragged and shivering beggar stood an equal chance with myself, to receive the most exalted marks of divine favour in the kingdom of heaven. He plainly told me, that a person of the most loathsome and offensive appearance might, in the sight of God, be among the excellent of the earth, and be ranked by omniscience with his most chosen saints.

If all this had been delivered as doctrine merely, I should have been content. What my preceptor offered to my consideration would have passed as words, and I should have been a good Christian upon as cheap terms as most of my neighbours. But Hilkiah did not stop here. It may be that he was actuated towards me by a parental affection; certain it is that he commented with great rigour upon my supposed defects in this nature; and what was worse, in a style so general and loose, as conveyed no distinct ideas to my mind. If my preceptor had so designated my faults, that I could have had a clear apprehension where the error lay, I have that conviction of my own candour, particularly at this early stage of human life, as to be persuaded that I should have ingenuously and sedulously applied myself to the remedy. But it is so easy to rail, and so delightful to the majority of declaimers to unburthen themselves "in good set terms,"[1] and yet with a rea-

---

1 Shakespeare, *As You Like It*, 2.6.17.

sonable absence of thinking and precision, that it is not to be wondered at that Hilkiah became tickled with the speciousness of his discourse, without adverting to that radical defect, which made it wholly unsusceptible of being applied to use. The discourse of my preceptor, though shaped, it may be, into specious and well sounding periods, was vague and indefinite. If I desired to correct myself in conformity to its admonitions, I knew not where to begin. I understood that it was querulous and severe, but that was all. It inspired into me painful emotions; but it furnished me with no light to direct my course. I regarded my tutor as censorious and cynical; I believed him to be unreasonable and unjust; and by degrees came to view him as an enemy, that misconstrued my dispositions, that traversed my pleasures, and sought to rob me of that self-complacency which is the indefeasible adjunct of an honourable mind.

It must be admitted that I was not at this time uncharacterized by a certain loftiness of mind and disdainfulness of spirit. Whether these features were consistent with the purity of a gospel religion, I must leave to the casuists.[1] No doubt this frame of soul in me was rendered somewhat more palpable and systematical, by the habitual gravity of my character. By that gay and frolicsome mood which is for the most part incident to our early years, it would in some degree have been smoothed down; and, amidst the bursts and sallies of a buoyant spirit, I should often have forgotten my self-respect, and dismissed the idea of my own importance. But to the uniform sedateness, not to say sadness of temper, which characterized me, this self-oblivion was more difficult. I was proud, because I felt my value. I was conscious that my intellectual powers far exceeded the common rate; I was not unaware of the quickness of my apprehension, and the clearness and subtlety with which I distinguished the differences of things; I felt ambition, and the secret anticipation of a high destiny, which subsequent calamities have at length succeeded to extinguish within me; I felt the ardour and generosity of my spirit, which, as I believed, made me capable of great things; I felt an inborn pride of soul, which, like an insurmountable barrier, seemed to cut me off for ever from every thing mean, despicable and little. My bosom was fraught with that principle which Pythagoras[2] so

---

1 Those who reason from individual cases rather than principles; used pejoratively to describe those who use specious and opportunistic arguments.
2 Pythagoras (c. 570–c. 490 BCE): Greek philosopher, mathematician, and mystic.

emphatically recommends to his pupils, of self-reverence,—a determination of mind by which he who has it, is irresistibly impelled to reject whatever might stain the integrity of his spirit, or oblige him to part in any degree with the approbation of his own heart. When my preceptor, with that primeval simplicity and innocence for which he was so remarkable, pointed to the beggar-boy or the scullion, and bid me ask myself, What was I better than they? I perceived my soul revolt from the ignoble comparison, and believed I must dismiss all the discernment with which my reason inspired me, before I could subscribe to the humiliating conclusions which he called on me to draw. It is not impossible that my birth and fortune, my being heir to the honourable name and opulent property of Mandeville, contributed their share to the disdain with which my bosom swelled against Mr Bradford's insinuations.

One of Hilkiah's whims was, that in order to subdue the carnal pride of an unregenerate nature, it was good for me to be called occasionally to the exercise of those vulgar offices, which in the houses of people of family are ordinarily reserved for menials. Why should not I brush my own clothes, or black my own shoes? The Saviour of the world condescended to wash his disciples' feet; and the pope (though this was no recommendation to my preceptor) has his anniversary, when he observes the same ceremony to this day. To the evangelical motives for this discipline, Hilkiah added others drawn from the stores of philosophy. Nothing could be more precarious than the favours of fortune; and, if I might some day fall into the situation of being obliged to subsist by the exertions of my own industry, why should I not now, in the pliant years of youth, anticipate this necessity? I was a man, before I was a gentleman; it was good therefore, that I should not be wholly ignorant of the true condition of man on this sublunary stage, that I should be somewhat acquainted with his plain and genuine state, and not only with the refinements of artificial society. We lived in the midst of the confusions of a civil war; who could tell at what point all this violence might terminate? As the presbyterian had subdued the episcopalian,[1] and the

---

1 Episcopalian and Presbyterian refer to different forms of church polity with implications for political government. An episcopal church, deriving from the Greek "episkopes" (overseer), puts power in the hands of the clergy and is hierarchical; it has bishops (and sometimes archbishops), with a presiding (arch)bishop at the top. Examples are the Catholic and Anglican churches. At the other extreme is congregation-

independent the presbyterian,[1] might not the fifth monarchy-man finally get the start of all, and level the proud fortunes of the noble and the gentleman with the dust?[2] Was it not good to be prepared for these changes? The most enviable character that could fall to the lot of man, was independence; this was the goal, however mistakingly pursued, which men aspired to, when they sought after wealth, and "joined house to house, and field to field,"[3] with insatiable greediness. But the man of true independence is he that suffices to himself, and stands in no need of another. And this doctrine my preceptor illustrated by the known

alism, where the local congregation has control over its church (e.g., the Baptists). The Presbyterians represent what Godwin calls the "middle way." Deriving their name from the Greek "presbuteros" (elder), their churches are governed not by a single bishop but by a group of elected elders. But since these elders, in turn, are governed by synods which oversee several congregations, Presbyterianism remains a top-down form of church government.

1   In the course of the First Civil War (1642–46), members of the Long Parliament became divided over whether they should negotiate with the King or defeat him militarily. Though alliances were fluid and lines hard to draw, the Presbyterians were the "peace party," while the Independents wanted to defeat the King. The point is that while the Presbyterians had been the progressive group in relation to the Episcopalians, they now became the more conservative group. In *HCE* Godwin allies himself with the Independents or "republicans": "They were a set of men new in this country; and they may be considered as having become extinct at the Revolution in 1688" (1.5).

2   The Fifth Monarchists were among a number of democratic and sometimes extreme groups in the Civil War period, including the Levellers, Diggers, and Ranters. A non-conformist Dissenting group that wanted a reformed religious state, they were influential from 1649 to 1661 and initially supported Cromwell but then turned against him. They took their name from a prophecy in the Book of Daniel that four monarchies (Babylonian/Assyrian, Persian, Grecian/Macedonian, and Roman) would precede the fifth monarchy or new spiritual kingdom of Christ. Their proximity to the year 1666, the last three numbers of which were identified with the Biblical number of the Beast in the Book of Revelation, made them believe that the Fifth Monarchy was close at hand, to be followed by the return of the Messiah. While Hilkiah does not speak as a Fifth Monarchist here, he shares their obsession with the number 666. His rhetoric of levelling may also recall the Levellers, a more moderate group led by John Lilburne (1614–57) which played a role in Parliament and the Model army, and which was criticized by the Diggers: "True Levellers" who did not believe in private property.

3   Adapted from Isaiah 5:8.

story of Diogenes, who, when he was told that Menas, his slave, had turned runaway, exclaimed, "Aha! can Menas do without Diogenes, and cannot Diogenes do without Menas?"[1]

It may seem but a childish tale; but I cannot express with what loathings I was seized, when I was called upon to put in practice this lesson of humility. I remember an occasion when it was necessary to remove some logs of wood from one side of the farmyard, the only creditable and well arranged appendage to our mansion, to another side. This appeared to my preceptor a desirable opportunity for the practical illustration of his lessons. I was yet a mere urchin; and the task assigned me was considerately apportioned to my strength.—After all, this was certainly an injudicious mode of inforcing moral truth. An accountable and voluntary being cannot be made better, but by enlightening his understanding. Morality has nothing to do, but with actions chosen by their performers. Where there is absolute command on one side, and unconditional submission on the other, a useful result as to external circumstances may be achieved; but there cannot be a particle of good moral sense implanted by what is thus done under the bare influence of authority.

No doubt I was a proud creature; and, as I have already said, I never was a boy. As I did not appear born to feel the hard hand of necessity, I expected to bend only to my own will, and to consult my own judgment, in every thing I did. I understood something of the importance of lessons, and I willingly complied in whatever related to that point. I was desirous of possessing all the advantages of education, and all the information that falls to the lot of an ingenuous youth, destined to fill an honourable station in life. And lessons, a progress to be made in languages or in science, possess all the character of a system of mechanism, and accordingly are as readily submitted to, as the order of our meals, or the putting on of our clothes. It is principally where the caprice of him who has authority shows itself, where the wand of command is exhibited in abrupt nakedness, that the heart of the proud one revolts. Whatever proceeds in unvaried uniformity, or in stated and regular progression, we subscribe to without a murmur. What is thus prescribed, we acknowledge to be intended for our benefit; and the reason of the thing having once been known, or supposed to be known, we continue to act upon

---

1 Diogenes of Sinope (c. 400–325 BCE) was the founder of the Cynic philosophy. He makes this comment about his slave Manes (not Menas) in the section on himself in *Lives of the Eminent Philosophers*, Book 6.237.

that reason, without insisting that it should be submitted to an examination perpetually to be repeated. But when Mr Bradford, no longer seated in the chair of the pedagogue, issued his imperious mandates of Go there, or Do this, whenever what he required related not to my abstract advantage, but to the common usefulness of life, my spirit refused to submit; I felt convinced that I was treated in a manner unbecoming and unjust; and, my neck never having been bowed to the condition of a slave, my whole soul revolted at the usurpation. Hilkiah saw something, but imperfectly, of the state of my mind on these occasions; but, instead of modifying and adapting his proceedings to my tone of feeling, he took the contrary course. He held it for "stuff of the conscience" that he should subdue my refractoriness, and bring down a stubbornness of soul, so opposite, as he imagined, to the temper of a true Christian. Alas, good man, he little understood the tendency and nature of the task he had undertaken! My pride was not perhaps so great, that it would not have yielded to severe calamity, or to ferocious and unmitigated tyranny: I cannot tell. But there was no power that could be exercised by Hilkiah, who was a man substantially of a gentle temper, and under the roof of my nearest relation, that had any chance of rendering him victorious in this contest. I submitted indeed outwardly, for my nature did not prompt me to scenes of violence; but I retained the principle of rebellion entire, shut up in the chamber of my thoughts. If at any time I manifested tardiness, (and how could it be otherwise, when the soul was averse?) this called down from my preceptor a bitterness of remark, or a dryness of irony, that filled my bosom with tumults, and was calculated to make me understand something of the temper of a fiend. Hilkiah, as I have said, felt disposed to multiply his experiments in proportion as he found me restive. And it grieves me to confess that this ill-contrived and senseless proceeding, at length drove me into a rooted aversion of heart from this good man, to whose industry and care I owed so much, and the parity and zeal of whose intentions entitled him still more to my regard. It was Hilkiah, that first made me acquainted with the unsavouriness of an embittered soul. From time to time he filled all my thoughts with malignity. I can scarcely describe the frame of my temper towards him. I would not have hurt him; but I muttered harsh resentment against him in sounds scarcely articulate; and I came to regard him as my evil genius, poisoning my cup of life, thwarting my most innocent sallies, watching with a jaundiced eye for faults in me which my heart did not recognize, and blasting that sweet complacency, in which a virtuous mind is delighted to plunge itself and to play.

I said little; but this circumstance only deepened the effect on my mind. "Give sorrow words," says the great master of the human soul.[1] Whatever sentiment finds its way to the lips, and vents its energies through the medium of language, by that means finds relief. "Out of the abundance of the heart the mouth speaketh";[2] and we feel satisfied, if we have told, even to the desert air, but much more in the hearing of an intelligent creature, the story of our griefs. But my silent nature was an ever-living and incessant curse to me. My displeasures brooded, and heated, and inflamed themselves, at the bottom of my soul, and finding no vent, shook so my single frame of man, like to an earthquake.

I know there are rugged and brutal natures, who would interrupt me here, and cry out, that there is an easy remedy for all this. The boy whose thoughts are here described, was too much indulged; an effusion of wholesome severity would soon have dispersed these clouds of the mind, and have caused him to know, that there was nothing but ground for congratulation, where he found so much occasion for complaint. And let these brutal natures go on in the exercise of their favourite discipline! There will always be crosses, and opposition, and mortifications enough in the march of human life, from the very principles upon which society is built, and from the impatience our imperfect nature is too apt to conceive, of the imputed untowardness and absurd judgments, of those that are placed under our control. But let those of happier spirit know, that this imperious discipline is not the wholsome element of the expanding mind, and that the attempt to correct the mistaken judgments of the young by violent and summary dealing, can never be the true method of fostering a generous nature; in a word, that to make the child a forlorn and pitiable slave, can never be the way to make the man worthy of freedom, and capable of drawing the noblest use from it!

I have said that I was habitually a visionary. My visions were frequently of long duration, and branched out into a variety of minuter circumstances. In these moods I sometimes imagined that every thing around me was engaged in a conspiracy against me, that I was, in some inexplicable way, a captive, whose

---

1   Shakespeare, *Macbeth*, 4.3.209.
2   Matthew 12:34.

genuine destiny led to higher things, but who, like some imperial bird that had fallen into the hands of lawless men, was shorn of its strongest feathers, and deprived of its genuine and heart-awakening element, shut out from the sublimer scenery for which its nature fitted it, and robbed of that mysterious and inestimable freedom in which it could feel at home, at its ease, and resting, so to express it, upon its proper centre.

However strange it may appear, I am almost inclined to say, that the boy, particularly in these visionary moods, feels a more earnest aspiring than even the man, after true freedom, with all its adjuncts and retinue of inexplicable events. The comparison is the same, as between the colt, whose mouth has never known control, who frolics in a thousand wild gestures and attitudes, and has nothing to do but to prance along the plains,—and the horse. Man by degrees has bowed the neck to the hard yoke of necessity, has looked through human life and the conditions of existence, and has reasoned himself into submission, to those distasteful, but inevitable evils which are inseparably interwoven in the web of mortal life. Not so the boy: he has seen nothing of this; nor have any considerations occurred to his mind, leading him to choose subjection, and voluntarily and resolutely to resign the sweets of liberty.[1]

I am aware, that in what I now record I am relating a strange story; but it is necessary to the illustration of my future life. The moral of Aesop's fable of the lion and the man is applicable here. We see every where the monuments of human achievements; but the lions have no historians and no statuaries of their own.[2] All those persons who have produced practical treatises on the art of education, have been men. The books are always written by those who are the professors of teaching, never by the subjects. Every author indeed was once a boy; but he seems to abjure the recollection of what he was, when he puts on the manly gown, and to have no consideration and forbearance for that state through which every man has passed, but to which no man shall return. I have been obliged, by the tenour of what I have to record, to take

---

1 See Godwin's "Of the Rebelliousness of Man" (Appendix G3a).

2 Aesop (c. 620–560 BCE) was a Greek or Ethiopian who wrote animal fables. In the fable of the man and the lion, a man insists on the superior strength of men and shows the lion the statue of Hercules as evidence; the lion retorts that this proves nothing since the statue was made by a man. The moral is that the powerful construct the truth to suit their own purposes.

a contrary course. It has been necessary for me, to resume the character of my early years, and to forget for the moment that those years have passed away. I have committed to paper what, during those years, passed through my mind; I have nothing to do with either vindicating or condemning that of which I am the historian. I may thus perhaps have performed a task of general utility; it surely is not unfitting, that that which forms one considerable stage in the history of man, should for once be put into a legible and a permanent form. Far be it from me to impute my own feelings during this period, to every youth that is placed under the direction of a preceptor. I know that my feelings were solitary, unsocial, exaggerated, wicked. Still I regard myself on the whole as a member of the great community of man; and I cannot be persuaded that feelings, which were so familiar and habitual with me, do not under some modification exist in the majority of human minds during that period of life which in my own case I have been attempting to describe.

But to return. I may sum up the view of my situation, so far as Mr Bradford is concerned, by saying that it consisted of two features principally. I had the most unbounded deference for this good man in all his speculative decisions. His religion was my religion; his prejudices were my prejudices. As an essential characteristic of my nature was energy, I could have died for the faith in which he had instructed me; I could not bear to hear his tenets contradicted or opposed. At the age of which I am speaking I was but little of an intellectual gladiator; I therefore made up in zeal, what I wanted in skill; my blood boiled, my flesh trembled, and my indignation exceeded all ordinary pitch, when I heard sentiments uttered, which my education had taught me to regard as the pernicious suggestions of a blasphemous spirit. Yet, at the same time that I regarded Hilkiah in this point of view with unmingled reverence, I never wished to behold his face. His countenance, his figure, his gestures, the very tone of his voice, were all subjects of aversion to me. My understanding, my opinions, were at his devotion: but my heart took a different course. "It came not into his secret; and to his counsels it was not united."[1] In all that was most cordial and consolatory to the spirit it stood off from him, as wide as the poles from each other. In my wishes and cherished visions he had no part. This was a

---

1   In Genesis (49:6), Jacob calls his sons together, and says of Simeon and
     Levi, "O my soul, come not thou into their secret; unto their assembly
     ... be not thou united: for in their anger, they slew a man."

peculium[1] that I carefully shut up in my own bosom, and of which no creature that lived was a partaker.

CHAPTER VII

Such was the monotony of my life during the years in which I resided under the roof of my uncle. Few were the occasions that were calculated to awaken in me the social affections, in their purest and most fascinating tone. To all this however there was one exception. I have already said that I had a sister. This sister I had scarcely seen; and I almost forgot that she existed. One morning Hilkiah communicated to me the intelligence that she was expected on a visit; my uncle had invited her to spend a week or ten days under his roof. It cannot be imagined what pleasure I derived from the information. The entrance of one stranger, and that stranger a visitor, under the battlements of our mansion, was an event as memorable, as a congress of half the sovereigns of Europe, and all the splendours of their reception, would be to the fashionable and the gay.

My sister was one year younger than myself. She had regular features, a transparent complexion, and a most prepossessing countenance. "Her pure and eloquent blood spoke in her cheeks."[2] Her eyes were dark and expressive; and her smiles were bewitching. Her form was light and airy, like that of a sylph. Her motions had a *naiveté* and grace, that I cannot conceive to be exceeded. She made me a painter. Whenever I shut my eyes, I saw her; whenever I let my thoughts loose in imagination, I pictured to myself her gestures and her air. The tone of her voice was thrilling; and there was a beauty in her articulation, that made my soul dance within me, and without the labour and weight of emphasis, gave to every thing she said an impression beyond the power of emphasis to convey. Oh, Henrietta, thou dearest half of my soul, how can I recollect thee, such as I now saw thee, without rapture!

There is something in the prejudice of kindred, that has an uncontrolable power over the soul. I was alone in the world; I had

---

1   That which is "one's own"; in Roman law, a property over which the master grants the slave rights that can be withdrawn at any moment, or a sum of money that a father grants his son during his minority. The word, of course, also has the connotation of something peculiar.

2   John Donne, *The Second Anniversarie* (1612), 244–45.

neither father, nor mother, nor brother; but Henrietta was father, and mother, and every thing to me in one. We had a thousand things to talk about; and it seems to me, at this distance of time, as if we had possessed a power of dividing and multiplying the thoughts we expressed, and of giving to every one a fineness and subtlety, that the grossness and earthiness of more advanced years can never reach. We delivered our ideas with frankness; we had none of the false reserve, that makes older persons warily examine the recollections and sallies that press to the tongue, and throw away one, and mangle another; lest they should say any thing, that should subtract from the consideration they aim at, and of which afterward they might see reason to repent.

We walked together; and wherever we walked, the place seemed to invest itself in inexpressible charms. Nothing could be more dreary and desolate than the scenery in the midst of which I lived; but the presence of Henrietta gave to it the beauty of the Elysian fields;[1] and when she was gone, yet I could not visit the well-known haunts without their reviving in me the same ravishing sensation. She talked; and my soul hung on the enchanting sounds. To the little tales of the place from whence she came and its inhabitants, I could listen for ever. Her observations were so unlike to any thing I had ever heard before. What a contrast to Hilkiah, and my uncle, and the gloomy and formal establishment of Mandeville House! My sensations were not less surprising, than those of Shakespear's maiden in the desert island, when first she saw and contrasted the features and figure of the graceful Prince Ferdinand, with those of the aged Prospero and the hag-born Caliban.[2] I seemed now for the first time to associate with a being, with whom I felt an affinity, and whom I recognized as of the same species as myself. This was indeed a memorable era in my existence. I was never weary of my sister's company; no sooner by any accident did I lose it, but I instantly felt as if some insupportable period of separation had intervened, and I sought her presence again with uncontrolable eagerness; by night in my dreams Henrietta was sure to appear, and in some way to be the principal personage in their incoherent and fantastical drama.

---

1 In Greek mythology, the place where the virtuous go after death.

2 Shakespeare, *The Tempest* (1.2), where Miranda, brought up in protected isolation by her father Prospero, meets her future husband, Ferdinand of Naples, and contrasts him with Caliban. Caliban, the half-human offspring of the witch Sycorax, is the original owner of the island and subsequently Prospero's slave.

The character of my preceptor was entirely artificial, and yet of an artifice difficult to express. Nothing on earth could be more void of what is commonly understood by artifice and design; he was of a simplicity the most perfect and unsoiled; he stood defenceless and unarmed, the ready prey of any one who should think it worth while to play upon the unsuspiciousness of his nature. But his character was the creature of colleges and of books, of monastic discipline and theological debates, and bore little resemblance to nature, as she shows herself in those parts of the world, or those classes of society, where these causes have no operation. My uncle was a mere shadow, the semblance of a man, where nothing seemed to bear the impression of substance. But the sallies of Henrietta were the pure effusions of an unsophisticated spirit, and were like the first breathings of the morning in nature's sweetest climate; they carried with them the freshness of untainted air, the mild moisture of the dew, and the resistless charm of a thousand odours and perfumes, I know, that in thus describing them I may seem to rave, and that the majority of readers will consider all this, as mere bombast, and high sounding words without a meaning. But, in fact, the sensations I felt were such as all words that I have the power to command, must sink under the endeavour to convey to another.

My uncle, being duly informed of the arrival of his niece, in a day or two after sent to summon her to his apartment. Henrietta, curious about so near a relation, the representative of the elder branch of our family, tasked me to give her a faithful account of his manner, his character, and all those peculiarities of which she had not failed already to hear so much. They had of course been greatly the object of my youthful wonder and remark; and, to gratify so dear a friend, I conquered the natural brevity of my sentences, and placed before her in a vivid light, those circumstances, which had impressed so strong a picture in my mind. When she received the summons I have mentioned, she exclaimed, "Must I go alone? And will not you, Charles, accompany me to my uncle?" But she was speedily convinced, that his directions must be literally obeyed, and that his spirits were too tender to enable him to sustain an interview with both of us at once. When Henrietta was introduced to him, he uttered a few short sentences, with apparent effort, and with intervals between, "You are welcome"—"I am glad to see you"—"A fine girl!" while the singularity and mournfulness of his manner bereaved her of speech: and thus the interview ended.

Some days after, my uncle made the cardinal and mighty effort of receiving us both together: but this was never repeated. He looked at us tenderly. "Love one another," he said; "be a comfort to each other; assist each of you the other in the various trials of life!"

"What a man!" said Henrietta, as we left the room. "I am sure I love him. It is impossible to feel any other sentiment towards him. How much he must have suffered! What a life! Poor, dear uncle!"

"But, Charles," she proceeded, "we must be all in all to each other. We have no parents; we have no relation in the world, but the owner of this house. And he lives among the dead. I cannot think of this mansion, but as of one of the Pyramids of Egypt; and its master is like a deceased prince I have somewhere read of, whose body rose at a certain hour every night out of its coffin, and having passed through several apartments of state in silence and sadness, returned to its place, and laid down again in death, till the same hour came round on the following night.[1]

"Our poor uncle! He has done with the world. All his thoughts and hopes are buried in the tomb. Though he exists on the face of the earth, he has no longer any concern or interest with the inhabitants of the earth. But we, Charles,—we are young. It is the fate of all living creatures, to have at some periods quick feelings and a heart unwounded; and our turn is to come. We know not what destiny is reserved for us. But we shall meet it with quick imaginations and a beating bosom; and the disappointment of all that have gone before us, will not prevent us from anticipating joy, with as sanguine a spirit, as inspired the first man, before history had yet written one solitary page of warning and example."

Swift flew the hours during this ecstatic visit, and the ten days limited for its duration were speedily at an end. The day before the departure of Henrietta, and the day before that, we began to look towards the misery of separation. For a time however this recollection merely gave bitterness to a moment; and we seemed to use it, only to give zest to our never-ending conferences, and as an inducement to plunge so much the more desperately into the sweets of each other's society. Gradually it became otherwise. The morning of the last day we were to spend together made us sober; and as we watched the setting of the sun that evening

---

1 Referring to the legend of the vampire.

beneath the ocean-wave, without speaking a word, the eyes of both of us filled with tears.

"Well!" said Henrietta, rousing herself, "it cannot be helped; we must submit to our fortunes. The day, I am confident, will come, when we shall meet again; no one knows how soon; no one knows for how long. At this moment I feel that I do not love any human creature so well as my brother; the recollection of you, my Charles, will charm away many a sorrow, and will speak consolation and pride to my heart. Still too we have something left; we can write letters. You will write to me, will you not? And when I have the pen in my hand, and my chattering vein comes upon me, with which I have already tried your patience, I will think you are present. You know I have always been the principal talker, and you have answered me with silence or few words; so I will think I have got you beside me, your arm under my arm; that will do very well, will it not? I see by your looks, that you think it will do but poorly; I know that too, Charles. Heigh ho! but we will make the best of it, and be glad of that, when we can get nothing better."

Was not this charming talk? and could I help loving such a sister as this? I could not talk thus; I could only look the things, which she clothed in such bewitching words. But, oh! every syllable and every articulation penetrated to my heart. No, I cannot but think, that never creature loved as I loved. And the innocence and simplicity of our affection, which was all soul, and had no alloy of grossness, turned it into a purer, a brighter, and a more heavenly flame. We loved, as the angels may be supposed to love above the cerulean[1] sky.

Some persons will affirm, that the sentiments and ideas I express are above the age of the actors. It may be so: I only know that all I have related comes far short of the reality. It was with us, as it is said sometimes to be with a person at the point of death, who already breathes of heaven, who seems to have put off this cumbrous load of flesh, and to partake by anticipation, of the prophetic spirit and the unearthly vision that characterise the state of saints above. The situation was new to us, to me especially; and what was felt by one of us, was imparted as it were by electricity to the other. My life had been so monotonous, and its course had had so little in it to awaken the finer feelings. If I dared hazard an idea, which after all may not be true, I should say, Henrietta talked best, but I loved the most. But in both of us the situation was such, that it awakened in us faculties which oth-

---

1   Deep blue, sky-blue.

erwise might have slept for another climacteric.[1] We leaped a gulf of years, and seemed to understand, what ordinary mortals do not understand till they have celebrated many more anniversaries at the altar of life.

CHAPTER VIII

My sister had not long left us, when Mr Bradford was seized with a distemper, that threatened to put a speedy end to his life. A physician was called in from the nearest town, and all proper assistance was afforded. But it speedily appeared that the disease was too strong for the power of medicine to baffle; and its virulence was such, that in a few days it put an end to the life of this venerable and innocent being. In one of those intervals which afforded him a comparative degree of composure and ease, he caused me to be called to his bedside. He desired me to sit near him; and he took one of my hands in his.

"My dear Charles," said he, "in the solitude in which we have lived, you have been for years the principal subject of my anxiety. Your parents you lost early by the most dreadful calamity; the state of your uncle's health and spirits have long incapacitated him from supplying their place; Providence seemed to have cast you entirely on my care. I have done my duty according to the best of that light that was afforded me; and I am thankful that I have been spared so long for that purpose. It is now the will of the Lord, that I should be taken from you; and it is not given to me to foresee what will be your destiny, when I am no more with you. All that remains is, that I charge you, 'in the sight of God who quickeneth all things, and before Jesus Christ,'[2] that you hold fast the truth that has been committed to you. I foresee that great trials are yet reserved for the people of this unhappy land. The power of Antichrist is not at an end; and the cup of his enchantments still retains all its pernicious ingredients. There shall come a falling away and an apostacy, even in this chosen land of Great Britain. But be you fast in the faith. Eschew the

---

1   In astrology climacterics were critical years in a person's life, marking turning-points and changes in attitudes to life, and occurring in years that were multiples of seven. There may also be a connection here with the falling asleep and rewakening described with reference to the Seven Sleepers in Godwin's Preface (see p. 61).

2   Adapted from 1 Timothy 6:13.

persuasions of the 'scarlet whore that sitteth upon the mountains.'[1] Let not your soul come into her secrets, neither be you a partaker in her blasphemies.

"For myself I go to the blessed few, whom Christ has chosen out of the world. I go to the little flock of his saints, whom he shall bring with him in his glory. There I shall see my excellent namesake, who when threatened with the flames, defied the power of the evil one.[2] There I shall associate with the glorified spirits of Wishart and Hamilton, who amidst the pangs of death, with pious fervour predicted, the one the assassination of his judge, while the other summoned his accuser to meet him without delay before the judgment-seat of Christ. Where I am, no pope, nor cardinal, not one member of the vast Antichristian hierarchy shall ever come.

"But I do not so far rejoice in the glory that awaits me, my dear Charles, as to make me in any degree unmindful of whatever appertains to your welfare. I have endeavoured to do my duty by you; but at this awful moment, when I am compelled to review for the last time what I have done, I am filled with apprehensions and fears, lest, with the sincerest anxiety for your good, I may at any time have chosen erroneous means. I may have assumed an undue authority; I may have mistakingly awakened evil passions in your bosom. If I have done so, I ask your forgiveness. We are all of us fallible creatures, and ought at all times to fear the errors we may commit. Do not then, my sweet Charles, remember these things against me; treasure up only those truths I have delivered to you for your everlasting benefit. Remember me as your friend; and let the eye that looks upon my tomb, and the tongue that I have taught to repeat the lessons of human and divine learning, continue to bless me!"

My heart melted at the ingenuous confessions and the earnest affection of this venerable man. I recollected all the displeasure and the animosity I had felt against him, and I was ashamed. The eye that had darted at me glances of reproach, was now closed in death; the tongue that had overwhelmed me with sharp rebuke and bitter homilies of reproof, was silent for ever. I shed a torrent of sincere tears over his remains. I accused myself of a perverse and a wicked nature, that where all was meant so sincerely, I could have harboured such stormy resentments.

---

1   Revelation 17:1.
2   Referring to the Protestant martyr John Bradford (see p. 113, note 4).

This good man, the friend of my earliest youth, did not many hours survive the last admonitions and expressions of kindness he had addressed to me. I looked on his insensible corpse; it was the first time I had ever viewed the human form, after death had already extinguished the intellectual spark; and it was an awful meditation to me—to me, more than to many others; for the habit of my soul was endless rumination, in which the tongue was chained up in silence, and the limbs almost forgot their office, but the thinking part of the machine worked incessantly, like the members and wheels of a vast machine, or like the eternal descent of the waters in a foaming cataract.

The funeral of Mr Bradford followed soon. Though the nearest market-town was at a distance of seventeen miles, we had a diminutive parish church and its little churchyard, that was only six miles from us. I had seldom visited it; for Mr Bradford, while he lived, filled the joint offices of my preceptor in learning, and the chaplain to Mandeville House; and every Lord's day duly pronounced a discourse, and became the organ of the houshold in prayer, in a little chapel, which was preserved in a state of decent repair for that purpose. I knew the church however; it had occasionally formed a centrical point in my rambles; I was not unfamiliar with its unpretending architecture and its scanty congregation of graves. At the west end, near the outer wall of the chancel, was a vault which had been built by one of the ancestors of the Mandeville family; and to this repository were the remains of Hilkiah conveyed. The steward of my uncle marshalled the ceremony; a hearse was procured for the occasion; and the mourners, myself in chief, followed on horseback. The day was gloomy; the whole hemisphere was wrapped in a thick grey cloud, yet without rain. My soul became satisfied in this seeming harmony of the elements with the melancholy of the scene.

I have described the feelings which succeeded within me immediately upon the death of my preceptor. But these feelings were temporary. While the grave of Hilkiah was freshly closed, and his last scene was vividly impressed on my memory, I repented most truly of all the anger I had conceived against him. But when the impression of his last moments was somewhat faded, and what passed at that time only ranked with the other recollections of our protracted intercourse, my original notions returned to me. While the remembrance of his last benedictions was new to me, I loved him; at all times, in a certain sense I honoured him; but finally the habit returned to me, of considering him as the being, who had poisoned the first pleasures of my infancy, and who had first caused me to feel the pains of mortification and contempt. His image, the figure which my fancy conjured up of his person and his countenance, was displeasing to me. In my dreams the idea of Hilkiah always came associated with painful sensations. Yet, along with this, he was not the less my oracle and guide, the master of my theories, and the regulator of my faith.

CHAPTER IX

It has sufficiently appeared that my situation was a solitary one, while Hilkiah lived: what did it become when my venerable preceptor was no more? If freedom could make happiness, I was free. My uncle was a mere cypher in the economy of his own houshold. Having already reached the twelfth year of my age, and being considered as the immediate heir to the Mandeville estate, none of the servants had the boldness to control me in my caprices. Happily those caprices were neither violent nor adventurous. Still more happily for me, this period of my interregnum[1] was short. What effect would have been produced, if the interval in which I was my own master had been protracted, I can scarcely venture to say. I shut my books. This had been the case during the short season of Hilkiah's mortal sickness. But then my thoughts were much occupied with his precarious state, and the melancholy catastrophe that seemed to impend. When that was decided, and still more when the remains of my preceptor had been finally carried forth from the mansion in which he had enacted so considerable a personage, I felt that I was entering on a new epoch. The apartment in which we had sat together, was now entirely mine. The easy chair, in which in his character of my pedagogue he had delighted to repose himself, was vacant.

I shut my books. Probably after some interval, if the experiment had been tried upon me, I should have returned to them. But for the moment I was delighted with the change. That which had for years been imposed upon me as a task, could not immediately convert itself into a pleasure. Greek and Latin, the historian equally and the poet of antiquity, avaunt![2] It was the badge

---

1 The interregnum was the period of parliamentary and military rule by Cromwell (1649–60). Like the references to slavery, this fleeting metaphor makes Mandeville's dissident energies available to the "other" side that goes politically unrepresented in the novel.

2 Go away, begone.

of my liberation, that I no longer pored upon pages, rich with the spoils of time. This short period had a memorable effect upon me. If before I had been a lover of liberty, and had felt the deepest repugnance to every species of contradiction and control, I now seemed to myself to have actually entered upon the privileges and immunities, that are the just inheritance of the maturer part of my species.

For a few days I was contented with the simple fruition of these privileges. To savour the condition in which I was placed, to me was happiness enough. But, after a short time, this pleasure became familiar to the sense, and stood in need of further excitement to give it pungency. How far did my liberty extend? I went into and out of my uncle's house as I pleased. But was this the boundary of my discretion? Could I wander no farther than my legs could carry me; and were my rambles confined to so much as might be accomplished between sun and sun?

It was my own voluntary choice, that brought me back each successive evening, to the house in which I had resided ever since my escape from Ireland. I might emancipate myself from this restriction whenever I pleased. I might contrive the scheme of a secret elopement. But, if I desired to use my freedom with this additional enlargement, would elopement be the wisest way of accomplishing that? Might I not form a project of departure and absence, to which it should not be difficult to obtain my uncle's consent? When I thought of absenting myself for a time from this scene of my early years, the first suggestion that offered to me was that of paying a visit to my beloved sister. How much further the genius of romance, when I had put myself under his guidance, might conduct me, I could not tell. But, if I were enabled to execute any part of the project that now rose to my thoughts, I determined that the first stage in my journeyings, the first branch of the inheritance of pleasure I proposed to myself, should be, once again to embrace my dear Henrietta.

I endeavoured in another way to anticipate the events of my future history. I was left to my own devices. No one of the household had the presumption to talk to me of my future destination; and the silence and reserve of my own nature prevented me from inviting them to enter on the topic. But was my education ended? I was not so ignorant of the rules of political society, as not to know that ten years more must elapse, before I should be acknowledged by the laws of my country as my own master. How was this period to be filled up? Should I receive no more instruction in learning? Would some reverend divine, hitherto a stranger, be introduced as the successor of Hilkiah, to superintend my studies, and keep alive the devotions of Mandeville House? This was a very anxious question to me. If the authority and the magisterial rebukes of Mr Bradford, familiarised as I had been to them from my earliest years, had proved an intolerable torment, with what patience could I think of being subjected upon the same terms to an entire stranger?

These reflections, as of a bird escaped from his cage, that seems to ask himself to what woods and coverts he shall presently make his resort, and that, while he flutters his wings, has the whole cope of heaven[1] before him to dart himself to the east or the west as he pleases, were speedily put an end to in my case, by a communication from the steward, that it was my uncle's determination to send me to Winchester school. I had once seen Winchester, and its cathedral, the venerable repository of the remains of our Saxon kings.[2] I was not displeased at the new scene of life that was now chalked out for me. I had made a sufficient experiment of the system of a private education, and I detested it. I easily conceived that, in a numerous school, the masters were in some sort a mere appendage to the establishment, and that the whole was a species of commonwealth, in which each member had his own rights of equality, or claims of empire, to assert, and each supported either the one or the other as he could. I had never had experience of a similar scene, and knew not how I should find myself adapted for the combat. My imagination sparkled, and my blood tingled, at the thought of it. But I did not shrink. I felt that I was at the age for experiments; and I did not find myself willing to pass through the scene of existence inglorious, without once having asserted myself, or dared to mix among my equals.

I only suggested one condition, at the price of which I was willing to yield without a repining word, to my uncle's decision; this was, that I might first be permitted to spend a few days on a visit to Henrietta. My request was immediately granted. The place of her residence was in the New Forest, not far from the Southampton Water. It is not possible to conceive any thing more beautiful than the surrounding scenery.[3] To me, who had been

---

1 Over-arching vault of heaven.

2 Winchester College, founded in 1382, is the oldest public school in England.

3 The New Forest was a royal hunting area in the south of England created in 1079 by William the Conqueror.

accustomed for years to look only on sands and morasses, and all that was dreary and neglected, it was transporting.

I entered the New Forest by way of Lymington, and penetrated to Beaulieu.[1] It was in the neighbourhood of this charming village that my sister resided. The whole of the ride, which was of nine miles in extent, was exquisitely beautiful. It was a lovely evening towards the latter end of summer; and the recollection of the purpose of my journey was scarcely necessary to heighten the delight of the senses, though that certainly bestowed upon it an additional zest. The country was luxuriant, and richly covered with wood. Through a great part of the way, the road lay among a thousand venerable trees, that seemed for ages to have defied the rage of the element, and whose branches were barely sufficiently apart to afford an opening, amidst multiplied meanders, for the traveller to pass. Sometimes however a rising ground over which the road conducted me, opened a more extensive prospect, and I viewed the Isle of Wight, with its fields, its towns, and its variegated scenery, and the arm of the sea which flowed between, and divided me from this seeming terrestrial paradise. The stilness and silence of Sowley Water, a freshwater lake by the margin of which my road partly conducted me, agreeably contrasted with the eternal mobility, and never ending murmur, of the majestic tide beyond. Further on, a considerable extent of ruins presented itself, known by the name of Beaulieu Grange, which formerly afforded residence to the cultivators, and storehouses for the produce, that belonged to the monks of Beaulieu Abbey.[2] One wall in particular, eighty feet in width, and of proportionable height, appeared to have formed the gable end of a vast barn, and was now mantled with ivy in vast profusion, the clusters of which depended[3] thick and wide from the edifice which formed their support. At length I discovered the village upon the banks of a romantic stream, which owes its name to the beauty of its situation.

---

1   Beaulieu (French for beautiful place) is a small, and still unspoiled, village on the edge of the New Forest national park in Hampshire.

2   The abbey was a wealthy Cistercian abbey founded in 1203 and peopled by 30 monks sent from France. It escaped the dissolution of the monasteries under Henry VIII, but was forced to surrender to the government in 1538, and the abbey itself was given to the 1st Earl of Southampton, who demolished the church but made the gatehouse the core of his new Beaulieu Mansion.

3   Hung down.

My sister lived with a family of the name of Willis. The husband had been in the sea-service, but having sustained considerable injury from an accident, became a cripple for life, and had retired on a small pension. The wife had been a schoolfellow of my mother's, was a very notable woman, possessed various accomplishments, and was eminent for her intellectual powers. She had however been a girl of no fortune, and was considered as having married beneath her pretensions.[1] The friendship that had begun between my mother and her at school, had continued through life; Mrs Willis had paid us a visit in the summer immediately preceding the Irish rebellion, and having conceived a romantic affection for the little Henrietta, and having no children of her own, had prevailed on my mother, to allow her to take the child over to England with her on her return. It was probably owing to this circumstance that I now had a sister. After the dreadful convulsion in which my father and mother perished, my uncle Audley Mandeville, as the representative of the family, had taken their children into his protection, and myself having been received under his roof, he paid a handsome pension to Mrs Willis for the maintenance and education of Henrietta.

The cottage in which the Willises resided was the most beautiful I had seen, in the whole course of my excursion. It was ornamented throughout by the taste and manual ingenuity of its mistress; and nothing could be more lively and agreeable than the whole of its finishing and furniture. It struck me like a tenement in fairy-land. Of one room the walls were entirely covered with feather-work; the soft plumage of the swan, the partridge, the goldfinch, and the bullfinch, being interspersed with the master-feathers of the peacock, the ostrich, and the pheasant, so as to compose a thousand ingenious figures, with the softest and the most brilliant tints, that nature in all her prodigality ever engendered. The disabled sailor, though his accident had unfitted him for strong and athletic exertions, was fully capable of amusing himself in his own petty domain, and under the instructions and superintendence of his wife, had become an admirable gardener. The parterres, the arbours, and the little orchard, appended to his cottage, exhibited every kind of beauty and rustic wealth of which such a domain was susceptible. The garden was terminated on the bank of the Beaulieu river; and here Mrs Willis had erected a grotto of several compartments, cool, shady, and refreshing, a most agreeable retreat from the meridian heat of an

---

1 Potential rank.

August sun, lined with many-coloured spars[1] in a thousand fantastic forms, which sparkled like a mighty assemblage of jewels and diamonds.

The reader must not suppose however that all this splendour in any degree depraved and stained the character of simplicity, which so well accorded with this obscure and solitary retreat. The wealth I observed around me, was nature's wealth, uncorrupted by the hand of man, not bought with the tears, and groans, and blood of a hundred miserable victims, as cheap and ordinary in its materials, as it was beautiful from the elegance and taste of the hand that had arranged it. The trees were unshorn; the walks were neither straight, nor forced into strange serpentizing involutions, but simply accommodated themselves to the inequalities of the surface. Every thing was tended with an exquisite neatness; yet the hand of art never protruded itself, but was employed with that modesty which so well becomes it, as the silent and observant hand-maid of nature. The poultry-yard was well stocked with fowls of various sorts; and whichever way I looked, all appeared clean, healthful, blithsome, and contented.

My soul was harmonized to almost paradisaical joy, as I alighted at the door of the cottage. To have seen my sister, whom I so entirely loved, would have been to me a happiness, ample and overpowering. But I could not be insensible to the quiet contentment, the cheerful tone, and the alacrity of kindness, of Beaulieu Cottage, so opposite to every thing I could remember to have seen. Here every thing seemed to rejoice in the mere feeling of existence; there (at Mandeville House) all was formal and slow; and you would have thought they continued to live, from mere apprehension in lifting the latch of the door which dismisses man from this mortal stage, or want of that energy necessary to the individual who shall resolve to die. What I saw gave me a new existence; my blood circulated with a brisker flow; my eyes sparkled; my cheeks glowed; and I felt as if this were the first day in which I had known what it was to be truly alive. Not that I had not experienced mighty pleasures in my rambles and reveries during the life of my preceptor; but they were of so different a nature! They were solemn; they were even sublime; but they were deeply steeped in, or rather entirely penetrated with, melancholy. What I now felt, appeared to be similar to the sensations that might have been habitual to all mankind, if Adam had never fallen, and if the human species had universally retained the innocence in which they were originally created.

---

1 Crystalline minerals.

Mrs Willis was a perfect royalist. Not that she was much accessible to the angry, and not at all to the malignant passions. But loyalty to her was of the same nature and substance, as her religion. She had learned both from her father and grandmother, and she would have felt it like sacrilege to call either in question. She felt that neither of them produced in her any but the best feelings; and as she stood in need of a God to look up to in Heaven, so it was a solace to her mind to think of the king, as the protector and compassionate father of his people. The saint-like simplicity of Charles the First (at least as she read his character), and the exemplary purity of his domestic morals, particularly fitted him to till the place in the scale of being, which her imagination had previously provided for him: and Mrs Willis had in one instance been deeply implicated in a contrivance to free him from his imprisonment in the Isle of Wight.[1]

The understanding, the accomplishments, and the principles of this admirable matron, all of them strongly recommended her to the acquaintance and friendship of the loyal nobility of these times. Lord Montagu of Boughton was her nearest distinguished neighbour; and though his more splendid and magnificent residence was in Northamptonshire, yet he spent a few months of every year at his rustic mansion of Beaulieu.[2] The elder Lord

---

1 Charles was imprisoned in Carisbrooke Castle on the Isle of Wight from 1647 to 1648.

2 Beaulieu became titularly associated with the Montagu name only in the century after the novel's setting. The house came into the Montagu family through marriage to a member of the Southampton family in 1675, and the first Earl of Beaulieu, Edward Hussey-Montagu (1731–1802), was in turn a Montagu by marriage and was created Baron Beaulieu in 1762 and Earl in 1784. Both titles became extinct on his death in 1802 (though a descendant was created Baron Beaulieu in 1885). The Beaulieu titles are listed in *The Peerage of Great Britain*, which Godwin read in 1800, indicating that his details are based on fact even when he seems to be writing in the mode of romance. But although there were Barons Montagu of Boughton during the period of *Mandeville*, they had no link to Beaulieu until later. The anachronism, in combination with the reduction of the abbey to a country-house, contributes to a sense of Beaulieu as an abiding and almost middle-class place of sanctuary from the ravages of political history. In Godwin's own anonymously published *The English Peerage; Or, a View of the Ancient and Present State of the English Nobility* (London: G. and J. Robinson, 1790), there is a Henry Montagu who was created Viscount Mandeville in 1620 and has a son called Edward who was opposed to Cromwell, (*continued*)

Montagu, by no means a public character, was however reported to have expressed himself in terms of so strong censure of the proceedings of the parliament, as induced them to issue an order that he should be brought up a prisoner from Northamptonshire, though already eighty years of age, and committed to the Savoy in London. As he was on the road near Barnet, he chanced to meet the Earl of Essex, commander in chief of the parliamentary forces, who was newly setting forward on his expedition, and who expressed a wish to pay his respects to this venerable character; but Lord Montagu, understanding who it was that approached, roughly ordered his coachman to drive on, with the bitter remark, that "this was no time for compliments!" The elder Lord Montagu died in confinement in 1644:[1] and the present lord, who lived entirely retired from public affairs, was principally distinguished for the beauty, the promising character, and high expectations men formed, of his children.[2] Lady Montagu, daughter to Sir Ralph Winwood,[3] formerly secretary of state, was Mrs Willis's most intimate and particular friend.

This, and other similar connections of the mistress of Beaulieu Cottage, were of the greatest service to Henrietta. She was not like me, a wild and undisciplined savage, with that mixture of timidity and spirit that is to be found in an unbroken colt; but, being accustomed to the best and most polished society, was herself, in proportion to her years, a pattern of whatever was most perfect in that kind. Yet, as I have already shown, the cultivation she had received was far from having converted her into a courtly automaton. She expressed herself with the greatest ease; her sentiments were unparrotted and unstudied; and they were uttered by her with the utmost gaiety, grace and unreserve.

One part of the scenery at Beaulieu I have not yet mentioned: the ruins of the Abbey. Several portions of this formerly immense structure, were still applied to useful purposes; what had been the

---

but here too Beaulieu becomes associated with the name Montagu only in the following century (85–86, 448–49).

1 Edward Montagu, 1st Baron of Boughton (1562/63–1644). The episode is described by Echard, *History of England*, 544.

2 Edward Montagu, the 2nd Baron of Boughton (1616–84). He was in fact significantly involved in politics on both sides from the Commonwealth period through the Restoration, but Godwin may want to create a space in the novel insulated from politics and contention.

3 Sir Ralph Winwood (c. 1563–1617) was a diplomat and politician who became secretary of state in 1614. Again Godwin has done his research carefully.

refectory, was now the parish-church; and the house of the prior was still a dwelling-house, tenanted by one of the best families of the vicinity. These circumstances took away the feeling of desolation, which usually accompanies a heap of ruins; and the recollection of the devotion, the habits, and the vast undertakings of past ages, was pleasingly mingled with the neatness, the activity, and the civilization, that continued to occupy the scene. Thus, whether I sat in the well-economized apartments of Mrs Willis's house, or wandered amidst the hanging woods which cast their brown and solemn shadows upon the expanded stream beneath, or reposed among the ruins themselves, every thing was soothing and agreeable, and strikingly addressed itself to the better and more beneficent passions of the soul.

My visit to my sister and her protectress was short; but it has often occurred to me since, to imagine what a different being I should have been, if it had been my lot to have been brought up at Beaulieu Cottage, instead of at Mandeville House. As it was, I belonged to no one; I hung loose upon society, or rather had never entered into its circumference; never, except in one instance, and that for a very short time, had I seen a friend, a creature that irresistibly called forth my sympathies and my confidence. I ran wild in the woods; I told no tale; I uttered no sound that partook of equal communication; every thought I harboured in my soul, was a reverie; every passion was a monopoly, and fled from partnership, as from a pestilence. Oh, had I spent my early years at Beaulieu, had I passed a part of every day with Mrs Willis, a woman whose every word was a spark detached from the storehouse of wisdom, whose every look was benevolence, who had that grace for ever attending her, that won your confidence, and with an irresistible power drew forth your soul,—had I lived with my Henrietta, had I associated with the noble scions of the house of Montagu, and the respectable family that dwelt at the priory, I also should have been a human creature, I should have been the member of a community, I should have lived with my fellow mortals on peaceful terms, I should have been as frank, as I now was invincibly reserved, suspicious, and for ever disposed to regard my neighbour with thoughts of hostility! I should then have been amiable; and I should have been happy! But my fate was determined, and my character was fixed.[1] The effects of

---

1 Godwin is famous for the view that "the actions and dispositions of mankind are the offspring of circumstances and events, and not of any original determination that they bring into the world" (*PJ* 1.26). However, the combination of "accidents" that determine (*continued*)

living under such a master of a houshold as my uncle, with such a preceptor as Mr Bradford, and in the midst of such an establishment as that of Mandeville House, will never be obliterated, as long as one thought exists within this brain, and one pulse beats within my frame of man.

I passed an entire week at Beaulieu; and, if I had passed an eternity, it would have seemed like a single day. Every thing I saw was amiable; and I threw myself without apprehension into the arms of every one I met. Every thing I saw was frank, and easy, and communicative, and sensitive, and sympathetic. It was like the society of "just men made perfect"[1] where all sought the good of all, and no one lived for himself, or studied for himself. Mr Willis, the owner of the cottage, had been bred, as I have said, to the sea-service: but he retained nothing of his original profession but its ingenuous, unvarnished manners, and a bluntness, in no way connected with indifference to another's feelings or another's happiness, but that served only to convey in a more unequivocal manner the truth of his benevolence. He had been instructed by his wife; and, as he regarded her with a love approaching to adoration, he was in some sense a copy of this exemplary matron, with inferior intellects, and whimsically qualified and dashed with the phraseology and gait of an English sailor. His very lameness seemed to give him an additional interest with the spectator: the goodness of his heart blended, in a way I am not able to describe, with his infirmity; and you loved him the more, because he was feeble and helpless, and joined the sentiment of a true philanthropy, with an apparent want of power, as well as of will, to do you harm.

The Montagus were at Beaulieu the whole time of my visit; and the two sons of Lord Montagu in particular seemed to me a perfect specimen of all that is most admirable in character, and most engaging and excellent in boyish years. Edward was particularly praised for the beauty of his person, the united fire and sweetness of his disposition, and the gallantry of his temper. He contributed afterwards in an eminent degree to the bringing about the Restoration, and was slain, at twenty-five years of age, in the attack on the Dutch East India ships in the port of Bergen in Norway, under his kinsman, the Earl of Sandwich. Ralph, the

---

a man's character is so unique and individual that "at the moment of birth man has really a certain character, and each man a character different from his fellows" (1.42).

1 Hebrews 12:23.

younger brother, was a no less perfect creature, but of a different cast.[1] While Edward was all fire and activity, with an arch, yet affectionate smile for ever coming and going on his lovely features, while he played, and danced, and fenced, and rode, like a creature that never knew satiety or fatigue, Ralph was sober, calm and reported, equable in temper, but more prone to meditation and study and the gratification of a liberal curiosity, than to the exercises of the field.

But it is in vain that I dwell on the Willises and the Montagus. These amused me for a moment, and produced a temporary improvement to my temper. But Henrietta was the whole world to me. In every thing I thought of her approbation; and I resolved to accomplish myself in whatever was praise-worthy, because I felt that she was capable of being my umpire and my judge. I knew that she would be a friendly and a partial judge; but I was resolved against the interference of partiality; I fixed it as my purpose to satisfy her most enlightened discernment. Henrietta was the universal subject of eulogy to all that knew her; the daughters of the house of Montagu yielded her the superiority without a repining thought. Her gaiety was more irresistible, her *naiveté* more touching, her carriage more graceful, than that of any of her companions. She sung with a more thrilling and heart-felt tone, and danced with a more sylphlike and etherial air. What should I do to make myself the worthy mate of such a sister, was therefore the perpetual burthen of my thoughts.

CHAPTER X

From Beaulieu I proceeded to Winchester. This was a scene no less new to me; but how different from that which I had just quitted! Dr Pottinger, the head-master, had been the acquaintance and fellow-collegiate of Mr Bradford.[2] He felt therefore some respect for me on that account; but still more perhaps

---

1   Edward Montagu (1635–65) acted as an intermediary between his cousin Admiral Montagu (1625–72), Earl of Sandwich and interestingly a former supporter of Cromwell *and* Charles II, with a view to bringing about the Restoration. He was killed in battle in Bergen, Norway, at a young age. Ralph Montagu (1638–1709) was 3rd Baron and 1st Duke Montagu. Again, his alliances from the Restoration through the Glorious Revolution were expedient, thus casting doubt on the illusion of a space outside politics projected in this chapter.

2   John Pottinger was headmaster of Winchester from 1642 to 1653.

because I was the sole presumptive heir to the property of Mandeville. He examined me in my progress; he assigned me a class, and provided me with the implements of study. The school-room was a spacious and lofty building, and I looked round me, astonished at every thing I saw. The pupils were about one hundred and fifty; and never in my life had I seen so numerous an assembly. But this was not an assembly, thrown together promiscuously and for a moment; but an assembly (subject to those changes incident to all human societies), with which I was to associate, with few interruptions, for several years to come. Some of the boys had already reached the full stature of manhood; and others were so young, that they seemed to hold their books with a faltering and uncertain hand, and rather to lisp, than articulately to pronounce, the inflections of their accidence.[1] I also admired the garb of the scholars on the foundation,[2] who wore black gowns of crape, and, when they went out into the air, placed upon their heads trencher-caps,[3] like those belonging to the students in the universities.

This was indeed a busy scene. The murmuring labours of the boys, proceeding, as it did, from the half-closed lips of one hundred and fifty human creatures, produced a united sound, low, monotonous, indistinct and perpetual, unlike every other sound, but more resembling the rustling of the waves under the dominion of a moderate breeze, than any thing else to which I can compare it. The loud, authoritative, stentor voice of the master, in its sudden impulses, made me start again, till practice had accustomed me to this abrupt breach of the ambient air. The character personated by the director of a great school, if referred to the nature of man, is wholly artificial; but in him it becomes in a short time a second nature, which it is almost impossible for him ever after to lay aside. The withdrawing of the head-master at any time, produced a sudden revolution; and the voices from every quarter became more acute, with a stirring and lively note. The government of a seminary of this sort is a curious theme for meditation: its subjects are for the most part the most elastic, wild and thoughtless animals that can be conceived; yet they are governed, if you regard external appearances only, much like a machine; the machinist has to touch a spring only, and the whole is obedient.

---

1 The part of grammar that deals with word inflections.
2 The founders of colleges such as Winchester reserved a number of places at the school in perpetuity for members of their families.
3 Mortar boards.

After a few hours' labour, the assembly was dismissed. All care was then at an end; the signal was given for universal thoughtlessness and hilarity. The elder boys had an air of erectness, fearlessness and independence, that you would have thought they had never known restraint. But, in reality, their gait and their air were in part the growth of the restraint they had passed through. They were prisoners, dismissed indeed, but with some links of the chain still adhering to them. Their motions had not the ease and the grace of a creature in the state of nature; they had a stamp of pertness and insolence and petulance, that said, We are servants, but this is our *Saturnalia*.[1] They had felt the weight of the yoke upon their own necks; and they were resolved to retaliate their sufferings at the expence of the first victim they met. Thus they played alternately, from hour to hour, the parts of the despot and the subject, the commanded and the commander.

I, as a new comer, was exposed to a thousand ridiculous questions. The inquiries were wanton, and the inquirers had small care of the answers they received. All that I experienced in this sort was frolicsome; it had little consideration for the feelings of the person to whom it was addressed; but I must on the other hand confess, that it had little in it of malice or deliberate cruelty.

Many readers will consider the detail I have here given as frivolous and commonplace. Who has not had experience of the interior of a numerous school? The proposition however insinuated in this question, is not true. One half of the human species (the female sex), to which I may add a considerable portion of the other, have had no opportunity of experiencing what I have described.[2] But it is not for that reason that it is introduced here. It is the express purpose of the narrative in which I am engaged, to show how the concurrence of a variety of causes operate to form a character: and if I were to omit any circumstance that possessed a very strong influence on my mind, the person into whose hands this story may happen to fall, would have an imperfect picture of the man who is set before him, and would want

---

1 Roman festival celebrated in December in honour of Saturn, who was associated with the Golden Age of everlasting spring when there were no laws. It is characterized by role reversals and behavioural license: thus slaves could mock their masters and be exempt from punishment.

2 The comment about the exclusion of women from education is out of character and an instance of Godwin's more enlightened voice of Rational Dissent being intertwined with Mandeville's.

some of the particulars necessary to the developement of the tale.

Another circumstance made a very essential part of the scene into which I was now introduced. I was entered a student of Winchester College in August 1650. Parties at this time ran very high in the English nation; nor was the society of which I was now a member without its share of this spirit. A year and a half before this period king Charles had passed through Winchester in his journey, as he was conducted from Hurst Castle[1] to London for his trial. In this ancient city in particular, he had been received with great respect; the mayor and aldermen had waited upon him in form, as if this had been the period of his highest prosperity, to present him with the keys of the town; and the neighbouring gentry had flocked from all sides to welcome him, some out of curiosity to see him, but more out of zeal, either from original affection to his person, or compassion for the low estate into which he was fallen. This was a memorable period at Winchester school. The boys had asked and obtained permission to become spectators of the scene. And the melancholy catastrophe that so shortly after followed, caused the whole to make an indelible impression on their memory. People had but a confused idea why the king was conducted to London on the present occasion. It was sufficiently known, that the power was at this time in the hands of his bitterest enemies. But so many negociations had been entered into by all parties in turn, for his being restored with a limited power, that no one, out of the secret, could prevail upon himself to look upon him as any other than the king. It was therefore with astonishment and terror, that they heard of his being brought to the block; and it was with effort, and by dint of meditation, so to express myself, that they could be induced to believe the news. Mankind is so weak an animal, that they cannot be prevented from looking upon a king as a species of god; comets appear in the heavens to illustrate his birth, and the world labours with tempests and earthquakes when a monarch dies; that violence should be exercised on his person, that he should be imprisoned and put to death, is a thought to which the vulgar imagination can never reconcile itself; and when such a profanation is actually committed, men feel as if a violation was perpetrated on our general nature, that they were "themselves amiss, and did not

---

1 A fort built by Henry VIII on the south coast of England. During the Civil War it was held by the parliamentary forces and was Charles's last prison before his trial.

know it," and that the "fountain of their blood," the source from which they derived their existence, was "stopped."[1]

There was not I believe one boy in Winchester school that was not a royalist. By this I mean no more, than that we all felt indignant at the fate of Charles the First, and were friends to the house of Stuart.[2] It was otherwise with public sentiment, even in that class of society to which we for the most part belonged, some few years afterwards. Men are commonly governed, even in the opinions they shall entertain, by feeling and imagination. In this respect the fate of king Charles took strong hold on the mind. He was a tyrant; he had no consideration for any human being, beyond the circle of his own family, and a few personal connections to whom he was partial. Meanwhile, the decorum of his manners, the equability of his temper, his apparent mildness and resignation, totally free as they seemed from the least imputation of cowardice, were qualities that exactly fitted him to be the hero of a cavalier or a woman. But the recollection of the last scenes of the life of this unfortunate monarch gradually faded from the mind; and the successes of the republic, and still more the splendid character of Cromwel, as a statesman, and a firm assertor of the honour of his country, subsequently balanced the feeling I speak of, and seemed hastening to obliterate that popular sentiment of loyalty, of which a few continued to be proud. Cromwel appeared to be a monarch of Nature's own appointing; no one that ever wore a crown, knew better how to speak the language, that became the representative of a mighty nation.[3] It was at the time to which I allude, that Cowley wrote his celebrated Preface,

---

1   Adapted from *Macbeth*, 2.3.197–99.
2   The Stuart dynasty ruled Scotland from 1371 to 1714. Under James VI of Scotland, who became James I of England, the two countries were united in 1603. Except for the interregnum from 1649 to 1660 (the Commonwealth, 1649–53; the Protectorate under Oliver Cromwell, 1653–58; and the Protectorate under his son Richard, 1658–60), the Stuarts technically also ruled England from the Restoration of Charles II until 1714.
3   Oliver Cromwell (1599–1658), leading Puritan general of the parliamentary army and Lord Protector (1653–58). The final volume of Godwin's *HCE* is a sympathetic, though not unbalanced, history of Cromwell's reign, and the views expressed here are those of Godwin rather than Mandeville. On the other hand, the critique of Cromwell in the next paragraph is more representative of Mandeville—an indication of Godwin's nuanced and multi-perspectival understanding of the history of this period.

disclaiming all opposition to the government established.[1] The death of Cromwel however in the flower of his age, which speed-ily followed, and perhaps some untoward circumstances that occurred in the contention of the representative system and the protectoral power, overturned to the very foundation that fabric of government which he had so ably begun to erect.

There was not a boy in Winchester school that was not a roy-alist. Yet political party ran very high among us; and the con-tention between opposite sentiments was animated and fierce. The master was a Presbyterian. The civic sentiments of the Pres-byterians are well known. They were the original stirrers of the war between the king and the parliament. They were indignant against the acts of arbitrary power and cruelty, by which the king and his ministers seemed to intend to break the spirit of their opponents. Their leaders were deeply studied in the theory of government, and had firmly resolved to place the privileges of parliament, and the rights of the people, on an immoveable basis. In the early part of the war they ran a splendid career. But they were in the sequel outwitted by the independents. Cromwel and his cabal, with infinite dexterity and address, finally engrossed all power in their own hands.

From this time the purpose of the cavaliers[2] and the Presbyte-rians became nominally the same, the restoration of the monar-chy in the family of Stuart. But the nearer they drew to a seeming agreement, the greater was their fundamental antipathy to each other; at least it was so within the walls of our college. The cava-liers devoutly aspired to the object for which they had fought in the beginning, the establishment of the monarchy, unshorn of its beams, and invested with all the prerogatives of an eastern sultan. They scorned to take less than that, for which they had con-tended in the field, and bled on the scaffold. The Presbyterian on the other hand, true to his original principles, aimed at the estab-lishment of a constitutional monarchy, without any other alter-ation, than what should consist in clearly defining those public

---

1 Abraham Cowley (1618–67): Royalist poet who went into exile but returned to England in 1656. His unfinished Royalist epic poem *The CivillWarre* was not recovered until 1973. It is referred to in the Preface to his *Poems* (1656), where he renounced the Royalist cause.

2 The name given by Parliamentarians to the Royalists during the inter-regnum. Initially it was a term of contempt because of its association with an ornate and effeminate mode of dress (vs. the shorter hair and simpler clothes of the "Roundheads" or parliamentarians).

rights, which naturally grew out of the feudal system when accommodated to the changes that had arisen in the order of society, which had been with no equivocal voice asserted under the house of Lancaster,[1] and the sentiments of which had been strongly inforced by the event of the Reformation.[2]

It is astonishing with what abhorrence and contempt the cavaliers at this time regarded their new allies. They charged them with being the first authors of all the calamities that followed, and held them as more criminal than the independents, who had merely stepped into the scene which the others had begun, and conducted it to its natural conclusion. They spoke with the utmost asperity of those, who had first drawn their swords against the king, and then pretended to be his friends. The tears which the Presbyterians affected to shed for the catastrophe of Charles, they compared to the tears of the crocodile, which are said to overflow with every demonstration of tenderness, while the heart of the animal is remorselessly bent upon cruelty and blood. The Presbyterians on the other hand, as no party is wanting in common-places for setting their own conduct in the fairest point of view, regarded the cavaliers as unnatural children to their mother-country, as men who, when every privilege to the inheritance of which they were born was trampled on, and when the sagest and gravest plans were put forward for preserving their birth-rights, yet abetted the tyrant, and drew their swords to put down the cause of freedom. Such men, they held, were a curse to their brethren, and by their own admission deserved to be slaves. In addition to this, they were persuaded that the cause of popery and slavery were intimately united. The cavaliers therefore were a party, who were willing to barter away that sacred freedom in matters of religion, for the assertion of which so many of their ancestors had died at the stake,—to return to the flesh-pots of Egypt, and tamely to receive "the mark of the beast in their foreheads."[3] The Presbyterians, according to their own account, had embraced that middle and temperate course, which best became

1 The House of Lancaster ruled from 1399 to 1461, and was followed by the Yorkists (1461–85, with a brief Restoration of the Lancastrians from 1470 to 1471), and then by the Tudors and Stuarts.
2 The Reformation is not so much a single event as a series of religious changes across Europe, which in England took the political and personal form (motivated by his desire to remarry) of Henry VIII's separation of the Church of England (thereafter headed by the monarch) from the Roman Catholic church (headed by the Pope).
3 Adapted from Revelation 14:9. Mandeville here speaks in a voice inflected by that of Hilkiah.

the character of Englishmen, steering alike clear of that self-abandonment and sycophancy which marked the cavaliers, and the extreme, equally worthy to be abhorred, of republicanism. And they would easily have succeeded in their generous plan, had not the senseless and self-destroying measures pursued by the cavaliers afforded scope to the artifice and conspiracy of the independents. But the wisdom of the measures of the Presbyterians, was not to be judged of by a momentary failure: they had not indeed been crowned with success; but they had merited it. The system upon which they had acted was alone worthy of Englishmen, and must finally prevail. It will presently be seen in what way these political discussions influenced my fate in Winchester College.

CHAPTER XI

I no sooner became a personage in this moving and busy scene, than among all my school-fellows one individual instantly fixed my attention and observation. His name was Clifford. To me, who had seen so little of the varieties of human character, he was an extraordinary creature indeed. He seemed both to attract all eyes, and to win all hearts. There was something in him perfectly fascinating and irresistible. His countenance was beautiful, and his figure was airy. The bloom of health revelled in his cheeks. There was a vivacity in his eye, and an inexpressible and thrilling charm in the tone of his voice, that appeared more than human. His gaiety was never-ceasing and eternal; and it was sustained by such lively fancies, such whimsical and unexpected sallies, and so inexhaustible a wit, that

> The air, a chartered libertine, was still;
> And the mute wonder lurked in men's ears,
> To steal his sweet and honied sentences.[1]

For a short time envy itself was disarmed; and I, like the rest, admired a spectacle, so new to me, and so beautiful in itself, that I was wrapt in self-oblivion, and possessed no faculties, but an eye to remark his graces, and an ear to drink in every sound he uttered. The illusion lasted for days, and I returned to the feast with an appetite that seemed as if it would never be sated.

---

1   Adapted from *Henry V*, 1.1.48–50.

But this was a brief intoxication. The solemn tone of my true character speedily returned to me; and, though for a time I relished the vein of Clifford with a genuine zest, it was in the main too alien from the settled temper of my mind, for it to be possible I should enjoy it long. It held me in an unnatural state of feeling; and my thoughts soon fell back to the train to which they had been accustomed. My rooted habits were those of reflection, silence, and reverie. To follow, as I had done at first, the brilliant sparklings of Clifford's wit, had an effect upon me similar to that produced by the rattling progress of a vehicle at full speed. It made my brain giddy, and my head ache, with its violence. And, when I looked back upon the pleasure I had for a time enjoyed, I scorned or imagined I scorned, the cause that produced it. Was man made for no higher a purpose, than to laugh, be amused, and wonder at the jugglings and dexterities of another's wit?—I did Clifford injustice. His wit was rational; and his most sportive sallies were worthy to abide the test of examination, and were pregnant with discrimination and good sense.

I have called the feelings, which thus at second thoughts arose in my mind, by the name of envy. The root of my sentiment however was a sort of moral disapprobation. I considered Clifford as a kind of mountebank,[1] debauching the character of his equals, and destroying that sobriety and concentration of soul, without which there can be no considerable virtue. I looked into myself, and was conceited enough to imagine, that I was a better sample of our general nature than he. I felt therefore, that much false judgment was made, and much injustice committed. I sat silent and obscure in my nook, and was silly enough to be angry, that the common route of my schoolfellows crowded round Clifford, and neglected me. If any one desired to be amused, to whom did he ever think of resorting to gratify that desire, but to Clifford? If any one wished to be directed in his choice of amusements, or to obtain a just solution of any of those knotty points that are the subject of a school-boy's noisy controversies, still Clifford was the only person that was thought of. If the business was to get some crabbed passage in a lesson explained, or even to have an exercise performed for some boy who was too lazy or too dull to achieve it himself, Clifford was sure to be the resource and the oracle. The talents of Clifford were equally adapted for every thing that was required of him; and his good-nature and kindness did not fall short of his talents. His wit was sportive and good-

---

1 A person who deceives others; a charlatan.

humoured; and it was an unknown thing for him willingly to give pain to a human creature.

There was another boy in the school, whose name was Mallison. He was very unlike Clifford, and yet he was perpetually found in his train. He was of a dark, sallow complexion. It was Clifford's foible to be too fond of amusing others and himself, and to say things surprising and unexpected, yet always, as I have observed, with the most innocent intentions, and without the most distant thought of wounding or humbling another. Mallison, on the other hand, had a singular gratification in seeing his fellows writhe with mental pain. His conduct was something like what I have heard related of a village-satirist, who in reading the Whole Duty of Man,[1] found means to turn that upright and honourable work into a collection of libels, by writing in the margin of the different vices, prodigality, avarice, extortion, cruelty, lying, lewdness, which the author innocently declaims against, the names of different persons, his neighbours and fellow-parishioners. Just so, Mallison possessed the art to turn the careless and good-humoured effusions of Clifford into lampoons, and the devilish chymistry, from honey itself to extract a poison.—I will give some instances of this.

Clifford, though descended of a noble family, was immediately of a very impoverished branch of that family. The marriage of his father and mother was entirely a marriage of love. She had been extremely beautiful; but she brought no portion to her husband. He had entered a volunteer into the king's service at the beginning of the civil wars, and was among the slain in the first battle, of Edgehill near Keinton in Warwickshire.[2] His widow was left with this one son, totally destitute of provision, either for his education, or her own subsistence. Such was her affection for her husband, and her tender regard for this his only child, that she

---

1 A Protestant devotional work, a sort of catechism, published anonymously in 1658 and influential in the eighteenth century.

2 The first pitched battle in the Civil War (October 1642), which pitted Cavaliers against Roundheads. This, combined with the emphasis on Clifford's wit and gaiety, may suggest that he is from a Cavalier family, which would explain Mandeville's emphasis in the preceding chapter on the tensions between Cavaliers and Presbyterians as something that influenced his "fate" at Winchester. Clifford's gaiety reminds us also of the Cavalier poet Robert Herrick (1591–1674), best known for his line "Gather ye rosebuds while ye may," epitomizing a *carpe diem* ("seize the day") attitude. Presbyterians were generally Puritans; Cavaliers were often Episcopalians (as Clifford is), but never Puritans.

could never be prevailed upon again to enter into the ties of wedlock. In more prosperous times, no doubt, some stipend would have been assigned for the widow and child of a gentleman-adventurer, who had fallen fighting for his king. But amidst the public disasters of her country, she had been much overlooked; and almost the only thing done for her, was the obtaining a nomination for her son upon the foundation of Winchester College.

The situation therefore of this wonder and ornament of our establishment, was what would have been vulgarly felt as depressing. But it was not so to Clifford. He was in the midst of the sons of noblemen, and wealthy knights and franklins.[1] His prospects and his expectations for the years of maturity and manhood, were nothing. But his soul was elastic; and the spring that kept all his thoughts in activity and motion, was always working, and never went down. How did he maintain this incessant gaiety and carelessness? Not as a school-boy might be expected to do, by the oblivious draught which the sports of that period so readily supply. No, he looked the enemy in the face, and threw out a bold defiance to his host of terrors. He wantoned with sorrow, and laughed at those things which break the hearts of many.

"Well"; he would say; "I am destined to be poor. And what is poverty? As long as my blood flows cheerily in my veins, and a light heart dimples in my cheeks, I shall be the truly enviable man. I know, some will tell me, riches are the genuine means of independence and liberty. But it is all a cheat. The rich man is the only slave. He cannot move without scores of menials to attend him. He cannot dine without twenty dishes before him. He cannot sleep, but on thrice-driven beds of down,

> Under fringed canopies of costly state.
> And lulled with sounds of sweetest melody.[2]

He calls himself the master of all these, and he is the slave of all. He cannot go forth, and take the air, until his servants please. He is at the mercy even of his horses. If one of them meets with an accident, or is taken sick, the rich man is immediately a prisoner, and at best must wait till a relay of fresh horses is procured. Upon

---

1 Freeholders: in the Middle Ages they were neither nobles nor serfs tied to nobles who owned land; later they became a class of property owners ranking below the landed gentry.
2 Shakespeare, *Henry IV, Part 2*, 3.1.13–14.

what an accumulation of circumstances does the tranquillity of every day of his life depend! How is every climate under Heaven searched and put under contribution, before his slightest meal can be supplied! And, if the minutest of these circumstances goes wrong, how is your fancied god immediately turned into a wretch! How does he fret and frown, and how is his peace of mind puffed away by the weakest breeze! Take my word for it, the rich man is the veriest slave that lives.

"But does nature require all these things? No: a wholsome crust of bread, and water from the spring, give the freest health, and the most elastic mind. He is the truly independent man, that has the fewest wants. He fears no change of fortune, has no anxieties about the sufficiency of his income, the honesty of his dependents, the strength of his locks and chests, the security of goldsmiths, the uncertainty of the elements, or the revolution of empires. Every state and clime will supply him with what he needs. Nor is he the slave of any habits or indulgencies. What he had to-day, he can dispense with to-morrow. He can wake when others sleep, and eat at whatever hour that the occasion offers to him. He can rest as well in a cabin as a palace, and as soundly, covered with his cloke on the naked earth, as on beds of sattin, and under canopies of velvet.

"This man is the only free man. He starts from his flinty couch, and dresses himself. No ceremony more; and he is ready to perform whatever his mind impels him to do. He does not wait, till the train is ready that is to accompany his march. He is not subservient to any man's humour and caprice, and is not obliged to calculate the ability or convenience of his dependents, two conditions, from neither of which the lordliest despot is exempt. His legs are his footmen; and his arms are ever ready and prompt to perform all he wishes. His eyes are his *avant couriers*,[1] and make plain the road for him wherever he desires to go. Fancy is his charioteer; and health, the best physician, maintains the evenness of his spirits through every stage of his journey. Appetite is his cook; and thirst his butler. Of this miscellaneous houshold he is thoroughly master, and has all his passions under subjection.

"What a state is that of mortal man in every civilized climate! The earth supplies us freely with her productions, and industry multiplies them. These productions are then divided among the inhabitants of the earth. But how divided? One man gets the share of ten thousand, which he wastes and dissipates in thought-

---

1   Advance runners in an army.

less profusion, as far as he can, and then gives away the remainder with niggard hand, to the pining and anxious wretches to whom the whole was indebted for existence. I have heard it said, If the rich man could but know the miseries, the agonies of pain, the anguish of heart, and the dreadful paroxysms of despair, that are going on, perhaps in the next poor street to that which his lordly palace occupies, he would find but little relish in his dainties. But I wish that were the worst of it. He is not only the neighbour of misery; but he is the author of innumerable instances of it. Every costly morsel that he eats, is mixed with the tears and the curses of the poor by whose labours it was procured. What right have you to the share of ten thousand? Would I could muster up and marshal the legion, by whose oppression you are so delicately fed!

> If every just man, that now pines with want,
> Had but a moderate and beseeming share
> Of that which lewdly-pampered luxury
> Now heaps upon some few with vast excess,
> Nature's full blessings would be well dispensed
> In unsuperfluous, even proportion,
> And she no whit incumbered with her store.[1]

For my part I am determined always to live so, that

> No widow's curse cater a dish of mine;
> I'll drink no tears of orphans in my wine.

"And do you think my enjoyments will be the fewer for that? How senseless a distinction is that which the world has agreed to express by the word, property![2] When we go to an inn, do we enjoy ourselves the less, because the walls were not raised by our ancestors, and we are no one of us the landlords of the house? On the contrary, we regard the landlord as a laborious drudge, overwhelmed with business and fatigue, that we may enjoy ourselves at our ease. The landlord it is true he is; but I, his guest, am the master of the house. Can any truth be more self-evident, than

---

1   Milton, *Comus* (1637), 767–73.
2   Clifford's long speech has little to do with the later development of the character. However, in contrast to the Levellers whom Hilkiah evokes, his emphasis on poverty (quite inconsistent with his support of the monarchy) is hedonistic rather than a matter of self-discipline.

that he that most perfectly enjoys a thing, is the real possessor? Well then; if I am the guest of some noble lord, the proprietor, as it is called, of a magnificent mansion, who is the true possessor of the luxuries that offer themselves to my acceptance? Why I, the occupier, or the consumer. His lordship is no more to me, than the landlord of an inn, the patentee of a play-house, or the tenant on lease of a set of apartments for concerts, balls, and masquerades. His is the labouring oar; his business it is to provide whatever may give me pleasure; his is all the care, the anxiety and foresight; that I may enjoy the whole without troubling myself about the matter.

"But I do not chuse to be his guest. I like simple pleasures, better than luxurious ones; and I know that the landlord who does not make me out a bill, may put an end to my visit, not when I please, but when he pleases. My lord's house is completely decorated with costly furniture, and the galleries are adorned with landscapes, history-pieces and statues. I like a plainer furniture better, and feel more at my ease with it. My taste is so uninstructed, that I have more pleasure from a landscape of Nature's painting, than even from those of Rubens or Claude.[1] Fair weather is the joy of my soul; when the sun bursts out in all its splendour, and flings its radiance on the neighbouring hills, my mind is tuned to rapture; and my bosom is sweetly soothed, by the rosy dashes of light, which so beautifully streak the clouds in a summer's evening. When I am lost in the leafy maze of trees in the New Forest, I do not envy a minister of state in the midst of his crowded levee. And my heart decisively prefers to all the brilliancy of a ball room, a serene ramble in a fine night, with thousands of stars sparkling over my head, that by my rule I look upon as part of my possessions, not without some indignation at the tastelessness of mankind, who run the race of life without once adverting to[2] its real enjoyments.[3]

"Another cursed thing which rises from this inexhaustible source of evils, called wealth, is that every man thrives by the ruin of another, and that death, which sweeps away all of us in our turn, and is in contemplation one of the main stimulants to love, and in approach one of the greatest incitements to sympathy, is

---

1   Peter Paul Rubens (1557–1640): Flemish painter; Claude Lorrain (1600–82): French landscape painter.
2   Turning attention to.
3   [Godwin's note:] Guardian, No. [Godwin's note doesn't specify which number.]

changed into an object of aspiration, and an occasion of joy. Thank God, I am not the son of a wealthy father! If I were, I believe I should abhor my own soul every morning that I rose. My father fell in the battles of his king; but my mother still lives; and long and peaceful may her days be upon earth! Filial affection is one of the purest of all sentiments; and my father was one of the noblest creatures, that God ever made to beautify his creation withal. But, if he were living, and possessed ten thousand a-year, how am I sure, that, as I grew up, and became twenty, thirty, forty years of age, I should not wickedly think that he had enjoyed his property long enough, and that it was time my turn was come? For ten thousand worlds, I would not connect any source of joy, or find any balance of good with the sacred sorrows of a father's death-bed! Oh, how treacherous is the human soul, and how much selfishness insidiously mingles itself with our kindest and most generous feelings! And, if such were *my* lot once, I must expect thereafter, that the tables would be turned, and that, when stooping in the vale of years, the lingering of *my* decay would be looked on askance with an impatient eye! Though I am a boy, I can put myself forward in fancy into future time, and imagine that I have that solace of human vicissitudes, a child of my love. And shall I mix that solace, with believing that my child grudges me those added years that the bounty of nature gives, and that he is in heart and inclination the murderer of the parent that begot him? Oh, how sacred and how lovely are the charities of kindred and blood, to the humble sons of Nature!

"But, of all the evils with which a human being can be afflicted, not being born to wealth, I will not involve myself in the guilt and meanness of pursuing it. What, shall I devote my life to trade, and barter away my honesty and my soul for the turning a penny? Shall I decry the thing I want to buy, and praise the thing I want to sell? Shall my whole soul be devoured with the anxieties of gain, and my precious hours of solitude be devoted to calculation and computing? And for what? That, when all the finer sensibilities of my nature have evaporated, and there is nothing left of heart within me, but what is as dry and impenetrable as an Egyptian mummy, then truly I may sit down, and enjoy myself.

"But there is another and genteeler recipe, I have been told, for turning a poor man into a rich one; and that is, by worming himself into the affections of the wealthy and the great. Oh, this is admirable indeed! The supple expectant at the board of a great man, is the slave of a slave, and is even a much more wretched thing than his master. His eyes, and his very thoughts, are not his own, and are wholly devoted to a gilded, nauseous, ill-odoured idol. How his hopes and fears rise and fall with the insulting good and ill humour of the animal he worships! How omnipotently he must hate the being he affects to reverence and value!

"For, what is this wealth and rank, that the world agrees so obsequiously to bow down to? Fortune distributes her favours blindly. Most estates have their beginnings in griping commerce, or, what is infinitely worse, in the confiscation and ruin of thousands, that their possessions, freighted with the curses of those who are stripped of them and turned out to beggary, may be conferred on some courtier, as worthless as he is servile. The king bestows nobility; he is the fountain of honour. And, I take it for granted, he means well: but his favours are dispensed here and there, not as he would choose, but by the breath of cabal and the basest intrigue. There is but one true nobility, and that is bestowed by the Almighty ruler of the universe. It has its seat in the soul. It is that inspiration, that makes the generous man, the inventor of arts, the legislator of the mind, the spirit formed to act greatly on the theatre of the world, and the poet who records the deeds of such spirits. Put one of God's nobility by the side of one of the king's: who does not laugh at the comparison? They are not of the same class of beings, scarcely belong to a common nature. Turn the former out naked to the world! His worth is intrinsic; his qualities are such as must excite reverence, wherever there is sense to perceive, or discernment to judge of such qualities. The king cannot bestow this: it cannot come down to a man by hereditary succession: it descends from Heaven alone."

I feel, while I am putting down these discourses of my schoolfellow, how much injustice I am doing him. I am aware that, as they stand upon paper, they will read vapid and tedious. I must observe here, as Aeschines did, when he recited to a circle of auditors the speech of Demosthenes[1] that had procured his own banishment, "What a piece of work you would have thought it, if you had heard it from his own lips!" So these discourses of Clifford, while he spoke them, appeared almost divine. He charmed, as it were, our very souls out of our bodies, and might have led us through the world. It was like what is fabled of Orpheus; mute things seemed to have ears; and you would have expected the very beasts of prey to lay down their savage natures, and obey him. There was something in the very nature of his sentiments,

---

1 Both fourth-century BCE orators and statesmen.

calculated to waken a responsive chord in every human bosom; and the melody of his voice, and the sportive gaiety with which he uttered them, made them altogether irresistible. Set down in cold lines and paragraphs, they may appear long-winded and pedantic; they may be judged beyond the feelings of his age; but, if ever there was a creature void of affectation and the desire to shine, Clifford was that creature. He talked like one inspired. He spoke, because he could not help it, and to give vent to his full bosom. And his discourses were always so well timed, so aptly rose out of the occasion in hand, and were so animated and pithy, that every one longed for the occasion, and were delighted to listen to the magic of his tongue.

It was wonderful the effect that this system of thinking wrought upon the scholars of Winchester school. Wealth in their eyes became dross; and instead of considering it, as others do, as a ground for vanity and arrogance, those who had the greatest pretensions to it became ashamed of them. I have heard that in other schools wealth and rank are very much overlooked, and that a sort of golden age of levelling and equality prevails. But with us it went one step farther. The captain among us boasted of his poverty and was proud that he was born to nothing. And, with that spirit of imitation so remarkable among human creatures, poverty accordingly became the fashion; and those among us who were born to other expectations, pined for this blessed inheritance, and held that they carried about them a brand of slavery. This extraordinary course of sentiment was the more easily introduced among school-boys; for school-boys have not yet learned the bitter evils which poverty sometimes introduces.

I, I alone, felt no pleasure, and refused to feel pleasure from the discourses of Clifford. In the first place, I was strongly impressed with the notion of their fallacy. How I came in my own mind to reason differently from my comrades I know not; but such was the fact. I looked upon Clifford as an enchanter, who hurled

> His dazzling spells into the spungy air.
> Of power to cheat the eye with blear illusion,
> And give it false presentments.[1]

I confessed to myself that wealth was pregnant with mischief, both to the possessor, and to society in general. But I did not look

---

1 *Comus*, 154–56.

upon poverty with the same eyes that Clifford did. I saw that man was not formed like the animals, to whom uncultivated nature supplies every want. Man is not, like them, a stationary creature, as perfect in one generation as in all that are to succeed, but is capable of infinite improvements. He then, that is so adapted to receive and engender arts and sciences, to adorn the earth with the works of his skill, to scan the heavens, and penetrate into the abysses of his own nature, ought not to be exposed to unmitigable poverty. In the solitudes of Mandeville House, and in my propensity to reveries, I had thought more of the condition of human beings, than school-boys usually do. I saw that in civilized society, the only state that appeared to me worthy of man, he could not subsist but upon the fruits of others' industry or of his own, and that the very attempt to supply himself subjected him in various ways to the caprice of his fellow-creatures, and was in various ways precarious. I saw that the poor man was strangely pent up and fettered in his exertions, whether their purpose might be to unfold the treasury of intellect in the solitude of his closet, or to collect facts and phenomena by wandering on the face of the earth. I saw that, when he suffered himself to contract the dearer ties of husband and father, poverty and an uncertain subsistence might depress his heart, and corrode his vitals. I saw that, if riches made a man a slave, entire poverty did the same, and perhaps more effectually. It is perhaps within the compass of possibility for a rich man to be free (though almost as hardly, as for "a camel to pass through the eye of a needle"); but the poor man must always wear the marks of his bolts about him, and drag at every step a heavier and more intolerable chain. I saw that poverty was environed on all sides with temptations, urging and impelling a man, to sell his soul, to sacrifice his integrity, to debase the clearness of his spirit, and to become the bond slave of a thousand vices.

All this I knew: but I was not like Clifford. I could not put my soul into my tongue, and witch all hearers with my eloquence. Envious nature had denied to me this privilege. But I felt my deficiency with fierce and burning impatience. Why should this youth steal away the souls of his companions with glozing[1] words, and I have no tongue to check his mistakes, and expose his sophistries? Why should error thus intrepidly bolt forth its apophthegms,[2] and I sit timidly in my corner, unable to utter the truths

---

1 Fawning.
2 Short, cryptic remarks containing some generally accepted truth.

that were fermenting in my bosom? It appeared to me that the system of the universe was in fault, and that the sacred cause of truth was iniquitously and unfairly dealt by. Jealousy thus, day by day, established its empire in my bosom; and Clifford was the maleficent wizard by whom I was hag-ridden, and the nightmare, under whose weight I lay at the last gasp of existence.

Sure I was (no matter how erroneous my opinion), in the secret calculations and combinings of my own thoughts, that my merits fully balanced the merits of Clifford, and that, weighed with the beam of a just estimation, my scale would prove the heavier. He that spends his days in solitude, and is seldom corrected in his determinations by the collision of another, has almost always an overweening opinion of himself. Clifford and I were two luminaries that could never shine in the same sphere; but I could not bear the idea of being under a perpetual eclipse, and that they who admired my competitor, should never turn a glance of passing approbation upon me.

This was rendered inexpressibly worse to me by the mischief-making temper of Mallison. The greatest gratification, as I have said, of this seemingly unnatural being lay in giving pain to another. The coruscations[1] of Clifford's wit were a harmless lightning playing in an evening sky; but Mallison's unremitted aim was to furnish the bolt, that should succeed as surely, as the report follows upon the flash. It fell to his office, to turn all Clifford's innocent sallies into personal satire. With the acuteness that malice perhaps always gives, he saw that I was the most sensitive lad in the school, upon whom his spurts of ill humour would be least in danger to be wasted. It happened, that the estate to which I was heir, was perhaps larger than that which any other youth in the establishment was entitled to look to. God knows, I thought but little upon this. But there was a gravity in my carriage, a sort of inflexible sadness of gesture and tone, which Mallison wickedly perverted into the crime of being purse-proud. If my manner was somewhat cold, reserved and uncommunicative before, it certainly did not lose any of these defects under the smart of his lashes. There is something in the temper of the unreflecting and grosser crowd, that always leads them ambitiously to join in a hunting of this sort. Under the tutoring of Mallison, they voted me a *prig*, a *frump*, a *fogram*,[2] and qualified me with all the disparaging epithets, that a familiar acquain-

---

1 Sparkling and glittering.
2 Old fogey.

tance with the vulgar tongue could supply to the glibness of their eager speech. Mallison barbed all these with the appellation of Presbyterian. To his malicious fancy there was an odd discordance, between the multiplied manors that were to descend to me, the remnant of a thousand dazzling exploits and achievements of chivalry, and the melancholy and mournful carriage of the adherents of this celebrated sect. He would contrast, with impressive strokes of description, the advantageous air, and frank and commanding language of the *preux chevaliers*[1] that had gone before me, on the one hand, with the ambitious plainness, the demure and nasal twang, the fixed eye, and the drawling *yea* and *nay*, of the persons to the inheritance of whose tenets I was bred.

It may be imagined with what writhings and contortions of soul I stood all these attacks. Figure to yourself a being, just escaped from the magnificent and moss-grown ruins of Mandeville House, from a life of silence and reverie, and now thrown among all the rude clatter and gabble of these unmannerly assaults! In the whole course of my former life I had never been spoken to familiarly by any human creature, and certainly had never felt pain from the familiarities of any one, except of the venerable Hilkiah. Now I was pointed and sneered at, as I passed. A significant winking of the eye, or a contemptuous shooting of the lip, the various mows and gibes of a school-boy's prolific and wanton malice, pursued me. The consciousness of this withered my heart, and gave an ungraciousness and constraint to all my motions. What was I? Why was I thus formed? And by what perverse and malignant destiny was I thrown on so intolerable a scene? I had stood out to my own apprehension, as a being choicely gallant and great; in the elation of my heart I had almost been ready to exclaim like the great Roman orator,[2] "Oh, fortunate generation of Englishmen, whose lot it has been to have me born your contemporary!" And here, within the walls of Winchester College, I was treated as nothing, a flouting stock and a make-game, a monstrous and abortive birth, created for no other end than to be the scoff of my fellows, their sport, and their joy, when they stood in need of an object to spend their brutal and unthinking mirth upon.

Tremendous were the convulsions and earthquakes, which these trials produced in my bosom. Sometimes I shut myself up in the circle of my own thoughts, and scorned to mingle with, or

---

1 Gallant knights.
2 Marcus Tullius Cicero (106–43 BCE).

to remark, the empty fools who purposed to humble me with their contempt. My brow contracted a scowl; my soul embosomed a ferocity; and in my own determined spirit I dug a broad and a deep foss,[1] and threw up an intrenchment, to cut me off from creatures wearing the human form, who seemed to me unworthy of my love, beneath my hatred, and to whom it was an error and a weakness to extend even my notice.

But this was an effort and struggle, perhaps beyond the nature of man, certainly beyond the strength of a school-boy. At other times I came down from my precarious elevation. I resolved to assert myself, and to put my opponents to rout. It was in vain that I endeavoured to do this by words; nature, as I have said, denied me this faculty. There is another resource, well understood among the retainers of an academic life. Words, few, but resolute, were to be inforced by all that corporal confutation and rebuke, which the unaided and imperfect strength of a stripling's arm can inflict. I was defeated; I was conqueror by turns. By practice my skill became more useful to its master, more formidable to the adversary. On such occasions I delighted in the sight of blood. Whether it flowed from the person of my competitor or from my own, in the one case no less than the other, it seemed to lighten and dilute the impure and substantial fluid that weighed on my heart. I gained some, but an imperfect relief to the injustice I felt. Few things in the scholastic circle obtain for their possessor more respect, than courage and power evinced in this species of contention. My equals became more cautious in provoking me to this retaliation. Even those of higher standing began to entertain a more tolerable opinion of me, and mechanically to refrain from those aggressions, which they saw I so well knew how to repress and to punish in such as were in any degree my match.

But what a situation was this for me, for the solitary wanderer of the bleak and majestic domains of Mandeville House? I disdained the position in which I stood. As I have just said, the subduing of an opponent gave relief to the depression under which my spirit laboured. But this was but momentary. I purchased a constrained and half-felt respect. But by what means? Not by any qualities I had been accustomed to honour: but by the mere force of muscles and sinews, by that in which the most brutal rustic, nay the very beasts of the forest, might overmatch me. When I saw myself and my competitor, with arms and bosom bare, prepared for the disgraceful contest, what feelings of disgust and

---

1 Ditch.

loathsomeness would rise in my soul! Hot tears, in spite of pride, not tears of cowardice, but of impatient indignation, would sometimes swell to my eyes. But I dashed them away with scorn, and strung myself for the task which I had not the liberty to avoid.

Habits of solitude had given me a peculiar turn. I had no respect for the limbs and members of my body, and viewed them but as an incumbrance upon the activity of my spirit. They were mine, not me. My arm was but an implement and a tool, of the same nature as a hooked stick, and of no value but for the commission in which it was employed. My creed was akin to that of Anaxarchus, of whom it is related that one of the Grecian tyrants having ordered him to be pounded in a mortar, he cried out under the execution, "Beat on, tyrant! Thou hast no power but on the case of Anaxarchus; himself thou canst not hurt":[1]—though I will not boast that I could have carried the principle of the philosopher to the same extent, as my master. Thinking thus, I detested the necessity I lay under, of being the captive of my body, and that by this means the soul of Mandeville, that free spirit that could wander unfettered from pole to pole, should be liable to the dominion of others.[2] The injuries of my body therefore seemed to be but the mark of my slavery; and its triumphs afforded me no consolation.

Guided by these principles, I bitterly felt that the walls of our college were not my home. The scene in which I was placed, was in utter discordance with the character of my spirit: And the consciousness of this, daily increased in me that concentrated and misanthropical spirit, which to a certain degree had subsisted within me from the earliest period of my remembrance.

CHAPTER XII

Clifford was a royalist to the core, and would often talk affectingly, yet cheerily, of the unfortunate Charles. Loyalty had been one of the lessons instilled into him from his cradle; and the ten-

---

1 Godwin tells the story in his essay "Of Body and Mind" in *Thoughts on Man* (1831): "Anaxarchus ... we are told, was ordered by Nicocreon, tyrant of Salamis, to be pounded in a mortar" and "in contempt of his mortal sufferings, exclaimed, 'Beat on, tyrant! Thou dost but strike upon the case of Anaxarchus; thou canst not touch the man himself'" (11).

2 See Godwin's "Of the Rebelliousness of Man" in *Thoughts on Man* (103–04; Appendix G3a in this edition). The essay often echoes Godwin's descriptions of Mandeville's early years.

derness of his heart would have led him to sympathize with the adversities of this victim, if he had not been a king,—and a prince, according to his creed, that from his birthright, and for his virtues, all Englishmen were bound to defend to the last drop of their blood. As he talked, gaily, but eloquently, on this favourite topic, a tear would sometimes start into his eye, which he dashed away, and smiled as he did it, in such a sort,

> As if he mocked himself, and scorned his spirit,
> That could be moved to weep at any thing.[1]

Clifford had been brought up in reverential ideas of kingship and prerogative, and with a hatred of republicanism. He admired the principles of chivalry, and those high notions of honour and generous fidelity which grew out of these principles. He was the creature of love and the affections. The splendid descriptions he had met with of tilts and tournaments caught hold of his fancy; and the various expeditions on record, in which the nobility and gentry of different countries associated themselves, to put down oppression, or to rescue the country and tomb of Christ from the hands of the Infidels,[2] were his amusement and his joy. All this inspired him with a congenial relish for whatever was grave, solemn and magnificent, either in the rites of religion, or the conduct of civil affairs, and a boundless contempt for the cold and unattractive simplicity and nakedness, which had been patronized and diffused by the adversaries of the late unfortunate monarch.

His talk of this sort, as I have already observed in another case, was without premeditation and formality, in starts and effusions of the soul, bursting from him as the occasion prompted. And, when he detected himself in a vein of this sort, he would turn away immediately from the thought, crying out, "But what am I talking of? I, who am but a school-boy? Older and abler heads than mine have laboured, by day and by night, in season and out of season, to amend these things, and see what it has all come to!"

At another time he would comment on his own thoughts in a different fashion, and exclaim, "Well, well, the world will have its way; and what can I do? I am born indeed in an iron age, and have been called on to witness, or to hear of, a multitude of

---

1 Shakespeare, *Julius Caesar*, 1.2.206–07.
2 Alluding to the Crusades (1095–1204).

crimes: but for all that I will not play the weeping philosopher.[1] What I cannot alter, I will learn to endure. I have but one life, and that, as far as I can without injury to others, I will make a happy one. When a few years have passed over my head, I shall never again be a boy. I shall but once be a man; and when that time comes, I will try to play a man's part in the world. I cannot have an universe made on purpose for me; so I will even make the best of that upon which fortune has thrown me. Then, hey, boys for a game at foot-ball!"

Such was the state of things among us, when an accident occurred to me, the impression of which will never be effaced from my mind. Among the other scholars at Winchester school, we had with us the eldest son of Sir William Waller, the famous parliamentary general.[2] Sir William, when he had been dismissed from his command by the parliament as a Presbyterian, received as the reward of his services the Castle of Winchester with its appurtenances, upon which he had some claims on the score of family alliance. This of course rendered him a great man among us: and it is well known that the brilliancy of his services in one period of the war, gained him with his party the familiar appellation of *William the Conqueror*. Nicknames at all times furnish a favourite sport to school-boys; and as young Waller was indisputably, as far as the rank and station of his father was concerned, the most eminent of the Presbyterian boys of Winchester College, his fellow-pupils, by general consent, fastened upon him in raillery and contempt the appellation which his father had earned by his exploits. It somehow happened that I contracted a particular familiarity with this boy. I can scarcely now account for the selection I made. My native taste, as I have already said, would have led me to Clifford. But such are the caprices of human intercourse!

Clifford was beautiful and prepossessing. Nothing could exceed the sweetness of his disposition, or the warmth of his

---

1 Heraclitus (c. 540–c. 480 BCE), known as the weeping philosopher.

2 Waller (c. 1597–1668) was a Presbyterian and prominent supporter of Parliament during the First Civil War and drew up the plan for the New Model Army. Later, after 1644, he supported the Presbyterian-Royalist opposition to the Protectorate and was imprisoned several times. He was active in forwarding negotiations for the Restoration of Charles II. He did have a son called William, who became an MP in 1680. Godwin read Waller's "Vindication" of his having taken up arms against the King, first published in 1793 (*Diary*, 6 and 7 October).

heart. Yet I shrunk from Clifford, and attached myself to Waller. The solution of this, lies in what I have already delineated of my character. I was by nature solitary. Therefore Waller suited me, and Clifford did not. Waller was a lad of diminutive stature, and his complexion was a deadly pale. His eye sometimes glistened; but not with kindness. He knew not what it was to love any creature but himself; the occasional, rarely occurring, lighting up of his looks, was from conceit, the triumph, when such triumph fell to his share, of an abortive specimen of manhood over his happier fellows. To finish his portrait, he was in some degree, though not violently, deformed in his person. Such was the *William the Conqueror* of Winchester College!

It was disdain, and the unsociableness of my nature, that dictated this choice. I could not unbosom my thoughts; I could not come into contact with another being of the same species as myself. Once I had done so, and yet but imperfectly, with a creature of another sex, my sister. But in the groupes and the busy scenes of Winchester school I felt that this was impossible. Clifford, as I have said, was the subject of my first and my sincerest admiration; but I could not court him. All beings were to me tools that I was to make use of, or foes whose destiny it seemed to be to thwart my purposes, or to subvert my tranquillity. Yes; I could court, and accommodate myself to the foibles of another, but not as to an equal. At the time that I descended to him, I must feel that it was the sport of my humour, not a necessity to which my inferiority impelled me. In a word, pride, a self-centred and untameable pride, was the inseparable concomitant of all my actions.

It was this feature of my nature, that drove me to reject Clifford, and any other of the talented and high-minded pupils of Winchester College, and to chuse Waller. I chose him, because my sullen nature would not admit of a friend. I could have him by my side, when I did not prefer to be alone, and could say to him just what I pleased, and no more. There was no danger in him of any sally of the mind, any spark of an electrical nature being struck out, that should set the whole man in a blaze. My sobriety, and the solitude of my soul were perfect. I had a figure pacing step by step along with me, with which I could amuse myself as I pleased, without losing the advantage, as to every material point, of being totally alone. I chose this lad, because I could manage him as I pleased. There was nothing commanding or masculine in his turn of mind. I was not afraid that he should run out of the course, and make me the unwilling associate of any freak of his own suggestion. He was of a timid and pusillanimous nature, and by no means likely to abound in his own sense, or to prove stubborn and uncontrolable to the mandates of one whose superiority he felt. Such at least was my interpretation of his character.

But, to return to the incident I was about to relate. A book of prints was found in my apartment, of the most odious nature, and least of all to be forgiven within the walls of Winchester School. It must have been the collection of some person, a deadly foe to monarchy (or, as it was then called) the government of a *single person*, and to the House of Stuart. The first print represented Henry, Prince of Wales, and his brother Charles, yet an urchin; Prince Henry being in the act of flouting and upbraiding the other, pointing at his crooked legs, with a label from his mouth, "Never mind; that is a good child! We will make thee a bishop, and thy petticoats shall hide them":—while Charles was in tears, weeping at the bitterness of the taunt.[1] The next print represented Osbaldiston, the master of Westminster School, at a time when there were above fourscore doctors of the three great faculties in the two universities, who gratefully acknowledged their education under him,[2] set in the pillory in the front of his own school; while Laud and the king were seen laughing and in triumph at a neighbouring window. [This scene never really took place; as Osbaldiston absconded and hid himself from his sen-

---

1 [Godwin's note:] Osborn: James I. § 45.

2 [Godwin's note:] Echard. [The reference is to Echard, *History of England*, 461–62. Lambert Osbaldistone or Osbaldiston (1594–1659), Master of Westminster School, was sentenced on the order of the Star Chamber to the pillory, fine, and forfeiture, because of a letter allegedly written to Dr. Williams, Bishop of Lincoln in 1638. Echard describes how, after the Bishop had been imprisoned in the Tower, the letter from Osbaldiston "in which there were some Enigmatical Expressions" was found among his papers. Though the Bishop denied receiving the letter and Osbaldiston convincingly explained it, the latter was sentenced. He managed to escape (hence Godwin's comment that the incident never took place), but lost his position at Westminster and lived in obscurity until his death just before the Restoration. Godwin's description of his influence on "Doctors of the three great Faculties" in Oxford and Cambridge is taken almost verbatim from Echard, 752. The episode of planted evidence parallels Mandeville's own predicament. According to Echard (752), Osbaldiston later became a Royalist, an indication of the fluctuating politics of the time.]

tence, till the period of general emancipation.][1] Another print represented Charles with a sword drawn, a dragon with many heads opposite, and Strafford standing near the king, to lend him his aid. The dragon erected its crest with conscious superiority, and thrust out its forked tongue; while the king shrunk frightened at his own temerity, and seemed preparing to seek his safety in flight. Underneath was written, "As for that hydra, the parliament, take good heed! You know I have found it here cunning, as well as malicious."[2] The next print was of the irresolute and ill-fated prince, immediately before his attempt to seize the five members, the queen standing over him in his closet, in a contemptuous and threatening attitude, with these words, "*Va-t-en, poltron! Arrache moi ces coquins-là par les Oreilles, ou ne me voir plus de tes jours.*"[3] Another represented Charles in the act of finishing his letter to the House of Lords, intreating them to save the life of Strafford; to which the queen was seen, with her right leg extended, and her left hand clenched and firmly pressed on her hip, compelling him to add the memorable postscript, "If he must die, it were charity to reprieve him till Saturday."[4] Another print

---

1 William Laud (1573–1645) was Archbishop of Canterbury from 1633 to 1645. A chief adviser of the King, he tried to impose uniformity in religion, and his episcopal practices, edging towards Catholicism, brought him into conflict with the Puritans and the Scottish Presbyterians. Laud took the lead in prosecuting Bishop Williams. His support for the King resulted in his beheading in 1645. He was the subject of numerous satirical cartoons and pamphlets.

2 [Godwin's note:] Strafford's Letters: Charles to the Lord-Deputy, April 1634. [In Greek mythology, the hydra was a many-headed snake slain by Heracles.]

3 [Godwin's note:] Echard. "Begone, coward: pull me those rogues out by the ears, or never see my face again." [In January 1642, Charles considered arresting Lord Kimbolton from the House of Lords and five leading parliamentarians from the Commons, including Godwin's heroes in *HCE*, John Pym and John Hampden. The King was nervous about putting his plan into execution, whereupon the Queen taunted him with the comment quoted here by Godwin. Lady Carlisle, who was present at the argument between the King and Queen, alerted the parliamentarians before the King could put the plan into execution (Echard, *History of England*, 520). They escaped to the City of London, which refused to surrender them, and returned to Parliament.]

4 [Godwin's note:] Burnet. [Gilbert Burnet (1643–82); see Appendix D4, pp. 489–90.]

represented Charles on horseback, in the act of receiving a distasteful petition, the petitioners being on their knees, while the king turns his horse suddenly upon them, with the purpose to throw them prostrate in the mire.[1] In another he was represented thrusting his head between the bars of a window in Carisbrook Castle, with a boat and horsemen in the distance to aid his escape, and these words, "Alas! where my head would go through, who would have thought that my shoulders would stay behind?" The king stuck in this attitude, so as to make a considerable force necessary to extricate him from it.[2] There were other prints not less satirical than these.

The book was found by Mallison, and shewn to Clifford. The prefects of the school (a denomination assigned to the boys of the sixth, or head form,) at this time twelve in number, held a *concio* or assembly, on the subject, to deliberate as to the way in which it was proper to proceed respecting so flagrant a delinquency. It was one of the maxims of this senate, that they were in no case to call in the interference of the masters respecting any thing that was not a school offence, and that they were a body, perfectly capable of redressing their own wrongs, and administering justice among themselves. Such was the spirit of loyalty at this time in our establishment, that no boy, excepting the two I have mentioned, so much as looked on the book. It was enough that it was reported to the sitting as infamous, by two credible witnesses. A jury of virgins would as soon have thought of satisfying themselves by minute inspection, that a set of prints of another sort was obscene. The heart revolted at the thought; and they believed that no patience, where the mind was yet undepraved, could sustain the examination.

Before this awful body, I was myself summoned, together with Waller, to account for the possession of this book. It was found under such circumstances, as were thought clearly to prove that it belonged to one of us. The nature of the book was briefly

---

1 [Godwin's note:] Traditional, from Mr Thomas Hollis.
2 [Godwin's note:] Firebrace, *apud* Herbert. [Henry Firebrace (1619–91) attended Charles during his captivity in Carisbrooke Castle in 1648 and tried to help him escape. Baronet Thomas Herbert (1606–82) was Charles's Groom of the Chambers, and also attended him during his confinement at Carisbrooke and then at his death in 1649 (Echard, *History of England*, 646, 660). Herbert's reminiscences of Charles's captivity were published as *Memoirs of the two last years of the Reign of Charles I* (1702, 1813).]

explained. We stood there as two persons, between whom at present the charge equally lay; but who might very probably, one of us be guilty, and the other innocent.

I was as ignorant of every thing that related to the affair, as the child unborn. I stood therefore in mute astonishment. I looked upon Waller, and saw that he was extremely distressed; he turned pale, and was scarcely able to support himself. I pitied him from my soul. It was not my business to speak to justify myself and still less to cast the charge upon him; and I left my companion to explain the matter as he could.

Our judges like me, observed the greater distress of Waller, and therefore applied themselves principally to him. He stammered, looked wild, and seemed hardly able to bring out a word. At length he somewhat recovered his composure. He intreated that he might not be urged any further; he protested his own innocence; he begged to be excused from speaking. The manner with which he expressed himself, turned the inquisitive gaze of all upon me. He was told that all false delicacies must be put aside in this case; the offence was a crying one; and it must be sifted to the bottom.

Waller now apparently roused himself with an effort. He confessed, that he was not wholly unacquainted with the matter. He said, the thing had been introduced to his knowledge by me.

"By *me*!" I uttered an interjection of astonishment merely.— But what an age of experience and horror was in that moment communicated to me!

Our intimacy, or rather the frequency with which we were in each other's society, was known; and he stated, that in one of our private walks, I had boasted to him with much apparent complacency, that I had such a book in my possession. In proportion as I had explained to him its contents, he had felt shocked, and had constantly refused so much as to cast his eye upon it. He remonstrated with me on the indecency and wickedness of giving harbour to or preserving such an article, which I had at first appeared inclined to dispute; but afterwards he had succeeded in convincing me of my error, and he sincerely believed it was my intention to have destroyed it.

Waller now seemed frightened at what he had done. He expressed the utmost distress. He appealed to themselves, whether they had not extorted the confession from him; he trusted that they would not stamp him in the records of the school with the odious character of an informer; and he intreated, that if not for my sake, who he was sure had seen my error, at least for his, and that he might not labour under so base an imputation, they would pass over and dismiss the offence.

It is impossible to utter the feelings with which I witnessed this detail. That Waller of all creatures should have dared to set himself in opposition to me!—that I should [have] been infatuated enough, to have nursed such a viper in my bosom!—was to me a thought insupportable.

I was not eloquent. My nature refused to supply me with the stream of a copious discourse on any occasion. But, had it been otherwise, could I have stooped to make an elaborate defence against an infamous charge, which I felt within myself to be void of the slightest foundation? Inexperienced as I was, and unknowing in the mazes and perplexities of the human heart, I believed that no one could be deceived with regard to the innocence of another, but he that was wilfully deceived. I therefore simply answered, but with the emphasis of truth, *that the book was not mine, that I had never seen it,*—and I expected my judges instantly to credit my assertion.

What then was my astonishment, when I plainly saw that the whole assembly leaned to the story of Waller? Could any thing indeed have been more unavoidable? His speciousness, his distress, his fervent intercession in my favour, had the greatest weight with them. Add to which, the gentlemen of Winchester school knew nothing of my family or connections. But the celebrated Sir William Waller, the father of my antagonist, and who still bore the style of governor of Winchester Castle, had for years been the firm and acknowledged leader of the presbyterian royalists, and was at this moment a prisoner for his adherence to the king's party. It was not to be believed therefore, that his son should be in possession of a scurrilous republican libel, and pamper himself with the record of royal imbecility and dishonour.

But all this I did not at the time understand. I could not put myself in the place of my judges, and estimate the various presumptions that guided their decision. I remained in my own place, and saw only the justice of my own cause. Agreeably to the misanthropical and savage character of my mind, I could see nothing in all that was passing but a combination to disgrace and to injure me. I could not conceive, that they should not know my innocence, when I told them of it. The picture therefore to my mind was, that all that I saw was a trick, that the book had been maliciously procured for the purpose of fastening the guilt that related to it on me, and that the whole scene of the trial, the accusation, and the impending judgment, was preconcerted, with a view to trample me in the dust.

In this situation my misanthropy was no shield to preserve the severity of my mind. My nature was ambition personified. All my habits had been those of self-reverence. I felt that ardour and generosity of spirit, which, as I believed, made me capable of great things. I felt that inborn pride of soul, which, like an insurmountable barrier, seemed to cut me off for ever from every thing mean, despicable and little. With all this pride, I could not endure the thought of a slur or an inglorious imputation, and, as is said of the ermine, I could die for very spite and shame at the bare idea, that any thing sordid and vile should pollute the whiteness of my name.[1] And now "the thing which I feared was come upon me!"[2] Was this to continue? Was this to cramp and control all my future efforts, and put an end to my aspiring thoughts for ever? I cannot express the agonies of my soul.

It is true, that in a certain sense this was no disappointment. Habitually I shut myself up in the storehouse of my own spirit; and intuitively I expected no justice from the world, whether a wider or a narrower world, in the midst of which I lived. No matter! For a human creature to find his worst imaginations confirmed—imaginations, wantonly formed in all the luxuriance of a gloomy spirit, to which, while bodied forth, the heart refuses its assent, and which seem conjured up in wilful determination to exceed the possibilities of an actual scene—to find these realised, I say, in their utmost extent,—is no lulling and tranquil sensation. On the contrary, the very notion of having met with the thing before, amidst the incoherent creations of delirium, or in the fancy-formed rout of hell broke loose, seems to give to its sudden and perfect existence a more exquisite pang.

The whole of the evidence having been gone through, Waller and myself were ordered to withdraw. We remained alone in an adjoining apartment. I looked upon my accuser; I could not speak. I examined curiously whether he had the lineaments of a human creature, and even, with a vulgar superstition, looked down at his feet, to see whether the demon did not betray himself by his cloven heel.

At length I recovered the power of utterance. With a haughty and imperious accent I said, "Waller, am I guilty of the crime with which you have charged me? Or what have I done, that you should fabricate so foul an accusation against me?"

---

1   The ermine, white except for its tail, was thought to be willing to die rather than be polluted by dirt.

2   Job 3:25.

He replied: "I cannot ask you to forgive me. You have done nothing to me; I bear you no malice. But—you are endowed with courage; and I am a coward. The guilt is mine. I saw the book in the house of a bloody regicide, whither I had been allowed some time ago to attend some messengers of my father; and, while they sought grounds of another kind to criminate the owner, I made prize of this. With a boyish love of amusement, I studied it at home, and brought it to the school. I thought the prints well done, and I laughed at the witty malice of the rogue that made it, without suspecting that I was doing any thing wrong. But when I found that the book had fallen into the hands of the prefects, and that they considered it as an affair of so heinous a nature, I could not own it; and I threw it upon you, because I had no other way of clearing myself."

"Well, Sir, and now go instantly to the prefects, and repeat all you have just said to me."

Waller drew back with the greatest terror.

"Oh, for God's sake!" said he, "The imputation will do you no harm; you are accountable to nobody. But my father, if it were known, would resent my fault so much, that he would turn me adrift to the world, and never speak to me again."

"Take then," answered I, "the results of your folly. I am innocent; and I will not submit to the consequences of being pronounced guilty."

"Oh, Mandeville," replied Waller, "indeed you must. The original charge of having such a book in my possession I could not support; and what will become of me now? If now I am exposed, I shall not only be found to be the real criminal, but shall further labour under the complicated dishonour of being a false accuser, of having with cool and unabashed effrontery told a tale, no word of which was true, and that with the fixed purpose of transferring a fault to you, of which I was the real perpetrator. It is all over! I am ruined for ever! I shall be hunted out, not from the Wiccamists[1] merely, but out of the world. My father, my brave and gallant father, will break his heart to think that he had such a son. I shall have a brand upon me like Cain, to mark me out to every creature that lives. I shall have a stain, that no penitence or penance can ever remove.—Yes, Mandeville, do your pleasure with me! I have deserved it. I am entitled to no mercy. Let me perish in

---

1   Members of Winchester College, which was founded by William of Wykeham (1324–1404), Bishop of Winchester and later Chancellor of England.

unimagined torments, so that the least hair of your head may go uninjured!"

I know not what came over me at this moment. This was a worthless fellow. His act had been that of a finished scoundrel, and showed that there was no rational hope, that he could ever prove a credit to his species. Yet I determined that I would be his preserver. There is something in the accent of genuine anguish, that a well constituted human heart (and yet mine was not such!) can scarcely resist. Much of the emotion he expressed was allied to virtuous feeling, and struck upon a chord that is unbounded in its potency. Add to this, he was in my power, and therefore I could not resolve to use that power against him. I would not be his destroyer. I would not have that to recollect. However small might be his chance to act an honourable part in human society, I would not deprive him of it.

Beside that, there was something gallant, that at this time suited my savage temper, in braving the imputation of guilt, when secretly, in the chambers of my own heart, I knew, that I was innocent, and more than innocent. It accorded with the disdain which, without yet knowing why, I entertained for my species. I could brave the imputation of guilt, when it was in my choice to do so, though, when the imputation appeared unavoidable, it struck me as the greatest of calamities. I could "doff the world, and let it pass." I could "make mouths at the invisible event."[1] There appeared to me, while I thought of it, a sort of lordly delight in standing the scorns and reproaches of my companions, when all the time in my own reflections I smiled contemptuously at their error, and rose serene above the clouds in which their misconstructions sought to envelop me. It will presently be seen that I overestimated my own powers.

I said, "Waller, be satisfied. You have acted a foul and ignominious part: but I will carry you through."

I had scarcely uttered the words, before we were called to appear again before the council of the prefects.

"Mandeville," said Clifford, "the act of which you have been found guilty, is unworthy of a subject of Great Britain, and still more of a Wintonian; and the character of the college requires that it should be expiated."

"Shame on the wretch!" said Mallison. "To trample upon the ashes of a fallen monarch! secretly to find delight in contemplating the scandalous lies, that have been invented against the name

---

1 Shakespeare, *Henry IV, Part 1*, 4.1.96–97; *Hamlet*, 4.4.50.

and reputation of a murdered king! I vote that he be required to eat the book on the spot."

I started. I had been far from anticipating the possibility of such ingenuity of malice and degradation. My countenance sufficiently showed, that to persist in such a sentence would be to no purpose. Even the generosity of boys of noble and honourable birth, such as were those that tried us, was alarmed at the idea of awarding against me, of whom they knew no other fault, any thing so brutal and so detestable. I already began to repent of the concession, which in the vehemence of my compassion I had made to the wretched Waller.

"No," said another; "let his punishment be with his own hand to commit it to the flames."

"Prefects!" cried I, with uncontrolable impatience, "it is in vain that I am treated with this ferocity of contempt. How the book came here, it is no matter. I am as free from any disloyalty of sentiment as the best of you. I acknowledge nothing unworthy or mean. My limbs and the members of my body are my own. One and another of you may dishonour yourselves by such barbarous and uncivil suggestions: but you cannot dishonour me. I cannot truly suffer disgrace and ignominy, unless by my own act."

While I spoke thus, Clifford caught up the book, the subject of our debate, thrust it in the fire, and in a moment it was in flames. He then turned to me.

"My lad," said he, "you put on here something too much of the brave. You should be conscious of your fault, and appear a little humbled for it. You should remember that you were so sensible of it at first, that at first you denied it. But let this be your punishment; not that with your own hand you commit it to the flames; but that with your own eyes, as is fitting, you see it consumed."

This to me was a heart-breaking trial. When I found myself pressed by the agonies of the wretched Waller, I had thought, like a boy, only of the thing immediately before me, and had yielded to his intreaties. I deemed, as I have said, that there was something gallant, and well suited to my disdainful temper, in suffering in silence the imputation of a guilt, from which I secretly knew myself to be free. But my imagination had proved sluggish on the occasion. I had taken the thing only in gross. I had not shaped out to myself the idea of actual punishment, and still less had conceived all the insulting words and things, that might be addressed to me. I flinched and writhed with anguish at these, as they successively rose before my unanticipating spirit; and, to say the truth, utterly repented the generosity I had practised. I would have given the world, to have published the undisguised truth at once. But it was too late. I had returned to the *concio* with all the rashness, but not with the firm resolution and deliberate desperateness, of a martyr.

That any creature that breathed, should have dared to give words in my hearing to the idea of my being condemned to eat by compulsion the substance of that by which my fellows had been offended, a degradation that at any rate could be awarded only against the most abhorred and recorded coward, was an insult that could only be expiated with blood. That I, descended from one of the first families, and in immediate succession to one of the largest estates in England, should have been addressed with this indignity, was a thought that could never be blotted out from the record of my brain; by day and by night it accompanied me; in solitude and society it haunted me; it mixed with all my dreams and all my reveries; if a moment of festivity or peace came over me at unawares, it was presently poisoned by the withering recollection—"I am a blasted branch—the tremendous gale of public disgrace has passed over all the buds of my promise, and I am nothing!"

It will hardly be thought how fierce a havock this event made with my constitution. It was exactly as if an envenomed arrow had entered my flesh. My blood boiled within me. The whole surface of my body burned, so that every one that approached me, and touched my flesh, suddenly snatched away his hand, as if it had been scorched with fire. I was in a raging fever. Before the close of the day I was conducted to my bed, which I did not leave for weeks. My agonies, and the distress both of my mind and body, were insupportable. And, when at length my disorder subsided, as it seemed, for want of further fuel to feed on, I was totally an altered creature. My colour and my flesh were gone. I seemed like a meagre, unlaid ghost. All my motions were languid, and all my thoughts were spiritless.

But what was most strange, and will be thought altogether unaccountable and perverse, the whole force of my resentment fastened upon Clifford. His part in the scene I have just described, was really a generous one. He saw how hardly some of his brother-prefects were disposed to bear on me; he was shocked at the inhuman suggestion of Mallison; and by seizing the book, the subject of debate, and thrusting it in the fire at once, he was really sparing my feelings, and putting an end to my misery.

But I could not persuade myself to view it in that light. His act was the crown and finishing of this whole; and the scene, as it stood in my memory, melted all into one mass, and belonged, without reserve or distinction, to the individual that had consummated it. Why did Clifford, thus unreasonable and unjust were my reflections on the subject, join in the cry against me? Was I not already brought low enough? Was not the whole school united, as in one faction, against me alone? How inhuman then, that he should have spoken to me after the same tone,—that he should have acted, what they only threatened!

My nature would not permit me to hate the rabble, the mere chaff and refuse of the threshing-floor. Waller and Mallison came not near me. They might deport themselves as they would; what was that to me? It is true, while the scene was actually passing, I thought otherwise; but they flitted away, as fast as the living scene in which they acted a part; and it must be something of more muscle and substance, that should fasten itself on my memory. Clifford was a name with which my soul could grapple: he was an obstacle interposed in my path that must be removed; or else all that I loved to contemplate and dream of for future time, was lost to me for ever. For these reasons, all the offences I received from inferior opponents, left the figures and features to which they properly belonged, and centred in him.

My pride was unbounded: what stood in the way of that pride? It was perhaps but an ill regulated and abortive passion. My temper was reserved and sullen; my speech was slow and sparing; I hardly communicated myself to a human creature: what chance had I for popularity and admiration? If all had been smooth and level before me, if no eminence had interposed itself through the vast plain of my existence, my hopes would, very likely, not have been the less abortive. No matter: whatever I was compelled to admire, I was compelled to hate. I was a disappointed and discontented soul; and all the wholesome juices and circulations of my frame converted themselves into bitterness and gall.

Clifford was the great luminary of the sphere in which I lived. Every one admired him; every one hung on his accents. He bewitched all that knew him by the nobleness and gallantry of his spirit. He charmed, without a purpose to charm; the walk of his soul was free and unconstrained and graceful; his happiest impulses expressed themselves with such tranquillity, and so without an effort, that you wondered in what their happiness consisted. It is like what we hear described of the benignity of the Deity, that diffuses life and enjoyment every where, and produces the astonishing miracles that even the very "angels desire to look into"[1] and understand, in perfect repose, and is as one, in doing every thing, that does nothing. What then was I? A dark and malignant planet, that no eye remarked, that fain would shine, but that, as long as the sun of Clifford was above the horizon, was cut off from every hope of gratification.

At this distance of time I can sit down, and deliberately calculate my small hopes of success, even if Clifford had been removed from the scene. But such were not my reasonings at the moment. It seemed to me, that he was my only obstacle; that he was my evil genius; and that, while my merits were in reality more sterling than his, he always crossed my path, and thwarted my success, and drew off all eyes, not only from perceiving my worth, but in a manner from recognising my existence.

Is it not surprising that all this should have ripened into hatred? What enormous and unmeasured injustice! What had I to do to hate him? He never injured me in the minutest article. He never conceived a thought of injury. Yet all my passions seemed to merge in this single passion. I must kill him; or he must kill me. He was to me, like the poison-tree of Java:[2] the sight of him was death; and every smallest air that blew from him to me, struck at the very core of my existence. He was a milstone hanged about my neck, that cramped and bowed down my intellectual frame, worse than all the diseases that can afflict a man, and all the debility of the most imbecil and protracted existence. He was an impenetrable wall, that reached up to the heavens, that compassed me in on every side, and on every side hid me from my fellow mortals, and darkened to me the meridian day. Let this one obstacle be removed (so I fondly thought), and I shall then be elastic, and be free! Ambition shall once more revisit my bosom; and complacence, that stranger, which, like Astraea,[3] had flown up to heaven, and abandoned me for ever, shall again be mine. In a word, no passion ever harboured in a human bosom, that it seemed so entirely to fill, in which it spread so wide, and mounted so high, and appeared so utterly to convert every other sentiment and idea into its own substance.

---

1 1 Peter 1:12.
2 The Upas tree, which was thought to be so poisonous that it destroyed life for miles around.
3 Goddess of justice who, in Greek mythology, lived on earth during the Golden Age but later fled to heaven to escape from man's wickedness.

MANDEVILLE.

A TALE

OF THE SEVENTEENTH CENTURY

IN

ENGLAND.

BY WILLIAM GODWIN.

And the waters of that fountain were bitter: and they said, Let the name of it be called Marah.

Exodus, Cap. xv.

IN THREE VOLUMES.

VOL. II.

EDINBURGH:

PRINTED FOR ARCHIBALD CONSTABLE AND CO.
AND LONGMAN, HURST, REES, ORME, AND BROWN,
LONDON.

1817.

CHAPTER I

I dwell too long on the scenes of my boyish years. Now, when the winter of age has shed its snows on my head, the mind finds a strange delight in meditating on times long past, and in living over again the turbid visions of its youth. Willingly would I lose the memory of the fresher sorrows that have succeeded; and, if I yielded to the impulse of my own thoughts, I should rest for ever upon these remoter seasons, though the days I passed at Mandeville House must be acknowledged to be sad, and those I spent at Winchester College to have been full of ungrateful accidents, and of sharp chagrin. But grief, when mellowed down by time, and seen obscurely through the atmosphere of added years, loses its more rigid and distressful features, and is not unaccompanied with a sedate and melancholy pleasure.

What I have recorded however may serve as a specimen of that portion of my existence, which I passed in the establishment of William of Wykeham. The rudeness of school-boy intercourse was ill suited to the sensitive temper of my soul; and almost every day brought along with it its freightage of pain. By dint of being perpetually in society, my disposition seemed to grow more solitary. In the majority of my school-fellows, I could find nothing to love; and in the few in whom I could not but recognize admirable qualities, these qualities, seen through my distempered organ, changed their nature, and became the nourishment of hatred. By their brilliancy I was obscured; and the purity of their temper seemed to be given them only, that they might wound me the more deeply, and pierce to my very heart. Pride, the infirmity through which the angels fell, was my ruin also.[1] But for this baser alloy in my character, I might have looked on at the busy scene around me, and have been both instructed and amused. If now and then I too had been jostled with and elbowed, if in the unthinking and wanton sports of the school-boy I had been made a jest of in my turn, what was I, that I should be exempted from the lot, which at one time or other falls upon all? But it is in vain to moralize. Man is so constituted, as always to take his joys and his sorrows, not as they are in their abstract nature, but as they accord well or ill with his own particular frame and constitution. At least it was thus with me: and trifles, which a gayer and more

---

1 Alluding to the phenomenon of Romantic Satanism, in which Milton was thought to be really "of the Devil's party," secretly valorizing the perverse energies of Lucifer.

vigorous mind would have shaken off, and forgotten like the successive clouds of fleecy seeming that are hurried along by the freshness of the breeze, clung tenaciously to the surface of my spirit, struck their roots like the corroding cancer, and ate into the substance of my soul.

From Winchester I removed to Oxford. But I had not long been there, before a sudden summons appeared to call me from these haunts of contemplation, and to demand my presence in a busier world. Cromwel had by this time ascended to the supreme height of power, and was in the close of the year 1653 proclaimed Lord Protector of the Commonwealth of England, Scotland, and Ireland. Secure in his "pride of place,"[1] and contented perhaps if he could have been generally and approvingly recognised as the first servant of the state, he called together a parliament upon a new model, and which promised to be a fairer representative of the nation, than she had ever enjoyed under her kings. But this parliament began with questioning that very condition, under which alone Cromwel purposed to allow their deliberations. The country was divided into royalists, presbyterians, and independents; and no one of these parties was disposed to subscribe to his usurpation. Cromwel's situation was therefore embarrassing and uneasy; and, after a considerable period of contention, he thought proper to put an end to the sittings of the legislature, sometime before the season actually arrived, which he had prescribed for its close.

The scene which was thus taking place, tended to weaken the security of the protector's government, and to blow up afresh the hopes of a party, which, however they appeared for a time inactive and supine, had their wishes and their hearts perpetually bent upon the restoration of the exiled family. In the commencement of the year 1655, a conspiracy was set on foot for that purpose, which extended its ramifications through the greater part of the kingdom, from the county of York north, to the western extremities of Devonshire and Cornwal. The Earl of Rochester, father to the celebrated poet and libertine,[2] came over from the continent for the express purpose of conducting it; and Charles II removed from Cologne to Middleburg, that he might

---

1   *Macbeth*, 2.4.12
2   Henry Wilmot, 1st Earl of Rochester (c. 1612–58), was father of the 2nd Earl, John Wilmot (1647–80), the poet. Charles II was at this time in exile.

be at hand to take advantage of such occasions as might arise.[1]
The hopes of the royalists were wound up to the highest pitch.
They saw that the yet green and unmatured usurpation of
Cromwel was the object of general disapprobation; and they naturally thought that all those who were enemies to the protector,
might be counted upon, especially when the project of the insurrection was once auspiciously commenced, to be their friends. It
was believed that Cromwel was so unpopular even in the army
itself, that he would not dare to call them to a general rendezvous, lest, as they had on former occasions erected themselves
into a deliberative body, and voted down those who were negoci-
ating with the king, so now they might vote down their commander-in-chief, and set up king Jesus (the favourite language of
these enthusiasts),[2] as the only supreme magistrate in their spiritual theocracy. It seemed therefore as if the enterprise now on
the eve of breaking out into light, once well begun, might be considered as good as finished. Could any concurrence of circumstances appear more favourable? Every one who was a friend to
the ancient constitution of the English government, felt inspired
with something more than hope, and believed that a little precaution and patience must necessarily lead to the most brilliant
results.

This occasion, as I have said, served to summon me also from
the haunts of the Muses. At the university I had for a fellow-
student a distant relation of the celebrated Sir Anthony Ashley
Cooper.[3] At college I was still the same character as at Winchester; and this youth originally engaged my partiality and affection
by his infirmities. When he first became known to me, his health
was extremely delicate; and it soon was sufficiently obvious that
he had within him the seeds of a confirmed consumption.[4] He
was therefore a person that could scarcely at any time give me

---

1 During 1654 two underground political parties, the Sealed Knot and
   the more militant Action Party, were plotting to bring the exiled Charles
   II back to power. When 8 March 1655 was selected as the day for coor-
   dinated uprisings (of which the Penruddock Uprising in the novel was
   one), Charles moved from Cologne in Germany to Middleburg in the
   Netherlands, with the aim of crossing over to England once the uprisings had gained momentum.
2 Religious fanatics, though the word was also used loosely of anyone with
   fervent beliefs.
3 Later 1st Earl of Shaftesbury (1621–83).
4 Pulmonary tuberculosis.

umbrage, or appear in the light of my rival or competitor. I pitied him; and my pride was gratified, while I played towards him the part of a guardian genius, supplying his wants, soothing his infirmities, and endeavouring by unremitted attention to mitigate his sufferings. I scarcely know when I was ever more happy, than in performing these offices. The reader has sufficiently perceived, that I had something within me, which appeared irresistibly to cut me off from the enjoyments of social life. Yet every man is formed with some appetite for these enjoyments; and it was therefore no small acquisition to me, when some extra-ordinary concurrence of circumstances, as in this case, seemed to enable me for a short period to be the vanquisher of my fate. As his disease advanced towards its last stage, I was almost continually, day and night, by his bed-side. What had been the character of this poor youth in a period of entire health, I can scarcely determine. But, as he lay on his death-bed, he was uncommonly mild and amiable. The disease contributed to give fire to his eyes, quickness to his conceptions, and a celestial sweetness to the faint smiles with which he seemed to thank me, when his voice was inward, and he could with difficulty articulate a sentence. He expired in my arms.

Sir Anthony came to Oxford to visit his kinsman, a short time before he died. He was desirous to have removed him to his own seat at Winbourn, that every possible effort might be made in his behalf. But it was found no longer practicable. The youth was profuse in his acknowledgments of the services I had rendered, and the constancy of my humane attentions; and Sir Anthony, with that graceful and winning manner for which he was remarkable, expressed his anxiety for an opportunity to show how deeply he and his family felt themselves indebted to me. I attended the remains of my friend to Winbourn, where they were deposited, and afterwards spent some weeks under the roof of the hospitable baronet.

It was during my residence at Winbourn, that the intelligence reached me of a design upon the eve of execution, for putting down the protector, and setting up the king. I learned it at the house of a royalist, where I accidentally visited, and where the son of the house, in all the unsuspecting warmth of youth, and believing that no person of an honourable race, like myself, could form any other wishes than he formed, dropped some hints that I could not misunderstand, and which I pressed him further to explain. I was myself at this moment a thousand times more a partisan of the exiled house of Stuart, than I had ever been. The disgrace I had endured on their account at Winchester, produced this effect upon me. I felt as a young man of the military profession might have done, who having betrayed some alarm in his first encounter with the enemy, would make it the passion of his soul to seek a second, where he might amply wipe off the slur he conceived himself to have sustained. Just so, the blemish that had passed over my name, glowed and smarted, and festered in my remembrance like a wound; and I was driven, to sacrifice myself, if necessary, in the royal cause, by a zeal, fervent, yet not altogether pure; for it was the torment of the reflex act of the soul, eating into itself, that furnished the spark that lighted up my flame.

In Sir Anthony I traced a character compounded of strange and discordant elements. Ambition was the ruling passion of his soul. But his mind was fluctuating, and unstable and unresolved; and the turbulent scene of the times in which he lived, tended to increase this defect within him. He had set out in life a royalist: offended by some transaction in which he conceived his merits to be undervalued, he turned parliamentarian: and, shortly after, he endeavoured to organise a third party, which should over-power and dictate to the other two. When Cromwel ascended to the chief magistracy, Sir Anthony seemed for a short time to be fascinated by the splendour of his talents and his fortune, and to have devoted himself, heart and soul, to the Lord Protector. He became one of the council of state, appointed as the advisers of Cromwel; and he had before this disgraced himself in the public eye, by being an active member of that motley assembly, called Barebones' parliament.[1] But nothing could long satisfy the aspi-

---

1 Just before and after the execution of Charles I, the Rump Parliament (consisting of Independents, Presbyterians who had tolerated the execution of the King, and gentry) passed a number of acts creating the legal basis for a republic; a Council of State then took over the executive functions of the monarchy. On 20 April 1653, Cromwell dismissed the Rump. It was replaced in July by Barebones Parliament (named after the Baptist merchant Praise-God Barbon), a nominated assembly that Cromwell felt would be easier to control. This parliament, which included Fifth Monarchists, moderates, and conservatives, was dissolved in December 1653, with Cooper voting for dissolution. Cromwell then became Lord Protector under Britain's first written constitution, known as the Instrument of Government, which was replaced by the Humble Petition and Advice (1657). While Royalists dominate the "history" in this novel, and while Cromwell appears on the fringes of the action, except for this reference Godwin says little about the Independents or others who resisted Cromwell on the left.

rations of his spirit: Whatever distinctions and honours were bestowed on him, he deemed all of them to be infinitely beneath the magnitude of his claims. During these fluctuations of his conduct, he did not the less maintain an uninterrupted correspondence with the royal party, and thus, keep open for himself a constant door of retreat, though this could not be done by him but at the hazard of his life. Add to this restlessness and temerity of nature, the most consummate address, with an eminent portion of penetration and daring; and you have then no inadequate portrait of Sir Anthony Ashley Cooper, afterwards Earl of Shaftesbury.[1]

One of Sir Anthony's favourite pursuits was the developement of the varieties of human character, as they presented themselves before him.[2] He condescended to employ his sagacity on me; and he soon "plucked out the heart of my mystery."[3] I wanted the

---

1 In 1659 General George Monck (1608–70) recruited Sir Anthony in his campaign to restore the monarchy, and he was among those who travelled to the Netherlands to persuade Charles II to return. After the Restoration Sir Anthony was made Chancellor of the Exchequer (1661–72). He was created Earl of Shaftesbury in 1672 and was Lord Chancellor (1672–73). He initially supported but then opposed Cromwell. While Mandeville and later Wagstaff represent him as a turncoat, S.R. Gardiner, a leading nineteenth-century historian of the Civil War period, says his "shrewdness" stemmed not from "personal ambition" but from a sense of how the tide was turning that resulted from a "sympathy with the main tendencies of the day ... he may fairly be credited with the principles which formed a thread of continuity in his devious career, a dislike of clerical domination, and a belief that the forces of a State are increased rather than diminished by the practice of toleration" (*History of the Commonwealth and Protectorate 1649–1656* [1894–1901; rpt. New York: AMS P, 1965], 3.3–4). After the Restoration, Sir Anthony, a patron of John Locke, espoused toleration and frequent meetings of Parliament, for which he spent time in the Tower of London (1677–78). He was a supporter of the Exclusion Bill, which was designed to prevent the king's Catholic brother, James, from succeeding Charles II. He was also one of the founders of the Whig Party, which was born during the Exclusion Crisis, which pitted Tories who opposed the bill against those who feared a return of absolute monarchy. During the Tory reaction after the failure of this Bill, he was arrested for high treason in 1681. He was acquitted, fled to Amsterdam, and died shortly afterwards.

2 The description links Sir Anthony to his grandson, the 3rd Earl of Shaftesbury (1671–1713), and author of *Characteristics* (1711).

3 *Hamlet*, 3.2.373–74, describing Rosencrantz and Guildenstern's manipulative attempts to probe Hamlet's inner recesses.

courage, or I wanted the frankness, that should have induced me to lay out my soul before him, and to have intreated his assistance. But, when I saw this extraordinary man, with an art that I could not sufficiently admire, make his way to the inmost recesses of my thoughts, and, like a skilful angler with a fish, give me line, and seem by turns to dismiss me from his reach, only that he might more securely bring me within his power, I gave up all resistance, and joyfully made him my confident, who already without my concurrence was master of my most secret ruminations.

I found that Sir Anthony knew better than I, and more fully in detail, the conspiracy that was going against his late patron, the Protector Cromwel. He told me, that he could not be of the service to me in the object of my desires that he otherwise would, because, though the purpose of the conspiracy had his sincerest wishes in its behalf, yet there were reasons, with which he would not trouble me, why he could not appear in the affair. He however furnished me with a letter of introduction to his neighbour, Colonel John Penruddock of Compton-Chamberlaine in the county of Wilts, who was destined to take a leading part in the enterprise in the west of England.[1] In this letter he recommended me as a person extremely well qualified, in his judgment, to conduct the correspondence of the enterprise, as secretary to the commander-in-chief, with such other military appointment as it might be thought proper to bestow upon me. I was delighted with this opening to the fortune to which I aspired. I was not yet fully seventeen years of age. At so early a period of life, to have obtained the recommendation of so eminent a man, and to look forward to a station in which I fondly hoped my abilities might be of no small service to the cause, was a degree of prosperity in the outset, with which I could scarcely have flattered myself.

I did not think proper to communicate to my uncle the prospect that was thus opened before me. With his character the reader is already acquainted. The details of affairs with which he was most nearly concerned, were very sparingly laid before him.

---

1 John Penruddock (1619–55), an English Cavalier during the Civil War. The Penruddock Uprising is given much more space here than in *HCE* (4.167–69). The larger insurrection of which it was a part also comes across in the novel as a purely Royalist plot, whereas in *HCE* Godwin stresses the alliance between the Royalists and Republicans disillusioned with Cromwell's treatment of Parliament and "the new usurpation to which they were subjected" (4.160).

Upon the accounts of his steward he could scarcely be prevailed on to bestow the slightest inspection. All business that was offered to his consideration he did not indeed repel with violence; but he shrunk from it with invincible obstinacy. He ordinarily required that every thing of this sort should be submitted to him on paper: and this paper he gave back sometimes, but not always, the next day, either with no postscript, an indication that he was resolved not to take any part in the matter, or with a short remark added in his own handwriting, pointing out what he desired should be done. I was the only male heir to the Mandeville estate in the direct line; and I took it for granted that my uncle, unenterprising as he was in his own person, would object to my hazarding myself in an insurrection of this sort, particularly at so premature a period of my existence; and I deemed, that I had a sufficient excuse for being silent, in my uncle's habits of neutrality and seclusion. For the same reason I determined not to communicate my secret to any member of the establishment at Mandeville House. Sir Anthony, at his own suggestion, undertook to supply me with any sum of money, that might be necessary for my immediate purposes.

CHAPTER II

Furnished, therefore, with whatever the occasion seemed to require, I proceeded with my own servant and horses from Winbourn to Compton-Chamberlaine. Here I was informed that Colonel Penruddock was from home; and by enquiries among his attendants, my servant learned that he was gone to the house of Colonel Hugh Grove,[1] a gentleman of the same county. Hither I followed him, the house of Mr Grove lying at the north-eastern extremity of Salisbury Plain. On my arrival I perceived an unusual bustle and activity; and it was plainly to be seen at the residences of both these gentlemen, and through a considerable part of my journey, that something extraordinary was in agitation. I will not pretend to determine what was the cause that the officers of civil administration in the neighbourhood, seemed to take no notice of these preparations; whether it was that they were impressed with indifference and alienation from the government of the protector; or that it might be the policy of his

---

1   Royalist beheaded in 1655 along with Penruddock.

administration, to ripen the plots of the royalists to a certain height, that his authority might be strengthened by their suppression, and his coffers enriched by their forfeitures.

Having enquired for Colonel Penruddock, and sent in my message, that gentleman immediately came out to me, the house being almost entirely filled with officers and their attendants, who had resorted hither, as to a secret rendezvous and consultation. The mansion of Colonel Grove had been found most convenient for this purpose, on account of its remote and solitary situation. I was immediately struck with the appearance of the man to whom my letter was addressed. He was above the middle stature, in the vigour of youth, and of a grave and noble aspect. His eyes and his hair were dark; his forehead capacious; his cheeks colourless; and the general cast of his features firm and sedate. His countenance bespoke the purity of his heart, and expressed in striking lineaments the steadiness of a martyr. I afterwards understood, that he had had two brothers, older than himself, who had fallen in the civil wars, fighting for the late king; and he therefore regarded himself as a person consecrated and set apart, to avenge their fate, or to follow their illustrious example. The voice and language of Colonel Penruddock were in the highest degree both sweet and manly; and he seemed born to be the ornament and benefactor of any country, where true patriotism was held in esteem.—What mystery is there in the frame and constitution of political society, that it should be thought necessary for the general welfare, that such a man as this should be brought out to the gaze of senseless multitudes, that in the sight of men he may suffer an ignominious death, as a person unworthy to live?—But I am hurried into scenes, that did not occur till some months after the period I am describing.

Colonel Penruddock drew me aside, and immediately opened the letter I had brought from Sir Anthony. He seemed pleased with my appearance, and struck with my youth. He said, Sir Anthony gives you here, young man, a liberal and a full commendation; and I will do what I can to serve you. He then ordered a youth, to be called, a cousin of his, of the same name, and desired me to remain with him, till we should all return to Compton-Chamberlaine together. He added, "The writer of this letter desires that I would commit it to the flames, as soon as read. I ought therefore to do that in your presence. I have not the instant opportunity of doing so. Take it, young man; to you it was intrusted at first; and I therefore devolve on you the office of fulfilling the injunctions of him who sent it."

In the evening of the same day I returned, in company with Colonel Penruddock and several of his followers, to his own country seat. Here we continued for the most part for the week or ten days next ensuing. During this time he had several conversations with me. He set before me in the most candid light the hazards of the enterprise he had undertaken. He advised me to think better of my situation, and return to the university. He observed, that the name of Mandeville had never been engaged on either side in the late calamitous wars, and that, particularly at my early period of life, I should do more wisely to hold myself neutral, and to enjoy, as I had a right to do, the protection of the civil government of my country, whatever that might happen to be. He felt, he said, as sensibly as any one, the blessings of a private life. He had a plentiful fortune, was married to an excellent woman, and was happy in his family and his children. But his situation was extremely different from mine. His family was already deeply engaged in the royal cause; and he felt, that the ashes of his brothers loudly called on him not to desert a loyalty, for the testimony of which they had perished.

I was deaf to the advices of my excellent monitor. The more he displayed in them of the admirable qualities of his mind, the more I rejoiced that so favourable an opportunity had offered itself to me, of launching upon the busy scene of the world. This, I felt, was a man that I could follow to the earth's extremest verge. He was neither pedantic, like Hilkiah, nor broken-hearted and incapable of exertion, like my uncle. Sir Anthony Ashley Cooper had honoured me with his particular notice, had made me a thousand professions of friendship, and whatever he said to me was adorned with all the grace that the most polished manners could bestow. But this was far from being so touching to me, as the noble frankness of Colonel Penruddock. There was something in his demeanour, that carried a conviction of his sincerity directly to the heart. And his dissuasions from committing myself were so unaffectedly earnest, as to impress me with a feeling that now for the first time I had found a friend. The earnestness that I had felt to prove my devotion to the royal cause, gained a double strength by my predilection for the leader, and thus mounted into an uncontrolable passion.

The growing attachment I experienced for Colonel Penruddock, seemed to be in some degree mutual. The zeal I expressed, had a certain correspondence with the sentiment in his own bosom; and, as I turned a deaf ear to the suggestions of prudence, so he felt convinced in his heart, that he was leaving an enviable scene of domestic felicity, for the precarious success of an adventure, where his life was "set upon the cast." The very obstinacy with which I resisted his counsels, awakened within him a sentiment of pity and esteem. He conversed with me repeatedly, and was pleased with my qualifications. I was of a family that commanded respect; and my education and my talents sufficiently fitted me for the station to which I was recommended.

The day was now approaching, in which it was agreed our enterprise should move. I became enrolled a gentleman-volunteer in Colonel Penruddock's own troop. I had equipped myself with certain habiliments expressive of my destination; and such is the lightness and vanity of the human mind, particularly at my period of life, that I had no sooner put on somewhat of the appearance of a soldier, than I felt like one, and became persuaded that there was no vocation on the face of the earth so glorious and so enviable.

Colonel Penruddock, Colonel Grove, and the other gentlemen of Wiltshire, who had associated for the present undertaking, were in daily expectation of the arrival of Sir Joseph Wagstaff,[1] who had come over from the continent with the Earl of Rochester, had for some weeks concealed himself in London, and was destined to take the command of the king's forces in the west. I listened eagerly after the character of this officer, who had distinguished himself honourably in the royal cause, under Prince Rupert,[2] and the other commanders of the times. His presence was much desired: he was spoken of as a gallant officer, a perfect gentleman, and a person of the greatest companionableness and courtesy of manners. A scheme of the boldest nature was formed, for entering the city of Salisbury at the period of the approaching assizes, seizing the judges and the sheriff in their beds, who were expected there the night before, taking from them their commissions, and compelling them to proclaim King Charles the Second in the public market-place. A master-stroke like this, it was sup-

---

1 Wagstaff (c. 1611–66/67) was a soldier of fortune who in 1642 was major in an Irish regiment in the service of France. Later in 1642 he was on the Parliamentary side, but on being taken prisoner by the Royalists in 1643, he again switched sides and accepted a commission to raise a regiment for the King. After the defeat of the Penruddock Uprising he fled to Holland, and survived the Restoration.

2 Prince Rupert, Count Palatine of the Rhine and Duke of Bavaria (1619–82), was General of Horse in the Royalist army from 1642 to 1645.

posed, would tend beyond any thing, to overawe the disaffected, and encourage those who wished well to our purposes, to rise as one man in our favour.

Two days before the time fixed for the execution of the project, it was announced to us that Sir Joseph had arrived at the house of a gentleman residing a very few miles from Salisbury. Colonel Penruddock immediately hastened to pay his respects to him, and took me with him. We slept at the house of this gentleman for that night. In the evening I was merely introduced in my character of a volunteer, and received in the most polite and encouraging terms. The next morning Colonel Penruddock mentioned to his now superior officer the particular appointment I had been induced to expect.

The courteous and obliging manners of Sir Joseph became instantly altered, the moment this was mentioned. He civilly desired me to withdraw for a few minutes, and leave him and the Colonel alone. The following particulars of what passed I did not learn immediately, but I became acquainted with them in no long time after.

"Colonel," said Sir Joseph, "this is no slight thing you ask of me, and must not hastily be granted. Why, the young fellow you have brought to me, is scarcely more than a school-boy. Have you sufficiently reflected, that whoever shall be appointed to the office of secretary to the commander-in-chief, will necessarily be in possession of all our secrets, and may make what use of them he pleases?"

"Granted, Sir Joseph," replied Penruddock. "But you must allow me to say in return, that I have not proceeded without reflection, and that, if my recommendation is not hastily admitted, neither will it I hope be hastily rejected. You say, he is young. Believe me, fidelity, and a sincere discharge of the trust reposed in us, are not always the growth of years. Youth has often a generous confidence, and an ardent attachment to men and principles, that might put persons of maturer life to the blush. Experience, such are the impure paths of mortal life, as often instructs men in cunning, as in plain dealing. I have talked largely with this youth, have heard his sentiments, and proved his character; and I will answer for him with my life."

"How long have you known him?"

"Almost a fortnight."

"A wondrous term of observation for so bold a reliance as you are disposed to place in him? How came you by his acquaintance? Who recommended him to you?"

"He brought a letter of introduction, couched in the warmest terms, from Sir Anthony Ashley Cooper."

"Very well, Sir, and have the goodness to tell me, who trusts Sir Anthony Ashley Cooper? Who pretends so much as to understand his character? A man without faith, and destitute of common honesty. He is a being, to whom principles and consistency are playthings and mockery. Young as he is, he has given himself by turns to all sides, and has betrayed them all. He does not even trouble himself with the smallest decency, in the strange fluctuations of his conduct. His pride seems to be, that no man shall trace him in his complicated evolutions, and that no sagacity shall be able to foretell what he purposes to do next. Sir Anthony, Colonel, is the very man against whom we should be most on our guard, and this stripling is exactly the sort of person that such a fox would choose, by means of whom to worm out our secrets, to obtain intelligence for the enemy, and to have us all in a string, to hang up whenever he pleases. Besides, Sir Anthony is a presbyterian, and the family of this Mandeville is presbyterian also."

"And who, Sir Joseph, have of late years shown themselves more devoted to the royal cause than the presbyterians? The enterprise in which we are embarked, is intended for a general rising of the kingdom, in the east and the west, in the north and the south. Our hopes are, to show this imperious upstart, who, after having accomplished the murder of our last sovereign by his artifices and hypocrisy, has had the audacity to seat himself in the chair of our kings, and fancy that all England will wait upon his nod,—to show this Cromwell, I say, desolate and forlorn, naked of almost a single supporter to abet his profligate cause, defeated without a battle, and as low and contemptible in the eyes of all the world, as he now holds himself pompous and magnificent, lording it over his country, and bullying the nations around. And can this be done, without moderation and forbearance towards those, who differ from us in some points, but agree with us in the main object for which we are engaged?"

"I am not of your opinion, Colonel," replied Sir Joseph. "We will make use of these presbyterians. We will take advantage of the preference they entertain for the king whom they hate, over the protector whom they abhor. But they shall have no part in the conducting our holy cause. We are ourselves sufficient for that. Ours shall be the project, and ours the triumph. It is enough for them, that, as long as they demean themselves quietly, they shall be allowed to enjoy the redemption which we shall have brought in. I should think the pure feeling of a cavalier violated, if a single man of those who first stirred the rebellion, was permitted to put his sickle into this harvest.—Beside, I have promised the office of secretary already."

"Pardon me, Sir Joseph; you should have told me that from the first. The command is yours; and no man can dispute your right to appoint your own staff. You need not have cast a slur upon my recommendation in this case; it was enough for you to have put your negative upon it.—And who is the youth for whom you reserve the appointment?"

"His name," answered Sir Joseph, "I am unacquainted with. But he is expressly recommended to me for the office by Lord Bellasis, one of the six loyalists residing in London, known by the denomination of the *Sealed Knot*,[1] who have had the secret management of every attempt for the restoration of the king, since the day of the martyrdom of his royal father. I expect the young man for whom the appointment is reserved this very hour."

During this conversation between Sir Joseph and the colonel, I remained in the antechamber, walking up and down in anxious expectation of the result of their conference. Till this moment, with the confidence that inexperience never fails to inspire, I had not entertained the smallest doubt, that the office for which Sir Anthony named me, and which Colonel Penruddock had in a manner promised, was substantially mine. There were several other persons as well as myself in the antechamber; but I took no notice of them. My mind was engrossed with its own thoughts.

While I remained in this position, the door leading to the staircase opened, and a young man entered, who put a letter into the hand of one of Sir Joseph's *aides-de-camp*. The officer looked on the letter, and immediately took it into the inner room. He was scarcely absent a minute when he returned, and invited the stranger to enter. The interval was so short, that the new comer had not leisure to seek for any occupation to fill it, and had not even looked round upon the persons present. Not such was the case with me. By accident, my attention had been roused by the first opening of the door; ardent, like the most romantic lover, for the success of my suit, I was smitten with the sentiment ever atten-

---

1 John Bellasyse (c. 1614–89) was one of the six founding members of the Sealed Knot, a secret Royalist organization dedicated to the Restoration of the Stuart monarchy during the interregnum. The Sealed Knot made six attempts between 1652 and 1659 to bring back the monarchy, the most famous of which was the Penruddock Uprising.

dant on a fearful and apprehensive lover, jealousy. Every fresh object alarmed me. The new comer was a youth of a most graceful and prepossessing figure: I looked up in his face. It was Clifford!

CHAPTER III

I had entirely lost sight of this adversary of my peace, since I left Winchester. I had enjoyed a season of comparative tranquillity at Oxford: it was because I had seen and heard nothing of my dreaded tormentor. Now, the hurricane within my soul, that had slept for a while, was instantly set in action. I had an instinct that told me, that the sight, and the very name of Clifford, was the precursor of some terrible reverse in my fortune. I recollected the altered manner of Sir Joseph, when I was mentioned to him for his secretary; and the truth instantly flashed upon me: The place is reserved for another, and that other is Clifford!—It was so.

It is hard for a young man to digest his first disappointment. I was barely seventeen; but already I counted myself for man. I had suffered disappointments, and I had suffered mortifications. But that was as a boy. There was no need of a wise man and a prophet, to tell me that, under every state of civilised society, a boy is a slave. Having escaped therefore from that condition, I was willing to count for nothing all the checks and stripes, and scorns, and contumelies of that immature period. I said, they cannot dishonour me. A boy is not held responsible for his conduct at the most awful bar of manhood; but is disciplined and controled in another way. I puffed them from me therefore, and bid them pass. Now I was placed under the recommendation and countenance of honourable men, and had to play my first scene upon the theatre of real life.

And what a scene? I had thanked Sir Anthony for his letter in the fulness of my heart. I had been transported with joy at the attention and partiality I had now for ten days experienced, from Colonel Penruddock. I had been last night received by Sir Joseph, with that affability and cordial manner for which he was so much distinguished. And for what was all this? For nothing. I was to be a gaping stock and a scorn to all the young volunteers, with whom I had for some days associated, and to whom in the thoughtless innocence of my heart, it seemed to me, that I had assumed the airs of Mr Secretary.

In reality I had done little of this. It was not in my nature. My spirit was too reserved and too concentrated. But it was all one.

At this early age, I felt as if they could read my heart, and knew all my thoughts. I know not that I had assumed any airs of superiority; though silence and reserve are always construed for such, and to a certain degree make enemies of all by whom a contrary procedure is expected. But I knew that I could not bear humiliation. If I had not shown my comrades that I looked down upon them, I had done so in my heart, and I could not bear to be reduced to the vulgar level.

And that all this should come from Clifford! I said to myself, I have but one enemy in the world, or but one enemy who is worth my care. But then that enemy is a host. He divides himself into a thousand parts, and meets me at every point. I feel that one world cannot contain us both. In the world where Clifford lives, there is no room for me.

Colonel Penruddock might in some degree have softened my disappointment to me. There were obvious topics for this, particularly the recommendation of Lord Bellasis, prior in time, and paramount in authority. He might have assured me, that no slight or offence was in any respect intended to me. He might have soothed my feelings, have exhorted me to patience, and told me that no doubt an opportunity would shortly offer, to make up to me for my present disappointment. He did nothing of this. Colonel Penruddock was one of that sort of men, whom a perfect sincerity disqualifies for some of the kinder offices of society. He was by no means rugged and blunt. His air was humane, and his manner conciliating. But he held it for a sacred duty, to tell the plain and simple truth. This is the misfortune of the moral virtues. Whoever acts them scrupulously, overacts them. The topics I have named, and which Colonel Penruddock did not use, were all of them true. By omitting them, he told but half the truth, and did not know it.

I have said, that Penruddock told me but half the truth; but there was an obvious reason for this. He saw but half the truth himself. He was considerably chagrined by the repulse he had experienced from Sir Joseph Wagstaff. His creed and that of Sir Joseph were of a very opposite tenour. Penruddock's heart overflowed with all the kindliest feelings of our nature. He was incapable of being any man's enemy. He was incapable of concurring in a severe and sanguinary proceeding towards any one. He loved his country; and to her cause, as he understood it, he devoted himself. He had been bred in an affectionate regard to his king; and that regard was greatly increased by the uninterrupted series of calamities which befel Charles the First. The males of his family had successively fallen martyrs in the royal cause: and this he conceived to be his destination in life, either by his energies to contribute to the victorious restoration of his master, or to seal his loyalty with his blood.

But he was not formed so much as to understand the littleness of party distinctions. The denominations of episcopalian or presbyterian were nearly alike to him, provided the men by whom they were borne, sincerely loved their country, and appeared willing to cooperate with him in the great enterprise of restoring her ancient constitution. He proved the urbanity and sweetness of his character, when a few weeks after, upon the scaffold, he expressed himself respectfully towards the protector, for the overthrow of whose government he had sacrificed his life, and by whose unjust forcing of the law (as Penruddock understood it) he was condemned to die. The Colonel therefore believed, that nothing could be more unwise and ill-timed, than the distinctions he saw his superior officer ready to set up, and the proscription that was extended against every one that bore the name of presbyterian.

The fault, in the affair with which I was concerned, originated with Sir Joseph Wagstaff. He might, as Penruddock had hinted to him, have pleaded the superior recommendation of Lord Bellasis, without mixing any personalities against Sir Anthony Ashley Cooper who had written in my favour, or any attack generally against the presbyterians to whom he considered me as belonging. Penruddock felt the impropriety of all this, and was offended accordingly.

The offence he felt, he communicated without qualification to me. He joined me immediately, took me by the arm, and led me into an obscure walk of the grounds. There he unburthened his whole heart to me. "Sir Joseph," he said, "had negatived my appointment." He added, that he saw, an illiberal proscription was intended to be set up against every one that was not of the old church, that is, as things then stood, against a great majority of the people of England. He spoke with great feeling, of the discouragement that was meditated to be exercised against the concurrence of such a man as Sir Anthony. He perceived, that the project of Sir Joseph was diametrically opposite to his own. Sir Joseph proposed to put down the government, and the neutrals that lived under its protection, by a small party, whose tedious sufferings and adversity had filled them with ideas of acrimony and persecution against all by whom they had at any time been baffled. The consequence of this, even if it had any chance of success, was to introduce a civil war more obstinate than the last, and to reduce every one to despair, who had at any time given aid to the parliament, since its commencement in 1640. His plan, on the contrary, had been to obtain the general concurrence of Englishmen, in every part of the island, and of every sect and denomination, and to convince the government and its abettors, that they were but an insignificant handful of the population at large. The king might thus, he sanguinely believed, be restored, without a struggle, and almost without shedding a drop of human blood. In my case, which was principally to be regarded as giving a foretaste of what was to follow, I was rejected, because I was a presbyterian, and Clifford was taken, because he was supposed to be an episcopalian in the narrowest sense, and his relations were papists.

Penruddock was yet speaking, when a messenger advanced in all haste, to summon him to wait on Sir Joseph Wagstaff. But for this accident, our conversation doubtless would not have terminated in this abrupt manner. Penruddock would probably have pointed out to me some gratification to be looked to, now that the secretaryship was gone, and would have given me some advice for the regulation of my conduct. But the summons was peremptory, and he hesitated not a moment to obey.

I no sooner found myself alone, than all the horrors returned upon me, which are to a certain degree almost always suspended, when man stands in the presence of his fellow-creature. I traversed the walk in which Penruddock had left me with a rapid pace; I beat myself with my clenched fist upon my forehead. It was no doubt early days, for me to break off all commerce with my kind, and to shut myself out from human life. But so I was constituted: such was the effect that this incident produced upon me. I felt that the door of manly existence had just been opened upon me, that I had been permitted for a moment to contemplate prospects that appeared to me delicious and rapturous (for what sensation exists more rapturous, than that which a young man experiences, when he feels for the first time, that he is counted for something substantive in the *dramatis personae* of society, that his voice is numbered, that his opinion is listened to, that some eyes are turned upon him to remark the part he shall act?)—and that then the door was suddenly and violently clapped in my face. I was left alone, in the narrow line between being and no-being; the impenetrable door of exclusion, framed of the most hardened and the thickest oak, clamped with iron, and thick studded with the largest nails, before me, and the precipice of annihilation behind me. I had not an inch of ground to stand on. I looked round; my head turned giddy; I fell.

"No," I said: "I have nothing to do with human life. Never again will I enter its circle. I will fly the face of man. I can lead the life of my uncle. I can shut myself up on the termination of a thousand heaths, and on the edge of the breakers of the ocean. I was ill fitted for the scene at best. Fool that I was, to be tempted within its verge! But let me grow wise at once! No doubt, there are men, that can struggle with disappointment, and rise again when they have been beaten to the earth. They are like the pliant reed; and, when once the tempest has spent its fury, they remember it no more. Not such am I! I cannot bend: I can break. Every wound of contumely pierces through all the defences of my soul; it corrodes and festers; the wounds are more durable and tremendous than those of arrows dipped in the gall of Lernaean Hydra; not Machaon and Podalirius, nor even Apollo himself, can ever cure them!"[1]

I know not whether I make myself understood; and it is no matter. There are, who will think the check I received was no great affair, that I had only to rally my spirits, and wait for a more favourable opportunity. Blessed are they in their insensibility:— not less blessed, than if all their limbs were palsied, and all their members were dead! But I envy them not. No; amidst the protracted sufferings and excruciating agonies I have endured, still I lay my hand upon my heart, and again I repeat it,—I envy them not.

I saw with an unerring judgment,—I saw, however minute was the sketch, and however faintly touched, in this one incident the whole history of my future life. I felt, with the spirit of prophecy, that all the various events that were to happen to me, would but be repetitions of this. I was confident, that Clifford and I were linked together for good or for evil (no, for evil only!), and that only death could dissolve the chain that bound us. I saw as plainly

---

1   All characters in Greek legend associated with healing and/or trauma. Apollo is, among other things, the god of healing. When Heracles killed the Hydra, he dipped his arrows in their blood, making their wounds incurable; but here it is the arrows themselves which are wounded, suggesting that conqueror and victim cannot be disentangled in the trauma of war. Machaon and Podalirius were sons of Asclepius (son of Apollo and a skilled surgeon, but born from the trauma of being wrenched from his mother's womb when she was being burned for infidelity). The two brothers were physicians to the Greeks in the Trojan War, and when Machaon was killed his brother was wild with grief.

the records of the BOOK OF PREDESTINATION on this subject, as the Almighty being in whose single custody the BOOK for ever remains.[1] There was no obscurity, no ambiguity, no room for an uncertain or a doubtful meaning. The letters glowed and glittered, as if they were written with the beams of the sun, upon the dark tablet of Time that Hath not yet Been.[2] It was my destiny for ever to shun, and for ever to meet him. I could no more avoid the one, than the other. I was eternally to engage in the flight, and eternally to meet the encounter.—Was not this a dreadful fate? Was this indeed the trifle, that required of me no more, than to shake it off, to rally my spirits, and to wait a more favourable opportunity?

I hastened into the house. My determination, as I have said, was taken. It was my fortune, that I no sooner entered the hall, than I perceived Clifford. Sir Joseph was by his side; and I saw had just been presenting him to the officers and gentlemen-volunteers of his battalion, in his new character of secretary to the commander-in-chief. I looked upon him: he was a head taller than when we last met, and was radiant with youthful beauty. I withdrew my eyes in confusion: all the demons of hatred took their seat in my bosom. I looked again: a spell had passed over him, and every feature appeared aggravated, distorted and horrible. "Oh, yes!" cried I to myself, "I see the sneer of infernal malice upon his countenance. How odious is the vice of hypocrisy! How much more honourable the honest defiance of unmitigable hate! Yes, Clifford, yes! let us shake hands in detestation, and pronounce a vow of eternal war. Tell me fairly at once, 'Wherever I meet you, I will hunt you; I will do you every mischief in my power; I will ride over you in triumph, and tread you down to the pit of hell!'"

Clifford came up to me. "My dear Charles," he said, "I should have been glad rather to meet you on any other occasion, I am

---

1 The book containing the full record of men's lives, to be opened on the day of judgment (Revelation 20:11–12).

2 Godwin may be recalling Isaiah 30:8 in Bishop Lowth's translation (1788): "Go now, write it before them on a tablet; / And record it in letters upon a book: / That it may be for future times; / For a testimony for ever." But Godwin gives the relation of present and future a uniquely recursive curvature that makes the future more unreadable than in predestination. Cf. P.B. Shelley whose *Defence of Poetry* (1821) describes poets "as the mirrors of the gigantic shadows which futurity casts upon the present" (*Shelley's Poetry and Prose*, ed. Donald H. Reiman and Neil Fraistat [New York: Norton, 2002], 535).

truly sorry for my appointment, since it is a source of mortification to you. Believe me, I would gladly withdraw from it, if my retirement would secure its being bestowed on you. I set no value on the treasures of ambition. My temper is careless and gay; and you, with a sensibility all trembling and alive, will find it hard to bear disappointment. But Sir Joseph, I plainly see, is resolute against your pretensions.[1] Bear with me then, my friend, and let us be friends still. This rivalship is as momentary, as it is accidental; and glad I shall be to march by your side, in still increasing harmony, through the journey of life. Charles, your hand!"

Was not this infernal malice? I know not. To me it appeared so. He triumphed over me every way. Oh, Clifford, wear your honours modestly! What needed all this strut and ostentation, this "pomp, pride, and circumstance"[2] of boastful success? This was the very root and kernel of the mischief of which I complained. I was to be eclipsed, after every fashion in which inferiority and contempt could be thrown upon me.

If it had been pure goodness of heart, that impelled Clifford to this apology and these professions, why did he not follow me out of the room, and utter them between him and me alone? But, no: it was too plain, that his purpose was to render me despicable, and in the elation of his heart pronounce over me an oration of intemperate and unmeasured victory!

I endeavoured to answer the lordly and disdainful speech that had been addressed to me. I thanked Clifford for his consideration and sympathy. I wished him joy of the success he had obtained.—The words died away on my tongue. I stammered and grew inarticulate. My voice faltered; my colour changed. I felt a film come before my eyes, that I could see no object distinctly. I was hardly able to support or to guide myself. I left the room in a confusion, that must have been too visible to every one that was in it.

"What a happiness it is to be alone!" I exclaimed, as soon as I found myself in the open air—"to have no eye, observing my looks, and measuring my gestures! to move as I please, and think what I please! to be in a world of my own, in the midst of a moral desert, and independent of my fellow men!"

I had no sooner muttered these words, an effort to relieve the misery under which I laboured, than I felt some one tap me on the shoulder. A man, that had just thrown away his dagger drop-

---

1 Claims.
2 Shakespeare, *Othello*, 3.3.54.

ping with the gore of a recent murder, would have felt exactly as I then felt. I shivered with preternatural horror. I looked round: it was Clifford! My face was turned full upon him; and he drew back three steps, at the sight of the passions that were working in it. His hand, which had been extended to grasp mine, fell nerveless, like a dead thing, to his side.

"Leave me," I said, with a voice, hollow, inarticulate, and inward. "I am miserable enough; leave me!"

Clifford made an effort to speak.

"If you address a single word to me, I shall live no longer! Consolation!" and I shook my head despairingly as I spoke, "ay, consolation is a glorious thing! Kindness! keep it, keep it to yourself! Hug it to your heart, and applaud yourself that you have so much humanity, and so much friendship! I will not hear you! I never will hear you more!"

Saying this, I burst from him impetuously, and fled with the rapidity of lightning, I found a stripling, a rustic, and sent him, to order my servant to attend me with my horses, a mile forward on the road. I returned immediately to Oxford.

Why did I get the better of Clifford, so to express it, in this interview? Because my breast was more fraught with an almighty energy of passion, than his. He came to me, spurred forward by all the purest sentiments that can inform a human heart. He pitied me; he loved me. Clifford was a being of no mean discernment; and he had had ample opportunity of observing my character at Winchester. He had generously resolved, that I should not perish by any mistake that it was in his power to set right. But the passion of Clifford, beautiful as it was, sunk into nothing, before the eddy and whirlwind of mine, I was worked up to the height. Ocean itself could have set no bounds to my fury. I had pent up my rage to the furthest minute in the quarters of Sir Joseph Wagstaff; and now I felt, that the presence of all the kings of the earth would have controled me no longer.

It was not long before I learned the unfortunate issue of the enterprise, in which I was to have borne a part. The surprise upon Salisbury was successfully conducted. The judges in their robes, and the sheriff, fell into the hands of the insurgents. The royalists were complete masters of the town. But all, after this, proceeded in the most unhappy train. A controversy immediately broke out between Sir Joseph Wagstaff and Colonel Penruddock, as to the disposal of their prisoners.

Sir Joseph and the mere military men insisted, that the judges and the sheriff should be hanged on the spot. This was the only way to secure the success of the enterprise. In the commencement of an insurrection, the insurgents are always irresolute. They ardently wish to obtain the object they have in pursuit: but for some time they are in doubt; they cast a wistful eye behind them; they can hardly persuade themselves that they have no retreat left. What was necessary therefore, was to pass the Rubicon.[1] By putting these men to military execution, the royalists would be convinced, that there was no room for negociation, and that they had offended the existing government beyond the hope of forgiveness.

The arguments of Sir Joseph were thrown away, upon the gentle temper and well-turned disposition of Penruddock. The country gentlemen sided with the colonel, and the general was outvoted in council. This was the root of the mischief; Sir Joseph lost all confidence in his own enterprise. The next step was more fatal. Salisbury had been appointed the place of general rendezvous; there was no body of military within a moderate distance; reinforcements of insurgents from the western and the southern counties might be expected daily; the occupation of the town was a measure of perfect safety. In this situation it was determined, for what reason I could never discover, to evacuate it. The royalists entered Salisbury at five in the morning; they quitted it at two. It was impossible to have devised a measure of more irreparable discouragement. They fell back on Blandford, and from Blandford on Southmolton, where Penruddock, and as many as kept with him, surrendered, as they supposed, on terms of quarter.[2] But the executive government decided otherwise. Penruddock and Grove were beheaded at Exeter; eleven were hanged there; five at Salisbury; and several at other places. Sir Joseph Wagstaff escaped to the continent. Thus ended the secretaryship of Lionel Clifford.

CHAPTER IV

At Oxford I had few acquaintances:[3] my habits were never of a sociable turn. But I had some. Human nature is so constituted,

---

1 To take an irrevocable action: by crossing the Rubicon, the river that formed the boundary between Republican Italy and Gaul, Julius Caesar decided to declare war on Pompey and the senate in 49 BCE.
2 Terms of clemency.
3 Cambridge was represented in Parliament by Cromwell, and according to S.R. Gardiner had been reformed by the Presbyterians (*continued*)

that, till the propensity is cured, as mine has been, man naturally seeks the society of his like. I found a young man of a cast of mind similar to my own. His thoughts were all gloomy; his countenance was perpetually sad. Some persons are said to love by contrast; the melancholy to associate with the merry, and the fantastic with the severe; and thus to find mutual comfort and relief. But we loved by sympathy. We spent whole evenings together in silence: but, if thus we did not amuse each other, at least we had a mutual understanding, and did not the one torment the other by ill-applied attentions and civilities. We found a social pleasure in looking in each other's faces, and silently whispering to our own hearts, Thank God, I have a companion, that hates the world as much as I do!

The name of my companion was Lisle, son of that Sir George Lisle, who, together with Sir Charles Lucas, was shot to death by the republicans in cold blood, after the surrender of Colchester in 1648.[1] Sir George Lisle is described by the historians, as the bravest and most amiable of all the champions of the royal cause in the civil wars. He left behind him a widow, and this one son. Lady Lisle devoted herself, as long as she lived, to the recollection of her husband. She shut herself up from all society, except that of one female friend, whose history was nearly similar to her own. There was but one tie that continued to attach her to this world; and that was, the living representative that her dead husband had left behind him. It was her daily purpose, to fill his bosom with her own sentiments, and those of his deceased father.

All this had a strange effect upon his youthful mind. His mother spoke to him every day of the parent he had lost, and never without tears. A thousand times, while a child, he had mingled his tears with hers, from the mere uncontrolable force of sympathy. Sometimes he did not weep, for his recollections of his father could not be altogether so vivid as his mother's were. And

---

and was more progressive (*History of the Commonwealth*, 4.22). But Oxford was firmly Royalist, having had Laud as Chancellor from 1630 until his execution in 1645. This may provide a context for Lisle's subsequent conduct to Mandeville.

1   Sir George Lisle (d. 1648) was a loyal supporter of the King, and his dragoons participated in the Battle of Edgehill during the First Civil War (1642–47), in which Clifford's father was killed. During the Second Civil War (1648–49) Lisle was one of the leaders of the Royalist uprising at Kent suppressed by General Fairfax, who had Lisle and Sir Charles Lucas (1613–48) executed.

yet the difference was less, than it was almost possible to suppose. He saw scarcely any one but his mother, and her narratives were so frequent, so minute, so faithful, so animated, and so pathetic, that the child might say with Hamlet, "Methinks, I see my father!" though, alas! it was with his "mind's eye" only that he saw him.[1] When he did not weep, still his voice was tremulous and almost seemed to weep, when he looked up in his mother's face, and uttered some brief and artless remark, the comment of her story. Another of his daily exercises was, that she led and set him before his father's portrait; while the sight of the limning[2] drew from her a particular strain of commendation, expressly awakened in her by the object they contemplated.

I have said that she endeavoured to fill his bosom with the sentiments of his deceased father. The royal cause therefore, in her painting, was the most illustrious of all causes; and her panegyric[3] of the great martyr was not exceeded, in devotional spirit, and utter prostration of soul to his attributes, by all the thirtieth of January sermons[4] that ever were preached. Her ideas of Cromwel were framed after the same fashion. He was the special pupil and ward of the prince of devils. There was no crime in which he was not thoroughly accomplished; there was no depravity that was not an inmate of his heart. His hypocrisy furnished her with a copious theme. Cromwel was a man so constructed that he had no delight but in wickedness. Lady Lisle seemed to have borrowed many of the colours she employed in his portrait, from Shakespear's Richard the Third. But, as he had no illustrious blood in his veins, and could occasionally accommodate him to the lowest vulgarity, so there was something in his hypocrisy, more round and finished, more like a serpent entangling his victim in his folds, more like the sea-monsters of Africa, the Lamiae,[5] that with a thousand inticements and flatteries lure

---

1 *Hamlet*, 1.2.184–85.
2 Drawing of the outlines of forms rather than objects.
3 Formal public speech containing high praise of some person or thing.
4 Charles I was beheaded on 30 January 1649. Thirtieth of January sermons commemorated his martyrdom.
5 Although Lamia in Keats's poem of that name is a beautiful woman with a serpent's body, a seductress but possessed of a certain pathos, she is also sometimes identified with the monstrous sea-goddess Keto, and made the mother of Scylla and Akheilos, who was transformed into a shark by the goddess Aphrodite.

their victims to their ruin,—in a word, more consummately loath-some and detestable,—than the deceitful condescension of a man, by his birth neighboured to a throne, could possibly be. Cromwel, according to this lady's description, was a man, "whose spirits toiled in frame of villanies." He had a natural appetite for blood, and was like those wretches we sometimes read of, who are said to be guided by a strong and unconquerable instinct to the commission of murders, and the destroying their fellow crea-tures by lingering torments, for the disinterested pleasure they reap in the contemplation of misery, and in the consciousness, of having themselves produced it.

Such were the amusements of young Lisle from almost his ear-liest infancy. It was part of his mother's idea of widowhood, that she never, from the catastrophe of Sir George, allowed herself to behold the light of the sun. Her apartment was always hung with black, and lighted with tapers. She permitted her son to resort every day to a neighbouring school; but he returned to his mother constantly in the evening. It is common enough, that a lad at a certain age should regard his school as a drudgery, and his home as a sort of luxury that succeeds and repays it. And yet one would hardly have expected that, in the particular case of young Lisle. But habit is the sovereign empress of the human mind. He looked with scorn and aversion upon the sport and merriment of his fellow-pupils, and returned with eagerness and impatience to the sable apartment of his parent. The talk that she loved, was his choicest delight; of the talk in which she indulged herself for ever, he felt that he could never have enough. There was a sort of grandeur in it, that was dear to his pride. There was a solemnity and a tragedy, that pampered his imagination. That to which he had been for ever accustomed, seemed to become as necessary to him as his daily bread. King Charles the First was his God, and his deceased parent the most splendid of heroes. They filled much the same place in his conceptions, as Charlemagne and Orlando are found to occupy in the tale of Roncesvalles;[1] with this advan-tage, that the Grand Rebellion and the siege of Colchester were, to the apprehension of young Lisle, the main realities of life. If at any time his mother seemed to ebb in the stream of her narratives, the boy would cry, Oh, now tell me something of my father! If she

---

1 Referring to the medieval French romance, the *Chanson de Roland*, about the defeat of the army of Charlemagne (c. 742–814) and the death of his most famous knight, Roland. Orlando is another name for Roland.

had no new stories, he would call for some favourite incident over again; and his questions, and thirst to know still more and more of the circumstances, could never be satiated.

Such was my present favourite and companion in the university of Oxford. Sometimes we would sit silent together for hours, like what I have heard of a Quakers' meeting;[1] and then, suddenly seized with that passion for change which is never utterly extinguished in the human mind, would cry out as by mutual impulse, Come, now let us curse a little! In the art of cursing we were certainly no ordinary proficients; and if an indifferent person could have heard us, he would probably have been considerably struck, with the solemnity, the fervour, the eloquence, the richness of style and imagination, with which we discharged the function. The fulminations of Lisle were directed against Cromwel, his assistants and abettors, against Bradshaw and the regicides,[2] and against the whole body of the Republican and king-killing party. The favourite object of my comminations[3] were the pope, and the cardinals, and the jesuits, and all those, who, from the twelfth century downwards, had devoted the reformers, and the preachers of the pure religion of Christ, to massacre and the flames. My companion recited, with all the sacred emotions of revenge, the massacre of Sir Charles Lucas and Sir George Lisle; while I, with equal agitation of feature and limb, commemorated the last fatal day of my father and my mother, and swore to avenge their catastrophe, upon every the humblest adherent of the Catholic religion that should ever fall within the sphere of my power. While we were thus engaged, we seemed to ourselves to be discharging an indispensible duty; and our eyes sparkled, and our hearts attained a higher degree of complacency, in proportion as we thus proceeded, to

1 The Quakers, or Society of Friends, founded c. 1648–60 by George Fox, were another Dissenting group, emphasizing a personal and direct experience of Christ without elaborate forms of worship. They saw themselves as bringing back the true Christian Church after centuries of apostasy. Despite strong patriarchal elements, they believed in the spiritual equality of women and later the abolition of slavery, and so are part of an allusive network that links Mandeville to potentially more radical social energies.

2 John Bradshaw (c. 1602–59), Lord President of the High Court of Justice in the trial that led to the execution of Charles I, and later Lord President of the Council of State for the English Commonwealth.

3 Acts of threatening revenge or punishment; in Anglicanism prayers that include a list of God's judgments against sinners. Mandeville is indiscriminate in his denunciations of both the Protestant and Catholic side.

"unpack our hearts with curses." Lisle however, I must with contrition confess, was much my superior on these occasions. Not in feeling; but he was blessed in a surprising degree with copiousness of speech, in which faculty I was deficient. So that we were something like Queen Margaret, and the mother of the two young princes, in the play of Richard the Third: when the first had poured forth her astonishing and heart-withering execrations, the other could only say,

Though far more cause, yet much less speech to curse,
Abides in me: I say Amen to her.[1]

In this respect however the comparison failed. If the torrent of his curses was louder and more foaming, mine certainly did not come behind them in bitterness.

But the conformity of disposition I have remarked between myself and my companion, by no means superseded the contrast of character, that grew out of the different methods of our education. Lisle had been nurtured and cherished with all the tenderness of a delicate mother. His misanthropy therefore had a strange mixture in it of the gallant and the *chevaleresque*. He loved and hated like a gentleman. Love was in his bosom the main spring and vital principle of his hatred. It was the intensity of his affection for King Charles, and for Sir George, and his mother, and the cause to which they had devoted themselves, that gave direction and strength to his dislikes. He hated therefore with generosity and defiance; and whatever sentiment revelled in his bosom, it alike swelled with warmth, and panted with the frankness of enterprise. His misanthropy, so to express myself, had an alloy of tenderness in it: and he felt like a lady; or like one the *preux chevaliers* of old, who learned their principles and the rule of their actions from the bright eyes of the fair.

My education had been extremely different from his. I may be said never to have known father or mother. There were certain muscles of my intellectual frame that had never been brought into play; there were arteries of my heart through which the blood never rushed. My character was withered: not chilled; but dried, and stiffened, and changed to a yellow, death-like hue, like the confected carcases of ancient Egypt.[2] It was scorched with

---

1 Shakespeare, *Richard III*, 1.1.197–98.
2 Referring to the Egyptian practice of mummifying dead bodies to preserve them.

too much heat; a heat that operated, not like the life-giving beams of the sun, but like the suffocating, pestilential sirocco[1] of the desert. I had never seen a female, with whom I had held frank and familiar intercourse, till the visit of Henrietta. My education I had derived from a formal, rigid, pedantic, pharisaical[2] priest. Other inmates of the roof under which I dwelt I had had none, except my unfortunate uncle, and his servants, who were more like *automata*, than human beings. I had conversed only with the hills and the clouds. I had lived in my reveries only; and those reveries were modelled by the very circumscribed course of my experience, and by the tragical events which filled the earliest section of the records of my memory. The consequence of all this was, that, of Lisle and myself, perhaps equally inspired with death-dealing sentiments, Lisle was under the guidance of an impulse, similar to that which urged on the ancient crusaders in their expeditions against the Saracens, while my disposition resembled rather that of the Old Man of the Mountain,[3] the redoubted adversary of these Christian adventurers, whose weapons were known by their deadly effects, while the hand that guided them was never seen.

As both Lisle and myself were copious and abundant in execration, so by indulgence we grew wanton in our imaginations and projects respecting it. One of these projects was of a misanthropical club, where the knot that bound the members together, and the feature that they held in common, should be a disappointed and embittered spirit.[4] But this plan was never carried in execution. A mere vulgar misanthropy was not sufficient to satisfy either of us. We demanded also a refinement of taste, and elegance of sentiment, in whoever should be made our comrade; we never could entirely convince ourselves of the eligibility of any stranger; and we never added a third member to our society.

Now, that I look back on this through a vista of years, and see it with all the lights that my own tragical history has thrown upon it, I could alternately weep over the folly, and rave against the presumption implied in the conduct in which we thus indulged ourselves. What were we, that we should turn an eye of supercilious

---

1 A hot wind.
2 Hypocritically self-righteous.
3 The Sheikh-al-Jabal or supreme ruler of the Assassins, a Shiite sect (fl. eleventh to thirteenth centuries), known for secret assassinations of its enemies. They are the subject of a short story by Percy Shelley (1814).
4 Likely a reference to the Sealed Knot; see p. 204, note 1.

abhorrence and implacable animosity upon mankind, or any large body and diversified multitude of mankind? What constituted the fancied eminence from which we looked down upon our own species? Were our virtues so resplendent, or our merits so superior, as to give us these rights? What but the accident of birth or education had made us to differ from those we loathed and despised? And had not that accident given us rather a motiveless contempt and abhorrence for others, than any real advantage over them? Oh, that man should be so constituted, as to harbour these malignant passions against his brethren, instead of compassionating, and patiently suffering, and endeavouring to rectify them, as the laws of all true ethics would require him to do! But, alas, this moralizing, in my case, comes too late!

It would seem, from what I have here stated, that I opened my heart, and unloaded the secret sorrows of my bosom, to my youthful companion. Alas, I did no such thing! This was a relief, from which the very vital principles of my character for ever debarred me. I frowned, my nostrils would dilate, and my eyes would seem to start from their sockets; you might discover in me all the indications of a genuine rage, I clenched my fists, and strode up and down the room in which we sat, with the frenzy of impatience. But I never mentioned Clifford. His name was to me like the incommunicable name of Jehovah to the Jews, which they never pronounced, but substituted in its room that of Adonai, the Lord. The expressions of my hatred confined themselves to generals; it seemed as if there was an impassable gulph, that prevented me from descending to particulars. I could speak of my father and mother: but that not without the greatest difficulty, and with a feeling as if I was somehow violating a secret, which it was the most flagitious[1] of crimes to violate. I spoke of them with a voice, low, tremulous, hollow, and death-like. I cast my eyes round as if to guard against surprise, and approached close to the ear of my hearer. Every word seemed to shake my frame; and I spoke, hardly resolved to go on, and hardly conscious of what I did. But the sorrow that related to my father and mother was somewhat softened by time; it seemed like the narrative of a former age; the transactions were so long passed as to have become the legitimate topics of history:—they could find their way to the tongue. Oh, if I could have pronounced the name of Clifford, if I could have told the griefs that had flowed to me from him, if I could have given vent to the various emotions he had

---

1 Villainous.

excited within me, I should have become a different man; I should been lightened of

A weight of woes, more than ten worlds could bear;

I should have leaped, and bounded, and given loose to my limbs, "like man new made"; I should have felt like Prometheus,[1] upon the supposition that the adamantine chains that Vulcan forged for him, could have been dashed to the earth, and the vulture that fed for ever on his liver, could have been chased away, and banished from his sight.

CHAPTER V

Such was the character of my acquaintance with young Lisle: but, during the period I have been attempting to describe, my mind did not fail to be greatly disturbed with the recollection of the scenes through which I had lately passed. To a careless observer they may appear to have contained nothing very extraordinary; but it was not so to me. The events that had occurred to me in Wiltshire, constituted what I may call my first entrance into the scene of the real world. When they were over, they were not to me as things that were passed. Waking and sleeping, by day and by night, I actually saw them—the courtesy and noble nature of Penruddock; the extent of my disappointment; the conduct and language of Clifford, whether intended to soothe or exasperate I could not determine. In my ordinary frame of mind, I decidedly imputed to him the latter intention; though I could not always prevent the intrusion of a fairer and more candid interpretation.

For some time the course of succeeding events operated to give renovated strength to the agony of my spirit. Rumours and intelligence of things that occurred, did not fail to reach Oxford; nor did I fail to be for ever anxious to be more fully informed. When I first heard of the promising and impressive commencement of the enterprise, my emotion was great: I said to myself, "This is the most splendid and magnificent adventure the island of Great

---

1 Greek god who stole fire from the gods and gave it to man; in punishment, Zeus had him chained to a rock where a vulture ate away at his liver. A favourite of the Romantics, he was the subject of Byron's poem "Prometheus" (1816) and Percy Shelley's play *Prometheus Unbound* (1820).

Britain ever saw; and, but for Clifford, I should have had my share of its glories, and the first stage of my inscription in the roll of man, would have been illustrious." When on the other hand I heard of the reverses that followed, my compunction was unbounded. "Was this a time," I said, "when I should have withdrawn myself, or have suffered any personal consideration to have prevented me from taking my share, of the disasters and dangers naturally attendant on such an undertaking?" It may therefore easily be supposed with what feelings I listened to the conclusion of the story, and the undaunted and heroic behaviour of Penruddock and his associates, in the public, final scene of their human existence. I procured copies of their trials and their dying speeches. They furnished me with a theme of endless rumination. Had these men been guilty of a crime? I laid my hand upon my heart, and from my soul pronounced, They had not. Had their conduct that characteristic, the *malus animus*, the malignant intention, which the law pretends to require, before it pronounces any man a criminal? Their intentions had been of that purity and virtue, that is rather the indication of an angelic nature, than of so mixed and imperfect a creature as man. A man must be some time a member of human society, and accustomed to the regulations of administrative justice, before he can be thoroughly reconciled to the idea, of bringing his fellow mortal to a violent death on a public scaffold, in the midst of full peace, for his virtues only.

But I was speedily roused from the train of my solitary reflections on this subject, by an incident which I have next to relate. One day, as I passed, after my usual manner, careless and unobserving, along the High Street, my eye accidentally caught the figure of Mallison. This somewhat disturbed me. Though he had been deeply concerned in all that had been most distressing to me, previously to my arrival at Oxford, I did not do him the honour to hate him, as I hated Clifford. He appeared to me a being "out of my sphere"; and however we might revolve in the varied orbit and circle of our lives, we could never, in my estimation, clash and jostle with each other in our progress. But, though the sight of Mallison did not violently disturb me, every thing would have given me for the moment an uneasy sensation, had it been a chair or a table merely, that should have served to remind of the scenes in which he had been concerned. Stung by the circumstance, I could not refrain from directing some enquiry to be made, as to the phenomenon of his appearance. I found that he had come on a visit to a relation of his in the town, and after a stay of three days only, had again quitted the city.

Insignificant as this incident may appear, such was the perverseness of my fate, it was pregnant with the most memorable effects to me. My intercourse, as may well be supposed, with my fellow Oxonians was very little. From nature I had hardly the disposition to court them, to display affability or courtesy in relation to them. And such is the constitution of man, that when this has been sufficiently ascertained, our fellows are sufficiently inclined to repay us in our own coin, and to apply to us the same airs of superciliousness and neglect, which they have experienced at our hands. This had grown up into a sort of implied compact between my contemporaries and myself. Yet little as our intercourse was, I could not now help observing a striking alteration in their demeanour towards me. Agreeably to the variety of their turns of mind, they would either cross to the other side of the way, or almost elbow and jostle me as they passed, with manifest tokens of incivility. One would scowl at me with a significant sneer; and others would seem to whisper words of contempt, with a haughty carelessness whether or not they reached my ear, or awakened my resentment. I was upon the point of resolving to bring this insufferable mystery to an end, by singling out one of the most offensive of these impertinents, and demanding of him an explanation; when the evil was brought home to me in a more direct form.

I had not seen Lisle for three days, when I chanced, in an obscure and remote street (such streets were often my favourite resort), to perceive him advancing towards me in the opposite direction. At the same moment that I saw him, he appeared to catch my figure, and suddenly turned back, retraced his steps for a short distance, and then struck down a narrow alley, and was immediately out of my sight. This, at another time, would have made no impression upon me. He, as well as myself, was of a wayward disposition, gloomy and fantastical, often inclined to solitude, and averse to the society of his nearest associate. Neither of us, on such occasions, were very punctilious in our mode of avoiding the thing that thwarted us. But I could not help combining this incident in my mind, with what had already occurred to me from other quarters: and I instantly determined, if the action of Lisle sprung from the same source, to obtain the explanation from him, which I had been on the point of seeking elsewhere. My nature was too gloomy and concentrated, to allow me to delight, as some unhappy beings have done, in noisy altercation and defiance. I infinitely preferred seeking the information I needed, from the lips of my friend.

A young man is new to every thing; and every thing out of the ordinary routine makes a deep impression upon him. As I walked towards the apartments of Lisle, I said, "I am going to learn something from him. It can be no small thing, that seems to prompt every man to shun me, and, if I conjecture rightly, is about to sever me from my nearest ally. I care but little for society; the ordinary intercourse of the world, has slender charms for me; but I have ambition; and ambition is a passion, that cannot have its proper scope in a world of my own imagination. I care but little for the world; but I shall be ill satisfied with the reverse of this proposition, that the world should not care for me. I will not endure its censure; I will not endure its contempt; I am formed to feel any slur that is cast upon me, not like a wound, but like fifty mortal swords, each of them striking at something infinitely beyond my life."

I mounted the stairs that led to my friend's apartment, with a solemnity of feeling I had scarcely ever experienced. Every muscle of my frame seemed to move, and to be prepared to start into a new and several existence. I know not whether I make myself understood. I was one man, all my powers collected and centered in one thought: and yet I seemed to feel within me a quantity of life, enough for a thousand men.

I knocked at his door: no one answered. I paused for a minute, and knocked again, I listened: I heard him pacing up and down in his chamber. I knocked a third time. The door flew open before me with passionate violence. My friend stood a few steps within the door.

"What do you come here for?" he said. "You saw I was desirous to avoid you."

"Lisle," I replied, "if you entertain a different opinion of me from your former one, you are bound, as a soldier and a gentleman, to account to me for that difference."

"You were, not long ago, absent for several weeks from the university. You told me that you spent that time at Sir Anthony Ashley Cooper's. Why did you impose upon me?"

While these few questions and rejoinders were passing, I advanced further into the apartment, and shut the door as I advanced.

"You question me somewhat rudely," I answered. "The reason of my silence was, that the adventure I had passed through was a painful one; and I know of no right that any one has to demand the history of another's sorrows, unless so far as he chooses to disclose it."

"Your adventure was a painful one! Call it by a fitter name, and say, It was disgraceful. I do not complain of your silence; I complain that you deceived me. But I am in the wrong to mention that. Your adventure, as you call it, has fastened upon you irretrievable infamy; and why should any man be called on to be the historian of his own dishonour?"

"Your language is too harsh, Sir. It is true, I have suffered much: my lot has been to encounter injustice, bitter, barbarous, inexpiable. But then Sir" and I struck my hand upon my bosom as I spoke, "I have no fault of which to accuse myself."

"Humph! Yes, I have been told that every man has a way of colouring his own actions, so as to make them to himself as bright as the sun, and as beautiful as the rainbow.

"But you say, I am bound to account to you for my present opinion. I will therefore ask a few questions. Did you not go, and offer to enlist yourself in the troop of the illustrious unfortunate, Colonel Penruddock? Were you not received for a time, and afterwards, upon further information, were you not dismissed from the troop?"

"No, Sir, I was never dismissed. I withdrew myself."

"Oh, you were only a deserter! And you hope to found the vindication of your character, upon an allegation, that you, coward-like, withdrew from this generous, immortal band, a short time before they fell victims, in the purest of all causes, to the foul tyranny of Cromwel? An admirable account you give of yourself! that you enlisted yourself under the royal banner, and, a few days after (before the shock and conflict came), repented of your loyalty! that, like that noble animal, the rat, you had an instinct, that apprised you beforehand, of a falling cause! Sir, in the troop of the heroic Penruddock there were no deserters: they were all patriots: they resolved, to a man, to succeed in the enterprise they had undertaken, or to sink with a sinking state.

"But I am a little better informed respecting your engagement with Penruddock, than you are apt to imagine. They found you out to be a spy of the protector, they discovered, that your motive for becoming so zealous a loyalist, was, that you might be the better enabled to give information to your employers, of all the motions of the insurgents. You wished, forsooth, to be secretary to the commander-in-chief; and you brought a letter from that well-known character. Sir Anthony, recommending you for the employment. But, fortunately, the gallant Clifford came just in the nick of time, and disclosed the reputation you had acquired at Winchester College. He told the story of the pictures, Sir,—the pictures!

"The step you have taken, Mandeville, can never be recovered. The ambiguous adventure in which you have been involved, admits of no honourable explanation. Choose which side you will, between the alternative of treachery and cowardice. You were either a spy, always a king-killer in your heart, and prepared at the pupil age of seventeen, to play the part of a fox, eluding the most wary observation, and of a serpent, piercing with mortal sting the bosom that cherished you: and that is the interpretation in which I firmly believe. Or, you skulked away in the hour of danger, and hid your inglorious head from the chance of military warfare, and from the honourable sentence, which the usurper's courts of justice award against the honest, and which every man who draws his sword in the cause of virtue should be prepared to meet with dauntless serenity. On the day that Penruddock entered Salisbury, you returned to the university. On the day that his head rolled on the scaffold, you, totally careless of these things, were employed in practising your deceits on me, and endeavouring to make me believe you every thing the reverse of your real character."

I listened with astonishment to the invective of Lisle. I had made things, I thought, bad enough for myself in my secret ruminations. I had even a confused, unaccredited suspicion that I was guilty of exaggeration. I doubted that that was the leaning of my temper. How greatly was I deceived! My gall rose as he spoke; my mouth was filled with its bitterness, loathed the sight of the insolent youngster that dared thus to address me; I loathed the light of the sun; principally, I loathed myself, and the perception that I existed under all this. I would not have consented to live another hour, but that my death would have given advantage to my calumniators.

Most of all, I thought scorn of the idea of vindicating myself, of making appeal, as to the scales of a balance, casting the foul aspersions to which I had listened into one scale, and my own explanations and protestations into the other, and carefully watching which way the beam would turn. This, of all things, was the most contrary to my temper. Fierce impatience was the ruling passion of my soul. He that did not understand me from the impulse of his own mind, that did not find in his own heart the explanation of my conduct, and the true estimate of my thoughts, was unworthy to hear me. Slowly to win one's way by special pleading into the good opinion of those who regarded one with aversion, was, I deemed, the basest of all degradations.

I gazed upon Lisle with eyes that sparkled with fury. "It is well, Sir," I said. "I am glad of it. Misanthropy at least, the God that I worship, is the gainer. You hate me, because I am calumniated; and I hate you, because you are unjust. The hatred that existed this morning, has spread its empire wider, and has gained two additional subjects to exercise itself upon." Saying these words, I burst away from Lisle, and saw him no more.

Since that time, I have often thought what would have been the conduct of an ordinary young man at college, under my situation. Lisle had called me treacherous, and had called me a coward: he had given me my choice between these two characters. The vulgar expedient in this conjuncture would have been, to have dared him to the field, and to have vindicated my honour with my sword. I call God to witness, that it was no lurking sentiment of fear, that restrained me from this proceeding. But, Good Heavens! how cold and inadequate a remedy did this appear in my eyes. The little appointments and arrangements of a duel, the measuring of weapons, and the display of skill, with all the technical science of a master of fence, might have suited a colder character, but were altogether discordant and intolerable to a temper like mine. Then, what should I have gained by defiance and a duel? Would that have cleared up my loyalty and integrity, or have dissipated the foul aspersions, that had by some means been so successfully propagated against me? If I could have thought of a duel, or of my sword buried to the hilts in the life's blood of an antagonist, as a consolation, how enviable and how happy, would my condition have been! But I was incapable of being the dupe of so wretched a fallacy.

I stop myself for a moment in my narrative, to say, that Clifford was entirely innocent of having contributed in the slightest degree to the glosses on my conduct, which had reached the ears of Lisle. They were the sole production of the fruitful ingenuity of Mallison. But such was my fate, and thus I was hedged in on every side. I had a Clifford to cross all the prospects and views of my existence, a Mallison to ground on my disappointments the grossest calumnies, and a Lisle to give energy, and sharpness, and a venomed point, to all that Mallison had forged. It was still therefore against Clifford that my hatred was directed. He was the source, the primal cause of all: and without him, such at least was my interpretation of the scene, neither Mallison nor Lisle would have had the power to disturb my serenity.

As I receded from the apartment of Lisle, I felt more and more distinctly that Oxford was no longer a place for me. The calumnies, which Lisle in such pitiless array had spread out before me, were universally propagated: I had seen that in the countenances of multitudes: Lisle had been the last straggler of the long file of demons prepared for my damnation.

But, if not Oxford, then was not England, then was not the world, a place for me. I was not the insignificant person, that could go into some new and obscure corner, and be no longer connected with the thing I had been. I was heir to estates of immense value. It is the nature of all civilized communities, that the aristocracy of the country, the few who are greatly elevated by rank or station, form a tribe by themselves, as distinct from the rest of their compatriots, as the tribe of Levi among the descendants of the rest of the twelve patriarchs.[1] The cities of London or Paris, for example, contain, according to one mode of calculation, half a million of inhabitants respectively;[2] but in another view, and in relation to the aristocracy of these capitals, they contain but a few hundreds each. London and Paris therefore, to the rich and the noble, are but two narrow villages; and the pest so often complained of in a village, the industrious propagation of scandal, and the malicious watchfulness of one neighbour over another, are equally to be found there. A man may hide himself in them; but a lord cannot. Strange condition of this gaudy and envied race of men! A lord, while he lives, is a great thing, with all the advantages, and all the miseries, attendant upon greatness. Death only abates the nuisance. This Omnipotent Phantom almost singly obtains the power, to turn a lord into nothing. What a remorseless tyrant, what a mighty leveller of all these extrinsic distinctions, is Death! How true is that solemn *dictum* of theology, "Naked I came from my mother's womb, and naked shall I return to the dust!"[3] To instance in my own contemporaries only. Dryden dedicates his plays in a style of servile adulation to Lord Vaughan, and Lord Haughton, and Sir William Leveson Gower; Otway to Lord Viscount Eland, while he revelled in the frosty sunshine of the favour of Lord Plymouth; and Butler was happy in the countenance of Mr Longueville.[4] And now, what place is

---

1 One of the groups constituted by the division of the Jewish nation among the twelve sons of Jacob, the Tribe of Levi was designated for a special role in the divine service. It is interesting that Mandeville allies himself here with the Jews, who were being shown greater toleration by Cromwell, but were not able to practise their religion in England.

2 Godwin's numbers are correct, though by his own time London's population had tripled.

3 Job 1:21.

4 John Dryden (1631–1700), Thomas Otway (1652–85), and Samuel Butler (1612–80) were all Restoration writers. Godwin voices his

occupied by these luxurious and pampered lords, and what place by the retiring and obsequious Dryden, Otway, and Butler? Truly, oh, Death, thou hast the attributes of a God, pulling down the mighty, and setting up the humble; and the pillars of the earth are in thy hands!

To return. Could I submit to live an exile in a foreign clime, like a man charged with some enormous crime, the name of which nature revolts at? If I could, surely the reputation of my crime would pursue me. In this respect, the whole world is but a large village: and no foreigner can come and live in opulence and splendour in a country not his own, but that the enquiry will be bandied about, "Why has he abandoned his native soil?" But what had I done to deserve this? My action with regard to Waller, was virtuous, at least it was generous: and, as to the affair with Penruddock, was I not driven away, by a loathsome necessity imposed upon me, from a place, where I felt it utterly impossible to remain an instant longer? Could I then sink, palsied and unresisting, under this oppression? Ambition, as I have said, was the vital spirit, that fed my life, and preserved my corporeal frame from putrefying. I looked forward to something great, and something good. I felt within me powers answerable to this destination. I could not therefore, if I might, retire into a corner. I would not bind myself, so my heart whispered to my head, to a vegetating, inglorious life. Better, a thousand times better were it, not to be at all. What; that I should walk about, a tarnished thing, a petty rascal that had had the word VILLAIN branded upon his forehead in the dock of a court of justice, or like Cain, with a mark set upon me,[1] "lest any one finding me kill me," and that I might live out my appointed years of expiation!

---

contempt for this period in "Of History and Romance," where he describes it as a period of "negotiations and tricks" (Appendix B, p. 465). That Mandeville refers to these writers as his contemporaries means that he would have to be at least 52 at the time of writing, since Dryden's *Amphitryon* was dedicated to Leveson Gower in 1690. Despite being an adherent of the House of Stuart, Mandeville appears to share Godwin's contempt for their servile Royalism, which Godwin reiterates in *Thoughts on Man* (85–86).

1   The first murderer in the Bible, Cain is a frequent hero in Romantic texts such as Byron's *Cain* (1821). Mandeville paraphrases Genesis 4:15, when God sets a mark on Cain. The reference also anticipates Mandeville's "branding" at the end of the novel.

Such was the wretchedness and misery of my condition; and what was the cause of this? It all lay, I repeated a thousand times to myself, in one man. Fate, I was fully persuaded, had bound Clifford and me together, with a chain, the links of which could never be dissolved. "Marriages," it is said, "are made in heaven." The power that moulds us all according to his pleasure, divided the human species into male and female, and decreed that it was not good for man to remain without his mate. In his Providence he has fitted to every variety of the masculine character a female adapted to afford him satisfaction and felicity; and happy the man, to whose encounter fortune shall present the fair, that by the eternal decree was designated to become his partner. In the same manner as, in the world of human creatures, there exist certain mysterious sympathies and analogies, drawing and attracting each to each, and fitting them to be respectively sources of mutual happiness, so, I was firmly persuaded, there are antipathies, and properties interchangeably irreconcilable and destructive to each other, that fit one human being to be the source of another's misery. Beyond doubt I had found this true opposition and inter-destructiveness in Clifford. Mezentius, the famous tyrant of antiquity, tied a living body to a dead one, and caused the one to take in, and gradually to become a partner of, the putrescence of the other.[1] I have read of twin children, whose bodies were so united in their birth, that they could never after be separated, while one carried with him, wherever he went, an intolerable load, and of whom, when one died, it involved the necessary destruction of the other.[2] Something similar to this, was the connection that an eternal decree had made between Clifford and me. I was deeply convinced, that his bare existence was essentially the bane of mine. Had he not extinguished me, from the first hour that we saw each other? Had not his wit, his gaiety, his perennial flow of amusement to others, and the angelic

---

1 Mezentius was an Etruscan tyrant known for his cruelty, particularly his practice of binding live men to corpses, face to face, so that they died a lingering death. See Introduction (p. 36) for Godwin's use of this striking image in connection with Ireland.

2 The image of conjoined twins, the related inverse of the previous reference to Mezentius, is used in *Caleb Williams*: "The pride of philosophy has taught us to treat man as an individual. He is no such thing. He holds necessarily, indispensably, to his species. He is like those twin-births, that have two heads indeed, and four hands; but, if you attempt to detach them from each other, they are inevitably subjected to miserable and lingering destruction" (408).

sweetness and urbanity of his temper, drawn all his fellows after him, as with a medicine, and left me to loneliness and contempt? Had not his poverty, and the charming way in which he declaimed respecting it, made my expected wealth, the unalterable gravity of my manners, and my sparingness of speech, the topics of endless derision? Because he was bred an adherent to the English government in church and state, was not I despised as a poor-spirited wretch and a presbyterian? Then, in the affair of the pictures, to which Lisle had just alluded, had not he come off with additional and redoubled honours, while I sustained a blemish that could never be removed? Oh, the weary and loathsome days and months and years that I had passed, for his sake, within the cloisters of William of Wykeham! If it had ended here, I knew too well that the tortures then endured, had left a gaping and agonizing wound, had broken and disabled the members of my soul, in such a manner as no time could ever assuage or make whole. When however I quitted those hated walls, hated only because he had been an inmate there, I indulged a vain hope, that I had performed my penance, and that Clifford would approach me no more. How fond and senseless a dream! He had approached me; he had approached me as a rival, as a successful and resistless rival; he had driven me from the field I sought, driven me with ignominy, with the bifronted imputation of cowardice and treachery; he had revived against me all the miseries of my youth; he had made me the outcast of mankind.

CHAPTER VI

I quitted the apartment of Lisle, and hastened to shut myself up in my own chamber. "At seventeen years," says Old Adam in the play, "many their fortunes seek."[1] I was arrived at seventeen years; but my fortune was ended and done. I had no place in the world of mankind. I took to myself no accusation of vice or crime; but a sentence of prescription had gone out against me, and could never be revoked. As I rolled these considerations desperately in my mind, I felt myself successively a theatre for sensations before unknown. Lightnings flashed from my eyes. My head throbbed; my senses became giddy; all was confusion and uproar within me. Involuntarily I uttered loud cries and piercing shrieks. Again, I looked up, and saw the objects around me.

---

1   *As You Like It*, 2.3.73.

Books, placed regularly on shelves, or thrown carelessly, after having been consulted, on the floor, a desk, papers, and the implement of study, with maps orderly arranged against the walls: What have I to do with these? I said. This is no place for me! Instantly I rushed from my chamber; I passed along with winged rapidity; I sallied out at the eastern avenue of the city, and presently plunged myself in the wildest and most savage recesses of the forest of Shotover.[1] I felt ease, in proportion as I withdrew from the haunts of men. "Ah," said I, "here I have room to be miserable! Man, that accursed thing, no longer hedges and represses me with the tyranny of his eye; and I am surrounded with Nature's productions only, not with doors, and locks, and walls, and streets, the artifices of human ingenuity."

I remember no more. The first sane and lucid sensation that followed, was that I saw myself in bed, and my sister seated by my bed-side. That sight had over me a magic empire. I was languid, and scarcely capable of exertion. I looked at her for some time in silence, and thought, "Surely I am not altogether a wretch; is it possible—is it possible, that this lovely creature should be watching my health, and pouring out the aspirations of her soul for my safety? It is," exclaimed I;—"it is my Henrietta!"

"My brother!" returned she. "Ah, you know me now!" I put out my hand, and took hold of hers. "While I have life, I can never cease to know you!"

"And yet," said Henrietta, "I have sat for weeks by your bed-side without your seeming to know me!"

I had wandered into the forest of Shotover in a state of mind the most pitiable. All the events which preceded, had prepared me for distraction; and distraction presently followed. I roamed about in this desolate scene, till I was completely fatigued. I plunged into thickets, and climbed to the summits of rocks. In this occupation I had been observed by two or three wood-cutters; but I had drawn from them a very uncertain attention. They were accustomed in some degree to the frolics and vagaries of the younger students; and, though they wondered, and perhaps thought that I exceeded the usual limits of eccentricity and daring in persons of my class, they did not conceive themselves called on to interfere.

The next morning I was found by one of these woodmen, stretched at my length at the bottom of a pit, extenuated, vacant, scarcely able to help myself, yet with a grim expression of restless

---

1 A hill and forest near Oxford.

ferocity in my countenance. The uniform of a student, upon a person in this situation, carried more fully to the rustic's mind, that I must not be so left, and that I stood in need of help. He was however frightened at the strangeness of the phenomenon, and went back to call another labourer to his aid. I no sooner saw them, and was aware of their purpose, than, weak as I was, I suddenly started from the ground, and endeavoured to rush by them, and escape. They seized, and detained me. I instantly became furious, struggled with them, and once more obtained my liberty. "Man shall never have power over me!" I exclaimed. There were other labourers however a little further onward; and I was overpowered.

It happened, that at Cowley, at no great distance from this spot, there was a receptacle for lunatics;[1] and thither they conveyed me. The master, seeing my condition, willingly admitted me, till intelligence and enquiries could be dispatched to Oxford. In this matter there was little difficulty, as a pocket-book was found about my person, containing my own name, and that of the college to which I belonged. One of the tutors immediately came to visit me; and having made his report to the principal, a deliberation was held as to the proper mode of proceeding. A messenger was dispatched to my uncle; and, as it was known that my sister was one of my most frequent correspondents, another message was forwarded at the same time to the New Forest. By directions from home it was ordered, that for the present I should be continued an inmate of the house to which chance had conveyed me.

I have said, that I remember no more, and that the first sane and lucid sensation that followed, was when I saw my sister seated by my bed-side. It is true. I seemed to myself at that moment, like a person waking out of a long and sound sleep, or rather suddenly recovered from a state in which he had lain apoplectic and senseless for days and weeks. Afterwards however, I recovered by degrees the recollection of many things that had passed, in this interval that had at first appeared a blank. A thou-

---

1 While asylums for the insane were a late eighteenth-century phenomenon, private madhouses did exist in the seventeenth century. They became subject to licensing only in 1774, and were custodial rather than curative institutions, unlike the more humane institutions that were being introduced in Godwin's own time. We should not identify Mandeville's confinement with the latter, even though the benign Henrietta and Mrs. Willis are kept apprised of it.

sand hideous visions had perpetually beleaguered me. All that had ever occurred to me of tragic in the whole course of my existence, had beset me. Ireland, and its scenes of atrocious massacre, that one might have expected to be obliterated from the tablet of my memory, presented themselves in original freshness. My father and my mother died over again. The shrieks, that had rent the roofs of Kinnard fourteen years before, yelled in my ears, and deafened my sense; and I answered them with corresponding and responsive shrieks. I forgot the lapse of time that had passed between; I did not advert to the circumstance, that I had then been a child; and I put forth my virile strength, and uttered my firmer expostulations and threats, to save the lives of him who begot, and her who bore me. The scenes of unspeakable distress that I had witnessed in my journey from the north of Ireland to Dublin, all assailed me, in their turn. The cries and struggles even of the poor Judith, from whose arms Hilkiah had so unjustifiably torn me, were once more heard and seen by me, in their original Hibernian[1] energy. Then came Penruddock and Grove, and the many victims that had fallen by the sword of the law in the conclusion of the late enterprise, at Exeter, at Salisbury, and elsewhere. I saw their heads roll on the scaffold; I saw the blood spouting from the dismembered trunk; I saw the executioner, as he advanced, with his hangman's and gore-stained hands, to the edge of the scaffold, holding by the hair the head of the illustrious victim, and crying, "This is the head of a traitor!" These visions ate into my inmost soul, and exhausted my strength in misguided and empty exertions.

All this came mixed to my recollection, with the violence, the cords, the harsh language, the blows, it had been judged necessary to employ, for my restraint, or my cure.[2] I had been turned into a coward, the veriest slave that lives, trembling at a look. At first the blows inflicted on me, only awakened in me additional ferocity. I met them with indignation and rage; I strung and stiffened my sinews, in a degree that no man in his senses can form a conception of; for a man in his senses calculates, and anticipates results in his violence; but mine was pure, simple, undefecated[3] rage, that did not dream of controling itself, that scorned all consequences, and filled my whole frame with the venom and the

---

1   Ancient Irish, Celtic.
2   The phrasing recalls Mandeville's traumatic memories of Ireland in Volume 1, pp. 109–10.
3   Unrefined, unpurged.

malice of myriads of blaspheming demons. My teeth were ground almost to pieces; my head shook, and my mouth scattered foam, like that of a war-horse in the midst of the din of arms. Perhaps I am in the wrong, "to unfold the secrets of my prison-house."[1] Perhaps I suffered no more, than is commonly incident to that sort of madness, which expresses itself in fury. Enough: to this condition of man I was reduced by Clifford.

Yet may I not say, All this I suffered for want of a friend? "A faithful friend is the medicine of life." There was a critical moment—If a true friend had taken me by the arm, as I came from the apartment of Lisle, and had poured the balm of wisdom into my wounds, it had yet perhaps been in time. No man needs a friend, so much as he who is under the slavery of a domineering passion. A friend is like Time, the master of us all, or like boundless Space. He removes us to a due distance from the object, which we see falsely and distorted only because we are too near to it. He makes us view it in the light, in which the generation yet unborn shall view it. The mere communication and common discussion with a sober and healthful mind, of what sovereign power are they! Silence and sequestered thought have a magic charm, sometimes for good, often for harm. The dreams of the poet, while yet they lie "in sacred secundine asleep,"[2] ere yet the power of the master has

> Turned them to shapes, and given to airy nothing
> A local habitation, and a name,[3]

perhaps cannot be communicated without the danger to perish. There are certain holy and mind-exalting conceptions of the solitary wanderer, that will not bear the touch of a second individual. But all that is disease in the soul, is, by this gentle exposure put in a train of cure. I can hardly describe to my friend the thing that torments me, in the wild and exaggerated way in which I view it with closed doors. What I deliver to him, is a compounded notion, made up partly of the impression I have myself entertained, and partly of the temper of his mind, and of

---

1   *Hamlet*, 1.5.14, where the ghost of Hamlet's father says that he cannot divulge his punishments in the afterlife.

2   Abraham Cowley, "The Muse." Secundine: in botany, the outer seed coat; in medicine, the placenta, umbilical cord, and membranes of afterbirth.

3   Shakespeare, *A Midsummer Night's Dream*, 5.1.16–17.

my anticipation of the way in which he will regard the facts I have to relate.

Yet how exceedingly rare is this phenomenon, a friend! The true definition of a friend is, he to whom I can bear to speak and whom I can bear to hear! But where am I to look for the qualities of a genuine friend? In the man whose assistance I want. The patience required of me, is his attribute, not mine. Were I but once convinced of his ability and his sincerity, did I but know the soundness of his judgment and the frankness of his nature, were I assured of his love for me, and that it was his love that spoke, in a word, could I meet with a man of sufficient purity of heart and fervour of spirit, to dare on all occasions to tell me all the truth that my welfare required, I could not be impatient if I would. Had I encountered such a friend at my greatest need, I should never have gone mad. It was that that broke up all the caverns of my soul, and merged[1] my better understanding for twenty-four years.

I never had a friend. Advantages of earth and dross[2] I was endowed with in plenty, by the accident of my birth. What good have they done me? Well says the wise man, "Exchange not a friend for any treasure; neither a faithful brother for the gold of Ophir."[3] I have been acquainted, it may be, in different degrees with fifty thousand men, have been able to call them all by their names; but, among all this multitude, never has my hand been pressed in the hand of a friend. For this want, and this want only, I have become a monument for human misery, and a villain.

I remained for several weeks under the discipline of men, whose trade it is to superintend persons in my unfortunate condition. In my uncle's houshold there was a menial, whose special office it was, to open all letters directed to the master, and to exercise his own discretion, as to what it was that was requisite to be communicated. The intelligence respecting me was suppressed. My uncle, it was not doubted, notwithstanding all the forms of apathy and neutrality he had cultivated, was deeply interested in my well-being. It could scarcely be, where there was only a single male in the next generation to himself, the representative of his family, and the heir of his property, that he should not be under the domination of the common human feelings in

---

1   Submerged.
2   Dregs, waste.
3   Isaiah 13:13. Ophir is a region mentioned in the Bible, famous for its
    riches.

so obvious a case. But my uncle was wasted to a shadow. As he never put forth any thing that, in the ordinary language of men, is called an exertion, so it is probable he had finally lost the power of such exertion. For years he had not breathed the fresh air, or looked upon the face of day but through an artificial medium; he had not gone out of his chamber, or put on his shoes. It was therefore universally believed in Mandeville House, that, as he advanced in age, any violent and unexpected shock would kill him on the instant, and he would go out, like a lamp in which the last drop of oil had been dried up and exhausted. It was prognosticated, it seems, from the symptoms of my case, that my alienation of mind would be but temporary; and it was therefore concluded, that the affair was not of that sort that required to be communicated to the head of the family, at the extreme risk with which that communication would be attended.

A correspondence however had for some years been kept up between the official minister of affairs at Mandeville House, and Mrs Willis, who seemed entitled to this distinction, on account of the relation in which she stood to my sister, and the high character she bore for judgment, discretion and virtue. Mrs Willis gave her sanction to the suppression of the circumstance, which was adopted in the present instance. She hastened however to give me all the personal attention in her power, and, with my sister, actually took lodgings in the village of Cowley, that she might be at hand to watch all the variations of my disease. An attempt was at first made to forbid her from judging of my state by actually seeing me. But Mrs Willis was a woman of too firm a mind, and too zealous a spirit of affection, to be baffled by the customary pretences that are played off upon the mob of those who may happen to be the nearest relations or friends of the insane. The master of the madhouse understood that she was no relation, and that a very slight and casual acquaintance had subsisted between her and his patient; and he believed that little danger was to be apprehended from an interview. In fact, as has already appeared, I took no particular notice of her, and was not even aware that any stranger had approached me. Both Mrs Willis and the keeper were of opinion, that it was necessary for the present to keep my sister out of my sight.

By degrees, as was predicted, the violence of my disorder abated. One of the first favourable symptoms was that I slept soundly for hours together. Henrietta, my dear Henrietta, was inexpressibly anxious for the safety of her only brother, who was also in a manner her only relative. Forbidden, as she was, to see me by day, she was most importunate in her petition, to be allowed to visit me when asleep. This indulgence was conceded to her. She viewed my lineaments, and revived every tender emotion to which our former intercourse had given birth. She was painfully impressed with my pallid hue and emaciated form. She turned back the bed-clothes, and discovered that my neck and chest had suffered as much from the effects of my disease, as the lineaments of my face. She wiped away with her handkerchief the cold moisture, which occasionally broke out upon my skin. She watched the twitchings and contortions of my features. Sometimes I mumbled inarticulate words in my sleep; and she moved her ear toward my lips, to try if she could gather up their meaning. At other times I uttered the names of Bradford, and Judith, and O'Neile, of Penruddock, and Clifford. Then I would suddenly start and scream, and vent myself in fierce and terrible ravings. In these cases it was contrived, that the bed-curtain should be instantly interposed between me and the sight of Henrietta. On some occasions they forced her out of the room. But this was peculiarly distressing to her; and in a short time she obtained, to be permitted to remain in her concealment. It was a tremendous trial to her, thus to be made a witness of my degradation, my fury, and my misery; but she commanded herself with unalterable constancy. And by this means, with the discernment with which affection and talent conspired to endow her, she was enabled to penetrate to the very heart of my disease, with an accuracy that no other resource could have supplied.

Generally, when I awoke, it was by degrees. I stretched myself; my breast rose and sunk with quick heaves and pantings; there seemed to be a struggle and pause between the new visitor to my eyelids, Forgetfulness, and the painful, and confused, and embarrassed state of my waking thoughts. This was for some time the signal for Henrietta to withdraw. Once it happened that I awoke so imperceptibly, and with so little disturbance, that, till I spoke as asking for something, she did not perceive the change. She sat opposite to me, and I looked towards her. But my state was so languid, and my observation so feeble and vacant, that I had not the smallest conception who it was that was before me. "Give me some drink," I said. Henrietta, according to her compact, arose to withdraw; but it was little less than agony to her, to think that I had looked at her, and spoke to her, and no longer knew my Henrietta.

This happened several times. At length she obtained permission to retain her attitude in silence, and see what effect that would have upon me. It was then, as I have said, that I gazed upon her for some time in silence; and gradually, like the dispersion of a mist, or the removal of one veil of the thinnest gauze after another, I knew who it was that sat beside me. She was nothing to me, a mere stranger, an attendant; next she was a beautiful vision, or like a magic picture, made by the fantastic play of sun-beams on a cloud, that it was refreshing to the senses to dwell upon; by degrees she was an acquaintance, a friend, a sister! "Surely," thought I, "I am not altogether a wretch; a lovely creature sits beside me, watching my health, and pouring out aspirations for my safety!" At last the truth came over me, and I spoke aloud. "It is, it is," I said "my Henrietta!"

This was the moment that seemed to determine my convalescence. My health and my sanity now improved by rapid strides. It was happy for me, that every thing about me was new, that nothing existed to remind me of the fountain of my disease. If the first object that met my sight upon returning recollection, had been the walls of my college, I should almost infallibly have relapsed, or rather should never have recovered. But of the house in which I resided every thing was new to me. As I grew better, they removed me into a more cheerful apartment; and presently after, I was considered as sufficiently restored, to be dismissed from the infirmary, and to take up my abode in my sister's lodging. My next remove was to Beaulieu, where I had spent some days immediately before I was placed at Winchester, and which place I had visited once or twice since that period.

CHAPTER VII

It has already appeared what a fascinating power my beloved Henrietta possessed over my mind. It had lately been all tumult, and tempest, and supernatural rage. But her voice was like the song or incantation I have read of, that could "still the wild waves as they roar," and hush the maddening winds.[1] Where she built her nest, and paid her watchful tendance, the place seemed sacred from the storm, and no boisterous and unmannered passion dared intrude.

She talked to me of love, and my heart was tuned to the sweetest emotions of the human soul. She told me tales of her own daily experience, and the earthly paradise of Beaulieu; and all

---

1   *Comus*, 87: comparing the attendant Spirit to Orpheus.

that has been fabled of Arcadia[1] seemed to me spiritless and vapid in the comparison. She drew a bewitching portrait of an obscure and rural life, a path through the vale of existence, that leaves no traces behind it, and the traveller in which, unknown to the trumpet of fame, is contented with happiness. The being that passes through this tranquil scene, hears nothing of kings, and ministers, and the intrigues of a court, sits him down quietly by the margin of the rippling brook, and is never told of the factions and wars to the right hand and the left, in which men tear one another to pieces with a thousand barbarities. Him every morning's sun wakens to new enjoyment; and no cares, misfortune, or disappointment ever cloud his brow, or plague his heart. He dates his years from no public epoch, the rise and fall of kings, but marks the lapse of time only by the succession of the seasons. And at length he sinks into the grave by a gentle decay, without the recollection of one crime that had stained his spotless life, or of one day that he would wished to have been other than it was.

All this was fiction, a fiction of the visionary poets that Henrietta loved, and not adapted to real life. Man is not one of the different species of animals that we see, that can sleep away life upon a sunny bank, unless when roused by the imperious cravings of nature, and those having been supplied, immediately sleep again. Man is a creature, as a celebrated philosopher has remarked, one of whose most constant characteristics is a sense of uneasiness; we yawn and are wretched in the absence of excitement, and cannot be satisfied and content, except as we are engaged in some earnest pursuit. But however the Arcadian pictures drawn for me by Henrietta, might be imperfect in a general view, they were accurately adapted to my disease. I was just recovered from a state of fearful perturbation; the very principles and foundations of humanity within me, had been shaken; and music was the restorative my condition required. Never was there so consummate an artist in this respect as my Henrietta. Her voice was melodious; her sentiments were all one mighty scheme of harmony; and the gay, yet peaceful and serene pictures, with which she amused me from morning till night, gave me a new sort of existence, to which I had hitherto been a stranger.

The first effect which all this produced upon me, was like the song of the Sirens.[2] It lulled me into forgetfulness. I was all ear:

---

1 Synonymous in Roman poetry with the idealized world of pastoral.
2 In Greek mythology, female spirits whose enchanting music lured sailors to shipwreck on the rocky coast of their island.

every other sense was suspended; or was made tributary and sub-ordinate, to assist the impressions that the sense of hearing conveyed. At one time Henrietta led me to the woods, the banks of the murmuring stream, or the neighbouring ruins: in the heat of the day we reposed upon a bench in the grotto I formerly described: it was all one: every thing that Henrietta did, was right; every thing that Henrietta said, was best. Why could not I have lived thus for ever? How infinitely more delicious was this indolence and oblivion, than the revelry of the voluptuous, the accumulation that avarice pursues, and the dreams of mad ambition?

By degrees Henrietta talked to me of the views of my future life. She reminded me that my uncle had lately been much shaken by a disease, that was supposed to partake of the nature of palsy. She observed, that existence with him hung only by a thread, that very shortly he would be no more, and that then I should by necessity succeed to his vast estates. She excited me to reflect now, on the conduct I should then think proper to pursue. In consequence of the neutrality and melancholy state of the present proprietor, every thing had been neglected, every thing had been trusted to the management of hirelings. It was true, that however soon my uncle died, I should not come into the administration of the property, till I had completed the age of twenty-one. But that period would soon arrive; and it was proper that my education and my studies now, should all of them be directed to fit me for the station to which I was destined by my birth. In the opinion of Henrietta, the proprietor of a large estate was merely a steward for the benefit of others. All wealth, when accurately examined, resolved itself into a certain quantity of human labour; and they who performed the labour, whatever were the artificial regulations which society, wisely or otherwise, adopted on the subject, were entitled to the benefit. The proper office of every landed proprietor was to make them easy and to make them happy. Nor was this the whole of the duty incumbent on him. He not only ought to consider himself as a sort of father to his tenants and labourers. He was, beside this, in the present distribution of the civilised world, the member of a state, important, in some degree, in proportion to the extent of his property. He was therefore called upon to study for the general advantage of the whole state. He was bound to encourage among them arts, and sciences, and knowledge, and virtue, and liberty, and good government. For these purposes it was incumbent upon him to be munificent, without being either luxurious or prodigal.

The mansion-houses, as well as every thing else that belonged to the family-estate, had gone to ruin under my uncle Audley. Henrietta and I talked over the character of these houses. We had seen one or two, and had heard of others. We discussed which of them it might be proper for me to choose for my principal residence. This was a complex question, partly to be governed by the beauty of the situation, and partly by the consideration of which was the place in which I could be most useful. We decided in favour of a house that we had both of us seen. We then set about planning the improvements that would be eligible and necessary. The house we pitched upon, had a spacious and admirable saloon;[1] but each of us suggested alterations, by means of which it would be rendered more complete. We also thought of new arrangements for the chambers; nor were the grounds omitted in our consideration.

Sweet and soothing was the tone of mind that these agreeable speculations engendered, and well did it dispose me for impulses of a generous nature. If Henrietta was disposed to study my happiness, I was not less anxious to contribute to hers. How could I do enough for such a sister? The most pleasing vision I could frame to myself, was of our living together, and having the daily fruition of her society. Our delicious wanderings, as at Beaulieu, might then be made perpetual; and, under the fashioning care of my Henrietta, I could not fail to become peaceful, virtuous and happy. Why had we ever been separated? Because our respective educations required it. Alas, how erroneous a conception! Had any preceptor, could any instructor, teach me lessons half so valuable as those of Henrietta? Should I ever have suffered what I had suffered, or fallen into such mistakes as I had committed, if I had had her for ever at my elbow?

Devoutly I wished that we might be separated no more. But I was not vain and selfish enough to desire to make Henrietta my slave. She might have different views and a different vocation in life. She might be destined to become a wife and a mother. Was there ever a creature so admirably formed to grace the duties annexed to that character? Who but must regret that such a being should die, and leave no model of herself behind? No: for a time she might be my inmate; afterwards, I might be contented to retain her for a friend. At all events I determined to render her independent; to endow her amply with the means to follow the impulses of her soul, wherever they might lead her. I told her this;

---

1 The centre room of a suite of formal rooms.

and endeavoured to plan out the scheme by which it might most fully be effected.

After a time Henrietta ventured, but with a timid hand, to approach more near to the seat of my disease. My error was misanthropy; she endeavoured to inspire me with a contrary principle. She believed she could not do better, than begin with authority. She turned me to the works of a favourite writer, and intreated my attention to the following passage:—[1]

"He who justly proves himself a friend, said I, is man enough; nor is he wanting to society. A single friendship may acquit him. He has deserved a friend, and is man's friend; though not in strictness, or according to your high moral sense, the friend of mankind. For, to say truth, as to this sort of friendship, it may by wiser heads be esteemed perhaps more than ordinary manly and even heroic, as you assert it: but, for my part, I see so very little worth in mankind, and have so indifferent an opinion of the public, that I can propose little satisfaction to myself in loving either.

"Do you then, rejoined the philosopher, take gratitude to be among the acts of friendship and good-nature? Undoubtedly: for it is one of the chief. Suppose then that the obliged person discovers in the obliger several failings; does this exclude the gratitude of the former? Not in the least. Or does it make the exercise of gratitude less pleasing? I think rather the contrary. For, when deprived of other means of making a return, I might rejoice in that sure way of showing my gratitude to my benefactor, by bearing his failings.

"Consider then, what it was you said, when you objected against the love of mankind, from the consideration of human frailty, and seemed to scorn the public, because of its misfortunes! For, where can generosity exist, if not here? Where can we

---

1   Godwin's note on this passage is at the end of this volume (p. 310), where he alludes to Shaftesbury's *Characteristics* (1711; rpt. 1790), from which only the first three paragraphs are adapted. Not only has Shaftesbury's ancestor been portrayed in a dubious light, the self-confessed "anachronism" of citing the third Earl (1671–1713) marks Henrietta as an Enlightenment figure: a future that seems quaintly out of date in the much more pressing present of the Civil War. By putting his note so conspicuously at the end of the volume, Godwin may also be suggesting that we not use any other anachronistic references to texts written after the Glorious Revolution to argue that Mandeville lives on, a sadder and a wiser man, into a period that has overcome the traumas of British history.

even exert friendship, if not in this chief subject? To what should we be true and grateful in the world, if not to mankind, and that society, to which we are so deeply indebted? What are the faults or blemishes, which can excuse such an omission, or, in a grateful mind, can ever lessen the satisfaction of making a grateful and kind return?"

Setting out from this text, Henrietta sought to inspire me with principles of benevolence. She said, that we were all "children of one God, and therefore ought all to consider ourselves as members of one great family. Our natures, our wants, and our desires are alike: as Shakespear says, 'Has not a Jew eyes? Has not a Jew hands? organs, dimensions, senses, affections, passions? Is he not fed with the same food, hurt with the same weapons, subject to the same diseases, cured by the same means, warmed and cooled by the same winter and summer, as a Christian is? If you prick him does he not bleed? If you tickle him does he not laugh? and, if you poison him does he not die?'[1] We are formed for mutual sympathy, and cannot refrain from understanding each other's joys and sorrows. By the very constitution of our being we are compelled to delight in society: 'it is not good for man to be alone': we are all exactly fitted to contribute to the good of all; and it is by each carrying his respective amount to the general bank of human happiness,[2] that each is enabled to draw most largely for his private accommodation.

"If man could meet man in an uninhabited island, how would he rejoice in his good fortune! If he met his fellow for the first time, and had never seen his like before, how would he admire the miraculous kind of being that stood before him! We may travel into distant countries, to measure the height of mountains, or gauge the depth of caverns, we may analyse the substances of which the earth is composed, or study the different characters of the animals by which it is peopled. But man is the master-piece of the creation, and the ornament of the world; and without him the whole globe on which we dwell, would be a mighty blank, a speechless desert, a dreary scene, that smiled on nothing, and on which nothing smiled. Oh, then, how should beings of this wonderful structure, hail each other's presence, love each other's good, and strain their utmost nerve to defend each other from injury!"

---

1 Shylock in *The Merchant of Venice*, 3.1.59–66.
2 The utilitarian emphasis on general happiness recalls Godwin's *Political Justice*. Inserted into Henrietta's ventriloquized patchwork of thinkers, it suggests the limitations of easy platitudes, including Godwin's own.

From love, my heavenly monitress proceeded to speak of hatred. And, as she illustrated the one from human strength, so she inveighed against the other from the consideration of human weakness. "'Man cometh up as a flower, and is cut down; he fleeth also as a shadow, and continueth not.' Is this frail creature, that is blown away by every wind, the proper subject of our anger? We are like 'the grass of the field, which to-day is, and to-morrow is cast into the oven.'[1] We are beset with infirmities on every side; every limb has its appropriate disease; every wind wafts pestilence on its wings; every element is pregnant to us with the means of destruction. Shall man, the compound and receptacle of so many frailties, become the tormentor and the enemy of man? Is no human life sufficiently freighted with sorrows, that we must each of us endeavour to increase the other's burthen? In the child of an hour old, I can see in the anticipations of fancy the ancient father trembling with years, tottering with weakness, sinking, even now scarcely half-alive into the darkness of the grave. Is this frail and ephemeral existence the fitting subject of rage, abhorrence, indignation and revenge?

"Consider, that man is but a machine![2] He is just what his nature and his circumstances have made him: he obeys the necessities which he cannot resist. If he is corrupt, it is because he has been corrupted. If he is unamiable, it is because he has been 'mocked, and spitefully entreated, and spit upon.' Give him a different education, place him under other circumstances, treat him with as much gentleness and generosity, as he has experienced of harshness, and he would be altogether a different creature. He is to be pitied therefore, not regarded with hatred; to be considered

---

1   Job 14:2; Matthew 6:30. The unsourced quotations that follow in Henrietta's speech come from the Bible, a curious feature that adds to the patchwork quality of her speech, given that using Biblical language is more her brother's style.

2   The reference could be to the French philosopher Julien Offray de La Mettrie's *Man a Machine* (1748), which is not so much a reduction of man to mechanical determinism as a use of materialism to unsettle a purely rationalist approach to human nature. But the figure of the machine is also throughout *PJ*, in which Godwin sees man and society as a "machine" but also questions this reduction. In the remainder of the above passage Godwin also has Henrietta parrot his own necessitarianism (the view that man is arbitrarily formed by circumstances that can be changed). In the following paragraph, however, Henrietta takes the opposite view: her harangue is a contradictory patchwork of various sources.

with indulgence, not made an object of revenge; to be reclaimed with mildness, to be gradually inspired with confidence, to be enlightened and better informed as to the mistakes into which he has fallen, not made the butt and object of our ferocity.

"It is the prerogative of man, to look on outward circumstances with scorn. We are placed amidst a thousand inferior natures; we are surrounded with many causes adapted to produce in us sensations, pleasurable and painful; our lot is cast for us between 'life and death, blessing and cursing.' But we have the source of our satisfaction or unhappiness within us, and are the masters of our own fortune. The colours under which things are seen by us, are not in the things themselves, but derive their brightness or their deadness from the eye of him that looks upon them. It is the glory of a man, to stand unmoved the shock of ill fortune. He that is truly worthy of the powers with which nature has endowed us, is of no thin and airy substance to be turned by every wind that blows, is no cameleon to take the colour of every substance upon which he may happen to be placed. He is full and complete within himself. The hand of fate may strike him; the hand of death must strike him at one time or other; but it will never take him by surprise; it will never quail his heart, or make him less than the man he ought to be.

"Oh, my brother, forgive me if I ask what you have been, compared with this best and noblest standard of man? 'a reed shaken with the wind'; a character with no intrinsic erectness, but yielding to every impulse, and at the mercy of every one, great or small, ignoble or honourable, that has come in contact with you. Why is this? You have talents; you have education; you have virtues; you are even amply endowed with the goods of fortune. Who shall be happy, if you are a wretch? Where shall we look for stability and honour, if you are a prey to every noxious breath that sweeps across your atmosphere? Justify better, my brother, the ways of heaven! Show that all the blessings that have so abundantly been showered upon you, have not been poured down upon a thankless soil!

"My brother, you have told me that you loved me. He that loves, is willing to do something for the object of his love. In you I 'have garnered up my heart'; my affections are centred in you; you are the only creature in the world, to whom I intimately, and by the closest ties, belong. Give me then the joy I am most capable of receiving, the joy to see you happy. Indulge me in the weakness, if weakness it is, to be proud of you. Do not wither up my young spirits, by seeing you a monument of misery, a spectacle of woe. I foresee, with a distinctness that nothing can deceive, that, if I am ever to be a memorable victim of calamity, it will come from you. Perhaps I ask too much of you, to do all this for me, to restrain the excesses of your nature that I may be happy. But remember, my sweetest Charles, that this is certainly a virtue, a generosity, that will prove its own reward!

"Surely, my brother, you should consider yourself as a being in the hands of God, and as that reasoning species of creature, who has his resources within. Can any man command you to do this or that? Can you not dispose of every day, and every hour in the day, as you please? If you desire improvement, are not the sources of improvement open to you? If you desire to travel, and see men and manners, the means of doing so are in your hands. If solitude and meditation and study are objects of preference to you, who is there that can invade your solitude? If you wish for society, have you not the means of calling about you companions, as numerous, or as select, as you please? If you prefer a philosophical, a frugal and temperate mode of living, who is there to control you? If you desire luxuries in any moderate and beseeming degree, luxury is within your reach.

"What then can be more unjust, than that he who possesses every external and internal means of satisfaction, should suffer his serenity to be disturbed at the caprice of others? Does any thing displease you? Leave it. If you cannot immediately withdraw yourself from it, rise above it. If you have done nothing wrong, appeal to your own conscience; be satisfied that that approves or acquits you, and despise the mistake and misconstruction of another. Why should I place my happiness as a deposit, in the custody of my neighbour? Who gave him an empire over me? In what market did he buy me for his slave? Where is the indenture by which he claims to dispose of me? Independence is the best birthright of man, and that which each of us ought to cherish beyond all earthly possessions.

"I will tell you what a slave is, and what is a freeman. A slave is he who watches with abject spirit the eye of another: he waits timidly, till another man shall have told him, whether he is to be happy or miserable to-day: his comforts and his peace depend on the breath of another's mouth. No man can be this slave unless he pleases. If by the caprice of fortune he has fallen as to externals into another's power, still there is a point that at his own will he can reserve. He may refuse to crouch; he may walk fearless and erect; the words that he utters may be supplied by that reason, to which the high and the low, the rich and the poor, have equally access. And, if he that the misjudging world calls a slave, may retain all that is most substantial in independence, is it possible, that he whom circumstances have made free, should voluntarily put the fetters on his own feet, the manacles on his own hands, and drink the bitter draught of subjection and passive obedience?

"What a wretched thing is anger, and the commotion of the soul! If any thing annoys me, and interposes itself between me and the objects of my desires and pursuit, what is incumbent upon me is, that I should put forth my powers, and remove it. How shall I do this? By the exercise of my understanding. Wherein does my power emphatically reside? In the rational part of my nature. To the employment of this power, a cool and exact observation is necessary. I must be like a great military commander in the midst of a field of battle, calm, collected, vigilant, imperturbable: but the moment I am the slave of passion, my powers are lost; I am turned into a beast, or rather into a drunkard; I can neither preserve my footing, nor watch my advantage, nor strike an effectual blow. Did you never see a passionate man and a temperate pitched against each other? How like a fool did the former appear! How did his adversary turn and wind him as he pleased, and show like some God controling an inferior nature! It is by this single implement, his reason, that man governs the brute creation, that he trains horses and camels and elephants to his hand, that he tames the lion of the desert, and shuts up the hyena with bars."

Such were the divine discourses with which Henrietta sought to heal the ravages which circumstances had inflicted on my soul. The wisdom which she uttered, was beyond her years; but she had imbibed its lessons under an unrivalled instructress. How different were the sermons of Henrietta, from the homilies of Hilkiah, of which I had so long been an auditor! Hers was a religion of love: his was a religion of hatred. His sectarian spirit justified disdain and abhorrence in its disciples, and enlisted all their bad passions in the service of the Almighty. It was his delight to contemplate the chosen few which were elected and separated from the world; and his principles taught him, good man! (for a good man he was) a sovereign aversion to the great multitude of the children of the common Father of us all.

CHAPTER VIII

While I was at Beaulieu, I renewed my acquaintance with the noble family of Montagu, whose members have been commemorated in the early part of my narrative. The boys were now, each of them, five years older than at the time of my first visit, and were consequently more interesting, their manners more formed, and their sentiments better entitled to attention and deference. Edward was now fifteen, and Ralph two years younger. But the sobriety and sedateness of the character of Ralph, raised him nearly to an equality in point of judgment, with his more volatile brother. At another time I should have been apt enough, like the generality of youths whose cheeks are beginning to be clad with the first down of manhood, to disdain companions who were still of a school-boy age. But my present state of precarious convalescence made me somewhat more humble. Henrietta, and the matron under whose guardianship she was placed, earnestly recommended to me, to unbend from the severity to which my constitution was inclined, and to mix in the lighter pursuits and amusements of persons younger than myself. The progeny of Lord Montagu, both male and female, made a groupe, that might almost have tempted a winged messenger of heaven, if he had passed that way, to suspend his flight, and to fix on this place as a scene of short repose, "though bent on speed."[1] Henrietta, as I have before said, was the favourite visitor of this circle; and the daughters of the house of Montagu observed her superiority without one repining thought. For myself, my character and temperament was different from them all. I could not divest myself of my reserve, the unsociableness of my habits, and the perpetual activity and fermentation of my solitary thoughts. But I was willing to become their pupil. I was like one performing his noviciate in this school of juvenile philosophers. While I looked on, it seemed as if the infirmity of my mind, however twisted up with and inseparable from its original elements, quitted me. And I have sometimes been surprised to find it happen to me, that for a moment I also grew frolicsome, sportive and fantastical, by the charm of the irresistible contagion.[2]

---

1 From *Paradise Lost*, where the archangel Michael, "Though bent on speed," pauses "Betwixt the world destroy'd and world restor'd" (12.2–3).

2 Note the description of the healing powers of Beaulieu as a "contagion."

I have mentioned that the character of Ralph Montagu was sober and sedate. In that respect it was somewhat contrasted with the active and animated natures of Edward and Henrietta. But it would be a great mistake to imagine on that account, that his temperament bore any resemblance to mine. His eye was steady, and his front serene. He was not easily ruffled with passion, or moved to any impetuosity of voice or gesture. In that respect he might be said, in the phrase of the nursery, to have been "born a judge." But his look was frank; his forehead was broad and open; his voice was melodious; and his temper kind and considerate towards all. It has already appeared that that was not my character. "Care sat on my faded cheek";[1] seldom I smiled; my thoughts were solitary; and whatever passed in my bosom, with difficulty manifested itself, and was for the most part carefully locked up in the recesses of my heart. My words were few, and seemed as if pumped up, one by one, out of my breast. My voice had no insinuation; and the expression of my countenance—bore no resemblance to that of a courtier. I lived in human society, like a creature that no way appertained to it; but as if I had strayed from a remoter sphere, and was a mere stranger and foreigner on earth. The desert was my country; and gloom and asperity the element in which I breathed. Such was the stripling, who was fated to reap the ample inheritance of Mandeville, whom Henrietta loved, and whose history these pages are destined to record.

Great pains were certainly taken by the virtuous dwellers upon the New Forest, to reconcile me to the world, and to reconcile me to myself. Lord Montagu and Mrs Willis had heard of the adventure of Clifford: they were interested by the question of the strange madness that had seized me: and they successfully applied themselves, to sift out all the circumstances of my intercourse with this extraordinary rival. It struck Mrs Willis in particular, that now was the desirable time for effecting a perfect cure of my malady. My disorder she pronounced to be somewhat in the nature of a gangrene, or mortification in its incipient state, while yet the part retains some sense of pain, and a share of natural heat, but which, if not then acted upon, will speedily infect the whole man with its putrifying tendency, and be out of the reach of medicine to cure. Lord Montagu, in particular, reasoned on the subject like a lord. I was likely to be of some importance in my country; and Clifford was at least my equal by birth. We might therefore, his lordship thought, by a thousand acci-

---

1 *Paradise Lost*, 1.601–02, describing the Archangel Lucifer or Satan.

dents be called into the same field of action; and it might be of consequence, that no ill blood should be bred, that we should, neither of us, feel a personal objection to the other, but be at all times ready to cooperate for any honourable purpose.

Cromwel, having sacrificed as many victims, as he thought necessary to expiate the guilt of the insurrection, did not refuse to make some of those who were dipped in it the objects of his clemency. Among these Clifford had received a free pardon. When he was at Winchester school, he was a stranger to the indulgences of wealth, and he professed to despise them. But, since that time, a distant relation of his, an adherent of the Catholic faith, had lost his only son, and now showed himself disposed to extend that protection to my rival, no particle of which could before by any importunity be extorted from him. In this case a round[1] sum of money was disbursed to the protector, to secure the young man's discharge from all reckoning and trial. My own immunity was more easily accomplished, as I had been induced, though from no political considerations, and no calculation of consequences, to desert the cause of the royalists almost as soon as I was enlisted in it.

It was now resolved by Mrs Willis and Lord Montagu, that a formal reconciliation, between me, and the youth who had been the cause of all my sufferings, should be effected, and that for that purpose Clifford should be invited to spend a few days at Beaulieu. Henrietta was deputed the ambassadress to prepare me for the interview. I have already related her divine discourses, how she applied her admirable leechcraft[2] to the gaping wounds my mind had sustained, and with what earnestness she sought to inspire into me the principles of philanthropy, suavity of sentiment, and a true and heroical philosophy. I listened to her topics, for there was a charm in them against which no human bosom could be shut; I listened to the speaker, for she had an empire over my soul that no mortal perverseness could limit. She cast down all the intrenchments and bastions which my wilful passions had set up for my ruin, and entered with triumphant wheels the fortress of my heart.

She saw her time. She "took once a pliant hour,"[3] when heaven and earth smiled upon her undertaking. She found in me an

---

1 Large.
2 Leeches, a kind of worm, were (and indeed still sometimes are) used to drain blood from patients.
3 *Othello*, 1.3.150, on Othello's wooing of Desdemona.

unwonted tranquillity and peace. We sat beneath the shade of some venerable elms, just on the bank of the stream, which fell with murmuring sound over some large stones, that seemed unavailingly to endeavour to choke the current. A gentle breeze played among the foliage. A single linnet from a neighbouring spray, poured forth its rich and melodious notes in joyous and endless succession. No sounds, but those of nature, and that befit the most sequestered retreat, were to be heard. A balmy incense reached us from some odoriferous shrubs, that grew on the further side. The sunbeams played, through the ever moving foliage, on the lawn beneath. Henrietta broke the charm that had hitherto sealed our lips, and pronounced the name of Clifford. I involuntarily shuddered.

"And why should not he be loved too?" said Henrietta. "Nature is love. See how the bending branches kiss the stream! Each portion of nature nourishes its neighbour portion; and hence are derived health and vigour and harmony to all. See how the fawns upon yonder hill sport and gambol and frisk with each other! They have no reason to teach them this; but they derive from surer instinct the principle of mutual gaiety and love. And shall man, the lord of the creation, be less tender to his brother, man?

"Say, What has Clifford done to be shut out of this general bond of brotherhood? Ask yourself, and answer truly, Has he any bad passions that should exclude him from this benefit? The general fame respecting him is, that he is one of the kindest, the most simple-hearted and affectionate creatures that live: complacent in aspect, in his person lovely, and graceful in all his actions. Is this a being to be hated? Shall he be proscribed from the universal league? No; my Charles is too just and too honest for this."

"Henrietta," I cried, "take me, and mould me as you please. I can refuse you nothing. I will be the friend of Clifford!"

"Ah, Charles," she rejoined, "you are now my genuine brother. There wanted but this. You had a fault: who is exempt from error? But I see your nature purifying, all that was distorted and deceitful in the glass of your perceptions disappearing, and the whole converting into a fair and transparent medium, through which every thing shall be seen, not according to your preconceptions and prejudices, but as they are.

"Do you know, Charles, it was not for nothing that I introduced the name of Clifford! You have friends here, most anxious for your welfare, most watchful for your reputation, most profoundly concerned for your happiness and peace. Clifford will arrive upon a visit at Beaulieu House the day after to-morrow."

Why was it that I felt a serenity and a calm during this awful crisis, that I had never before experienced at any period of my life? The soul of Mandeville seemed to have left me, and the soul of Henrietta to have entered my bosom in its stead. The moroseness of my temper, the gloom of my complexion, were gone. I no longer knitted my brows, or clenched my fists, or folded my arms: actions which before were almost habitual to me. I walked in air. I found nothing that seemed to oppose itself against the specific gravity of my frame, but all the elements were the ready and obedient ministers of my will.

It was, that I was satisfied with myself, I felt that I had made a gallant determination, and that all the world was in duty bound to look on and approve. Obstinate, firm, inflexible I had been before; but never satisfied. A cursed disposition is its own punisher. My natural temperament was gloomy, unsocial and ferocious; the creed of Hilkiah was the prolific mother of a thousand malignant impulses: I yielded to these; I formed them into a system; I framed a multiplicity of ingenious reasonings recommending and applauding them: but they did not make me happy. I still had a bad conscience. The whole college of the Jesuits, with assiduity unrivalled, may form for man a code of artificial morality: nature will almost inevitably, at some solitary and sequestered hour, interpose her voice, and vindicate her insulted rights.

I was happy for these two days in a degree that I never experienced before. Alas, I am talking a language that hundreds will be found too fortunate to understand. They are perhaps daily and perpetually and for ever happy, because for ever full of that sweet accord, which I enjoyed for a moment. That which I harboured for two days, is their eternal inmate. That which was to me such unlooked for and celestial ravishment, is the element they respire. How must their angelic natures laugh at my grossness, if in reality they are not moved by the diviner impulses of condolement and pity!

To some, on the contrary, it may seem surprising, that I persisted for two whole days, to contemplate with pleasure the scene that Henrietta had opened before me. How came it, that old habits did not once intrude, that old wounds did not fester, and smart, and throb within me? Partly it was for the reason already given, that the views Henrietta suggested to me, were new. These views, are they not beautiful? Where is the heart so hard and unsusceptible, that can contemplate them without some delight? For my own part, I was never tired of listening to such divine precepts. Partly it was, that I felt that "the day of my redemption was at hand."[1] I had given myself up to despair. I was like what we read of the fallen angels, that could approach to Heaven's gates, that could image to themselves the songs and the joy to be found within, but against whom a sentence of unmitigable and eternal exile had been promulgated. Was it nothing to me, to suppose, that even I might yet be admitted within the pale[2] of my species, and that the joy that Henrietta had victoriously lighted up in my bosom, might be made of equal duration with my life? I saw the atmosphere of hell, in which I had been wrapped up, and almost suffocated for as long as I could remember, and which had thickened about me from year to year, gradually retiring, and sinking away into the distance, so that that Egyptian darkness[3] which had enveloped my whole horizon, now seemed "a cloud, no bigger than a man's hand."[4]

But the principal cause why the gladness and ease I now experienced, was without mixture, or recession into any thing of an opposite nature, was Henrietta. How could I be unhappy, when my guardian genius was for ever near me? When I rose in the morning, I met Henrietta. We partook of our light and healthful refections[5] together.

> Together both, ere the high lawns appeared
> Under the opening eyelids of the morn,
> And, till the star, that rose at evening bright,
> Towards heaven's descent had sloped his westering
>   wheel,[6]

we talked, or read, and rambled, and smiled. When I retired to rest, and was closed in my chamber, Henrietta was still with me. As long as I waked, I repassed the theme of our communication, and saw again in fancy her airy motions, and her bewitching attitudes. And, when I slept, still my dreams were full of Henrietta. What a change from the madness, wherein late I raved!

---

1 Mandeville refers to the season of Advent, which announces that a new day is dawning but has yet to come.
2 Determined bounds.
3 Referring to Exodus 10:21–22 and God's promise to Moses to deliver the children of Israel from Egypt. Cf. the allusion in the epigraph to Volumes 1 and 2.
4 1 Kings 18:44.
5 Refreshments.
6 Quoting from Milton's pastoral elegy *Lycidas* (1638), 25–31 (with two lines omitted).

The day approached. I went with Henrietta to the mansion-house, with the certainty of seeing my rival. My features were composed to serenity; all was sunshine within, I examined my own spirit, and was assured that the conquest I had gained was complete. The noble owner has skilfully contrived, that our meeting should take place on a day of solemn pomp. It was the anniversary of his Lordship's marriage; a mask[1] was ordered to be performed by the younger branches of the family; and Sir William Davenant[2] had come from London to superintend it. It was in the following year, that Sir William obtained permission from the existing government, to exhibit his musical entertainments in the nature of dramatic representation, publickly in Charter-House Yard.[3] An idea had been entertained of assigning me a part in the present performance; but it was an occupation too irreconcilable to the turn of my mind: and Henrietta declined taking an active share, from delicacy, thinking it would be most agreeable to my humour that she should refuse. It was finally arranged, that there should be no performers but the children of the family, assisted by a few persons who had been accustomed to pursue such employments for the sake of its profit.

The company assembled in a saloon, previously to the theatre being opened. Here it was that I saw Clifford. Here, as every where that he appeared, he seemed to me to fix all eyes, by the superior elegance of his person, gracefulness of his manners, and sweetness of his countenance. Lord Montagu took him by the hand, and led him towards Henrietta and me. "I think I have never given you cause of offence, Mandeville," said Clifford. "I hope," replied I, "that you will allow me to say as much on my part." "Then let us be friends," cried my beautiful adversary, "friends, now and for ever!" "It makes me happy," interposed our host, using the action corresponding to his words, "to join the hands of two young men of such distinguished merit and rank."

---

1 Masque, a form of courtly entertainment.
2 Poet and dramatist (1606–68), and supporter of the King during the Civil War. Because most dramatists were patronized by the aristocracy and monarchy, and because the Puritans disapproved of entertainment as sinful, the theatres were officially closed from 1642 to 1660. Davenant therefore staged his opera *The Siege of Rhodes* (1656) at his own house. The reference also indicates that we are still in the year 1655, when Volume 2 of the novel begins.
3 Rutland House in Charterhouse Yard was the mansion leased by Davenant.

Saying this, he led his guest away, as he had brought him to me. Clifford was the stranger, and Lord Montagu condescended to introduce him to the most considerable of the persons present.

CHAPTER IX

It was well for me that our interview had been brief. Henrietta joined some of her female acquaintance, and I was in a moment alone. She probably thought it best to leave me for a short time to myself, and believed that any comment she might make on what she had seen, and how she felt, would for the instant be impertinent and unacceptable. I followed Clifford with my eye. It was still the same glistering vision that had for ever thrown me into shade. Presently he disappeared. I drew back all my intellectual powers into the chambers of my bosom. I examined anew the state of my heart.

I had met Clifford at his first advent, if I may so express it, valiantly. I bid the young and busy devil, that seemed with more than ordinary quickness to "tickle up and down my veins," lie still in my heart. I mastered myself, and thought, that I was as calm as a lake, when not the smallest breath stirs on its surface. Presently I caught myself breathing hard and with difficulty. "Away! away!" said I to the half-formed and embryo emotion. The whole interview occupied but a few seconds; and at the same instant Henrietta, my guardian genius, left my side. At that moment I felt like one of those animals, that are said to derive from nature a mortal antipathy to some other species. I was first sensible to a sort of disturbance in the presence of my adversary, that I could not account for. I firmly believe that I should have felt the same, if Clifford had been present, with my back turned towards him, and without my knowledge. Instinct would have told me, The being is near, within whose presence thy "genius sinks rebuked." But, to return to the animal I mentioned. He is first disturbed; he shakes his mane; his hairs grow erect; he snuffs and snorts; his nostrils dilate themselves; his eyes emit sparkles of fire; he lashes his belly with his tail on this side and on that, with still augmenting fury; his wrath becomes at length too vast to be controled; and "the smoke of his nostrils is terrible."[1] Such was I. So fierce was my antipathy; so dreadful were my struggles; so did hatred rise in my bosom, till it almost "burst with its fraught."[2]

---

1   Job 39:20.
2   *Othello*, 3.3.49.

We passed from the saloon into the theatre. I took care to place myself at a distance from my enemy; I endeavoured to be calm; I sought to fix my whole attention on the performance. Yet, ever and anon, before I was aware, my eyes would withdraw themselves, and seek out Clifford. When I had found him, I started then, and drew them back as fast.

The entertainment being over, I withdrew, and walked by myself in the park. I turned my steps to the least frequented part of the inclosure.

"Mandeville!" said I, "you are a fool. What," I proceeded, "shall I suffer the worst part of my nature to get the better of me thus? Shall the gall that is within me overcome, and taint with its infection, all the wholesome and life-giving juices of this frame? No!

"I came hither this morning with resolutions, the purest and the most firm. Shall all this melt away in a moment? Is my whole frame so diseased, that it cannot bear the slightest touch of what is medicinal and healing? To-day I was a man, kind in my heart, and in my purpose lovely. Shall this goodness and honesty of my nature last but one day, and all the rest of my life be spent in the service of those demons, that exist only for the plague and torment of the human bosom? It is well worth my while, an honour indeed to this soul that informs me, to have pledged me to resolves, that I cannot adhere to for a single sun!

"Mandeville, be just! Did a lovelier vision ever manifest itself to mortal eyes, than the whole figure and physiognomy of Clifford? Was not this the impression you received the first moment you saw him? And do not his character and dispositions fully answer to the promise of his countenance? Is not this the universal verdict of every one that knows him? Even to yourself, who seem to have conceived such an animosity against him, has he ever purposed an injury, has he ever acted any thing but kindness?

"Yes; I have suffered tremendous agonies; the blood has seemed, once and again, to start from my forehead, and trickle down my cheeks, by the interference of Clifford; I confess that. Well then, it is my function and my task to forgive. Magnanimity is the crown of a man, is the befitting ornament of a gentleman, upon whom the partial course of society has heaped up vast possessions, that he may show a more generous spirit than the herd of his species. And, if I have still a part to act upon this mortal stage, my course, even in bare prudence, is to forgive. If I remember, the world also will remember, my disgraces at Winchester, and in Wiltshire. But, if I wipe them out from the records of my memory, I may reasonably expect that the world will reward my generosity with a reciprocal oblivion.

"And then, to whom is it that I have solemnly promised, to take Clifford to my bosom? Is it not to Henrietta, the empress of my fate, my only consolation on earth, that better part of my soul, for whom and by whom only I live? Yes, I have sworn, and it shall be performed!"

I had no sooner arrived at this calm-giving and peace-inspiring conclusion, than I saw Henrietta in the distance. She had come out into the park to seek me. We rushed toward each other. She hastened to meet me, because she had been alarmed at my disappearance, and the savage disposition that she feared was implied by my plunging into solitude. I flew into her arms, proud of the feelings into which I had reasoned myself.

"Why have you gone away?" said Henrietta. "Where have you been?"

"The worst is past," answered I. "Clifford and I have met. That cost me a little more than I expected. That was nature's struggle. Every succeeding interview will be an easier task, till at length pain will turn into pleasure. You may be sure of me now."

"My brother!" replied Henrietta, "you cheer my heart. I have committed my soul upon this venture. You must not deceive me in it. No, I see plainly you will not."

She led me towards the house. The representation had been given by day-light; and it was now succeeded by a sumptuous entertainment. In passing to the hall where the dinner was spread, Clifford and I crossed each other. He gave me his hand. I pressed it in mine. It cost me less than in the former instance. The "mother" within me (as Shakespear calls it)[1] was less obtrusive and troublesome than before. "I am glad," said I, "—very glad,—that we have met thus."

After dinner, the dishes were removed, and the conversation became general. One of the most considerable of the neighbouring gentry, who was not in the secret of the generous plot which Lord Montagu and Mrs Willis had formed in my behalf, now addressed himself to Clifford, and requested him to favour the company with the particulars of the extraordinary manner in which he had covered the flight of Sir Joseph Wagstaff, after the miscarriage of the royalists at Salisbury.

Clifford appeared a good deal embarrassed, at the way in which he was thus singled out by a gentleman of so much con-

---

1 *King Lear*, 2.2.56.

sideration. He begged, for particular reasons, to be excused from entering into the subject at present.

The gentleman who addressed him, though a man of much importance in the country, and who had formerly been a main pillar of the royal cause, was in other respects a mere sportsman, illiterate in his habits, and utterly a stranger to any refined notions of delicacy.

"Pooh, pooh, young man!" resumed he: "we all of us know why you are backward in entering into the subject. But modesty here is out of the question, and is often the most beggarly and back-handed friend that merit can have in its pay. If you have known how to do a noble thing, you must be condemned for your pains to tell all how and about it. There are no spies, my lad, in this company, but all cavaliers to the back-bone: therefore begin. Here are several gentlemen near me who have never heard the story; and I do not myself know all the rights of it. I think myself lucky, to have met with the young fellow who made so extraordinary a figure in the business; and I will not be cheated of the opportunity such a meeting gives me, to learn more of the matter."

Clifford cast upon me a look of supplication and distress.

It may easily be supposed that I felt a little alarmed at the first mention of Sir Joseph Wagstaff. The morning on which I had been introduced to that officer had been the most unfortunate of my life. But, at the instant I describe, I was a new man, and my bosom beat with the most virtuous resolutions. The time had been, when the bare mention of this name, and that as the prelude to a story, and before so numerous and respectable a company, would have driven the colour from my cheek, and have deprived me at once of speech, of hearing and sight; I should by turns have glowed like fire, and been covered from head to foot with a deathlike dew. But now I strung myself against these invasions of a mere animal nature.

The moment after Clifford had cast upon me the glance I have mentioned, I turned my eye upon Henrietta. I saw in her countenance the index of her sufferings, and that she would have given the world for some accident, that should have suddenly turned the attention of all to a different subject.

What I saw, infused into me new animation and energy. The distress of Clifford was a homage he paid to my feelings; that of Henrietta was my alarm to courage and heroism. "I will no longer be an object of pity and indulgence to others," said I internally; "I am capable of a higher and more honourable vocation; and to show that I can endure what requires much fortitude to endure, is the proper way to enter upon this career."

"It would give me pleasure to hear the story," said I across the table to Clifford, in, a low, composed and distinct voice.

Clifford signified his assent to my request by a slight gesture of the head, and began:

"The unfortunate issue of the gallant undertaking of Sir Joseph and Penruddock," said he, "is sufficiently known. It began under the happiest auspices; but unfortunate differences that arose between the leaders, speedily led to the most disastrous reverse.

"After our retreat from Salisbury, we halted for a short time at Blandford, and there caused King Charles to be proclaimed in the market-place. This was however the last show of prosperity that attended us. We had the good wishes of many; but insurgents that appear to be on the retreat, are not likely to be recruited in their numbers. The characters of Penruddock and Sir Joseph were strongly contrasted with each other; the former had every quality that could do honour to a gentleman, but he was not thoroughly penetrated, as Sir Joseph was, who had learned the rudiments of his art in the wars of Germany,[1] with the principles of the military profession. At Salisbury our principal commander had conceived a plan of proceeding of the most decisive sort, the only one that could have led to a successful termination; and in this he had been counteracted by the humane scruples of Penruddock. As Sir Joseph knew how to take advantage of the tide, when it was at the highest; so the same perspicacity of judgment led him instantly, to perceive when the chance of benefit was gone. On our leaving Blandford, and even before, he was thoroughly aware that our case was desperate. He called together the officers, and told them this, earnestly pressing them not to throw themselves away upon a vain point of honour, but to do, as became men engaged in the service of their king, to save their lives from the vengeance of the tyrant, and reserve their zeal and their talents for some occasion, where they might be of substantial advantage. Penruddock on the contrary, being once engaged, could not endure to throw up the undertaking, and urged that, by going further westward, we should try what yet could be done

---

1 Wagstaff served in the French army during the last phase of the Thirty Years' War (1618–48), a pan-European conflict that was initially religious but then became a struggle between the Habsburg and Bourbon dynasties for political supremacy.

with the gentlemen of Devonshire and Cornwall. Here then the leaders of the expedition divided: Sir Joseph, and the most distinguished military characters withdrew, and sought their safety in dispersion, the country-gentlemen and their followers kept together, reached Southmolton to the number of about two hundred,—and met the reward of their perseverance on the scaffold.

"I continued with Sir Joseph, to whose person I was by virtue of my appointment attached. I will not trouble you with any of our adventures, till we came to the house of a Mr Landseer near the coast of Devonshire, whose wife was a distant relation of my mother. Landseer was himself an adherent of the existing government; his wife was strongly attached to the exiled family. It happened that Landseer had been absent for some years, on a commission which the republicans had given him to one of the northern courts, but was expected on his return in a few weeks. The fugitives from Salisbury were now chased almost from house to house; they were disappointed of a vessel, which they had expected to have found at Lymouth, ready to carry them off; captain Unton Croke[1] in particular, a man wholly destitute of honour and humanity, was most assiduous in hunting them out from their hiding-places. It happened in one instance, that Sir Joseph having already nearly exhausted the protection of the loyal houses in the neighbourhood, seemed to be driven in a manner to the last extremity. In this conjuncture it occurred to me to think of Mrs Landseer whose house would be less exposed to the jealousy of the military, on account of her husband's being in the employment of the present rulers. On my representation I was commissioned to repair to this lady, and, confident in her loyalty, to propose without any disguise, that she should receive Sir Joseph Wagstaff into her house, till one of the vessels should be discovered, which were known to be hovering on the coast for the purpose of carrying off the fugitives to France. Mrs Landseer readily entered into my proposal, and observed, that the most effectual way in which she could serve this gentleman, was to receive him as if he had been her husband. She added, that none of the servants in her house knew Landseer's person, he having taken with him in his embassy two or three of those that had been longest established in the family. Her house was too small to afford her any means of concealment; but, if she received Sir

---

1 Judge and politician (1593–1671) who supported the parliamentary side in the Civil War.

Joseph in this open manner, it would be impossible for any one to conceive that he was a malignant in disguise. With this proposal then I hastened back to my principal, by whom it was accepted without an instant's hesitation. I was further concerted that Sir Joseph should sleep in the house of a neighbouring tenant, on the pretext that the political differences which had arisen between Mrs Landseer and her spouse, indisposed her, at least for the present, from receiving him with the unreserve and cordiality of a wife.

"This was a busy day with us. Sir Joseph was no sooner installed in his new character, than Captain Croke arrived in pursuit of him, satisfied that he was somewhere in this very neighbourhood. Sir Joseph had just had time to put off his travelling disguise, and to equip himself in the habiliments of the person he represented, which were in the highest style of puritanical formality. Among the many convivial qualities of my patron, one was that he was an admirable mimic; and he assumed the drawl and canting language of a thorough Brownist[1] in such perfection, as upon a less critical occasion would have risqued that Mrs Landseer and myself should have died with laughter. Captain Croke was completely the dupe of the scene. He warmly congratulated the supposed Landseer on his unexpected arrival; asked him many questions respecting the court he had visited, to all which Sir Joseph, who had seen the world, answered with consummate address; and in fine, earnestly enquired how soon he would set out for London, to give an account to his employers of the success his embassy. My principal, who thoroughly enjoyed this scene, and would hardly have been prevented from enjoying it, if he had seen a scaffold prepared for him the moment he quitted it, went on to overact his part. He pressed Captain Croke so earnestly to dine with him, that at last the republican yielded. He said he would first make a circuit of some of the neighbouring mansions, in search of that villain, the rebel commander, and would then return; leaving in the meantime one of his serjeants with us, as security for the performance of his promise.

"Croke had no sooner turned his back upon us, than a courier arrived, with the unwelcome intelligence, that the true Landseer had taken land at Ilfracombe, and might be expected to reach his own dwelling in the course of an hour. The serjeant was luckily in

---

1 Follower of Robert Browne (c. 1550–1633), founder of Separatism, a form of religious Dissent. "Separatists" in this period were synonymous with Independents, who were allied with Cromwell's government.

the stables at the receipt of this message, and was therefore unacquainted with its import. Sir Joseph and I, now thoroughly alarmed, prepared for immediate departure. The conjuncture was portentous. Croke would be back in less than three hours, and would then detect the cheat that had been imposed upon him. The serjeant, if he were a fellow of any adroitness, would discover the trick sooner; and he and the true Landseer would set on foot a pursuit after us, before we had almost commenced our flight. We cursed the hour when we entered this dangerous abode, and still more the ill-timed and ill-indulged humour of Sir Joseph, that had fixed upon us the return of that notorious rebel-hunter, Croke.

"Landseer, however, instead of following his *avant-courier* in an hour, arrived in a few minutes after him, and to our utter confusion entered the parlour, just as we were taking our sad and hurried leave of his wife. The Serjeant had now caught up the intelligence, that another person, claiming to be the owner of the house, had arrived; and, as in duty bound, he entered the parlour at the same time with the stranger, that he might see every thing with his own eyes, and draw his own conclusions. An extraordinary scene ensued. Here were two Mr Landseers, both dressed in the same habiliments, and each asserting his rights as master of the house. The newly arrived demanded, with a haughty and a furious tone, what was the meaning of all he saw? Sir Joseph, with admirable composure, and with the most edifying and saint-like tone and gesture, requested the intruder to moderate his anger, and to quit a dwelling where he had not the smallest right to be found. Mrs Landseer was appealed to, and decided for Sir Joseph as her true husband. After much wrangling and violence, I proposed that the serjeant should retire to the outside of the door for a few minutes, till the dispute was settled. I then desired Sir Joseph to withdraw into the inner room and leave me and my cousin alone with the new-comer.

"This arrangement was no sooner effected, than I lost no time, in laying before Landseer the true state of the case, and imploring his compassion. I told him, that his unexpected guest was no other than the gallant Sir Joseph Wagstaff, who had been totally defeated in his insurrection, was flying before a merciless enemy, and desired no more than to escape with life to his master in France, whose cause was now totally desperate and hopeless. I put it to him as pathetically as I could, whether he could reconcile it to the honourable disposition I had ever known in him, with his own hands to deliver up to the scaffold a gentleman, who claimed the sacred hospitality of his roof. I flattered him for dispositions for which he was not remarkable, that I might wake the embers of humanity in his breast. My cousin joined her intreaties to mine; but he was steeled against all she could say, from anger that, at first meeting after an absence of years, she should have denied that he was her husband. I interposed here. I observed that, Croke's serjeant being present, this was a cruel necessity imposed on the lady, and that, if she had faltered in the least, it would have cost a gentleman his life, who had thrown himself upon her generosity. It fortunately happened, that I had more than once spent some weeks, while quite a boy, under the roof of this Landseer; and had always been his special favourite. He ended therefore with confessing, that he could deny nothing to his old playfellow, who had made him merry a thousand times, when his heart was most a prey to constitutional melancholy.

"The next question was, how my commanding officer could be most effectually screened from his blood-thirsty pursuers. And here I boldly suggested, that no method could adequately answer the purpose, unless that of supporting and carrying through the deception that had already been practised: Sir Joseph must still be affirmed to be the true Landseer. 'And what then am I?' rejoined the republican. 'Consider, my dear Sir,' said I intreatingly; 'it is but for a day; and it is for the life of a gentleman in distress; What good will it do you to take away his life?' 'And what then am I?' repeated my kinsman with impatience. 'Why you, Sir, must personate Sir Joseph.'

"Landseer started back three paces at the proposition. 'And shall I, one of the known champions of the liberties of England, for an instant assume the name, and act the person of one of its destroyers? of a cavalier? of a malignant? of a reprobate? No, Lionel; no consideration on earth shall induce me to submit to such a degradation. Let your general be gone; I will do him no harm; I will use no means for pursuing him.'

"'Do not deceive yourself, sweet kinsman,' rejoined I. 'If you do not protect him, if you do not lend yourself for a few hours to his preservation, you are his destroyer. The infernal Croke is within a short distance; his serjeant is on the other side the door. No earthly power can save us from the tyrant.'

"While I was yet speaking, Sir Joseph opened the door, and came out of the inner room. 'Thank you, Clifford,' said he; 'a thousand thanks to this good lady; I thank you too, Mr Landseer, for as much kindness and forbearance as you have professed towards me. But life is not worth accepting on these terms; I will never disgrace the master whose livery I wear; whether I live or die, it shall be with the gallantry which, I trust, has hitherto marked all my actions. Clifford, call in the serjeant!'

"'No,' replied I. 'For this once I must take upon me to disobey you, Sir Joseph. If this gentleman' pointing to Landseer, 'is inexorable, at least the deed of surrendering you, a stranger, under his own roof, shall be his.' And, as I spoke, I advanced towards the bell, that I might order the serjeant to be called in. 'This is the gentleman,' added I, turning to Landseer for the last time, 'whose head you are by your own act to cause to roll on the scaffold.'

"There is something in the sight of a human creature, upon whom you are yourself called on to pronounce a sentence of death, that produces the most terrible recoil in every human bosom. A man ought to be a judge by his office, that can do this, and then sit down gaily, and with a good appetite, to his dinner. But Landseer had never been a judge. Sir Joseph Wagstaff stood before him. I thought I had never seen so perfect a gentleman, with so frank and prepossessing a countenance, and an air so unassuming and yet so assured, as was presented before me at that moment. The self command, by no means resembling a stoical apathy and indifference, but inspired by an unexaggerated view of all the circumstances, combined with what he felt due to his own honour, that displayed itself in his visage and attitude, was deeply impressive. There was but a moment, a slight articulation of the human voice, that remained between him and death.

"'He shall not die,' said Landseer. 'Do with me as you please. He shall be Landseer; I will be Wagstaff. I have only this morning set my foot on English ground after an absence of years, and my first home-act shall be one, that it may please me at other times, and in the hour of my own agony, to recollect.'

"This capital point being settled, the rest was easy. We called in the serjeant, but for a different purpose than had been spoken of an instant before. Landseer stated to him, that he was in reality Sir Joseph Wagstaff; that, hearing that the master of the house was absent on the continent, and being in the greatest distress for a hiding-place, he had thought this a good opportunity, for prevailing on a lonely female to afford him a brief protection. But all his hopes had been blasted, by finding the master of the house arrived a few hours before him, who was too much devoted to the protectoral government to consent to give him the smallest harbour. He was therefore reduced to make a virtue of necessity; and, delivering his sword into the hands of the officer, he added, 'I am your prisoner; use me well.' The serjeant repeated to him the deceitful cant that had been employed to the other prisoners, and told him that he had nothing to fear, for he would find himself included with Penruddock, in the capitulation that had been made at Southmolton.

"The arrangement of the affair was now in our own hands. Landseer was constituted a prisoner, as Sir Joseph Wagstaff; and we of course took care to secure for him as good treatment as we could. The place of his confinement was a summer-house in the garden, with one centinel, Captain Croke's serjeant, at the door, and another, who was really one of his own servants, beneath the single window of his apartment. This was one of his new houshold: the old servants had remained with his baggage, when he pressed forward on the spur, and had come home alone. Captain Croke speedily arrived from his cruise without any success; but he was transported to find the commanding officer in custody at his return. We sent the prisoner his dinner from his own table; and in the course of the afternoon Captain Croke and Sir Joseph, who, as I before said, was delighted with his talents for mimicry, and who had caught some fresh hints from the brief intercourse he had had with his original, became the best friends in the world. The next day we learned that the vessel we had been in search of was ready; and we embraced the opportunity to depart, while Croke was out for his morning's ride. We took a brief and constrained leave of Landseer, whom Sir Joseph emphatically thanked for his generous self-denial and clemency. I had the pleasure to see my commanding officer safe on board: here my commission ended: I returned straight to my mother, and am therefore unable to tell you how Croke and the ambassador settled their accounts, when the necessity for deception existed no longer."

CHAPTER X

The narrative of Clifford was listened to with great eagerness from all sides. Every one expressed astonishment at the admirable dexterity, firmness and presence of mind which had thus been displayed by a youth of nineteen. Nor were they less struck with the beautiful simplicity with which he related the adventure, rehearsing every thing that passed in the most direct and unaffected manner, and seeming to be himself wholly unconscious of those fine qualities discovered in his own conduct, which every one else contemplated with wonder and delight.

Words cannot express what passed in my mind during this trying scene. I had begun to be virtuous. I had just entered upon a new career. I had found my own frailty in the first encounter of Clifford. I had retired into solitude, and had resolutely engaged in the conquest of this frailty. I possessed that, which divines have described as the most important qualification for a victory over our corrupt nature, a clear perception of my own weakness. The preparation I had thus passed through, appeared to be of the greatest service to me. I sat unmoved, as if I had been a statue hewed out of marble. If painful reflections sometimes obtruded themselves on my mind, as the narrator proceeded from point to point, I suppressed them, with the same austerity which Ulysses manifested, while he listened, in his disguise, to the pathetic complaints of his loved Penelope; of whom the poet says,

> The hero much was moved to see her mourn,
> Whose eyes yet stood as dry, as iron or horn,
> In his untroubled lids.[1]

And when the story was finished, I yet commanded myself sufficiently to join in the general applause. I however soon took an opportunity to withdraw.

My walk was no longer confined to Lord Montagu's park, but plunged me into the wildest parts of the forest. Not like my morning's walk, was my roving after dinner. That had served to tranquillize my tempestuous feelings. It was the presence of Clifford that had then disturbed me; and when I had got beyond the extent of his atmosphere, I appeared to grow calm again. But that was in a moderate and imperfect state of my disease; it was gone beyond that now. The more I thought, the worse I became. I was but half a demon, when I came out at the park gate, and set my first step into the forest. But now my better angel, my new-found virtue, was driven from my side as with a puff of wind; and Mandeville was himself again—the same pernicious creature that the preceding sheets have described him!

---

1 [Godwin's note:] Chapman. [George Chapman (1559–1634) was a Renaissance poet; Godwin refers to his translation of Homer (1616), and to the scene in the *Odyssey* (Book XIX) in which the hero Ulysses (or Odysseus), still wandering the world, returns to Ithaca disguised as a beggar, and observes the attempts of his wife Penelope to ward off the various suitors who are tormenting her in his absence.]

"For what end," said I, "was this story related in my hearing; could not the wretched vanity of this animal have curbed itself for a single day? Must that very point in the kalendar, that brought us once more together—must it also witness this sanguinary insult?

"Yes, yes, I see well enough what was intended. What a contrast between the secretaryship of Mandeville, and the secretaryship of Clifford! Mine was no sooner begun, than it finished: and it is imputed to me, that I withdrew from my duty and my faith, and sheltered myself in ignominious safety. The secretaryship of Clifford was persisted in to the end; and, brief as was its period, it did not conclude without fixing on his brow, now and for ever, the imperishable honours, of an inventive spirit inspired from the heart, a presence of mind that no peril could overawe, and a fidelity that was proof against every danger. Clifford, like myself a mere stripling, and lately my school-fellow, succeeded in leading his principal unhurt through the midst of his foes, saw him in safety on board the vessel that was to bear him to a hospitable shore, and returned to his domestic roof and his fireside, exulting in the consciousness of his heroism and his worth.

"He that does a good and an honourable deed, is worthy of praise. But he that constitutes himself the historian of his own merits, and the puffer of his own worth, is entitled to contempt only. All posterity have shown their sense of that, in the character of Cicero.[1] The oriental sultan, that styled himself 'King of Kings, and Lord of Lords, Emperor of Babylon, Steward of Hell, Porter of Paradise, Constable of Jerusalem, Flower of the Universe, and Cousin to the Great God,'[2] might be a man, robust of frame, and powerful in intellectual resources; but, having thus announced himself before he appeared, how wretched and pitiful a creature, in the eyes of any one of sound judgment, must his person have looked!

"And is Clifford any thing of that extraordinary nature, that he gives him out to be? I repented of my candour of the morning. It is true, his skin is smooth, and the contour of his body is sleek:

---

1   Roman philosopher, politician, and orator (106–43 BCE) who was criticized for his autobiographical poems, *De Consulatu Suo* and *De Temporibus Suis*, in which he sang his own praises.

2   [Godwin's note:] This is literally copied from a record in the Heralds' College, of a letter addressed to King Henry VIII. [The College of Arms, or Heralds' College (founded 1484), is a royal corporation that grants coats of arms and records pedigrees.]

but this is not the index of real salubrity; it is the emblem of that overweening and venomous self-conceit by which he is inflated. I see the insolence of his gait, assumed to trample on all merit, but his own. I see the falseness of his eye, personating all softness, all tenderness, all consideration for another, and then suddenly snatched away in the unfeelingness of triumph, and the congratulation of having well deceived. I see the insidious curl of that lip, that to a discerning eye expresses volumes. The sound of his voice makes me start again with the hollowness and treachery of its cadences. Yes, I feel an instinctive antipathy to the wretch: but it is the voice of God, warning me of my danger; it is founded upon reasons and indications as infallible as the pillars of creation. He has indeed a superficial grace, well adapted to ensnare the thoughtless and unwary, that thinly veils his Satanic soul. But is it not strange, that minds even of moderate discernment, do not perceive what I see so clearly, the hostile gesture that effectually betrays the secret soul? Conspiracy, and that only, can explain the mystery. They see it as plainly as I do; but they bely their senses, and will not own to the truth!"

I recollected Henrietta: Henrietta, that had hitherto seemed to possess the master-key of my soul. But the time was past for that now. My condition was like that spoken of in Job. An attempt had been made to "shut up the ocean-tide with doors."[1] For a moment the object was attained. But the indignant waters roared and chafed, and grew white with portentous foam. At length they burst the bounds that would have confined them, and bore away every impediment.

> Swept with them houses, herds, and flocks,
> And trees entire, and broken rocks,
> Making the woods and mountains roar.[2]

Such was the present condition of my soul. It was a vehement and a terrible effort that I had made, to suppress my nature, to substitute mildness for my native ferocity, to be kind, and forbearing, and benign, when it was my nature's hint to be restless, and stubborn, and dark of soul; and, in proportion to the exertions that it had cost me, was the vehemence of the recoil, when

---

1 Job 38:8.
2 [Godwin's note:] Horace, by Sir Richard Fanshaw, Book iii, Ode 29.
[Quintus Horatius Flaccus, Roman poet of the first century BCE, translated by Fanshaw in 1652.]

the bough that had been bent was constrained no longer. Philosophy, how specious is thy name, and how mighty thy vaunts! Preach it to a man at his ease; and he will think that you have furnished him with a machine framed for all occasions, and an engine, such as Archimedes boasted of, that might move a world.[1] But the passions of the human mind laugh at philosophy; and the events that the course of affairs brings forth to torture us, render its boasts as impotent, as the menaces of a man that had lost the use of his limbs.

I said that I wanted a friend; and I defined a friend to be, "he to whom I can bear to speak, and whom I can bear to hear." Why could not Henrietta be my friend? She could speak with eloquence divine; and I could bear to hear her; and, while she spoke, my soul became her prisoner, and all her accents had over me the power of enchantment. But, unfortunately, the converse of the proposition totally failed. I could not speak to her in return. I pined for her approbation. It will hereafter sufficiently appear that I could do things that would excite her discontent. But I could not speak them. No; nor could I have acted them in her presence, with the chance, that in doing so I might glance the expressive lines of her countenance, and that the beam of her resistless eye might be bent upon me. How then could I premeditatedly lay bare my bosom in her sight, and expose all its blackness and deformities? My reasons, while they passed before me in tremendous array in my solitudes, and I dwelt upon them in all the fervours of an agitated spirit, were unanswerable: but, oh! I know well enough what judgment she would pronounce; I had a secret inspiration that lighted me in to her soul, and showed me, or ever I spoke, how she would censure my crimes, or, which was worse, despise my weakness. My lips therefore were, in this regard, for ever closed in her presence; and, in a question of such vital importance, I had no benefit from her love.

One thing I determined on,—that I would see Clifford no more. The world was wide enough for both of us. Let him, the beggar! hide himself in his hovel; let him keep far from the terrace, where I mean to read! I was in some degree improved, from the latest feelings I experienced at Winchester School. No; I would do him no harm! I retained still so much of Henrietta's philosophy. The world was stored with a thousand blessings! The

---

1 Archimedes of Syracuse (c. 287–212 BCE) was a Greek mathematician, engineer, and inventor who made this boast in a letter to the then-ruler of Syracuse.

splendours of prosperity offered themselves to my acceptance. What would not wealth purchase? What might not talents achieve? All I asked was, that Clifford would stand out of my sun. That surely was a small matter. If by fair means he would not yield to this, I might obtain it by force. With the resources which fell to me by inheritance, I might cause him to be kidnapped, and transported to the American plantations.[1] Then I should have elbow-room. Was I not indeed a happy man, since there was but one thing existing on the face of the earth, that offended me, and of which I could not endure the approach?—So idly I reasoned! So little was I aware of the cogs, the sockets, and the teeth, by which the different parts of the social system are connected with each other, and are made to act and react in perpetual succession, and to sympathise to their remotest members!

CHAPTER XI

Having formed my plan, I instantly hastened home. There was no one in the house but a servant. I took pen and paper, and wrote to Henrietta, to say, without assigning any reason for my conduct, that I was going for a few days on a visit to a franklin near Winchester, at whose house I had once been boarded during a fit of illness, while I was at school, and who, having succeeded to the inheritance of a distant relation, had been very importunate with me to spend a few days under his roof, and partake with him in such rural sports as his neighbourhood afforded.

This visit seemed to be of considerable service to me. I studiously accommodated myself to the manners of my host, who, with no small independence and firmness of character, cared little for what was passing among kingdoms and their rulers, was still less acquainted with the refinements of literature, and shut

---

1 There were plantations in New England in the early seventeenth century (notably the Plymouth Plantation, actually intended to provide a haven for Dissenters), and Britain did transport (i.e., deport) criminals to North America from the 1620s until the American Revolution. However, penal transportation to American *plantations* (implied here) is later, and indeed the Transportation Act (which tied transportation to a period of indentured labour) was not passed until 1718. Taking us back to the earliest colonial plantations in Ireland at the beginning of the novel, the anachronism symptomatically links the seventeenth century and Godwin's own time within a discourse network of literal and metaphoric slavery that returns in the novel's final sentence.

up his thoughts within that circle to which his station in life obviously destined him. He was hardy and robust from nature and from discipline; and I joined in his exercises from choice, for I persuaded myself that this change would prove the medicine of my mind. When we returned from our pursuits in the fields, he was cheerful, sociable and agreeable. He was not destitute of fancy, though this faculty within him was unmoulded and uninstructed by any rule. Whatever he had once seen, he seemed to have considered with no unobservant eye, and he could describe with accuracy, vivacity and humour. This was the more amusing to me, because it had all the raciness of originality, with no spark of imitation in it.

How long this uncultivated scene would have pleased me, I know not. It was totally alien to all my preceding habits, and therefore, I take it for granted, it would not have pleased me long. But for the few days I continued here, I was thoroughly satisfied. I was sick of that fretful and turmoiled existence I had lately experienced, and I sought repose. The fresh feel of the morning air, when we went out with our dogs and our guns, breathed new life into me; and the plenteous board, and the flowing cups, undebauched with rude intemperance, which marked our evenings, seemed the very emblem of cheerfulness. Once or twice we were joined by the rural neighbours of my friend; they came home with us, and each man cracked his joke, and told his tale:— all but myself. The same taciturnity still followed me here, as elsewhere. But they forgave me. They made allowance for the university-man. The less I said, the more room there was for the rest to hear themselves speak. I was inoffensive; I seemed good-humoured; and I was the stranger, whom every one appeared desirous to consider, and to make easy.

What a life was this! Was it possible to pass the whole of the short term of human existence in this tranquil scene? Here no cares appeared to intrude; no vexations to break the midnight slumber; scarcely any thing even to distinguish the events of one day from the events of the next. This seems of all things most exactly to answer to the idea of the poet,[1] of a life spent in dulcet idleness, forgetting all, and by all forgotten, wrapt in happy, yet unenviable obscurity, full of enjoyment, yet leaving no marks behind it that it had ever been.

The night before I quitted the house of my Hampshire farmer, suggested to me the notion, that I had been over sanguine in the

---

1 [Godwin's note:] Horace.

prognostic I entertained of my future tranquillity. I dreamed of Clifford. Long was the scenic controversy in which we were engaged, and various the actors. Henrietta was joined in inflicting on me the torture that distracted my sleeping thoughts. Some charge was made upon me, the particulars of which, after I awoke, I could never exactly recollect, but which had fired my blood, and distended every fibre of my frame. Some misconstruction was made of my words, some foul and calumnious accusation started against me, void of the remotest foundation in truth, but which all the asseverations[1] I could make were ineffectual to remove. I threw myself upon my knees with impassioned vehemence, and uttered the most dreadful imprecations upon myself, if there were a particle of truth in what was alleged against me. My hair seemed to me, as I slept, to stand erect, and my eyes to have their balls enlarged, as ready to burst from their sockets. Scarcely ever, when I was awake, and engaged in the heartappalling realities of life, had I experienced an equally tumultuous commotion of soul.

Such was my dream. It brought me down from the brutish philosophy, and disdainful indifference of spirit, in which for a few days I had indulged. "No," said I to myself, "Clifford is my fate. Present or absent, waking or sleeping, I can never get rid of him. What matters it then, if I were to ship him for Virginia, or banish him to the regions of Japan?[2] He is part of myself, a disease that has penetrated to my bones, and that I can never get rid of, as long as any portion of consciousness shall adhere to the individual Mandeville. If I were to sharpen my dagger's point, and send him to the grave; from the grave he would haunt me, and my crime would prove utterly unavailing. Still I should see him, when I slept; still I should think of him, while I waked; and he would be the unexhausted ingredient, that turned the cup of my existence into poison."

When the next morning I again made my appearance in my farmer's hall, the apartment was no longer the same, and the air of the persons I saw in it was wholly altered in my eyes. The farmer bade me good-morrow; but I had no spirits to return his salute. The dogs bounded into the room, and fawned upon me.

---

1 Claims.
2 There were indentured labourers in Virginia (white and black) from 1616 onwards, who worked in the tobacco plantations, and Virginia was a major recipient of transported convicts. But once again, this occurred in large numbers only later.

Oh, how loathsome to my changed soul was every thing I saw! I was astonished at myself that I could for a moment have been made the dupe of such idiot avocations. I took a hasty and a melancholy leave of my host; and turned my horse's head once more to the village of Beaulieu.

I saw Henrietta. She immediately remarked my haggard eye, my pallid cheek, and my altered demeanour. She marked it, but she made as if she marked it not. Most judiciously she refrained, from saying a single word of Clifford, and from offering at the smallest inquiry respecting my abrupt departure and my sudden return. Clifford, whose visit it was originally purposed should be a short one, had departed before I came back. Henrietta conceived that the wisest thing she could do, was to engage my attention with some indifferent subject. She had just been reading Sir Walter Raleigh's Narrative of his First Voyage to Guiana; and she asked me what I thought of it. We both of us agreed, that this statesman and philosopher was one of the most extraordinary and illustrious characters, that our native island had produced. Yet, how reconcile the narrative of his first voyage, with the contents of the second; the splendid description of the kingdom and city of Manoa, equal in magnificence to any thing that oriental imagination had ever figured, and that was to be found in the centre of the South American continent,[1] with the poor story of a mine to be opened near the mouth of the river Oronooko, that made the subject of his second narrative? Was it to be conceived, that a man of so lofty a genius, and so proud a spirit, would sink himself to the wretched level of a traveller, the deliberate inventor of lies?[2] From Sir Walter we passed to the other mighty men,

---

1 [Godwin's note:]   The yet unspoiled
                        Guiana, whose great citie Geryon's sons
                        Call El Dorado
                              MILTON.
   [Godwin is referring to *Paradise Lost*, 11.409–11, where the Archangel Michael shows Adam the kingdoms of the earth.]

2 Sir Walter Raleigh (1554–1618): Elizabethan statesman and explorer. In 1595 he led an expedition to Guiana in search of El Dorado, a place of fabled wealth which has never yet been found, and wrote a narrative of the journey which claimed that Manoa was El Dorado. In 1616, in a second quest for El Dorado, he persuaded James I to release him from a thirteen-year imprisonment in the Tower of London to lead an expedition to a goldmine near the Orinoco River in Venezuela. The expedition ended disastrously and Raleigh was beheaded in 1618. The second narrative that Henrietta mentions is probably his *Apologie for his Voyage to*

the ornaments of the reign of Elizabeth, the statesman Walsingham, the philosopher Bacon, the accomplished Sidney, the chivalrous Essex, the patriarch of luxuriant description and fancy Spenser, and, more than all, the omnipotent Shakespear.[1]

I found Henrietta almost equally well-informed upon all these subjects; and her unerring judgment was, if I may so express myself, so beautifully relieved by the *naiveté* of her language, and the originality of her remarks, that the whole constituted an inexhaustible spring of amusement and delight. Yes; Henrietta was all, and more than all, she ever had been. But, oh, I was no longer the same, as when I paid my first visit to Beaulieu! Henrietta did not now possess the same unlimited power over me as at first. She could not, or, if she could, it was for very short intervals, make herself the despotic mistress of my faculties, and carry me away from all my recollections, my associations, and my griefs. I had not then seen Clifford. Now, wherever I went, I had still the head of the fatal arrow sticking in my breast, that throbbed and smarted and rankled within me, and from time to time occasioned me paroxysms of indescribable anguish.

But Henrietta was a physician, the ardour of whose attentions no discouragement could quell. She plied me from day to day with interesting topics and cheerful discussions. She considered me in fact, as a person whose intellectual health had unfortunately been shaken, and who stood in need of a peculiarly delicate and forbearing treatment, to restore him to that constancy which the vicissitudes of human life might require. She discarded that more frank and direct mode of proceeding which she had at

---

Guiana (not published until 1650). Henrietta's evocation of Raleigh alongside Bacon and Sidney keeps him in a literary Arcadia removed from real history: one whose darker underside is evident in her brother's recent reference to American (tobacco?) plantations. For not only did Raleigh, who held estates in Munster, participate in the suppression of the 2nd Desmond Rebellion in Ireland (1579–83), he also carried his project of an English settlement in Munster over to Virginia in 1584 and is credited with developing a taste for tobacco in England.

1   Of the eminent figures mentioned here, Sir Francis Walsingham (1532–90) was Elizabeth's Chief minister and secured the execution of Mary Queen of Scots in 1587. Sir Philip Sidney (1554–86), son-in-law of Walsingham and author of *Arcadia* (1590), was the son of Sir Henry Sidney, twice Lord Deputy of Ireland during the reign of Elizabeth I, who suppressed the first Desmond Rebellion. Edmund Spenser (1552–99), author of *The Faerie Queene* (1590–96), was involved in suppressing the 2nd Desmond Rebellion and, like Raleigh, was given lands in the Munster Plantation.

first adopted, and now sought to cure me, less by remedies immediately applied to the source of the disease, than by diverting my
attention to indifferent objects. In the execution of this plan she
had considerable success. I grew every day less disturbed in my
thoughts, and gradually exhibited a degree of serenity, which did
great credit to her skill.

CHAPTER XII

For some time after my return, I absented myself from Lord
Montagu's, and even felt a repugnance to all society beyond the
circle of our own cottage. When about a week had elapsed,
Edward and Ralph Montagu called one morning together at the
cottage, and pressed me and my sister to dine with them that day.
They particularly talked in raptures of a young Marquis de
Gevres, who had just arrived from France, and was now on a visit
at their father's house. He had been introduced to them as the
perfect paragon of the court of the young king (Louis XIV), who
had lately been declared major, had gone through the solemnity
of his coronation, and had made his first campaign in Flanders.[1]
They swore to us that he was the most elegant young man, with
the most graceful carriage, and the easiest and gayest conversation they had ever seen. To this they added, that he had an
uncommon nobleness of air, and that the good sense of his observations upon every thing that he had heard or seen, was altogether wonderful. Henrietta joined in their importunity that I
would accept the invitation. I was myself not without an inclination to comply. The Marquis de Gevres spoke French only. But
we were none of us to seek in that accomplishment. I had always
possessed a peculiar facility in learning languages, and had taken
care at Oxford to supply myself with an excellent master. In my
distempered state of mind, I felt as if I were sick of "the old familiar faces," and wanted a certain infusion of novelty, to restore me
to a fresh and robust habit of soul.

---

1 Louis XIV (1638–1715), King of France from 1643, was declared to
   have reached the age of majority in 1651 (when he was thirteen), but
   assumed personal rule only in 1661 on the death of Cardinal Mazarin.
   His first campaign in Flanders, which was the scene of a long struggle
   between France and Spain, was in 1654, after which France made an
   alliance with Cromwell against Spain, ending in Spain's defeat in 1658.
   The recent 1654 date suggests that we are still in the year 1655.

The Marquis by no means disappointed the expectation, which the two young noblemen had excited respecting him. Lord Montagu gave a dinner to the persons of highest rank and fashion in the vicinity of the Forest, with a view to produce in his distinguished guest as advantageous an idea as he was able, of the gentry of England. The Marquis himself was accompanied by two of his equals in rank and age from his own country. The company that sat down to dinner consisted of nearly twenty persons.

After various enquiries respecting the king of France, and the cardinal, and the Prince of Condé, and Monsieur Turenne, to all of which the Marquis answered in the most intelligent manner, some one turned the conversation to the exiled family of England.[1] That topic was a melancholy one. The court of Versailles had for years been engaged in the civil war, known by the name of the *Fronde*;[2] the young king was repeatedly expelled from his capital, and made thoroughly acquainted with the discipline of adversity. The ministers had been involved in the greatest embarrassments, and driven to much difficulty to support the little shadow of their pageantry. They had been able therefore to do little or nothing to support the house of Stuart. The Marquis however spoke with the greatest attachment of the members of that house. King Charles, he said, was a young man of infinite vivacity and wit, and bore his misfortunes with a gallantry to which no words could do justice. The Duke of York[3] was a person of unquestioned bravery; and the sobriety and sedateness of his manner gained him a thousand friends. He next spoke of the

---

1   Cardinal Jules Mazarin (1602–61) was Chief Minister during Louis XIV's minority. Louis II de Bourbon, Prince de Condé and Henri, Vicomte de Turenne were French generals. Charles II had lived in exile in France until July 1654, when he left in anticipation of France's more cordial relations with Cromwell.

2   Reference to the civil wars (1648–52) in which *parlements* and nobles challenged an emergent royal absolutism in France. The word *fronde* means sling, a weapon that Parisian mobs used to break the windows of Mazarin's supporters. Unlike Charles I, Louis XIV triumphed over his enemies, and the divine right of kings prevailed in France until the French Revolution (1789). But as against insular readings of Britain's history that see her as having overcome the dissensions of the seventeenth century, this chapter, with its emphasis on the troubles in France, puts Britain back into a more global history where those conflicts still remain unresolved in Godwin's own time.

3   The future James II (1633–1701), King from 1685 until he was deposed in 1688.

widowed queen and her only surviving daughter. King Charles and his brothers, he said, had often been reduced to pecuniary straits; but the queen dowager, particularly at one time, was in the most lamentable condition. He remembered an instance, in which he had himself been commissioned to wait on her in the depth of winter, when she received him in a room without a fire, and confessed that her daughter, the princess Henrietta,[1] then about nine years of age, (afterwards the resplendent Duchess of Orleans) was still in bed, that being found the most convenient way, for fuel they had none, of maintaining in her the requisite animal warmth.

The conversation of the Marquis fixed the attention of every one present. No person now uttered a word, unless for the purpose of asking him a question, and exciting him to be more copious in his communications. Lord Montagu had chosen his company so well, that the circumstance of the French language being our sole medium of intercourse, produced no inconvenience to any. We were all of us, before, well affected to the royal cause; but so interesting was the picture that was made by the Marquis, of the different members of the family that had a claim of right to the throne of England, that every one became more a royalist, as he spoke.

Having satisfied our enquiries on these subjects, the marquis proceeded to talk of our present chief magistrate, the lord protector of England. He abhorred him as a regicide, and he despised him, as having, in his estimate, none of the qualities which constitute a gentleman. He deplored however the way in which he had succeeded in corrupting individuals, among the most seemingly zealous adherents of the royal cause, so that no one scarcely knew how to trust his nearest ally, and all were surprized to find Cromwel in some manner or other apprised of their most secret consultations. He particularly mentioned the recent case of Manning, who had been confided in with the utmost security; but who was detected in a correspondence with the protector's secretary, Thurloe, and had been condemned accordingly in Germany to be shot, by the sentence of a council of war.[2]

---

1 Henrietta (1644–70), fifth child of Charles I.
2 Henry Manning, son of a Royalist colonel, turned out to be a double agent in the pay of John Thurloe, secretary to the Council of State under Cromwell. When he was found out as a mole in 1655 he was shot by the Royalists in Cologne, Germany, where Charles was then in exile.

The Marquis de Gevres seemed himself to be well acquainted with the counsels of King Charles. He had seen the Earl of Rochester and Sir Joseph Wagstaff, a few days before they took their passage to England, for the purpose of countenancing and forwarding the insurrection projected by Penruddock and others. He mentioned a very dangerous scheme of which he had received information, that had been plotted for the purpose of making Cromwel master of the consultations of the insurgents here, as he was already, through Manning, acquainted with the leading particulars of what passed at the little court of king Charles at Cologne. He said, it was well known, that a youth of seventeen, of one of the first families in Great Britain, though he could not recollect his name, had had the baseness to submit to be made a tool for this purpose. He had been introduced to the commander of the western army for the purpose of being appointed secretary to the expedition; and, had it not been for the vigilance and caution of Sir Joseph Wagstaff and Lord Bellasis, this infernal design would have succeeded.—

It was speedily perceived by my zealous friends, the Montagus, what course the disquisition of the Marquis de Gevres was taking, and they hastened to interrupt him. Several of the persons present were aware of my unfortunate adventure in Penruddock's army, and a considerable degree of confusion took place in the company. It may easily be imagined what I felt.

The good Lord Montagu himself, with the utmost promptness, entered into my vindication. He told the Marquis, that the young gentleman whom he had so hastily censured, was one of the present company, as he, the Marquis, would probably have observed, had he not, as he had just mentioned, forgotten the name of the person against whom he had pointed his accusation.

Lord Montagu then turned to me. He said, he was sincerely grieved that such harsh and ungentleman-like terms had been applied to me in my presence; but added that, if I reasoned justly on the circumstances, I should rather be disposed to count it fortunate, as it afforded him an opportunity of amply clearing the misapprehension, which had in some way been entertained respecting my conduct. Lord Montagu then assured the Marquis de Gevres, that I had always been well disposed towards the royal cause, that my father had fallen in the service of the late king in Ireland, and that the whole of the story to which his guest had alluded, was a mere question of priority of appointment between me and another young gentleman, my competitor, and by no means implied the slightest reflection on my loyalty, which was unquestioned. He further requested the Marquis upon his return, to clear up this mistake to king Charles, and to assure his majesty, upon his authority, and that of one or two other persons of distinction at the table, to whom he pointed, of my unshaken fidelity and generous devotion to the royal cause.

The foreigner was profuse in the expression of his regrets to me, for the offence he had unwarily committed. He assured me, that nothing could give him sincerer pleasure than the distinguished testimony which had that day been borne to my honour: and he hoped it would not be long, before I should give him an opportunity of proving in his own country the particular esteem he entertained for me; and he trusted, that from that day I would confer on him the favour of admitting him into my friendship. He added, that he would make a point of seizing the earliest opportunity of reporting what he had that day heard, to my Sovereign, to whom, and to some of whose confidential servants, he saw that my character had been much misrepresented.

Some men in my situation would perhaps have been well satisfied, with the generous vindication of Lord Montagu, and the ample apology of the Marquis. It has been seen what an effect the same accusation had produced upon me, when uttered by the son of Sir Charles Lisle. It was then delivered obscurely, in the brown and unornamented apartment of a college student, with no creature near, except him who spoke, and me who heard. The same story was now repeated, in the sumptuous hall of a revered peer of Great Britain, before some of the first personages of the country, and by a nobleman of France, who had been introduced to me as the adequate representative of that illustrious kingdom. Why was this? What had I done? Was I that loathsome and detested thing, an informer? Had I sold myself to the destroyer of my country? For ever had I been the votary of truth. The solitariness of my first education had entailed on me the most unsuspecting simplicity and singleness of character. I can scarcely recollect that once in any instance I had averred a falsehood, except when, moved by the intreaties and agony of Waller, I generously took his offence upon myself. I was not prepared therefore to be the victim of calumny, and to lie for ever oppressed under a mountain of malignant forgeries.

But, it will be said, I was no sooner accused on the present occasion, than my character received the most ample vindication. Alas! vindication in these cases partakes of the same qualities, that Homer ascribes to prayer. Slander,

Strong, and sound of feet,
Flies through the world, afflicting men:[1]

but vindication, lame, wrinkled and imbecile, for ever seeking its
object, and never obtaining it, follows after, only to make the
person in whose behalf it is employed, more completely the scorn
of mankind. The charge against me would be heard by thousands; the vindication by few. Wherever vindication comes, is not
the first thing it tells of the unhappy subject of it, that his character has been tarnished, his integrity suspected, that base
motives and vile actions have been imputed to him, that he has
been scoffed at by some, reviled by others, and looked at askance
by all? Yes; the worst thing I would wish to my worst enemy, is
that his character should be the subject of vindication. And what
is the well known disposition of mankind in this particular? All
love the scandal. It constitutes a tale that seizes upon the curiosity of our species; it has something deep, and obscure, and mysterious in it; it is whispered from man to man, and communicated
by winks, and nods, and shrugs, the shaking of the head, and the
speaking motion of the finger. But vindication is poor, and dry,
and cold, and repulsive. It rests in detections, and distinctions,
explanations to be given to the meaning of a hundred phrases,
and the setting right whatever belongs to the circumstances of
time and of place. What bystander will bend himself to the drudgery of thoroughly appreciating it? Add to which, all men are
endowed to a certain degree with the levelling principle, as with
an instinct. Scandal includes in it, as an element, that change of
fortune, which is required by the critic from the writer of an epic
poem, or a tragedy. The person respecting whom a scandal is
propagated, is of sufficient importance, at least in the eyes of the
propagator and the listener, to be made a subject for censure. He
is found, or he is erected into, an adequate centre of attack; he is
first set up as a statue to be gazed at, that he may afterwards be
thrown down, and broken to pieces, crumbled into dust, and
scattered to all the winds of heaven.

It was sufficiently observable, even according to the admission
of the Marquis de Gevres himself, that king Charles, and some of
his confidential servants, had already formed their sentiments
respecting me. Should I stoop to the misery of being set right in
their opinion? What a prologue was this, to the "swelling theme"

---

1 Untraced.

of imperial ambition![1] The meanest creature that lives, is entitled to set out in the drama of life unblown upon, and, if unrecommended, at least left to work out his way in the intricacies of human society, according to his faculties and his inherent resources. My character was blotted in England; it was blotted in France. My countrymen had heard ill of me at home; my king, and his generous followers in exile, had received that impression of me abroad. The same bitter thoughts returned to me, that had attended upon my first hearing this unmerited reproach at Oxford. "If I take the wings of the morning," said I, "and dwell in the uttermost parts of the sea," this calumny shall pursue me! "If I say, surely the darkness shall cover me, behold, the night shineth as the day, and the darkness and the light are both alike!"[2]

It has already been seen, that all the agony and passion that I suffered from the diversified circumstances that persecuted me, terminated in Clifford. In the present conjuncture I said within myself a thousand times, It is enough on any occasion for Clifford to be interposed, to render life a burden to me too great to be endured. I never knew what misery was, till I met him at Winchester. How often and how deeply on that spot did he cause me to drink of the cup of agony! I left Winchester, and was again at peace—till in fatal hour he crossed me again in my excursion into Wiltshire. And now these busy Montagus, and the officious Henrietta, the moment I had obtained an interval of tranquillity, put themselves forward, forsooth! to effect a reconciliation between us. Yes, such reconciliation there shall be, as between fire and gunpowder, or between the tiger and the lamb! Might they not have been contented with things as they were, without interposing this ill-omened mediation? Had I not already gone mad for Clifford? Was not this the man, for whose sake I had undergone whips and chains, a dark chamber and ignominious cords? Had he not by his machinations reduced me to the condition of a beast? Oh, yes, it was a precious invention, that I should meet this man in peace, should return him smile for smile, profess myself his eternal friend, and undertake to walk with him, hand in hand, through the weary pilgrimage of life?

Hatred, bitter and implacable hatred, became now more than ever the inmate of my bosom, I lived but for one purpose, the extinction of Clifford. This was the first object of my existence,

---

1 Adapted from *Macbeth*, 1.3.128–29.
2 Adapted from Psalms 139:9, 11–12.

the preliminary, the *sine qua non*[1] of all my other pursuits. I devoted myself to this end, as Hannibal,[2] by the instigation of his father, at nine years of age, swore upon the altar of his country, deadly and eternal enmity to the Romans. If, from this time forward, any creature that lived addressed to me one syllable in favour of Clifford, that creature, be his claims upon me in other respects whatever they might, entered into the fief[3] of my abhorrence, and became included in the savage sentence of his extermination. On other subjects I might have a heart of flesh, I might be accessible to tender and humane feelings; but on this I was the iron man,[4] with ribs of steel, described by Spenser: no compunction, no relenting, no intreaty, no supplication could approach me: I was deaf as the uproar of conflicting elements, and unmelting as the eternal snows that crown the summit of Caucasus.[5]

CHAPTER XIII

It was at this time that I received a summons to the house of my uncle. A letter was addressed to me by the steward, the person through whom all communication from that quarter reached me. The present letter however was entirely confidential, and the good man spoke in it purely from his own feelings and apprehension! He informed me "that my uncle's health was visibly in a declining state," and observed that, "from the extreme frailty of his frame, and delicacy of his constitution, it might be expected that, when he was once going, it would be all over with him very rapidly." My old friend added, "that he held it to be the more his duty to give me suitable advertisement on the present occasion; as, to his great mortification and surprise, there was a new comer, totally a stranger till now at Mandeville House, who had lately

---

1 Indispensable condition; literally "without which nothing" (Latin).
2 Celebrated general (247–c. 182 BCE) who led the Carthaginians against Rome in the Second Punic war.
3 An estate held on condition of feudal service.
4 Talus in Book V of Spenser's *The Faerie Queene*, who is the hatchet-man of Artegall in what is often seen as an allegory of the subduing of Ireland.
5 A mountain range where Prometheus was chained to a rock by Zeus as punishment for giving humankind the gift of fire. Here and elsewhere, Mandeville's identifications with literary characters are deeply contradictory.

established himself a constant visitor, and came there almost every day." This visitor was one Holloway, an attorney, a man of the worst character; "and," continued the steward, "in the way that my poor, dear master is in, knowing nothing of worldly affairs, and seeing nobody, it is surely very alarming, that such a fellow as this Holloway should have his ear, and be able to do with him whatever he pleases." "I know not," proceeded my correspondent, "what he can do—the estate is entailed,[1] and you cannot be deprived of it—but I know, that such a scoundrel as this ought to have no power, and that we cannot too soon be rid of his company."

It may well be supposed, that it was by no ordinary stretch of dexterity, that this Holloway introduced himself to the presence and conversation of Audley Mandeville. Many years had elapsed, since my uncle had seen any one out of the circle of his own family: thus he had lived; and thus he desired to remain, till time should finally close his eyes on all things terrestrial. Holloway had duly considered all this, had made every preliminary enquiry, had searched minutely into every circumstance of the Mandeville estate, and finally determined that he would instal himself the confidential adviser of the melancholy Audley.

With this purpose he addressed a letter to my uncle. The contents were drawn up in a professional style. He said that he wrote by the direction of Josiah Hampole, esquire, (a vulgar and conceited Roundhead, who had lately taken possession of an estate about seven miles from Mandeville House) "to announce that, in looking into the writings of the estate, he had found that he had a right to the fishery of the coast, for twelve miles upward and downward, and that he had determined to avail himself of this right, as one of the signories of his domain." The letter added, that, "as Mr Hampole was desirous of doing nothing unbecoming by a neighbour of my uncle's consideration, he had given him this previous information, that it might not be imputed to him that he had proceeded in any way by surprise."

This letter, like all others addressed to Audley Mandeville, was opened by Mr Norton, the steward. It had long been considered as one of the functions of his office, to intercept all letters addressed to his master, and to communicate their contents in whole or in part, or to suppress them altogether, according to his discretion. Happily the Mandeville estate, owing partly to the

---

1 Restriction of property by limiting inheritance to the owner's lineal descendants (usually the eldest son).

antiquity of the claims, and partly to the moderation of the desires of its possessors, had been exempt from all litigation, perhaps for centuries. This letter therefore was of a totally different tenour, from those which usually fell into Mr Norton's hands. He was a good deal puzzled how to proceed in the case. He laid it before Mr Tomkins, the official solicitor to the Mandeville property; and they jointly consulted what was to be done. Mr Tomkins was just such a solicitor as might be expected to an estate wholly unknown to litigation. He could draw (that is, transcribe) a lease, and talk, very technically, and very sapiently,[1] upon subjects that fell within his every day's experience. But he had never heard of this fishery. He went home, and looked at his books, and returned that day week, exactly as wise as when he last quitted Mandeville House. It was however determined between him and the steward, that my uncle should be allowed to know nothing of the matter. Tomkins in the meantime made some enquiries respecting Mr Hampole, with the hope that the matter might be amicably accommodated, but found, to his utter dismay, that that gentleman had just set out upon a journey into Scotland. No notice therefore of any sort was taken of the letter that had been received.

Mr Holloway, having waited what he thought a sufficient time, one morning mounted his horse, and turned the head of the animal towards Mandeville House. He rode up to the great gate of the mansion, and had already tried by a variety of noises to rouse its lethargic inhabitants, when at last a rustic servant-maid appeared, who told him that, if he desired to gain admission, he must ride round to the postern. Having done so, and with an air of much importance announced that he wanted to see Mr Mandeville, he was ushered into the steward's room.

"My business is with Mr Mandeville," said Holloway.

"May be, you are a stranger in these parts," replied the steward, "and do not know that my master sees nobody."

"My name is Holloway; I come on business from the beloved in the Lord, Josiah Hampole; and I must see thy master."

The very communication by which Mr Holloway intended to strike his hearer with awe, produced exactly the opposite effect. Though Mr Norton and his privy-counsellor had returned no answer to the letter that had been received, it had however induced them to inform themselves more fully respecting the character of the writer; and they had had no difficulty in learn-

---

1 Knowledgeably.

ing, that he was an accomplished scoundrel, and the disgrace of his profession. Poor Norton had never suffered under the talons of the law, either for himself or his employers, and therefore did not feel the proper degree of respect for such a gentleman as now stood before him.

"Give me leave to tell you once for all, Mr Holloway," replied the steward, "you will never see my master as long as you live. He never does any business; and therefore, if you have any thing of that sort to treat upon, your best way is to communicate it to me."

"I shall never see your master as long as I live! Now I tell you—and mind what I say—I will see him, and talk to him in person, before either of us is a fortnight older. In the meantime you may tell him—or you may let it alone, if you please,—that I come to him once more on the part of Josiah Hampole. And, what is more, I come as a friend, and might perhaps have settled the business for him as a friend, if he would have heard me. Good morning to you, sir!"

Finding the difficulties that had thus far intercepted his progress, Holloway determined to proceed by a *coup de main*.[1] It would not have answered his purpose to have entered into a negociation with any one but my uncle in person. Three mornings therefore had not elapsed after the visit I have described, before a number of boats arrived off the coast, at the nearest practicable point to the windows of Mandeville House, and with them a very considerable quantity of planks and workmen, seemingly for the purpose of constructing huts for the fishermen who were henceforth to be stationed there. There was a creek and a landing-place near, sufficiently convenient for the accommodation of a few fishing-boats. Care appeared to be taken, that the greatest possible noise and disturbance should attend this invasion of the family-estate.

Yet, from the description I afterwards obtained of the affair, I should have thought Holloway's measures very inadequately calculated to obtain the purpose he had in view. The event however proved, that he had considered the matter more judiciously than I should have done. His fishermen and labourers were at a considerable distance from the house; and whatever clatter and vociferation they made, would, to most men's ears, have died away before they reached the mansion. The waves of the sea for ever beat against the rock upon which the house was built; the sound

---

1 A stroke of the hand.

of the dashing waters was eternal, and would have been very annoying and very depressing to any one that was unaccustomed to it. But my uncle, more than almost any human being that lived, was the creature of habit. The dashing of the waves, no less than the pulsations of the heart, was necessary to his existence; silence in this particular would have been as awful and distressing to him, as the invasion of an enemy, or the firing of a thousand cannon. This monotonous and hoarse voice of the waters however, was the only sound that ever entered the ears of Audley Mandeville. Double doors and matted galleries cut him off from the knowledge, through that organ, of the existence of his family. Every one about him was aware of his infirmity, and respected it; and the falling of a pin unexpectedly, would have created a sensation through the whole houshold of this venerable mansion. Audley was master of the entire territory, as he believed, for miles around; and, had it been necessary, which it never was, he could have suspended any process or operation that had been going on, by the turn of his finger.

My uncle therefore was exceedingly surprised, and beyond measure disturbed, by the sounds, which a coarse ear perhaps would hardly have adverted to, so distant was their source, that assaulted his auditory nerves. The unloading the planks, and casting them successively on the shore, was attended with considerable clash. It was something like what Homer describes, of the preparations for the funeral of Patroclus.

> Loud sounds the axe, redoubling strokes on strokes;
> On all sides round the forest hurls her oaks
> Headlong. Deep-echoing groan the thickets brown;
> Then, rustling, cracking, crashing, thunder down.[1]

My uncle rang his bell; and a servant entered. Poor Norton had been sufficiently aware of the confusion that was about to take place, and had hastened with the earliest intimation of what was going on, to the scene of this unhallowed industry. He found only the workmen, with a master-carpenter superintending them. He enquired respecting the meaning of what he saw. The answer he received was, that they were there by the direction of Mr Holloway. "Where was Mr Holloway?" "He was not there: perhaps he

---

1 From Pope's translation (1715–20) of Homer's *Iliad*, Book 23. Patroclus, friend and companion of Achilles, was slain by Hector during the Trojan War.

would be in the course of the day; perhaps not." The carpenter showed to the steward the plan of the range of huts, that was to be erected for the accommodation of the fishermen. Mr Norton expostulated. He told the man, there must be some mistake, and required him to suspend his operations, till Holloway should arrive, and the error be cleared up. The carpenter was exceedingly sorry, if what he was about should be found offensive to a gentleman, who had so long honoured the country with his residence among them; but his orders were peremptory. He offered to attend the steward to the great house, and make any explanation and atonement in his power; and this offer was accepted.

Norton was no sooner returned home, than he met the footman, who told him that his master wanted to see him immediately. The poor fellow added, that Audley was in a most alarming state, sometimes almost raving at the invasion that was taking place, and at other times subsiding into a fit of insupportable despair. Norton entered his apartment alone. My uncle pathetically, in the mildest, but the most earnest manner, intreated to know what all this meant, reproached the steward for suffering such a mischief to come upon him without any previous notice, and desired, that it might be removed with the utmost possible diligence. The steward was now obliged to detail to his master, what had passed between him and Mr Holloway, in the letter and visit that gentleman had addressed to Mandeville House. He said, he could not in any way understand the pretensions that had been set up: he had consulted Tomkins, who was no less in the dark than himself. Hampole, the claimant was in Scotland; therefore he had not entertained the smallest apprehension that any immediate measures would be adopted. And he concluded, as the speediest remedy, with offering to raise the tenantry, and drive by main force the invaders from the ground they had occupied by surprise. My uncle would not hear of this. He saw, that the remedy would be worse than the disease, that he should be immediately placed in the midst of a scene of tremendous confusion, and that it was impossible to foresee where a transaction, commenced with force and arms in this manner on both sides, would terminate.

Audley Mandeville, except in one single instance, where he had been forced into contention with his own father, had never, from the hour of his birth, been engaged in so much as a debate with any living creature. He took it for granted, that Hampole must have some pretensions to the right he appeared to claim in so summary a way; and he was aware that to settle such a claim by process of law would be a tedious affair. He therefore saw no safety, but in flight. He had three or four other houses, delightfully situated, in different counties of England; and he must take refuge in one of these.

This however would be a wearisome process. There was not one of them, that would not require various alterations and improvements, to adapt them to his particular habits. Then what an undertaking was it, for such a man as my uncle, to remove! The life he had led for more than twenty years, was less that of an animal, than a vegetable. He had constantly been surrounded with the same objects. He had not gone out of his chamber, or put on his shoes. The very roaring of the ocean, as I have said, and the dashing of the waters, were no less necessary to his existence, than the pulsations of the heart.

Such were the incidents of the first day of Mr Holloway's campaign. On the morning of the second day, a new fleet of boats arrived, and a new gang of workmen, to reinforce the operations of the former. My uncle's distress was wrought up to the height. The work had already been proceeding for four hours, when the mighty master of the spell, the great Holloway himself, arrived at our postern. He was immediately received with a reverence and homage, almost amounting to prostration. Every servant of Mandeville House sympathised most sincerely in the agony of the master. The quietness of his temper, and the inoffensiveness of his manner, that gave annoyance to no one, had the effect of causing every one, from the steward to the scullion, to be devoted to his pleasure. They gathered round Holloway: they intreated him to have some consideration for the feelings of their master, and to put an end to the nuisance. They asked him, as if each had been suing to save his father or his brother from capital and ignominious punishment! "Lead me to your master!" was the authoritative and laconic reply.

The character of Audley Mandeville was totally changed by what had now occurred. For some hours you would have looked in vain in him for that lethargy and listlessness of demeanour, for which he had been many years distinguished. The more he thought of removal from his sea-beat dwelling, the more it appeared to be an experiment impossible to be endured. On all sides he saw nothing but despair. This, it might have been expected, would have reduced him to imbecility and helplessness. But every fresh fall of a plank, or shout of the workmen, for the purpose of exactly timing their united effort, smote upon his brain, and convulsed his whole frame. Contrary to the established practice of Mandeville House, the great event that had taken place, the arrival of Mr Holloway, was instantly announced to the chief: and my uncle, stung with desperation, as with a scorpion, desired immediately to see him. Just as the lawyer entered the secluded apartment of the master, a shout and a crash, louder than any that had preceded, seemed to shake the roofs of the mansion; and my uncle fell at once, like a stone, upon his couch.

Holloway instantly dispatched a messenger to stop the operation of the workmen; and by a sort of enchantment, that it may seem difficult to account for, without regard to the laws of time and space, not one sound, of all those which had lately given so much annoyance, was heard, from the moment that the order had passed the lips of the director of the scene. Holloway had now gained the point he aimed at; he stood in the presence of Audley Mandeville; and all else seemed easy to the mastery of his skill.

He began with a profusion of declarations of the sorrow he felt, for having been the innocent cause of any disturbance to the gentleman in whose presence he stood. If he had had the least suspicion that such would be the case, he would have eaten his fingers, or laid down his life, rather than it should have happened. He had just heard something about it accidentally from the carpenter, and had instantly turned his horse to Mandeville House, to set every thing right. If the establishment of the fishery which had been meditated, would be in the slightest degree disagreeable to my uncle, he would undertake for it, upon the forfeit of all the character he had in the world, that it should be for ever given up.

The lying accents of Holloway instilled themselves gently into the ears of Audley, like the wholsome dews into the thirsty and indurated[1] soil. They gradually revived him. He could not believe in his good fortune, that the calamity, which a moment before he had thought it beyond the reach of human powers to remedy, was thus in an instant removed. He was first barely attentive, and then listened with greater and greater eagerness, fearful that his senses should deceive him, or that somehow he did not rightly understand the meaning of the words that were addressed to him.

My uncle said, that he would willingly agree to give any sum of money that should be required of him, to purchase his redemption from an evil, that he was sure would in a short time put an end in the most deplorable way to his existence. Mr Holloway would not be outdone by Mr Audley Mandeville in the display of his generosity. He assured my uncle, that the object he

---

1 Hardened.

desired should never be permitted to cost him a single penny. He would open the question to Mr Hampole; and he flattered himself, that his credit with his client was sufficient to settle the question without difficulty. In the mean time, till he had heard from that gentleman, every operation should be suspended, and the planks should all of them rot on the ground, rather than any annoyance should be complained of, either from their being applied to their original purpose, or even from their removal to the place from whence they came. Mr Holloway was as good as his word. From the hour of his visit, a deathlike silence prevailed in the late active scene of industry. As many of the materials, as had not yet been disembarked, were carried off, without so much as a whisper. The planks that were already on the shore, and it somehow happened that these were extremely few, remained where they fell, a monument of the masterly operations of the attorney. Mr Hampole was found to be an antagonist not less accommodating than his solicitor; and the dispute was settled in the briefest and most satisfactory manner.

It is scarcely necessary to add to the preceding narrative, that Mr Hampole had never heard any thing, from first to last, of the fishery in question. The whole was bred in the prolific brain of Holloway. He took his time, when one of the parties was in Scotland. He relied on the singular character and inaptitude of the other party. He previously informed himself sufficiently of the habits of Norton and Tomkins; and had confidence enough in his own resources, to believe that he should find means to defeat all the skill and activity, that were likely to be brought into the field against him.

CHAPTER XIV

The most extraordinary part of this whole transaction was the complete success of the operator, which reflected immortal glory upon his sagacity and foresight. From this moment Audley Mandeville seemed to have conceived the most singular affection for the person of Holloway. To any other individual this incident of the fishery would have been a momentary vexation only; and, as soon as the evil was removed, the benefit would have been forgotten. Not so with the representative of the house of Mandeville. From the hour that he had become lord of the domain, nothing had happened to contradict his will; and, though his pleasures were few, the pains inflicted on him by others might almost be said to be none. His recollection therefore of this agony of twenty-eight hours, never in the slightest degree decayed in his mind. Add to which, Audley Mandeville, like all other sentient beings, wanted something to love, and felt a vacuity and uneasiness from that want, without being able to account for his pain. The whole affectionate capabilities of his nature had once been centred in Amelia Montfort. She had been suddenly and violently removed from him; and his heart had died at their separation, and been buried in her grave. Since that time, his love can scarcely ever have been said to be excited, except towards myself and my sister. Her he hardly knew by sight; and, as to me, my tender years had disqualified me to be his companion, and there was a savage unsociableness in my nature, that incapacitated me from paying him those insensible attentions, which might in time have conciliated him. Such a gentle being as he was, might seem formed to love and be loved; but his heart was dead in his bosom, and he could never get through the preliminaries of a friendly intercourse. One peculiarity of his history was, that he had never known a benefactor; and, therefore though his obligation to Holloway was slight, or none at all, it did not appear so to him. He could not chaffer[1] with his duties. If the affair had related to another man than himself, he might have been able to calculate the lawyer's motives, and so to reduce his generosity to its proper dimensions; but, upon the present occasion, he took it whole, and did not apply the analysis of distinctions and subtilties to separate its elements. Holloway therefore never came into his presence, but the poor deluded solitary looked up to him like a God. He considered him as a being, who had secured to him the inestimable privilege of sinking quietly and insensibly into his grave. Whenever the name of the scoundrel was announced, it appeared to communicate new life to Audley Mandeville; his countenance assumed a faint radiance of cheerfulness and good-nature; and he said to himself, "Here comes a man, to whom I have contracted a 'debt immense; still paying, still to owe.'"[2]

Holloway had a further hold upon the being whom he destined for his prey. He found out (God knows on what foundation he built the assertion) that his mother was a Montfort. He had the courage to pronounce that talismanic name in the hearing of my uncle, and the skill to do so with success. According to Holloway, there never was a being that bore the name of Montfort,

---

1 Dispute the terms of, bargain over.
2 Satan, resentfully describing his debt to God in *Paradise Lost*, 4.52–53.

that had not something in it above the standard of human excellence; his mother was a paragon of women; and he promised himself, as soon as he should find leisure for the luxury, to part with the name of Holloway, and assume that of Montfort. By degrees the tongue of the dumb man was loosed; the revolutions of the sun that had passed over the grave of his beloved, had something assuaged the sorrows of Audley; and he could now bear to pamper his soul with the repetition of "Amelia." The infatuated lover believed that he had found a sympathetic spirit in the breast of the attorney; and his hard-hearted betrayer seemed to drop tears, while the despairing celibataire descanted on his "whole course of love."

Holloway having made his lodgement good within the fortifications of Mandeville House, had now to consider how best to improve the advantages which his valour had achieved. He meditated no less than to divert the whole property annexed to the name of Mandeville into the house of Holloway. He found no difficulty in excluding the feeble Tomkins, from all participation in the counsels of his employer. He engrossed the ear of Audley exclusively to himself. He possessed himself, as a lawyer should, of all the title-deeds of the Mandeville estate. There was not a scrap of paper or parchment, evidencing the entail and descent of the property, that was not carefully removed from the great house, and duly arranged among the treasures of Holloway's closet.

Thus far it was well; and the ground seemed duly prepared for the achievements that were to follow. It is inconceivable with what art, and by how insensible degrees, Holloway entered upon his great master-stroke, the causing my uncle to sign a will, which with all proper ambiguities, obscurities, and circumlocutions, to veil its real drift, should occasion the main substance of the Mandeville estate, as he would contrive the matter, to descend to the family of Holloway and their heirs for ever; they having first duly assumed the name, style and armorial bearings of the house of Montfort. This will having first been duly executed, the honest attorney was prepared immediately to consign to the flames all evidences of the entail.

I grieve to say, that, with all the masterly management of the accomplished Holloway, he was never able to achieve this favourite purpose. My uncle had a fund of clear understanding, beyond what his able solicitor had calculated upon. He had also a deep and unalterable sense of what he owed to his ancestors that had gone before him, and to their posterity that was to come after him. Audley Mandeville was, as to external appearance, of so quiet and passive a nature, that poor Holloway was utterly deceived, and thought, because his client betrayed no symptoms of dissatisfaction, for these the attorney watched for with the eyes of a lynx, that he drank in all the suggestions that were offered him, as naturally as milk.

This was not the case. Though the limbs and features of my uncle were motionless, his understanding worked. When Holloway drew to the conclusion of an harangue, that might have baffled all the rules of Aristotle[1] to discover a defect in it, and hugged himself upon the profound silence and deference with which it appeared to be received, my uncle refuted it with a single monosyllable—"No." The attorney returned to the charge. He varied the mode of attack. He seemed to set out from a different point, and to drive at a different conclusion. Still the victorious monosyllable, like a warrior clad in the arms of the invulnerable Achilles,[2] came to defeat and put to rout all the forces of this veteran and his art's-master attorney.

Audley Mandeville took his leave of the sagacious Holloway, on the day on which he had broached his grand scheme, with the same mild and complacent tones that had marked his farewels on former occasions. The solicitor congratulated himself. He considered, as he rode home, "It is not so bad as it may seem however. The rich old fogram has not fallen into my snare at once, as I expected. But it is something to have opened the scheme. He has heard it without starting, or one gesture of disapprobation. I am glad I have broken ground upon the subject. Seeing the poor valetudinarian every day, and taking care, as I shall, that nobody else shall see him, it will be hard indeed, if perseverance does not carry the point, which I have failed to gain by surprise."

Holloway was miserably mistaken in his calculations. The proposition of a will that he had made to my uncle, was not forgotten. But the oftener it was thought of, the greater aversion it excited. Audley Mandeville had begun with regarding the solicitor as his only friend; and if Holloway had not taken a step of so unequivocal a character, the illusion would never have vanished

---

1 Greek philosopher (384–322 BCE) who wrote, among other things, an influential treatise *On Rhetoric*.
2 A leader of the Greek side in the Trojan War. As an infant he was dipped in the river Styx by his mother to make him invulnerable (except in the heel, by which she held him).

from his eyes. Nor, as it was, did the change take place at once. My uncle wrestled with the idea that his new lawyer was a villain, as in some sort a want of fealty and faith towards a man to whom he owed so much. The next time he saw Holloway however, he saw him with less pleasure. Poor Audley had a great fund of natural penetration, unaided by experience, though he seldom gave himself the trouble to put it to use. Every time now that the attorney came to him, he discovered in him new indications of a gross and selfish character. His visits, instead of awakening, as they did at first, a gleam of cheerfulness in the heart of his client, gradually changed their nature, and became a disturbance and a burthen. My uncle said to himself in the bitterness of despondence, "I see the truth; I must go out of the world, as I have lived in it, without a friend."

After a due interval, and having interposed abundance of precautions, Holloway ventured once more to allude to the subject of the will. Audley Mandeville shuddered. A slight degree of convulsion disturbed and agitated the features of his face. After a pause, he spoke in a deep, slow and solemn tone of voice.

"Mr Holloway, I am under the greatest obligations to you. I have chosen you for my agent; I have put all my affairs into your hands; I cannot repent that I have done so. But if you mention this proposal again, we are no longer friends."

It was with extraordinary effort, and allowing himself much time between the clause that went before and the clause that succeeded, that my uncle was able to utter these few sentences. Holloway was filled with confusion and alarm. He declared that he was totally misunderstood. He had believed, that it was his client's intention to bequeath him a trifling legacy, in consideration of his having the honour to be descended from the house of Montfort. But, for all that the world could bestow upon him, he would not impair the descent of the estate to Mr Charles Mandeville, the true heir. If my uncle would have the patience to hear the thing over again, he would perceive that he had totally misapprehended it.

More Mr Holloway would have said, had it not been that his client, without uttering another word, rose from his seat, walked out of the room, and shut and bolted himself into his closet. The next time Holloway came, my uncle apologized, and said he was afraid his behaviour had been uncivil. But there was something in his manner, that was the farthest in the world from inviting the lawyer to renew his subject. His carriage was austere, and spoke a recollection of dislike.

My uncle had now one additional displeasure, weaning him from all attachment to the world. He had thrown himself so hastily and unsuspectingly into the hands of Holloway, that he was in a manner his prisoner. Neither yet did he entertain by any means so ill an opinion of the lawyer as he deserved. He retained indelibly in his mind the vast obligation, as he conceived it, that he had received from him. He still felt the fascination, that had been produced in him by his maternal name of Montfort. He recollected, that he had opened to this execrable Holloway, in a way that he had never done to any other living creature, the cherished and sacred emotions of his soul. But what poor Audley Mandeville wanted, was a being in whom he could repose confidence. And the proposal about the will had convinced him once and for ever, that he had not found such a being in Holloway. His feelings about this unshrinking invader of his privacies, were contentious and distressful. Whenever his step was heard in the gallery, for the lawyer had dismissed the ceremony of sending up his name, my uncle called upon himself for a feeling of pleasure, but discomfort came in its stead.

There were times when Audley Mandeville seriously debated with himself, whether it were not better to get rid of the new comer altogether. But his nature did not qualify him for peremptory measures. He feared that there might be consequences attendant on the change, more distressful than the evil that change purposed to remove. The Hampole fishery haunted him by day and by night, and was for ever before his eyes. Might not that pretension be again brought forward, if he ungratefully parted with the man, who had miraculously delivered him from it? Better it seemed, much better, not to disturb what already was well. All that the poor solitary aimed at, or hoped for, was quiet; and quiet he already had. In addition to which, there was nothing that my uncle dreaded more, or for which he was more absolutely incapacitated, than exertion. What an uproar would it produce, equal in his imagination to an anarchy of the elements of nature, to dismiss Holloway, from the situation into which he had intruded himself? Nor, if he were ever so much inclined, had my uncle a friend in the world to help him in the arduous achievement.

But what added the last bitterness to the calamity I am describing, was the perennial flow of Holloway's eloquence. My poor old tutor, copious as had been his rhetoric whenever he addressed any other individual, became a mere Spartan, almost a

Pythagorean,[1] in the presence of Audley Mandeville. For twenty years my uncle had never witnessed the birth of a sentence of more than six or eight words. This misfortune, as it regarded Holloway, was little adverted to in the beginning. The melancholy recluse had first seen the solicitor of Hampole, under a peculiar exaltation of soul, and as the bearer of tidings scarcely less joyful, than if he had been a winged messenger from heaven. Audley could hear, and Audley could even speak himself, on that memorable occasion. Then came the lawyer's master-stroke, the claim of kindred with Amelia Montfort. That had acted upon the recluse like witchcraft. The dumb man learned to talk; and he who had been silent as a corpse laid out for the funeral, on all points in which his feelings were concerned, began to unfold the secrets of his soul in the ears of a stranger.

But that fit was temporary. The topic even of Amelia was at length exhausted, and my uncle felt that he had unburthened his heart. The host relapsed into silence; and the stranger found room to display his habitual garrulity. While he was engaged in what seemed the necessary explanations about the fishery, and when he dwelt upon the virtues that attended upon the very name of Montfort, my uncle did not repine. But, when, failing these, he spoke of ordinary and indifferent topics, of the many contentious suits in which he had been employed, with all their bad passions and quirks, and of the private history of the various families in the neighbourhood, then the trial came. In this only the usual policy of the solicitor deserted him. Circumspect and cunning he was in all other respects, to the utmost extent of sublunary perfection. But he had this frailty, marking him for a descendant of our mother Eve, that he "tied his ear to no tongue but his own," and so unaffectedly admired his talent for narration, in which he did not suspect that Livy[2] himself could excel him, that all symptoms of weariness and aversion in his hearer were thrown away, and passed wholly unheeded by him. Till now, Audley Mandeville had been surrounded by persons that owed him implicit deference: but he had met Holloway in the first instance as a benefactor, and with overwhelming gratitude; and it is astonishing what airs of independence and equality were upon this circumstance assumed by the attorney. Nor was this alto-

---

1   Adjectives connoting restraint and self-discipline in utterance, both derived from classical Greece.
2   Roman historian Titus Livius (59 BCE–17 CE).

gether without design. Holloway purposed to make himself necessary to his client, and in a certain sense to hold him in awe.

Nor was it merely the endless stream of Holloway's eloquence, that proved deadly to his auditor. Audley Mandeville was a being of elegant taste and great intellectual refinement. The world is full of deformities. Many things in it are squalid, many are loathsome, many are shameless, profligate and monstrous. He, who shall pass through the divisions and precincts of a great city, and enter into its courts, its alleys, and less obvious recesses, may easily convince himself of this. But Audley Mandeville had never set his foot over the threshold of the world; and was as ignorant of what passes on the "seamy side" of this terraqueous[1] globe, as if he had been the inhabitant of another planet. Now, whoever will give himself the pains to observe it, will find that every historian puts much of his own character into his work; and a skilful anatomist of the soul, before he reaches the perusal of the last page, will have formed a very tolerable notion of the dispositions of the writer. I, who am penning this series of events to which I give my name of Mandeville, shall have shown, and should have shown, if they were the memoirs of a stranger, to a penetrating reader many secrets of my own heart, which modesty, or, it may be, a feeling of moral right and wrong, would have prompted me to conceal, if I had been aware what I was doing. It may easily be conceived therefore what a piece of work Holloway made, while he was painfully putting together this collection of anecdotes, which he compiled for the use of my uncle. His unfortunate hearer did not exactly understand it in the way I describe. He never thought of studying it as a sample of the mind of its author. But, without making the inferences which might justly have been drawn, to Holloway's disadvantage, he felt himself extremely uncomfortable. In the unhappy lawyer's narratives there never occurred any thing, to cheer the heart, and make the feelings glow with elevation. Contrasted with the daily nourishment of his client's mind, antecedently to this unhallowed intrusion, it was as if, in the feast of the modern Apicius,[2] you had taken away from him unobserved his *Tokai de la Reine* and *Lachrymae Christi*,[3] and stealthily substituted in their room an agreeable

---

1 Consisting of land and water.
2 A celebrated Roman gourmet of the first century BCE.
3 Both fortified sweet wines.

variety of sour small beer, and an infusion of *assa foetida*,[1] and water from the common sewer.

The life of Audley Mandeville, as has already been said, hung but by a hair; and it was foreseen, that any sudden and unexpected change would infallibly kill him. There is no doubt that Holloway brought that life to a premature conclusion. The days of Audley had before been quiet; they were now comparatively tumultuous. The silence of his studies, and the religion of his melancholy, were almost daily broken in upon by this vulgar and insolent intruder. Nothing now seemed to be, as it had been, almost without variation, for the last twenty years. It is incredible what an effect this produced upon the tender and fragile susceptibility of my uncle. What his feelings were in the presence of the wretched Holloway, have been sufficiently anticipated. The rest of his life was spent in digesting the potion which his lawyer had administered, or in savouring beforehand, in the morbid activity of his fancy, the drench[2] that was to be administered in the course of the following day. It was not many weeks, before the effect of this regimen was visible to the most careless observer. My uncle became every hour feebler and feebler: before, he was incapable of having his mind engaged and interested by the things around him; now he actively loathed them. Existence became insupportable. He took to his bed entirely; and it was clear to every one that he had but a short time to live.

CHAPTER XV

It was in this conjuncture, that I received from the steward the letter above-mentioned, announcing to me the actual state of affairs. Immediately upon the receipt of it I did not fail to set out for the residence of my youth, that I might at least use the information of my own senses on the subject of which it had treated. The diversion of my mind to matters of a totally different nature, was fortunate for me, after the indescribable wretchedness I had experienced from the events at Montagu House.

I arrived without accident at the seat of my ancestors. But, previously to my arrival, a totally new arrangement had taken

---

1 A resinous gum that is ground to a fine powder and used in Indian cuisine.

2 Draught (perhaps of an unsavoury medicine).

place within the walls of this ancient fabric. Holloway became aware of the very precarious state of his client's life; and he considered it as essential to the plans he had at heart, not to suffer any one to enter into the presence of Audley Mandeville, of whose subordination to his own views he could not be perfectly secure. For this purpose he had fixed for himself a temporary residence under this very roof. How could this be hindered by the modest and timid members of the Mandeville establishment? Holloway ordered things as he pleased, with an air of authority that would not submit to be parlied with.[1] The servants, from the highest to the lowest, well knew that their master was not to be spoken with by them, least of all upon any subject that might lead to the discomposure of his mind. Within the circle of this mansion, the law had long since been promulgated, that quiet was the first duty of its domestics, and an anxiety for the interests of its master only the second. Holloway therefore, as I have said, now constantly slept at Mandeville House, without the ceremony of any previous knowledge or consent on the part of the proprietor. And, that he might be exposed to no counteraction or mischief, in periods when he might unavoidably be obliged to absent himself for a short time, he also fixed his nephew as his joint inmate (for he had neither wife nor child), together with a fellow that sometimes officiated in the character of a clerk, and sometimes simply of a servant. The name of his nephew was Mallison, the same identical individual, whose character has been delineated at large in my history of Winchester College.

It was not Mallison however, but Holloway himself, that it was my lot to encounter upon my arrival at the family mansion. The frequently commemorated postern was now never opened but by the lawyer's own servant. The first face that met me therefore, was the face of a stranger. But, as, in such an establishment as this, a portion of every domestic's time is spent in idleness, one of the houshold caught a glimpse of me, as I waited for a moment in the hall, by the desire of him who admitted me, while he hastened to announce my arrival. In an instant the whisper ran through the servants' apartments, that Master Charles was come. The next minute, no fewer than ten or a dozen were assembled round me, to welcome me. Their countenances were dismal: they gave me but a poor account of their master; and it was easy to see that they were greatly dissatisfied with the present administration of affairs. But pleasure struggled with

---

1 To talk with an enemy.

grief in the countenances of all, at my much desired entrance into the hall of my fathers.

The servant of Holloway returned, and desired I would walk into the parlour. It was the very apartment, where I had been accustomed to receive the lessons of Hilkiah, but which was much more endeared to me, as the spot upon which I had first met the embraces of Henrietta. I looked round upon the furniture and arrangement of the room: every chair and table, and all the figures of the tapestry, were my old acquaintances.

Mr Holloway entered.

"I have the pleasure of speaking to Mr Charles Mandeville?" said he.

I nodded assent.

"Pray, Sir, be seated."

And the worthy gentleman drew his own chair to the fire, and left me to follow his example.

I was astonished, and in no small degree shocked, at this supercilious reception. I however seated myself.

"Your uncle is in a very bad way, Mr Charles—very bad indeed. He sees nobody. You cannot see him."

"Sir," replied I, "I believe I know your name, and that is all I know of you. I must therefore be satisfied by other evidence than yours, that it is improper for me to see my uncle. What is more, asleep, if not awake, I will see him. I am come here to judge with my own eyes."

"Since you say you know nothing more of me than my name, it is proper that I should inform you, that I am here as Mr Audley Mandeville's authorised agent, to take care of his affairs, and to preserve his tranquillity. You seem equally to stand in need of the information, that you are what the law denominates 'an infant.' Sir, your uncle stands greatly in need of protection, and he has chosen me his protector. Whatever may be your dispositions in other respects, your age is that of rashness and inconsideration; and I shall take care, Sir, that your thoughtlessness does not turn you into the destroyer of my patron."

And he struck his hand on the table, as he spoke; intending by that vulgar ornament of his rhetoric, to give greater impressiveness to what he said.

I smiled.

"Mr Holloway," I said, "a little explanation may be of some use in this case. I have come alone, because, whatever you may be pleased to say of my youth, I feel myself fully competent to every thing I wish to effect. The friends from whom I come, Lord

Montagu and the rest, advised me not to come alone, and were anxious to aid me with their countenance.

"I am perfectly acquainted with your views, Mr Holloway. You are not the first gentleman of your class, that has put himself forward by uncommon means to get possession of the person of a man of great property in his dying moments. I am not aware how much your plan may enable you to effect. But I will set you at your ease at once, thus far. My concern is with the health and comfort of my uncle, and nothing else. This house has been my home from almost the earliest period of my memory; this uncle has been in a manner the only parent I ever saw. I know my duties to him, and I will perform them. For his property, at least so far as I am myself concerned, I value it not. I had rather wander a beggar through the world all the days of my life, than make the last days of this revered relation days of discomfort. And now, Mr Holloway, it depends upon yourself, whether we shall proceed hand in hand in this melancholy crisis, or the contrary. You may have me for a friend, if you chuse it; or, if you prefer me for an enemy, I shall equally know how to deport myself in that relation."

This was one of the few long speeches I ever made in the course of my life. To utter uninterruptedly a number of words to this amount, was in the highest degree adverse to my nature. But I found, in this, and one or two other instances, that I was not wholly incapable of this conquest over myself. On the present occasion every principle within me was worked up to the highest bent. I felt that, if I failed in my duty to a being, who, as I figured it to myself, had taken me up upon the wild waste and harbour-less desert of the world, and made me—the wretched thing I was!—I should be the most despicable of mortals. Yes; it was true, I was wretched; but I was not unjust enough to impute that to Audley Mandeville. He had meant every thing that was friendly and parental; his plan for me had been superior to all exception; and it was an original taint in my nature only, that had turned all that he designed for blessings, into a curse.

From this moment Mr Holloway and myself, to express it in the ordinary language of mankind, were "the best friends in the world." He saw that I was romantic and silly enough, such were his conceptions of the matter, to be not at all dangerous as a friend, and he was by no means sure that I should prove equally harmless as an enemy. Therefore he resolved to pay me every degree of attention, and to make the most strenuous professions of an unalterable fidelity to my interests.

These professions did not deceive me for an instant. At least for this time, I saw things precisely as they were. I knew perfectly, that Holloway was a man whose conduct was under no restraint of principle, and that his object in having thus strangely established himself an inmate of Mandeville House, was to make the utmost advantage of every power that his profession afforded him, and of the weak and unprotected situation of the present proprietor of the estate.

Yet what could I do? The proceeding which the nature of the contest seemed to require, was, that I should call in the assistance of some of my most respectable friends, that I should expel Holloway from the sanctuary he had so ungraciously invaded, and turn the attention of my uncle to the real dangers that assailed him from within and without, and to the remedy which those dangers called upon him to adopt. But this conduct I could never prevail upon myself to pursue, I knew that the powers of Audley Mandeville would not stand the shock. And I had resolved, as I told Holloway, to submit to every personal evil, rather than plant one thorn in the pillow of my uncle, or shorten his existence by a single hour. This however I could do; and upon this determination I proceeded. I could plant myself on the spot; I could with my own eyes observe from day to day what was going on; and I could extort from the fears of his generous "protector" some information as to the extent of the sacrifice I was called on to make.

One bitter pill which Holloway was called on to digest, was of an incidental nature, and such a one as, I believe, neither of us anticipated, till the occasion actually presented itself. According to the new administration which the present *chargé des affaires* had introduced, a table was provided every day for Mr Holloway and his nephew. A civil message was sent to me, a few hours after my arrival, inviting me to make a third in their party. Many men in my situation would have thought this a very simple thing, and would have submitted without a murmur. But my whole soul boiled at the proposition. I was just come from being half an inmate at Lord Montagu's, where three tables were every day provided for the three different ranks of its inhabitants. And that I should sit down to dinner with an attorney and his clerk, so in my own mind I denominated them, my young blood rejected with disdain, and my towering pride revolted against as inexpiable dishonour! I ordered a separate cover to be placed for me in another apartment.

This, as I have said, was a grievous mortification to the honest solicitor. His original project had been, to divert the whole property of Mandeville into his own possession, and to have turned me adrift, a beggar, upon the wide ocean of society. Nor had he yet altogether resigned his hopes of this. At all events, he very naturally considered every thing that was to come to me, as the free gift of his own generosity and forbearance. Was it then to be endured, that I, a sort of charity-boy to be subsisted by his bounty, should dare to assert myself his superior, and look down upon him, as a vassal, a retainer, and a sort of menial? Beside which, he had other projects, hereafter to be explained, to which such a state of things was decisively hostile. But he digested the affront as he could. "Lowliness is young ambition's ladder."[1] And he flattered himself that the time should come, when he would take ample revenge for every dishonour that was now imposed upon him.

I was impatient to appear in the presence of my uncle; nor did Holloway any longer oppose my desire. The attorney preceded me, and announced my visit. I followed close, and the poor invalid turned upon me a smile of satisfaction. He was in his bed, from which he no longer rose. His face seemed to be composed of bones only, with a thin and inexpressibly delicate covering of colourless skin. His eyes glistened, in a manner which is often seen in patients, when the principle of life is insensibly wasting away. There was something in his countenance, which, at least to my perception, had inconceivable persuasion and beauty. Nothing that was gross, and nothing that was ill in human nature, could be conceived to take up its abode in those features. It was a celestial spirit, informing a body that was no longer earthly. Love, as I saw it at least, was still there, the only dweller through all the regions of that face. The person I beheld was incapable of inflicting harm, and was therefore to every just conception inviolable and sacred.

As I looked on, I could not prevent those reflections arising in my mind, which were congenial to my misanthropy. "What is human nature made of," said I, "that an object like this, should immediately become the theme of its speculation, and the magnet of its cupidity? Man, civilized man, gathers round this object, as the beasts of the forest round their prey, or the savages of North America about their devoted victim. Happy is he who can catch the last opportunity, of guiding those fingers to subscribe a legal instrument, or of collecting the articulations of that

---

1 Shakespeare, *Julius Caesar*, 2.1.22: Brutus comments on Caesar's feigning of humbleness to get ahead.

breath for a donation. Selfishness and avarice engrosses all. The beautiful contemplation I now entertain, the sense of something too pure and aerial for our mortal nature, is wholly lost upon the hardened heart of him who lies in wait for a provision."

The lips of my uncle moved. "Charles!" said he. That was all. "God bless you, Sir," I replied. I sat down by his side. "I am come on purpose to visit you: I will not leave the house till you are better." He made no answer. He shut his eyes, and his body was without motion.

I spent much of my time by my uncle's bed-side, seeing myself, unseen for the most part by the patient and unrepining sufferer. I cannot express how much benefit I appeared to derive from this position. My nature, or my circumstances, seemed to have made hatred my ruling passion. Here, the impulse that was perpetually urging me, was love. I was like the high priest of the Jews, as he sat, or as he kneeled, within the tabernacle, that was constructed to receive the ark of the Lord.[1] A simple curtain of linen was often all that he, and all that I saw, affording excitement to the acts of a religious faith. But behind that curtain, he felt, was placed the sacred symbol, which, as a pillar of fire and a pillar of cloud, by night and by day had in past times proved an unfailing guide through the waste and savage wilderness. He meditated on these things, and worshipped. Placed amidst similar objects, I also was impressed with similar feelings. A sacred quiet came over me; a quiet, not in my case unattended with sadness, but far removed from the vulgar cases of the world. It stifled my passions; it drove far from me the violences of a perturbed spirit; and it filled me with a sense of self-approbation, a welcome visitor to my distracted heart.

Mr Holloway judged it expedient, to make me a confident of the main secrets of his office, and the contents of my uncle's will. He believed, that this was the only way to secure my passiveness, and to prevent my residence under the roof of Mandeville House, which he could not resist, from being fatal to his machinations. On my part, I was well pleased to have the opportunity of obtaining this information. For, though I believed that no earthly consideration could induce me to disturb the last moments of my beloved uncle, yet I was glad to be able to satisfy myself, that

---

1   The Ark of the Covenant was a chest that contained the tablets on which the Ten Commandments were engraved: God orders the Jews to build a tent for the chest and to carry it with them in their wanderings (Exodus 25).

there would be nothing that the world would call incurable frenzy, in my supineness.

Before I state the particulars which Mr Holloway communicated to me, it is necessary to take up a few past circumstances in the history. My uncle, as it has been seen, imposed a severe silence on his lawyer in this question. A short time after however, he delivered into Mr Holloway's hands a paper, purporting to be instructions for drawing a will. A letter was annexed, in which Audley Mandeville undertook to express his present sentiments of his solicitor's character. He said, "Mr Holloway, I believe you an honest man. As to the outline of a will which you suggested to me, and which I rejected, I cannot account for that. You considered its meaning as one thing, and I thought it another. It struck me too as unnecessarily wordy, complicated and obscure. It may be, I was wrong; I am no lawyer. I cannot however deliberately admit the persuasion, that it was dishonestly intended. Our acquaintance began with your conferring on me an inestimable benefit. I am also deeply impressed with the idea you once expressed, that nothing villainous can connect itself with the stem of Montfort. I therefore confide in you. But I expect you literally to observe the inclosed instructions, and to express them in the simplest words that your profession will allow. And, if you have any observations to make, materially affecting the dispositions herein contained, I require you to communicate them in writing. I retain, I cannot help it, an unpleasant sense of our oral discussions on the subject, which makes me resolve they shall not be renewed."

When Holloway read this paper, he felt a considerable struggle in his own mind. His first impression was that of joy. "I still then retain the favourable opinion of my patron. He thinks me an honest man. I was afraid it had been otherwise. I was afraid that he only wanted strength of muscle and nerve, to get rid of me. But, since he continues my friend, what may I not hope for? I have been a pupil of Machiavel[1] to little purpose, if I cannot yet 'wind me into the easy-hearted man, and hug him to my snare.'"[2]

Thus boldly did Holloway feel at the first perusal. But as he reflected more deeply on the subject, his courage diminished. He dared not venture on the experiment again. The good opinion of his patron had been shaken, not overturned, it seemed, by what

---

1 Reference to Niccolò Machiavelli (1469–1527), Florentine political theorist whose name became synonymous with cynical manipulation.

2 Holloway quotes Comus's plan to entrap the lady in Milton's poem (163–64).

had already passed. What might be the consequence, if the trial were repeated, he had not firmness enough to contemplate. He also felt it a different thing, to express his suggestions in writing, as he was required to do, from the mere act of giving breath to his devilish insinuations and perplexities, which in the latter case might be distinguished away, and substantially altered, by the change of an apparently insignificant word, if necessary, till no certain accusation remained against the venomous suggestor. Thus, veteran subtlety shrunk before the understanding of one, whom at first he had considered as no better than a child; the lawyer's "higher knowledge," in the presence of honest simplicity, "fell degraded"; his "wisdom, in discourse with it, shrunk back, discountenanced,"[1] and showed that it was folly.

The instructions were, that Charles Mandeville was to be recognized as heir-general to the entire property, after the discharge of a certain number of legacies. The principal of these were thirty thousand pounds to my sister, and ten thousand to the attorney on his taking the name of Montfort. My uncle further manifested the sweetness and generous temper of his soul, by liberal bequests to the different members of his houshold.[2]

The coward Holloway ventured no further observations on this sketch, than to suggest that the testator had omitted to name an executor for his will, and a guardian and trustee for myself and my sister. The poor, deluded Audley allowed the name of the attorney to stand for both these. There was another clause of the will, which had crept in I know not how, providing that my sister should not marry without the consent of her guardian.

Holloway not only described to me my uncle's testament, but showed me the instrument itself. He observed, that it was already fairly engrossed,[3] and duly executed. He added however that it was the last thing in the world that he could wish for that any question of form should stand in the way of the exercise of my discretion, or prevent the writing from bearing ultimately the provisions that should be most to my satisfaction. He begged me

---

1 *Paradise Lost*, 8.551–53 (Adam describing Eve).

2 The Mandeville family must have been fabulously wealthy. According to the National Archive Converter, Holloway's legacy, presumably a fraction of the estate, would have been worth £1.7 million in 2005. Even by Godwin's own time it would have been equivalent to £419,200.

3 Drawing up a written deed or contract involved working out a rough draft and then having the final terms of the instrument "engrossed" or copied out legibly.

to take it to my closet, and ponder it maturely. If there were any points that appeared to me to require elucidation, it would give him the greatest pleasure to afford me his assistance. He knew that he was totally unworthy of the magnificent bequest that his patron had made to himself, and he had omitted no expostulations to prevail upon the testator to alter it. He had not been aware, that he was likely to have had the advantage of my known good sense and reflection to advise with in so momentous an affair, or he would on no account have allowed the proceeding to have been closed without me. That however was of no consequence: the testator was still living; he was in perfect possession of his intellectual faculties; and if there was any thing that struck me as wrong, partial, or inequitable in the clauses, Holloway added that he would take upon himself to prevail with my uncle, to cancel the present will, and to execute another.

The only provision that my mind dwelt upon with some degree of scruple, was that which directed that my sister should not marry without the consent of the executor. It was loathsome to my soul, to think that such a scoundrel as this, should come near the most perfect of the inhabitants of earth, in the most important transaction of her life. But what could I do? The same rule applied here, which I had already used in the general question, that the last moments of the most innocent of human beings must not be disturbed. Such an alteration, as my own wishes would point out to me, perhaps could not be made, without much discussion, and the chance of great uneasiness. My objection really rested upon the unworthiness of Holloway: but how could so cardinal a consideration be obtruded upon the mind of the dying man? And, after all, what chance was there, that Holloway should think he had an interest in obstructing the marriage of Henrietta, or should dare to set himself in opposition on that point, to the judgment of her respectable friends? In fine, whether it shall be considered as weakness, or duty, or humanity, I decided that the peace of the dying man should not be interrupted.

The end of Audley Mandeville now rapidly approached. Having never thought of him as a being dowered with the common imperfections of humanity, this event affected me strangely. It felt somehow as if an abstract principle, one of the capital articles of my creed, was destined to die. The same thing happened in the case of my uncle, which I have since repeatedly had occcasion to observe in other men, that the creature was never more perfect than in the period when the heart was on the point of ceasing to beat, the intellect never more clear than when it was just ready to be merged in insensibility, the flame never burned more brightly than when the extinguisher of death was descending to quench it for ever. In all the cycle of human events there is nothing more strange than this, the point, the indivisible instant, in which divine intelligence is converted into a clod.

On the day on which this amiable man expired, a few hours before his lungs ceased to heave, myself and Mr Holloway, the most sincere, and the most hypocritical of men, stood, each of us at his bed-side. He looked, first at one, and then at the other. "Farewel, my son!" were the last ravishing accents he addressed to me. To my companion he said, "Remember, your name is Montfort!" At that moment we were both honest; we could neither utter a word. A few minutes later his lips moved; he pronounced the name, "Amelia"; it was his last.

His death was without convulsion, without a groan, or a sigh. It exactly realised those beautiful lines of Donne: Thus

> — vertuous men pass mildly away,
>   And whisper to their souls to go:
> While some of their sad friends do say,
>   The breath goes now; and some say, No.[1]

Audley Mandeville was certainly not the most useful of mankind. He was engaged in no illustrious acts, either of intellect, or philanthropy. If you ask his history, the reply may be made in the words of Shakespear's Viola, "A blank"; and much of the lines that follow, might with the strictest propriety form the epitaph on his tomb.

I will not enter into the detail of the scenes that immediately followed, which the reader may easily imagine, but not to the life. It is difficult to conceive the impression of pure innocence and inoffensiveness, when they are the attributes of hands, that might, if so the heart had pleased, have been employed in giant-work, to injure and to crush. Never was a master more truly lamented by his domestics. Several of them had never seen him, but they knew where was the unviolated sanctuary, in which the arbiter of their condition visibly resided.

The body of Audley Mandeville was conveyed with all due solemnity, from the sea-girt mansion where he had spent his latter years, to the beautiful manor near the centre of England, where he and his Amelia had passed the spring-time of their lives. Amelia

---

1   John Donne (1572–1631), "A Valediction: Forbidding Mourning," 1–4.

had died near this place: my uncle had ordered her to be entombed in the chapel of the mansion, and a sumptuous monument to be erected over her grave. Other lovers would have delighted themselves with examining different designs for this monument first, and afterwards with sedulously visiting it. Audley Mandeville could not do this: the pressure on his heart had sunk too deep. The sculptor had brought him different designs for his choice. He was not able to allow the portfolio that contained them, to be opened in his presence. He only directed, that all devotion should be expressed, and no expence should be spared. He once gave orders for a journey toward this mansion, in which he was born; but he completed no more than the first stage, and returned. The images in his mind were of that living and perpetual force, that refused to mix with external impressions which might be brought in their aid. The coffin of Audley was placed by the side of that of her he loved.

I was now, more than ever, a detached creature on the face of the earth. Relationship is a bond of almost irresistible power; and, solitary as was my nature, it was not without its influence over my feelings. The death of Audley Mandeville therefore produced a revolution in my mind, and is to be regarded as forming an epoch in my history. Still there remained one thing, that I loved beyond all names of love, and that had an empire over me, such as I thought all obstacles and limitations would have in vain sought to control. This was Henrietta. Hers was the master-string, that alone could wake the soul of harmony in my rugged bosom. Beyond all goods to myself, beyond all gratifications, beyond existence, I valued her. I lived in her alone. And, when I was most agitated in the whirlwind of my passions, I turned to her image, and was (sometimes, not always) content. Who would have thought, that this affection would not prove the salt, preserving me from the corruptions of the world, and the malignant operation of my own character? It was not so. The destroying angel was too strong, and took from me all occasions of my safety.

Note on page 137.[1]

I own, I have been guilty of an anachronism in making this quotation, and have nothing but the beauty of the passage to plead in my excuse. It is to be found in Shaftesbury, Vol. II. Essay II.

---

1 Godwin's note to page 137 of the 1817 edition (p. 310 of this Broadview edition) refers to the passage from Shaftesbury's *Characteristics* quoted by Henrietta on p. 243.

MANDEVILLE.

A TALE

OF THE SEVENTEENTH CENTURY

IN

ENGLAND.

BY WILLIAM GODWIN.

From either host
The clink of hammers, closing rivets up,
Gives dreadful note of preparation.[1]

SHAKESPEAR.

IN THREE VOLUMES.

VOL. III.

EDINBURGH:

PRINTED FOR ARCHIBALD CONSTABLE AND CO.
AND LONGMAN, HURST, REES, ORME, AND BROWN,
LONDON.

1817.

---

1 *Henry V*, 4.Chorus.13–15.

CHAPTER I

During the last illness of my uncle, I had kept up a regular correspondence with my sister; and he had no sooner expired, than,
with the approbation of Mr Holloway, I invited her and Mrs
Willis, to superintend with me such details as might be necessary,
on the demise of the head of the family. Audley Mandeville, in the
last period of his life, had expressed no wish to see any absent
connection or relation; and it was therefore thought advisable to
defer the visit of Henrietta, till after the melancholy event of his
death. It was so arranged, that the arrival of my friends took
place, on the day subsequent to my own return from the solemnity of the funeral. I had just completed the eighteenth year of my
age.[1]

Deep and solemn were the emotions with which we now met
each other, beneath the postern in the desolate court-yard of
Mandeville House. Henrietta gave me her hand, and motioned
me to lead her to the apartment of Audley. Her acquaintance
with him was exactly of that degree which made the contemplation of these things soothing. She viewed with a wistful eye the
chair, in which he had sat when he received her visits, and the
chamber and the bed in which he expired. She burst into a
stream of tears. Shortly after, she soothed the sadness of her
mind, by enquiring into the particulars, from hour to hour, of
the last days and nights of the inoffensive deceased; and this
detail, however common, or however fastidious it may prove to
an indifferent and uninterested person, is always dear to the survivor, who knows that he shall see the subject of the narrative no
more.

I felt, that, after the agonizing circumstances that had occurred
during my last residence at Beaulieu, I could not soon have
visited that place again. It was therefore doubly soothing to me,
to receive Henrietta in the domain where I had passed almost all
my early years. My feelings towards this darling sister on the
present occasion were inexpressible. The death of my uncle was
in my eyes an event of the greatest magnitude. Its effect to my
conceptions strikingly resembled that, when the spectators in the
house of Dagon saw the pillars of that spacious fabric bend
beneath the grasp of Samson, and felt the first reeling of the
edifice, but did not yet know in what manner the terrible phe-

---

1   The year is therefore 1656. We are also told on p. 419 that Audley died
    in 1656.

nomenon would end.[1] My connections and the bands which united me to the world were almost nothing; I saw that which was, in the vulgar acceptation, the chief of them, suddenly removed; nor could I guess what would be my situation under, what appeared to me, this mighty revolution. I had no experience to guide my judgment, of the removal of one of those cherished objects upon which my affections leaned; and the idea that impressed me, was as if an essential part of myself was buried in the grave of Audley Mandeville. I turned therefore to Henrietta, with a sentiment a thousand times more tender than ever. I was like a mother of two darling sons, between whom her heart was divided, who, if she loses one of them, feels that she loves the survivor, more fervently than she had before loved the two together. Beside which, all that I had suffered in the wretched question of Clifford, rendered my heart but the more tender, where any tenderness remained, and raised my affection for Henrietta into a something exclusive, that admitted no rival, that allowed of no partner, and that told me, "Here, and here only, can I truly love."

We resumed the talk, in which we had engaged early in my last visit to Beaulieu, respecting our plans of future life. The house we then selected for my fixed residence was that which had been the abode of Commodore Mandeville, and in the neighbourhood of which the line of my ancestors, and latterly Audley and his Amelia, lay buried. The projects we had then formed, were now one step nearer to a reality. The last proprietor of the estate was gone; and it seemed certain that, if I lived three years longer, I should be absolute lord of the whole. The speculation therefore was more interesting, than it had been, a few months before, at Beaulieu. Henrietta loved to engage me in such topics, because

---

1   The story of Samson, blinded and enslaved by the Philistines after he tells Delilah that the secret of his strength lies in his hair, is in Judges 16. But Godwin must have in mind Milton's *Samson Agonistes* (1671), which focuses on the captive Samson's final, suicidal destruction of the temple of the Philistine god Dagon, and which some date back to the Civil War period, while others see it as expressing his despair over the Restoration. Samson's vengeance combines with the new epigraph to Volume 3 (from *Henry V* instead of *Exodus*) to suggest a turn to action; but Samson is both agent and victim of his violence. Here it is Audley's death which unleashes what Gordon Teskey calls the "delirious violence" that "cancels the Philistine hallucination of a unified and harmonious world" (*Delirious Milton: The Fate of the Poet in Modernity* [Cambridge, MA: Harvard UP, 2006], 7) and that culminates in Mandeville's assault on the marriage coach at the end of this volume.

she well knew that schemes of future life, which, by the nature of the case, are much subject to the empire of the imagination, and we can make of them what we please, are perhaps the best emollients that can be devised, for such wounds as the past may have inflicted. While I considered in detail what I should be, or desired to be, my attention was in a great degree distracted from the mortifications I had already endured. Add to this, that topics of this sort, or of any sort, fell with tenfold impression from the lips of Henrietta. Whatever was the subject of her discourse, came to my ears inexpressibly improved, by the harmony of her voice, the gracefulness of her diction, the lustre of her eye, and the undescribable vivacity and ease of all her motions. Still it is true, a deadly grief lay rankling in my bosom, which I could scarcely at any time forget, but which with unremitting firmness I forbad, ever, even in a whisper, even in an inarticulate exclamation (that cry of nature from which the heart at all times derives ease), to find its way to my tongue.

I had now with me under the roof of Mandeville House, Henrietta, the idol of my soul, Mrs Willis, to whom Henrietta was materially indebted for some of her noblest accomplishments, and two wretches, Holloway and Mallison, for whom my soul confessed the most unbounded contempt. Yet could not these latter be wholly excluded from our counsels. We kept them indeed at a sufficient distance, a distance which was intolerably galling to our guardian and my uncle's executor. It was necessary however that he should be in some degree advised with. My residence for the next three years could not be fixed without his participation. Wretch that he was, he was in some sort my master, and what the law seems to regard in the light of a parent, during the remainder of my minority. The only adequate check that existed upon his abuse of these authorities, was the desire he would naturally have, if I lived to the age of maturity, and ultimately became possessed of the estate, that I should, if possible, be induced to think of him as a friend.

It was the wish of Henrietta that I should reside near the most spacious and considerable of the mansion-houses that descended to line, that in which my grandfather had spent his latter years, and that my mind should be in some degree occupied in digesting those improvements, which could not be fully realised till I came into possession. I was resolute against returning to Oxford; and the abode in which I could be most retired, and which should have the additional recommendation of turning my thoughts to subjects, most flattering to my ambition, and the anticipation of my future importance in the world, seemed to be in all respects the most beneficial.

Holloway, to whom I and my sister occasionally communicated the outline of our projects, willingly lent himself to this idea. Nothing could exceed the obliging behaviour, or I may rather call it the obsequiousness, of the attorney. Upon the first suggestion of the scheme, he proposed to ride over to the family-seat in Derbyshire, and enquire out a dwelling in which I might be agreeably accommodated. In a short time he returned, with information of something that seemed exactly to correspond to our notions. It was a house within two short miles of Mandeville Place, now tenanted by a farmer, but which not long before had been the residence of an unfortunate cavalier, with a patrimony of a few hundreds a year, who had fallen in the civil wars. This house contained several apartments in a better style, for which the farmer had no occasion, and which he was willing to appropriate to my use. Here I could be received, together with two menservants; and the farmer offered the assistance of his wife and the female part of his establishment, to supply my table, and conduct the inferior parts of my economy. The proposal was readily accepted. I set off with my sister and Mrs Willis, that we might judge of the whole with our own eyes. Every thing appeared to possess the necessary recommendations: I assembled my books and the implements of study about me; and I proposed to relax myself every fine day with a walk or a ride about some part of the park or the neighbouring country. Thus easily every thing that Henrietta and I had projected, as most conducive to the restoration of my intellectual health, appeared to be fully accomplished. It was judged necessary, that my sister, and the guide of her early youth, should return to the vicinity of the New Forest; but, before they left me, they had the satisfaction to believe, that whatever the most sagacious foresight could require for my welfare was provided, and that there was every prospect that I should pass the remainder of my minority in tranquillity.

No sooner was I alone, than a train of reflections crowded in upon me. How different a creature is man in society, and man in solitude! By society I mean, where a man meets with persons of like dispositions to himself. The savage man probably, wherever he encounters a being of his own species, encounters a companion. The artificial distinctions of civilised life he knows not; and every man in the savage state, is in the main particulars like every other man. They have all the same appetites; they all delight in motion, and delight in rest; they are pleased with sunshine, and are pleased with shade; they love and they hate; they derive agreeable or disagreeable emotions from whatever appears the precursor of pleasure or pain; and they regard in almost all instances, with sympathy, and a certain lightness of heart, the countenance of their fellow-man. Not so in the countries of civilised Europe: "as this world goes," he who claims to be my companion, must be "one man picked out of ten thousand": he must have a disposition to laugh when I laugh, and to cry when I cry; he must have with me a similarity of tastes, and a consonancy of studies; he must be prepared to enter into those associations of thought, that are valuable in my eyes, and to appreciate those sentiments that are dear to my heart. As long therefore as I had Mrs Willis and Henrietta with me, I was in society; but, when I had only the farmer and his family, and his servants and mine, I was alone. It is true that, when I mingled with these beloved associates, that did not always preserve me from thoughts of anguish; I had secret misgivings and sinkings of soul in the midst of my most valued enjoyments.

> For where's the palace, whereinto foul things
> Sometimes intrude not? Who has a breast so pure,
> But some uncleanly apprehensions
> Keep leets, and law-days, and in session sit
> With meditations lawful?[1]

But, when these my better angels left my side, then was the sabbath of my unhallowed cogitations. Then was the tempest and whirlwind of the soul. Then I was wholly delivered up to hatred, disappointment, and remorse, and all those darker emotions that lacerate and tear in pieces the human heart. I looked round upon my implements of study, I looked from my windows upon the rich and heart-reviving prospects they commanded, and I cast upon them a smile of bitterness and contempt. I said all these meadows, and hedge-rows, and streams, this forest-land, and these woods, as far as the eye can reach, are mine. What matters it? I carry a poison in my bosom, to which they afford no antidote. I bear about with me a blemished reputation, a wound that not all the arts of medicine, and all the incantations of witchcraft, can heal. What avails it then for a man to be rich, who knows that he is destined to be miserable?

---

1 *Othello*, 3.3.137–41. Leets and law days are meetings of local courts.

I could not meanwhile be for ever engrossed with thinking. I ate, and drank, and slept, like other men; that is, I performed all these functions, however imperfectly. I walked, and rode—sometimes even talked; for I could not attend to the projected improvements of my property, which I had prescribed to myself as one of my special occupations, without some communications with others. When I returned home, I took down the books from my shelves. I resolutely discarded that loathing of study that had risen in my mind. I placed before me maps, and globes, and charts, and various delineations of cities, of buildings, and of fortified places. I resolved to become acquainted with the history of the world. I read the admirable details of political affairs which ancient Greece and Rome have handed down to us, and illustrated them with the biographical records of the venerable Plutarch.[1] I even made considerable proficiency in these studies. I grew enraptured with the virtues and the elevated minds of antiquity; and Themistocles, and Aristides, and Socrates, and Plato, and Fabricius, and Scipio, and Cato, and Brutus became to me a sort of Gods.[2] I was not "lost in loss itself."[3] I still retained something of the best characteristics of our human nature. My heart panted with admiration, and glowed with exalted sympathy. I was even vain enough to imagine, that I felt within me the capacity to have been like one of these.

But, in the midst of all the fervours of my soul, there was mingled a sadness. An undefined recollection haunted me, even when I was most rapt out of myself. "There is some reason,—what is it?—why I must be wretched." I shut my books; I started away from my studies; I plunged into the most desolate and the obscurest of the neighbouring scenery. My heart seemed ready to burst from the chamber that held it; tears, precious, life-giving

---

1 Greek historian (c. 46–120 CE) who wrote parallel lives of famous Greeks and Romans.

2 The names mentioned are those of statesmen, military heroes, and philosophers from the republican periods of Greece and Rome. Godwin's *History of Rome*, written for children under the pseudonym of Edward Baldwin (1809; rpt. Baldwin and Cradock, 1895), takes up Scipio, Fabricius, and Cato as part of a history that "contains the finest examples of elevated sentiment and disinterested virtue." Noting that "Youth is not the period of criticism," Godwin writes: "If these narratives are to be destroyed, let that task be reserved for a riper age" (iv–v).

3 In *Paradise Lost* Satan's followers are relieved to find him "not lost / In loss itself" (1.525–26). The phrase is repeated on p. 354, strengthening the association between Mandeville and a Romantic, Byronic Satanism.

tears, would sometimes roll down my cheeks. Words would be altogether vain to describe the agitations, the agonies, the bitter repinings, and satanic rebellions of my soul against the God that made me. I said, "What a glorious world is that, which produced such beings as I read of! The times of old Greece and Rome shall come round again: nor has even England been destitute of some characters, that latest times may look on and wonder at. What an admirable nature is this of man, that can think such things, and feel such things, and act such things! Well then, I have been reading a portion of the history of the world. But of this world I form no part, I am cut off from it for ever. Reputation, that good which is beyond all wealth, which embalms and consecrates all virtue, and without which there can be nothing worthy and excellent, I have lost; and, once lost, it can never be restored to this frame of Mandeville, so long as one fibre of that frame remains even in the caverns of the grave."

Nor could I admit (and here lay the sting of my reflections) that I had done any thing to deserve this loss. I seemed to myself to be able to conceive the pleasures of guilt. If I had been really a traitor, if I had trampled upon those boundaries which morality prescribes to the liberty of man, I should have had a sullen satisfaction in my disgrace. Morality is a sort of limit, which the policy of society sets to the active powers of the individual, for the interest of the general. But man has a natural delight in the exercise of his active powers, and is apt sometimes to feel indignant against that mandate, which says, "Thus far shalt thou go, and no farther."[1] We covet experience; we have a secret desire to learn, not from cold prohibition, but from trial, whether those things, which are not without a semblance of good, are really so ill as they are described to us. And prohibition itself gives a zest, an appropriate sweetness, to that which a wiser being than man might have scorned. If then I had stained the first dawn of my manhood with licentiousness, if I had been a traitor to my duties and my country, if I had involved the life of innocence and beauty in shame, contempt and remorse, if I had in my actions bid defiance to the world and its most solemn and unalterable decrees, if I had imbrued[2] my hands in brother's blood, I should have at least contemplated my own audacity with a gloomy delight, and felt a bastard pride in having trampled on all ties, divine and human. But mine was the punishment, without the crime. I had

1 Adapted from Job 48:11.
2 Stained.

austerely conformed to whatever society requires, and sought no enjoyment that conscience forbids. My life had been blameless; at the same time that my name was rendered a by-word, an astonishment, and a curse.

It is true,—and, with the wretched tale I have to unfold, I may be allowed to do myself that justice—though I could conceive the pleasures of guilt, I had no taste for them. There are undoubtedly, history sufficiently confirms it, souls of so strange a texture, that their first passion seems to be, to walk in the purlieus[1] of guilt, to have contemplations that ask no participator, and refuse to be vented in articulate sound, men, who would be less pleased to be loved than to be feared, who revel in the sink of sensuality, careless of the sensations of their victims, who are gratified to spread around them anguish and despair, who have no instinct for kindness, and stand,

> As if a man were author of himself,
> And knew no other kin.[2]

But I was not one of those. I had a heart for love, Oh, for what transports and turbulence of love! My education, all the first scenes and instructions of my youth, had been full of ideas of God and duty; and from earliest childhood I never lay down to rest, without having every wilder impulse subdued by the remembrance of a life to come. I therefore could not think of the excesses of an unbridled spirit without horror; and it is bitter constraint alone, that has forced me to become—what I am! But, for that very reason, it was doubly hard, that I, who sought not, who desired not, any thing that was ill, should suffer all the consequences of the most shameless vice.

But was every thing so hopeless with me, as I painted it to myself? If I were blemished in the great world, I might still perhaps live among my tenants and my country-neighbours, and be respected. Now and then some stranger might pass my gate, and say, "here lives the man, of whom they tell strange stories about Penruddock and the western insurrection." But the humbler vicinage would scarcely have heard the tale; and those who had, would allow a life spent in unambitious beneficence to obliterate its deformities. Nay, upon the same terms I might go out into the world at large. Even my king and my country would

---

1 Areas nearby.
2 Shakespeare, *Coriolanus*, 5.3.36–37.

perhaps admit my services, and provide me with an opportunity by some honourable achievement to cast a shade upon my unfortunate beginning. I might gain a patched-up and a passable character. My name would be like a garment of price, whose original colours were tarnished and gone, but it is sent to the dyer, and in receiving a new tint, becomes possessed of a second-hand and half-faced beauty. It would be like a human body, covered with wounds and marks of its former hardships, hardships not met with in the career of honour, but which are now skinned over and healed, and it is again capable of a sort of halting and disabled duty.

No: this was a compromise that I could not think of for an instant. My conception of fame was too pure, to admit of such an anomalous and questionable existence. I was ambitious: but it was Ambition's self, that fixed my mind upon something resplendent and illustrious; and, if I could not shine in what I deemed my proper sphere, I could not accept of less. Next to the pride of being great, was the pride of being nothing. I resolved to shut myself out from the world, to think of my studies only, to be unknown to, and unseen by any human being, except the bare members of my own houshold. This appeared to be my only chance for tranquillity.

Such were some of the reflections that passed in my mind, under the roof of my Derbyshire farmer. Undoubtedly this was a falling off from the state of my thoughts, immediately before I was summoned to the death-bed of my uncle. Then I had felt that I had but one vocation in life, the destruction of Clifford. I knew, too well I knew, that that would be no cure for my misery. But at least it would be some consolation to my insupportable anguish, to bathe my arms to the very elbow in the blood of my rival. I should then say, "At length he is extinguished! he can never harm me more! It is true, I must perish, but he shall not look on, and exult over my ruin! When I am made one monument of wretchedness, he shall not, while I live, and after I die, have his luxuries, gratifications and enjoyments, his bosom shall not beat with pleasure, and his eye shall not sparkle with gladness!" I had formed therefore a solemn vow, that I would have no other pursuit and occupation in life till this was fully effected, that I would devote to it my days and nights, and consider nothing but how it was to be most speedily and certainly consummated. Meanwhile my mind was all a chaos: I had formed no plan; I was incapable of digesting any settled design; I was conscious to nothing, but one overwhelming passion, one inextinguishable and infuriated desire.

Events have over us a power, that seldom any operation of the mind within itself reach. My thoughts were called off from this uproar and carnival of diabolical suggestions, by the summons I had received, to come over, and see my uncle die. My journey in obedience to this summons, all I had witnessed on this awful occasion, and the new situation in which the death of the proprietor of the Mandeville estates placed me, made a different man of me. I studied; I surveyed my estates; I meditated, and digested a variety of improvements. The tenseness of all my muscles, which preceded, was relaxed. The horror of my purposes was suspended.—Aye! suspended only, not annihilated. I still felt the "*injuria alta mente reposta*."[1] I never forgot the calamity of my condition. Clifford still haunted me. But it was like a thin and unsubstantial ghost, half melted into air, and dispersing itself, as it were, in the elements. But the time was coming, in which he was to revisit me in his original horrors, to resume his gigantic and irresistible force, and to clutch in his terrific grip all the powers of my being.

CHAPTER II

I had not been long alone under the roof of my farmer, before I received a visit from Holloway. It is sufficiently obvious with what feelings I met him. Toleration, and a search for topics of favourable construction, was no part of my character. He approached me with an air of great self-complacency. His figure was what is commonly termed portly, though the activity of his thoughts gave to it occasionally an unexpected adroitness; and it was clothed upon this occasion with an ample portion of drapery, his pockets being further swelled with accounts, inventories, leases, and bonds.

"Well, Mr Mandeville," said he, "we have begun with being excellent friends. You have had sufficient occasion to observe the frankness and directness of my character. I have sought no mysteries; I have laid every thing before you with the utmost explicitness. I have scorned to take refuge in the idea of your being a minor, and incompetent to the management of your affairs. For my share, I have never done any thing that I have reason to be ashamed of; and therefore it is my desire to take you along with me, and receive your opinion upon every thing I am called on to do. Your judgment is far above your years; and it will be great

---

1 Injury stored deep in the mind (adapted from Virgil, *Aeneid*, 1.26).

advantage to me at present, and honourable acquittance here-after, to consult it."

Saying this, he caused a large table to be brought into the middle of the room, and properly displayed. He next began to unload his person, pocket after pocket, of the heterogeneous cargo with which it was enveloped. He then called to his servants, to bring in five or six cloak-bags of formidable dimensions, well stuffed with similar materials. One by one, these were each extracted from its "concealing continent," and scattered, and classed, and piled upon this portentous table.

I looked on in silence at the long-drawn preparation. My sensations were none of the most comfortable. I considered with great truth that this was in some sort a trial what I was to be for years, perhaps for the rest of my life. I had the worst opinion of that integrity of the solicitor, of which he vaunted so loudly. I knew that, if I would be the conscientious administrator of that property, which the order of society was placing under my control, I must at some time become a man of business; and, if at some time, perhaps the sooner the better. I know not that there did not rise up in my bosom, mingled with these sage and virtuous reasonings, an alloy of youthful vanity, proud to be called in to the administration of an ample revenue, and resolved to show to my guest that I was equal to the task, which I should otherwise have suspected that in derision he had set before me.

Mallison was now introduced, as our assessor, and the assistant of his uncle in the task which impended. He was just of my own age; but he had already been initiated in the details, to which I was utterly a novice. He had been accounted a dull boy at school; but, I know not how it is, there are some businesses for which dulness seems to be a qualification. There is a sort of labyrinthian progress, and circuitous drudgery, in which it has a thousand times been found, that a blockhead is fitted to make the more brilliant and luminous figure.

I sat down to my task with these choice and amiable companions. "Yes," said I, "I will be a man of business; I will understand my own affairs; I will exercise a perspicacity, that no subterfuge and trick shall be able to elude."

I adhered to this resolution for three whole days. It is inconceivable what I suffered during this period. Holloway was a master in his art; he knew how to "perplex, and dash maturest counsels,"[1] and to congregate a cloud that should baffle the

---

1 *Paradise Lost*, 2.114–15, describing Belial in the Council of Hell.

acutest vision; and Mallison, with his tedious elucidations, dictated by an apprehension, that groped in the dark, and was yet to seek in the very elements of the subject which with inexhaustible flounderings he undertook to explain, was still more intolerable than his leader. What I should have made of the questions before me, stranger as I was to every thing of the sort, without their perverse assistance, I am unable to pronounce. But, entering upon them as I did, the further I investigated, the more ignorant I grew.

I bore all this with the horrors of the damned. Such is the nature of the human mind (I speak at least for myself) that no train of thinking goes on in the brain, however earnest and overwhelming, that there are not at the same time subordinate trains and episodes, that perform their peculiar revolutions, without seeming to interrupt the larger and more comprehensive machinery. When I studied the pages of Homer, of Dante, or Ariosto, conceptions that related to Penruddock and Clifford would obtrude themselves, uncalled for and unwelcome, without appearing to require any reference or association from the ideas of the author, to introduce them. I could talk, or I could write with earnestness, amidst visitations of this kind, without any danger that the abhorred intruder should mix with or interrupt what I wrote or what I said. Its torments were secret, and my voice and my pen disdained to confess them. But it is worst of all, when you are occupied with an ungrateful theme, which seems to answer no other purpose than to chain the body and the mind in a constrained stilness, I never thought of Clifford, and my past mortifications, and all that I believed was in store for me in future, with such depression and wretchedness of mind, as when I was employed in auditing the accounts of Holloway, and listening to his ample explanations of base fees, and fees simple, and fees in tail, and all the complicated jargon that successive centuries have caused to grow out of the feudal system.[1]

Meanwhile, in the midst of the sublime obscurities of Holloway's explanations, he contrived to chequer the darkness with

---

1 The word "fee" derives from "fief," which is a feudal landholding. It is unclear if the terminology with which Holloway tries to confuse Mandeville pertains to what Mandeville owes the farmer who has been made his landlord to put him in a position of dependency, or to what the Mandeville estate owes its landlord (the government). Base fees are owed by a peasant to his lord and "fees simple" refer to estates held by absolute ownership. Fees in tail relate to estates regulated by conditions made by the donor, but since the Mandeville estate is entailed there can be no conditions relating to its passing to Mandeville.

now and then a solitary coruscation, adapted to show his exactness in accounts, the conscientiousness of his detail, and the purity of his administration. Whatever a man greatly desires to believe, it is no difficult task for him to persuade himself is true. Detesting these details as I did, feeling more and more every hour the impossibility of my sustaining the burthen, I willingly yielded to the idea, that what I was now called on to do, was not less superfluous, than unpleasing.

I knew that Holloway was selfish; I well understood the cause and the circumstances of his connection with my uncle; but there was something to my apprehension so plausible in his statements, and so clear in his official details, that I repeatedly said within myself, "At least he is honest here. Man is a being of a mixed nature; and, as there is no integrity without its flaws, so is there no man so knavish, but that in some things he may be trusted."

In a word, my artful solicitor and guardian completely carried his point. I threw up the question of being my own steward in despair; I owned my weakness; and even intreated him to take all trouble of that kind upon himself. I pushed away my chair from the well incumbered table, caught up my hat, sallied forth among the breezes and the objects of nature, and bid adieu to accounts, and the intricacies of management of an estate, for the most part, for ever. The recollection of these three days of torment, of an occupation so different from any thing to which I had been previously accustomed, with objects so repulsive, and persons so alien to my taste, at no time by any length of interval faded from my memory.

Holloway and Mallison took their leave, and I was once more alone. I could see marks of a greater degree of communication between them and the farmer, my landlord, than I could exactly account for. As I kept up the punctilio[1] of never receiving them at my own table at the period of meals, this forced upon them a certain degree of intercourse with the family. There was nevertheless a deference and even servility expressed by the farmer towards this limb of the law, more than well accorded with my ideas of an English yeoman, especially in these republican times.

Now however I was once more alone; and the sad and solemn tone of my character became still less interrupted. Whoever looked upon me might see, that I was a human creature cut off from my fellows, and blighted by some awful visitation. Seldom I spoke; still seldomer I looked any other man in the face. If, in my solitary

---

1 Exactness in the observance of formalities.

rambles, the veriest rustic crossed my path, I struck away into some other direction, and avoided him. My brow became habitually knit; my eye was wild, roving and fierce; my manner grew in a striking degree morose and repulsive. I perceived that, wherever I appeared among my inferiors or dependents, I produced a sort of terror: if they could have seen my heart, they would have soon been convinced, that I was better entitled to excite their pity than their fear. My flesh gradually wasted from my bones; my skin for ever glowed and burned with the fever of my mind; my nights were restless, vexatious and wearisome; and I became so acutely sensitive, that almost the dropping of a pin discomposed me.

CHAPTER III

I was in this frame and temper of mind, when a small packet was one morning brought me by the arrival of the post. It contained nothing but a number of the *Mercurius Politicus*, a weekly newspaper of the times.[1] There was no writing of any kind in the packet; and I could never tell with certainty from whom it came. For my part, I was no hunter after news. It was a thought alien from my condition, which I regarded as cut off from the congregation of the living world. The only histories, as I have said, that arrested my attention, were those of the nations of antiquity. Wherever I perceived the word England, I seemed to myself to behold the names, Penruddock, Wagstaff, and Clifford. My senses dazzled; my eyes saw double, or rather fluctuated in a vision, where every thing danced, and nothing was distinct; and my mind was turned into uproar, confusion and anarchy. The arrival of this newspaper to my address, was a singular circumstance; and I cast my eye over its columns, with a feeling of something between curiosity and listlessness, to see whether I could readily discern why it had been brought me. My eye was true to my disease; and I presently saw in Italic letters the terrifying words, "Lionel Clifford." The paragraph was to this purpose.

---

1 A newspaper published by the parliamentarian side, for which Milton also wrote, and one of the only two newspapers permitted by the government. Since Volume 3 begins in 1656, this must be an old issue, as we are told on p. 401 that Clifford converted in the midsummer of 1655 (not November), and that in the light of his new found fortune Henrietta's guardians had already agreed, before Audley's death, to his future marriage to her.

"It is with great concern that we announce to our readers the following melancholy fact. On the 24th of November last, George, Earl of Bristol, who, under the name of Lord Digby,[1] made so notorious and disgraceful a figure in our civil wars, to the precipitate commencement of which he by his evil counsels mainly contributed, together with six young gentlemen of considerable families in England, made a public renunciation of the Protestant religion, and were reconciled to the Romish communion in the cathedral of Ghent. The bishop preached a sermon on the occasion; and the day was observed by the inhabitants with every demonstration of joy." Among the names of the six gentlemen, satellites of the Earl, was that of my ancient adversary.

Certainly this was a material piece of intelligence to those who, like me, regarded themselves as adherents of the house of Stuart. The Reformation had become the established system of the church of England for about one hundred years. The adherents of the Romish faith however, throughout Christendom, possessed in a formidable degree the advantages of combination and policy, and had never lost sight of the design, to restore this important branch of the commonwealth of Europe to the obedience of Mother Church. The reign of Elizabeth had been incessantly disturbed with plots and conspiracies; and the memorable Gunpowder Treason[2] sufficiently showed what had been the temper and thoughts of the zealots of the Romish faith in the beginning of King James. The expulsion of the royal family, and the abolition of monarchical government in England, were melancholy events to the lovers of our genuine political constitution, but had been the occasion of infusing fresh hopes into the mind of the true Catholic. "God, by the finger of his Providence," he said, "had conducted the royal family of England, three young princes of the highest hope, to countries where the Romish religion predominated, for their education." From this moment all Jesuits and zealots for this cruel religion, had considered it as their choicest vocation, to reconcile these young princes to the creed, which had constituted the faith of the church of Christ for so many ages. They never entertained a doubt that the ancient government and royal family of England would speedily be restored; and they fondly believed that this calamitous train of

---

1 Digby, Earl of Bristol (1612–77), was a Royalist general known for changing sides. He may have converted to Catholicism in 1656, but the date of September 1658 is also given.
2 See p. 81, note 4.

events had been chosen by the Almighty, as the effectual means of bringing back his beloved people of this island to the flock of Christ. From the first they had had the queen-mother, not only for their sincere, but their indefatigable partisan: it was suspected by many who had the best means of information, that the Duke of York was gone over to the enemy; and the greatest alarm was entertained, lest the king and his youngest brother should equally fall victims to the pernicious arts of the Romish priesthood.[1]

It may easily be supposed what a melancholy anticipation this afforded to me. "After the straitest sect of our religion, I was" bred a Protestant.[2] I looked upon Popery as the lowest pit of disgrace and calamity, into which human beings could fall. I was more convinced, that the adherents of that faith laboured under the everlasting wrath and displeasure of God, than I was of the condemnation of the idolatrous heathens of former ages. "The corruption of the best thing becomes the worst"; and Popery was the corruption of that adorable dispensation, in which the second person in the Trinity had assumed flesh, and died on the cross for the salvation of men. It substituted for divine truths the inventions of men; it changed the meek religion of the holy Jesus into a stupendous engine of pride, insolence and oppression, and his pure precepts into a cover for licentiousness, and a method of compromising with our basest lusts for the gain of the spiritual treasury. Such were my sentiments respecting it, whenever it prevailed. From this yoke of ignominy and mischief my countrymen had been gloriously delivered. They had not only cast off the authority of a foreign usurper over the souls of men: they had beside disengaged themselves from the tyranny of an episcopal hierarchy, that last remnant of the corruptions of Rome. No people so well understood, such was the conviction of my mind, the principles of true religion, and the "liberty with which Christ has made us free," as the people of England. What a calamitous presentiment then must I entertain, of the attempt of a Popish king and royal family to bring us back to the subjection, from which we had so illustriously and so providentially escaped! My mind was distracted, like that of many other presbyterians of this

---

1 Duke of York: the future King James II. The youngest of the three surviving princes was Duke Henry of Gloucester, who actually became a Protestant but died of smallpox in 1660, aged 20.
2 Because of Clifford's "apostasy" this chapter has many quotations from the Bible, some of them made up and given the authority of sounding Biblical.

time, between attachment to my King, and a longing desire to see him restored, on the one hand, and a fear of nameless and incalculable mischiefs from this source, on the other. Had the apostacy[1] of the house of Stuart from the principles of the Reformation stood before my mind as a fact, I know not how my sentiments of loyalty would have borne up against it: but I could not allow an hypothesis and a possible mischief, to outweigh my duty as an English subject, however that very possibility might fill me with anxious forebodings for the future.

Such were the feelings, as they regarded the public, that were excited in my breast, by the perusal of this memorable intelligence. But my feelings, with respect to the public, were quickly swallowed up by the consideration of the individual. This is for the most part the nature of the human mind. Abstractions and generalities are subjects of our moral reasonings: while we contemplate them, we are conscious of a certain elevation, that is flattering to the mind of man: but it is only through the imagination, and when we apply our reflections to an individual, when the subject upon which our thoughts are occupied, comes before us clothed in flesh and blood, and presents a set of features and a sensible reality, that our passions are roused through every fibre of the heart.

Clifford then was the figure upon which my thoughts rested. Clifford, the apostate! Clifford, the renegade! One would have imagined, that such a tale of the man that I hated would have been gratifying to my inmost feelings. It was not so. My mind was all confusion and uproar. I was pleased, and I was displeased. Hatred, when the cause that creates it is felt to be most substantial, is the farthest on earth from being a soothing and a consolatory sentiment.

An apostate was to my ideas the being most worthy of inextinguishable abhorrence. To him, who, "after having received the knowledge of the truth," falls away, and deserts the divine fountain of mercy, "there remains no more sacrifice for sin, but a certain fearful looking for of judgment."[2] And such was Clifford! He had been bred in the pure Protestant faith. I saw well enough what was the cause of his profession of the Roman Catholic religion. The head of his family, the man from whom he expected the succession of an ample estate, was a Papist; and this was the con-

---

1   A person who deserts his former religion or more generally reverses his principles.
2   Hebrews 10:26–27.

dition upon which he was to be allowed to inherit this wealth. He was not deceived; he was puzzled by no ambiguities; he was misled by no sophistries; he sinned against the clearest light, and the most certain knowledge. Clifford had sold his expectation in the world to come. There is one memorable instance on record in the Scriptures, of a man who bartered his redeemer for certain pieces of silver: and the name of that man was Judas Iscariot. An action, how wretched, and how vile! "What shall a man be profited, if he gain the whole world, and lose his own soul; or what shall a man give in exchange for his soul?" This is the crime, over which the blessed Jesus paints himself as triumphing with pious exultation: "He that shall deny me before men, him also will I deny before my Father, and before all his holy angels."[1]

Religion is the most important of all things, the great point of discrimination that divides the man from the brute. It is our special prerogative, that we can converse with that which we cannot see, and believe in that the existence of which is reported to us by none of our senses. Such is the abstract and exalted nature of man. This it is that constitutes us intellectual, and truly entitles us to the denomination of reasonable beings. All that passes before the senses of the body, is a scenic exhibition; and he that is busied about these fantastic appearances, "walketh in a vain show, and disquieteth himself in vain." Invisible things are the only realities; invisible things alone are the things that shall remain.

What then is he that stakes at the basest game, this first of human considerations? All other vices, crimes, profligacies, call them by what name you please, are trifles to this. What care I in the comparison, for the plunderer, the ravisher, and the homicide, for him that sacks whole cities, and lays waste a whole generation of mankind? The apostate does what in him lies to murder the God, that made him and all of us. He expresses in action, much more emphatically than the atheist in words, that there is no Almighty. Poor, senseless, groveling wretch, who knows nothing but what he sees, and is affected by nothing but what feeds his appetites, or pampers his vanity! This is the true disgrace. I thought myself disgraced, because it had been said of me by a few mistaken men, that I was disloyal to my King, unfaithful to my engagements, a liar, and a hypocrite. What was this, compared with the ignominy of Clifford? All mankind have agreed to regard with the foulest abhorrence the man, that deserts the religion in which he was trained, and, by making light

---

1 Matthew 16:36; 10:33.

of his allegiance to heaven, convinces us at what price he will estimate all meaner bonds of duty, veracity, humanity and honour.

In one respect I will own my very heart was lightened, by being
enabled to consider Clifford under this new aspect. The bitterest
agony perhaps I had hitherto felt, arose from a struggle between
the certainty that I hated him, and the secret suspicion, from which
I could not free myself, that he did not deserve to be hated. To me
he was odious, he was loathsome. But I saw plain enough, that
other men regarded him with complacency, that his presence made
a little holiday, and that the very doors flew wide, and leaped from
off their hinges, to give him entrance. I knew full well, that all the
miserable sufferings I had ever experienced, came to me from Clifford, that his intervention had blasted my days, and devoted my life
to horrors without end. Yet no man, and especially no very young
man, is guilty of a crying injustice, but his conscience smites him,
and his heart quails at the thought. At times I felt myself compelled
to admire Clifford, and to subscribe to his innocence and his
worth; and this was to me the consummation of miseries.

"Thank God," I said to myself, "all that is at an end! I may
now hate him as much as I please with a safe conscience. He now
looks 'lovelily dreadful' in my eyes, even as he would look, if he
were going, smeared with the blood of both his parents, which he
had just shed, hardened and blasted with impenitence, to be
broken on the wheel. Thank God, he has thrown off the mask,
and shown himself for what he is! Yes, I always knew him; an
unerring instinct always showed me the exact measure of his
worth. But he walked about in false colours, cloked and disguised
from the world's eye, and passed himself for a virtuous man and
a hero. What a relief is sympathy! What a burthen insupportable,
to be penetrated with a sentiment and a passion, in which no
human being partakes! Yes, I am a man again: I can once more
walk abroad among my species: and, whatever secret wound I
may bear about me in other respects, I need no longer conceal my
hatred. I can say to every one I meet, *Do you not see that Clifford?
Do you not in your heart pass upon him the same judgment that I do?*"

Strange as it may appear, with this new aggravation of his
deformity, I nevertheless in some degree pitied him. He was
blasted by the eye beam of God, even as the unfortunate victims
we read of in the heathen mythology, who by one glance of the
visage of Medusa[1] were turned into stones. His power was

---

1   In Greek mythology, one of the Gorgons: the sight of her glaring eyes
    and serpent-hair turned men to stone.

nothing; a judgment had fallen upon him, that unthreaded all his joints, and pulverised his sinews. Poor wretch! what could he do? whom could he trust? He had a voice that could persuade no man, and that, like what I have somewhere read of the "Palace of Truth," when he uttered all his glosings[1] and varnished tales, turned them, unconsciously to the speaker, into mockeries, and warnings that no man should believe. Who would be his ally? All men would fly him with horror; they would fear some horrible mischief growing out of his bare presence; they would gaze, with "hairs upstaring stiff, dismayed with uncouth dread,"[2] and then fly from him, as if all that was deadly to our nature was to be avoided by their escape. I had read the "Relation of the Fearful Estate of Francis Spira"; and such a man I accounted Clifford. Spira told those who visited him, that he was "for ever accursed from the presence of God, and that there remained for him nothing but everlasting damnation"; and I believed him. For the space of eight weeks he slept not, day nor night; he ate not; he was burned with a consuming fever; yet was all the time in a tremendous state of sober understanding, capable of reasoning and discussing with whoever approached him. Who but must pity a man fallen into "the Fearful Estate of Francis Spira?"[3]

Even so I pitied Clifford. Yes, I mourned over him; but it was with the pity of a bigot. I sorrowed for his affliction, even as Bellarmine or Saint Thomas Aquinas[4] might be supposed to sorrow for the irreversible sentence of the prince of devils. I sorrowed with the true sympathies that were felt by the persecutors of John Huss and Jerome of Prague,[5] who consigned their bodies to be burnt for their heresy, and prayed God, if in his unerring justice he saw fit, that he would have commiseration of their impenitent souls. Well said the inspired Psalmist of old, if I may be allowed so to accommodate his phrase: *"The tender mercies of the bigot are cruel."* "Who

---

1 Ingratiating and fawning phrases.
2 *The Faerie Queene*, 1.9.22.
3 Nathaniel Bacon, *The Fearfull Estate of Francis Spira* (1638). Spira (d. 1548) was an Italian lawyer who converted to Lutheranism, was summoned before the Inquisition, and then recanted. Tormented by what he had done, he became incurably and despairingly melancholic and died.
4 Cardinal Bellarmine (1542–1621); St. Thomas Aquinas (1225–74): scholastic theologian and philosopher.
5 Jan Hus (c. 1369–1415): Bohemian (or now Czech) reformer who was a precursor of the Protestant movement. His burning at the stake led to the Hussite wars (1419–34). His follower Jerome (1379–1416) was also burned.

are we," say such men, "that we should blasphemously murmur against the righteous judgments of the All Merciful?"

I make it a law to myself in this narrative, now when all is over, and hatreds and heart burnings are at length buried in the silence of the grave, not to relate any thing to the disadvantage of Clifford, without at the same time producing his side of the question, and stating, not merely how I saw the things that exasperated me, but also what they were in themselves. This is the least expiation I can make. All that I have said of his having been trained in the clear light of Protestant principles, is gratuitous. He was indeed descended from an impoverished, and by some accident a Protestant, branch of a great family, whose leading members had never in any instance swerved from the ancient faith. But his friends were few; and the virtues by which he was distinguished, rather drew their birth from the admirable predispositions with which nature had endowed him, than, from any pains that had been taken with his moral education. He had scarcely heard any thing more of religion, than was contained in the public service of the church, and in the regular, but to him somewhat uninteresting, precepts and expositions of a pedagogue. His mother had done nothing more for him, than obtain him an exhibition[1] at Winchester College, that he might be a gentleman, and watch over and cherish him daily with the anxieties of her widowed love. The affection she bore him was ardent and unalterable, and amply did he return it; but the extent of her intellectual powers bore no proportion to the strength of her regard.

In the course of the present year it had happened, that a distant and wealthy relation of Clifford had lost his only son, and became anxious respecting the succession of his estate. Within no long period he had been the father of four children; but, together with his wife, they had all died within a short time of each other, and left him the solitary survivor of a once cheerful and affectionate circle. In the pride of his prosperity he had treated all applications relative to my late schoolfellow with disdain, and had even refused to contribute the most scanty pittance to fit him out in the world. But calamity had softened the old man's nature. He looked out for an heir: the praises of this youth, to which at the time he seemed to turn a deaf and unconceiving ear, now came fresh and unimpaired to his thoughts, as if they had this moment been uttered. He sent for Clifford, and found him all, and more than all, his fondest wishes had anticipated. The old man was like

---

1   Scholarship given to a student by a school or university.

a reverend and time-worn oak, upon whom a thousand tempests had wasted their fury; and now he seemed to find, in this adopted stranger, the only prop that interposed between him and entire prostration. The loss of all his children had nearly produced the effect of snapping the thread of his existence; and one memorable change it effected in his character. He had hitherto shut up his affections in his domestic circle, and been hard and unfeeling to all the world beside. Now he felt the full retribution of this, and found the necessity of having something to love, and by which to be loved, elsewhere. His fondness for the youth whom he protected, mounted to the utmost extravagance; he thought he could never do enough for him; he could scarcely bear him out of his sight. There was one thing however that still clouded the old man's days, and saddened his heart. It was the pride of his race, the distinction they set up between themselves and the herd of these degenerate days, that they had never swerved from the religion that Augustine,[1] the monk, had planted in the island more than a thousand years before, and to which Archbishop Becket and Sir Thomas More had fallen illustrious martyrs.[2] He was miserable therefore, till Clifford should be reconciled to his Holy Mother, and assume the sacred symbol and proud distinction of his progenitors.

For the young man himself, it was impossible for any one to be more free from the spirit of a sycophant, or less disposed to be a hunter after ample legacies and a rich inheritance. It has already been seen, and will be seen still more hereafter, that he was careless to an extraordinary degree about the advantages of wealth, and had devoted himself, heart and soul, to the love of independence. But his nature was penetrated with the tenderest sensibilities. He could not resist the old man's demonstrations of fervent attachment; he felt that he owed to his love, though not to his rent-roll, every deference it was in his power to express. He ruminated with compassion upon his patron's hard situation; his children, genuine adherents to the religion of their parent, had

---

1 St. Augustine (d. c. 604) was sent to preach the gospel in England in 597 and was the first Archbishop of Canterbury.

2 St. Thomas à Becket (c. 1118–70), Archbishop of Canterbury (1162–70), was murdered as a result of hints dropped by Henry II. More (1478–1535), Lord Chancellor for three years and author of *Utopia*, was beheaded by Henry VIII for refusing to swear to the Act of Succession, which legitimized Anne Boleyn's children, and the Oath of Supremacy, which made Henry head of the Church of England.

grown up "like olive plants about his table"; and now he had no one to console himself with in their room, but a kinsman six times removed, and over whose spiritual estate he wept daily as a heretic. Clifford was however slow to change, and meditated the act with frequent hesitations; but the consideration of the old man's peace at last decided him. The priest, who resided as chaplain in the family, was a person of great integrity and simplicity of character. He was deeply read in the controversies between the two churches: and what with the superiority of his knowledge of the subject, the strength of his reasonings, the goodness of his heart, and the pure Christianity of his temper, Clifford found himself powerfully beset. All these at least served for no contemptible allies, in recommendation of that conduct to which his affectionate nature so strongly prompted him.

CHAPTER IV

I had continued only a few months in my Derbyshire retreat, when Holloway and Mallison once more made their appearance. This time it did not seem as if their visit was principally intended to me; they were rather guests to my landlord, the farmer. Holloway paid his respects to me, enquired whether every thing went on well, or there was any thing I wished should be otherwise; but seemed anxious to make his visits short and unobtrusive. At another time Mallison came in, and, after salutations given and received, informed me that he was going to ride over next morning to the nearest market-town, and asked whether there was any commission he could execute for me. This went on for days. I thought it strange; but I felt a repugnance to enquiring into the matter. After all, I was not the master of the house, but merely the tenant of a certain part of it; and I had no right to call the farmer to account, as to what visitors he chose to receive at his own board. Still I should have been glad, that his guests, if guests he had, should rather have been persons that were entire strangers to me.

After some time I perceived further operations. Various articles of furniture were brought in, in carts, and in waggons. Carpenters and other workmen arrived; and it was plain that some alteration was in hand as to the appropriation of certain parts of the building. One room I could perceive was in the act of being fitted up in the manner of an attorney's office, with desks, and shelves, and compartments for the reception of deeds and leases and other documents of legal importance. Still I looked on, undecided in mind, sometimes full of indignation that such measures should be pursued without the smallest intimation or deference towards me, and sometimes, heart-sick as I was of the fooleries and fopperies of the world, disdaining to consider what such reptiles and worthless animals might think proper to imagine or to act. The drama advanced, and the *denouement* at length became plain: the farmer and his family, who were the mere creatures of Holloway, finally disappeared; and my guardian, and his retinue, whether of a domestic sort, or appertaining to his craft, were established in their room. The procedure all together, reminded me of the irregular way in which this same person had obtruded himself as an inmate of my uncle's residence in Dorsetshire; and I could not help applying to him the denomination which I have seen somewhere appropriated to a distinguished theological mummer, of "the most impudent man living."[1] I however felt deeply convinced in my heart, that I was not yet such a one as my unfortunate uncle, and that this blushless mountebank should never make a property of me.

Every thing being completed to his mind, Holloway now waited upon me in person to give me an explanation of the whole. He said, that he perceived I had no turn for the drudgery of business, and he had therefore been casting about in his thoughts, how he could most effectually free me from the intrusion I abhorred. His obligations to my late worthy uncle were of so unspeakable magnitude, that he should feel no sacrifice too much, to advantage his successor. He had therefore determined to give up his professional connections in Dorsetshire, valuable as they were, that the industry of himself and his nephew might be wholly devoted to my accommodation. At the distance at which we were otherwise placed, applications of a disagreeable nature might be obtruded upon me, which it would now be in his power to intercept; and I might stand in need of consultations, for which it would be in many ways inconvenient to me to wait the return of the courier. With any other person, he should doubtless have felt it his duty to submit his project for approbation previously to its being carried into execution, and to have governed himself by the decision of his principal; but he saw plainly the propensity of my mind, and he had thought it became him to conform to it. I

---

1   Referring to Viscount Bolingbroke's *A Familiar Epistle to the Most Impudent Man Living* (1749), an attack on William Warburton (1698–1779), Bishop of Gloucester.

was melancholy; and he hoped by substituting himself, who was wholly devoted to my service, and his nephew, my old school-fellow, for my neighbours and inmates, instead of the farmer and his men, to benefit me that way. I did not love business; I did not love to be called on to form a resolution: and he had accommodated himself to both these peculiarities, by doing in this instance what my interests manifestly required, without giving me the trouble to be consulted in the matter.

This harangue, notwithstanding all I had previously observed, took me so much by surprise, that I did not choose to commit myself, by instantly giving the answer which arose to my lips. The very idea of so intimate an alliance with persons so little agreeable to my disposition, was hateful to my soul. I had resolved to cut myself off from every thing that wore the human form. It was sufficient, in conformity with that resolution, that I suffered the attendance of the servants of my landlord, the farmer. I was not exactly prepared for the condition of a hermit, living on roots, and passing my days in one uninterrupted train of contemplation; and therefore some service from other men was necessary to me. The situation in which I was placed on my arrival in Derbyshire, was such as my wishes pointed out to me. I might use the persons that approached me, as mere machines. I neither knew, nor desired to know, any thing about their history, their occupations, or their feelings. They were to me like a dumb waiter,[1] or the instrument constructed by the smith, and by courtesy called a "footman":[2] they did what I required, and I was no further concerned with them. But with my guardian, and my ancient school-fellow, I could not feel thus at my ease. I might resolve to treat them with superciliousness and disdain, and to take no notice of them as they passed: but they stood in such relations to me, that it would be difficult to maintain this form of behaviour, without feeling a sort of contention within, no less hostile to my peace than the utmost degree of familiarity would have proved.

Though I returned therefore no answer to Holloway, when he announced to me the plot he had formed, I was not the less seriously bent upon defeating its execution. I could never consent, I thought, that this presumptuous pettifogger[3] of the law should hold me in his shackles. Was it to be endured, that he and his

---

1 A small elevator meant to carry objects (such as food) rather than people.
2 A stand on which to put a kettle.
3 An inferior legal practitioner, especially one who uses dubious practices.

kinsman should intrude upon me whenever they pleased, that they should watch every thing I did, and be acquainted with all my motions? I might as well be a prisoner at once. My condition would differ from that of a captive in nothing but the name. The poorest peasant is in a certain degree at liberty to choose his own domicile, and to have no other person dwelling under the same roof with him, except such as he had previously contemplated and subscribed to: and should I allow myself to be placed in a situation more servile than that of a peasant? My whole soul rose against the thought. Nor did the insolent manner in which Holloway's purpose had been effected, by any means tend to make it more palatable to me. I saw therefore in its genuine light the character of the solicitor, and the nets with which he was preparing to entangle me.

In the mean time I did not immediately perceive how I was to free myself from my perplexity. If my guardian had proceeded in a manner less audacious, and had signified to me his project before it was carried into execution, I should undoubtedly have declared myself against it in a manner the most strenuous and inflexible. But every thing was finished, before an obvious opportunity to do so was thrown into my hands. The farmer and his family were gone, and the newly arrived were already installed in their appointments. I could not expel Holloway; I could only withdraw myself. To do that in the most becoming way, it seemed necessary, that I should begin with presiding my own future habitation. Affronted, as I conceived myself to be, by the extraordinary behaviour of my guardian, I could not quite reconcile it to my ideas of propriety, in this manner to throw down the gauntlet, while I continued to reside, and did not know how long I should find it necessary to reside, in the same house.

My mind was full of perplexity and tumult. I shut myself up, more than I had ever yet been accustomed to. When my occasions or my inclination prompted me to go out of my apartment, I asked myself, "Now, the moment I open the door, shall I not meet these scoundrels?" My first impulse was to watch, or to enquire, that I might avoid the encounter. But my second thought was, to disdain such subjugation and slavery. I sallied forth, desperate and contemptuous. Often I saw nothing of them: when I did, for the most part I scowled, and turned away in silence. On their side, they well knew the cue it became them to follow. They did not obtrude themselves. In the generality of instances they adopted the behaviour my carriage seemed to prescribe.

What is there so offensive, to which habit has not the power to reconcile us? I knew not how to proceed in the migration I contemplated. I was young and inexperienced. Should I take my horse, and, riding about among the neighbouring villages, endeavour in the first place to ascertain by ocular survey, what situation I could discover that would be most agreeable to my inclinations? I did so. I never went out, without being attended by a servant on horseback. I entered once or twice into conversation with the servant, the consideration in my own mind being, "Where shall I now fix my abode?" and endeavoured to elicit such hints from his exacter knowledge of the vicinity, as should direct me in my choice. Still my purpose was, to take Holloway by surprise, even as he had surprised me, and that he should know nothing of my plan of removal, till every thing that related to it was fully arranged. With this view it was necessary, that I should lead my servant to speak up on topics connected with my secret mind, without allowing him to penetrate into its workings. I used the same policy with certain persons, who were engaged in plans for the alteration and improvement of my estate. Alas, how vain and fruitless were my precautions! The profound sagacity of Holloway enabled him to read my most covered thoughts; and, while I, with the gravity of a privy counsellor, set myself to elude his observation, he was considering and settling in his mind, how the whole might best be caused to terminate in the manner he wished.

I returned from my excursions, perplexed and undecided. When I alighted from my ride, it was contrived by this master-craftsman, that nothing should occur to exasperate my uneasiness. His plan was, that, without seeming to be in the slightest degree conscious of my dissatisfaction, his nephew and he should exert themselves to the utmost of their power, to soothe my humour, and reconcile me to the change that had been effected.

The character of Mallison had by this time become entirely the reverse of what it had appeared when he was a school-boy. At school he seemed to have no pleasure so great as that of giving pain to another; and there was a disinterestedness in his malice, that was truly exemplary. He tormented his fellows from the express relish he felt in the faculty of tormenting; and the writhings and anguish they betrayed under his knife, were the sole harvest he sought. With admirable coolness and presence of mind he engaged in his favourite sport; and the transports it internally afforded him, never ruffled one feature of his face, or imparted the slightest vestige of impetuosity or emotion to one articulation of his voice. I have called it sport, nor can there be a more appropriate term. He had all the keenness of a sportsman, joined with all the composure and *sang froid* of the most consummate general in the heat of an engagement. In the pursuit of his game he lost sight of all incidental considerations. He spared neither friend nor foe. To vary the metaphor, he thought not at all of warding his own person from danger, so he might make one successful home-thrust at his adversary.

Since the time that I had lost sight of him, he had fallen under the tuition of the accomplished Holloway; and Holloway was a preceptor of quite another order, than Dr Pottinger, the headmaster of Winchester College, in modelling the character of an ingenuous youth. He opened upon the apprehensions of his nephew a system of morals, quite different from any he had had a previous conception of. Holloway was a sort of *amateur*, and assimilated every thing to the laws of natural history. He taught Mallison, that the world of mankind was made up of two distinct species of beings, which he denominated, by one extensive classification, "wise men and fools," and that between these two there was a natural war, the one being destined to become a prey to the other. A wise man, according to Holloway's definition, was one, who kept a steady eye to his own interests, was fruitful of expedients to promote them, and restrained by no weak scruples in their employment. The wisdom of all other sets of men he regarded as folly; the vaunting pretensions of science and philosophy, in comparison with this, were the drivellings of an idiot.

"The whole world," he said, "the civilised world, was a scene of warfare under the mask of civility. Every man grasped for himself what he could, and every man oppressed his neighbour. The rich man oppressed the poor; and that was his supreme delight. Such a man came into the world with a token of good fortune on his forehead; and he was a lord over his fellows, merely because chance so decreed it. For the rest of mankind, who were born to nothing, they must kick, and scramble, and snatch the good things of the world as they could, or be content to pine for ever in degradation and misery. Honesty was a starving quality, set up by powerful villainy for its own ease and safety. It was in reality an imaginary existence, like truth, much talked of, never to be found. The rich man made no scruple to consume upon his unnatural appetites, what, diffused, would produce health and comfort to hundreds; and the laws, which were framed by the rich exclusively for the protection of their monopoly, bore them out in this. But the injustice was much more glaring and beyond controversy, than that of the man, who took by force the property of another on the highway, and gallantly ventured his neck for the supply of his wants.

"But our lot is 'fallen to us in pleasant places, and verily we have a goodly heritage.'[1] It is no longer necessary for him who wishes to possess himself of the good things of this world, to the disposal of which he is not born, to sally forth with guns, and swords, and the various instruments of offence. There is one little instrument with which he opens the purse of his neighbour with much less risk of miscarriage, than with staves, and cutlasses, and bludgeons,—a smile. This is the engine, by means of which the smooth shopkeeper behind his counter, contrived to enrich himself at the expence of his customers. Flattery is the art, that makes him who is accomplished in it, the master of the masters of the earth. Tickle the palm of the rich man, and the gold falls from his gripe, and is all your own. And of all professions and callings on the face of the globe, the lawyer is most advantageously disposed, to enable him to sweep the wealth of the world into his coffers. But for this purpose he must be master of his passions, and perfect in the art of self-control. Nothing must irritate him; nothing must divert his eye from the object of his pursuit; nothing must turn him aside from the steadiness of his aim. Go on coolly and resolutely, in the path that I have trod before you; regard mankind as your implements merely; you will say, they have a soul and sense; but have no consideration for that, except so far as by those feelings they may be made the more subservient to your purpose. This is the true philosophy, never to be turned aside by any meaner suggestion from the great end you have in view. What the ancients styled philosophy was a mere name, pursued for ostentation and vain-glorious purposes only; but the principle I recommend, has for its destination and its haven, not a phantom, but a substantial reality."

Never was a pupil that did more honour to his preceptor than Mallison. He drank in these lessons of sublunary wisdom, as the young poet has been feigned to quaff the Heliconian streams;[2] and his very soul was refreshed. In fact, his methods of action according to this creed, were the same as those with which nature had instinctively inspired him; his end only was changed. As a school-boy, he had always been dispassionate and collected,

---

1 Psalms 16:6.
2 In Greek mythology, Mount Helicon had two springs that were sacred to the Muses.

watching where to plunge the murderous knife with most desperate effect, and exploring the nerve where torture might be most powerfully awakened. His hint was now, to cringe, to fawn, and to flatter; but with the same impassive observation of the effects he produced, and the same supernatural deadness of emotion to the interests and the happiness of those respecting whom his projects were conversant.

CHAPTER V

Things were nearly in this situation, when an incident occurred that marvellously helped forward the project of my guardian and his kinsman. I have sufficiently painted the disturbed and unhinged condition of my mind. To the man who has a spring of uneasiness in his own bosom, external sources of emotion are often peculiarly grateful. Yet the difficulty is to find those, that a mind diseased can bear. I could not go into the world; I could not bear the intercourse of my species. I could not endure to seek the abodes of distress: for, in doing so, I should be annoyed with the observation of others; and I should have to encounter that, which, perhaps of all things in the world, in my frame of thinking I most irresistibly shrank from, the thanks and the praise of those who witnessed my actions. The emotion I required, was that which should demand no effort on my part, and which no annoying spectator should stand by and observe. One species was brought to my thoughts by accident, which had all these qualities; and I immediately seized on it with eagerness.

This was the act of riding; the simply mounting upon my horse, and pushing him along the downs and the forest-paths at a rapid pace. I could not bear to join in the chace, or to make my appearance any where in the resorts of men. But the motion of a horseman was agreeable to me; it communicated a new alacrity to the circulation of the blood; it excited the animal spirits; and the way in which hills and plains and the clouds of heaven fly away and succeed each other, to him that travels swiftly, had something in it that brought nameless relief to my wearied spirit. The very fatigue that I felt resulting from this exercise, was grateful; and, while engaged in it, it often happened to me, though not always, that I forgot Clifford, and Lisle, and Penruddock, and every thing that again and again had planted a dagger in my soul.

From a love of the exercise of riding, I came, by a very natural transition, to a love of the animal by whom this pleasure was communicated to me. When once my mind had taken this turn, it produced a sensation soothing to my misanthropy. I said to myself, "At length I have found a noble animal, that has none of the vices of my own species. He will never flatter and deceive me; he will never form plots for my undoing; he will never conspire with the treacherous and the base, to rob me of my fair fame, and to level me without cause with the vilest." When I was not on horseback, I would often go out into the fields, on a sort of visit to the creatures for whom I had conceived this partiality. My harassed spirit was not in a tone to make the first overtures to this species of friendship; but it somehow happened, that my favourite mare saw me at a distance, uttered a neigh of pleasure, and trotted up to the spot where I stood. I was pleased with the circumstance, and determined to improve upon the opening that thus presented itself. I repeated my visits frequently about the same hour, patted the animal's neck, and brought with me, sometimes one thing, and sometimes another, which the creature eagerly and proudly accepted at my hands. Perhaps all gregarious animals are imitative; the other horses in the field followed the example of the first, and seemed to emulate each other in courting my favour.

The more I addicted myself to horses and horse-exercise, the more curious I became in my choice of the animals I rode. The servant, who always accompanied me in my excursions of this sort, was himself an expert jockey. This circumstance produced a considerable degree of familiarity between us. I loved to speak of any thing that was not man; and the gnawing pain which the trials I had sustained produced in me about the region of the heart, was soothed, and its anguish suspended, while I talked, and heard this fellow talk, of this quadruped, his noble nature, and his extraordinary merits. My groom was of course not less charmed with a topic of this levelling sort, in which he was at least as good a man as I, or was in reality decisively my superior.

My love for this species of amusement (thanks to the communicative temper of my attendant!) soon became notorious through my own and several adjacent hundreds. Many a dealer in horses, when he conceived he had got an animal of more than ordinary value, came and offered his beast to the heir of the opulent house of Mandeville. My taste in this respect however was extremely limited: I never partook in the pleasures of the chace; I had no share in the passion felt by many of my wealthy contemporaries for the sports of Doncaster or Newmarket.[1] I was

---

1 Both places had racecourses, but not until the early eighteenth century.

therefore in no danger of falling into any injurious excess of expenditure.

One day an animal of this sort was brought to me, the most beautiful my eyes ever beheld. His figure was light; his limbs graceful; his coat of a bright chesnut, and of an uncommonly smooth and glossy appearance. His eyes seemed full of intelligence and fire; and the curve of his neck was peculiarly expressive of a proud and spirited character. He was young, and had hardly yet been sufficiently reduced from his coltish wildness. I bought this horse; and he became my favourite. There was something in the intellect of my new four-footed friend, superior to that of any of his species that I had possessed before. By practice among these animals I became more skilful in my manner of addressing them, and knew better how to adapt my approaches to their taste. This young thing was of a nature peculiarly affectionate, and showed his attachment to me in a variety of ways that I had never witnessed in his fellows. Our mutual partiality had this effect, that he became more docile and conforming to all my wishes, and I the more completely understood his dispositions, and knew how to avail myself of them with gentleness and good humour. It was a spectacle that won the admiration of the rustics, to see me mounted on this beast, so spirited, and yet so tractable. The animal himself, as I have said, was uncommonly beautiful; nor did his rider any way mis-become him. My figure was slender, and my limbs tapering; loving the exercise, and confident in my skill, I sat my horse well; my locks shadowed my forehead and cheeks in wavy ringlets; the uncommon seriousness and sensibility of my temper gave a romantic interest to my visage; all together, I believe I may venture to say I was no ill model of a cavalier, at this period, when among multitudes a cavalier was held to be a name for the very abstract and quintessence of honour.

The admiration of strangers did not much incommode me, for by the assistance of my *monture* I could easily escape from it; and my delight was in solitudes. It happened however unfortunately for Mallison, that this was the occasion, upon which he ventured to make his first essay of that system of flattery and insinuation that he had laid down to himself. He thought, poor, senseless coxcomb! that he understood the human heart, and how to take advantage of its weakness. As I excelled in horsemanship, he took it for granted that I was vain of my accomplishment, and he had learned from his precious instructor, that "flattery direct, seldom disgusts." How true this maxim holds of others I cannot pretend to decide. I only know that the compliments of Mallison on this occasion excited in me inexpressible loathings, and that I manifested in a way sufficiently intelligible what was passing in my mind, I was astonished, that such a reptile should dare to profane my ears with his praise. I remembered, in an indistinct way, the gibes and scoffs and insults he had a hundred times tried to put upon me, when we were school-boys together. I say, in an indistinct way; for it has sufficiently appeared, that even at that time I never did him the honour to hate him. Yet, huddled and confused as the recollection was, it did not fail to spring up in my mind; and I was struck with no little wonder, that he, who a few years before had tried in vain to rise to the distinction of being my enemy, should now, without sinking into the earth with shame, venture to accost me with his nauseous approbation. But Mallison could say, like Shylock in the play, "Patience is the badge of all our tribe." He stomached the contempt with which I loaded him, and lost no whit of the serenity of his countenance, and the smiles of complacency and adulation with which he was at all times prepared to meet me.

I had already for some months addicted myself to this exercise, when an accident happened, which served, at least for some time, to suspend its indulgence. I was riding rapidly along by the side of a bank, surrounded with osiers,[1] and on the further side a hay-field. The haymakers, it seems, were reposing themselves for a short time in the shade, from the fatigue of their employment. One of them happened to catch a glance of the young squire and his favourite gelding, and named it to the rest. Four or five started up at once, stepped up the bank at the foot of which they were reclining, and began a sudden rustling among the osiers. My horse was frightened at the sound, leaped violently to the other side of the road, and I was thrown. This was no specimen of my good horsemanship. But it was the peculiarity of my nature, to be frequently wholly absorbed in reveries. At this moment I happened to be engaged in a thousand melancholy reflections on my condition, and had no consciousness of any of the objects by which I was actually surrounded. I was as little capable of helping myself upon this sudden emergency as a man asleep. My servant hastened to my assistance, and found that I had broken my leg. My horse stood motionless by my side, in an attitude the most expressive of grief and shame that could be conceived. I was not far from my home: a sort of litter was speedily procured; and the animal who without the least ill intention

---

1 A small willow that grows in wet habitats.

had been the cause of my casualty, followed the vehicle without a leader, with no less appearance of mourning than Homer describes in the horses of Achilles, when Patroclus had fallen beneath the spear of Hector.

This was the incident, that threw me at once into the hands of Mallison. I was for several weeks confined to my bed under the care of the surgeons. Mallison tended my couch with unwearied care; nor was there any species of tenderness and attention left by him undischarged. Oh, wretched condition of poor humanity! that all those demonstrations of love and attachment which the most ardent affection can prompt, should be so perfectly imitated by a creature without a heart, conscious only to the basest self-ishness, and prompted by the most sordid motives that satire in all its bitterness could desire. Such is the condition of the rich. They can scarcely ever know the real inward workings of soul of the people about them. They live in the midst of a stage-play, where every one that approaches them is a personated actor, and the lord himself is the only real character, performing his part in good earnest, while the rest are employed in a mummery, and laugh in their hearts at the gross delusion they are practising upon him.

For fourteen days from the time I was conveyed to my bed, I was required to continue in one attitude, my body straitened, and my face turned toward the zenith. It is difficult for any one, who has not passed through an experiment of this sort, to conceive the tediousness, the weariness of spirit, and the restlessness and intolerable itching of the limbs, which such a situation produces. Human nature is capable of exhibiting a hero. But then heroism is a thing, that for the most part requires that the fire within the hero's breast, should be cherished by the presence of one or a greater number of spectators; or, if not that, at least it is neces-sary, that the conception existing in the actor's or sufferer's mind, should be of something energising and great. It is less difficult to bear with serenity the bite of a scorpion, than the stinging of a thousand insects that are nearly invisible. It is next to impossible, that what wears away and utterly dissipates the electrical fluid within us, should leave in the human heart a sense of loftiness and pride.

If such will be found the actual experience of every one that has been placed in my situation, it will easily be imagined how grievous it was to me. I bore a wound in my heart, to which the fracture I had sustained in a limb was nothing. My mind was dis-turbed; the chambers and compartments of my understanding were broken up; and twenty times a day I had been accustomed to find it necessary, by change of place to dissipate the pressure of my inward agonies, and by the violence of bodily exertions to overcome, as for a short time I was generally able to do, the sufferings of my soul.

I know not how humiliating the confession may be considered by others, but I must ingenuously own, that my innate pride was wholly subdued and laid prostrate for the time, by my situation. I was unable to relieve myself even by the act of reading. The poorest creature, that would have come near me, and soothed me by his attentions, would have been received with an animated welcome. One of the gossips, that are hired in savage countries at so much an hour, to recite legendary stories, would have been hailed by me as an angel of light. Elaborate as are the distinctions of rank set up in civilised countries, and deeply as they are grafted into the hearts of their envied possessors, there are many other adversaries, besides Death, by which they are liable to be crumbled into dust.

In this situation Mallison, the wretched Mallison, became a favourite with me, and I was uneasy if he left my bed-side but for a moment. This fellow must be acknowledged to have been an admirable artist. He personated, as I have said, the utmost watchfulness and tenderness. He did not value my "life at a pin's fee"; yet the part he acted proceeded from a passion as real and as deep, as if the term of his existence had been linked to mine, as closely as Meleager's to the brand of Althea.[1] All that he did was subordinate to an end; and every syllable that he uttered, was supplied by as profound a feeling as the most disinterested friendship could have inspired. The same study furnished to him as effectually, the means of amusing my weariness, as of soothing my paroxysms. We had both been bred at the same school; and every one who has had the experience of it, knows that there is a topography of language and topics—so that every Wintonian[2]

---

1   Godwin's own account is that at Meleager's birth the Fates blessed him with various gifts, but foretold that he would live only as long as a brand on the hearth was not consumed. His mother Althea snatched the brand from the fire and extinguished it to prevent its burning out, but when he killed his envious uncles in the hunt for the wild boar of Calydon, she set it on fire and her son died (*Pantheon: or, the Ancient History of the Gods of Greece and Rome* [London: M.J. Godwin, 1806; 4th ed. 1814], 141–42).

2   Student of Winchester College.

talks the same jargon, and to a certain degree thinks the same thoughts. It was not long enough since I had resided there, for me to have lost a particle of these recollections, or of my school-boy identity; at the same time that the scenes were sufficiently distant in months and years, to give the repetition of them a greater zest, and to interpose more of an aerial or poetic perspective between, than they would have had if recited to me in the first term after my admission at the university. In this respect my enjoyment was similar to that, when Englishman meets Englishman on the further side of the globe. Mallison likewise, though he had a mind wholly eunuch[1] and ungenerative in matters of literature and taste, had retained with sufficient fidelity the discourses of Dr Pottinger, and could harangue like an accomplished commentator, upon the urbanities of Aristophanes, and the fragments of Menander.[2] I have met with, though rarely, a memory of the same class as that of my present companion, a person who could recite words in all their identity and primitive arrangement, without seeming to have a particle of feeling of the spirit they contained. My memory in the affair of minuteness, was certainly very inferior to Mallison's. I therefore felt grateful to him for reviving impressions, which had once been pleasant to me, but the traces of which in my mind had become indistinct and obscure; and for the sake of the pleasurable sensations he afforded me, I felt as if it would be a sort of injustice in me, not to believe that the sound observations I heard, were the genuine growth of the speaker's understanding. By the same tenaciousness of memory he could also repeat to me many of those passages of the classics, which he had been accustomed to hear most highly applauded. Mallison too added to his other accomplishments, that of being an excellent mimic. In the pride of my soul, when in vigorous health, I had scorned so inglorious and plebeian a talent; but what will not a sick-bed reduce us to? Add to which, there is something in mimicry that is irresistible; and the generous hearer will sometimes find himself surprised by it into convulsions of laughter, even while he despises and hates himself for the degradation. Dr Pottinger himself, and all the inferior masters in turn, by this means passed in review before me; and it is perhaps an invariable rule, that schoolmasters, with their mock dignity, and self-satisfied airs of importance, furnish the richest field for this species of imitation. If there is a fund of real worth

---

1 Emasculated.
2 Comic dramatists of ancient Greece.

and superior understanding behind this curtain, it subtracts nothing, but on the contrary gives an additional richness and relish to the exhibition. To my great surprise I found Mallison abundant in anecdotes; and the dry, sarcastic, unemotioned, and seemingly half-unconscious way in which he detailed them, in some way operated so, as to bring out the striking points more completely in relief. He had certainly a genuine talent for humour and comedy. And the malignity, which lay as a corner-stone of all his faculties, helped his performances. That malignity formerly found its favourite occupation in molesting my peace; now it was the smooth, and specious, and silky side of his nature, a side indeed which was purely the creature of the severest discipline and art, that was turned upon me; and the malice was all employed for my entertainment, serving perhaps occasionally to betray what its owner "could do, an if he would."

Shall I say, that the helpless state to which this incident reduced me, sunk me below the genuine attitude of man, or that it merely brought me down to the true level and standard of my species? Before, I held myself aloof from the human race, and disdained their assistance; or, if I admitted it for the necessities of animal life, I sternly repelled it so far as related to our consolations and our pleasures. I was like a person, who, having read the narrative of some poor shipwrecked mariner, condemned to dwell for years in an uninhabited island, should buy himself a vessel, or procure himself a passage, and say, "I will be that man's successor." But now I came to the sound human feeling, and said, "It is good to have a companion. My companion shall be from among 'the excellent of the earth,'[1] if I can procure such, shall be a being who awakens all the best sentiments and the purest delights of our nature, shall be Henrietta, or the counterpart of Henrietta in my own sex, if that be possible: but still I know that a companion is necessary. I will therefore abstain from all romantic and Arcadian speculations; and if my companion is homely, thick in his apprehensions, and grovelling in his temper, and I can get no other, I will be content with that."

Well then, I had Mallison, and no one else, except now and then his uncle, with the servants, and the periodical visits of my professional attendant, that came near the couch to which I was confined. By dint of studying my associate, I discerned in him powers and accomplishments of which I was not previously aware. The faults that he had, by familiarity became less offensive

---

1 Adapted from Isaiah 4:2.

to me. I did not find them such "black and grained spots, as would not leave their tint."[1] On the contrary, they presently ceased to be shocking to my taste, and by degrees seemed, like the dark parts of a picture, to add their share to the total excellence. They constituted the style of the artist, which had been a thousand times connected with agreeable sensations; and I should as soon have thought of finding fault with Rembrandt for the deepness and breadth of his shadows,[2] as with Mallison for the hard and unsympathetic tone of his conversation. It is thus, that the chances of human life, as well as its "miseries, make us acquainted with strange companions";[3] and many a man, by the mere control of time and place, has poured out his soul to another, and made him the partner of his bosom, who would certainly never have admitted him to that function, if it had depended upon his spontaneous election.

Mallison observed with an acute and steady perception the progress he made in my favour. He was certainly by nature a man of no great talents; but he was of that class of mortals, no very rare one, in which interest sharpens the faculties, and brings out a species of capacity that had before lain idle and unemployed. He improved by exercise. He saw that the time was come, when he might venture to flatter me. His experiment in the case of my horsemanship was most unfortunate; but the situation was very different now. It is not every one, to speak from my own observation, that can safely venture to become a flatterer. The flatterer's is a delicate task. When any one praises me, I am inevitably reduced to examine, "But is what this person affirms of me real and just?" And very often I am compelled to confess a doubt, or more than a doubt, that he is dealing in fiction, and that at best, if he is not a deceiver, he is himself misled. It is true, that most men can sit with decent composure to hear themselves praised for an attribute, of the existence of which they are wholly unconscious. We are perhaps more fastidious, when the commendation is employed on our real qualities. Then, he that commends us, too often employs terms, that appear to us too low, and not in unison with the worth of the subject; or he praises us for a quality that we do not value, and that we would have thought it more

---

1 *Hamlet*, 3.4.91–92: Gertrude, describing her guilt over her infidelity to Hamlet's father and complicity in his murder.

2 Rembrandt van Rijn (1606–69), Flemish painter famous for his *chiaroscuro*, a technique involving light and shade.

3 Adapted from *The Tempest*, 2.2.39–40, referring to Caliban.

honourable to us that we should have been given credit for in silence; or he is a person of no weight and character himself, and we are less gratified with the sweet applauses with which he endeavours to crown us, than offended with his presumption, that he should dare to importune us with his judgment.

I had been one of the best grounded of all my contemporaries in Winchester school. I have said, that I was constitutionally ambitious. It is fatally but too true, that ambition is incident to human beings, in whom there exist no powers by which the appetite can be appeased. This is undoubtedly the case in every department of mortal eminence, but is no where so conspicuous as in the passion for literary fame; because this sort of ambition does not address itself to a patron merely, but exposes its essays in a certain degree to the whole world, and they possess, if abortive, a portion of what I may call, *fugitive permanence*, for the "hand of scorn, to point its slight, unmoving finger at."[1] How many men have been "smit with the sacred love of song,"[2] who never in their lives could construct a poetical line? But such was not my case. I was ambitious; and I had in me naturally the power which seemed best calculated to procure the gratification of my ambition. My talent was not showy, but, if I may venture to say it, profound. I could not, like Clifford, leave the shore at once, and dash into the mighty ocean of classic lore. I was not born with the talent of an ancient bard, and could not pour out in copious and unexhausted streams, the unpremeditated verse. On the contrary, I was like the lawgiver of the Jews, "slow of speech, and of a slow tongue."[3] Diffidence, the offspring of haughty self-respect and disdain, sealed up my lips. Once or twice, in a hot fit of youthful pride and ostentation, I had not failed to make the trial. But my self-possession deserted me. I fell into blunders inconceivable; all that I knew before seemed to have left me at the moment it was wanted; I could never command the recollection of things, in the interchange of defiance and debate, that were most fully at my disposal in the cool element of meditation. The dullest boy in the school could often put me down. And, when I once felt mortified and ashamed, it was all over with me. "Man but a rush against Othello's breast, and he retires." Such was the aukward and ineffective figure I made at Winchester school. Yet it was known, that I really possessed powers that I wanted the skill

---

1 Adapted from *Othello*, 4.2.54–55.
2 *Paradise Lost*, 3.29.
3 Exodus 4:10, continuing the parallels between Mandeville and Moses.

to bring into play. When my "co-mates and fellows" in the form triumphed over me most unmercifully, they knew that Themis[1] was not there, and that the whole was a pageant, in which the shadow triumphed over the substance. Even Clifford himself, with all his "dazzling fence,"[2] was always ready to acknowledge that I was intrinsically his equal.

This was Mallison's cue, the principle that guided him in the attack he was now directing against me. He spoke freely and effectively, because honestly, of my real strength, and my absolute resources. Yet even this he did not venture upon, but with judgment and caution. To my unfaithful memory and envenomed imagination Winchester was all one tissue of mortification and disgrace. But the industry of Mallison brought out scenes of an opposite character, and examples in which I was myself compelled to confess that I had appeared to more advantage than I was aware. These were doubly gratifying to me, because they were unexpected. He told of situations, in which my secret powers were drawn out, in which I had myself played the principal character, but which, neither at the time, nor since, had I apprehended in the sense in which he displayed them.

I began comparatively to like Mallison. The man who, whenever you see him, puts you in good humour with yourself, will past all doubt be found, after no long trial, a welcome visitor. This sort of fair understanding being established between us, Mallison now ventured, when his stock of anecdotes and panegyric began to run low, to ask my opinion of men and things, of periods of literature, and the great heroes and colossal personages of the intellectual world. I was naturally no copious talker. It was fear, and pride, and a doubtful anticipation of the effects to be produced, that made me silent. But I know not how it was, I never felt so unrestrained of speech, as at the period I am now describing. No, not the presence of Henrietta herself, and the charm of her society, ever gave such a loose to my tongue. I secretly stood in awe of her judgment. I knew she had an independent mind, and an instinctive discernment of right and truth, which, while I adored it, almost made me tremble lest she should discover the extent of my infirmities. But Mallison was so implicit, bowed so completely to all my judgments, and drank in all my suggestions,

---

1 Greek goddess of justice, who ensured that things were in their place in human affairs.
2 The Lady on the sophistries of Comus (790). Mandeville often compares Clifford to Comus.

that it was a pleasure to talk to so accommodating a pupil. There was another thing that produced a material effect in my intercourse with him: his mind was totally vacant of all moral discernment. We could not be always talking of abstractions, of literature, and authors. I had relapses, when I was any thing but a hero. If I had at any time an attack of pain, if I was wretched, or was peevish, I no more thought of suppressing the first symptoms of these conditions in the presence of Mallison, than if I had been alone. I played the querulous fool without constraint, and spread out my nature before him in its most pitiful and degrading imperfections. He had absolutely no sense of these things, and seemed to know no difference between what was illustrious and what was contemptible. If I had conceived any "villainous, inglorious enterprise"[1] of the basest fraud, or if I had laid a scene of murder for fiends to shrink at, it seems to me, that I should have disclosed it to Mallison without reserve, and that he was too entire a friend to have given harbour to the least uncivil scruples on the occasion. As he discovered himself to me at this time, he seemed to have no object but my gratification, no study but of what would be acceptable to me, and no standard of good, but what depended on my will.

The company of Mallison was in some measure to me like the song of the Sirens. They complimented Ulysses in ravishing strains upon the profoundness of his discretion, and he could scarcely be restrained from showing himself a fool.[2] This was the first time for many years that I had regarded myself with any absolute complacency. That feeling, almost the only one that makes human existence felt as a blessing, had long been a stranger to me: and I welcomed it, in somewhat the same manner as an affectionate father would hail the return of a long-lost son. It was doubtless in part the weakness which resulted from the tedious recovery of my limb, that made me receive with so true a relish so poor a praise as Mallison's. It must however be considered, that it had been in a singular degree my lot, to live with honest men. In my childish residence at Mandeville House, nobody had spoken to me any thing but the truth, or what the speaker considered as truth. There was no one,

---

1 Otway, *Venice Preserv'd*, 2.2.
2 When passing the abode of the Sirens, Ulysses had the ears of his men filled with wax and had himself tied to the mast of the ship to avoid yielding to their blandishments.

> — under fair pretence of friendly ends,
> And well-placed words of glozing courtesy,
> Baited with reasons not unplausible,
> To wind him with the easy-hearted boy,
> And bring him into snares.[1]

At Winchester every one was too full of his own fancies, and the pursuit of his own gratifications, to flatter another. Even Mallison, the earth-born and false-hearted Mallison, felt there a greater propensity, to sting his neighbour with flouts and gibes, than to smooth him down with tickling praise. There was beside a *sombre* reserve and a forbidding haughtiness about me, that seemed to dash the first accents of applause; and in this way it might easily have happened to me, to have sunk into old age and the grave, without once having heard the fawning voice of adulation. But Mallison had both motive and opportunity in abundance to enter upon the unpromising task; and accordingly he was too gallant and high-minded, to be deterred by the very unfavourable attempt with which he had commenced his career.

I am ashamed to own, that this was to me a period of unwonted enjoyment. Strange is the nature of that anomalous creature man, that even so pitiful an animal as I held Mallison to be, should have had the power to make me happy. But it should be considered, that the breath of dishonour had passed over the first buds of my youth like the pestilential wind of the desert, and had blasted the whole harvest of my hopes. All my solitary reflections had been full of dismay; every morning that I awoke, the first flavour upon my fasting palate had been bitterness. I was so accustomed to look on the dark side of things, that I hardly suspected that one ray of light could penetrate my gloom. It was with me, as when "the sun shall be turned into darkness, and the moon into blood, and the stars shall fall from heaven."[2] All therefore that Mallison told me of the trophies of my youth, the speculations and conjectures that he drew from me, and the profound attention with which he appeared to receive them, was like a welcome intelligence brought to me from the remotest corner of the earth. I began to say to myself, "I am not lost in loss itself. There is still enough left of me to make a worthy. I am still capable of exciting the approbation and wonder of my species;

---

1 *Comus*, 160–64.
2 Alluding to the breaking of the sixth seal in Revelation (6:12–13), which unleashes cataclysmic events.

and the sentiments of our fellows concerning us, are an unfailing mirror, refracting the beams of pleasure, and awakening in our hearts self-respect and self-reverence. Yes; I will form a new system of life; and hope, the welcome stranger, shall again visit my breast."

I have no doubt, that this interval of serenity and pleasure had another cause, beside that which I adverted to at the time. This was, the state of my animal system: I had been for fourteen days required to continue in one unvarying attitude. My spirits were worn out with the dismal monotony; and though, excepting a slight fever at first, I cannot be said to have been in ill health, my confinement produced upon me most of the effects of sickness. My lassitude, and the tediousness of my days and nights, but for Mallison's attentions and the amusements he supplied to me, would have been insupportable. The pleasure I felt, when I was rescued from captivity, when I was first permitted to rise from my bed, and to go out into the garden, was such as cannot easily be expressed. As I had for many days had no real sickness, and suffered only a compulsory confinement, my situation perfectly resembled that of a prisoner, restored at once from a strict constraint to his liberty. My blood literally danced in my veins. I snuffed the free and wholesome air of the blue heavens, and exclaimed, "Ah, this is indeed to be happy!" The restoration of these prerogatives, so little valued by man till he has felt the loss of them, came to my senses blended in point of time with the ingenious cajoleries of my novice-lawyer; and whether I looked on the one side or the other, to the exhilaration I derived from the sunshine and the breeze and the face of nature, or to that which came to me from the artful flatteries of my newly-admitted companion, I equally exclaimed, without attempting any nice investigation of the cause, "Ah, this is indeed to be happy!" To say every thing in a word, I imputed the whole of what I felt to Mallison, and considered him for the time as my better angel.

The man who leaves his apartment, where he has been attended by the sons of Hippocrates and Galen,[1] where pain has been his companion, and lassitude his bed-fellow, where every morning he prays for the night, and every night for the morning, has infallibly something of the feeling which belongs to the commencement of a new life, and which Adam may be supposed to have had, when first he opened his eyes on the groves and the fountains of Eden. Sickness, after it is passed through and ended,

---

1   Ancient Greek physicians who influenced modern medicine.

is like a gap in existence. It is one of the characteristics of the sick man, that when he is at the worst, his mind is shut up within the circle of his actual sensations, a sort of deadness as to external things comes over him, and the world is nothing to him; its vexations and embarrassments are absolutely annihilated and forgotten. His recovery therefore is something like the state of a man accustomed to carry heavy burthens, but who feels his load no more. He enters the world with new thoughts, new projects, and new hopes. Such was my condition at this time; such my elasticity and the renovation of my nature. And I owed the advantage very much to Mallison. He had somehow in a very great degree reconciled me to myself. For the moment, I forgot the mortifications and agony by which I had been so long depressed. For the moment, they appeared to exist no longer. He had brought my hidden virtues to the light of day. He persuaded me that every thing was not so desperate with me as I had imagined. He stirred up once again in me the fire of ambition, that fire which seemed to be in me the first principle of existence, and which, though raked up, and hidden with ashes, could never, I thought, be utterly extinguished, while one pulse continued to beat within me.

CHAPTER VI

The mighty master smiled to view
　　The triumphs of his art:
And, while I heaven and earth defied,
Changed his hand, and checked my pride.[1]

In the openness of my heart, which was a violation of my nature, and which I had never felt before, I talked to Mallison of my new projects and purposes. I said, "I am but nineteen:[2] What should ail me, that I should think the world at an end with me? I have health; I have youth; I have a plentiful estate. You, Mallison, by

---

1　Significantly turned around from Dryden, "Alexander's Feast" (1697), 69–72: "The master saw the madness rise / His glowing cheeks, his ardent eyes / And while he heaven and earth defied / Chang'd his hand, and checked his pride." The date of Dryden's poem could mean that Mandeville is 59 when he writes his memoir, but there are other anachronistic quotations in the text that exceed any normal lifespan.

2　We are now in the year 1657.

your kind and cordial communications, have made me feel, more vividly than I ever felt before, that I have talents, the materials out of which a patriot, an ornament of his species, a benefactor of mankind, is to be formed. If I have done wrong, or rather if I have been misconstrued and calumniated, the world is not so unjust, as to allow no return to honour, to a youth of nineteen, who possesses all internal, and all accidental means, of courting its favour, and loading it with benefits. If then the world has not passed a decree of exclusion against me, neither will I. I will neither desert myself, nor hide what I am in a napkin. No: that which it is in my power to do, I will do strenuously. I have not yet fully digested what; but the task of human usefulness is a solemn office, and shall be well ruminated by me, before I buckle on my harness, and descend into the field."

Mallison shook his head.

"All this would be well," said he, "were it not for Clifford. No being that lives, ever possessed greater advantages than you, or has been endowed with a more gallant spirit, to improve those advantages. I frankly own that. You might turn the pages of Greek and Roman story, and choose out the character that you would imitate, or rather that you would rival. You might be the pride of the island that gave you birth. The concentration and reserve of spirit, of which you have sometimes been disposed to complain, are of infinite service in that point of view. A noble soul like yours does not waste itself in idle efforts, and boil over in trifles and things of no value till its best powers are evaporated. Such a one as you, where he devotes his attention, strikes; and the blow is a master-blow, that at once astonishes the bystander, inforces obedience and sympathy, and quells opposition. It is not possible, without the profoundest sorrow, to see such a fountain of general refreshment and usefulness, choaked up and stifled in its source: but, alas! my dear sir, you are not aware what a general prepossession has gone out against you. Remember what Lisle told you; remember what you heard from the Marquis de Gevres. Oh, my dear Mandeville, the world is much more unjust, and much more unrelenting, than you imagine. Your chance for making a splendid figure, and playing an illustrious part among your contemporaries, is at an end. You are like some majestic oak in the forests of your country, that the thunder hast past over, and has scathed it. There it stands in all its giant size and original dimensions; every one may see what it might have been; every one may gaze at its stupendous outline; but upon its bared branches there remains not a single leaf to adorn them; the bark is peeled away at the root from the naked stem; and the heart of the tree, so late the boast of its native soil, is daily crumbling into dust.

"Revenge therefore, hatred and revenge, is all that is left you. Your pleasure, it is true, must be a gloomy pleasure; but dark and church-yard contemplations have their sublimity and their satisfaction. Remember what you are, and meditate what you might have been: all this shall fill you with a mournful and heart-breaking delight. You cannot live for the world: no, that is past. But you may live, like Charles the Fifth, to solemnize your own sepulchral honours, and to recollect the path which nature and the election of God seemed to destine you to tread.[1] You may in imagination fill your ears with the anthem and the dirge, and all those solemn sights and sounds, with which we are accustomed to bid to the great ones of the earth an everlasting farewel. Yes, God assigned to you a high destiny, and to leave a trail of glory behind; but a malignant demon has passed over your intended orbit, and has driven you infinite leagues away from the path in which you ought to have moved, into the desert waste of space. Nothing therefore remains for you, but solemnly to revolve what you might have been, and to retaliate largely and with interest upon the enemy that has destroyed you. Even so Achilles slew twelve of the choicest of the Trojan youth upon the funeral pile of Patroclus."[2]

The reader may be surprised to find such ideas flowing from the lips of the wretched and worthless Mallison. But, if he is, I have failed in conveying to him the idea of his character. I have said that Mallison was an admirable mimic. He was an excellent actor, or indeed more than this, since he could compose the phrases and the sentences of the part he had to play. Without being any thing in himself intrinsically, superior to the dirt upon which he trod, he had that pliancy of disposition, that he could remove himself for the moment into the person he wished to represent, with a power something similar to that, with which Fadlallah in the Persian Tales, could shoot himself into any organized body that lay inanimate before him.[3] By dint, in a certain degree,

---

1   Charles, Duke of Burgundy, Holy Roman Emperor (1519–56), abdicated for health reasons and lived in a monastery for his last two years.

2   In Homer's *Iliad*, Achilles desecrates Hector's body before cremating Patroclus' body.

3   Godwin tells the story in his *Lives of the Necromancers* (1834); Fadlallah, King of Mousel, learns from a young dervish the skill of projecting his soul into the body of a dead being; while the King is thus out of his own body, the dervish takes possession of it and tries to steal the King's position and kingdom (117–19).

of imitating the tones and gestures of another, he could come to think his thoughts. Nor indeed is it at all uncommon, though not much observed in the world, that intensity of purpose shall, for the given occasion, convert a mere oaf into a man of wit and sagacity. When Atys saw a soldier raise his scymetar against the life of his father Croesus, the dumb man spoke;[1] and assuredly an overpowering crisis has often loosed the tongue of the intellectually dumb, and made him discourse with a propriety and energy, of which the most favoured son of genius needed not to be ashamed. In the present instance, Mallison's proceeding would have been impotent to his purpose, if he had not thought my thoughts, and expressed himself in my idiom.

The language thus held to me by Mallison was like a stroke of thunder. A thousand circumstances had communicated to my spirits an unaccustomed buoyancy. I had just recovered the free use of the members of my body, and could proceed to the right or the left, with a swift or a slow motion, as I pleased. I was like what I have somewhere read of a person issuing forth from the *Thermae*, or hot-baths of Egypt, where, after a copious perspiration, various attendants had been employed with a strenuous friction, in removing the various obstructions that usually stop up all the pores and outlets of the body. I felt, as if the power of gravitation that binds material substances to the earth on which they are placed, was removed, that my limbs and my whole frame had lost their cumbrousness, that I was in danger of mounting up in the air, and could sail as I pleased, sustained and cushioned upon the clouds of heaven.

Such was the state of my corporeal feelings; and the style in which Mallison had talked to me for weeks, wonderfully harmonized with the freedom of my spirits. I felt in my heart, though I confessed it as little as I could, that his language was that of a flatterer. But, for this very reason, I the more relied on its consistency; since, in this sense, you can never be sure of a man who speaks the truth, but you may depend upon a liar. On Mallison's plan, as I understood it, he had nothing to do with the real phenomena, and the absolute merits of the case: he spoke from a principle, and steadily pursued a certain end that he proposed to himself. This it was in reality, that compensated for his want of

---

1 Croesus, King of Lydia, had a dumb son for whom he had little regard, but who saved his life during the battle of Sardis in the way described. Atys was the subject of an Italian opera, a German popular play, and a French opera by Jean-Baptiste Lully (1632–87).

sincerity. The human heart naturally revolts from delusion and imposture, from the impudence of the man who, with unabashed and unaltered front, asserts the thing that he knows to be false. But then this species of intercourse has its advantages. We are not more sure that wholsome food will nourish, and wine will intoxicate, than that the tongue of the flatterer will speak agreeable things. Nothing therefore could be more shocking to me, than the abrupt manner in which my companion now set before me the most loathsome and heart-appalling conceptions that ever were offered to the attention of a human being.

I made a strenuous effort to throw off the weight, with which Mallison was thus unexpectedly endeavouring to overwhelm me.

"No, no, my good fellow," said I, and a smile of bitterness came over me as I said it, "that is past. Perhaps you have not heard that Clifford has become reconciled to the church of Rome."

"Oh, yes, that fact is public and notorious."

"Well then, sir, the fate of every man that is put on his trial, depends on the character of the witness that is brought against him. I have suffered under certain enormous and unfounded accusations: but who is my antagonist? Oh, Mallison! you can have no conception what relief that has brought to my mind. Yes; I thank God, Clifford has settled the controversy between us. I have been charged with secreting and delighting myself with certain inhuman libels against our late illustrious and murdered sovereign. I have been accused of selling myself to the usurper, for the purpose of ruining Penruddock's generous attempt to restore the royal exile, and of betraying this band of heroes to the scaffold. I will not talk of the malignity and the falsehood of these accusations. But what is all this, compared with the turpitude of Clifford? My antagonist is down, and I am up, for ever. You talk of revenge. But what place can there be for revenge against one, who has blotted himself out from the roll of living men and of honest reputation! He walks blasted among his fellow creatures; he bears on him the mark of reprobation; he is reserved for the wrath of God, and his case is beyond the reach of hope; the colour is driven from his cheeks, and his skin is already parched up and embrowned by the fire of hell that burns within him. Who will associate with an apostate? He is cut off from the common benefits of society: no one will harbour him; no one will give him a morsel of bread to eat, or a drop of water to drink. His very touch is contamination; and to breathe the same element with him, is to insure our destruction. His condition is similar to that which our ancestors awarded to a leper, who with a bell and a clap-dish[1] warned those who passed by, not to approach, but to cast their alms by the road-side, which the afflicted sufferer was not allowed to gather up, till the traveller was already gone."

"My dear Mandeville," rejoined my companion, "what you say is certainly of great weight; and all that can be alleged against it is, that the fact is otherwise. I doubt not, there was a time, when men were directed in their treatment of others by ideas of right and wrong, and apostacy was considered as the abhorred thing you so justly describe it. But unfortunately we do not live in those times; and the court of the exiled king, which will soon become the court of London, is the focus of all sorts of latitudinarianism[2] and licentiousness. Lord Digby and his six companions immediately repaired from Ghent to king Charles at Cologne, where they were received with open arms, and almost stifled with the fervent embraces that were bestowed upon them. Clifford in particular was distinguished from all the rest: the large property he is destined to inherit, the beauty of his figure, the enchanting tone of his conversation, the elegance of his manners, the frank simplicity of his disposition, and the brilliancy of his wit, were considered as entitling him to this distinction. The persons principally trusted by king Charles are indeed for the most part Protestants; but there seems to be a general opinion at his little court, that the Protestant episcopal religion is the faith that becomes an English politician, while the Catholic is the religion of a gentleman. There is no other creed to be found at the courts of Versailles, Madrid, and Vienna, the great receptacles of all that is magnificent and brilliant in civilised Europe; while the new religion is fain to take refuge with a beggarly and wandering sovereign, or in still more homely and shop-keeping republics."

It is impossible to express what I felt, while Mallison related these particulars. It was as if my brain-pan had been laid open, and all the conceptions and knots of ideas which had been stored there, were given to irretrievable confusion. Man is the creature of experience. From infancy to age we accumulate from year to year a certain knowledge which serves us for the guide of our actions. We observe the succession of day and night, summer and winter, seed-time and harvest, and regulate our conduct by the

---

1   A wooden dish, with a lid that could be clapped to attract attention.
2   Latitudinarians were seventeenth-century theologians who followed the Church of England but believed that differences over doctrine, liturgy and church government were not crucial.

belief that that succession will take place in future. We conceive that fire will burn, and that water will drown. And there are certain expectations that we form respecting our fellow-men, their treatment of us, the power of motives, and their approbation and disapprobation, upon which we no less confidently rely, than upon these phenomena of nature. But, if what Mallison told me was true, all that I had learned, and the inferences I had been accustomed to draw from it, were to go for nothing. "The moon had come more near the earth than she was wont, and made men mad."[1] Or rather, the whole harmony, and all the constellations of heaven, were moved from their place, and chaos was come again.

I know not that I can make any one that reads these pages, understand the sensation that thus came over me. From the day on which the *Mercurius Politicus* reached me, I in reality obtained a new life. To change one's condition, from darkness to light, from imprisonment to liberty, from a sandy and sterile desert to all that nature pours out of profusion and resistless beauty on her most favoured spots,—no, these are metaphors, and do not at all come near the thing I would record. It was utter and entire hopelessness from which I had escaped, it was Tantalus's thirst,[2] it was the dream of the man who distinctly sees all that is most dear to him perishing before his face, and feels his joints innerved as by some magician's spell, and himself incapable of stretching out a finger to save them.

Till I was thus unexpectedly delivered, I did not understand the extent of my misery. Human nature does not enable us to suffer beyond a given point. When there is no longer hope, our sensations become deadened, our power of apprehending is benumbed, we are the statues of despair, and no more. A slow and a nerveless fever comes over us; the skin is dry; the tongue is parched; the heart sinks within us; and every principle of life is deprived of its tension and its elasticity. We scarcely know this; we do but half lament it. But, once open the door of hope, once let in the fresh and living breeze to which the face of earth is indebted for all its graciousness, how we gasp and pant with the feeling of renovated existence! Then we perceive how wretched we were, and are astonished we should not have known it. Then

---

1   *Othello*, 5.2.190–91: frequently cited in this volume; referring to the accumulation of catastrophes towards the play's end.

2   In Greek mythology, the gods punished Tantalus by putting him near a pool of water that receded whenever he tried to drink from it.

first we apprehend the full meaning of all that can be expressed by the word Misery.

Well then; the obstacle that stood between me and the career of glory was removed. I was once more vested with the rights of man; and all that man, with talents, with favourable circumstances, and with diligence, could achieve, I might hope for. Clifford and I had changed places. It was thus that I understood the situation. But all this, if the report of Mallison were to be believed, was utterly reversed.

Now it was, that I truly hated. Now it was, that I felt that Clifford was my fate, and that, as long as he existed, I must give myself up to the last despair. For me the order of the universe was suspended; all that was most ancient and established in the system of created things was annulled; virtue was no longer virtue, and vice no longer vice. This utter subversion related to me, and me alone; every where else, in every corner of the many-peopled globe, things went on right; I, and I only, was shut out of the pale of humanised society. Whatever I might do, how pure and virtuous soever, was to be the meat for calumny to feed on: whatever Clifford might do, he was a privileged person; a circle of glory for ever surrounded his head; he might

> — trace huge forests, and unharboured heaths;
> Yea there, where very desolation dwells,
> By grots, and caverns, shagged with horrid shades,[1]

he might pass on unhurt, like queen Editha among the burning ploughshares,[2] or the three children in the fiery furnace, when "not a hair of their head was singed, nor the colour of their garments was changed, and the smell of the fire had not passed upon them."[3] A condition like this is to be found only in the wild creations of fancy, or in the legends of a credulous and spectre-haunted superstition. But I can imagine how a champion would feel, who found his frail and human conditioned limbs staked in

---

1 *Comus*, 423, 428–29.
2 In an apocryphal story, Queen Editha (or perhaps Emma), wife of Edward the Confessor (King of England 1042–66), was accused of too close an intimacy with the Bishop of Winchester, and walked over red hot ploughshares to prove her innocence.
3 Shadrach, Meschach, and Abednego were Jews saved by divine intervention from the Babylonians' attempt to kill them by putting them in a fiery furnace (Daniel 1–3).

mortal combat against one who "bore a charmed life."[1] And such feelings were mine. Preternatural horror, and deep despair; a rebellious spirit, blaspheming against fate and the Lord of all things, and fearfully impressed with the unjust and unequal measure that was dealt out to me. The blows I should strike seemed to be unaccompanied with the slightest hope of effect; but I was on that account, only incited to strike with more resolved aim, and a more desperate fury.

CHAPTER VII

I pass over a considerable period of time in which I was a victim to the machinations of this precious pair of devils, Holloway and Mallison. They had me in their hands, to play upon me as they pleased. By turns they soothed, and by turns they irritated me. Their admiration of my high qualities knew no bounds: their professions of devotion to my service exceeded those of the most fervent loyalty, in that period of feudal history, when the vassal conceived himself born for no other end, than the use, the pleasure, the defence, and the glory of his lord. To do justice to the ardour of their attachment, these gentlemen, my guardians, or my keepers, found themselves reduced to borrow something of the language of religion, and to speak almost as a creature to the Creator.

All this affected me strangely. I never ceased to see these men in their true colours. For ever and for ever I hated them. I understood their motives. Never for an instant did I ascribe one particle of sincerity to their professions. They talked this well; their protestations were ample, full of energetic phrase, and rich in sentiment and adoration. Yet they stood before me as two finished scoundrels. I knew that they thought only of themselves. I knew that they were incapable of one impulse that did not centre on their own interests. I knew that this was not only the original constitution of their minds, but that they had worked it up into a system, that it was a principle by which they elaborately regulated all their actions.

Yet, such is the nature of the human mind, I received pleasure from the song of these hollow-hearted hypocrites. It required however an introduction and a prelude. When it had at first been addressed to me abruptly, I repelled it with scorn. For a long time

---

1 Macbeth referring to himself (5.8.12).

I kept these abject wretches at a sufficient distance. I believe they would never have carried their point, if it had not been for my accident, which seemed to throw me, naked and defenceless, into their hands. By this my heart was "subdued even to the very quality"[1] of my keepers. I stood in need of Mallison, and could no longer do without him. He "took my pliant hour, and found good means"[2] to wrap me round with his snares. And it happened in this, as it does in a thousand other instances to frail human nature, that familiarity altered the appearances of things. What I had before thought of with impatience and contempt, I now learned to endure. The aggravated features, that had lately excited my aversion, by frequent perusal became less disagreeable. I listened; and the more I listened, the more the tale grew acceptable to me. At last the attentions and the flatteries of Mallison became necessary, and were a flavour and a diet that I knew not how to dispense with. I was like Mithridates, the celebrated King of Pontus, who is said by his perpetual labour to neutralise the effects of poisons upon him, to have found nourishment at last, in that which had originally the most virulent tendency to destroy.[3] Praise is agreeable to every human organ. However fastidious we may be in the beginning, if we will persist in swallowing the draught, we shall presently become passive and resigned. It will then exercise its natural attribute to soothe and to titillate. It matters not from whom it comes; it matters not, however much we may be internally convinced of its insincerity and its falsehood; the pleasure will by degrees more and more predominate over the pain, till the unpleasing sensation is finally merged in that which is of an opposite character.

They turned and winded me at their pleasure. When by their flatteries they had laid me most naked to be assailed, that was the moment they chose to aim at me the most deadly wound. And I am ashamed to say, that experience scarcely made me wise in this point, and that I was weak enough to be again and again the dupe of their machinations. They told me tales of my future greatness. They told me what the family of Mandeville had been, and what it was qualified to be again. They convinced me, that no one was

---

1 Desdemona: "My heart's subdued / Even to the very quality of my lord" (*Othello*, 1.3.245–46).

2 *Othello*, 1.3.151, referring to his courtship of Desdemona.

3 In an early form of inoculation, Mithridates VI (134–63 BCE), who feared being poisoned, ingested small doses to develop immunity. Godwin gives the story a new twist.

ever so largely endowed with powers to carry him forward in the paths of glory and of usefulness, as I was by nature. They told me tales of Clifford. They carried him from country to country, from employment to employment, and from honour to honour. I could not discover whether the things they described were real, or were the pure creatures of invention. I had no means of ascertaining; I had first voluntarily shut myself out from the world, and was now "benetted round with villainies."[1] First I believed all they related to me; then, upon revisal, the whole appeared so romantic, that I could not refrain from suspecting that I was made the dupe to a series of the grossest impostures. After that, circumstances came to my knowledge, sometimes by the public prints which were thrust in my way, and sometimes from other sources, which proved a few of the most material points, and scarcely left me power to doubt of the rest.

The comforters of the patriarch Job have grown into a proverb.[2] But they were drivellers, compared with the two practitioners, inmates of the roof under which I resided. They had no such means, and no such opportunity to torment. These were, as I have said, my sworn and devoted friends. They lived but to oblige me. When they told of what I might have been, they spoke the language of an ardent admiration. When they related things that tortured me to agony, it was with the most fervent protesting, that with contentions inexpressible they conquered their unwillingness to distress me, but that with severity and stoicism they compelled their feelings to give way to their duty. At other times they contrived, that I should see they were suppressing something too terrible to be communicated. When they consoled me, phrases and insinuations were sure to creep in, that reduced me to a much more pitiable situation, than if I had not been consoled at all. They gave me no rest, day nor night. I cannot help believing, that, as regularly as the morning returned, they consulted together, as to what electuary[3] of viper's flesh should be administered to me to-day, that the darkness of the days that had gone before, might not laugh at the whiteness of this. Their object was to reduce me to so helpless and pitiable a state of mind, that I might finally be a passive instrument in their hands, to do with me whatever they pleased.

---

1 *Hamlet*, 5.2.29.
2 Job 16:2: while purporting to comfort him, Job's false friends undermined his faith in himself.
3 Medicine mixed with something sweet.

It was wonderful what an effect this had upon me. It is sufficiently visible from what has been already related, that I was no stranger to what misery was. But all that I had previously felt, was as nothing, compared with what I suffered now. Those dogmatists, who, in whatever religion, have endeavoured to make out the punishments of a future state, have shown themselves no mean masters in their art. The main ingredient in their delineation is, to be "tormented by devils." No climate of hell, however fierce, parching and intolerable, no flames, so intense that the wretched sufferer intreats for one drop of water to cool his tongue, no gnawings of conscience, no agonies of remorse, could be complete without this, the presence and incessant activity of the tormentor. I have read of a tyrant, who having exhausted all that his dungeons could inflict, at length hit on this refinement, that a centinel should call on the unhappy prisoner every half-hour, by day and by night, during the remainder of his existence, and compel him to answer, that he might never attain to a temporary oblivion of his sorrows. Nature in this respect is treacherous, and apt to allow the victim from time to time to forget that he is miserable. Nature is always at the bottom a friend to the unfortunate; and, if she does not relieve his sorrows, at least benumbs the sense.

> Our purer essence then may overcome
> The noxious vapour, or inured not feel,
> Or changed at length, and to the place conformed
> In temper and in substance, may receive
> Familiar the fierce heat, and void of pain.[1]

It needs, as in my case, some disinterested and never-sleeping friend, to rake the embers, to throw on new combustibles, and to blow the flames, if we would have the misery complete.

What was most strange, was, that the more these wretched beings tormented me, the more in a certain sense grew my attachment to them. They were like some loathsome deformity, or envenomed excrescence on the human body, which the infatuated man to whose lot it has fallen, cherishes with obstinacy, and would rather part with his life than be delivered from it. The effect was such as is related of the bird and the rattle-snake; the defenceless victim is bewitched by the eye of his adversary, and is necessitated to fly into his mouth, though by so doing he rushes

1 *Paradise Lost,* 2.215–19.

on certain destruction. Holloway and Mallison became in some degree a part of myself. I felt that day maimed and incomplete, in which I did not sup up my allotted dose of the nauseous draught they administered. I must have their company; I was miserable when alone; and, though I was more miserable with them, yet in their society I had the delusive feeling as if I had something to support me.

Rapid was the progress that these men seemed to make towards the accomplishment of their desires. My health wasted daily; my powers of action seemed reduced to almost nothing. A perpetual gloom beset me, like "a huge eclipse of sun and moon," while the affrighted elements laboured with fearful change.[1] My skin was dried up; my flesh perished from my bones; my eyes became unacquainted with sleep; my joints refused to perform for me the ordinary functions of a living being.

Yet, while "this mortal coil"[2] seemed fast wasting away from and deserting me, my mind was in a state of preternatural activity. I felt that I must do something,—what, as yet, I knew not—but that must be terrible, that must lay a scene of horrors; that must be responsive to the desolation I was conscious of within. My mind balanced between two tones, that of inexorable rage, and that of the lowest despondency. The former urged me to revenge; the latter to suicide. According to my idea, the wretches that attended me, were indifferent what catastrophe it should be that crowned their labours; all they required was something dreadful; something that should shock all those who lived within the knowledge of it, and that should entail upon me unmingled detestation.

Another thing that rendered my situation at this time more deplorable, was, that these men were my study of human nature. I saw no other persons with any sensations of intercourse; my servants were merely the animated implements of my accommodation. And, as I viewed these men in their proper deformity, as none of their disgraceful qualities ever came softened to my thoughts, it may easily be supposed what sort of a thing human

---

1   *Othello*, 5.2.99–100.

2   From Hamlet's famous soliloquy, "To be or not to be" (3.1.56–89), in which he debates between the introversion and will-to-death that so fascinated the Romantics in this character, and taking "arms against a sea of troubles." The reference resonates with Godwin's use of a new epigraph for the Volume 3: the call to arms in *Henry V* instead of the bitter exile evoked by the passage from Exodus used for the first two volumes.

nature appeared to me. It was entitled to none of my sympathies; I agnised[1] in it no kindred qualities; it merited only my aversion; pity and compassion appeared to me weaknesses, unworthy to be harboured; and bitter animosity, or merciless revenge, the only sentiments it could be honourable to me to cherish.

CHAPTER VIII

I have related how industrious this deserving pair, my guardian and his nephew, showed themselves, to obtain my good will, and make themselves necessary to me. Nor were they less assiduous in their attentions to my sister, and the admirable matron under whose protection she dwelt upon the New Forest. In the first arrangement that took place after the death of my uncle, Holloway resided in Dorsetshire, my sister at Beaulieu, and I myself had fixed my abode in Derbyshire. The New Forest therefore was but little out of the road of the worthy solicitor, whenever he found, or made an occasion of proceeding from his own habitation to mine: and at other times, when he did not purpose this journey, still the distance was but small from the petty fishing-town where he dwelt to the residence of Mrs Willis. Holloway took advantage of this, and was, as I have said, diligent in paying his court to these dwellers on the New Forest. His visits could not be objected to, nay, were agreeable, for they always appeared to be prompted by an anxiety for my interests. It has been sufficiently seen, that this hoary practitioner of the law, was no mean adept in the art of turning to his purposes the weak sides of human nature. He did not like to make a single step without Mrs Willis; he had the profoundest respect for her extraordinary penetration. He thought it right, that Henrietta Mandeville should be acquainted with every thing that was done in my affairs; she was my next of kin, and was besides endowed with a very superior understanding. She saw into things with the quickness of intuition, and her sagacity was still further sharpened by the strength of her affection for me. Mr Holloway also, in the most delicate manner, alluded to my late unfortunate distraction, and my continued melancholy. He observed, that I ought not to be left to myself, nor trusted entirely to my own guidance. In short he had the dexterity, whatever he desired to do, to obtain for it the previous approbation of these ladies; and even, in several instances,

---

1 Recognized.

to make it seem to have flowed from their suggestion. This is the third example, the first being that of my uncle, and the second of myself, in which this wretched Holloway, without precisely obtaining the good opinion of any one, made himself a person useful, and almost necessary, while his officious and left-handed interpositions were received, by each party in turn, with acknowledgments and thanks.

Holloway made Mrs Willis and my sister fully acquainted with the particulars of his first expedition into Derbyshire, his earnest exertions (for such he described them) to render me master of my own affairs in all the minuteness of detail, and the distressing way in which he had failed in the attempt. He contrived, by ingenious insinuations, and certain openings which seemed to come from him at unawares, to make the plan for his ousting the Derbyshire farmer, and substituting his own establishment in this man's place, appear to proceed from Mrs Willis herself. In a word, notwithstanding the vulgarity of his manners, and the meanness of his mind, his persevering obsequiousness won him some favour with the family of Beaulieu Cottage; and, if he had not the inward feeling of attachment to my welfare, he however so perfectly played the part, as to all outward demonstrations of solicitude in my behalf, that the ladies could not avoid expressing themselves in a certain degree grateful to him.

When Holloway and his establishment were once removed into Derbyshire, Mallison became in most instances the representative of his uncle, as an occasional visitor at the New Forest. The ladies were rather gratified with the exchange. Mallison had had a better education than the solicitor himself: he had recently come from keeping company with the sons of gentlemen at Winchester College: besides which, he had his youth in his favour. The habits of Holloway's mind were essentially brutal and base: he had indeed a natural talent for insinuating speciousness, and could with sufficient success make his party good, when his cue was merely to show to an individual, how earnestly he was bent upon that object as an end, as a generous and disinterested consideration prompting his deeds, which in reality he regarded with the most philosophical indifference, as a means only to promote his own advantage. But, when this respectable person endeavoured to play the gentleman at large, nothing could be more ignominious than his failure. It was the ass in the lion's skin;[1] it

---

1 In Aesop's fable, an ass puts on a lion's skin but is soon discovered for what he is.

was Moliere's *Bourgeois*[1] attempting to impose himself with the manners of a courtier. Every step was a blunder; every word came out in exact opposition to the purpose the speaker intended to effect. But Mallison was at that happy age, when the limbs are pliant, and the voice and the lines of the countenance more easily accommodate themselves to the will of their possessor. He studied the models on whose pattern he desired to form himself; and, though he produced but a bad imitation, you could at least see a dim and imperfect representation of the thing from which it was copied.

The purpose of these worthies was, as I have said, to make my nearest connections believe that I was a person dreadfully diseased, and to persuade them that the care of me could not on the whole be more advantageously confided, than to those who had me already in some measure in their custody. Notwithstanding all the artful suggestions of Holloway, my friends could not be induced to look upon my distemper as incurable; and it had been the first idea of Henrietta, that, at the period when I came of age, and took possession of the family-mansion, she would live under the same roof with me, and preside at my table. Till then, it was held most decorous that she should remain at her present residence in Hampshire. Alas, how vain are the pretensions of human foresight! How many disastrous events occurred, between the period when this purpose was conceived, and the time for which my poor sister prepared herself with so much contemplative tranquillity!

In the precarious condition in which I was judged to be, both as to body and mind, Henrietta and the guide of her youth were not contented with such letters as I might address to them, but thankfully accepted the offer made them by Holloway, of such private epistolary communications as might be made them from time to time by himself or his nephew. The worthy solicitor had private ends of his own in view through the whole, and did not fail to render this opportunity subordinate to his purposes. Those purposes required, that no occasion should be lost, of improving the familiarity and frequency of his intercourses with Beaulieu. Mallison generally held the pen on these occasions. Old Latitat[2] had so long bewildered himself in the jargon of the law, and it flowed so naturally to his mind when he took up a pen, that he could hardly by any effort get through a letter, without mixing up

---

1   Molière's *Le Bourgeois Gentilhomme* (1670) deals with a bourgeois's comical attempts to seem a man of quality.
2   The old lawyer.

in it some of this uncouth phraseology. But Mallison was fresh from the study of the classics; he had moreover the advantage of my conversation; and when he contemplated in his ignoble spirit the radiant beauties of Henrietta Mandeville, even his style, young as he still was, drew a comparative refinement from the subject of his thoughts.

In the way in which Mallison and his uncle painted my rejection of their lessons, as to the stewardship of my own estate, it was made to appear a symptom of that unsteadiness and inconstancy of mind, which are so often to be found in persons subject to occasional attacks of lunacy. They made no recital of the insidious artifices by which they had studiously rendered this sort of occupation disgusting to me, but described the whole as an ingenuous experiment for my welfare. The disdainful spirit in which I had at first rejected all their efforts at familiarity, were distorted and exaggerated. Give to any one the entire and sole custody of any human being, especially if that human being is of a hypochondriacal complexion, and allow his keeper to be from day to day the historian of his ward; and he must be a man of very little dexterity, if he cannot make those who do not approach the patient believe any thing he pleases, and if he do not weave together circumstances and incidents, in such a manner as to clothe his tale with an irresistible air of probability.

Henrietta was extremely delighted with the account that reached her, of the new passion I had conceived for mounting on horseback, and anticipated the happiest effects from the diversion and the health which was in this way likely to be procured to me. With equal vexation and chagrin she received the news of my unfortunate accident. On that occasion she paid me a visit; and this was the first interview I had ever had with my beloved sister, upon which I did not look back with entire complacency. Her visit continued only for a few hours. I need not say with what rapturous delight I fixed my eyes on her heavenly features, or how sweet to me were the thrilling tones of her voice. In this instance her habitual gaiety was somewhat subdued, by sympathy for the painful and wearisome state in which she found me; but the subdued tone it assumed, only added to it a thousand nameless graces, unknown before. I was in Elysium, as long as her visit lasted. But so unreasonable and monopolising was my temper, that I felt strange murmurings within me, when I found that she purposed to spend not so much as one night under my roof. She was proceeding to Lord Montagu's principal seat of Boughton in Northamptonshire; there was a wedding to be celebrated there;

the day was fixed; and the presence of Henrietta was impatiently counted upon, as one great ornament of the festival. Yet I was dissatisfied. I said to myself, "Theirs is the house of mirth. Multitudes will be assembled there, a bright *parterre* of beauty; their enjoyments and their gaiety are certain; they would not have leisure to regret the absence of Henrietta; they surely might spare her to the lonely and desolate couch of her suffering brother." These were the reflections that passed through my mind; but I sealed my lips; I scorned to complain. I thought, "If she has the unkindness to leave me thus, I will not attempt to detain her."

Mallison escorted her and Mrs Willis to the stage where they purposed to sleep for that night. The next morning they were attended by the young Montagus, who had advanced thus far to meet them. My sister felt the kindest sentiments for Mallison on this occasion. She was delighted to observe the familiarity which was at length brought about between me and my *quondam*[1] school-fellow. The assiduities he exercised towards me were a truly exemplary spectacle. I have already described them. He was constantly alive to my comforts; he lost no opportunity of rendering me every service, and procuring me every amusement in his power. Henrietta thanked him in the warmest terms for all that she had seen, and all that she had heard, of his attentions. She exhorted him to persevere in the course on which he had so auspiciously entered. She expressed with earnestness, how unspeakably she herself, and all that were connected with the Mandeville family, would feel indebted to him for a kindness so beneficent. What my sister said was delivered by her, not in the mere style of a graceful compliment, nor with the flattering condescension which a superior sometimes so successfully employs to an inferior, but with the true ardour of sisterly affection. There was a bewitching frankness in her manner, on all occasions, and to all persons: and, in what passed on this little journey, the animation of her soul from time to time made her almost forget who she was talking to; and, as it was a brother that occupied her thoughts, the cordiality of her discourse was such, that you would hardly have thought but that she was addressing a brother. Both the ladies spoke to the young man in the language of the heart, and communicated their approbation and their grateful feelings with the most lively sincerity. Poor Mallison, who had never done any thing in the whole course of his life to merit any one's approbation, was transported with the novelty of the situation. It was with the utmost difficulty,

---

1 Former.

and by means only of the severe habits of dissimulation to which he had addicted himself, that he could be prevented from breaking out into the utmost extravagance of youthful intoxication, and falling into disgustful and ruinous follies.

The pupil-solicitor was the more enchanted with the occurrences of this delightful evening, because they so precisely fell in with the plan which the uncle had formed for fixing the fortune of his nephew. This was one of the many projects he had conceived, for transferring the whole property of the house of Mandeville, to the house of Montfort, hitherto Holloway. The scheme I allude to, was no less than that of bringing about a marriage between Mallison and my sister. The youth indeed, however destitute of imagination and refinement, had all that impression of the distinction of ranks, which is often found to exist as completely in the dullest, as in the most elegant minds. He was therefore beyond measure astonished with his good fortune. Had he not been well fortified by the dextrous and persevering lessons of his uncle, assisted, as they fortunately were, by the invincible coldness of his own heart, he would infallibly have made a declaration in all the forms to Henrietta, before they parted; or, if his extravagance had stopped short of that, he would at least by ogling, by the languishing tones with which he addressed her, and by all the nameless indications of a lover, have betrayed the secret, not indeed of his heart, but which lay brooding in his brain. But, no: he scorned to be conquered by the frailer part of his nature. Mallison was a practical philosopher; and he had the honour to part from my sister on this critical occasion, without allowing her or Mrs Willis once to take notice of the thought that was uppermost in his own mind.

He returned to his uncle, and related the prosperous success which had attended the commencement of his suit. The old gentleman listened to the narrative with the most enviable sensations. Wealth was the ruling passion that predominated over all others in his bosom. Yet had not this passion so swallowed up the rest, but that he had still a corner in his heart for considerations of family and rank. He now began to look forward, by means of this marriage of his nephew, to the founding a family. He considered me, in some way or other, as inevitably cut off from the succession. Either I should fall a victim by death to the unhappy constitution of my mind, or I should subside into a permanent state of distraction or fatuity, "no son of mine succeeding."[1] Hen-

---

1 *Macbeth*, 3.1.63.

rietta would then remain the only representative of our ancient house; and her husband would be no longer a Mallison, no longer a Montfort, but the genuine successor to the honours of Mandeville. The doting solicitor began to look upon his nephew with other eyes than he had regarded him with before; he felt towards him a sort of commencing reverence and awe; and was seized with something of the same transport as Sir Giles Overreach in the play, when he imagined to himself in prophetic vision, his "honourable daughter," his "right honourable daughter!"[1]

The uncle and the nephew laid their heads together, to consult how the suit of the latter should be most successfully prosecuted. Poor Holloway lost his discretion in a great degree, under this new aspect of his fortunes. He no longer could discern in Mallison the overgrown schoolboy, the aukward and unimaginative attorney's clerk, with a blundering intellect, a lame and unprosperous carriage, and an illiberal disposition. To his inflamed and drunken conception he put him fully upon a level with me, with Clifford, or with either of the accomplished sons of Lord Montagu; or rather he figured him as riding triumphantly over all. He was therefore ridiculous enough, to be impatient to bring him into contrast with his equals in age, his inferiors, as Holloway fondly flattered himself, in all that is most elemental and considerable in man.

The family of Montagu was to return, after the festivities of the marriage of their kinsman were completed, from Northamptonshire to their seat upon the New Forest. Hither Holloway was in haste to send his nephew, that no time might be lost, and no cross accident might be suffered to intervene, to bar him from the golden crop he looked for. Accordingly, almost as soon as intelligence reached us that the family had left Boughton for Hampshire, Mallison was dispatched to carry news of my improving health to the ladies at the Cottage.

CHAPTER IX

Every thing happened in one respect, as the veteran solicitor would have wished: the ladies had been invited to dine the next day at the house of the noble baron. They had been much pleased

---

1 Sir Giles Overreach in Philip Massinger's *A New Way to Pay Old Debts* (1633), a play illustrating class conflicts of the Stuart period, in which Sir Giles, a wealthy man from a new mercantile background, aspires to have his daughter marry into the old gentry.

with Mallison, as I have related, in their late excursion into Derbyshire; they were still more gratified with the favourable report he now brought respecting me. The young Montagus called in, in their ride before dinner, to remind Mrs Willis and Henrietta of their engagement; and Mallison happened to be present. This hopeful suitor to my sister, as he presumptuously regarded himself, and these young gentlemen, had never met before. Mrs Willis, who was in high good humour, introduced him; not as the nephew of Holloway, my guardian, but as a *ci-devant* Wintonian,[1] and my particular friend, to whom they were under great obligations. The Montagus had never heard his name. They therefore invited him to accompany the ladies in their visit; and the invitation was no sooner given than accepted. To crown the scene, beside several visitors from among the neighbouring gentry, there was an unexpected guest: it was Clifford.

Mallison, encouraged by the warm hopes and the magnificent dreams of his uncle, had been presumptuous enough in accepting the invitation; but he had no sooner entered the avenue of Montagu House, than his heart misgave him. The spaciousness of the apartments, and the splendour of the service overawed him. He had seen a nobleman's house before, by a fee to the housekeeper when the master was absent; but this he felt to be quite a different thing. The venerable air and solemn courtesy of the old Lord Montagu and his lady, were a spectacle he had never encountered. But the constant presence of mind, the entire ease, the vivacious tone, and the light and graceful motions, of the young Montagus and of Clifford, were still more terrible to him. The saloon was also crowded with ladies in the most costly attire. Mallison shrunk back with fear; his manner grew every moment more and more ludicrous and sheepish; and he seemed to feel within himself what a scoundrel he was.

There was however another thing, which added inexpressibly to the tortures of his ignoble soul. He now for the first time conceived in his heart the passion of jealousy. Clifford, at least in the beauty of his exterior, and the nameless graces of his person, surpassed even the sons, as much as Henrietta eclipsed the daughters, of the house of Montagu. No unprejudiced stranger could have seen them together, without being struck with the thought that they were destined for each other. But Mallison believed that he remarked something more than this. He seemed to perceive an extraordinary degree of mutual understanding between them.

---

1   Former student at Winchester.

There was something in all their motions, which might best be described by borrowing the phrase of a great French philosopher, of a "pre-established harmony."[1] Their eyes followed each other; their highest pleasure lay in observing what either said or did; and, when their glances encountered, an increased animation was visible in his eyes, while a slight tinge of added colour flitted across her cheek.

The presentation of the hopeful Mallison at the drawing-room of Lord Montagu, was an event to which both he and his uncle had looked forward with eager impatience. The day came; but the event proved altogether different from what they had anticipated. The sensations of our ardent adventurer bore a striking resemblance to those of Phaeton, when he found himself irretrievably engaged in the career of Apollo.[2] Mallison, flattered by his uncle, and dazzled with the high destinies that he believed awaited him, had thought himself, as he sat in their oak-parlour in Derbyshire, equal to any enterprise. But, amidst the magnificent tapestries and the Persian carpets of Lord Montagu, his convictions were totally different. He was no sooner fairly entered, than he wished himself at the bottom of the sea. And, when he beheld the mutual partiality of the beautiful vision in the form of a woman, whom he had designed for the victim of his sordid ambition, and Clifford, he felt in his breast all the malignity of a demon. To do him justice, he was totally blind to all the extraordinary qualities of his rival. He believed that the success and the good fortune he witnessed, were entirely owing to one simple cause, an easy assurance. He lamented over the modesty of his own merit: for, while in his cool and calculating head he planned some attack to be made upon, or trifling service to be rendered to my sister, Clifford was sure to step in, and with a ready grace to do the thing, which he had only purposed.

---

1 The phrase is actually that of Leibniz (1646–1716), describing the accord between what he calls "monads," the infinitely multiple basic constituents of the universe (like atoms), each of which develops according to its own law but nevertheless are all in accord. But Godwin alludes to Voltaire's *Candide* (1759), which wryly mocks a related theory of Leibniz: that amongst many "possible worlds," God has given us the very best. Here again, Henrietta is associated with a facile Enlightenment optimism.

2 Phaeton, to assert his position as the son of Apollo, tried to drive the chariot of the sun and was burned to a cinder by the thunderbolt that Zeus hurled at him for his presumption.

He attempted to speak to Clifford, as his old school-fellow; and, I must confess it to the honour even of my adversary, the ingenuousness of Clifford's temper was such, as to make it impossible for him to design to put down any man, or wantonly to give him uncomfortable sensations. But the ease, the openness, and the grace, with which he met the salutation of Mallison, proved even more distressing, than reserve and haughtiness could have done: it made the embryo-lawyer savour to the very dregs, the utter contrast between the benignity and self-possession of Clifford, and his own wretched consciousness of foul thoughts and a base and groveling character. He could not thoroughly comprehend where the difference lay; but he felt that hope, like Themis of old, had spread her airy wings, and abandoned him for ever. In all probability, this feeling would not have been excited in him, but for the appurtenances and accidents of the scene; and accordingly, when that scene was removed, it will appear that at no distant period he recovered all his accustomed presumption.

Mallison returned with the ladies in the close of the day, and having seen them home, departed to a village-inn hard by. But they could not help remarking, that he seemed a totally altered being. Even Mallison, to whom they had considered themselves as so much indebted, appeared no longer amiable. His confidence and his self-complacence were gone. He was morose, sullen and silent. And you may think how Mallison's features, which at best had a sufficiently heavy and brutal expression, looked, when he no longer played a part, but surrendered himself up to the most unsocial passions.

When this promising youth returned once more to his uncle, he had a very different story to tell, from that which had gained him so much applause upon his preceding interview with Henrietta. But Holloway was a man not to be turned aside from his purpose. He was like Horace's personage "just and inflexible of soul":

If the cracked orbs should split and fall,
Crush him they would, but not appal.[1]

Or, to express the thing in a less poetical phraseology, he was not to be deterred by obstacles, but had an unabated confidence in his own resources.

---

1 [Godwin's note:] Fanshaw. [Translator of Horace.]

He saw however the necessity of introducing an amendment into his plan. He had begun with representing my state of body and mind in the most unfavourable light, that he might the more easily gain possession of my person, and that he might impress all my connections the more deeply with a sense of the obligations they were under to him. He now perceived that the surest card he had, was to endeavour to gain me over to his party, and bring me forward as the instrument of his purposes. He was aware how profound was my hatred to Clifford, and that he might safely rely on me as an abettor to prevent an alliance in that quarter. He did not know how far he would be able to use me as a direct accessory in his favourite purpose of joining the hands of Mallison and Henrietta: but confusion was his element; and he did not doubt, while all things were in a state of commotion and tempest, to find his advantage in the storm, or even that, when the battle was committed, he should lead me further than in the beginning I had ever contemplated.

It was Mallison's cue, to lay before me all he had observed in his late visit to Beaulieu. I was sufficiently shocked with the idea, that he had seen Clifford! All that he added to this, I frankly set down to his own gratuitous malignity. In my private estimate of the character of my inmate, I had never flattered him; and I gave him credit for his ingenuity, in inventing and laying before me the most diabolical idea that could be engendered in the thoughts of a human being, that of an ardent passion and an indissoluble union between this fearful and endless adversary to my peace, and the only person the love of whom still linked me to·the accursed scene of the world. But I took pride to myself in this, that I was not prepared to be the dupe of his hellish tale. "No, no," I said, "I have still so much of human intellect about me; I have so much of the health of the soul remaining, that I can shake off and puff away such a forgery with the contempt it deserves."

But what remained of the communication which Mallison brought, was sufficiently grievous. I had now in my presence a person, who, a few hours before, had breathed the same air with my arch-enemy. This seemed to give a reality and demonstration to the reports that had been brought me, of the favourable reception of Clifford in society, since the event of his apostacy: and to me, who fondly calculated the number of reporters through whom the former stories of Mallison had reached me, and who counted each reporter in the series as a new ground authorizing me to doubt of the truth of the whole, that was by no means immaterial. Mallison stood before me like a person arrived from a town infected with the plague, and who had performed no quarantine: it seemed as if his clothes were poisoned, and the odour and the very sight of him were deadly to me. Then add to this; where had he seen Clifford? At Lord Montagu's table, where I had so often sat with cordiality and joy: in company, with Lord Montagu's sons, whose conversation and amity it had been delightful to me to recollect. I was no friend to what is vulgarly called toleration and liberality, but felt that I partook of the mind which Homer ascribes to Achilles, who says,

— Nor fits it the respects
Of my vowed friend, to honour him that hath dishon-
    oured me;
It were his praise, to hurt with me the hurter of my
    state.[1]

But least of all, (though I put away all the other malignant insinuations of the historian of the scene) could I bear to think that Henrietta, heart of my heart, and soul of my soul, had sat at the same board, with this disgrace of his species, and plague of my existence. Mallison was not a little irritated at my incredulity upon the point which he principally laboured, and resolved that I should not long hug myself in my present security.

Shortly after his return, I received a visit from the two sons of Lord Montagu. It was seldom, as I have already shown, that my solitude was disturbed by the intrusion of strangers; yet I could not refuse to show some symptoms of pleasure, in receiving the compliment implied by the appearance of guests of so much distinction and worth. It will hereafter be seen that their visit was not an affair of compliment merely; but that the purpose was to remark me more nearly, and to verify by their own personal observation what degree of credit was to be given to the statements of Holloway and Mallison respecting me.

My soul was fraught with a rooted partiality to these young men, on account of a thousand excellent qualities with which they were endowed. Yet could I not forget for a moment that they had lately seen Clifford, that they had received him with civility, and that, whatever marks of confidence and distinction they now extended to me, he had reaped the crop that preceded mine, and that what I got, that would otherwise have been grateful to me,

---

1 [Godwin's note:] Chapman. [From Chapman's translation of Homer's *Iliad*, Book IX.]

was by that circumstance rendered faded and worthless. I was like a jealous lover. I required that the friendship that was offered to me, should be a virgin and a first love. I could not ally myself with

> a common laugher, one who used
> To stale with ordinary oaths his league
> To every new protester.[1]

They had received Clifford, and by that act had shown a want of true moral discrimination, a deadness of soul, that made all the preferences and partiality they could express not worth the having. By this reasoning I shut up my heart against them; I wore a moodiness of mind upon my brow; and the tone of my voice was bereaved of all the notes that emphatically express cordiality and affection.

We talked of a hundred miscellaneous subjects. They tried me with literature and with questions of ordinary life. They spoke of the sports of the field, and of all the amusements congenial to a rural life. They talked of horsemanship, of the various qualities with which this noble animal, the best servant of man, is endowed, of his instinct, and the points in which his memory and sagacity approach most nearly to human understanding. They enquired with great interest respecting my late accident, and speculated, playfully, yet affectionately, upon the tediousness and want of amusement that must have attended my cure. They made sport of the characters and qualities of my present inmates, and laughed at the very ingenious manner in which they had introduced themselves to that situation. They talked of my family-mansion, of the many advantages which they heard it possessed, and of the great taste of the improvements that I had meditated or had begun. Every thing on their part expressed kindness and the most perfect sympathy; but they could not conquer me. No allurement, not all the siren music which they touched with so admirable a skill, could tempt me to pass beyond the reserve in which I had obstinately intrenched myself.

But, with all the ease which these admirable young men seemed to use in their conversation with me, there were a variety of topics that they sedulously avoided. They knew the sore places of my soul, and were careful not to touch upon any thing that might seem calculated to awaken in me painful remembrances.

---

1 *Julius Caesar*, 1.2.72–74.

The last thing in which they would have allowed themselves, was to make any mention of Clifford. They said nothing on politics, the present government of the protector, or the hoped-for restoration of the king. At the moment they spoke, it was understood that Cromwel was dying; but they made no allusion to that important event.[1] They remembered how painfully matters of this kind had operated in my short experiment of human life, and that they had afflicted me with a temporary privation of reason. Yet, a great part of the object of their visit, was, in the most delicate and tender manner, to probe my soul; and they could not with any propriety put an end to it, till they had in some way performed the purpose for which they came.

During the earlier part of the interview, these young noblemen, though not entirely satisfied with my manner, if tried by the laws of friendship, yet by no means saw enough to justify the representations that had been made by Holloway and his nephew, that I was in the condition of a person not competent to the ordinary business and intercourses of human life. They accordingly expostulated with the solicitor on the subject, and reproached him sharply (particularly Edward, who was much the more impetuous of the two), insinuating a fear that he had had some crooked and dishonourable design, in describing me, in a way that the appearances they had observed by no means justified.

Holloway, as I have said, began by this time to repent of the representations he had made respecting me, and to think that the purposes he had in view required from him a different mode of proceeding. The present occasion afforded to so masterly a politician a most desirable opportunity of retracing his steps, and recanting all the disqualifications with which he had loaded me. He seemed to have nothing to do, but to fall in with the suggestions of the Montagus, and to compliment them on the infallibility of the judgment they had formed. But this profound statesman was for once seduced from the great principles of conduct, by which his life had been governed. He was irritated (such is human vanity and frailty) by the contradiction which these young gentlemen presumed to give to his assertions; he was offended with the insinuations they threw out against the unimpeachableness of his motives; and he resolved upon a triumphant refutation of their error. He told them plainly, that they were little acquainted with the subtlety and deceitful appearances presented by a mind in the state in which mine was, and that nothing was

---

1 The year must therefore be 1658.

more common, even among the inhabitants of a house appropriated for the reception of lunatics, than to find a person, whose intellect was sane, and his conversation rational, upon all topics but one.

The Montagus proceeded upon the suggestion of Holloway. They conceived it absolutely necessary that they should not return home, without the satisfaction they had come hither to seek; and they determined for once, to lay aside their delicacy and forbearance, for the accomplishment of their end. Very little contrivance happened to be necessary on their part. They began with the mention of the Earl of Bristol, whose high talents, whose accomplishments, and whose unstained loyalty they commemorated in lofty terms.

This was enough for me. They touched the master-key, that made most discord and tumult in my bosom. A thousand terrible recollections rushed upon me at once. The last time I had met with the name of Lord Bristol, was in the memorable recantation-scene at Ghent. I knew little of him beside, and what little I did, did not prepossess me in his favour. To hear this man applauded therefore, was to me a whole volume of blasphemies and execrations at once. They uttered the name of Bristol; but I heard nothing but Clifford. And every word they pronounced was such an overturning of all moral principles and sacred truths, that I could not sit still and tamely witness it. My mind however, from some cause, must have been in a peculiarly inflammable state; or else I could not have broken out at once with such inconceivable violence as I did. Upon many occasions I have mastered myself, I have checked the "climbing passion" within me, I have braced my eye-strings, and governed my tones and my words. But it was not so now.

I said, that Lord Bristol was the pest of the human species, and I would not endure to hear him named in my presence. I raved of the whore of Babylon,[1] and the beast which St John had seen in his desolate exile in the isle of Patmos.[2] I said, that all other crimes were whiter than innocence compared with that of him, who returned again to the filthiness his forefathers had abjured, and endeavoured to set up afresh the image of Dagon, which God with his thunder had dashed into fragments. I prayed fervently, that I

---

1   See p. 120, note 1.
2   The Beast seen by St. John has "seven heads and ten horns, and upon his horns ten crowns, and upon his heads the name of blasphemy" (Revelation 13:1).

might live to see such recreants and misbelievers made memorable examples and unperishable monuments of "the wrath of the Lamb."[1] I talked of the fire from heaven, by which Sodom and Gomorrah[2] of old had been reduced into ashes, and were made a pool, exuding noisome and stinking vapours to latest generations. I knew that hell had in reserve a receptacle of fiercer and more devouring flames than was the inheritance of ordinary reprobation, for such unheard of monsters. While I spoke, my face blackened with rage, my eyes seemed starting from their sockets, and the saliva gathered upon my lips in an abundant foam.

The Montagus became seriously alarmed at the effect of their experiment. They addressed me in the most soothing tones; they essayed every artifice of humanity to calm me. It was in vain. I would not hear them. The interposition of the gentlest obstacle, only served to work me into a more tremendous rage. I poured along a stream of maniac eloquence, that knew neither suspension nor end. I did not stop, till the organs of respiration refused to furnish me any longer with voice; and I then sunk into a state of almost total insensibility. It must be confessed, that this was neither more nor less than a genuine attack of frenzy.

My visitors were now satisfied as to the point, upon which they had previously been sceptical; and the malignant and treacherous insinuations of Holloway were terribly justified. They had no inclination to prolong their visit any further; and they staid till the evening, upon a feeling of humanity merely, and that they might not desert a poor creature whom they had themselves thrown into so alarming a state, without waiting till he was tolerably recovered. They however thought it advisable for a time not to exasperate me by their presence, and left me in the hands of my familiar, Mallison. When I saw them again, I apologized for my violence, and said that I was far from being in a healthful state either of body or mind; but neither they nor I felt inclined to enter on the subject anew.

CHAPTER X

It is time that I should proceed to explain the relation that at this time existed between Clifford and Henrietta. They had first met, in the interval that occurred between my leaving Winchester and

---

1   Revelation 6:16.
2   Cities consumed by fire and brimstone; they have become synonymous with sin and divine retribution.

the expedition of Penruddock, I being then a student in the university. Henrietta was on a visit to a friend of Mrs Willis at Petersfield on the confines of Sussex, and Clifford's mother was a resident in the same place. The town of Petersfield, though accustomed to the privilege of sending two members to parliament, was of small dimensions; and such of its inhabitants, as were raised in any degree above the lowest class in the community, were habituated to live in much harmony and good neighbourhood with each other. The lady at whose house Henrietta now resided for a few weeks, and Mrs Clifford, were old friends. My school-mate, who at this time had left Winchester, and whose destination in life was yet unsettled, was for the present under the roof of his mother. He was advertised, as I have since heard, of the expected visit of Henrietta, and warned to be upon his guard not to lose his heart to her, as he was an adventurer only, and she was an heiress. Such warnings will often be found to fail of producing the effect which their prudent authors have in view. In a country-town the merits of a young person, especially if she be fair, and combine a certain dignity of understanding with a conspicuous frankness of heart, will be apt to be exaggerated. The merits of Henrietta could not be exaggerated. Every assembly and every tea-table in Petersfield resounded with her praises, for a whole week before she arrived. On the day that was fixed for her coming, the town was in commotion. Clifford and his mother were at the dwelling of her hostess when she alighted; and if his expectations of the beautiful stranger had been raised before she appeared, his feelings now were like those of the Queen of Sheba in holy writ; "Lo, I believed not the report that I heard, until I saw; and behold, the half was not told unto me." If the reader has in any way entered into the portraits I have attempted of Clifford and Henrietta, he need not be told how improbable it was, that a petty town, like Petersfield, should contain an individual that could in the smallest degree vie with either. In the meantime, as it was an adjudged case, that Henrietta was a being "out of the young man's sphere," and as Clifford was notorious for a disposition the very opposite of sordidness and intrigue, it was not considered as in any way necessary to put a bar to their intercourse.

Clifford himself was influenced by the same considerations, that governed the proceedings of those who were naturally the guardians of the young persons. He felt the impossibility of supposing that he could be any thing to Henrietta but a friend, and therefore trusted himself to the fascinations of her society with a fearless confidence. He believed that he could

Enter the very lime-twigs of its spells,
And yet come off.[1]

He took many a solitary walk with my sister by the hills and the
meadows in the neighbourhood of Petersfield. He talked with her
of her connections. The circumstance that he and I had been
school-fellows together, served in some degree as a bond between
them. He spoke of me in terms of liberal praise. It was impossible to suspect from what he said, that there had ever been any ill
blood between us, as indeed on his part there had not. On the
contrary, Henrietta loved him for the warm and affectionate
terms in which he expressed himself, of her dear and only
brother. They spoke also of the Montagus. And here my sister was
delighted to enlarge upon the worth and the merits of persons, to
whom her companion was at this time a total stranger. The tone
of conversation between Clifford and Henrietta was, for some
reason, extremely different from that which had so often
occurred between her and the Montagus. To the intercourse of
these gallant youths she had been accustomed from her childhood; but Clifford was a novelty. With Clifford she was again and
again engaged in solitary rambles; but them she seldom saw apart
the one from the other, for indeed they were almost inseparable.
And it was, I believe, the judgment of all indifferent spectators,
that his attractions were superior to theirs. There was in Clifford
that nameless something, that indescribable charm, that no
female heart can resist; and even when, as in this case, he purposed no conquest, the affections of the unfortunate fair one
were not the less prostrated at his feet. They wandered together,
unconscious of any thing, but the pleasure of each other's conversation, and the mutual approbation of each other's sentiments, and drank in the fascinating draught, without being aware
of the nature of its ingredients, or the effects it would leave
behind. They were both of them penetrated with the purest feelings of human charity: and, though their power of relieving the
distresses of their fellow creatures was but small, it so happened
that the demands made upon it were comparatively trivial; and
they found, what every one in the more refined classes of society
may find when he pleases, that compassion, and attendance, and
sympathy are more grateful offerings to the forlorn and the poor,
than those gifts that the careless hand of wealth sometimes osten-
tatiously condescends to impart. Thus Clifford and Henrietta saw

---

1 *Comus*, 645–46.

in each other the mirror of the mind of either; and each admired in the other what, when viewed at home, in the silence of retrospection, hardly assumed the name of merit.

This is a very simple tale; but its ultimate consequences were memorable, tragical and tremendous. The time limited for Henrietta's visit to Petersfield soon drew to a close; and the moment of parting discovered to this amiable pair a secret which, till then, neither had suspected. Their farewell was affectionate; they protested to each other an everlasting remembrance—friendship. Each of them had known friendship before; and on either side they could hardly divine why the feelings of this friendship should be so essentially different, from any that experience presented to their recollection. A mind disciplined in the levities of ordinary youth, would soon have taught them to give an appropriate explanation to what passed in their bosoms; but they were full of primitive purity and innocence; and the practice of the head, and an initiation in grosser conceptions, did not assist either, in giving point and a premature character of activity to the mysteries of the heart.

When Henrietta returned to the roof of her earliest friend, this clear-sighted and affectionate matron immediately perceived a material alteration in her fair charge. Henrietta had been the gayest of the gay; her spirits inexhaustible; her innocent levities the perpetual amusement of all that approached her. She was now grave and silent, given to reverie, fond of solitude, her fine, beaming, conscious eye perpetually turned on the ground. Mrs Willis several times surprised her in tears, and Henrietta knew not why she wept. Henrietta, the sincerest of her sex, could give no explanation. Mrs Willis enquired anxiously the particulars of her visit to Petersfield, who she saw, and how she had spent her time. My sister answered ingenuously to all the questions that were proposed to her; her matron-friend had never heard the name of Clifford, but her discernment, and her maternal regard for her charge, presently occasioned her to remark the greater glow of countenance, and the superior animation of voice, with which Henrietta always spoke of the companion of her rambles. Yet it was strange: she never mentioned him of her own accord; she never reverted to the subject, but when it was forced upon her; and ever and anon, in the midst of her warmth, she would check herself, and falter in her voice, without meaning any harm, and from the force of an intuitive modesty.

Well did Mrs Willis understand the phenomena that were presented to her observation. Never, but on this one occasion, had she trusted Henrietta out of her sight; and bitterly did she repent that she had ever done so. She made a point of learning all the particulars she could respecting Clifford, and was informed without difficulty, that he was of a good family, of an unblemished character, but a beggar. One thing Mrs Willis was particularly on her guard against, the being made the confident of Henrietta's secret. Upon another point she was not less circumspect, carefully to avoid every thing that might lead her young friend to a clearer knowledge than she yet had, of her own mystery: both of them errors into which an ordinary woman in Mrs Willis's situation would immediately have fallen. She endeavoured to give full occupation to the mind of her charge; she knew that idleness and *desoeuvrement*[1] are among the most effectual fosterers of the passion of love. She insensibly led the ideas of my sister to speculate on the mechanism of civilized society, the distinction of ranks, and the variously modified duties which society prescribes to the king and the beggar, the lord and the peasant, the woman of high birth and the lowly shepherdess. All this pointed in Mrs Willis's mind to the subject of a prudent and honourable discretion in marriage, though the direct notion was never suffered to intrude in her discourse. This sensible matron was strongly impressed with the thought, that, by skilful management on her part, the impression Henrietta had received from her intercourse with this fascinating youth, might be converted into a fugitive impulse merely, might be skinned over and obliterated.

If Henrietta did not forget Clifford, and frequently encountered him in her dreams, neither did the recollection of my sister fail to subsist in the most vivid colours in the mind of this gallant adventurer. He however was not backward to reason with his love, and set himself earnestly to combat an unavailing passion. He was glad at least, that what he felt was shut up in his own bosom, and that he had been too honest, by the remotest hint ever to betray his secret to the object of his affection. His honesty had gone beyond that. As I have already said, it was the very moment of separation that first discovered the secret to himself. If he had suspected it earlier, earlier would he have set himself to contend with his infirmity. He would instantly have started some pretence for absenting himself; he had no right by indulgence to nourish his own disease. And Clifford had quite sense enough to know, that passion, however concealed and immature, seldom fails to produce some effect on the person towards whom it is

---

1 Being without occupation.

directed, and, if it does not excite aversion, is apt to give birth to an image of itself.

These were the first thoughts of Clifford; but he presently came to see the subject in a different light. The admiration he had conceived for Henrietta was his primal lesson in the school of human society. Hitherto his imagination had run riot; and whatever was brilliant and prepossessing in its aspect, whatever savoured of independence and grandeur of soul, was sure to have him for its advocate. I have recorded his school-boy theorems on the subject of poverty and wealth. Now first the romance of a lover's feelings made him descend from the romance of abstractions. "I love Henrietta," he said to himself. "If I love her, why should not I win her? False diffidence is out of the question. Have not I the qualifications and endowments that might enable me to stand as a candidate for her affections? I dare not flatter myself that I have made any deep impression upon her, or that this angelic creature would feel uneasy in being deprived of me. But neither can I dissemble, that she liked my society, and was partial to my conversation. I know they will say, I am not her equal, no suitable match for the daughter of a prosperous and an illustrious house. What is a man, but his body and his mind? But grant it, I am not her equal. All else may be supplied. No, I will never be the occasion of disgrace to Henrietta! I will never solicit her to do that for which any one shall have a right to reproach her. I will seem therefore to forget her; but I will never really forget her for a moment. She shall be my pole-star, the light by which I will steer my bark, the end that I will propose to myself in all my pursuits. I have seen hundreds of young men about me ambitious; I will also enlist myself under the standard of ambition. They are ambitious, for what? An empty name, a fluttering ribband, a sash with graceful folds, a feather, a gaudy title; or perhaps, in the hope that they may retire in the end of their days with all the accommodations of an ample fortune. I have a higher prize in view; and shall not my ambition be more successful than theirs? Yes, I will take my leave of Henrietta; but upon some glorious and happy day I will return, confessedly worthy of her love, and will claim her hand in the face of my country. I know not yet what shall be the express path I will elect; but I also will engage in the career, and I will not doubt of my prosperous success."

Clifford had a young friend, in whom to a certain degree he reposed his confidence. Not that he ever named Henrietta to him; that he would have considered as a breach of delicacy and honour. If the communion between him and my sister had gone so far, that in the glow of youthful sincerity and affection she had confessed herself partial, would he have had a right to violate her maiden modesty, by imparting that secret to another, which assuredly she would not so have imparted? But in this respect Henrietta was not in his power. He however would have thought that he was guilty of an undue levity towards her, if he had made her name a theme of talk with his young friend, by confessing, what he had but just begun to confess to his own heart, that the first wish of his soul was that Henrietta should be his. But, though upon this point he was not communicative to Calvert, yet, in the dear cordiality of unbending freedom, Clifford acknowledged to his friend, that he had lately somewhat altered his views of human life. He no longer looked upon it with the disdain of a Zeno, or the carelessness of an Aristippus,[1] but was desirous to mix in its business, and be counted for something. He also had caught the flame of a generous ambition, and was resolved to record his deeds upon the column of fame. Calvert smiled at this resolution in the mind of his associate, and could not but feel some curiosity about the cause of the change. At length, he so far wrung the secret from Clifford, that he was in love, and that he was impatient to render himself worthy of the object of his affection. But the name of his adored fair the amorous youth would by no means communicate.

Calvert was of course desirous to assist this young man, who was beloved by all that knew him, myself only excepted, in the object of his wishes. Among other means for an advantageous introduction into life, he mentioned the name of Lord Montagu. That name awakened in Clifford's bosom no ordinary degree of commotion. He knew that that nobleman's house at Beaulieu was within one little mile of the residence of "her whom his heart loved." What should he say to the proposal of an introduction to Lord Montagu? Should he refuse it, because it might possibly lead to a renewed intercourse with Henrietta? He ought not to desire to entangle her affections. It would be a breach of all decency, that, he should at present propose himself as a match for her: and, as to the course of prosperous achievements that he meditated by way of rendering himself worthy of her, in that he might be finally disappointed. He had already resolved that he would not profess himself her lover till the day of his purposed triumph; and true honour and virtue required, that, in the painful interval, he should not so much as see her.

---

1   Greek philosophers representing the opposites of stoical austerity and hedonism respectively.

This was one view of the subject; but Clifford had not fortitude enough to adhere to that. His soul was too fervent; his passion too impetuous. "Why should not I see her? The severest morality cannot forbid that. I purpose a long separation; surely I may allow myself just to bid her adieu. I will not talk of love. No; sooner will I be torn in a thousand pieces. I will never cause to her gentle heart one moment's uneasiness. But I will talk to her, believing her to be my friend. I will tell her the views I have formed, the projects I have conceived. I will prepare her for my absence; I will lead her to expect that we may meet again. That, without doing her any harm, may serve to prevent her from entirely forgetting me."

Laying "this flattering unction to his soul,"[1] Clifford thankfully accepted the kind proposal of his friend. The conversation I have related took place in London, and Calvert was going in a few days to make a short visit at Beaulieu. He proposed to the lover to seize the present opportunity, and accompany him: such a deviation from the usual route would add nothing worth speaking of, to the distance from London to Petersfield. The consultations between young persons, where the fancy is in any way engaged, are seldom of long duration; they are not liable to the scruples and precautions of mistrustful old-age. It will easily be conceived, whether Clifford were not highly pleased with a project, which promised him a speedy and unlooked-for interview with his mistress.

The two friends arrived promptly and without accident at Lord Montagu's at Beaulieu. My school-fellow was introduced for the first time to the noble proprietor and all his family. All were enchanted with his appearance, his manners, and his conversation. But Clifford had not been many hours under the roof of this nobleman, before he found an opportunity of stealing away from the company, and sallying forth alone. Henrietta had the most extraordinary talent in conveying a vivid picture of whatever she described, to the mind of any one that listened to her. If you heard her account of any strange place, and afterwards visited it in person, you felt as if you had previously seen it, and every thing came successively before you with a sense of reminiscence. I know not in what this art consisted, for she never seemed tedious and minute; all her delineations were composed of a few master-strokes only. The rest was to be supplied by the imagina-

---

1 *Hamlet*, 3.4.145.

tion of the hearer; but she chose her points so skilfully, that it must be a very dull hearer indeed that missed his way. "Each lane, and every alley green, dingle or bushy dell,"[1] lay as in a map before him.

Clifford set out, with Henrietta's power of delineation, and the inspiration of love, for his guides. He did not miss the true path. He turned to the right at the corner of the park, and to the left at the end of the wood, just as he ought to have done. But the God was not this day a niggard of his bounty. By some wonderful chance, before Clifford was well within sight of the Cottage, he perceived Henrietta in the footpath, advancing in the opposite direction. Her eyes were on the ground, and she seemed deep in meditation. Clifford withdrew a few steps under cover of the wood, that she might not observe him from a distance. As she proceeded, a little dog that attended her steps, barked at him. Clifford advanced, and saluted my sister. Her first emotions were simply those of surprise, trepidation and joy; and, as she was in the habit of giving utterance to her sensations, she expressed both her surprise and her joy in no equivocal terms.

Presently however she recollected herself, and wore a look of displeasure. She asked him gravely, to what she owed the seeing him, and what purpose he had in view? This was easily explained. He told of the introduction that had been offered him to Lord Montagu, and that after dinner he had strolled out in the domain. He ingenuously owned however, that a desire to see Henrietta once more, had joined with other motives, to induce him to accept the proposal. He told her of his altered views of life, and of his determination never to rest, till he had obtained for himself honours and distinction. He spoke frankly of the forlorn and unprovided way in which he entered the career of life, and with sanguine assurance, that he would tread all obstacles under his feet. He added, "Henrietta, you are my friend; I am sure you are. You have listened with complacency to the little detail of my boyish sentiments. The approbation of innocence and beauty in your sex, is necessary to sustain ours in arduous undertakings. You are the only one of the guardian inspirers of manly virtue, to whom I have ever ventured to pour out my thoughts. I could not therefore set out upon this voyage, without obtaining from you the indulgence of a few moments to unfold my views. Give them your sanction! When I go forth, do you invoke the blessing of heaven upon my purposes! I ask no more."

---

1 *Comus*, 310–11.

Henrietta's conceptions of honour and right conduct were more lively and animated, than those of any other person I ever knew. It has been seen how she talked to me of the sentiments I ought to entertain, and the conduct it became me to pursue; nor was the clearness of her soul less conspicuous in this interview with Clifford. Her eyes sparkled, while he spoke of the ambition that pervaded him, and the projects he had formed. "Go on," she said. "Just such resolutions as you now express, I expected from you. The times have need of young men, so gallant and high of soul as you are. England shall again be restored; and other Raleighs and other Falklands shall refresh her annals.[1] Clifford, I will not forget you. My thoughts shall follow you; my enquiries shall collect your memorials. And in the end, or in the intervals of your achievements, remember to come to me again. The means of our meeting will easily be found; I know not how, but my prophetic soul tells me, we shall see each other hereafter. Clifford, I have considered you with an observing eye, and I approve you." And, saying this, she drew a ring from her finger, and placed it on his, with the motto, "*Je n'oublierai pas.*"[2]

Much more passed in this accidental conversation. Clifford thanked her in a more expressive way than mere words would convey, for her approbation. He smiled a thoughtful and heart-beaming smile, while he said, in the language of elder times, that he would be her knight. He looked with transported thoughts on the ring he had received from her hand, and kissed it.

The interview in which Clifford and Henrietta thus saw each other alone, was short, but its effects were memorable. They parted, considerably altered in sentiments and rumination, from the frame in which they met. Clifford became convinced, that, if the attachment he had conceived for Henrietta was ardent, his was not a solitary sentiment. He was now more deeply read in the language of love, than the last time they met. Then he had not the clue, he did not know the state of his own heart. It is surprising how a circumstance of this sort quickens the apprehension: Each little, nearly imperceptible indication on the part of Henrietta, of what passed within her bosom, was like a note struck upon one of two musical instruments set to the same key: it drew a sound from the corresponding string in Clifford's bosom; and knowing in himself the meaning of that, it enabled him to read without mistake in the heart of his mistress.

---

1   The second Viscount Falkland (c. 1610–43), a Royalist.
2   I shall not forget.

"Why too," he said to himself, "did she express herself angry in the beginning of the interview? If I had been indifferent to her, what right had she to be angry? It showed that she understood more, than simple decorum would have bid her own she understood; and how came the idea in her head?"

Clifford was transported with the discovery he believed he had made. "Does she condescend to cast an eye of favour on me; and shall not that make another man of me? Am I of importance to her; and shall not that make me considerable in my own eyes? Are the peace and happiness of this divine creature in any degree dependent on me; and will I not take an especial care that no harm results to her from so unmerited a condescension? I was ambitious before; but now I feel that the strength of twenty men nerves this arm, and new strings this soul. Urged by this powerful thought, all obstacles disappear, mountains sink into plains, 'to make what cannot be, slight work.'"[1]

CHAPTER XI

In the minutes that Clifford and Henrietta walked together, they had insensibly drawn nearer to the cottage. Mrs Willis was walking in the garden, and perceived her beloved charge engaged in earnest talk with a young man of a very noble and prepossessing air, whom Mrs Willis herself had never seen before. Their gestures to an experienced eye told I know not what of partiality and confidence. It occurred strongly to Mrs Willis's mind, that this could be no other than Clifford. Poor Henrietta had been wholly unaccustomed to precaution and disguise; she lived with Mrs Willis as a friend only, and not as a person by whom she was to be controled; and her innocence taught her, that she had nothing to conceal, and nothing to fear. She did not therefore regard this interview as a furtive one; and the thought did not occur to her, "Let us take care, and set proper limits to our walk, that we may not be seen."

When Henrietta returned to her own roof, she appeared more than usually absent and thoughtful. Mrs Willis gave her time to recollect herself, that she might see whether my sister would of her own accord enter into an explanation of what the other had just seen. She did not. When Henrietta spoke it was upon indifferent subjects, and with the air of a person whose mind was not

---

1 *Coriolanus*, 5.3.61–62.

in what she talked of. At length the elder lady put the direct question, "Who was the young cavalier, with whom I saw you engaged a few minutes before you came in?" Henrietta blushed with an expression of some complacency in her countenance, she said, "Did you see him? Why, that was Clifford, the gentleman, whose society and conversation gave me so much pleasure at Petersfield."

This was a moment, that inflicted a very unusual degree of pain upon Mrs Willis. She saw, from Henrietta's blush, and her distracted air, if she had not been convinced of it before, that Clifford had made a very dangerous impression on the heart of her charge. The most injurious and unworthy suspicions at this time rushed into the mind of Mrs Willis. "What had produced this interview? How came Clifford in the vicinity of Beaulieu Cottage? What am I to understand has previously passed between him and Henrietta? Was this meeting a concerted one? Is it possible that, by means that have escaped my penetration, there has been a regular clandestine correspondence between them?"

The thing meanwhile that occurred to her, as first to be done, was to question Henrietta on the subject. She received in return a very clear and unequivocal explanation. The moment however was critical. The veil with which Mrs Willis had hitherto covered her thoughts, was removed. In the perturbation of her spirit, she instantaneously changed her mode of proceeding. She spoke to Henrietta at once, and in direct terms, of the state of her heart. She told her that it was necessary, that she should call up the firmness of her soul, and dismiss a weakness which, if it were not checked, might prove fatal to her peace.

Henrietta was shocked that it could be imputed to her, that she could do, or feel any thing, contrary to the strictest laws of propriety. The mode of conduct which Mrs Willis now adopted, was inconsiderate. It is dangerous, particularly where you have to do with an innocent and inexperienced mind, hastily to impute a fault. We live in a great measure, almost all of us, in the opinions of others, especially of those we respect. While I am thought incapable of an error, I shall find it difficult to fall into one. Most of all, I shall be little disposed to regard with indulgence and favour that deviation, which it is judged impossible I should ever commit. But, if you warn me, particularly in a tone which gives me credit for my frailty, you have already in some measure taken away my character. You have thrown down the barrier, which seemed to set me at an insurmountable distance from vice and folly; you have removed me, from that elevated ground, the possession of which is often the best security against dishonour.

Henrietta spoke of the plans and resolutions that Clifford had formed for the advancement of his fortune. "Not," as she prettily added, "that this is any thing to me. I assure you, my dear aunt, (this was an appellation of fondness that she frequently bestowed on Mrs Willis,) he has never made love to me; he has never uttered the word; I do not believe he thinks of any such thing. And I can tell you, I am not a girl to throw myself at the head of the first likely young man that comes in my way. But still I would not have him on my account suffer injustice, and be represented as nobody."

Mrs Willis took little notice of the pretty artifices and ingenious turns of thought, by which Henrietta vindicated herself from the imputation of falling in love with a man, who had never avowed a partiality to her. She only exclaimed against the infatuation, of giving a person by anticipation the fortune and the honourable state which he has set up a resolution to acquire; and she drew a vivid picture of the world, its ruggednesses, its acclivities and precipices, the obstacles that were thrown in the way of young ambition, the crosses and animosities it was sure to encounter, the innumerable accidents by which it was baffled, and inferred, that not one young man in five hundred, was lucky enough to realize the romantic visions of an inexperienced fancy. She concluded with a very serious remonstrance to my sister, that she should set herself to cure this infatuation, while yet there was time.

"My lovely girl," said this admirable matron, "you have always been my pride, and the wonder of all that knew you. Your accomplishments are extraordinary, and your understanding is of a very exalted class. I have at all times found in you the best dispositions. No one sees more justly into the different relations of human beings, or can read more convincing and unanswerable lessons of purity and propriety to every one for whose welfare you are concerned. Virtue is doubly virtue, when inspired and recommended by you; no one can listen to you, without feeling his whole soul penetrated with moral ambition and the most generous resolutions. The ears tingle that hear you; the heart beats with holy rapture; and men wonder that vice and infirmity should ever have found a moment's harbour in their bosom. I cannot even explain to myself whence this comes; but, in the various gifts of a superintending creator, some are born with endowments, that no advantages of birth and education can account for, and that to many those advantages can never impart. In your cradle, as in that of Plato, a swarm of bees seems to have gathered round your lips,[1] and the persuasion of moral wisdom and rectitude falls irresistible from your tongue.

"No, Henrietta, no; you must not, shall not, fall. The honour of your sex is bound up in you; the women of England, if they could choose a representative for the glory and crown of their entire community, would fix on you. With you they prosper, and with you decay. Their character for an entire age is gone, if you show yourself, lofty indeed in purpose, excellent while the object is only to talk this well, but in act characterized by the same frailty as the meanest, vanquished by the same follies, enslaved by the same passions, dictated to by the same caprice, governed by impulse, and incapable of dedicating yourself at the holy shrine of a principle."

Every word that Mrs Willis uttered, went to my sister's heart. She touched a string, that guided and controled every power of her nature. Henrietta saw the delusion into which she had fallen, and blushed. This you would think was a victory for Mrs Willis and discretion. But it was not so. Little was this amiable matron disposed to congratulate herself upon her conquest. Henrietta appeared like Patience herself. Never was she heard to utter a murmur. Least of all did she, like a vulgar love-sick girl, pity herself, play a double and a treacherous part, and, pretending to resist as much as she could, in secret open the gates to the enemy. No; she was a true heroine, brave, generous and unalterable. But the arrow had penetrated deep; her health seemed to give way under the struggle. Mrs Willis watched her with unceasing anxiety: she saw her hollow eyes, her sleepless nights, her serenity gone, her flashes of harmless gaiety, her light, tripping step that spoke the health and ease of her mind, appearing no more. Ever and anon, Henrietta would make a gallant attempt to sustain her former character; but, somehow or other, it always failed, before the effort was half performed. "Be under no uneasiness; I shall do very well," said my sister, with a forced cheerfulness. But Mrs Willis had a painful foreboding, that she would not "do very well."

---

1 Supposedly when Plato was in his cradle a swarm of bees alighted on his lips, marking him as a singular individual. But the reference could also be to his *Meno*, where Socrates asks Meno for a definition of virtue and then complains that Meno has shown him a swarm of bees instead of a single bee.

Hitherto no one but Mrs Willis was acquainted with the weakness of Henrietta's bosom; but an unfortunate accident more than half revealed it. One day they were dining, as was often the case, at Lord Montagu's table. My sister's spirits were in a diseased state, and her general health feeble and alarming, a subject of much anxiety, even to those friends, who were unacquainted with the secret hurt that seemed mining her constitution. This day she was a little worse than usual: but she scorned to yield like a coward, and, on the contrary, thought it became her resolutely to contend with and to vanquish her enemy. Solitude and pensive thought were evils that she had particularly to fear; and therefore, though scarcely fit for company, she preferred it to the treachery of reflection.

During dinner the conversation happened to turn upon the subject of some late very tempestuous weather. The storm had prevailed with particular severity at Portsmouth; and as it came on in a very sudden manner, it had not only done considerable damage among the shipping, but an uncommon number of boats had also perished. A gentleman, one of the company, who had just arrived from the spot, said, that among the number of lives that were lost, there was one young man who seemed to be particularly regretted, and whose name was Clifford. He had taken leave of his mother and several friends at Portsmouth, and had purposed to go over to the Isle of Wight, to the house of an acquaintance, by whom he was invited to a festival that was to be given on occasion of this islander's coming of age. The boat had scarcely made its way out of the harbour, when it was attacked with all the fury of the elements, and Clifford and all that were on board perished, in the very sight of his despairing mother, who witnessed the fatal event.—The intelligence of this stranger was premature. The boat indeed had sunk, and it was for a few hours believed that Clifford had been a victim to the storm. It was still believed, when the stranger left Portsmouth. But he escaped on board a vessel in the harbour, and was restored to his terrified and disconsolate friends.

The stranger was without apprehension pursuing his narrative, when the attention of the company was suddenly drawn off from his discourse. Henrietta fell back on her seat in a state of total insensibility; and, had not Mrs Willis, who took the alarm from the moment the stranger began his tale, been on the watch to support her, she would have fallen from her chair on the ground. My sister was taken from the table and led into the garden. The stranger stammered out a hundred apologies. He asked, if the young lady were any relation to the unfortunate Clifford? The Montagus wondered; and thoughts suddenly occurred to their minds, that had never been dreamed of before. The common excuses were made, that the young lady was in a poor state of health, and the room was hot; but there seemed to be something behind, that these excuses were hardly sufficient to explain. Henrietta herself, as soon as she recovered her senses, felt so ashamed and shocked at what had passed, that she begged she might immediately go home.

One night she spent in melancholy reverie on the tale she had heard. Death puts an end to all the distinctions of rank and fortune; and the chastest woman alive feels, as if without reproach she might love the dead. Henrietta gave a loose to all the tenderness of her nature. "He is gone," she said, "and I am now free to celebrate his obsequies. Yes; in my heart, Clifford, shall be thy grave; and in my memory, and my lonely reveries, thou shalt have a funeral procession, more splendid, and of a slower and longer march, than ever attended a monarch's remains. That beauteous form, those limbs whose motions might have charmed a seraph from his sphere, now lie at the bottom of the sea. Those eyes, so soft, so beaming, so expressive of the best emotions of the soul, are now vacant of their lustre and their meaning. No shroud shall cover, and no hearse receive thee. The whelming[1] waters shall roll over thy frame, and the restless tides shall float thee from shore to shore. No friendly hand perhaps shall afford even a little earth to cover thee; but thou shalt at least lie embalmed in my unperishing recollections. For ever shall thy image be before me; the eyes of my mind shall contemplate thy figure, thy voice shall be in my ears. Never have I regarded any youth with maiden affection but thee; and my virgin vows shall be consecrated to thy bones. The heyday of my life is past; and the rest of my years shall waste in mourning and in miseries. In this shall my heart find a hallowed luxury. No law forbids my union with the dead. No cool prudence comes in with its remorseless rules to interdict this junction; nor is there any danger here, that the tenderest regard should lead me into any false steps, such as the censorious lay in wait for, and enlarge on with envious delight."

Mrs Willis herself was led into the same error as Henrietta; and, when Lord Montagu in person came the next morning to enquire for my sister's health, her matron-hostess thought disguise no longer necessary, particularly with so respected a friend,

---

1 Surging.

and disclosed to his lordship in confidence the secret malady of her charge. Lord Montagu listened to the tale with the tenderest concern. As they talked however, the idea occurred to his mind, that the loss of Clifford was not to be considered as absolutely certain; and he resolved to send over an express to Portsmouth to ascertain the fact. The messenger speedily returned with the welcome intelligence, that Clifford was well, and had sustained no injury from the accident that had befallen him.

This information gave an entirely new turn to the ideas of Lord Montagu. He agreed with Mrs Willis, that the youthful passion of Henrietta was by all means to be discouraged; and, though this unforeseen accident had brought to light all her secret weakness, they both of them hoped that the passion which had surprised her at unawares, might yet be extinguished without injury. They had great confidence in the rectitude of her judgment, and the general healthfulness and strength of her mind.

Poor Henrietta was far from deriving benefit from the vicissitudes, at the mercy of which she had thus been placed. At first, when she thought that Clifford was dead, she had, at least to her own mind, thrown off all restraint, and dared frankly consider herself as a victim to the empire of love. Most sincerely, and from the bottom of her soul, did she rejoice at the news of Clifford's safety. Yet in one respect it occasioned a painful revulsion in her blood. He lived, the ornament of the world, the most beautiful of the works of God, the most gallant and generous of the sons of men; and that was indeed a subject for exultation. But that very circumstance brought back to her the necessity of eternal warfare against the sentiments of her heart. That for more than twenty-four hours she had avowed to herself that she was in love, that in the solitude of her chamber she had mourned for him, as a mother mourns for her only-begotten son, made a great difference to her for all her life to come. She had broken down the barrier, that had hitherto subjected the flood of her affection to the laws of propriety. She also learned from Mrs Willis, that Lord Montagu was no stranger to her weakness, and that he had been instigated by the knowledge of it, to send off his express to Portsmouth. That transgression, which we ought not to confess to our own hearts, it is peculiarly dangerous to us if we know that it has been made a subject of attention and remark to others. Henrietta evidently drooped; it was hardly likely she would ever be again the charming, fascinating, exhilarating creature she had been. She struggled indeed with edifying energy and fortitude; but her struggles were attended with a disproportionate success.

That one, single night, in which she had indulged uncontroled all the tenderness of her soul for the imaginary deceased, had produced a permanent effect on all her feelings; so dangerous is the shortest intermission in matters of this sort. When she looked up too, she saw the two most venerable beings she knew on earth conscious of her frailty. They pitied her: and there is something truly seducing in this consideration. If they pitied her, why should not she be allowed to relent over herself? Lord Montagu and Mrs Willis were unfeignedly distressed for her; this generous nobleman prided himself in my sister, perhaps even more than in his own daughters.

In no very long time after this incident, another revolution took place in relation to the same subject. It was about Midsummer in the year 1655, that Clifford's wealthy relation, having been left childless, declared his resolution to constitute the young man his heir. Intelligence of this sort is rapidly spread. Lord Montagu heard it, and eagerly conveyed it to Mrs Willis. They augured every thing good of it; they did not doubt of the truth of the young man's affections. They had before canvassed all the circumstances of the case; they were satisfied that his visit of introduction at Beaulieu, had been mainly prompted by the wish to obtain the conference that had occurred with Henrietta. Yet they waited with patient expectation that Clifford should declare that passion, which he had no longer any motive to suppress.

They waited not long. In a very short time the post brought the following letter from him to Henrietta.

"You doubtless remember, dear Henrietta, our last interview. I came on purpose to tell you, that I was resolved no longer to be contented with an obscure fortune. I had caught the sacred flame of ambition, and resolved to set out on a career, in which my better genius assured me, I should out of all doubt succeed. Why did I come to tell this story to you? That I did not avow to myself: in truth I did not understand myself. I said, that I came to ask your sanction and your prayers. But your answer was better than my request: ah, when have you not been better than all human kind besides? You answered, that you 'would not forget me'; that your 'thoughts should follow, and your enquiries be busied respecting me.' You gave me a ring; and the motto of that ring is a thousand times in my sight, and for ever in my mind.

"Henrietta, never was a soul more pure and innocent than yours; and I was myself as little experienced in the first disclosures of mutual affection between youth of different sexes, as you were. We both of us spoke a language that the very speaker understood not; we stammered the first uncertain accents of an eternal vow.

"Presumptuous Clifford, what are you saying? No; I have no confidence of any thing. I desire only to approach you as a stranger, and to receive the decree of lasting happiness or disappointment from your own lips. You are the sovereign mistress of you; and I am not foolish enough to advance any claim, or assert any title.

"The conclusion of this letter will hardly be worthy of the arrogant expectation excited in its beginning. You will have a right to conceive that I am come to redeem my pledge:—that I have performed glorious achievements, that I have gained myself a name, and that wealth and honour have combined to crown the lustre of my exploits. But there is nothing of this. I am as obscure as ever, unknown to the records of fame, and never having done aught to entitle me to any man's praise. Merit to boast I have none. The end of my communication is simply this worthless thing, 'I am no longer poor. I am not one of those sons of the earth, who flutter loosely on its surface, and have no inheritance, *but their good spirits, to feed and clothe them.*'[1]

"I dare go no further in this letter. I leave it maimed and imperfect. You perhaps will be able to piece out its defect: but, if not,—I will shortly come myself to the Forest, and lay the thoughts of my heart before you.

"LIONEL CLIFFORD."

In reading these lines, Henrietta scarcely ventured to flatter herself that she had understood their contents. She took the letter to Mrs Willis.

In the commencement of this ill-fated amour, my sister had made no communication of her thoughts to her beloved protector, the former of her mind. This had been partly the result of accident. The first acquaintance between Clifford and Henrietta, had been made at a distance from the domestic roof. Add to which, love will be found to be a subject (where the mind retains its natural bent, and the temper is bashful), respecting which a certain degree of concealment will take place, between friends the most cordial. Henrietta did not immediately understand herself. The first emotions of this passion are full of trepidation and flutter. Can we expect, when the butterfly is just evolved

---

1 *Hamlet*, 3.2.58–59.

from the chrysalis, that the fair one in whose secret chamber this work of nature is performed, will immediately seize on the just-appearing insect, and carry it to her friend, that she may hear a lecture in the forms upon its genus and its accidents?

But Henrietta had bitterly experienced the ill consequences of wanting an adviser. In all the unsuspiciousness of youth, she had given way to impulses, in which she knew there was no crime. She had given up the reins to her fancy, and indulged in all the prodigality of reverie, without once thinking it necessary to restrain its flight by cold calculations of probability, or comparing the dreams of an animated imagination with the realities of existence. Her life had nearly become the sacrifice of this mistake. Henrietta, I say, had bitterly experienced the ill consequences of wanting an adviser; and she was resolved for the future to steer her course under the direction of her faithful guide.

Mrs Willis read the letter with great delight, and easily explained to my sister those particulars, which the fervour and extacy of her lover had left in obscurity. Henrietta dismissed with one deep sigh the dejection of her mind; but she was too serious, and felt too much what was due to herself, to break out into the levities of joy. Serenity only, and a calm thankfulness to Providence, took place of that silent sorrow, which had seemed to be going fast to undermine his existence.

Mrs Willis took care that it should not be long before Lord Montagu was acquainted with the contents of Clifford's letter. They both congratulated each other most fervently, upon the revolution that had occurred. They mutually owned, that nothing could have been more unexpected; and, of consequence, that nothing could till then have been more hopeless than the passion, which these lovely creatures had conceived for each other. They set no bounds to the eulogiums they pronounced of both. They were convinced that Henrietta could no where else have met with a husband worthy of her excellencies. They augured a thousand blessings from their union, and with sighs and tears rejoiced over my sister, as a pattern of female worth restored to them from the tomb. Clifford soon followed his letter: and now the young Montagus, as they had watched with more than paternal anxiety the alarming symptoms that had appeared in Henrietta, were admitted to a knowledge of the favourable change that had taken place, and its cause. The whole circle of this excellent family were transported with joy at the good fortune that had fallen to the lot of Clifford, and received him into the midst of them as a brother.

In this narrative of the early loves of my sister and my school-fellow, I have introduced many things, which did not come to my knowledge for several years afterward, but the recital of which was necessary for the perspicuity of my tale.

CHAPTER XII

Up to this time not a whisper had ever been heard, of the ill blood that was secretly fermenting in my breast against Clifford. It was but just before, that the insurrection of Penruddock had exploded, an occasion that blew up the embers of my school-boy detestation of this accomplished young man, into a flame. Clifford had engaged in the insurrection from the sentiment he had recently professed to Henrietta, the resolution, that he would enlist under the banners of ambition, and that he would rest no more, till he had obtained for himself honours and distinction. It was not long after the defeat of this gallant handful of men, that the revolution took place in the mind of Clifford's kinsman, which promised to have as favourable an operation with regard to the dearest wishes of his heart, as could have resulted from the most successful progress in the hazardous paths of ambition. The dangers perhaps that he had incurred in this insurrection, and the gallant spirit he had displayed in every thing that related to it, combined with the influence of domestic calamity, to turn towards him the heart of his wealthy relation.

The circumstance of the mutual love entertained by Clifford and Henrietta for each other, when it came to my knowledge, furnished me with a clue to many things that I had not understood before, and set others in a light very different from that in which they had appeared at the time. Why had Clifford shown himself so earnest and importunate for my favour, on the day that I met him in the affair of Penruddock? Why, not contented with the apology he made to me in the quarters of Sir Joseph Wagstaff, did he follow me into the street, and press me again and again to be reconciled to him? I had never supposed that I was too indulgent in my construction of the actions and sentiments of Clifford: yet even I had in this instance given him credit for an admirable and disinterested generosity. Fool that I was! He acted from the basest and most ignoble motives. He was eager in a show of kindness to me, only because he desired the possession of my sister. It was thus I now reasoned upon an incident, that at the time had almost the force to shake the steadiness of my hatred.

It was but a few months after the insurrection of Penruddock, that I was seized with frenzy at Oxford, that I was shut up in a receptacle for lunatics at Cowley, and that my sister visited me there. Clifford and Henrietta loved each other; their love was approved by those who stood most nearly in guardianship to my sister; and, so approved, it was not doubted that it would obtain the sanction of my uncle Audley and of Clifford's protector, whenever that sanction should be demanded. But the lovers were yet very young. Their mutual suffering had been considerable when an unsurmountable bar seemed to be opposed to their union but, when that bar was removed, when their passion had the countenance of all those persons in the midst of whom Henrietta lived, when they might correspond as they pleased, and see each other as frequently as occasion offered; the young persons acquiesced in this situation of affairs, and yielded to the discretion of my sister's friends as to the retarding their union. Theirs was not the hot, boiling and furious passion of youth unacquainted with the refinements of sentiment, and undisciplined in the purest principles of morality and virtue. Their attachment was of the mind; they loved each other for qualities which appeared to them worthy of the most fervent admiration. Beauty indeed came in for its share: the speaking eye, the ingenuous countenance, the features which corresponded to and fascinatingly expressed the emotions of the soul, and the gracefulness of motion and form, all served to bind and corroborate the feeling; but these held a subordinate place only, while the root of the attachment was nourished in the soul. The flame that inspired them was bright and steady and pure; it was of that kind of fire which promises a long duration and inflexible constancy, but which does not exhaust itself in impetuous tumult and rage. The well-constituted mind looks forward with elevated calmness to a happiness, that is viewed as in certain prospect. The person so circumstanced says, "I am happy now, because I have in expectation the gratification of all my desires; and I am happy now, because I know I shall be ten thousand times happier." There is something in the nature of the human soul, that is strikingly in harmony with the office of building castles in the air: we revel and luxuriate in the envied task of painting out to our thoughts the things that shall be. It is by virtue of this principle, that the saints below wait, in edifying patience, and delighted serenity, "all the days of their appointed time, till the change come" that is to translate them from earth to heaven.

My sister visited me at Cowley. She sat by my bed side, during a great part of the period when my disorder was at its worst, and with incredible perseverance and affection relieved my sufferings, and soothed my woes. She listened to my ravings. Sometimes I talked of Bradford and Judith and O'Neile, and the scenes of my childhood. At other times I cried out in my exclamations upon Penruddock and Clifford. This last topic peculiarly engaged her attention; the name of Clifford, in particular, vibrated from her ear to her inmost heart. She strained all her attention to gather the hidden meaning of my words; but my discourse was so incoherent, that it was impossible to arrange it into any certain sense. When the words no longer struck her sense, she endeavoured by meditation to penetrate into my mystery. Clifford she had seen since the insurrection; but his whole discourse had been of the happy change that had taken place in his own fortunes, and the consequent removal, as he trusted and believed, of every rational obstacle that could be interposed to his addresses to Henrietta. Unassisted however as she found herself in developing my enigma, there was one thing of which the quickness of her feelings certainly assured her, that my tones were those of aversion.

This was painful to her, but not a cause of despair. It was distressing to find any defect of harmonious and responsive sentiment in the mind of one, with whom she had always lived in the most unexampled and uninterrupted accord. Poor Henrietta was far from understanding the depth of my passion. How could she? She was formed of nature's kindliest mould.

> Her life was gentle; and the elements
> So mixed in her,[1]

that the maker of us all, when he surveyed the works of his hands, might have fixed upon her, as the pattern of whatever is perfect in woman. But I was cursed from my birth. My feelings were all tempestuous and tumultuous; never did I look upon any thing on its fairest side, or make of any thing a candid or a generous construction; hatred was the element in which I lived, and revenge was my daily bread. No, Henrietta; neither now did you anticipate, nor to the latest hour of your existence, though suffering from me more than woman ever suffered, could you understand, my atrocious qualities, or the springs by which they acted!

But though she could in a very imperfect degree make out what I talked of, or whereto my discourse tended, my sister was not the less disturbed and distressed at the incoherent sugges-

---

1 Adapted from *Julius Caesar*, 5.4.73–74, describing Brutus.

tions which thus escaped me. She enquired of Clifford as to what related to Penruddock and he ingenuously told her all he knew. She set on foot an earnest investigation into the circumstances that had preceded my frenzy; and at length became acquainted with my unhappy altercation with young Lisle, and the reproaches with which he had loaded me. All this produced in her a great degree of pain and alarm; but it did not abate her confidence.

She prepared herself for a powerful struggle against the prejudices, which had polluted and eaten into my soul. She had a perfect confidence in the justice of her cause. She knew that Clifford was the most amiable of men. She knew that he overflowed with every generous affection and was incapable of harbouring a malignant thought against any creature that lived. She knew that he was born to command all hearts, and subdue the love of all men to himself. Nor was she less persuaded of the equity of my nature, and my accessibleness to the powers of reason. She was not unacquainted with the ascendancy she had over me. Though therefore she prepared herself diligently for the combat, and was aware of the mighty results dependent on the issue, she did not allow herself for a moment to doubt of the event.

It has been seen, with what more than human eloquence she expressed herself on the occasion. I was completely her convert; for the moment all resistance and every ruder passion was subdued within me. I considered her as preaching mere philanthropy; I regarded her as, purely by the energies of a virtuous spirit, giving a soul to morality, more than all the philosophers of antiquity had ever been able to impart, and clothing the simplicity of abstract truth in all the radiance of sunshine, and all the tints of the rainbow. Alas! I little knew, poor soul! that she was pleading for her life, and that the peace and contentment of all her days and nights to come, depended on her success in the enterprise to which she had vowed herself.

This was a moment of pure joy and exultation to the divine Henrietta. She looked in my eyes, and saw that the spirit of self-existent and everlasting benignity had descended upon me. She addressed me with the soul-ravishing words, "Ah, Charles, you are now my genuine brother. There wanted but this. You had a fault: who is exempt from error? but it is over now. I have committed my soul on this venture. You must not deceive me in it. No, I see plainly you will not!"

Henrietta's soul was at this time on her lips. When she put my hand into the hand of Clifford,—at that preternatural moment when she saw us looking at each other with the aspect of broth-ers—the secret had almost broke from her bursting heart, "Behold my husband!" But she conquered herself. She felt that now was not the time. The affair, she judged, was well begun: but it was here, as in what they relate of the mighty menstruum[1] that is to convert all baser metals into gold; the most unconquerable patience is necessary; the least precipitancy ruins the whole oper-ation. Henrietta held her breath; her eyes glistened with her secret thought; her bosom heaved; but she uttered not a syllable further.

How speedily was this auspicious beginning thrown down and demolished! I saw Clifford; I hailed him; I ate with him; I heard from his lips the story of Landseer. I constrained myself to hear that story with rigid and unaltered muscles. It was a terrible effort I had made, to conquer the savageness of my nature, and to feel all mildness and benignity and philanthropy. But the more strenuously the bow was bent, the more resistless was the recoil. It will be recollected, what strange fancies and furies at this time occupied my thoughts. I resolved that I would see Clifford no more. I ruminated ferocious ideas, that I would cause him to be kidnapped, and transported to the American plantations. To that state of mind a worse state succeeded. I said, "Clifford is my fate. Present or absent, waking or sleeping, I can never get rid of him. What matters it then, if I were to ship him for Virginia, or banish him to the regions of Japan?[2] If I were to sharpen my dagger's point, and send him to the grave; from the grave he would haunt me, and my crime would prove utterly unavailing. Still I should see him, when I slept; still I should think of him, while I waked; and he would be the unexhausted ingredient, that turned the cup of my existence into poison." It will easily be judged then, in what frame of spirit I was to receive him for a brother-in-law.

Henrietta did not see all this; such horrible conceptions filled all my thoughts in solitude; but I never uttered Clifford's name in her presence. What then? she was my true sister. She entirely sympathized with me; and by virtue of the secret and preternat-ural affinity between us, she read my inmost thoughts. There was no need of words to communicate to her the deepest workings of my soul. She saw that she could never be at once the bosom-ally of Mandeville and Clifford. What though I did not wound her ears with frenzied execrations, and all the deadly liturgy of my

---

1 Solvent used to extract the chemical compounds of metals.
2 Mandeville says the same thing on p. 273.

soul's hatred? It hung for that with only the more insurmountable weight upon the neck of her mind. Had I "unpacked my heart with curses,"[1] had I poured out the freight of my bursting bosom in all the exuberant rhetoric of vulgar abhorrence, there would have been hope. To the thus venting my passion, it were not unlikely that a comparative temperance might have succeeded. Beside, that, if I had spoken all that was in my mind, if I had given to my "worst of thoughts the worst of words,"[2] this would in some sort have operated as a dispensation to Henrietta. But the inviolable silence I observed acted like a spell; there was a sacredness in it, that she could not find it in her affectionate heart to trample upon. I stood before her as a figure over which the blast of heaven had passed; and there was something portentous in the dumb anguish that dwelt about me, that awed her very soul.

CHAPTER XIII

Sharp and terrible were the struggles of my poor sister's mind in this unlooked-for situation. There were two persons, between whom her entire heart was divided; and one of these was an irreconcilable enemy to the other. It is the law of morality, that a woman "shall leave father and mother, and all the kindred of her birth, and cleave unto her husband."[3] It is the nature of human feelings, that when the irresistible sentiment of love has been awakened in the youthful breast, all other considerations fade before it. It is true, we do not scruple to blame with severity those, who being once touched with this mighty passion, think of nothing but the gratification of their own partialities, and regard all other inducements and pleas, divine and human, as unworthy of their attention. However powerful, and however subtle may be the insinuations of love, a truly virtuous person will rather die, than yield to any unhallowed indulgence; and this very sentiment will often enable them, to "set at nought the frivolous bolt of Cupid."[4] But had not Henrietta passed through a sufficient ordeal? Surely her trials had multiplied, to a degree to satisfy the demands of the severest morality; and she was entitled to the reward.

---

1 *Hamlet*, 2.2.585–86.
2 *Othello*, 3.3.132–33.
3 Genesis 2:24
4 *Comus*, 443–44.

It was not thus however that my sister reasoned. She felt, that to part with Clifford now, was to tear away strings that had wound round her heart, and would require an effort, of which her life would very probably be the sacrifice. Yet she resolved at once, that this was the path she would pursue. "Mandeville is sick; and we are well," she said. "He is a banished and a blasted man. He has no friend but me; I am his only tie to mortal life; and never will I teach his tongue to curse me. Alienated from the rest of the world, he leans on me with unsuspecting confidence; shall I then be the person to inflict upon him a wound, more agonizing than even in all the exacerbations of frenzy he ever imaged to himself? I shall perhaps be the sacrifice. What then? Is there any end for which I wish to live, but to promote the gratifications of those I love? Can I be so sordid, as to count myself for any thing in this desperate struggle? If evil be the portion of him to whom I am most ardently attached, while I am myself unhappy, I shall not feel the bitter sting of reproach; but is it possible that I should think of obtaining peace and felicity for myself, by an act that shall plant mortal anguish in the breast of my nearest and most valued relative?"

Such were the virtuous determinations of Henrietta; but the agony of her soul while she formed them was excessive. It is sufficiently apparent, by the irresistible appeal she made to my feelings at first, that no one understood better than she did the true merits of the case. "How unreasonable are these prejudices of my brother! how inhuman the obstinacy with which he persists in them! and we are to be made the sacrifices of his error! It is thus for ever in this world, that vice triumphs over virtue, and imbecility over strength. Because we are right, therefore we must submit; because we are strong, therefore we must crouch, suffer all our just expectations to be disappointed, and our happiness to be blasted for ever. This is exactly the morality that is taught us when children, that the wise must yield to the foolish, and the sober to the tumultuous and ungovernable; and the same morality is still imposed upon us in our ripest years. What a triple knot of unrivalled happiness might be knit between me and my brother and Clifford? I see it all. They are all I ever loved in the world; and truly, most truly, do they merit the distinction. I might sit between them, blessed and cherished by each, fervently attached to both, and forming the indissoluble tie by which they were bound for ever to each other. All this is within our reach; every day would be peace; every day would be happiness; for every day would be uninterrupted love. Brother, brother, cannot you see this? Is there no power in the speech of man, that can make you understand it? That which I feel so intimately, and of which I am so infallibly convinced, can I by no means convey to your heart? I could tear out my tongue, that it is so powerless to communicate my sentiments. Will these scales never, never, fall from your eyes? Oh, how has the framer of this our human nature constituted us, that we have all happiness and joy within our reach, and that we are thus our own only enemies, and reject it, because we will reject it!"

At times Henrietta was worked up almost to frenzy at the thought of her destiny. She was like a captive bird, that has not yet lost the passion of its woods and its skies, the birthright that nature assigned it, and beats itself to pieces against its wires, and scatters all its most beautiful plumage at the bottom of its cage. At times she raved against me, and loaded me in her mind with every opprobrious epithet. In the tumult and tempest of her spirit, the affection of a sister was wrecked and almost dashed to pieces. She asked, Why, from infirmity merely, from obstinacy, from vice, I stood in the way of a scene of future happiness, which she imaged to herself as distinctly, as the external landscape is repeated by the mechanism of a *camera obscura*?[1] She sometimes thought she could be contented to see me dead. "I could have followed my brother's funeral, though I cannot consent to be the cause of his living anguish. Of what use is his life? He is an abortion merely, and appertains in no way to the scene of the living world. He never will be anything but miserable; and his existence answers no purpose but that of intercepting the happiness of others." At times she felt as if she hated me.

But all Henrietta's agonies did not even move, or in the smallest degree disturb, her virtuous resolutions. The thought that now occurred to her, was truly characteristic of the loveliness of her nature. "Mandeville!" it was thus she discussed the question in the secret chambers of her own heart, "you are my greatest enemy. It is your frowardness,[2] the unheard-of wilfulness and blindness of your character, that robs me of a prize, the most inestimable that can be drawn in the many-ticketed lottery of life. Oh, God, Oh, God, that there should be no remedy for this!

---

1 The camera obscura (literally "darkened chamber") is an optical device into which light is admitted through a convex lens, forming an image of external objects on a paper or glass. Used since antiquity, it eventually led to photography.
2 Difficult or contrary nature.

Henceforth, all the days of my existence are devoted to a twilight, more chilling and desolate than that of a Russian winter. It might have been otherwise. But my purpose is conceived; my resolution is taken. Most remorseless of brothers!

    Beautiful tyrant! fiend angelical!
    Dove-feathered raven! wolfish, ravening lamb![1]

since I cannot escape you, since I have no hope to move you, I will fly from your envenomed hostility—into your arms! You are my only destroyer! therefore I will love none but you! That shall be my revenge: so will I satiate all the just and deep resentment, with which your unkindness has filled me. You have struck a barbed arrow into my very heart, the smart and the anguish of which can never be asswaged. Therefore all my days and nights shall be devoted to the increase of your comforts. I will talk to you all day, and smooth your pillow by night. I will hide all my sorrows, and the bitterness of my disappointment, in the recesses of my own bosom. Never shall you have reason to guess at the true state of my feelings. No accent of mine shall ever betray it; not one disobedient muscle shall express the sufferings I underpass. It may be, that I am most worthy of pity, and have most need of consolation. But it shall not seem so. I will always have a cheerful word to soothe you; not a thorn that untoward fortune has planted in your pillow, but I will pluck it out; I will weep for your sorrows, when my heart is bursting with my own; I will invent for you a thousand tales of amusement, a thousand schemes to give variety and zest to the tedious day, while my frame is fast wasting to the grave. This is the conduct my heart prescribes, and my reason approves. I shall thus best secure my own approbation; I shall thus best insure something for my mind to dwell on with unwearied complacency. Naturally entangled as I have been, disappointed as I must be, I should no longer be of use to any, a mere incumbrance on the face of the earth. But thus I will defeat my cruel fate: and every day that I mitigate in any way the sorrows of a brother whom I love as my own soul, I will not think that I have lived that day in vain."

There was something in the greatness, the very extravagance of this sacrifice, that Henrietta felt as particularly consolatory. I had taken upon myself a sort of Hannibal-vow[2] for the extinction

---

1   Shakespeare, *Romeo and Juliet*, 3.2.75–76.
2   Legend has it that Hannibal's father made him swear eternal hatred to Rome.

of Clifford: I had sworn, upon the altar of my revenge, immortal hostility to him whom I regarded as the author of all my woes. Had I not gone mad for Clifford? Was not this the man, for whose sake I had been exposed to whips and chains, a dark chamber and ignominious cords? Had he not by his machinations reduced me to the condition of a beast? And would I ever forget this? Henrietta's determination therefore, that she would live with me, and employ all her thoughts for the service of her torturer, was a martyrdom, beyond any thing that we read of in the history of monastic vows, beyond the rules of the Carthusian order, or the discipline of La Trappe. It was as if the mother of the Scipios[1] should have consecrated herself, to the nourishment and anxious preservation of the springal[2] Hannibal. Could we suppose Cornelia[3] reduced to that situation, the daily reward of her pains would have been, to have heard the stripling's copious and diversified execrations of her beloved country. Every species of bigot abuse and recrimination against Rome, was no doubt familiar to his unbearded lip. Even in his dreams he repeated the fatal and portentous vow. His waking study, was to procure intelligence, the more to whet his enmity against Rome, or to discover her vulnerable part, and how she might most effectually be destroyed. What a situation are we imagining for the mother of the Scipios! In one respect the condition which Henrietta chose for herself was more bitter than this. I indulged my feelings indeed in no execrations against Clifford. Never, but when I had secured myself in the double night of impenetrable solitude, did I so much as pronounce his name. But there was something more fearful and heart-quelling in this silence, than in the most open and loquacious hostility. Henrietta could never look upon me, without having reason to say, "What murderous thoughts against Clifford may at this moment be engendering in his bosom!" She must have perpetually the impulse, to cover him with her mantle, or to throw her body between, to intercept the blows of the brain-created dagger, or the blood-dripping poniard,[4] which in imagi-

---

1 Scipio Africanus (236–183 BCE), best known for defeating Hannibal in the final battle of the Punic Wars.

2 Youth.

3 [Godwin's note:] There is a mistake here. Cornelia was the name of the females born of the Scipio family; that of the mother of Scipio Africanus is unknown. [It is not clear why Godwin introduces an error into his Roman history and then corrects it.]

4 A dagger with a slender blade of triangular or square cross-section.

nation I drew against him. A blessed life was this she chose for herself; to sit perpetually by the side of, and study all manner of kindly offices for, him in whose bosom rage and fierceness and inextinguishable animosity kept their revels and tumultuous sabbath against the youth she loved above the price of worlds!

These were the thoughts and purposes conceived by Henrietta, as soon as she understood the full extent and incurable nature of my animosity to Clifford. But from these thoughts and purposes she was afterwards turned aside. Never was a gentle and a tender nature so obstinately beset. Not by Clifford: he did not fall short of her, in the generosity of his temper and sentiments. This pair of perfect lovers would, I verily believe, if left to their own direction, have immolated themselves, willing victims, upon the altar of my prejudices. Clifford could not bear, any better than Henrietta, that his happiness should be built upon another's misery. The thought of the state that he had reduced me to, would have had the effect of causing his happiness to cease to be happiness. This lovely pair would have rested satisfied in eternal self-denial, and would have supported themselves with a consciousness of the integrity of the principle, in submission to which they should have formed the vow of immortal celibacy. They would have resolved to have seen each other no more, and have been contented exclusively to have cherished each other's image, comforted moreover with the unshaken faith that in this occupation their sympathy was complete. This, I have great reason to apprehend, would have been their destiny for the remainder of their lives.

They met once, to confirm each other in these sentiments, to pour out all the agitation of their spirits, and to meet no more. Despair was in the hearts of both. The interview was a long one. As their determination was fixed, and apparently irrevocable, they were in no hurry to part, and they thought it no crime to indulge in a full effusion of soul. So one might imagine the youthful tenant of a cloister to take his last leave of the world, and to enjoy the closing ball and closing dance with unrestrained intoxication, a few hours before the gates of his convent are to shut upon him for ever. So one might conceive Eloisa and Abelard to have drawn out the eloquence of their last adieus, if Eloisa and Abelard had not fallen the inglorious victims of human frailty.[1] My sister and her lover in this interview repeated the same things

---

1 A curious comparison, since Eloise's love for her tutor, the theologian Peter Abelard (1079–1142), adapted by Rousseau in the highly popular

again and again, and took no note of the censurable iterations and tautologies of which they were mutually guilty.

Thus in all probability would have ended this fervent and unrivalled attachment; but their friends would not allow of it. Lord Montagu, and Mrs Willis, and the rest, seemed in this respect to feel more for them, than the young people felt for themselves. They expatiated upon the unreasonableness of two persons, so formed for happiness, being made the sacrifice of one in such a state of disease as I was. Nothing could be more sense-less and unjustifiable, than the state of passion to which I had surrendered myself. I must be miserable: no human contrivance or exertion, as long as I persisted in my present feelings, could save me from that. I was necessarily an abortion. They sympa-thised with me, they pitied me from their souls. But no justice could require, and no justice permit, that Clifford and Henrietta, framed to be the ornaments of the world, the boast of the present age, and the wonder of posterity, beings, the occupation of every day of whose existence would be, to be happy, and to make happy, should be consigned to perpetual disappointment, for the sake of one who could never become useful to society, and whose existence would be a burden to his fellow-creatures. I must there-fore be considered as a person under the dominion of deplorable malady, to be treated with the most exemplary tenderness, while my prejudices and my groundless fancies were on no account to be permitted to become a law, to the sane and effective members of the community of mankind.

Henrietta had conceived the plan of living with me, and devot-ing all her great powers and wonderful qualities to the task of ass-waging my sorrows. But her friends undertook to prove to her, that that was impossible. It was, they said, the result of all expe-rience, that a human being in my state of disease, was best regu-lated, and most advantageously watched over, by strangers, persons who with calm and unaltered temper, and from a sense of the duties of their occupation merely, did whatever was neces-sary. Where the ideas and the passions of a man were in a state of vehement disorder, the presence of such as he was accustomed to regard the most affectionately only served as a signal to bring on the most frightful and injurious excesses. Beside, that the friends

---

Julie ou la nouvelle Héloïse (1761), crosses boundaries of propriety that the marriage of Henrietta and Clifford preserves. Throughout this chapter Mandeville sees his sister in his own Romantic and dissident terms.

of Henrietta could not endure that her splendid qualities should be confined to the occupations of a nurse. It was a high strain of generosity in her to have conceived such a thought; but it would not be the less censurable and immoral to carry it in execution. Had she properly figured to herself what it was to immure herself in a dark chamber, to have at all times nothing but painful sensations, to see but one object, and that object a person whom unfortunate circumstances had deprived of the better part of man? No; this was not the office and the destiny of a healthful human creature, least of all, of such a creature as Henrietta. The blood of Mandeville was not for ever to be disgraced, by exhibiting only a succession of hypochondriacal and melancholy solitaries. Formed as she was to grace the society of which she was a member, she must present herself in the lovely relations of a wife and a mother; my sister must show herself at the head of a numerous and honourable establishment, and be seen the protector and benefactor of all the tenants and dependents of a prosperous and illustrious husband.

Thus was the poor Henrietta beset with the advices of persons in the highest degree anxious for her honour and happiness. And it will easily be believed that she had a traitor within the fort, that inforced all their arguments, and was at all times ready to deliver up the garrison of her heart to the irresistible assailant. Still she held out with invincible obstinacy. Never were struggles more vehement and fierce than those she endured. "Talk not to me," she said, "of making others happy, of being a wife and a mother, of presiding over a numerous establishment, and affording a splendid example to all within the reach of my influence! The first duty of a human being is to do no harm. I will begin with innocence. Then, when I have taken care, that no creature shall shed a tear through any act of mine, that no one shall put on mourning on my account, that I will never do aught that shall occasion to any one a sinking or a paroxysm of the heart, then I will begin to be actively virtuous. You advise me to make a conspicuous and a dazzling figure in society. And, as the preliminary of this, I am to be the destroyer of my brother. Yes, I shall make a dazzling figure indeed, when first, covered with the magnificence of my robes, I have planted the sting of guilt within my bosom. I shall have spirits to discharge the duties of an honourable matron, when the worm of remorse is for ever preying on my vitals, and I shall always have before my eyes the intolerable accusation. Here is the wretched woman that ascended to the bridal couch over the murdered body of Mandeville! No; give me innocence, a clear conscience, and a light heart; let me take care to feel that within, which shall enable me to look serenely on all around, secure that I shall find nothing any where, to call up a blush upon my cheek, and to fill my soul with alarm, secret misgivings, and fearful confusion! I had rather be a milkmaid on these terms, than queen of the universe with an equivocal character, and a doubtful apprehension of the effects of my own doings."

CHAPTER XIV

Lord Montagu had from the first been extremely dissatisfied with the appointment of Holloway, as executor to my uncle's will, and guardian to me and my sister. This worthy limb of the law had practised his delusions successfully on Audley Mandeville, for Audley Mandeville was totally without knowledge of the world, or communication with his fellow-creatures. He had deceived the ladies at the Cottage, for they were of an ingenuous and confiding character, and whatever was told them with gravity and smoothness, whatever story was conveyed to them, that was constructed with art, and varnished over with unabashed speciousness and fluency, would perhaps at all times have produced in them conviction. Holloway was too fat and too smug to look, in their eyes, like a knave; and the silver-tongued and even-tempered Mallison they could hardly have prevailed on themselves to distrust. In a word, neither Mrs Willis nor Henrietta, though both of them gifted with a sound understanding and an exquisite taste, were formed to detect the wiles of the crafty, and to drive knavery and imposture out of the world. They had indeed, particularly Mrs Willis, their strong predilections in behalf of certain maxims and establishments in church and state. It would have been somewhat difficult to have inspired Mrs Willis with a cordial sentiment, for an Oliverian,[1] or a republican. But whatever did not strike at these foundations, was sure to be regarded by her, with a temper prone to favourable interpretation.

But Lord Montagu was a person of a different character. He had a manly understanding, and never allowed himself, either to put the change upon his own judgment,[2] or to permit other men to do so. He had less poetry in his constitution than the ladies at the Cottage, and more logic. He had in his disposition, a good

---

1   Follower of Oliver Cromwell.
2   Deceive his own judgment.

deal of the intellectual anatomist. He guided his dissecting knife with an unfaltering hand: and, though he might be said to be essentially a man of a soft heart, and who abhorred the thought of inflicting unnecessary pain, yet he never permitted any misgivings of temper, to divert him from the course of a strict and unalterable justice. Among the diversified sects and forms of enthusiasm, that so peculiarly distinguished the period of the civil wars, he had accustomed himself to put aside the draperies of external appearance, and acutely to discern the man as he was. This was not a sort of party, with whom it could be agreeable to Mr Holloway to have any concern.

Lord Montagu had become acquainted with the expedients, by which my guardian had first broken ground in the confidence of Audley Mandeville. He looked with no friendly eye upon the style in which he had placed himself under the same roof with me, and gained in a manner possession of my person. Roused by these hints, this venerable nobleman extended his enquiries farther. Holloway came out to be a man of nothing, who had never had any character, or any respectable practice. In one instance formerly, he had gained the ear of a man of property, as he had gained that of my uncle, and having been made the guardian of his infant heir, had found means to divert the whole estate to his own use. The case had been attended with circumstances of peculiar atrocity; the heir, born to the possession of a considerable domain, disappeared in a mysterious way, when a child, and was reported to be dead; the civil wars, which were just then breaking out, called off men's observation from an affair which no one felt to be his own, and for years the crime was successful; after a considerable interval the youth was found, under another name, and in the character of a simple hind,[1] engaged in following the plough; and a series of incidents, that seemed almost miraculous, led to the full establishment of his claim. Holloway was condemned to refund every shilling of the estate, and was covered with the blackest dishonour. This was a tale sufficiently secure from the discovery either of myself, or the ladies at the Cottage; but the intelligence and perseverance of Lord Montagu traced it to its minutest particulars. He resolved, that such a man as this should not remain in the administration of any thing that appertained to myself or my sister.

These things took a considerable time in ripening, and nearly two years elapsed, between the period of my uncle's death in

---

1 The female of the red deer.

1656, and the ultimate measures to which the course of my narrative now leads me. This interval was in a great degree occupied in arguments and inducements presented to Henrietta, as to the determination she ought finally to adopt in the choice of life. In one instance during this period, Henrietta paid me a visit. It was shortly after my fall from my horse, and the breaking my leg. Her visit lasted only for a few hours. Very far was I from suspecting the infinite artifices and contrivances, with which my guardian had prepared and conducted this visit. It was attended with a slender degree of satisfaction either to Henrietta or myself, and was in that respect inexpressibly unlike all our preceding interviews, from the days of childhood up to that very moment. Henrietta found me very different from all that she ever saw me before. She was bid to observe certain symptoms in me; and her terrified imagination and palpitating heart made her see, or think she saw, every thing that had been previously announced to her. On my part I discovered in my sister only the shadow and empty semblance of what she had been. We were both of us merely puppets, in the hands of the great conductor of the exhibition.

Previously to the final adjustment of the project that Lord Montagu had formed relative to my sister's destination, the young Montagus came over to pay me the visit which has been described in an earlier part of this volume. This step was taken with the concurrence, though not upon the suggestion of Henrietta. She entertained the most perfect confidence in both of them. It demanded all the steady nerves of Ralph, and all the quick and ever-wakeful sensibility of Edward, to produce such a report respecting me, as should be admitted for conclusive by her in so momentous a crisis. She earnestly recommended to them to use their best diligence, in a question that sank so deep into her heart. She adjured them, not to be swayed by any previous impressions, but to try it with all the impartiality, what would be due from jurors sitting upon an issue of life and death. She protested again and again, how much better she should be satisfied with a decision that restored to her her beloved brother, though it should cut her off from Clifford for ever.

The history of the interview between the young Montagus and me, has been detailed. They were terribly satisfied of every thing that had previously been related to them respecting me. They saw me in an access of frenzy, such as perhaps they might have read of in books; but human imagination is a tardy and lethargic faculty, in comparison with the impression produced upon us, by what is exhibited before our eyes; and the terribleness and violence of the scene they carried away in their recollections, infinitely exceeded any thing their fancy could have suggested to them. They made their report accordingly. The arguments of Lord Montagu were in the strongest degree inforced, by the representations founded on ocular evidence, that were now made by his sons.

The next step was a legal proceeding commenced in the court of chancery, for appointing a different person, or in the technical language a different "committee," for the two functions of "tutor of the person, and curator to the estate," in behalf of myself and of my sister. Lord Montagu was the petitioner in this cause, under the denomination of *prochain ami*.[1] The question was brought on before the Lord Whitelocke, first commissioner of the great seal to Richard Cromwel, lord protector.[2] Abundant evidence was collected of the unworthiness and profligacy of Holloway, and the record was appealed to, of the conviction that had passed upon him of fraud in the case of his former guardianship.

Meanwhile a course of this sort required, that due notice should be served upon the party, against whom the suit was instituted, and whom it was the purpose of the proceeding to overwhelm with dishonour. Holloway received this notice with a heart bursting with conflicting emotions. He saw at once that the tendency of what was on foot, was to disappoint him in every project, which he had so long meditated, and so carefully prepared. He could not believe the evidence of his senses. He had chosen his party, and given up every thing for gain. He had made it his signal and his device on all occasions, that every thing was lawful for him, which led to that as an end. He had studied, days and nights, how his purposes might best be achieved. He had betrayed himself by no precipitancy; but had gone on patiently, and step by step, as so important a business required. He had insulted nobody; he had been harsh and abrupt with no one; but had turned a face of smoothness, and suppleness, and the most submissive accommodation, to all. How then had he deserved this? How could he have expected to be undermined and blown up, in the manner with which he was now threatened?

---

1 Legal term for a person who, without being appointed guardian, sues for recovery of the rights of someone, often a minor, who cannot speak for himself.
2 Richard Cromwell (1626–1712) succeeded his father for the years 1658–59.

Where, the poor solicitor anxiously asked himself, might all this end? He had stood in the most enviable situation, and with the richest and most unrivalled prospects. He had had in his hands a minor of immense wealth, and whom he had not doubted, with a little of his management, to keep a minor all the days of his life. He had had a reasonable expectation of gaining possession of my sister by marriage, and would then have engrossed the entire direction of every thing that in any way belonged to us. He would have been Mandeville, as far as the property was concerned; and his nephew would have been Mandeville in rank and in name. An extinguisher would be put over the genuine family for ever. Thus it was that Holloway calculated his profits.

It was in this stage of the business, that Mallison for once resolved to take a step of his own. Many had been the conversations that had passed between him and his uncle, respecting the favourite project of advancing his family, by means of this hopeful young gentleman obtaining the hand of my sister. Mallison, always sufficiently conceited of his own gifts and graces, had never thought altogether so highly of himself, as since this proposition had been started. Of the trophies which mortals pursue, the most fascinating to a young man's eye, is to appropriate to himself a female, whose charms and whose beauty all are forward to confess. Mallison was really susceptible, however improbable it may sound, of a certain kind of admiration of Henrietta. Indeed he did not analyse the different sources of the impression made upon his too tender heart; beauty, grace, rank and fortune, all besieged him at once, all seemed to court his acceptance, and produced a united and overwhelming sentiment.

The thought that at this time occurred to him was, that it would be no injudicious project, to seek an interview with Clifford, and argue the case with him. He knew, that at Winchester Clifford had been king of the school, and that it would have been ridiculous in such a one as Mallison to dream of coping with him. But he had now looked a little into the world; and he saw that it was quite a different scene, from that which was perpetually passing within the cloisters of William of Wykeham. He saw that many a man, who at school had been set down incontestibly for a dunce, acquitted himself afterwards with great approbation. At school all was nature; in the world, at least in his world, all was art. Every man learned his part, and repeated it, as volubly and composedly as if it had been his catechism. At school hardly any thing was serious, and ceremony and forbearance were almost completely banished; the whole was constructed, like the ancient Greek drama, with a chorus that made an integral part of the piece, and the moral sentiments of approbation or contempt that were expressed in the ode, determined irresistibly upon the reputation of the characters. But, in the busy scenes of the world, every thing was conducted with suitable gravity; every man, engaged in any part of importance, knew what was before him, and what he had to do; and the most considerable matters were acted, either with closed doors, or with an audience drilled to the enervating and death-dealing laws of decorum. On this stage therefore, the presumptuous Mallison did not doubt to make good his part with Clifford. Beside, that he was perfectly convinced he had all the reason of the case on his side. He sought Clifford, and he easily found him.

"Mr Clifford," said he, "you and I are rivals. We are both of us in love with the sister of Mandeville."

Clifford smiled.

"I know that in some things you have the advantage over me. You are patronised and recommended by the family of Montagu. You have the advantage of keeping company with the young lady oftener than I can."

Clifford protested that he would make no unfair use of his opportunities. "Mallison," said he, "you are a young man of more spirit and enterprise than I took you for. I promise you, I will insinuate nothing to your disadvantage; I will not say a word about you, that you would yourself wish unsaid. We will start fair; and whichever of us shall win the maiden's good will, shall wear her."

Mallison stared; and in his own sordid and dishonest soul could scarcely credit so frank a profession.

"Well, sir, but that was not what I meant to talk about. You have heard, I suppose, that the young lady has thirty thousand pounds. But perhaps you do not know that that depends upon her marrying with my uncle's, her guardian's, consent. Now, that she will never have, except it is to marry me. My uncle is a firm and resolute man, too wise to be moved by a young lady's weaknesses, or a young lady's requests. I thought it but the part of an old schoolfellow to inform you of that. I should not like you to deceive yourself. You used to tell us at Winchester, how much you despised money; but you know better than that now. I do not think that you would knowingly be taken in to marry without a fortune. Now, as your wife, she will never have a farthing—not one farthing!"

Clifford thanked Mallison for his advertisement. He assured him that he took it kindly of him.

"It is true," resumed Mallison, "that Lord Montagu has formed a plan to deprive my uncle of the guardianship. But, Lord! they do not know my uncle. They might as soon think of turning the Thames. He has the law at his fingers' ends, with all its quirks and its cranks, and its ins and outs; and, if you could raise old William Noy[1] from the dead, I am sure he would acknowledge that Coke Holloway was a cut above him."

"I will remember what you say," answered Clifford. "You may rely upon my giving it every proper attention."

Mallison still hesitated. He was not sure that he had produced all the effect he wished.

"Mr Clifford," said he, "you and I were old rivals at school. There you carried every thing. You had Dr Pottinger and all the masters in your favour; and at Latin, and Greek, and themes, and verses, I must own I cannot pretend to cope with you. But the world is a different scene. You would hardly think it, but I doubt whether you would ever make so good an attorney as me. And, with my uncle to back me, I tell you once again, that all the world cannot stand before us. You may believe me or not, as you please; but, remember, I come to you for your good, and that you may not go on blindly, in the dark. I have now told you how the case stands; and I advise you, as a friend, to give up the thing at once, with a grace."

There was no affectation in Clifford's behaviour on this occasion. There was a genuine modesty and simplicity in Clifford, that he did not feel he had a right to elbow aside, or trample upon, any human creature. In some sense indeed he was aware, that he could have crushed this poor wretch in a moment, as one would crush a spider. But he had compassion on the spider, and suffered it to crawl to its hole. No one saw more distinctly the difference between honour and fraud, an elevated character and a presumptuous one; and no one had in a greater degree words and phrases at will, to do justice to his conceptions. He could have painted Holloway, and he could have painted Mallison himself, in such colours, as would have made the unfledged lawyer writhe in convulsions, and sink with confusion. But he checked the impulse, and refused the office. He dismissed him, as the lion dismissed the mouse in the apologue of Aesop.[2]

---

1 Noted jurist (1577–1634) and attorney-general under Charles I.
2 In Aesop's fable a lion magnanimously spares a mouse that has bothered him; later the grateful mouse gnaws the lion free from a hunter's net.

CHAPTER XV

Such had been the proceeding adopted by the hopeful Mallison. But Holloway's politics were of a deeper reach, and suggested by a much more subtle and persevering train of thought. He had gone on for some time representing me as insane, and suggesting that the wisest plan would be, to leave me, as such, under his control. He now saw that a different line of conduct was required of him. To make the most of the great advantage he enjoyed in the possession of my person, it was necessary that he should vest me in a certain degree in the robes of authority, and engage me to represent a part in the drama before him.

I had listened, as I have said, with obstinate incredulity, to the story of Mallison, and the vile insinuation that, during a dinner at Lord Montagu's, he had observed conscious glances, and the various indications by which the secret understanding of lovers manifests itself, between Clifford and Henrietta. I felt that every thing worth living for depended, as to me, upon the loyalty of my faith in this respect. I spurned the accusation from me with unbounded contempt. With a disdain that reached to the heart even of the case-hardened Mallison, I insisted that he should mention the subject no more. And, when he endeavoured to stammer out something further in support of his assertion, I overwhelmed him with a torrent of execrations and invective, that effectually closed up his lips, and drove him from my presence with terror. I was like a man walking on the top of the parapet of the highest building human hands ever raised, who knows that, if he allows himself to doubt of his safety, he will instantly lose the firmness of his footing, topple into the depth below, and be dashed into a thousand pieces.

Holloway was much more a master of his fence than Mallison, and perhaps he derived some instruction and warning from the scene I allude to. He did not once mention to me the names of the lovers. He only told of Lord Montagu's proceeding, and laid before me the notice he had received. This notice purported to call upon Holloway to show cause, why he should not be deprived of the guardianship, in both its relations, of the nephew and niece of the late Audley Mandeville. The paper said nothing of his unfaithful discharge of his trust in a former guardianship, or of any other imputation upon his professional character; and Holloway was of course sufficiently to be depended on for not furnishing me with any ground of disparagement against himself.

Having thus submitted the question to my consideration, the solicitor put on his most insinuating forms of address. He appealed to me, whether he had done any thing to deserve this refinement of cruelty, this deadly attack upon every thing that could be dear to a human being. He had given up every other engagement he had in the world, and had devoted his time, his industry, and his talents, entirely to my service. He trusted, I would stand by him, and not see him thus undeservedly trampled upon and destroyed. It was in my power to do every thing for him in this momentous crisis. If a question was excited, who was the properest person to be my guardian, I was at an age when I had a right to a voice on the subject; and if I were disposed to exert myself in his behalf, he would take care that voice should be heard. He added, that he was far from valuing the stewardship of the Mandeville estate: he acknowledged, that that would be attended with advantages, to which the person who faithfully discharged the duties that belonged to it, would be fairly entitled: but he solemnly averred, that he would give up that without a murmur, if he could be dismissed to the humble and comfortable situation he had left for it, unpursued by the malignant aspersions that some secret enemy was conjuring up against him.

I listened to this detail in a very different spirit from that in which it was exhibited before me. My pride, of which I had a very ample portion, was vehemently offended, that such a proceeding should be commenced, without the smallest communication with me on the subject. I determined to resist to the utmost of my power an interference on the part of any human creature, in a question that concerned me more than any one. The more I reflected on the affair, the more I was bewildered. Did they mean to treat me like a lunatic? If they did, for whose benefit was this to be done? I had been guilty of no extravagance; I had squandered no part of my property, either in possession, or in reversion; I had shown none of those dispositions, in consideration of which persons in any part of the world are treated as unfit to be trusted with their own affairs. There must be some deep meaning in this, very different from any that I had yet penetrated.

While I endeavoured by dint of persevering reflection, and turning the subject on all sides, to pluck out the heart of this mystery, the recollection occurred to me of that tale of Mallison, which I had originally thrown from me with such utter disdain. The affair of the guardianship, gave a sort of probability to what had at first seemed to me of all things most impossible. I named it to Holloway.

"My dear sir," said the solicitor, "it is the object nearest my heart, not to put you to pain. There are certain subjects that must not be mentioned to you: there are certain names that must not be articulated in your presence."

"Speak! speak!" I replied, with uncontrolable earnestness and emotion. "I must know all. This is no time for precaution, and half-measures, and temporising."

Holloway told me a story, so full of particulars, so entirely of a piece, so consistent, that I no longer allowed myself to doubt. He had taken much pains to obtain information; and he invented some things, so conformable to what was certain and irresistible, as to make all together a tale of terrible demonstration. I begged him to leave me; and he felt that he had done enough, to lay a complete foundation for what he intended should follow.

Oh, God, oh, God, what a being was I, and for what a fate was I reserved! I had pitied myself; I had held myself unfortunate! I never had been unfortunate, never worthy of pity, till now.

I was all made up of passions. My nature was composed of every thing turbulent, that is incident to man. But love, love, was paramount to all the rest. Love was like the God of the tempestuous ocean, that controled, and directed, and turned, like yielding gossamer in his hands, every wind that blew. I had never loved but one thing, and that was Henrietta. I found, or fancied in her, every perfection. She was my teraphim,[1] my idol; and before her semblance I prostrated myself every day in worship. She was my faith, the all I believed in with undoubting confidence. She was the whole world to me; and nature without her was one blank, one universal desert. She was the sun that illuminated all; and, when that sun was once extinguished in the heavens, I wandered for ever in darkness, and on the edge of precipices, where every step threatened to shiver me to atoms, or sink me in a fathomless abyss. Henrietta was a charm, that I hung about my neck, and wore next to my heart, blessed with a thousand prayers; and fierce and gloomy and dismal as was my nature, I had only to think of her, and I became "patient as the female dove, when that her golden couplets are disclosed,"[2] and as cheerful, as sea and sky and air, when the halcyon[3] sits brooding on her nest.

---

1 [Godwin's note:] Genesis, xxxi, 19. [Teraphim: a small image or idol of an ancient Semitic household god.]

2 *Hamlet*, 5.1.286.

3 A kind of kingfisher, fabled to calm the waters.

But human nature is full of inconsistencies. Though Henrietta on some occasions was to me like a God, that I worshipped at an awful distance, and that I communicated with, with the consciousness how infinitely she was my superior; yet at other times I demanded from her a complete sympathy, and a sentiment in all respects responsive to mine. It was my delight to believe, that she loved as I loved, that she would sacrifice herself as I would, that for all the world she would not be persuaded to an act that would give me pain, and that she was the sister of my soul. It was this human union, that filled up and completed the sentiment, and that made it, if I may be allowed to say so, beyond all the religions, that the most fervent enthusiast, in the depth of his impenetrable solitudes, ever dreamed of.

Henrietta was the rock against which I leaned, and was secure. Though the earth quaked around me, though "the sea saw it and fled," though the mountains were shaken, and the hills "reeled to and fro like a drunken man,"[1] here I reposed my confidence, and was inaccessible to fear. I was like that hero of antiquity, of whom it is related, that his whole body, all but one indivisible point, was incapable of a wound.[2] I was like the Capitol of ancient Rome, well fortified and defended by art and discipline, on every other side except one, for which nature seemed to have done enough, and where no assault was to be apprehended. Not that I was invulnerable in other points, as has sufficiently been seen: but that wounds elsewhere were not mortal, and might be healed; the blood retreated to the heart, and it was well; but a blow here must inevitably lay me prostrate on the earth at once. This was my stay amidst all my calamities; "Henrietta can never be my enemy."

Mandeville was born to be deceived. What signifies faith? Of what avail is confidence? Oh, that I had believed nothing, that I had expected nothing, that I had relied on nothing! I should then have sunk at once; I should have felt that I was unequal to the toil of life; all hope and uneasiness and struggle would have long been over with me; I should have laid down my head in the grave, and been a rest. It is this fond reserve, that I for ever made, amidst sorrows inexpressible, and that otherwise could never be endured which sustained me through all, and has made me a monument upon which every evil has been heaped that the heart of man can think.

---

1 Psalms 114:3; 107:27.
2 Achilles; hence the phrase "Achilles heel," meaning a point of vulnerability.

I know that fiction is a very ingenious thing; but I defy fiction in all its luxuriance to equal that, which I cannot yet tell that I can hold my pen to relate. I was wounded in every point where my soul most lived along the nerve; in religion, in frustrated ambition, in the hatred of disgrace which pervaded my every muscle, and most of all in love. Never did man receive so religious an education as I did, sanctified by the tall and solemn figure of my instructor, his colourless cheek, his inflexible muscles, his face, every feature of which spoke consecration and martyrdom. Solomon says, "The words of the wise are as nails, fastened by the master of assemblies."[1] Every one of these nails, in my case, was driven to the head, and clenched again on the other side, by means of the impenetrable solitude and wild desolation, amidst which all my early years were passed. This might have seemed precept and speculation only: but in the margin of every precept were painted the scenes of Kinnard, the murder of my father and mother and the whole assembly of those among whom they lived, and all the unspeakable horrors of the Irish massacre. The thing that my gorge most rose against with intolerable heavings, was a Papist; unless indeed in those rare and almost unheard of instances, where Popery was reinforced, and rendered more horrible and inhuman to look at, by apostacy.

Methinks I hated Clifford enough, before he turned Papist. I had no sooner quitted the desolation of Mandeville House, and been entered a member of the congregation of the living at Winchester School, than I saw him. He crossed me at every turn, and darkened me in all my lights. Whether I desired to be distinguished by master or scholar, it was impossible; for there stood Clifford. Wherever I placed myself, he was right before me, and I could not be seen. That he did this without the smallest tincture of malice, aggravated my grievance. If he had borne his honours insolently, that would have been a consolation to me. Every thing he did, I felt as a personal insult; and what most of all stained the point with a deadly venom, was the composure, the frankness, the innocence, nay, the air of benevolence, and all-beaming kindness and affection, with which every thing was done.

Would to God, when I quitted Winchester, I had lost sight of Clifford forever! But it was not so. He was born to thwart my ambition; and ambition perhaps never burned more fervently in any human breast than in mine. The evil did not stop here. He not only kept me down in all my hopes to rise; in addition to this

---

1 Ecclesiastes 12:1.

he overwhelmed me with disgrace. No; I felt that I was not born to the inheritance of disgrace. Never was a creature more innocent, more honourable, more plain and direct in all he did, more a stranger to the crooked dealings of a corrupt world. How therefore did I bear disgrace? It made me mad! I have said it repeatedly; I must say it once more; it was Clifford, that reduced me to the state of a beast, that added weight to all the chains I endured, and a rowel[1] to every lash I received from my inhuman keepers.

Well; Clifford had done all this for me. He had arrested me in my first step on the theatre of life. Perhaps the ruling passion of my soul was ambition, a generous desire to obtain the good opinion, the suffrage, the admiration of my fellow-creatures. He had put a violent close upon that. He had thrown me down the ladder, just as I was stepping on the stage, and laid me prostrate, maimed, and unable to help myself, on the earth. It may be, I could have borne that. Let me then be obscure; but let me not be dishonoured! He had followed me with disgrace, accumulated disgrace. I was accounted for a spy and a traitor. Like Jupiter in the war of the giants, he was not contented to sink me to the lowest depth; but, to keep me there, as the king of the Gods treated Typhoeus, he cast the whole weight of the island of Sicily upon me, Pelorus on my right arm, Pachynus on my left, and Lilybaeum on my feet.[2] He made me mad!

One thing only occurred to console me under these accumulated sufferings. Clifford turned Papist. Now it came to my turn to triumph. God had smitten him with his thunder. God had made him "an astonishment, and a hissing, and a perpetual desolation, to the nations round about." His star was set, and mine was risen. I might be any thing I pleased, resplendent, magnificent, illustrious, with no fear of being hindered by Clifford.

---

1 Diminutive of *roue* (wheel): a sharp-toothed wheel inserted into the end of a shank of a spur, putting Mandeville, who prides himself on his horsemanship, in the position of the horse.

2 In Godwin's account of the violent cycles of history that underwrite peace in the Greek world, the rebellion of the Titans against Saturn is followed, after Jupiter had overthrown Saturn, by the revolt of the Giants, "a sort of second brood." Typhoeus, "the most terrible," with dragons' heads growing from his shoulders, was said to "be the son of Juno without a father," and to be "so tall that he touched the East with his right hand and the West with his left." He was buried under the volcano Aetna, in Sicily with his body distributed across the three promontories as described above (*Pantheon* 69–73).

My customary ill-fortune pursued me. Clifford became an exception to all precedent and all rule, that anomaly, that monster in human society,—an honoured apostate! One confirmation after another reached me, that this was true.

Well; what was this to me? Disappointed as I had been, voluntarily as I had renounced all connection with my kind, I might shut myself up in my own pursuits and connections, and leave the world for him to gambol in. I could almost have said, "Take the rest of the inhabitants of the earth, and leave me Henrietta," I was in the plight of the poor man of whom Nathan spoke to David, who "had nothing, save one little ewe-lamb, which he nourished, and it grew up together with him; it ate of his meat, and drank of his cup, and lay in his bosom,"[1] and was all the world to him.

Clifford then was to marry Henrietta. I thought it too much that he lived; and he was to marry my sister—this hateful thing, this loathsome spider, this execration to latest posterity, this thing, not less hateful in the eyes of God, than of Mandeville. I would sooner have seen her spotted with the plague; I would sooner have seen her barked and crusted over with the foulest leprosy; sooner, ten thousand times sooner, I would have followed her to the grave—than that she should touch this man. If I had closed her eyes in death, if I had seen the king of terrors triumphing on her pale cheek, if I had looked at those beloved limbs inclosed in a shroud, and deposited in a coffin, if I had followed her hearse, and heard the stiffened clods rattling on the chest that contained her remains, that would have been a day of jubilee to me:—for she would have been uncontaminated. All stories of rape and violence, and the infinitely diversified excesses of human brutality, would have been tenderness, and beauty, and fragrance to this: for the mind of Henrietta was corrupted, and her will consented.

What a mockery is enumeration in a case like mine! At this distant period it is a sort of consolation to me, to analyse and count up the different ingredients of which my cup was composed; but, at the time itself, it was all one mighty drench of misery, in which nothing was distinguished. My soul was chaos. A thick cloud, the "dunnest smoke of hell"[2] came over me. I was wrapped round with fivefold darkness, a smother, that stopped my breath, and penetrated through all the coverings and integuments[3] of the body, and turned my very bones into jelly. Oh,

---

1 2 Samuel 12:3.

2 *Macbeth*, 1.5.51.

3 Natural covering of an organism or organ.

nothing so discomfiting, so helpless, and so hopeless, was ever felt by any other human being. Despair is a term altogether inadequate to express it. It overwhelmed me with the full sense of my misery, and left me without the power or conception, that I could any way relieve myself from, or escape it.

I was a sensible time in this deplorable condition. But then my soul, which had fled away and was gone, came back to me, I shook myself, and stretched my limbs, as a man might be supposed to do, at just coming out from a dungeon, where every thing was stagnant and poisonous, and where he seemed to have been consigned to eternal oblivion. I awoke from a sleep more deadly and oppressive, than that from which the whole world shall be roused by the last trumpet. I viewed my murderers, Clifford and Henrietta, trampling on my lifeless limbs with looks of scorn. I never saw such looks. Diabolical triumph sat on the lips of each. Inhuman laughter flayed and mangled my ears like a hundred lancets. The pointed finger, the gesture of mingled hatred and contempt, spoke their secret soul. I raised myself from the earth, and stood in an erect posture. At length they caught my eye fixed on them, and they suddenly became blank: they spoke not, they moved not, they uttered not a sound: their hue became ghastly, their features indistinct, their outline dim, they melted into air: I was left alone. All this I saw with a depth of apprehension, and a graduating of vision, that, as it appears to me, exceeded all the realities of my preceding life.

Full of this vision, my blood seethed and bubbled in my veins. I exclaimed with all the energy of rage: "They insult and despise me; they count me for nothing. Yes, I know they think, the moment I hear of their execrable crime, I shall become transfixed and insensible; my heart shall burst with a thousand flaws; I shall be like one struck with heaven's lightning, and turned at once into a brittle and marrowless cinder. They are mistaken. There is a vivifying principle within me, that they remember not: vengeance, inextinguishable vengeance! They think, that the world is theirs; that they walk, crowned with garlands, and welcomed with choruses of joy, that they have no enemy to contend with. By heaven, it is not so! I will pursue them for ever; they shall feel me. 'Sleep shall, neither night nor day, hang upon their penthouse lids';[1] through toilsome and insupportable years their flesh shall waste and be dried up with sorrow. They shall become as

---

1 *Macbeth*, 1.3.19–20.

miserable, if possible, as by their wanton and savage cruelty they have made the brother of Henrietta.

"Henrietta, I foolishly flattered myself, was bound to me by indissoluble ties of nature, flesh of my flesh, and bone of my bone. She has cast me off; she treats me as an alien to her blood; she regards me with indifference; she places her delight in inflicting on me the most dreadful injury. By heaven, I will not be thus treated with impunity. Thou hast rejected me; I also will reject thee. I renounce all kindred. All weakness, fondness, tenderness past, the nameless arts and endearments by which thou hast wound thyself round my soul, shall preserve no traces in the volume of my brain. I am vengeance, and nothing else. I feel that I have nothing of human nature left within me. 'My heart is turned to stone: I strike it, and it hurts my hand.'[1] I will pursue her for ever. If she has children—Ha! they will be the children of Clifford—living, substantial beings, in whom the blood of Clifford and of Mandeville shall be mingled together!—Can nature sustain such monsters?—Will not the demons themselves, tenants of the deepest hell, laugh with unhuman joy to behold them?—I will steal them from her; I will teach them to hate her; I will make them my instruments of vengeance. How it will delight me, what mitigation will it bring to the fire that burns within me, to see their infant fingers stream with their parents' blood!"

Such was the train of reflections that Holloway's intelligence produced within me. From the state of a man, palsied with astonishment and horror, which was the first effect, I mounted into supernatural energy. I commanded my horse to be made ready. My guardian had watched all my motions with the utmost stretch of anxiety. He saw my extraordinary sinking of soul: that was what he expected. Yet it went to so terrible an extreme, that it did not fail to alarm him. He saw the altered current of my feelings, which of necessity manifested itself in violence of action, and every possible contortion of the body. When I came forth to mount my horse, he approached me, but with hesitation and timidity.

"Whither go you, sir?"

"To Henrietta."

"Will you not allow my nephew to accompany you?"

"No; I will be attended by my groom only."

---

1 *Othello*, 4.1.182–83.

Holloway dared press me no further. Beside, that he was partly satisfied with this. My groom, as well as every one about me, was his implement.

Of my journey I remember nothing. I reached the Cottage of the New Forest, without any accident that could defeat my purpose. I saw my sister. I met her, as Clifford had done in his first visit to Beaulieu, and nearly on the same spot: it was one of her favourite haunts. I alighted, and gave my horse to the servant. Henrietta started as she beheld me, and almost fell to the ground. I supported her, and solemnly led to a bank. My voice had a depth, and a hollow, inward sound, like what we attribute to a ghost, returned from the mansion of departed spirits.

"Henrietta, this is a meeting, not like those I so well remember in the purlieus of the Forest. This is not like the meeting of a brother and a sister. I come to you for the last time.

"You add to my knowledge of human nature. I thought you an angel of light; I see in you a demon from hell. 'It was not an enemy; then I could have borne it: it was not he that hated me; then I would have hid myself from him: but it was thou my equal, my guide, and my acquaintance, from whose lips I have received sweet counsel'[1] I know not how oft, with whom I have worshipped God, and lost myself transportingly amidst the magnificence of nature.

"Henrietta, why have you deceived me? I was hardly born to love. It is my disposition to walk gloomily among my fellow-creatures, and scarcely waste a thought upon them. I shut myself up disdainfully in my own contemplations, and basked in the majesty of desolation. Why did you draw me out of this? What boots it,[2] that you are my sister? This is mere vulgar prejudice, the common stuff of the earth. It is dangerous to call forth the love of such a one as I am!

"You made me believe—what did you not make me believe? every thing that was lying and hypocritical—that you cared for me, that you loved me, that you were anxious for my welfare, that you sympathized in my joys and my sorrows, that you studied to prepare for me good counsel, and to lead me in the path of honour and happiness.—Pooh, pooh, there was none of this!

"It was thus that you laid bare my bosom to your dagger's point, that you stripped me of the armour with which nature had covered my bursting heart, and threw down all my defences. I

---

1 Adapted from Psalms 55:12–14.
2 What does it matter.

else had walked the world in safety, not untried, not untortured, not undistressed—but with such trials and tortures as I could have sustained."

Henrietta was surprised at the collectedness of my discourse; she knew she had used me unworthily; she was weighed down with the consciousness of guilt.

"But is this true?" I pursued, suddenly changing my tone. "Deny it! Fall, fall instantly on your knees, and swear it is false! You are not married? Who told me that you were? You are not the wife of—? Then must it never be!

"Oh, Henrietta, I adjure you by all that is holy, and all that is sacred! for my sake, for your own sake! eschew the greatest of crimes! Crime, as in itself it is; to throw away the paragon of creation, upon a miscreant, an apostate, the abhorrence and the refuse of universal nature! What will England think of you? What will your whole sex? What name or place will you retain in the diversified society of living men?

"And for the sake of this crime, this abhorred mixture, this unnatural pollution, this worse than incest, you would destroy your brother! Here I am. Dispose of me as you please. I do not set my life at a pin's fee. For any thing that would do you honour, and do you grace, I would die a thousand times. Nothing would give me greater transport, than to sacrifice all I have, and all I am, for you. Those eyes, that figure, that heaven-descended aspect, the smile I have seen on those lips, I value beyond a million of worlds. But, to see them consigned to every thing that is leprous, and that is horrible—that will I never!

"Henrietta, have you no purity? have you no shame? It is the crown of a woman, to do nothing that is equivocal, or ambiguous, to stand clear in the sight of all, to suffer no unhallowed breath for an instant to obscure the unsullied brightness of her name, to expose herself to no comments, never, never to subject her conduct to the discussion of the vulgar and profane.

"My sister, you had a father, you had a mother—have you forgotten them? They died Protestants. They died by the hands of blood-thirsty and barbarian Papists. They never would have suffered their daughter, to join in unhallowed union with the son of the destroyer. If they could know that such a thing was once meditated, or once named, it would stir them up from the rest of the grave. Think you see them before you! Think you see them, as they appeared in the last moments of their mortal existence. Their breasts streaming with gore shed by the accursed hand of Papists, their hands lifted up to heaven in execration of that cruel religion! Now, now, they stretch them forth to you, their daughter, and implore you, for heaven's sake, for religion's sake, for the sake of all that is holy, in consideration of all the ties of blood, in recollection of their lives, and of their deaths, to renounce this detested marriage!"

Henrietta was shaken by the solemnity of my address. Her resolutions in my favour had been strong, and of the most disinterested sort; her struggles had been sharp, and terrible, and severe; they had been almost too mighty for her tender nature to endure. Her language to the Montagus, when they set out on their late visit to me in Derbyshire, had been to recommend to them, "to use their best diligence in a question that sank so deep into her heart; to adjure them, not to be swayed by any previous impressions that might have been made on them, but to try it with all the impartiality that would be due from jurors sitting upon an issue of life and death. She had protested again and again, how much better she should be satisfied with a decision that restored to her her beloved brother, though it should cut her off from Clifford for ever."

She was therefore in a high degree surprised at the style in which I addressed her. She found in it energy unbounded, and the deepest pathos. She found in it the most fervent and high-wrought passion. What then? There was nothing to censure in this. It would have been absurd, if it had been otherwise. She found in it no touch of insanity.

This was a moment, that was worth more than all the mines of Golconda.[1] Henrietta, who was the jewel of the earth to me, and to whom all the rest of the world was only the crust and the setting, was mine. Her heart was mine. I could retire with her to any corner of the peopled earth that I pleased. Henrietta was saved, saved from pollution, from blasphemy, from the most execrable of crimes, saved for her sex, for her country, for her age, and for me. I never can recollect this moment without an agony, a frenzy, beyond all frenzy, and to which every thing else that bears the name, is like the mummery of a personated clown, and the antics of children. That moment is gone. Oh, that all the happiness and the virtue of the earth should depend on a moment! The clock points the hour; and man is yet as virtuous as our first progenitor before the fall;[2] he may challenge the arch-fiend, the great accuser of the creation, to point out one speck in the pre-

---

1   An ancient Indian kingdom famous for its riches.
2   I.e., Adam.

cious organ with which he looks on his God. The clock strikes; and all is over; the fatal deed is done; millions of worlds cannot buy it back again; oceans of tears cannot wash it away; the stamp is fixed; the decree is gone forth; the trumpet of the Almighty proclaims it to the universe, "An immortal soul is fallen!"

By me this precious harvest of spotless virtue was marred. What could possess me? My soul was wrought too high; and the cord by which every thing that was dear to me was suspended, could hold no longer. My understanding had once been unsettled; and it could maintain its balance only to a certain point. At this moment, this critical, this tremendous moment, my eyes flashed fire, my brain fermented like a vessel of new wine, placed for that purpose by the hands of the maker. I raved. I talked—I know not what, I spoke of the Duke of Savoy, the pretender to the crown of England,[1] whose claims were upheld by the infuriated and blood-thirsty Papists, the true successors to Guy Fawkes and to Garnet.[2] My reason was unsettled. In some wild and unaccountable way I conceived Clifford to be the Duke of Savoy, and Henrietta to be his queen. My gestures were furious; my motions were alarming; I was suddenly seized with all the demonstrations of the most rooted frenzy.

CHAPTER XVI

Having thus begun, I know not to what extravagance I might have proceeded, had it not chanced that, just at this instant, the young Montagus and their servants passed along in the road below. They were surprised at seeing me thus; they were alarmed at the vehemence and outrageousness of my gestures. I was alone with Henrietta. They alighted; and, accompanied by their servants,

---

1 [Godwin's note:] See Parsons on the Succession, 1594. [Robert Parsons (1564–1610) was a Jesuit and author of *A Conference about the Next Succession to the Crowne of Ingland* (1594), which traced the claims of five houses to the English throne, and argued that the line descending through the house of Portugal (and Spain) to the Dukes of Savoy (1562–1630) was the strongest. The Duke of Savoy referred to here is probably Charles Emmanuel II (1635–75), who led the massacre of Waldensians or Vaudois in 1655 referred to by Hilkiah, p. 116.]

2 On Guy Fawkes and the Gunpowder Plot, see p. 81, note 4. Henry Garnett (1555–1606), a Jesuit priest, gained knowledge of the plot but was prevented by confidentiality from disclosing what he knew, and was executed as a result. Garnett was educated at Winchester College.

hastened across a field, which lay between the road and the foot-path where we stood. I perceived them. By one of those sudden changes to which madness is often liable, the frame of my mind became totally altered. I in some way anticipated impediment and restraint from their arrival. I fled with the rapidity of light-ning; and, knowing where I had left my horses and my groom, was on my saddle in a moment. The groom, who, as I have said, had his instructions from Holloway, was aware how dangerous it would be to the purposes of my guardian, if, while suffering under an attack of frenzy, I fell into the hands of the Montagus, and seconded my purpose of escape with all his diligence.

The young gentlemen, seeing that by the opportuneness of their arrival they had driven me away, were not solicitous to pursue me, but turned their attention to my sister. She was in a state of the most distressful agitation. The unexpectedness of all that had passed, doubled the force of the impression it made upon her. She had been disconsolately meditating the trying circumstances in which she was placed, at the moment when I so unexpectedly stood before her. She had received the report of the young gentle-men upon the unfortunate state of my intellectual health. She had in some degree, with a sort of half consent, suffered it to be under-stood, that her decision waited upon the issue of that report. She was acquainted with the proceeding that had been commenced in the court of chancery, for putting an end to the guardianship of Holloway. Yet it might be said of her, in the most accurate sense of that phrase, that Henrietta did not know her own mind. Still she had great compunctions and misgivings of soul, leading her to an unreserved union with her brother. Her passions, all that precise state of feeling which nature herself so distinctly makes the portion of a female just entering upon the state of womanhood,—not a nature gross, vulgar, and depraved—but that nature which instinc-tively guides the individual to a proceeding which promises most to conduce to private and general happiness,—fought on the side of Clifford. Her reasonings leaned strongly towards me. On my side was that impulse of generosity, of self-sacrifice, and unam-biguous rectitude, which was so peculiarly suited to the constitu-tion of her character, and her habits of thinking. Most devoutly she prayed to the Almighty governor of the universe, that he would gra-ciously impart a light from above, to guide her in the difficult path she had to tread.

In the very breath that uttered this prayer, I unexpectedly stood before her. Yes; I have no doubt, that Providence itself took me by the hand, and placed me there, in answer to her prayer.

The suddenness of the event, the particular moment in which it occurred, overcame her spirits, and made her unable to stand before me. Oh, that the gracious purpose of a beneficent Providence, that the finger of God stretched out to point the path of rectitude, should have been so wofully defeated! She listened to me, with an attention that seemed to turn all her faculties at once into the single faculty of hearing. I have endeavoured to record the discourse I addressed to her. I have mentioned the effect it seemed to produce on her mind. I have spoken of the horrible start of frenzy, accursed revolution! by which all these blooming hopes seem to have been dashed for ever.

Henrietta listened with that perfect singleness of heart, which never fell to the lot of any other human creature. My passion became her passion; my sobriety her sobriety. Her feelings were of a mingled and a memorable sort. Her joy was great, in the evidence that seemed to pour upon her, of the sanity of her brother, that brother, whom if she did not love more than any other human being, she at least felt, in her single and unbetrothed state, to be the mark and proper goal of her most sacred and primal duties. So great was her joy, that it was only checked and held back by a confused sense of guilt, a persuasion that she had yielded too far to the young Montagus, and their noble father, and Clifford and every one around her, and had not examined enough for herself, and trusted to herself.

All this joy, this solemnity of soul, this new and serene beam of light that seemed to shoot through every fibre of her frame, served to render only more sharp and agonising what she felt, when I fell so unexpectedly into a fit of frenzy, as unequivocal as any human senses ever witnessed. I passed at once into a discourse the most incongruous and astounding. My gestures and actions were removed to the farthest distance possible, from those that could be incident to a being susceptible of the faculty of self-command. Henrietta observed me, with the utmost degree of terror, and the most poignant grief. She felt, that all was over, her hopes were terribly refuted, all the unfavourable reports that had been made of me were confirmed, in a way that smote her very heart. The greatest degree of misery of which she had a conception, was crowded into that moment.

Thus was the poor Henrietta delivered up into the hands of those who had already so fearfully misled her. Clifford was on the spot. They beset her together. They reproached her, that she had been so unjust as to doubt the reports that had been conveyed to her. They told her, that by all laws, human and divine, a maniac was to be considered as *non ens*,[1] a person *hors de cour*,[2] and not competent to exercise those rights, which may be claimed by every sane member of the community. They expostulated with her, that it would be hardly less than madness, to allow the sentiments of a person in my unfortunate situation, to influence the conduct of the more favoured and undeluded bystanders, in the most serious affairs of life. In brief, they urged, with all the strength of argument they were capable of, an immediate marriage. It was time, that so important a question should be set at rest, by being placed beyond the power of recal. This was a measure, not less due to me, than to herself. I was incapable of being the director of my own actions, and was in the hands of the most unprincipled of men, who were capable of using their power for the most dangerous and tragical purposes. My welfare and my safety required, that that power should be put an end to; and Henrietta's marriage would materially contribute to hasten that happy event. I should then, by the highest authority in the realm, be placed in the hands of guardians of character and respectability, well acquainted with my affairs, and incapable of being guided by sinister motives, and who would use every tender and considerate expedient, for alleviating my affliction as long as it endured, and for restoring me as speedily as possible to a healthful and sound state of mind, to the duties and enjoyments of a reasonable and well regulated human being.

In this sad and portentous moment Henrietta was lost. Every consideration that could terrify or seduce the human soul into error, was armed against her. She was beset by the arguments and intreaties of all she loved, and all that, by force of long habit, were accustomed to have authority over her. She was timid from a sense of error, and from the utter incapacity she felt, of being able to ascertain what system of conduct it became her to adopt. She had an impression that she had opposed herself too far to the friends in the midst of whom she lived, that she had been too confident and presumptuous on my side; and she had that sense of conscious shame, which is incident to every ingenuous mind, when that on which they relied, is suddenly shown to be utterly fallacious and unsubstantial. My authority with and ascendancy over her was never so little as at the present instant; for she had never on any other occasion been so poignantly impressed with the senselessness of my views, and the extravagance of my con-

---

1 A nonentity.
2 Beyond jurisdiction.

ceptions. The very circumstance, that, but a quarter of an hour before, I had assumed an almost omnipotent influence over her, made the matter worse. The fall on my part, from sublime eloquence, from a passion that seemed to have no commerce with human frailty, from that deep sobriety, that total collectedness and clearness of soul, which raises man most nearly to the idea of the God that made him, into the most ridiculous and inconceivable absurdities, was astounding beyond all precedent and all imagination. Nor is it to be counted for nothing, that Clifford stood before her, Clifford in all the radiance of youthful beauty, Clifford, whose eye seemed with mingled pride and tenderness to reproach her, for the wayward coldness and indifference with which he had been treated, Clifford, who had first won her virgin heart, and in whose behalf all its weaknesses pleaded, with an insinuation beyond that of the Sirens, which even "the man for wisdom's various arts renowned" could not have resisted, if his ears had not previously been stopped up, and his limbs had not been bound.[1] On the side of Clifford appeared all the realities of life, and its bewitching and most sacred charities; in me she had been deceived, and saw plainly that she could not find any sensible ground for reliance and a calculation of things to come.

The course of my narrative has now led me, by the regular succession and linking together of events, to that accursed moment, when, to my intellectual eye, the sun was turned into darkness, and the moon into blood.[2] No day-star, ever after this, rose, to disperse my gloom. No smile ever flitted across my cheek, no short interval ever occurred to break my anguish. I was born to love. My love was not a loose, general, effervescent sentiment, that in its tumult threw its spray in every face, and overspread whole provinces with its giant waves, and washed the barren sands far and near with the whiteness of its foam. But the more distinguishing it was, the greater and the fiercer was its heat. I loved, as never man loved. I poured out my heart and my soul, all my faculties, and all my thoughts, upon Henrietta. Early I learned to be dissatisfied with myself, and to despise myself. Disappointment cowered with its depressing and heavy wings over my cradle; and mortification hung round my childish steps, and waylaid me in my path. Early therefore I learned to go out of

---

1 Referring to Odysseus in Pope's translation of Homer's *Odyssey*, 1.1.
2 Acts 2:20 and Joel 2:31: referring apocalyptically to the Day of the Lord, a time of disaster and judgment for the wicked and of renewal for the just.

myself; and, like the dervise to whom I once before alluded,[1] in the Persian Tales, I left my own rejected and loathsome corse, to live in another, to feel her pleasures, and rejoice in her joys. To be defeated therefore in this witchcraft, to have this enchantment, dissolved, was an anguish—I throw away my pen—no words can describe it—it is mockery and insult to heap together a set of elaborate phrases, and then say, "It lies enshrined there!"—But I—I, not only lost the only thing that in all the world I prized; but I saw it given to my worst enemy, for him to play with as he pleased, for him to plant his kisses on that cheek, for him to count for his chiefest possession, for him to come home to, wearied with the business and the turmoil of the world, and to find his peace, his reward, and his consolation there!—there!

My feelings were tenfold embittered with the recollection, that this was a marriage. Of all the festivals that enliven the chequered scene of human life, marriage is the most genuine. The garland and the festoon, the sportive sally, and the festive dance, are all appropriate. The triumph of a conqueror is a forced and an atrocious spectacle. He comes home from fields of murder, from blazing towns, from every complication of human calamity and human profligacy, and he is welcomed with flowers. But the splendour and the gaiety of a marriage are unartificial. A youth and a virgin, in all the pride of unfolding beauty and hope, are brought together to be united in the most sacred bonds. This is the emblem and archetype of all that is most admirable in earth or heaven. Charity, the love of our country, and the love of our species, are copied from it. The mysterious union of Christ and his church, is unfolded to us in sacred writ, under the figure of the bridegroom and his bride. All the affections of human life grow out of marriage. Cicero says, they are all comprehended in the love of our country: it is more strikingly true, that they are all the just and infallible sequence of the nuptial tie. In the contemplation of this therefore, not only the parties rejoice, but all the bystanders dismiss their cares: wrinkles and anger are far from this scene, the sun shines brighter than was his wont, and all nature conspires to make a holiday.

Aye, my story is arrived at a festival; Clifford and Henrietta are one! May serpents and all venomous animals solemnise their union! May toads and aspics[2] mark their path with odious slime! May the sheeted dead arise, in every monstrous and terrific form,

---

1 See p. 358, note 3.
2 Small venomous snakes.

and squeak and gibber around them! May all the demons of hell celebrate their pomp in emblematic dance, and toss their torches on high, in testimony of their joy! Oh, that the festival of their marriage might be consecrated with such tokens and external gawds,[1] as might, however imperfectly, answer to what I feel within!

CHAPTER XVII

I cannot tell how Holloway and Mallison procured their intelligence; but they seemed to be acquainted with every thing that passed. The present situation of affairs took away all distance between us. I knew, that in them I should meet with concurrence, in whatever I should act respecting the point nearest my heart; and I knew not where else I should find it. The vehemence of passion that had animated me in my interview with Henrietta, the burst of frenzy that had seized me, had in a great degree subsided during my return from the New Forest into Derbyshire. I consulted with Holloway what was to be done in this momentous crisis. I shrunk from no violence, I was willing to engage in the widest scene of blood and devastation, rather than suffer that event to take place, which I regarded with more horror than the destruction of millions. It was the task of those within whose custody I was placed, to moderate me; and yet only so far to moderate me, as to render the blow more effectual, and the success more secure. They believed that the actual solemnity of marriage would not be attempted, till the legal power of Holloway had received its quietus[2] by the determination of the law: yet were they not so confident of that, as to neglect any devisable precaution that might be adapted to the intermediate period. Holloway diligently applied himself to the preparing his defence before the lords commissioners. For this purpose he was anxious to consult with and to instruct me, as to the part I had to act; and I was willing, for the important purpose of defeating the cabal that was formed against my peace, to conform to any instructions, to submit to any labour, and to compose myself to any face and air of sobriety, that might be prescribed. Holloway was also assiduous in the manufacture of deceitful affidavits, and the collecting a suitable portion of false witnesses. The course of the

---

1 Showy ceremonies.
2 Had been put to death.

question now to be decided, necessarily brought us to London. Lord Montagu and the other parties were also led to the metropolis by the same consideration.

I found, that my sister and the young ladies of this nobleman's family were on a visit at the house of Sir Thomas Fanshaw,[1] afterward Lord Fanshaw, at Barking upon the Forest, in Essex. This little town is about seven miles from London. One morning Holloway burst into my chamber with the intelligence, that the marriage was certainly to take place on the day after tomorrow, in the church of that place. I could not believe it, I replied, that they would questionless wait the decision of the lords commissioners; as the so doing was the only infallible way of securing my sister's fortune, which by the will of my uncle was made to depend upon her marrying with her guardian's consent. To this Holloway had no other answer, than that his information was such, as to entitle it to undoubted credit. He added, that, on the day before the marriage, the young Montagus, with Clifford and my sister, were to dine at Parslows, the residence of a younger brother of Sir Thomas, and to return in the evening.

This then was the moment in which something of the most decisive nature was to be effected. Holloway was perfectly willing to concur in whatever might prevent the marriage, with the reserve only, that he must not appear in any act of violence. I calculated the number of the party to return from Parslows, and resolved to provide myself with a force, sufficient to encounter them. I hired six troopers from General Lambert's regiment,[2] then quartered in London, and resolved to accompany them in person, and direct their motions. I decided, that no occasion could be so favourable for carrying off my sister by force, as on the eve of the very day that was fixed for consummating my misery.

I have expressed myself as if this plan was my own; and so it appeared to me. It was in reality Holloway's. He had constituted himself my guide, and, with an art worthy of a better cause, supplied me with ideas, engendered solely in his fertile brain, but

---

1 A Royalist (1596–1665), 1st Viscount of Dromore from 1661.

2 John Lambert (1619–84), a general who remained loyal to the parliamentary side, was imprisoned in the Tower of London in 1660, but escaped. Interestingly, around this time there was an abortive proposal that Charles II should marry Lambert's daughter: an example of the same Restoration expediency as in the marriage of Clifford and Henrietta.

which still seemed to me to spring from my own. He possessed in the utmost perfection the rhetorical figure of anticipation, and would often ask me whether thus and thus was not the way in which I purposed to act; while the suggestion was so apt and seemingly unavoidable, that I answered such indeed had been my purpose, and could seldom even bring myself to believe that it was not so. He had the absolute command of Mallison, of my groom, and of every one that approached me; and the drama in which I was destined to play a part, was, by the dexterity of my guardian, got up in a most masterly manner, whether as to the cast of the characters, the succession of the scenery, or the exact appropriation of the theatrical properties. Holloway had distributed his instructions, like a skilful general, for the battle that was in preparation, and had fixed upon the obscure retreat to which my sister was to be subsequently conducted. If this should afterward become known, he judged, that a *raptus*, or carrying-off, of a ward by her guardian, would find a very different construction, from the lawless enterprises usually known by that name. And he did not doubt, if Henrietta were once securely in our possession, that he should be able, by that contrivance which he had often made trial of in the most difficult cases, to bring the affair to that conclusion which his heart most eagerly desired, the lawful nuptials of his nephew and my sister.

We set out from London in the afternoon, and, having reached the Forest, withdrew ourselves into some of its most unfrequented haunts. My groom, by an extraordinary accident, had formerly lived in the service of Sir Thomas Fanshaw, and was fully acquainted with all the places that lay within the circuit of my expedition. As night drew on, one of the troopers advanced with the groom, that there might be one man to observe the motions of the enemy without interruption, while the other might pass and repass, to convey to us the necessary intelligence. The main body held itself sufficiently in the rear to be out of sight, but near enough to be called into action at a very short notice. We chose our post so judiciously, as to approach the very spot where the party separated, the young Montagus making the best of their way by the great road towards London, while the carriage, with my sister and one of Lord Montagu's daughters, struck into the by-path, which led to Sir Thomas Fanshaw's. The distance of Sir Thomas's house, was less than a mile from the place where the roads separated; and the young gentlemen might without inconvenience have escorted the carriage to the very roof where the ladies were to sleep. But an infatuation seized them. They apprehended no danger, and lulled themselves into perfect security. The night was considerably advanced; and it was agreed that the gentlemen should make the best of their way for London.

Before they came to the place of separation, I received notice that the party had already made its appearance; and, stationing the troopers in the thicket, I advanced so far, as without being observed, to enable me to reconnoitre their motions. There was a large tree, and a considerable quantity of underwood, between me and them. I witnessed, in patient stillness, and unconquerable silence, the parting. All those on horseback remained in the London road; the carriage turned off into the obscure and grassy lane. I followed it with stealing steps. I sent off the groom with notice to the troopers, at the same time requiring them to advance in the most cautious manner. By this time they had joined me; we surrounded the carriage; and in an imperious tone, I ordered the man that drove it, to turn round, and measure back his steps.

What was thus done, could not be effected so silently as to occasion no disturbance. The companion of Henrietta, whose thoughts were perhaps the more disengaged of the two, thrust her head from the window of the chaise, to enquire of the driver why he turned out of the road. As she did this, she saw that the carriage was surrounded; and she uttered a fearful shriek. The gentlemen by whom they had been escorted, were yet but at a little distance: with all my imaginary dexterity and wariness of proceeding, my motions had been too rapid; the moment I took off the curb by which the impetuosity of my mind had been restrained for a time, the fervour of my passion caused me to dash along the path with a vehemence that nothing could exceed. It is probable also that the trampling of the horses of my troopers had caught the attention of the party. They turned round, and advancing at a full gallop, speedily came up with us. One of the troopers shouted out *à l-arme*: and leaving the carriage, with one man well appointed at the horses' heads, we drew up in a line almost a stone's throw nearer to the parting of the road.

I called out to those who were advancing in the opposite direction, in a voice preternaturally swelled with passion, to stop, or they were dead men. I was answered with the discharge of a pistol. This was the signal. I ordered my men to fire. I was far past the consideration of how many lives might be the victims of my fury. There was a regular discharge of musketry on our side, and one or two men of the enemy fell. We then drew our broadswords. Clifford was the foremost of the defensive party; and, though the night was dark, by sure instinct I singled him out. We struck; we grappled; we fell from our horses, and came to the ground together. We rose, as if by a mutual consent, that had no need of words; and drew back again a few paces from each other, that we might once more clash with the greater fury. Clifford called out to me, not to force him to embrew his sword in the blood of the brother of his wife! That word drove me instantaneously to a towering madness. I cursed him in words of such bitterness and malignity as nothing but a passion like mine could furnish.—I remember no more.

I and my troopers were defeated. Each party carried off its wounded. There had been considerable effusion of blood; but no lives were lost. I received a cut of a sabre from the hand of Clifford, full across my eye and my left cheek: it descended even to my lips. It was given home; as all injuries ever have been, that came to me from that quarter. It threw me senseless on the ground. My body was defended by the soldiers, while the adversary rode off towards the carriage. It had been my strictest injunction to my followers, that, if the issue of our enterprise was unfavourable, my person should not be left, dead or alive, in the hands of the enemy; and they were faithful to that command, for they knew that their reward depended on its performance.

The word with which Clifford had thrust at my soul, the instant before he inflicted that terrible gash on my face, was true. The marriage had taken place on the morning of this day at Barking; and they had immediately proceeded from the church to Parslows. It had been arranged, that Clifford was to lay that night at Sir Thomas Fanshaw's; and his stopping with the young Montagus at the separation of the roads was accidental, he having recollected something, of which he wished to speak to them previously to their parting for the night.

Each of the Montagus received a slight wound in our midnight-encounter. Clifford alone was unhurt. He bore a charmed life. The blotches and stains which crusted his moral character, were no less sure a defence to him, than the cloud in which Juno is said to have carried off her favourite Turnus.[1] Let fall your blades on vulnerable crests; for none of woman born[2] shall damage Clifford! Of all appalling and maddening ideas, undoubtedly the cardinal one is the impassiveness with which hell sometimes dowers her votaries.

---

1 In Book X of Virgil's *Aeneid,* Juno actually distracts Turnus from the battle by forming a likeness of Aeneas out of mist, which he pursues.
2 *Macbeth,* 4.1.80.

It was otherwise with me. I had received a deep and perilous gash, the broad brand of which I shall not fail to carry with me to my grave. The sight of my left eye is gone; the cheek beneath is severed, with a deep trench between. My wound is of that sort, which in the French civil wars[1] got the name of *une balafre*.[2] I have pleased myself, in the fury and bitterness of my soul, with tracing the whole force of that word. It is *cicatrix luculenta*,[3] a glazed, or shining scar, like the effect of a streak of varnish upon a picture. *Balafré*[4] I find explained by Girolamo Vittori,[5] by the Italian word *smorfiato*; and this again—I mean the noun, *smorfia*—is decided by "the resolute" John Florio, to signify "a blurting or mumping, a mocking or push with one's mouth."[6] The explanation of these lexicographers is happily suited to my case, and the mark I for ever carry about with me. The reader may recollect the descriptions I have occasionally been obliged to give, of the beauty of my person and countenance, particularly in my equestrian exercises, when, mounted on my favourite horse, I was the admiration of every one that beheld me.[7] What was I now? When I first looked in my glass, and saw my face, once more stripped of its tedious dressings, I thought I never saw any thing so monstrous. It answered well, to the well-worded description of Florio. The sword of my enemy had given a perpetual grimace, a sort of preternatural and unvarying distorted smile, or deadly grin, to my countenance. This may to some persons appear a trifle. It ate into my soul. Every time my eye accidentally caught my mirror, I saw Clifford, and the cruel heart of Clifford, branded into me. My situation was not like what it had hitherto been. Before, to think of Clifford was an act of the mind, and an exercise of the imagination; he was not there, but my thoughts

---

1 French wars of religion, 1562–98.

2 A long facial wound, or the jagged scar it leaves.

3 Given as a synonym for *balafre* in Guillaume le Brun's *Dictionnaire universel françois et latin* (1760). Cicatrization occurs when a new tissue forms over a wound and contracts into a scar.

4 Someone who bears a scar from the above wound.

5 Seventeenth-century Italian lexicographer, who wrote a trilingual dictionary in French, Spanish, and Italian (1609). Vittori does not use the word smorfiato but rather "sfregiato nel viso."

6 John Florio (c. 1553–1625), linguist and lexicographer at the court of James I, published *A World of Wordes* (1598) which was reprinted and augmented several times. Florio does gloss the word as cited by Godwin.

7 See p. 344.

went on their destined errand, and fetched him; now I bore Clifford and his injuries perpetually about with me. Even as certain tyrannical planters in the West-Indies[1] have set a brand with a red-hot iron upon the negroes they have purchased, to denote that they are irremediably a property, so Clifford had set his mark upon me, as a token that I was his for ever.

THE END

---

1   During the reigns of James I, Charles I, and Cromwell, Irish slaves were sold in the West Indies, Virginia, and New England. There was no size-able black slave trade at the time, and under Cromwell's ethnic cleans-ing scheme Irish indentured labourers sent to Barbados were even derided by negroes as "white slaves," and the former were used to control the latter (Don Jordan and Michael Walsh, *White Cargo: The Forgotten History of Britain's White Slaves in America* [New York: New York UP, 2008], 143–81, 191). Godwin's reference is obviously a contemporary one, as slavery, abolished and reinstated and then again abolished in France during the period 1790–1815, was also a major issue in Britain during Godwin's time. The Slave Trade Act of 1807 abolished the slave trade but not slavery itself.

Appendix A: Godwin, "Fragment of a Romance" (1833)

[The fragment is thought to be the text alluded to in the Preface to *Mandeville* as the novel Godwin had begun eight years previously, the "germ" of which was taken from the story of the "Seven Sleepers" (see p. 61, note 3). Though written therefore about 1809, it was first published some 24 years later in *The New Monthly Magazine and Literary Journal*.]

I was born about the middle of the twelfth century from the birth of Christ, in an old and well-fortified castle in Spain, not far from the city of Talavera. My grandfather had served many a hard campaign under the Cid Diaz de Bivas, the thunderbolt of Spain; and the earliest lessons of my infancy were the songs, or *romances*, in which the exploits of this hero were celebrated with the blended enthusiasm of a *cancioneador*,[1] a warrior, and a Christian. My father, whose breeding had been in the tented field, delighted to tell that he had seen the Cid,—that he remembered the time when the aged warrior had held him in his arms, had seated him on his knee as the infant representative of his fellow-soldier, had stroked down the silken locks of his hair, and bade him fight bravely when he grew to man's estate, for the honour of Castille, and the glory of the Holy Cross.

Spain, at the time of my birth, was divided into two great portions, one of which was possessed by the Christians, and the other by the Moors. The Christians were masters of the northern and the middle provinces, under the respective sceptres of the King of Castille, the King of Arragon, the King of Portugal, and the Count of Barcelona. The fertile plains of Andalusia and Granada, together with Valentia and Estremadura, still continued in the hands of the Mahometans. The splendid reign of the Abdalrahmans, caliphs of Cordova, who for several centuries had rendered the Peninsula one of the eyes of the world, was passed away; and the petty princes, who ruled in the scattered fragments of their empire, had sunk under the gallant achievements and the hardihood of the Christian chivalry.

Another and a ruder power had succeeded to that of the Abdalrahmans, and had arrested, though with fitful and uncertain efforts, the fate of the Moorish empire in Spain. This was that of the Miramamolins of Africa. Two races of men, known by this title, successively

---

1 Singer or composer of ballads.

seized the empire of the Mahometans in this quarter of the world; and pretending to be immediately descended from the loins of the Great Prophet, challenged the submission of all true believers, as much for the sanctity of their lives, and their celestial destination to power, as the conquests of their sword. Their title imports this—which is correctly written—Emir-al-Mumenir, Commander of the Faithful; an appellation never applied but in the sense of religious supremacy. The metropolis of their empire was Morocco, a city which owes its foundation to their sway. The two families are known by the appellations of the Almoravides and the Almohades.

The sceptre of Castille had fallen, by the decease of Alfonso the Eighth, calling himself Emperor of Spain, into the hands of Sancho, his son, a prince only twenty-two years of age, when Abou Said, the second prince of the race of the Almohades, entered Spain with a numerous army. Taking advantage of the unsettled state of the kingdom, he captured several considerable towns, while the Moorish governments, hereditary in Spain, scarcely ventured to make a show of resistance against him. Partly converted by his pretensions to a divine commission and title, and partly perhaps awed by the success of his arms, the kings of Granada and Merida made a voluntary surrender of their crowns; while the citizens of Cordova and Seville, whose princes had shown themselves less docile to the representative of Alla, threw open their gates to the Mira-mamolin, and treated him as their deliverer.

Of the states here mentioned, the kingdom of Merida bordered most nearly on the place of my birth. The reigning sovereign, a prince considerably past the vigour of his years, was ordered by the Almohades into Africa, to pass the remainder of his days in a Mahometan monastery near the city of Fez. His two sons, Abenalhax and Omar, entered themselves among the troops of the victorious prince, and were soon numbered among the most gallant leaders of the Mahometan army.

Such was the state of my country. The prosperous reign of the Emperor Alfonso had given a degree of security to the hearts of the Spaniards, so that we scarcely felt that the soil of the Peninsula was divided between us and the enemies of our religion and our race. Christian and Moor sat down together with a temporary sentiment of harmony and peace. The temper of the two nations towards each other, in several essential respects, may easily be collected from one or two memorable incidents. Alfonso,—that Alfonso who seventy years before had wrested from the Mahometans the city of Toledo,—took to his bed the daughter of Benabad, the Moorish King of Cordova. Sancho the First, one of his predecessors, had for a time fixed his abode in the Moorish capital, and confided his person to the superior skill of Mahometan physicians, that he might be cured of a critical disease. The respective merits of the two people seemed to be adjusted; and it was admitted on all hands, that the Spaniards surpassed the Moors in military achievements and the warlike character, while the Moors left us at no less distance behind them in all the arts of elegance and refinement, in manners, in music, in poetry, and in philosophy.

My father, who was no longer young, reposed himself after the various toils of a military life, in his hereditary castle. My mother, who was of the illustrious family of Ponce de Leon, dedicated much of her care to the cultivation of my infancy, and was consummately well qualified for the task she had undertaken. My early years were passed in serenity and peace. I had heard of war: its thunders rolled at a distance, and I perceived their hoarse murmurs as if from the other side of the mountains; but it was a tale only, the report of which had been conveyed to my ears, while its realities had never offered themselves to the witness of my eyes.

Though I was very young at the time of the first great revolution in my existence, yet I remember somewhat of the scenes which preceded it, and I remember them the more perfectly from this very circumstance, which enables me to assign them an exact place in my history. I remember well the way in which the scenery around me first affected my thoughts. The country was mountainous, and the mountains were rugged and barren. It had very little to boast on the score of cultivation: my father and his dependents principally subsisted on the produce of their flocks. The castle in which we dwelt, was built for defence and retreat, and not for luxury. The light of heaven entered it only through narrow loopholes and perforations, piercing its massy and substantial walls. Most of the apartments were small, and the ascent to them by narrow and winding staircases; the hall only, the kitchen, and the stables, were spacious; in the former of which were daily spread two immense tables, where my father constantly sat down at the hour of noon with one hundred and fifty of his followers. The floor of this hall was spread with rushes, and the walls were hung round with shields, and spears, and swords, and all the various apparatus of war.

These things spoke to my childish soul a sufficiently intelligible language; and the tongue of my mother served further in the office of a chorus, explaining and enforcing their precepts and their eloquence. Christianity and war came united from her lips. The glory of the cross, the honours of Christian chivalry, the burning shame that was inflicted on knighthood and Spain by the multitude of mosques, and faquirs, and imans, that still overspread the land, was the daily burden of her thoughts. And deeply was she skilled in the art of adapting these topics to my comprehension, and bringing them into unison with my feelings. There was nothing dry, general, and vague in the discourses of my mother: it was all story and variety of adventure; it consisted of achievements glorious beyond the conception of a frigid and unanimated spirit; of the delivery of damsels from ravishment and slavery; of the undaunted assertion of justice and divine truth to the very teeth of the misbelievers; of everything that in the relation could thrill through my infant heart. The eye of my mother so glistened, too, when she spoke of the sacred triumph of the better cause; and her smile spoke volumes. That smile lives at this moment at the bottom of my soul; I retire into my inmost self, and I see it still: it was the smile of a mother, full of love, condescension, and hope. When she had fed her thoughts with the sentiments of a Christian and a Spaniard, the elevation melted down into a beam of unspeakable softness, that bended itself wholly and undividedly upon her son. I sprang to meet it; and the story and the lesson were sealed up with a kiss.

There was nothing in this period of my life to seduce my mind from the sole object of its attention. There was no luxury—or at least nothing that appeared to my recollection to be such—amidst the scenes of a very different character that were shortly afterwards presented to me. Whatever my father possessed, of costly materials, or exquisite workmanship, consisted of the spoils he had taken in different incursions against the Moors. I recollect, in particular, the chair of state in which my father sat on certain solemn days, when he gave law and regulation to his vassals. The substance of the chair was ivory, very curiously carved, and it was covered with carpets of rich and brilliant colours. Behind him, as he sat, was suspended a curtain of cloth of gold. But our possessions of this sort were scanty; they were barely sufficient to maintain a certain feeling of pomp and majesty, and were entirely void of that variety and profusion which might tend to relax the soul, and weaken the energies of its fortitude. All was grave, and solemn, and sedate. Whatever I saw, that addressed itself to my feelings of wonder and admiration, had a sort of military march in it. Peals of light and thoughtless laughter never met my ears, nor agitated my muscles. Infected by the character of everything around me, the very smiles of my infancy had a tincture of pride in them; and, like the smiles of my mother, were pervaded with sentiment and conscious elevation. The scenes of nature I beheld were in harmony with this temper. They were admirable,—for they were lofty and bold; and he that looked at them heard, as it were, the genius of the place bidding him awake and be a man. But we saw no laughing fields, no rich fertility, no copious exuberance of a wealthy soil, bidding the mind bask in the sunshine of prosperity, and be drunk with jollity and ease.

An incident occurred during this period which made a deep impression on my memory. My mother had a brother, ten years younger than herself, Signor Rodrigo Ponce de Leon. This youth had spent the greater part of his early years in the family of Don Sancho de Ximenes, which was reported to be the most perfect school in all Castille for the accomplishments demanded in a true knight. He however came more than once to spend a few weeks at a time in the castle of Torralva. My father was a soldier of high character, and worthy of his imitation; and the exemplary and heroic dispositions of my mother were such, that her stripling brother could not fail to drink in just and elevated sentiments from her lips. I am talking of very early times, concerning which I can scarcely trust the reports of my memory; but, to my recollection, Signor Rodrigo stands forth the very model of gallantry, ingenuousness, and good nature. Wise he was in my eyes, for I never saw anything in him but what was the emanation of purity; and whatever he said contributed to enlighten and enrich my infant mind. But what charmed me most in my squire uncle, as I called him, was the full and unsuppressed condescension with which he would often make himself my equal and my playfellow. There were no liberties I did not take with his person; and when I passed over in review the stories my mother told me, he would freely assist me to represent in action the defiances, encounters, and deliverances from bonds and oppression they recounted, and cheerfully join me in "playing at knights." A stick served us for a horse, and a thorn-bush for a castle to be beleaguered or surprised.

In one of Signor Rodrigo's latest visits, at the time when he had just attained the age of twenty-one years, his errand was to obtain the society of my father, together with that of his other relations, to do him grace to the court of King Sancho, to which he was summoned, with about twenty other young men of rank, to take upon him the character of a knight. My mother and myself, with the female part of the household, were for several days left alone in the castle, attended by no further guard than was judged necessary to defend us from surprise. After an absence of a few days my father and Signor Roderic returned, the whole party having agreed to partake of a social banquet at our table, as they were now on their journey from Toledo to the borders of Old Castile. The preparations were considerable. At a certain hour the centinel on the barbican[1] gave notice of the approach of the knights, and the gates of the tilt-yard were thrown open to receive them. Previously to their entrance, Signor Roderic alighted from his palfrey,[2] and put on a complete suit of armour; he then

1 Outer defence of a castle, often a tower at a gate or drawbridge.
2 A lighter-weight horse.

walked in solemn state, between my father and his father, followed by the whole troop of knights and squires, to the platform where my mother was seated, and where I, being now seven years of age, stood beside her. He no sooner reached her footstool, than he humbled himself on one knee before her. My mother rose, and threw a scarf she had in readiness over his shoulder. She then raised him with one hand, and fell on his neck, and wept. This ceremony had no sooner passed, than a war-horse was brought to Signor Roderic, on which he vaulted lightly with his armour on, and turning him about, wheeled round the court at full speed, and performed a variety of feats of horsemanship with an admirable grace. He then received a spear, which he brandished with great agility, and riding at the target, struck it full in the midst. After this, he tossed the spear to an attendant, and drew his sword, which he flourished over his head, and which was of so admirable a temper, that as the beams of the sun played upon it, it glistened with a brilliancy hardly inferior to lightning. The ceremony concluded with the whole company proceeding in full march to the oratory[1] of the castle, where a priest of considerable distinction delivered a short, but emphatical and impressive discourse upon the duties of a Christian knight, concluding with an exhortation to Signor Roderic to demean himself in a way worthy of his ancestry and his calling. The whole scene was calculated to make an indelible impression on my infant mind. One thing however did not fail to be afflicting to me. This was the being informed by my mother's favourite female attendant, that my squire uncle existed no longer,—that he had now entered into a very different order of persons, and that the sacredness of his present engagements would be dishonoured by his ever associating with me, and joining in my youthful sports as he had been wont to do.

The little all of my life hitherto had been peace. Every day was for the most part like the day before: my father was surrounded by his vassals; but as the countenances were generally the same, and the garments the same in fashion, and almost the same in colour, the impression made upon me was uniform. By repetition, the objects had hardly the effect of living things to me; they stirred up no semblance of tempest on the surface of my mind; the scene was to me "as idle as a painted ship upon a painted ocean."[2] But oh, how far was this from tediousness and lethargy! It was the luxury of sensation. It was the joy of a quiet and a satisfied spirit! a joy infinitely superior to that which is commonly to be found in turmoil and agitation. It was like breathing the purest and most health-giving element on the top of the

---

1   Room in a castle intended for use as a private chapel.
2   Coleridge, "The Rime of the Ancient Mariner," 2.35–36.

highest mountains. The mind rested upon its centre, as Adam reposed in Paradise, when the Lord God descended, and by insensible degrees caused a deep sleep to fall upon him,—a sleep that we may conceive to have been full of visions, in which he saw the things that were, even as if they were not. I sometimes viewed the pictures around me, leisurely savouring everything as it presented itself, and suffering each thing to make its own impression, while the mind remained sweetly and joyfully passive; and at other times, shut up in the rarities and fancies of my own spirit, I saw nothing of what was passing, but busily pictured to myself the scenes of an imaginary future, which, because they were childish, did not on that account fail to be interesting to me. I know not whether this will appear to others an exaggerated relation of the experience of six or seven years of age; I only know that it is the faithful history of my own childhood.

I dwell the more on these things on account of the sudden and dreadful stroke, by means of which they all vanished in an instant. Oh, scenes of my youth, how dearly once beloved, now fearfully vanishing for ever! In the subsequent narrative of my life, I shall sometimes have to tell of pleasures, more subtle, elevated, and refined, than those I have just attempted to paint; but there is a memorable difference dividing the one from the other. These were in one sense my truest pleasures. My mind was innocent; my heart was new. I had never known a pain but what was momentary, or sustained a blow that, so to speak, rased[1] so much as the skin of my soul. But, oh, what fearful gashes, what deep intrenchant scars, succeeded to this! Never did my heart recover the same pure and unviolated tranquillity. The pillars of my consciousness were shaken to their basis. The best of my after-life was like that of a man the bones of whose limbs have been broken, and though tolerably set and put together again, yet in the seat of each fracture there remains an unseen knot or protuberance, sufficiently marking to him that will be at the pains to visit it, where the injury had fallen. In my childhood the world to me was innocent; I saw in every form I met an image of myself; and did not doubt that every one was bland, and kind, and good, and void of harm and malice, as I was myself. But the injuries I am going to relate came from the hand of man; and, without pretending exactly to analyse the shades of error and guilt, I was compelled at a very premature period no longer to contemplate man, as such, with the same simplicity. I was driven to entertain sentiments of suspicion, jealousy, and dislike,—to consider human creatures as beings from whom in some cases no less injury was to be apprehended, than from a thunderbolt, a hurricane, or a conflagration. Nor was this speculation, or a tale made at pleasure, or

---

1 Destroyed.

related for amusement. It was brought home in the bitterest way to my feelings. The colour of my mind was tarnished; it was burned up and embrowned by the tropical sun of calamity. What I should have been, if the days of my youth had been protracted to the ordinary period, I cannot decide. But surely my having been forced in a certain sense to become a man, before I had well ceased to be a child, must have made me a very different being, from other men who have not passed through the same state of early suffering.

The visit of my knight uncle, as I was now bid to call him, was short. It was principally designed for my mother's gratification, who had an inextinguishable desire to behold this brother of hers in the new character which his king had conferred upon him. This passed, he hastened to place himself under the banners of Don Sancho Ximenes. The king, Don Sancho, had summoned all his peers and his chivalry to march against the Mira-mamolin. Abou Said advanced with a numerous army, and crossed the Guadalquivir between Baeza and Andujar. The Christian monarch was not less diligent in his preparations. Signor Roderic was to make his first campaign under the standard of Don Sancho, beneath whose roof he had received the education, and accomplished himself in all the exercises, which at that day were required for the military profession. My father was to lead forth his gallant followers in a band of his own. The campaign was looked forward to with much earnestness and enthusiasm. The Emperor Alfonso had sustained the Christian character in deeds of arms, in an uninterrupted career of glory, which far outshone the tracks of all his predecessors. Sancho, his son and successor, was just twenty-two years of age: and, though the invasion of the Mira-mamolin was naturally a subject of alarm, yet the superior prowess of the Spaniards to that of the Moors,—a fact sufficiently established,—and more than all, the elasticity and spring of a new reign, and the confidence entertained of the good fortune of a young prince of great hopes, and in the flower of his age, made every bosom beat with the expectation of a splendid and decisive success.

With what beautiful manifestations of affection did my mother take leave of her brother and her husband! She was a heroine of the genuine Castilian temper, and needed not have blushed for her sentiments, if she had been placed beneath the eye of a dame of Sparta or ancient Rome. Yet her heart overflowed with all the best and tenderest feelings of a woman. When she bade adieu to the partners of her fortune and her life, and to the beauteous youth who had now just entered upon the epoch of manhood, she knew that they were going to seek for honour in the ranks of danger and death, and that she might never again see them in the reciprocations of kindness and the erectness of life. But she knew that they were born for this. She was persuaded that every human creature, according to the place in which his lot was cast, had duties to perform; and that, without the discharge and the love of these duties, life was not worth the name of life. Every sentiment that could give grace to a human spirit concurred, in my mother, to sustain her, and throw a glory round her in this hour of her trial: the love of her husband's and her brother's honour, the recollection of an illustrious ancestry, the splendid feelings which chivalry nourishes beyond any other institution that man ever conceived, the zeal of Castille and of Spain, and the reverence and the pride attached to the standard of the Holy Cross.

She bade them adieu with the firmness of a resolved spirit. The priest pronounced his benediction upon them in the oratory of the castle; but though that was done in a seemly and impressive manner, and in a way that showed that the holy man was possessed with the spirit of his profession, yet that was nothing to the fervour with which my mother blessed them. When they rode forth from the gates, I went up with the marchioness to the tower of the barbican. Having proceeded to a certain distance on the plain, my father and my uncle turned round their steeds. My mother put forth her veil from the lattice, and waved it in their sight. The two champions bowed their heads, and after drew their swords and brandished them; having done which, they turned their steeds again, and went forward.

The departure of my father and my uncle took place in the first week of August, in the year 1158. My mother and I were left, as before, with a scanty guard; but that was a source of no uneasiness, particularly as, though there was war between the Christians and the infidels, the seat of contention, as I have already said, was removed from us, and every eye was turned on the side of the Sierra Morena, and the waters of the Guadalquivir. We rather seemed to be left at a distance in this busy scene, and to be called upon, while every nerve was strung for the arduous contention, to possess our souls in patience, and wait quietly for the result. The marchioness in the secret chamber of her soul was doubtless full of expectation and disquietude; but this had a singular effect on her outward behaviour. I never saw her so playful and so condescending: she appeared for the occasion to have laid aside the usual elevation of her soul, and to become an ordinary matron of lowly life or of quiet times. She told me stories; and the tales I now listened to, were not of heroism, but of fancy merely. She talked of fairies and enchantments,—of everything that soothed the imagination, and stole away the senses in a pleasing dream,—of all the wild inventions of the east, aided in its creations by a luxuriant climate, and by all the wealth and magnificence of Damascus or of Delhi. My pleasure was new; I had never found my mother so condescending, or condescending in this key. Lovely she always was; everything she said or did, at least so far as I was concerned, won upon the affections. But, at other times, the love I felt was mingled with admiration and awe. Now it was wonder, but wonder of a different family and class. I gazed on her as she spoke: my eyes glistened; but the ecstacy I felt seemed to draw me into her soul; I was filled almost to bursting with what I heard, but I was not afraid. Oh, moments of peace and joy! Far from war, or the idea that a man could exist that would shed the blood of man; full on the contrary of the feelings of pastoral life, and of the innocence and happiness of the golden age.

Tranquil was the slumber which followed close on a day like this. I committed myself to the arms of sleep, as to those of an assured friend; the period of my repose seemed like that reserved for the commemoration of some great religious event, upon which nothing ordinary and profane was to be feared to intrude.

The impressions of my mind were not those of a true augury. A few hours after midnight, when the silence and darkness of that period were yet at their full, I was startled from my sleep by the sound of the alarm-bell of the castle. In our deep and secure retreat, the night bore a very different character from that which it wears in a populous town. In cities the busy or the wayward mind of man in some individual or other is always awake; from time to time a solitary vehicle is heard rumbling along the streets; the oxen and the sheep with their lowing or their bleatings complain of their inexorable driver; the colloquy is heard of those that lie down late, or rise up early; or the careless song of the reveller rouses him who is vexed with sorrow or disease from his imperfect slumbers. But in a solitary, rural abode, nothing can be heard at certain hours that indicates the existence of man; nature herself seems to partake in the repose of her favourite son; and the few incidental sounds that occur from time to time are unconnected with each other, indicate nothing and lead to nothing, and appear, like the audible breathings of him who sleeps, to answer no other purpose, than to make the universal quiet a more distinct object of perception. The sound of the alarm-bell in the castle of Torralva was therefore doubly rousing.

I listened in silence; I never remembered to have heard the sound before; my thoughts were confounded. It was a loud and a deafening sound. It was not like the solemn and measured pace of the funeral knell; it expressed horror, and disorder, and affright—the eagerness to do something, with an uncertainty what was to be done. It was succeeded by the sound of steps, hurrying down the stairs of the castle.

I slept in a closet adjoining to the bed-chamber of my mother. By a certain rustling, and the sound of her voice, I perceived she was in motion. I crept quietly from my bed, and put on my clothes. As I opened the door of the closet, I perceived the marchioness passing out by the opposite door of the chamber, and I followed her in silence. She descended the stairs, and came down into the quadrangle. I then took hold of her hand. She had not perceived me before; but she did not repel my overture to join her. She cast upon me a look of encouragement.

Several of the attendants of the castle flitted about the quadrangle with lighted torches; and my mother, crossing the area, proceeded to the barbican and mounted the watch-tower. From thence we were presented with a dreadful spectacle; a town in flames. It was Oropesa, distant scarcely more than a mile from our walls. It had not long before been a flourishing seat of Moorish industry; but since it had been recovered by the Christians, it had fallen into decay. The castle of Torralva was erected for its defence.

The successive volumes of smoke that ascended, the flames, and the flakes of lighter combustible substance carried up with the smoke, were to me a terrible spectacle, and for some minutes fixed my attention. I then looked down into the plain between; which presented a still more intelligible and fearful scene of distress. The inhabitants of the town were seen flying in all directions, and in all directions were pursued, and goaded along and crossed by Moorish horsemen. Men, women, and children fled this way and that, and lifted up their hands, as they ran, with agony and despair. I gazed with earnestness and astonishment. How I hated a Moor! None but a Moor, thought I to myself, would drive the sons of quiet from their homes, would set fire to their houses, hunt, wound, and destroy them, and trample them under their horses' feet. These wretches have nothing human about them but their form; they are more ferocious than the wild beasts of the desert.

In the distance, and nearest to the flames, the Mahomedans and the Christians were mixed together in the wildest confusion; nearer to the castle we could see none but our friends, and persons that had a claim upon us for protection. It was true that the fortress itself had nothing to fear from a vagrant and accidental incursion. But Oropesa was my father's domain; its inhabitants were his clients and dependents. Every drop of blood that fell from them, and that it was in our power to have saved, was a violation of the great compact of society, by which the higher and the lower orders in Spain were bound together; every drop of blood that fell from them would be regarded by the marchioness as her own.

I looked at my mother; I saw a creature I had never seen before,— not different—not unlike her former self—it was the same character, exalted by the great realities, the terrible calamities and miseries, that beset the path of human life. It was an angel now, employed in an angel's office; before she seemed to have concealed what she was, and to have put forth but half her strength; now a ray from heaven played upon her features, and to my eye, a circle of glory, such as I had observed in the paintings of divine personages, surrounded her head. She issued a peremptory order, that the draw-bridge should be let down, the gates thrown open, and the fugitives admitted; with this precaution, over which from the tower she undertook herself to preside, that so many should come in, as could be received without danger that their pursuers should enter along with them, and that then the gates should be shut.

No sooner were the directions of the marchioness obeyed, than to her utter astonishment, a troop of Moors immediately rushed into the quadrangle. ✶✶✶✶✶

Appendix B: From Godwin, "Of History and Romance" (1797)

[Godwin wrote this essay for a possible second edition of *The Enquirer*, his 1797 collection of essays on "Education, Manners, and Literature," but the essay was not published in his lifetime. Bodleian Library, Abinger Collection, c. 86, fols. 23–28.]

The study of history may well be ranked among those pursuits which are most worthy to be chosen by a rational being.

The study of history divides itself into two principal branches; the study of mankind in a mass, of the progress, the fluctuations, the interests and the vices of society; and the study of the individual.

The history of a nation might be written in the first of these senses, entirely in terms of abstraction, and without descending so much as to name one of those individuals of which the nation is composed.... [It] ascertain[s] the causes that operate universally upon masses of men under given circumstances, without being turned aside in their operation by the varying character of individuals.

The fundamental article in this branch of historical investigation, is the progress and varieties of civilisation. But there are many subordinate channels into which it has formed itself. We may study the history of eloquence or the history of philosophy. We may apply ourselves to the consideration of the arts of life, and the arts of refinement and pleasure. There lie before us the history of wealth and the history of commerce.... We may follow the varieties of climates, and trace their effects on the human body and the human mind. Nay, we may descend still lower ... [and] apply ourselves entirely to the examination of medals and coins.

There are those who conceive that history, in one or all the kinds here enumerated, is the only species of history deserving a serious attention. They disdain the records of individuals. To interest our passions, or employ our thoughts about personal events, be they of patriots, of authors, of heroes or kings, they regard as a symptom of effeminacy. Their mighty minds cannot descend to be busied about any thing less than the condition of nations, and the collation and comparison of successive ages. Whatever would disturb by exciting our feelings the torpid tranquillity of the soul, they have in unspeakable abhorrence.

It is to be feared that one of the causes that have dictated the panegyric which has so often been pronounced upon this species of history, is its dry and repulsive nature. Men who by persevering exertions have conquered a subject in defiance of innumerable obstacles, will almost always be able to ascribe to it a disproportionate value.... Difficulty has a tendency to magnify to almost all eyes the excellence of that which only through difficulty can be attained.

The mind of man does not love abstractions. Its genuine and native taste, as it discovers itself in children and uneducated persons, rests entirely in individualities....

But the abstractions of philosophy, when we are grown familiar with them, often present to our minds a simplicity and precision, that may well supply the place of entire individuality. The abstractions of history are more cumbrous and unwieldy. In their own nature perhaps they are capable of simplicity. But this species of science is yet in its infancy. He who would study the history of nations abstracted from individuals whose passions and peculiarities are interesting to our minds, will find it a dry and frigid science. It will supply him with no clear ideas. The mass, as fast as he endeavours to cement and unite it, crumbles from his grasp, like a lump of sand. Those who study revenue or almost any other of the complex subjects above enumerated, are ordinarily found, with immense pains to have compiled a species of knowledge which is no sooner accumulated than it perishes, and rather to have confounded themselves with a labyrinth of particulars, than to have risen to the dignity of principles.

Let us proceed to the consideration of the second great branch of the study of history. In doing so, we shall be insensibly led to assign to the first branch its proper rank.

The study of individual man can never fail to be an object of the highest importance. It is only by comparison that we come to know any thing of mind or of ourselves. We go forth into the world; we see what man is; we enquire what he was; and when we return home and engage in the solemn act of self-investigation, our most useful employment is to produce the materials we have collected abroad, and, by a sort of magnetism, cause those particulars to start out to view in ourselves, which might otherwise have lain for ever undetected....

But let us suppose that the genuine purpose of history, was to enable us to understand the machine of society, and to direct it to its best purposes. Even here individual history will perhaps be found in point of importance to take the lead of general. General history will furnish us with precedents in abundance, will show us how that which happened in one country has been repeated in another, and may perhaps even instruct us how that which has occurred in the annals of mankind, may under similar circumstances be produced again. But, if the energy of our minds should lead us to aspire to something more animated and noble than dull repetition, if we love the happiness of mankind enough to feel ourselves impelled to explore new and untrodden paths, we must then not rest contented with considering society in a mass, but must analyse the materials of which it is composed. It will be necessary for us to scrutinise the nature of man, before we can pronounce what it is of which social man is capable. Laying aside the generalities of historical abstraction, we must mark the operation of human passions; must observe the empire of motives whether groveling or elevated; and must note the influence that one human being exercises over another, and the ascendancy of the daring and the wise over the vulgar multitude. It is thus, and thus only, that we shall be enabled to add, to the knowledge of the past, a sagacity that can penetrate into the depths of futurity. We shall not only understand those events as they arise, which are no better than old incidents under new names, but shall judge truly of such conjunctures and combinations, their sources and effects, as, though they have never yet occurred, are within the capacities of our nature. He that would prove the liberal and spirited benefactor of his species, must connect the two branches of history together, and regard the knowledge of the individual, as that which can alone give energy and utility to the records of our social existence.

From these considerations one inference may be deduced, which constitutes perhaps the most important rule that can be laid down respecting the study of history. This is, the wisdom of studying it in detail, and not in abridgment. The prolixity of dullness is indeed contemptible.... To read a history which, expanding itself through several volumes, treats only of a short period, is true economy. To read historical abridgments, in which each point of the subject is touched upon only, and immediately dismissed, is a wanton prodigality of time worthy only of folly or of madness.

The figures which present themselves in such a history, are like the groupes that we sometimes see placed in the distance of a landscape, that are just sufficiently marked to distinguish the man from the brute, or the male dress from the female, but are totally unsusceptible of discrimination of form or expression of sentiment. The men I would study upon the canvas of history, are men worth the becoming intimately acquainted with.

It is in history, as it is in life. Superficial acquaintance is nothing.... There must be an exchange of real sentiments, or an investigation of subtle peculiarities, before improvement can be the result. There is a magnetical virtue in man; but there must be friction and heat, before the virtue will operate.

Pretenders indeed to universal science, who examine nothing, but imagine they understand every thing, are ready from the slightest glance to decypher the whole character. Not so the genuine scholar. His curiosity is never satiated. He is ever upon the watch for further and still further particulars....

There are characters in history that may almost be said to be worth an eternal study. They are epitomes of the world, of its best and most exalted features, purified from their grossness. I am not contented to observe such a man upon the public stage, I would follow him into his closet. I would see the friend and the father of a family, as well as the patriot. I would read his works and his letters, if any remain to us. I would observe the turn of his thoughts and the character of his phraseology. I would study his public orations. I would collate his behaviour in prosperity with his behaviour in adversity. I should be glad to know the course of his studies, and the arrangement of his time. I should rejoice to have, or to be enabled to make, if that were possible, a journal of his ordinary and minutest actions. I believe I should be better employed in thus studying one man, than in perusing the abridgment of Universal History in sixty volumes. I would rather be acquainted with a few trivial particulars of the actions and disposition of Virgil and Horace,[1] than with the lives of many men, and the history of many nations.

This leads us to a second rule respecting the study of history. Those histories alone are worthy of attention and persevering study, that treat of the development of great genius, or the exhibition of bold and masculine virtues. Modern history indeed we ought to peruse, because all that we wish must be connected with all that we are, and because it is incumbent upon us to explore the means by which the latter may be made, as it were, to slide into the former. But modern history, for the most part, is not to be perused for its own sake.

The ancients were giants, but we, their degenerate successors, are pygmies. There was something in the nature of the Greek and Roman republics that expanded and fired the soul. [Godwin goes on to praise the ancients, contrasting the characters in the first-century BCE/CE Roman writer Livy and the fifth-century BCE Greek historian Thucydides with those in the work of his more immediate precursors, David Hume and William Robertson.]

What sort of an object is the history of England? Till the extinction of the wars of York and Lancaster,[2] it is one scene of barbarism and cruelty. Superstition rides triumphant upon the subject neck of princes and of people; intestine war of noble with noble, or of one pretender to the crown against another, is almost incessant. The gallant champion is no sooner worsted, than he is led without form of law to the scaffold, or massacred in cold blood upon the field. In all these mighty struggles, scarcely a trace is to be found of a sense of the rights

---

1 Ancient Rome's most celebrated poets, both first century BCE.
2 A series of dynastic wars for the throne of England, 1455–85; also known as the Wars of the Roses.

of men. They are combinations among the oppressors against him that would usurp their tyranny, or they are the result of an infatuated predilection for one despotic monster in preference to another. The period of the Tudors is a period of base and universal slavery. The reign of Elizabeth is splendid, but its far-famed worthies are in reality supple and servile courtiers, treacherous, undermining and unprincipled. The period of the Stuarts is the only portion of our history interesting to the heart of man. Yet its noblest virtues are obscured by the vile jargon of fanaticism and hypocrisy. From the moment that the grand contest excited under the Stuarts was quieted by the Revolution, our history assumes its most insipid and insufferable form. It is the history of negotiations and tricks; it is the history of revenues and debts; it is the history of corruption and political profligacy; but it is not the history of genuine independent man.

Some persons, endowed with too much discernment and taste not to perceive the extreme disparity that subsists between the characters of ancient and of modern times, have observed that ancient history carries no other impression to their minds than that of exaggeration and fable.

It is not necessary here to enter into a detail of the evidence upon which our belief of ancient history is founded. Let us take it for granted that it is a fable. Are all fables unworthy of regard? Ancient history, says Rousseau,[1] is a tissue of such fables, as have a moral perfectly adapted to the human heart. I ask not, as a principal point, whether it be true or false? My first enquiry is, Can I derive instruction from it? Is it a genuine praxis upon the nature of man? Is it pregnant with the most generous motives and the most fascinating examples? If so, I had rather be profoundly versed in this fable, than in all the genuine histories that ever existed.

It must be admitted indeed that all history bears too near a resemblance to fable. Nothing is more uncertain, more contradictory, more unsatisfactory than the evidence of facts. If this be the case in courts of justice, where truth is sometimes sifted with tenacious perseverance, how much more will it hold true of the historian? He can administer no oath; he cannot issue his precept, and summon his witnesses from distant provinces; he cannot arraign his personages and compel them to put in their answer. He must take what they choose to tell; the broken fragments, and the scattered ruins of evidence.

That history which comes nearest to truth, is the mere chronicle of facts, places and dates. But this is in reality no history. He that knows only what day the Bastille was taken and on what spot Louis XVI perished, knows nothing. He possesses the mere skeleton of history. The

---

1   Jean-Jacques Rousseau (1712–78), political philosopher and novelist.

muscles, the articulations, every thing in which the life emphatically resides, is absent. [Godwin goes on to describe the element of fable even in what seems to be history.]

From these considerations it follows that the noblest and most excellent species of history, may be decided to be a composition in which, with a scanty substratum of facts and dates, the writer interweaves a number of happy, ingenious and instructive inventions, blending them into one continuous and indiscernible mass. It sufficiently corresponds with the denomination, under which Abbé Prévost[1] acquired considerable applause, of historical romance. Abbé Prévost differs from Sallust,[2] inasmuch as he made freer use of what may be styled, the *licentia historica*.[3]

If then history be little better than romance under a graver name, it may not be foreign to the subject here treated, to enquire into the credit due to that species of literature, which bears the express stamp of invention, and calls itself romance or novel....

Romance then, strictly considered, may be pronounced to be one of the species of history. The difference between romance and what ordinarily bears the denomination of history, is this. The historian is confined to individual incident and individual man, and must hang upon that his invention or conjecture as he can. The writer of romance collects his materials from all sources, experience, report, and the records of human affairs; then generalises them; and finally selects, from their elements and the various combinations they afford, those instances which he is best qualified to pourtray, and which he judges most calculated to impress the heart and improve the faculties of his reader. In this point of view we should be apt to pronounce that romance was a nobler species of composition than history.

It has been affirmed by the critics that the species of composition which Abbé Prévost and others have attempted, and according to which, upon a slight substratum of fact, all the license of romantic invention is to be engrafted, is contrary to the principles of a just taste. History is by this means debauched and corrupted. Real characters are wantonly misrepresented. The reader, who has been interested by a romance of this sort, scarcely knows how to dismiss it from his mind when he comes to consider the genuine annals of the period of which it relates. The reality and the fiction, like two substances of disagreeing natures, will never adequately blend with each other. The invention of the writer is much too wanton not to discolour and confound

---

1 Author (1697–1763) of several historical romances, including *Manon Lescaut* (1731).

2 Roman historian and statesman (c. 86–34 BCE).

3 Historical license.

the facts with which he is concerned; while on the other hand, his imagination is fettered and checked at every turn by facts that will not wholly accommodate themselves to the colour of his piece, or the moral he would adduce from it.

These observations, which have been directed against the productions of historical romance, will be found not wholly inapplicable to those which assume the graver and more authentic name of history. The reader will be miserably deluded if, while he reads history, he suffers himself to imagine that he is reading facts. Profound scholars are so well aware of this, that, when they would study the history of any country, they pass over the historians that have adorned and decorated the facts, and proceed at once to the naked and scattered materials, out of which the historian constructed his work. This they do, that they may investigate the story for themselves; or, more accurately speaking, that each man, instead of resting in the inventions of another, may invent his history for himself, and possess his creed as he possesses his property, single and incommunicable....

The man of taste and discrimination, who has properly weighed these cases, will be apt to exclaim, Dismiss me from the falshood and impossibility of history, and deliver me over to the reality of romance.

The conjectures of the historian must be built upon a knowledge of the characters of his personages. But we never know any man's character. My most intimate and sagacious friend continually misapprehends my motives. He is in most cases a little worse judge of them than myself and I am perpetually mistaken. The materials are abundant for the history of Alexander, Caesar, Cicero and Queen Elizabeth. Yet how widely do the best informed persons differ respecting them? Perhaps by all their character is misrepresented. The conjectures therefore respecting their motives in each particular transaction must be eternally fallacious. The writer of romance stands in this respect upon higher ground. He must be permitted, we should naturally suppose, to understand the character which is the creature of his own fancy.

The writer of romance then is to be considered as the writer of real history; while he who was formerly called the historian, must be contented to step down into the place of his rival, with this disadvantage, that he is a romance writer, without the ardour, the enthusiasm, and the sublime licence of imagination, that belong to that species of composition. True history consists in a delineation of consistent, human character, in a display of the manner in which such a character acts under successive circumstances, in showing how character increases and assimilates new substances to its own, and how it decays, together with the catastrophe into which by its own gravity it naturally declines.

There is however, after all, a deduction to be made from this eulogium of the romance writer. To write romance is a task too great for the powers of man, and under which he must be expected to totter. No man can hold the rod so even, but that it will tremble and vary from its course. To sketch a few bold outlines of character is no desperate undertaking; but to tell precisely how such a person would act in a given situation, requires a sagacity scarcely less than divine. We never conceive a situation, or those minute shades in a character that would modify its conduct. Naturalists tell us that a single grain of sand more or less on the surface of the earth, would have altered its motion, and, in the process of ages, have diversified its events. We have no reason to suppose in this respect, that what is true in matter, is false in morals.

Here then the historian in some degree, though imperfectly, seems to recover his advantage upon the writer of romance. He indeed does not understand the character he exhibits, but the events are taken out of his hands and determined by the system of the universe, and therefore, as far as his information extends, must be true. The romance writer, on the other hand, is continually straining at a foresight to which his faculties are incompetent, and continually fails. This is ludicrously illustrated in those few romances which attempt to exhibit the fictitious history of nations. That principle only, which holds the planets in their course, is competent to produce that majestic series of events which characterises flux and successive multitudes.

The result of the whole, is that the sciences and the arts of man are alike imperfect, and almost infantine. He that will not examine the collections and the efforts of man, till absurdity and folly are extirpated from among them, must be contented to remain in ignorance, and wait for the state, where he expects that faith will give place to sight, and conjecture be swallowed up in knowledge.

Appendix C: Contemporary Reviews

1. From P.B. Shelley, Letter to Godwin (7 December 1817)

[This letter is the basis for Shelley's letter to Leigh Hunt's *Examiner* (see below, Appendix C2), but is less guarded in matters of taste. Shelley published the second and longer letter after Godwin had hastily published the first, private one in *The Morning Chronicle*, shortly after receiving it.]

I have read *Mandeville* but I must read it again soon, for the interest is of that irresistible and overwhelming kind, that the mind in its influence is like a cloud borne on by an impetuous wind—like one breathlessly carried forward who has no time to pause or observe the causes of his career. I think the power of *Mandeville* is inferior to nothing you have done; and were it not for the character of Falkland,[1] no instance in which you have exerted that power of *creation* which you possess beyond all contemporary writers might compare with it. Falkland is still alone; power is, in Falkland, not, as in *Mandeville*, tumult hurried onward by the tempest, but tranquillity standing unshaken amidst its fiercest rage. But *Caleb Williams* never shakes the deepest soul like *Mandeville*. It must be said of the latter, you rule with a rod of iron. The picture is never bright, and we wonder whence you drew the darkness with which its shades are deepened, ... The noun, *smorfia*,[2] touches some chord within us with such a cold and jarring power that I started, and for some time could scarce believe but that I was Mandeville, and that this hideous grin was stamped upon my own face.... Shall I say that, when I discovered that [Henrietta] was pleading all this time sweetly for her lover, and when at last she weakly abandoned poor Mandeville, I felt an involuntary and, perhaps, an unreasonable pang?

2. From P.B. Shelley, Letter to *The Examiner* (28 December 1817): 826–27

SIR,— The author of *Mandeville* is one of the most illustrious examples of intellectual power in the present age. He has exhibited that variety and universality of talent which distinguishes him who is destined to inherit lasting renown from the possessors of temporary celebrity.... *Political Justice* is the first moral system, explicitly founded

---

1 The antagonist of Godwin's first major novel, *Caleb Williams*.
2 See p. 447.

upon the doctrine of the negativeness of rights and the positiveness of duties, an obscure feeling of which has been the basis of all the political liberty and private virtue in the world. But he is also the author of *Caleb Williams*, and if we had no record of a mind but simply some fragment containing the conception of the character of Falkland, doubtless we should say, "This is an extraordinary mind...."

It may be said with truth that Godwin has been treated unjustly by those of his countrymen, upon whose favour temporary distinction depends.... Godwin has been to the present age in moral philosophy what Wordsworth is in poetry.... It is singular, that the other nations of Europe should have anticipated in this respect the judgment of posterity, and that the name of Godwin, and that of his late illustrious and admirable wife, should be pronounced, even by those who know little of English literature, with reverence: and that the writings of Mary Wollstonecraft should have been translated and universally read in France and Germany, long after the bigotry of faction had stifled them in our own country.

Mandeville is Godwin's last production. The interest of this novel is undoubtedly equal, in some respects superior, to that of *Caleb Williams*. Yet there is no character like Falkland, whom the author, with that sublime casuistry which is the parent of toleration and forbearance, persuades us personally to love, whilst his actions must for ever remain the theme of our astonishment and abhorrence. Mandeville challenges our compassion and no more. His errors arise from an immutable necessity of internal nature, and from much of a constitutional antipathy and suspicion, which soon sprang up into a hatred and contempt and barren misanthropy, which, as it had no root in genius or in virtue, produces no fruit uncongenial with the soil wherein it grew. Those of Falkland arose from a high, though perverted conception of the majesty of human nature, from a powerful sympathy with his species, and from a temper which led him to believe that the very reputation of excellence should walk among mankind, unquestioned and undefiled. So far as it was a defect to link the interest of the tale with anything inferior to Falkland, so is Mandeville defective. But if the varieties of human character, the depth and the complexity of human motive, those sources of the union of strength and weakness, those useful occasions for pleading in favour of universal kindness, are just subjects for illustration and development in a work of fiction, Mandeville yields in interest and important to none of the productions of the Author. The language is more rich and various, and the expressions more eloquently sweet, without losing that energy and distinctness which characterizes *Political Justice* and *Caleb Williams*. The moral speculations have a strength and consistency and boldness which has been less clearly aimed at in his other works of fiction.... It is the genuine doctrine of *Political Justice* presented in one perspicuous and impressive view. [Shelley goes on to provide conventional praise of Clifford and Henrietta, but finds the latter a disappointing character.]

But these, considered with reference to the core of the story, are extrinsical. The events of the tale flow on like the stream of fate, regular and irresistible, and growing at once darker and swifter in their progress;—there is no surprise, there is no shock; we are prepared for the worst from the very opening of the scene, though we wonder whence the author drew the shadows which render the moral darkness every instant more profound, and at last, appaling and complete. The interest is awfully deep and rapid. To struggle with it would be gossamere attempting to bear up against the tempest. In this respect it is more powerful than *Caleb Williams*; the interest of *Caleb Williams* being as rapid but not so profound as that of Mandeville. It is a wind which tears up the deepest waters of the ocean of mind. The reader's mind is hurried on, as he approaches the end, with breathless and accelerated impulse. The noun *Smorfia* comes at last, and touches some nerve, which jars the inmost soul, and grates as it were along the blood; and we can scarcely believe that the grin, which must accompany Mandeville to his grave, is not stamped upon our own visage.

3. From *Champion* (1817): 398

Mandeville is a novel full of strength, incoherence, and misery. The story is very simple in itself, and is told by the hero, with that homely force of style, those occasional bursts of tremendous pathos, those flashes of savage fury, which break through the cold gloom of the story, like lightning throbbing to a troubled night,—which so peculiarly mark the works of the singular, the powerful, and the appaling Godwin....

The style of Mr. Godwin is very peculiar, and we think very effective. It has no grace, no roundness, no airy lightness:—but it goes right on, sometimes staggering under the weight of the passion which it bears, at others pushing forwards.... It is a style of all others the most opposite to the diffuse;—perhaps, if any thing, it is too short and broken.... It has all the nerve of passion gathered into itself, and we feel that the language, like that it would convey, is decided and irrevocable....

Mandeville is intended to record the causeless birth, the gradual and deadly progress and the lonely effects of the passion of hatred. The hero, in the course of three volumes, records the events of his youthful life, up to the age of one or two and twenty. [The reviewer provides a brief plot summary.] The characters are for the most part finely drawn.... They are at times sketchy and imperfect, as though the author was bewildered in the labyrinth of his own imagination. Audley Mandeville is our favourite. He is a true picture of a delicate mind dashed to fragments by one rude and irrevocable blow from the hand of fate.... Henrietta is too highly coloured; and Clifford is made too pretty. Mandeville himself is all evil,—but passionate, imaginative, and intellectual. He recounts his swelling hatred with immense force, and dwells on his madness and his solitude with majestic and appalling ardour. His language absolutely quakes beneath the tread of his genius. Philosophy spreads her roll before him;—Poetry shews him her caves and her solitudes, Humanity withers at his touch. With all the power of this character, there are however great and lamentable defects in it.... The novel is however on the whole a deeply interesting and masterly one.

4. From [John Gibson Lockhart,] *Blackwood's Edinburgh Magazine* 2.9 (December 1817): 268–79

[Lockhart (1794–1854) played a key role in *Blackwood's* and was also Sir Walter Scott's biographer.]

... In the books of the ancients, the hero, in whose sufferings we are called upon to sympathise, is exposed to tangible dangers, and assailed by visible foes. He has to contend with the armed anger of his fellow-men, and with plagues, and tempests, and shipwrecks, and all the ministering weapons of offended deities. The main purpose of his legend was, to represent the stedfastness of virtue in resisting the worst attacks of external enmity, treacheries, and wrath.... The hero of a modern romance is not the victim either of implacable destiny, or of outward injury; the revolutions of his fate are all engendered within himself, and he has to contend with no assaults but those of his own wishes, prejudices, principles, and passions.... What was darkly hinted by the profound philosophers of old, is now familiarly illustrated by the most popular creations of female fancy; and it is at last universally recognized, that the world of thought is the proper theatre of man.

... The old writers of fiction are careful, as we must all have observed, to represent their personages as beings who preserve, in the midst of all their troubles, entire possession of their intellects. Nothing, on the other hand, is more common among modern authors, than to enhance the sympathy we feel for their heroes, by depicting them as having their reason itself shaken by the violence of their sufferings.... The peculiar fondness of our English authors for representing the thoughts and feelings of madness, is a subject which has often exercised the curiosity and ingenuity of foreign critics. That in this country, which displays in its laws and constitution the best specimen of practical reason, the greatest writers should take so much delight in depicting the vain dreams of fantastic or phrenzied imaginations, appears at first sight a very singular and inexplicable circumstance; that the taste of the great body of the English people should be so much habituated to this practice of their authors, as to dwell with the utmost intensity of devotion and attachment on these melancholy and bewildering representations, which it would seem more natural for national persons to abominate and avoid, appears, if possible, a thing more surprising....

There are two great English writers of the present day, whose works seem in a very peculiar manner to authorize this reflection—Lord Byron and Mr Godwin. The poet and the novellist have each given birth to a set of terrible personifications of pride, scorn, hatred, misanthropy, misery, and madness. Their conceptions are, in many respects, congenial. Gloominess and desolation, and Satanic sarcasm, are the ground-work of their fictions; but both (like their master, Dante)[1] have shewn, by many tender episodes of love and pity, that they might have given to their tales, had they so willed it, a very different complexion. In each of the heroes of Byron we think a partial delirium may somewhere be detected; but phrenzy, as an organ of excitement, has unquestionably been used with far greater freedom by the writer whose latest production is at this moment before us. What with other men is an ingredient, is, not unfrequently, with him the basis. He dares to introduce madness, not to heighten but to form the sorrow; and we gaze upon the whole world of his fictions with the same feelings of indescribable curiosity, awe, and terror, which accompany us in our inspection of a company of lunatics. [Lockhart describes the heroes of *Caleb Williams* and *St. Leon*; the latter sits like Prometheus, lifted above mankind upon his solitary rock, the victim of an undying vulture and an inexpiable curse.]

Mandeville is a being near of kin to Caleb Williams and St Leon. Like them he possesses a lofty intellect and many natural capacities for enjoyment. Like them his heart is originally filled with kindly and benignant feelings; and, like them, by a strange perverseness of circumstance and temper, he is afflicted with intolerable sufferings, in which we can scarcely fear that we ourselves ever shall partake, and which nevertheless command the most powerful of our human sympathies. He is more essentially and entirely a madman than either of his brethren. The raving of Caleb is produced by external tyrannies, that of St Leon by super-human gifts; the misery of Mandeville is the growth of the fertile but unassisted soil of his own gloomy thoughts.

1 Dante Alighieri (c. 1265–1321), author of the *Divine Comedy*.

Born to a princely fortune—surrounded with all the trappings of luxury, and the facilities of ambition—blessed with the unpolluted and reposing tenderness of a saintly sister—he seems, as if in disdain of external goods, to dive into the dark recesses of his own disordered spirit, and thence to drag into the light of day a fearful and self-created phantom, by whose perpetual visitations it is his pleasure to be haunted. A causeless *aversion* preys upon his soul; he gives up the whole energies of his nature to a hatred which seems to exert upon his faculties the sway of an instinct rather than of a passion; and in the effects produced by the unceasing influence of this demonly species of phrenzy, consists the whole interest of his tremendous tale.

[The reviewer summarizes the novel at length.] The very skilful manner in which this aversion [Mandeville's for Clifford] is developed, can only be appreciated by those who give the book much more than the casual attention of one perusal.... [The reviewer quotes several long passages from the novel and continues:] Such is the energy of the language in which he pours out the tale of his delusions and his sorrows, that we cannot peruse it without becoming at least, in so far, partakers in the very follies whereof we feel and pity the existence in the narrator. It required, indeed, no ordinary degree of management in the author to produce this mixture of apparently irreconcileable effects, to make us sympathize in the emotions without being deceived by the speciousness of his hero, and to feel as if our judgment were swallowed up in the dreams of one whom we know, almost all the while we are listening to him, to be the most incurable of madmen....

Mandeville, our readers have already seen, tells his story, like the rest of Mr Godwin's heroes, in his own words. Any other mode of narration would have brought much more into notice, what is nevertheless sufficiently apparent, and what constitutes indeed the chief defect of our author's novels—the want of all dramatic talent. His personages are described, not represented; we are informed of all they think and suffer, by their own free and voluntary confession to us, not by being admitted to draw our own conclusions from their words and behaviour, when they come into actual contact with the other characters in the fable. In this, as indeed in many other things, Mr Godwin resembles the German novelists more than those of his own country; but we need only turn for a moment to Waverley or Guy Mannering[1] to be convinced, that, if he had both ways in his power, he has certainly made an unfortunate election. We must not, however, allow ourselves to find fault with a great author because he chooses to give us his story in his own manner. The language of Mandeville is throughout nervous and manly. It has indeed many affectations; but these, as has always

---

1   Novels by Walter Scott, published in 1814 and 1815 respectively.

been the case in the writings of Godwin, vanish whenever he grapples with violent emotions. He is at home in the very whirlwind of terrors, and seems to breathe with the greatest freedom in the most tempestuous atmosphere. Now that his "talent of fiction" has been fairly awakened, we hope he will not again be so unjust to himself and to the world, as to suffer it to fall asleep.

5. From an Anonymous Response to Lockhart, *Blackwood's Edinburgh Magazine* 2.10 (January 1818): 402–08

The review ... of Mr Godwin's recently published novel of Mandeville, is written with ability, and its general principles seem extremely just; if it shall be thought (as I confess I think it) much too encomiastic,[1] one may pardon that error, from its being on the good-natured side....

Amongst the literary improvements of the present time, none is more remarkable than that of the novel.... Latterly this department of literature has assumed a very superior style; and under the guidance both of male and female genius, has risen to a rank in the world of letters, little, if at all inferior to the most dignified productions of scholars and poets.... [The novel is] the epic of ordinary life. Its range is among the passions as well as the manners of men.... It was not till a late period that novels left the common track of stories of sentiment, or of manners, to become delineations of *character*. In this northern part of the kingdom, an author who began to write not more than about forty or fifty years ago, gave one of the first examples of a novel purely of character, with no more story than was contained in a sort of journal of the private life of a Man of Feeling, interspersed with little incidents, which served to develope that character.[2]

The present work of Mr Godwin is of this kind, a novel of character; of character of a very peculiar sort, ... Mandeville is an anomalous sort of being, and that anomaly is of a kind that hurts our feelings as much as it exceeds our belief. Mandeville is the creature of metaphysical sentiment; and indeed every page of the book is filled with metaphysics, which are not always just, and often obscure plain truths by the subtlety of the language in which they are meant to be conveyed. [The writer criticizes Godwin's style, citing several passages.] Mr Godwin, I must agree with the critic in your last Number, is a man of real genius.... He is a skilful anatomist of the human mind; but it is its morbid anatomy which he loves to trace, and, like some curious dissectors, he prefers subjects of disordered organs, which ordinary life and nature do not exhibit, but which some anomalous and singular

---

1 Full of praise.
2 Henry Mackenzie, *The Man of Feeling* (1771).

structure have produced.

The German story, "The Sorrows of Werter,"[1] exhibits a man of singular construction of mind, of a morbid sensibility, resembling that of Mandeville, whose fate is also decided by one incident affecting his pride, and rankling in a mind, which, like that of Mr Godwin's hero, acts chiefly upon itself, and is not called out of its sorrows by external circumstances, which might dissipate the gloom of its distresses and disappointments. But the child of *Goethe's* imagination has more of the stamp of nature upon him, and, with the darkness of misanthropy, has much less of its weaknesses or its vices. The sympathy which it excites is of a kind which we can feel without pain or disgust. Our sympathy with Mandeville (if his character will admit of any sympathy) is of a sterner cast, and we can only conceive an apology for the direness of his thoughts, and the violence of his conduct, in that derangement of mind, of which, as your correspondent justly remarks, we may admit as a transient disorder, or the temporary effect of extreme anguish, but which we do not easily bear as itself the basis of the distress which is exhibited....

The era in which the author places his tale is sufficiently alluded to in its details, and the historical anecdotes are chronologically and characteristically correct. Except in one instance, for which the author apologises in a note at the end of volume second, there is no anachronism in the facts or quotations. But it seems to me that there is, through the whole work, a more generally pervading anachronism in the style, both of the sentiment and the language, which does not altogether accord with that period. The refinement of both seems of a much later growth; the turn of the sentiments, indeed, is more allied to the modern German, than to the ancient English school....

I am rather surprised that your last month's correspondent has not taken notice of the *conclusion* of this novel, a conclusion "so lame and impotent," that but for the words THE END, at the bottom of the page, we would naturally turn over the leaf for another chapter. I am aware of the stale and rapid winding up of many novels, by the marriage of the hero and heroine, the comfortable settlement of such of the persons of the drama as deserve it, with such punishments or mortifications for the wicked and the undeserving, *as* poetical justice requires; but to leave every thing unsettled, as in the conclusion of Mandeville, is to part with the reader on bad terms—is to leave an irksome feeling on his mind, which, if the characters have excited any interest, he feels an injustice both to himself and them.... In the conclusion, as it relates to Mandeville himself, we feel his character not

---

1   *The Sorrows of Young Werther* (1774; rev. ed. 1787), by Johann Wolfgang von Goethe (1749–1832) was highly influential in the Romantic period.

well supported, in the distress which he seems to suffer from the circumstances in which his violent and unjustifiable conduct has left him; a distress mainly arising from the scar on his cheek and mouth, which spoils that beauty of countenance which he has before described himself as possessing. In the description of this scar, too, he is *surgically* technical, which seems to agree as ill with the situation as with the character of the narrator; and in the midst of his severe affliction, he disentangles a point of etymology with all the elaborate coolness of a scholiast.

6. From *The British Review and London Critical Journal* 9.21 (1818): 108–20

Mr. Godwin has produced one novel of no common interest [*Caleb Williams*].... It is not easy to see on what ground the author could expect that [*Mandeville*] should please; since there is no gradual succession of events to keep our curiosity in suspense; and the malignant passions of Mandeville repel, rather than attract, our sympathy. Mr. Godwin will perhaps say, that, to relish his work, we must not peruse it with the views with which we read the frivolous productions of the Minerva press;[1].... We reply, that a novel which does not amuse is a bad novel, whatever metaphysical merits it may possess; because amusement is its primary purpose: and, secondly, that no useful knowledge with respect to the formation of character can be derived from such a work as Mandeville....

Besides the want of an interesting story, there are two faults in this performance which render it tedious. In the first place, it consists of an endless repetition of the feelings and sentiments of one disgusting individual. It is not what Mandeville does, but how Mandeville feels, that is in every successive page obtruded upon us.... Secondly, Mr. Godwin is every where prone to the most extravagant exaggeration. Mandeville's uncle is sunk in apathy: this apathy does not merely cut him off from the active pursuit of life; it is so extreme, that even the utterance or the hearing of a few words exceeds his strength. Mandeville must be brought up amid melancholy scenery, because such an aspect of external nature is, according to Mr. Godwin's notions, favourable to the character with which his hero is to be invested. It is not, however, a gloominess of a common kind that will satisfy him....

We have still another ground of dissatisfaction with this work. Mandeville is an historical novel. The intermixture of fictitious persons and incidents with the actors and events of authentic history is at least a

---

1 A publishing house at the time which became a byword for sentimental and Gothic fiction.

delicate if not a questionable mode of writing. Truth can never be a gainer by such an union, nor is it often that fiction can be made more attractive by it.... Mr. Godwin, we think, has by no means succeeded in blending history with his tale. The time of the action is laid between the Irish insurrection, at the beginning of the civil war, and the Restoration of Charles II.... But the historical part and the fictitious have no close connection with each other: the tale does not illustrate the manners of the age, nor are the events of the age intimately interwoven with the substance of the tale. The consequence is, that the historical passages appear as awkward appendages to the performance rather than as constituent parts of it. The first forty pages, for example, are occupied with a description of the state of Ireland in 1640, which has nothing to do with any of the subsequent pages of the book.... Were the whole of this expunged, the story would lose nothing, though the book would be deprived of its best-written chapter.

[The reviewer then takes issue with Godwin, often incorrectly, on points of historical and legal detail, "want of proper moral feeling," inappropriate citation of scripture and an "elaborate," metaphoric style.]

7. From [James Mackintosh,] *The Edinburgh Magazine, and Literary Miscellany; A New Series of the Scots Magazine* 2 (1818): 57–65

[The reviewer begins with remarks on the state of the novel as a genre.] We have been led to make these desultory remarks by the perusal of Mr Godwin's Mandeville.... He has amply availed himself of the extensive and undefined limits of novel writing,—but without aiming to attract the notice of his readers by topics of temporary interest; and he not only displays, in a very striking manner, the present fashionable indifference to the artful construction of a fable,—but has been content on most occasions to dispense with even the more essential parts of a fictitious narrative,—varied scenery, picturesque description, and surprising incident. There is nevertheless an obvious desire, on the part of this distinguished writer, to gratify the prevailing appetite for deep emotion.... The time he has chosen for the appearance of his hero, is one of the most interesting epochs of English history, and the rank to which this personage belongs, and the scene of his scanty adventures, bring him into immediate contact with some of the most important public characters of that tempestuous period; but ... it is no part of Mr Godwin's design to depict the everyday manners of the age, or the giant forms that then figured on the stage,
...
... Whenever we submit to take Mr Godwin for our guide, we are

sure to be led into the company of beings, who, whether innocent or guilty, are almost all of them either wretched themselves, or the cause of wretchedness in others. Yet it is not because he is unable to conceive or describe all that is amiable and virtuous, and dignified in the human character—for the characters of the wife of St Leon and their son Charles [in Godwin's novel *St. Leon*], and of Henrietta and Clifford in the present tale, forbid such a supposition—that he delights to explore the dark recesses of the heart. Still it is by this strange predilection that Godwin in prose, and Byron in poetry, are distinguished from all other writers of the present age, not less than by the eminent talents which both of them devote to this uninviting branch of the anatomy of mind.

It is of less importance, however, to inquire into the views with which Mr Godwin has exhibited such a character as Mandeville, as to consider with what success he has executed the arduous task of attracting the notice of the public towards a personage apparently so revolting and unnatural. Yet that he actually has succeeded, in no ordinary degree, is put beyond all doubt by the favourable reception which his work has already experienced. [The reviewer outlines the story and ends by wishing that Godwin would deal with more cheerful topics.]

8. From Jean Cohen's Preface to His Translation of *Mandeville: Histoire anglaise du dix-septième siècle* (Paris: Bechet, 1818), vii–x, xiii–xv; trans. Rajan

[Godwin's second wife Mary Jane Godwin had been in France in May 1817, trying to interest people in the novel.]

The publication of a new work by a celebrated author who, for a long time, has ceased to write, is an interesting event for all the friends of literature. The novel *Adventures of Caleb Williams* fixed the reputation of M. Godwin; and we must admit that this reputation was, in many respects, merited.... Unfortunately it also contained veritable heresies in politics and morality, and when we say that the translation of Caleb Williams appeared in France in the year 1795, one will easily judge that the success of this work was less due to its real merit than to the very paradoxes that formed its worse part. In effect, what could have been more attractive for the friends of the revolution, than to see an English author declaring that the inhabitants of England, who enjoy the freest constitution in the world, and civil laws that are the most favourable to individual liberty, are nevertheless just as much slaves as the subjects of the Sophie[1] of Persia? ... Be that as it may, the vogue for Caleb Williams was such that five thousand copies sold out in a

---

1 Shah or sovereign.

short space. Will the novel that we are offering today to the public have such a brilliant success? It is this that we dare not flatter ourselves about. The name of M. Godwin will not fail, however, to give it some interest. We cannot hide the fact that Mandeville is far from having the value of Caleb Williams; the basic conception is lacking, and curiosity finds nothing attractive here. The goal of the author seems to have been to show in all its details the progress of hate in an ulcerated heart and exalted imagination.... The progress of the work being extremely simple, too much perhaps, the repetitions cannot fail to be frequent.... however, one cannot fail to recognize here a great knowledge of the human heart, and energetic thoughts. The author has had less occasion than in his works to show his political sentiments.... The action is supposed to occur under the protectorate of Cromwell; all the actors nevertheless are royalists, and, in this regard, we cannot pass over in silence an observation that has particularly struck us in the reading of this work. The English people were then divided into three parties: the cavaliers, the presbyterian royalists and the republicans. The author apparently shares the opinions of the last; Caleb Williams leaves no doubt of this. Despite this, we see in Mandeville that all the perfectly virtuous characters are cavaliers; the presbyterians play a slightly less good role, and the only republican who appears here is a ridiculous man who inspires no interest. Is this a concession that the author has made despite himself to truth?

Appendix D: Historical Background: The Commonwealth, Cromwell, the English Revolution, and the Restoration

1. From Godwin, *History of the Commonwealth of England from Its Commencement to the Restoration of Charles II*, 4 vols. (London: Henry Colburn, 1824–28), 1.1–6, 77–78

The History of the Commonwealth of England constitutes a chapter in the records of mankind, totally unlike any thing that can elsewhere be found. How nations and races of men are to be so governed as may be most conducive to the improvement and happiness of all, is one of the most interesting questions that can be offered to our consideration.... In ancient history we have various examples of republics established on the firmest foundation, and which seemed in several respects eminently to do credit to that form of government. In modern times the republican administration of a state has been chiefly confined to governments with a small territory; the Commonwealth of England is the memorable experiment in which that scheme of affairs has been tried upon a great nation....

A war between the king and the nation, or its representatives, necessarily led men to a scrutiny into the first principles of government. The admission of one man, either hereditarily, or for life only, into the place of a chief of a country, is an evidence of the infirmity of man. Nature has set up no difference between a king and other men; a king therefore is purely the creation of our own hands....

Ideas like these unavoidably obtruded themselves into the minds of men engaged in a long and somewhat doubtful resistance against the encroachments and excesses of kingly power; and the result could not be otherwise, than that some men of a more cautious and unadventuring character, would be desirous as far as possible of retaining the elements of the old government, while others, more speculative and daring, would be anxious to seize so favourable an opportunity for reducing the state of their country to such a condition, as seemed in their eyes most agreeable to the simple dictates of reason....

Such was the precise state of the feelings of the two parties about the close of the year 1644; and it is of the republicans or commonwealths-men that it is the purpose of this work specially to treat. They were a set of men new in this country; and they may be considered as having become extinct at the Revolution in 1688. It will not be the object of these pages to treat them, as has so often been done, with indiscriminate contumely.[1] They were many of them, men of liberal minds, and bountifully endowed with the treasures of intellect. That their enterprise terminated in miscarriage is certain; ... the English intellect and moral feeling were probably not sufficiently ripe for a republican government: it may be, that a republican government would at no time be a desirable acquisition for the people of this country....

... It was their aim to new mould the character of the people of England. The nation had hitherto subsisted under a king; they were desirous to change the government into a republic. Nothing can be more unlike than the different frames of public mind demanded under these two forms of government. Wherever a court exists, and possesses considerable authority in a country, the manners and habits of the court will diffuse themselves on every side. In such a country there must always be a certain degree of frivolity and suppleness, an artificial character, and an outside carriage, not precisely flowing from the heart of the man who presents himself, but intended to answer a temporary purpose, and taken up with a design to win the good graces of him to whom it is addressed....

... The republicans in the Long Parliament were called upon to endeavour to substitute, for the manners of a court ... a severe, a manly, and an independent mode of feeling. If there were many religious enthusiasts among these leaders, on the other hand we well know there were men who were not the slaves of prejudice. The religious enthusiast himself, if he is a man of high capacity, will not by this particular bias of mind be robbed of his characteristic penetration.

2. From John Thelwall, *The Tribune* 43 (3 June 1795): 186–92

[Thelwall (1764–1834) had been Godwin's friend but they came to a parting of the ways over the latter's radical activism, which Godwin saw as precipitating violence. Thelwall's discussion of Cromwell is part of an argument for why the French Revolution will succeed where that of 1649 failed.]

... Persons who have read history superficially, observing the castrophe [*sic*] of the *English Revolution* in 1649, are inclined to suppose that a similar castrophe will take place in *France*; and that either the present Dauphin will be restored to the throne, like the son of *Charles* the first; or else that some other *dynasty* will be set up by the great men of that country, and royalty be again triumphant in that nation.... Were the revolution of 1649 in *England* and of 1789 in *France* produced by

---

1 Contempt.

similar causes? Are the circumstances of society in *France* now such as the circumstances of society in *England* were at that time? and have the same steps been taken or the same phenomena appeared in *France* during the present struggle as appeared in England during the struggle to which I am appealing? ...

Let us compare then the genius of the two revolutions.—The English revolution in 1649 was produced not so much by the luxury, the extravagance, and the profligacy of the court, together with a state of bankruptcy in the nation, as it was by certain causes, powerful indeed in their operation, but confined in their immediate action to a narrower sphere. The plain and simple truth is, that since the overthrow of our Saxon institutions [by the Norman Conquest of 1066], the sun of Liberty had never shone, with unclouded beams, upon this unhappy country....

When literature began to dawn over the western hemisphere, knowledge (though we were rather late in hailing the sacred beam) was not entirely neglected in England. In the reign of Elizabeth, who certainly was not less tyrannical than most of her predecessors, yet, as letters became considerably cultivated among particular classes of society, mankind began to awake from their lethargy; and though, under her vigorous administration, they were not strong enough boldly to demand their rights, yet the growth and progress of literature enabled them, under the succeeding reigns, to claim, with a firmer tone, a restoration of the ancient rights of *Englishmen*. They succeeded in a considerable degree, time after time, in the work, of political amelioration. Unfortunately at that time, however, the light of science was diffused only through a narrow circle: it had broken down, indeed, the walls of cloisters and monasteries: it had travelled beyond the studies of bishops and great peers; and the gentry of the country began to think that it was no disgrace to be able to read and write. But unfortunately the great mass of the people were not enlightened; and therefore we find that, in the reign of *Charles* the First, the people were only led forward by a few intelligent minds—men of great capacity and great personal courage, who led on the people, not so much by disseminating information, as by that dependance in which, on account of their large property, they continued to hold so large a portion of the country.

There was, however, a very *active spirit* of another kind among the people. They had light indeed (inward light) which, though it came not through the optics of reason, produced a considerable ferment in their blood, and made them cry out for that liberty, the very meaning of which they did not comprehend. In fact, the mass of the people were quickened, not by the generous spirit of liberty, but by the active spirit of fanaticism. Such, then, was the state of society at the time of the Revolution, that terminated in the first stage in 1649, and in the second stage with the restoration of *Charles* the Second. Among the leaders who stood forward, and signalized themselves in that cause,[1] there were certainly men whose virtues, courage, and transcendent talents, will demand admiration, so long as the *English* language shall exist. It is to be lamented, however, that all the characters in that revolution were not men of equal virtue. I need only name *Oliver Cromwell*; who, though he set out perhaps, with as large a portion of the love of liberty as was possible for a hypocritical fanatic, yet undoubtedly in the end proved himself to be, not a reforming patriot, but an ambitious usurper....

... What, then, was *Oliver Cromwell?* What was the size and capacity of his mind? and what were the projects in which he was engaged, and the nature of the system which he attempted to establish?—The acuteness of Cromwell's talents cannot possibly be denied. Every person who peruses the history of the period, will perceive that, through every stage of his political conduct, he always seized, and turned to his own advantage, every political event, whether in the first instance apparently prosperous or disastrous, that occurred. He had therefore a mind not only bold and enterprising, but capacious, versatile, and penetrating.... But *Cromwell* was always obliged to depend upon the expedients of the moment.... the whole *history* of his government—for I mean to shew you that there was nothing like system in it!—the whole history of his government is nothing but a history of expedients, to which he appealed under the particular circumstances in which he was placed.... Thus the *Protectorate*, or, as it is called, the Republic, continued as long as he lived, because the superior *activity* of his mind, the terror of his name, and that sort of fanatic eloquence which he possessed, kept all other persons in awe;.... But *Cromwell* had not a mind capable of calculating upon the passions of mankind in the mass, nor of viewing in distant prospect the events and causes likely to influence the politics of future years: he was therefore incapable of forming a system that could be rendered permanent, and contribute to the advantage either of his own particular family, or of the nation in general. Accordingly, we find that this government of expedients crumbled into dust as soon as he expired....

Thus, then, the revolution in 1649 was not the revolution of the great body of an enlightened nation, but a revolution produced in the first instance by a few intelligent minds, who stimulated the people to act upon principles which they did not comprehend, and was afterwards supported upon the shoulders of an individual, whose talents, though equal to the task of supporting the weight he had taken upon

---

1 Identified themselves with that cause.

them, were not sufficient to frame a system by which that weight could be supported, when he was taken away.

There is another circumstance also of considerable importance, relative to the revolution of 1649; and by means of which *Cromwell* was enabled to usurp the dominion of the country.

Citizens, there are two species of popularity upon which power may be built ... namely, the popularity obtained in the senate, and the popularity obtained in the field of battle.... these two kinds of popularity, for the benefit and advantage of the people, in times of revolution in particular, ought to be kept separate; for, when they are united, they throw so great a weight of influence into the hands of the individual so uniting them, that he always eventually possesses the power ... of overthrowing the liberty for which he appeared to contend....

Cromwell possessed this united popularity. He had spoken for the people, and braved all the dangers of being their champion, in the senate; he had exposed his breast, with manly resolution, to the daggers of courtiers.... In defiance of these, he had dared to step forward, to vindicate the insulted rights of Britain; and had been successful, in his senatorian exertions, in rousing the people to a manly and virtuous resistance. Cromwell also was a leader of armies: he fought for the cause for which he spoke....

Such, then, were part of the causes of the weakness of the revolutionary principle in *Britain*. Such were, in part, the causes of the power which *Cromwell* possessed, of usurping dominion in the country, instead of establishing liberty and justice.

Seeing, thus, what was the genius and nature of the revolution in 1649; and perceiving that it was propt in the first instance only by a few, and in the latter period only by an individual man, we cannot be surprized (the leaders of that revolution being cut off, and the great prop and support of it having fallen beneath the stroke of fate) that the revolutionary spirit became extinct; and that the house of *Stuart* was restored, with all those disgraceful appendages of unlimited power, which that house of *Stuart*, to its own destruction, exercised upon this harrassed and insulted nation.

3. **From Godwin, *History of the Commonwealth of England from Its Commencement to the Restoration of Charles II*, 4 vols. (London: Henry Colburn, 1824–28), 4.v–vii, 566–67, 579–608**

[The final volume of *HCE*, published in 1828, deals with the individual history of Cromwell within the general history of the Protectorate.]

The history of the reign of Cromwel is a difficult theme.... He abruptly dissolved the parliaments of 1654 and 1656.... He is affirmed tyrannically to have dismissed from their offices three judges of the land; and he sent three eminent counsel to the Tower ... He imposed taxes and made laws, solely by his own authority and that of his council.... Yet few have questioned the superlative talents of Cromwel as a statesman.... It has also been said, that Cromwel's life and all his arts were exhausted together, and that, if he had lived a short time longer, he must have lost the ascendancy he so surprisingly acquired. This assertion is here controverted.

... The object of the preceding [volumes] was to describe the unavailing efforts of virtuous and magnanimous men in the perhaps visionary attempt to establish a republic in England. The business of this is to delineate the reign of a usurper, who seems also to have had the idea of becoming a public benefactor, but who was not less unsuccessful in the issue of his design than they were....

... [Cromwel] had a frame of mind that no complication of difficulties could ever succeed to inspire with a doubt of his power to conquer them. The fertility of his conceptions, like the intrepidity of his spirit, was incapable of being exhausted. We seek in romance for characters, with qualities enabling them to achieve incredible adventures. In the Lord Protector of the Commonwealth of England we find a real personage, whose exploits do not fall short of all that the wildest imagination had ever the audacity to feign. [Volume 4 is some 600 pages; what follows is from the final two chapters.]

The death of Cromwel shortly followed upon that of his daughter. It was probably occasioned by the total breaking up of his constitution. Though he was only in the sixtieth year of his age, he had gone through that which might well try a frame, originally of the hardiest make.... The life of a man who purposes to found a new dynasty, is essentially different from that of a prince who succeeds to an hereditary throne. He had cares on his mind almost more than human strength could bear.... He was incessantly threatened with assassination....

Having traced the reign of Cromwel from its rise to its termination, it now becomes one of the duties of history to look back on the sum of the path through which we have travelled....

The government of a nation, particularly in such circumstances, is a complicated science, with difficulty mastered in theory, and with difficulty reduced to practice. It is comparatively easy for the philosopher in his closet to invent imaginary schemes of policy and to shew how mankind, if they were without passions and without prejudices, might best be united in the form of a political community. [Noting that the "character of Cromwel has been little understood," Godwin goes on to describe his concern for the poor, achievements in terms of reforming the law, supporting scholars, and protecting the universities; he emphasizes the problems Cromwell faced in the presence of a living King in exile and religious factions.]

A third thing of material importance to Cromwel, was the religious state of the community. In this respect the English nation was much divided. Many still adhered to the discipline and forms of the old episcopal church as patronised by Elizabeth: the bulk of the nation seems to have been wedded to the exclusive doctrines of presbyterianism: and a party by no means contemptible for either numbers or importance, were the strenuous advocates of independence and toleration. Cromwel courted the presbyterians, but secretly, and in his heart, was the friend of the independents.

The latter of these parties, with all their numerous divisions, demanded the greatest degree of attention, because of the fervour of their religious enthusiasm. A large portion of the independents, and the whole body of the anabaptists, were strenuous republicans, and more directly and openly thwarted Cromwel in their favourite projects, than any other set of men in the nation.

Nothing can be of greater importance in the state than the religious dispositions of its members. It not unusually happens that, when all other things give way, these will prove invincible to all the arts and the force that can be brought against them. The influence of the priesthood, the inspirations of fanaticism, and the salvation of souls, will often present an impenetrable barrier to the designs of the politician. And the influence of religious considerations was never so powerful as in the times of the English commonwealth.

... The lord protector of England had no friends, except the few that he made so by his personal qualities, and his immediate powers of conciliation. The royalists, and the votaries of liberty in general, the episcopalians, the presbyterians and the independents, the fanatics of all descriptions, and a great part of the army were his inveterate foes. He stood alone, with little else to depend upon, than the energies of his mind, and the awe which his character imposed on unwilling subjects....

Reviewing all [the] qualities and dispositions in the lord protector of England, we should be almost disposed to place him in the number of the few excellent princes that have swayed a sceptre, were it not for the gross and unauthorised manner in which he climbed to this eminence, by forcibly dispersing the remains of the Long Parliament, that parliament by which he had originally been intrusted with the command, and then promulgating a constitution, called the Government of the Commonwealth, which originated singly in the council of military officers. To this we must add, that he became the chief magistrate solely through his apostasy,[1] and by basely deceiving and deserting the illustrious band of patriots with whom he had till that time been associated in the cause of liberty....

How happened this? It was not from the want of talents and the most liberal intentions. But he was not free. He governed a people that was hostile to him. His reign therefore was a reign of experiments. He perpetually did the thing he desired not to do, and was driven from one inconsistent and undesirable mode of proceeding to another, as the necessity of the situation in which he was placed impelled him....

The result of all this was most unfortunate for the friends of a republican government, and for those who desired the establishment of monarchy in a new race of kings, and most favourable for the adherents of the house of Stuart....

What would have been the result, if Cromwel's life had been prolonged to the established period of human existence, or ten years longer than it was ... we should enquire. His character perpetually rose in the estimation of his subjects. He appeared to them every day more like a king, and less like the plain and unambitious descendant of the Cromwels of Hinchinbrook and Ramsey.... His capacity for government became daily more unquestionable. He looked into every thing; he provided for every thing; he stood, himself unmoved, yet causing every threatening and tempestuous phenomenon by which he was assailed, to fly before him.

... In a word, we are almost compelled to conclude, that, if he had lived ten years longer, the system of his rule would continually have grown more firm and substantial, and the purposes and ideas to the accomplishment of which he had devoted all the powers of his soul, would not have been antiquated and annihilated almost as soon as they were deprived of his energies to maintain them.

It was not difficult for a sagacious mind, rising above the atmosphere of prejudice, to foresee, from the death of Cromwel, that the Restoration of Charles the Second was inevitable. The details of what occurred in the interval may at some time be given; but whether by the writer of these volumes under the title of a History of the Restoration, is altogether uncertain.

---

1 Broadly speaking, reversal of one's principles. In this case, Cromwell began as a Republican and made himself virtually a monarch.

4. **From Gilbert Burnet, *History of His Own Time. From the Restoration of Charles II to the Conclusion of the Treaty of Peace at Utrecht, in the Reign of Queen Anne*, 4 vols. (1724; rpt. London: A. Millar, 1753), 1.63–69**

[Burnet (1643–1715), Bishop of Salisbury from 1689, was a religious moderate. His *History of His Own Time* was one of Godwin's historical sources.]

I will leave all that relates to the King's trial and death to common historians, knowing nothing that is particular of that great transaction, which was certainly one of the most amazing scenes in history. Ireton[1] was the person that drove it on: for Cromwell was on the whole in some suspence about it. Ireton had the principles and the temper of a Cassius in him:[2] He stuck at nothing that might have turned England to a Commonwealth.... The Presbyterians and the body of the City were much against it, and were every where fasting and praying for the King's preservation. There was not above 8000 of the Army about the town: But these were selected out of the whole Army, as the most engaged in enthusiasm: And they were kept at prayer in their way almost day and night, except when they were upon duty: So that they were wrought up to a pitch of fury, that struck a terrour into all people. On the other hand the King's party was without spirit: And, as many of themselves have said to me, they could never believe his death was really intended till it was too late. They thought all was pageantry to strike a terrour, and to force the King to such concessions as they had a mind to extort from him.

The King himself shewed a calm and a composed firmness, which amazed all people; and that so much the more, because it was not natural to him. It was imputed to a very extraordinary measure of supernatural assistance.... Thus he died greater than he had lived; and shewed, that which has been observed of the whole race of the Stuarts, that they bore misfortunes better than prosperity. His reign both in peace and war was a continual series of errours; So that it does not appear that he had a true judgment of things. He was out of measure set on following his humour, but unreasonably feeble to those whom

---

1 Henry Ireton (c. 1611–51) was Cromwell's son-in-law and a General in the New Model Army during the Civil War. Though he was not an extremist and was actually in favour of constitutional monarchy, he was a person of principle rather than expediency and compromise.

2 A character in Shakespeare's *Julius Caesar*. While opposed to Caesar's accumulation of power, he is also an opportunist, which is not how Godwin saw Ireton.

he trusted, chiefly to the Queen. He had too high a notion of the regal power, and thought that every opposition to it was rebellion. He minded little things too much, and was more concerned in the drawing of a paper than in fighting a battle. He had a firm aversion to Popery, but was much inclined to a middle way between Protestants and Papists, by which he lost the one without gaining the other....

... In the King's death the ill effect of extreme violent counsels discovered itself. Ireton hoped that by this all men concerned in it would become irreconcileable to monarchy, and would act as desperate men, and destroy all that might revenge that blood. But this had a very different effect. Something of the same nature had happened in lower instances before: But they were not the wiser for it. The Earl of Strafford's death made all his former errours be forgot: It raised his character, and cast a lasting odium on that way of proceeding; whereas he had sunk in his credit by any censure lower than death, and had been little pitied, if not thought justly punished.... But the recoiling of cruel counsels on the authors of them never appeared more eminently than in the death of King Charles the first, whose serious and christian deportment in it made all his former errours be entirely forgot, and raised a compassionate regard to him, that drew a lasting hatred on the actors, and was the true occasion of the great turn of the nation in the year 1660 [when the Stuarts were restored to the throne].

Appendix E: Religion and the Politics of Church Government

1. From John Milton, *Of Prelatical Episcopacy* (London: Thomas Underhill, 1641)

[Milton (1608–74), who was Cromwell's Secretary for Foreign Tongues, wrote a number of anti-prelatical tracts that attack the episcopal form of church government in 1641–42, as well as anti-monarchist works in 1648 and 1650.]

Epyscopacy, as it is taken for an Order in the *Church* above a *Presbyter*, or as wee commonly name him, the Minister of a Congregation, is either of Divine constitution, or of humane. If onely of humane, we have the same humane priviledge, that all men have ever had since *Adam*, being born free, and in the Mistresse Iland of all the *British*, to retain this *Episcopacy* or to remove it.... If it bee of *Divine* constitution, to satisfie us fully in that, the Scripture onely is able, it being the onely Book left us of *Divine* authority.... Through all which Booke can be no where, either by plaine Text, or solid reasoning found any difference between a Bishop, and a Presbyter, save that they be two names to signify the same order.

2. From John Milton, *The Reason of Church Government* (1642), Chapter 7

As for those many sects and divisions rumoured abroad, it is not hard to perceive that they are partly the mere fictions and false alarms of the prelates, thereby to cast amazements and terrors into the hearts of weaker Christians, that they should not venture to change the present deformity of the church for fear of what I know what worse circumstances.... If sects and schisms be turbulent in the unsettled estate of a church, while it lies under the amending hand, it best beseems our Christian courage to think they are but as the throes and pangs that go before the birth of reformation, and that the work itself is now in doing. For if we look but on the nature of elemental and mixed things, we know they cannot suffer any change of one kind or quality into another without the struggle of contrarieties.

3. From Godwin, *History of the Commonwealth of England from Its Commencement to the Restoration of Charles II*, 4 vols. (London: Henry Colburn, 1824–28), 1.42–43, 48–49, 80

The Reformation in England dates its commencement from the year 1532. It was conducted in all its early operations by that capricious and arbitrary monarch, Henry the Eighth.... Various causes contributed to render the progress of the Reformation in this country particularly fluctuating and uncertain; and the early reformers here were greatly divided among themselves.

On the continent the Reformation shewed itself in two forms. In Sweden, in Denmark, and in some parts of Germany, where the authority of the prince was most considerable, its principles were mitigated, and the policy of its conductors appears to have been, to banish the more glaring corruptions of the church of Rome, but to preserve the hierarchy and the forms of religious worship as nearly as might be the same. This mode of proceeding seemed best to accord with monarchical government. The church served to give lustre to the throne; ... In Holland, in Switzerland, and in Geneva, the process had been somewhat different. The reformers there, not being obliged to consult the inclinations of a potentate reigning among them, were less disposed to imitate the institutions of the church of Rome, and thought it more reasonable to consult the primitive pattern and simplicity of the Gospel. The consequence was the establishment of a parity among their clergy, ...

At the time of the meeting of the Long Parliament there were three modes of thinking prevalent among the English nation on the subject of church-government. The first was that of the king and hierarchy, the men who desired to retain the church-establishment such as it had been fixed in the reign of Elizabeth: ... The next party on the subject of church-government was that, which had studied the models that were offered in Scotland, Holland, Switzerland, and France, which considered this system best to accord with the precepts of the New Testament, and aimed therefore at no less than the utter abolition of the episcopal order. There was a third, but an inferior party, that preserved a medium between these two, and was disposed to preserve the order of bishops, but desired to retrench something of their pomp and political importance, and to elevate the presbyters, so as to give them a share in that authority which was now engrossed by the bishops alone....

... The presbyterian system of church-government was in many respects well adapted to foster republican sentiments;....

4. From Samuel Rutherford, *Lex Rex* (1644)

[*Lex Rex* means "The Law is King," which is also the book's subtitle. Rutherford (c. 1600–61), who was Professor of Divinity at the University of St. Andrews in Scotland, expresses the Presbyterian opposition to monarchy.]

[The Presbyterians] hold (I believe with warrant of God's word): if the king refuse to reform religion, the inferior judges and assembly of godly pastors and other church officers may reform [it].... Reformation of religion is a personal act that belongeth to all, even to any one private person according to his place.

All the forged inconsistency betwixt presbyteries and monarchies is an opposition with absolute monarchy, and concludeth with a like strength against parliaments and all synods of either side, against the Law and Gospel reached, to which kings and kingdoms are subordinate.

...The law saith there is no law of nature agreeing to all living creatures for superiority; for by no reason in nature hath a boar dominion over a boar, a lion over a lion, ... I conceive all jurisdiction of man over man to be, as it were, artificial and positive ... if you except that subjection of children to parents and wife to the husband.

... Nor is aristocracy anything but diffused and enlarged monarchy, and monarchy is nothing but contracted aristocracy.... And wherever God appointed a king, he never appointed him absolute and a sole independent agent.

... No society hath liberty to be without all government, for God hath given to every society ... a faculty of preserving themselves, and warding off violence and injuries.... We teach that government is natural, not voluntary; but the way and manner of government is voluntary.

5. From William Everard, Gerrard Winstanley, et al., *The True Levellers' Standard Advanced* (1649)

[The Levellers, referred to by Hilkiah in the novel (p. 127, note 2), were democratic politicians but did not go as far as the Diggers or True Levellers, who were radical democrats, as we also see from the reference to women. See also Introduction, pp. 33, 38.]

In the beginning of Time, the great Creator Reason, made the Earth to be a Common Treasury, to preserve Beasts, Birds, Fishes, and Man, the lord that was to govern this Creation. For Man had Domination given to him over the Beasts, Birds, and Fishes. But not one word was spoken in the beginning, That one branch of mankind should rule over another.

And the Reason is this, Every single man, Male and Female, is a perfect Creature of himself; and the same Spirit that made the Globe dwels in man to govern the Globe; so that the flesh of man, being subject to Reason, his Maker, hath him to be his Teacher and Ruler within himself, therefore needs not run abroad after any Teacher and Ruler without him....

But since humane flesh ... began to delight himself in the objects of the Creation more than in the Spirit Reason and Righteousness, who manifests himself to be the indweller in the Five Sences ... then he fell into blindness of mind and weakness of heart and runs abroad for a Teacher and Ruler ... and thereby the Spirit was killed, and man was brought into bondage and became a greater slave to such of his own kind then the Beasts of the field were to him.

6. **From *Encyclopedia Londinensis, completed, digested, and arranged*, by *John Wilkes of Milland House*, 6 vols. (London: J. Adlard, 1810), 6.668–74**

Since the times of Elizabeth, that religious sect had been gaining ground in England, which, from the pretended greater purity of their manners, were called *puritans*. Of all other sects, this was the most obnoxious to monarchy; and the tenets of it more calculated to support that imagined equality which obtains in a state of nature.... No period, since England had a name, could furnish so many instances of courage, abilities, and virtue as the fatal opposition called forth into action, AD 1642. Both sides, equally confident of the justice of their cause, appealed to God to judge the rectitude of their intentions.... The death of Laud[1] was followed by a total alteration of the ceremonies of the church. The liturgy was, by a public act, abolished the day he died, as if he had been the only obstacle to its formal removal. The church of England was in all respects brought to a conformity with the puritanical establishment.... Yet from the moment the puritans began to be apparently united, and ranked under one common denomination of Presbyterians, they began again to divide into fresh sects, each possessing different views and interests. One part of the house was composed of Presbyterians, strictly so called; the other, though a minority, of Independents, a new sect that had lately been introduced, and rapidly gained ground among the vulgar.

The difference between the two sects would be hardly worth mentioning, had not their religious opinions influenced their political

---

1 See p. 177, note 1.

conduct. The church of England has appointed bishops of clerical ordination and a book of common prayer. The Presbyterians exclaimed against both; they were for having the church governed by clergymen elected by the people, and prayers made without premeditation.... The Independents went farther; they excluded all the clergy; they maintained that every man might pray in public, exhort his audience, and explain the scriptures. The political system kept pace with the religious. Not content with reducing the king to a first magistrate, which was the aim of the Presbyterians, this sect aspired at the abolition not only of all monarchy, but of all subordination. They maintained, and they perhaps maintained right, that all men were born equal; but they alleged also, that no accidental or artificial institutions could destroy this equality; and there they were deceived. Could such a plan of government as theirs be practicable, it would, no doubt, remove all the causes of envy and jealousy among men; but this were impossible.

7. From Samuel R. Gardiner, *History of the Civil War, 1642–49* (1889), 2, 22, 45

... between the Presbyterianism of England and ... Scotland there was a great gulf. It is indeed possible to transfer the external institutions of a political or religious system from one nation to another, but it is not possible to transfer the spirit by which that system is animated.... The historical development of the Scottish nation favoured the predominance of the clergy, whereas the historical development of the English nation favoured the predominance of the laity.

It was therefore from no zeal for Presbyterianism as a divine institution that its English supporters rallied round it. It was to them chiefly an ecclesiastical form of Parliamentarianism, in which the Assembly was to work under the control of the Houses, and the parochial clergy were to work under the control of their lay elders.

The name "Presbyterian," in short, by fixing attention exclusively upon the ecclesiastical aims of the party which bore it, has been the source of much unintentional misunderstanding.... To make King and Church responsible to Parliament was the real aim of the Presbyterian party, and every year which passed after the Restoration made it more evident that, for the time at least, the most substantial gains of the long conflict fell to those who concentrated their efforts on this object.

It was inevitable that a party thus constituted should be intensely conservative, for the very reason that up to a certain point it had been driven to be revolutionary....

Presbyterianism had many faults, but at least its existence rendered impossible a return to a mode of government which had been tried and found wanting. It rested in the Church on an organisation proceeding out of the nation itself in the form of elderships, classes, and assemblies, rather than an organisation proceeding from the King. In the State it rested upon the House of Commons.... In the hands of men of expansive genius such a system may have acquired, at least for a time, a hold upon the nation itself. Its leaders were, however, by no means men of expansive genius.

[But] The Presbyterians had done their work. They had overthrown the monarchy, never, in the sense in which Charles understood the word, to rise again in England.... Whether Cromwell and the Independents would succeed where the Presbyterians had failed, in establishing a government which had the elements of endurance, remained to be seen.

8. From David Hume, "Of the Parties of Great Britain" (1741)

[Best known as a philosopher and the author of *A Treatise of Human Nature* (1739), Hume (1711–76) was also famous for his *History of England* (1754–62) which, unlike *HCE*, wants to put the Revolution of 1649 in the past and build on that of 1688. Hume's *Essays* were initially intended for a journal but published in book form in editions from 1741–54. His political essays, including this one, are a mixture of the liberal and conservative, and function as an extension of the *History* from 1688, where it ends, to 1740.]

This observation, concerning the propensity of priests to the government of a single person, is not true with regard to one sect only.... But if a prince has the choice of both, it is easy to see, that he will prefer the episcopal to the presbyterian form of government, both because of the greater affinity between monarchy and episcopacy, and because of the facility, which a prince finds, in such a government, of ruling the clergy, by means of their ecclesiastical superiors.

If we consider the first rise of parties in ENGLAND, during the great rebellion, we shall find, that it was conformable to this general theory. [Hume then describes the conflict between supporters of the king (Cavaliers) and those of parliament (Roundheads); see also Introduction, p. 32.] ROUND-HEAD and CAVALIER were merely parties of principle; neither of which disowned either monarchy or liberty; but the former party inclined most to the republican part of our government, the latter to the monarchical.... The commonwealth's men, and the partizans of absolute power, lay concealed in both parties....

... The established clergy were episcopal; the non-conformists presbyterian: So that all things concurred to throw the former, without reserve, into the king's party; and the latter into that of parliament.

Everyone knows the event of this quarrel, fatal to the king first, to the parliament afterwards. After many confusions and revolutions, the royal family was at last restored.... Charles II was not made wiser by the example of his father.... New parties arose, under the appellations of *Whig* and *Tory*, which have continued ever since to confound and distract our government. To determine the nature of these parties is, perhaps, one of the most difficult problems, that can be met with, and is a proof that history may contain questions, as uncertain as any to be found in the most abstract sciences. [Hume then describes, due to the difficulty of deciding which position really results in liberty, the overlaps, crossovers, and reversals between the positions of Tory and Whig from the Restoration to the Glorious Revolution and beyond. He concludes:] A TORY, therefore, since the *revolution*, may be defined in a few words, to be *a lover of monarchy, though without abandoning liberty; and a partizan of the family of* STUART. As a WHIG may be defined to be *a lover of liberty though without renouncing monarchy; and a friend to the settlement in the* PROTESTANT *line.*

Appendix F: Ireland

1. From Laurence Echard, *The History of England from the First Entrance of Julius Caesar and the Romans to the Conclusion of the Reign of King James the Second*, 3 vols. (London: Jacob Tonson, 1720), 513

[Echard (1670–1730) was a British historian and clergyman. His pro-English account of the Irish Rebellion, which Godwin read, can be contrasted with Godwin's more ambivalent account in Appendices F2 and F3 below.]

To compleat the Miseries of three Kingdoms, about three Weeks before the King left *Scotland*, there arose a sudden storm in *Ireland*, or rather an impetuous Hurricane that bore down all before it. It was a rebellion surprising and prodigious, as had been scarce known in any Age; such as can hardly be parellell'd for the numberless Acts of Perfidiousness and Barbarity; and the first Sound of it came like a most terrible Thunder-Clap to the *English* Nation, which prov'd of Infinite mischief to the King's Affairs. This astonishing Concussion broke out in all Parts of the Kingdom upon one Day, the 23rd of *October*; which by a close and deep conspiracy of the *Irish* took Effect after an unheard-of Manner. The Papists and old Natives, taking advantage of the present Posture of Affairs in *England*, resolv'd to destroy all the *English* Protestants, and to secure the Kingdom in their own Hands. Their Design upon *Dublin* was miraculously discover'd the Night before it was to be executed, and the Surprisal of the Castle prevented; and the principal Conspirators, who were to undertake it, as *Mac-Mahon, Mac-Guire*[1] and others, apprehended. But in the other Parts of the Kingdom, they exactly observed the appointed Day without hearing of the Disappointment of their Friends in *Dublin*: So a general Insurrection spread it self like a Deluge over the whole Country; in such an inhuman and merciless Manner, that forty or fifty Thousand of the *English* Protestants were massacred, without Distinction of Age, Sex, or Quality, before they suspected any Danger, or cou'd provide for their Defence, in Towns or elsewhere....

The chief Man and Ringleader in this Insurrection was Sir *Phelim Oneale*, a Gentleman of *English* Education, once a Protestant of Lincoln's-Inn, who with his Brother, and some others, carry'd on their

---

1   Hugh Oge MacMahon (1606?–44) and Conor Maguire (1616–45) were Irish landowners.

Designs with such Regularity and Secrecy, that no sufficient Discovery cou'd be made. And indeed at this time there was such outward Appearances of a settled Tranquillity, that scarce any Suspicion remain'd: For the ancient Prejudices and Animosities, which had frequently been shewn between the *Irish* and the *English*, seem'd now to have been bury'd in a Conjunction of their Affections and National Obligations. The two Nations had now liv'd together forty Years in Peace with great Security and Satisfaction, which had in a manner consolidated them into one body, fastned with all those Bonds of Friendship, Alliance and Consanguinity, as might have form'd a perpetual Union between them. Therefore it is more needful to inquire into the Causes of so sudden and strange an Alteration, and the Occasions and Inducements that these miserable People had to venture upon such daring Attempts, and run such desperate Hazards.

First, they observ'd, that by the *English* governors they were generally look'd upon as a *Conquer'd Nation*, and seldom treated like natural or free-born Subjects; and particularly complain'd, that upon the Account of the last Rebellion under *Tyronne*, six whole Counties were forfeited to the Crown, and very little restor'd to the Natives, though several of them were innocent, but a great Part bestow'd by King *James* on his Countrymen the *Scots*, who had made notorious Encroachments upon them.... Secondly, they believ'd their ancient Religion in imminent Danger; For they found that since the Beginning of the long Parliament in *England*, unusual severities were us'd against the Papists in *England*.... Thirdly, the Example of the *Scots* was a particular Incitement and Encouragment, as appear'd from the first Discoverers, who declar'd, *They did all in Imitation of* Scotland.... Fourthly, the taking off the Earl of Strafford[1] did not a little contribute to the ensuing Tragedy, whose Vigour and Vigilance kept them regular and obedient.... Lastly, the Army of Eight Thousand Men, rais'd for the Suppressing the *Scots*, being by the instance of the *English* Parliament disbanded, the Country was annoy'd by those Soldiers, who wou'd not return to their former Employments, but were ready for any bloody Enterprize: And tho' the *Spanish* Ambassadors desir'd to take them into the Service of their Master, the Parliament Leaders oppos'd it and defeated the Design; for which Piece of Service, Mr. Pym[2] is said to have receiv'd five Thousand Pounds from the *French* Ambassador. This ungovern'd Army, together with the encreasing Dissensions between the King and his Parliament, was the greatest Encourage-

---

1 See p. 66, note 3 and p. 68, note 2.

2 John Pym (1584–1643), critic of James I and Charles I, and a leader of the
   Long Parliament. Pym was one of the five men whose attempted arrest by
   Charles in the House of Commons triggered the Civil War.

ment of all, and caus'd the *Irish* not only to hope for an Inlargement of their Privileges, but a Breaking off their Yoak and Dependency upon the Crown of England.

2. From Godwin, *History of the Commonwealth of England from Its Commencement to the Restoration of Charles II*, 4 vols. (London: Henry Colburn, 1824–28), 1.213–39

[Unlike Echard, Godwin does not see Irish history as a digression from English history.]

The affairs of Ireland have not yet been mentioned, that, by drawing them together in a comprehensive view; the reader might the better comprehend the way in which transactions there operated upon what was going on in England....

The policy of James with respect to Ireland had been, to send over numerous colonies from Great Britain, with the alleged purpose of reclaiming the wild inhabitants, and improving the neglected soil, so as to render that country a valuable appendage to the empire. This had for a series of years had the effect to give an appearance of peace and tranquillity to Ireland.... But the real state of the people was not so favourable as it seemed. Beside all other prejudices, the natives of the island were Catholics, and the settlers Protestants, for the most part puritans and presbyterians....This was made worse by a vexatious and incessant inquisition into the titles by which estates were held, in which no length of possession was admitted to constitute right, but any flaw that might be found in the original patent placed the property again at the disposal of the crown, and accordingly it was given anew to such persons as were most favoured at court. The stern and unconciliating administration had lately aggravated all these evils.

Such was the state of Ireland a short time previous to the commencement of the civil war. Strafford was the only able, we might almost say the only zealous minister, at that time in the service of the sovereign. At the beginning however he saw nothing the king had to contend with but the resistance of the Scots; ... In Charles' first expedition against the Scots Strafford set apart a detachment of five hundred men from the Irish army to assist him....

But, though impotent to the purpose for which [this army] was raised, this act, placing arms in the hands of so numerous a body of Catholics, and instructing them in military discipline, did not fail to draw after it momentous consequences. [There follows an account of Charles's dealings with the Irish nobles and army, now said to be 8,000 men, in which Godwin unusually argues that the Catholic king actually authorized the Ulster rebellion for his own purposes.]

... Charles was aware, that the great mass of the population of Ireland, and a large portion of her nobility and gentry, adhered to the ancient religion, and that, if he wished for an ample military aid to his designs from that country, it was from this quarter that it must derive....

But the Irish Catholics were of a very different frame of mind from what Charles looked for. They were deeply impressed with a sense of intolerable grievances. No government was ever worse conducted than the Irish, almost from the hour that the English set foot in the country. It was a half-civilised nation undertaking to dominate over a people of savages. And yet neither were the Irish altogether savages. They had a tradition of ages of refinement and learning, which had existed in their island.... they could not endure the yoke of a master, who should assume to buy and sell them without in the smallest degree consulting their inclinations. They were as ferocious and unmitigable in their resentments, as they were warm and affectionate in their fidelity.

In addition to all other considerations in the present case, came in that of religion. The English despised the Irish too much to endeavour to convert them; and the Irish detested Protestantism the more because it was the religion of the oppressor. The fierce and unlettered Irish entertained Popery in its grossest and its rudest form, not soft-ened and refined, as it was in some countries on the continent, by the gradual progress of knowledge and civilisation. They were entirely under the direction of their priests, and the minds of these priests were enflamed and exasperated by seeing all the revenues of the church engrossed by ecclesiastics of a hostile religion, while they were exposed to every privation....

... the explosion of all these sentiments was terrible. [There follows an account of the Ulster Rebellion and its initially moderate intentions.] The idea entertained by some of the most sober among them, was that they would act towards the English, as the Spaniards had behaved themselves towards the Moors, conduct them out of the territory, and forbid them on pain of death to return[1].... [but] Violence led on to vio-lence. The priests in particular whetted the fury of their lay adherents, and goaded them to ferocity against the heretics.... It is one of the char-acteristics of bloodshed and cruelty, that the first step is viewed even by the perpetrator with uncontrolable repugnance; but the first step leads to another and another, till the offender even revels in his own enormity.

... All society is a sort of discipline that imposes chains upon the wanton impulses of many a wild and lawless spirit; and the Irish insur-gents now sought vengeance for the long restraint of moral and juridical

---

1   The parallel recalls Godwin's "Fragment of a Romance" (Appendix A, pp. 450–51), but reverses and confuses the simple opposition of Spaniards and Moors set up there.

law they had suffered.... The detail of murder by the club and the dagger speedily became too tedious to satiate the thirst for destruction.... At Portnadown one hundred and eighty persons were in one day goaded from a breach in the bridge into the stream, and shot at by the assailants as they rose to the surface. These executions were repeated again and again.... Forty thousand persons, and by some computations five times that number, are said to have perished in this undistinguishing massacre.

3. From Godwin, *History of the Commonwealth of England from Its Commencement to the Restoration of Charles II*, 4 vols. (London: Henry Colburn, 1824–28), 4.460–61

[Godwin does not spare the Republicans.]

Ireland has been for ever oppressed, perhaps more than any other nation on earth.... Its first misfortune is its position: a smaller island, overshadowed and overlaid by a larger, the government of that larger perpetually finding a fancied interest in keeping the inhabitants of the smaller, poor and helpless. The second misfortune was the difference in religion. The priests sought to avenge all the sufferings of the people of Ireland by keeping up their distaste to the faith of their more prosperous neighbours. The disadvantage arising from this difference of religion operated with double force under the rule of the English commonwealth. The Irish entertained the most invincible abhorrence of the creed of their conquerors; some of them fought for the dominion of a Catholic European sovereign; some for the house of Stuart: scarcely one could endure the ascendancy of the republicans, or of Cromwel.

4. From "Act for the Settlement of Ireland" (1652), in S.R. Gardiner (ed.), *The Constitutional Documents of the Puritan Revolution 1625–1660* (Oxford: Clarendon, 1889), 394–400

[Samuel Rawson Gardiner (1829–1902) was the leading nineteenth-century historian of the seventeenth century.]

Whereas the Parliament of England, after the expense of much blood and treasure for suppression of the horrid rebellion in Ireland, have by the good hand of God upon their undertakings, brought that affair to such an issue, as that a total reducement and settlement of the nation may, with God's blessing, be speedily effected, to the end therefore that the people of that nation may know that it is not the intention of the Parliament to extirpate that whole nation, but that mercy and pardon, both as to life and estate, may be extended to all husbandmen, ploughmen, labourers, artificers, and others of the inferior sort ... they submitting themselves to the Parliament of the Commonwealth of England, and living peaceably and obediently under the government; and that others also of higher rank and quality may know the Parliament's intention concerning them ... [There follows a list of those who are not "to be excepted from pardon of life and estate": specific people, Jesuit priests, and others involved in, or complicit in the Ulster Rebellion or of having borne arms against England, and even all Catholics who have not explicitly "manifested their constant good affection to the interest of the Commonwealth of England." These people are to have their titles revoked, and between one and two thirds of their property confiscated for use by the Commonwealth and the remainder given to their heirs, while only those having "no personal estate to the value of ten pounds" are to have the real chance of a pardon in exchange for an oath of obedience.]

5. From Godwin, "To the People of Ireland," signed Mucius, *Political Herald and Review* (1786), 268–75

[Godwin, who was at the time editor of the *Political Herald and Review*, frames his argument against the impending union of Great Britain and Ireland as a "letter."]

FREEMEN AND CITIZENS,
There are two nations in the present day, that have entered the career of heroism and liberty, and have boldly sought to inrol their names with the most illustrious periods of Athens and Rome. These two nations are America and Ireland....
... America holds the first place in the honourable field.... She began earlier and has done more. Ireland, however noble have been her beginnings, has not yet proceeded to the termination which she marked out for herself....
You have too [*sic*] objects to pursue, which, if it be desirable to unite, it is still requisite not to confound. Your objects are commerce and constitution.... [Godwin discusses the commercial incentives offered to Ireland by England, and concludes:] The present that is intended you by these men, will come to you no doubt under specious names and imposing appearances....
The principal circumstance that is calculated to impress the mind of him, who reflects upon this idea, is the very different situation of the two countries proposed to be united. England has run her career of glory, has suffered the gradual exchange of sturdy heroism for effeminate weakness and political profligacy....
From Great Britain, the center of empire, I turn my attention to

Ireland.... [England] has assiduously deprived you of the means of vigour. She has crushed all your efforts on behalf of liberty and commerce. She has desired to make your island a source of pension and emolument to her creatures.... The depression in which you had so long been held, seemed only to give you vigour and sternness. You spurned the yoke, and the elasticity you discovered, upon the removal of the weight that oppressed you, was equal to the most arduous objects.

Perhaps there could appear to the eye of the philosopher few objects more calamitous or more unnatural, than the union of two countries circumstanced as I have described. It is like that refined piece of cruelty, scarcely to be named by the tongue, or indured by the recollection of humanity, of tying a living body to a dead one, and causing them to putrify and perish together. All your efforts and your conceptions are to be crushed in the bud. You are to be hurried at once from the feebleness of infancy to the inanition of old age. The bloom of manhood, the firmness of maturity, all that is worthy of a rational being or a great nation, is to be proscribed you.... Is this an idea to be endured for a moment? ...

... I will not now urge you with the remark, that commerce would be an ill exchange for constitution; but I will ask you how reasonable is this plan for the acquisition of commercial prosperity? You are to reduce yourselves to a petty province of the empire of Great Britain.... You are to part with liberty, with constitution, with independence. And these are the lures by which you are to invite merchants to settle among you; these are the means of creating capital and attracting commerce. Is it by such pretensions that you are to be deceived?

6. From Godwin, "Ireland," *The Morning Chronicle* (25 December 1821)

[Godwin's letter is part of the population debate involving him and Malthus that sparked a series of countersallies. Godwin's point is that poverty brings about precisely the increases in population by a "geometrical ratio" that Malthus sees it as preventing.]

An intelligent Correspondent informs us that according to the late Census, which has not yet been published, the population of Ireland amounts to seven millions three hundred thousand. At the time of the revolution the population of that country was estimated at 1,200,000, nay, some writers set it down so low as 900,000, many of those writers expressing their regret that there were not enough people to cultivate the soil, whole tracts of which lay waste in consequence. But what an extraordinary change has since taken place. No nation in Europe has increased in population by any means in the same proportion—yet none of the same causes to which such increase is usually attributed, have at any time operated in Ireland: for the people (we mean the peasantry) have generally been little more than half-fed. Poverty has uniformly been their lot—they have never enjoyed comfort, nor seldom any internal peace; and of oppression and exaction they have always complained, as they have had but too much occasion.... How is it possible that six millions of people, of which at the least the Catholics consist, can patiently endure such an accumulation of insult and injury, and that they shall remain a proscribed class in their own native land? ...

But, if our Government determine upon continuing the old system of coercion and irritation in Ireland, how frightful the prospect for universal humanity, as well as for the particular interest of this country. Should the Bourbons be reconciled to the French people, or the French people be reconciled to the Bourbons, there can be little doubt that the old national antipathy of France to Great Britain would soon be set in motion, considerably inflamed, too, by a recollection of the events which led to the termination of the late war. The national pride of France received a wound upon that occasion which the French are but too anxious to heal by retaliation upon England; and should they, in the event of war, be able to convey only 10,000 troops to Ireland, with a due supply of arms and ammunition, how can it be conceived difficult, with such an immense multiplication of starving, and consequently desperate beings, to produce a separation between Great Britain and Ireland? and how long could the gigantic power or imperial greatness of this country survive such a separation?

Appendix G: On Extreme Phenomena: Cultural, Physical, and Psychic

1. On War

a. From Carl von Clausewitz, *On War*, trans. Colonel J.J. Graham (1832; London: N. Trubner, 1873), Book 8

[Clausewitz (1780–1831) is considered the first theorist of modern war in the wake of the Napoleonic conflicts. *On War* (1832), on which he began working in 1816 and which bears the impress of German Idealism in its perverse use of words such as "absolute" and "idea" to describe war, was unfinished at his death.]

We said in the first chapter that the overthrow of the enemy is the natural end of the act of war; and that if we would keep within the strictly philosophical limits of the idea, there can be no other in reality.... [T]here can be no suspension in the military act, and peace cannot take place until one or the other of the parties concerned is overthrown.

... [But] Most wars appear only as an angry feeling on both sides, under the influence of which, each side takes up arms to protect himself, and to put his adversary in fear, and, when an opportunity offers, to strike a blow. They are, therefore, not like mutually destructive elements brought into collision, but like tensions of two elements still apart which discharge themselves in small partial shocks.

But what is now the non-conducting medium which hinders the complete discharge? Which is the philosophical conception not satisfied? The medium consists in the number of interests, forces, and circumstances of various kinds, in the existence of the state, which are affected by the war, and through the infinite ramifications of which the logical consequences cannot be carried out as it would on the simple threads of a few conclusion; in this labyrinth it sticks fast, and man ... is hardly conscious of his confusion, unsteadiness of purpose, and inconsistency....

This inconsistency ... becomes the cause of the war being something quite different to what it should be, according to the conception of it—a half-and-half production, a thing without a perfect inner cohesion.

This is how we find it almost everywhere, and we might doubt whether our notion of its absolute character or nature was founded in reality, if we had not seen real warfare make its appearance in this absolute completeness just in our own times. After a short introduction performed by the French Revolution, the impetuous Bonaparte quickly brought it to this point.... Is it not natural and necessary that this phenomenon should lead us back to the original conception of war with all its rigourous deductions? ... [but] indeed, if we would be perfectly candid we must admit that this [mixed conception of war] has even been the case where it has taken its absolute character, that is, under Bonaparte....

According as we have in mind the absolute form of war or one of the real forms deviating more or less from it, so likewise different notions of its result will arise.

In the absolute form, where everything is the effect of its natural and necessary cause, one thing follows another in rapid succession; there is, if we may use the expression, no neutral space.... the end crowns the work. In this view, therefore, war is an indivisible whole, the parts of which (the subordinate results) have no value except in their relation to this whole.

... To this view of the relative connection of results in war ... stands opposed another extreme, according to which war is composed of single independent results, in which, as in any number of games played, the preceding has no influence on the next following.... If we keep to the first of these supposed views, we must perceive the necessity of every war being looked upon as a whole from the very commencement.... If we admit the second view, then subordinate advantages may be pursued on their own account.

[Clausewitz goes on to describe how the predominance through history of republics or states that are "an agglomeration of loosely connected forces" has hindered progress towards "absolute war" until recently. He concludes with a critique of "real war" as failing to realize the essence of war.] Thus war, in reality, became a regular game in which Time and Chance shuffled the cards; but in its signification it was only diplomacy somewhat intensified, a more vigourous way of negotiating, in which battles and sieges were substituted for diplomatic notes.... [Is not] this restricted, shrivelled-up form of war ... merely another kind of writing and language for political thoughts? It has certainly a grammar of its own, but its logic is not peculiar to itself.

2. On Wounds

a. From *The Complete Dictionary of the Arts and Sciences* ... (London: Wilson and Fell, 1764)

[The imagery of wounding appears throughout *Mandeville* and culminates in the protagonist's external wounding, p. 447.]

Wounds: *Vulnus* in medicine and surgery, is frequently defined to be a violent solution of the continuity of the soft external parts of the body, made by some instrument. Others take a greater latitude in defining it, and call every external hurt of the body ... a wound. On the other hand, some are of opinion that unless the injured parts of the body are divided by some sharp instrument, as by a sword or knife, it is by no means to be called a wound ... for a solution of the external parts by internal cause is not called a wound, but rather an abscess or ulcer; so when the harder parts of the body, as the bones, are broken by a fall, or a violent blow received from a blunt instrument, it is called a fracture.... The greater number of uses a part is intended for by nature, the worse will be the consequences of a wound upon that part ... there are many different kinds of wounds ... some are made with sharp instruments, others with blunt ones: with regard to their figure, some form a right line, others are curved, transverse, or oblique; with respect to their situation some are placed in the head, others in the neck, thorax or abdomen; and of these, some are internal, others external.... Since a wound is a solution of the continuity of the parts of the body,[1] the reunion of those parts seems to be the principal intention; but since wounds are of very different kinds, some slight, and others of great consequence, in proportion to this difference, so will the manner of prosecuting this intention differ. [The entry describes treatments such as sutures, plasters, and so on.]

b. From *The Works of John Hunter, F.R.S., with Notes*, ed. *James F. Palmer*, 4 vols. (London: Longman, Rees, Orme, Brown, Green, and Longman, 1835), 3.488

[Hunter (1728–93) would have been known to Godwin through the circle of the radical publisher Joseph Johnson (1738–1809), who brought out many medical texts and translations from German. Hunter was a pioneer in British surgical theory, and is representative of an emerging interest in war wounds.]

We come now to trace the operations of nature in bringing parts whose disposition, action, and structure, had been preternaturally altered, either by accident, or diseased dispositions, as nearly as possible, to their original state.... Nature, having carried these operations for reperation so far, as the formation of pus, she, in such cases, endeavours immediately to set about the next order of actions, which

---

1 [*Dictionary*'s note:] Solution of *continuity*, in surgery, is the separation of the natural cohesion of the solid parts of the body by a wound.

is the formation of new matter, upon such suppurating[1] surfaces as naturally admit of it, viz. where there has been a breach of solids, so that we find, going hand in hand with suppuration, the formation of new solids, which constitute the common surfaces of a sore. This process is called granulating, or incarnation.

3. On Madness, Dissidence, and Trauma

a. From Godwin, "Of the Rebelliousness of Man," in *Thoughts on Man, His Nature, Productions and Discoveries* (London: Effingham Wilson, 1831), 93–111

[This essay echoes *Mandeville* at several points.]

There is a particular characteristic in the nature of the human mind, which is somewhat difficult to be explained.

Man is a being of a rational and an irrational nature.

It has often been said that we have two souls.... The two souls of man, according to this hypothesis, are, first, animal, and, secondly, intellectual....

But our nature, beside this, has another section. We start occasionally ten thousand miles awry. We resign the sceptre of reason, and the high dignity that belongs to us as beings of a superior species; and, without authority derived to us from any system of thinking ... we are impelled to do, or at least feel ourselves excited to do, something disordinate and strange. It seems as if we had a spring within us, that found the perpetual restraint of being wise and sober insupportable.... A thousand absurdities, wild and extravagant vagaries, come into our heads, and we are only restrained from perpetrating them by the fear, that we may be subjected to the treatment appropriated to the insane, or may perhaps be made amenable to the criminal laws of our country....

There are two things that restrain us from acts of violence and crime. The first is, the laws of morality. The second is, the construction that will be put upon our actions by our fellow-creatures, and the treatment we shall receive from them....

The laws of morality (setting aside the consideration of any documents of religion or otherwise I may have imbibed from my parents and instructors) are matured within us by experience. In proportion as I am rendered familiar with my fellow-creatures, or with society at large, I come to feel the ties which bind men to each other, and the

---

1   Producing or discharging pus.

wisdom and necessity of governing my conduct by inexorable rules. We are thus further and further removed from unexpected sallies of the mind, and the danger of suddenly starting away into acts not previously reflected on and considered....

There are three principles in the nature of man which contribute to account for [rebelliousness].

First, the love of novelty.

Secondly, the love of enterprise and adventure. I become insupportably wearied with the repetition of rotatory acts and everyday occurrences. I want to be alive, to be something more than I commonly am, to change the scene, to cut the cable that binds my bark to the shore, to launch into the wide sea of possibilities....

A third principle, which discovers itself in early childhood, and which never entirely quits us, is the love of power. We wish to be assured that we are something, and that we can produce notable effects upon other beings out of ourselves. It is this principle, which instigates a child to destroy his playthings, and to torment and kill the animals around him....

Man is in truth a miracle. The human mind is a creature of celestial origin, shut up and confined in a wall of flesh. We feel a kind of proud impatience at the degradation to which we are condemned. We beat ourselves to pieces against the wires of our cage, and long to escape, to shoot through the elements, and be as free to change at any instant the place where we dwell, as to change the subject to which our thoughts are applied.

This, or something like this, seems to be the source of our most portentous follies and absurdities. This is the original sin upon which St. Austin [*sic*] and Calvin descanted. Certain Arabic writers seem to have had this in their minds, when they tell us, that there is a black drop of blood in the heart of every man, in which is contained the *fomes peccati*[1]....

Various obvious causes might be selected, which should be calculated to give birth to the feeling of discontent.

One is, the not being at home....

Home is the place where a man is principally at his ease. It is the place where he most breathes his native air: his lungs play without impediment; and every respiration brings a pure element, and a cheerful and gay frame of mind. Home is the place where he most easily accomplishes all his designs: ... Home is the place where he can be uninterrupted. He is in a castle which is his in full propriety....

---

1 In Catholic theology, the "tinder for sin" or the selfish human desire for an object.

In this sense every man feels, while cribbed in a cabin of flesh, and shut up by the capricious and arbitrary injunctions of human communities, that he is not at home.

Another cause of our discontent is to be traced to the disparity of the two parts of which we are composed, the thinking principle, and the body in which it acts. The machine which constitutes the visible man, bears no proportion to our thoughts, our wishes and desires. Hence we are never satisfied. We always feel the want of something we have not; and this uneasiness is continually pushing us on to precipitate and abortive resolves.

... Our nature has within it a principle of boundless ambition, a desire to be something that we are not, a feeling that we are out of our place, and ought to be where we are not. This feeling produces in us ... a restlessness of soul, and an aspiration after some object that we do not find ourselves able to chalk out and define....

It is this that, in less enlightened ages of the world, led men to engage so much of their thoughts on supposed existences which, though they might never become subject to our organs of vision, were yet conceived to be perpetually near us.... The most remarkable of these phenomena was that of necromancy, sorcery, and magic....

The original impulse of man is uncontrolableness.... There is a power within us that wars against the restraint of another....

This restiveness and impracticability are principally incident to us in the period of youth. By degrees the novelties of life wear out, and we become sober. We are like soldiers at drill, and in a review. At first we perform our exercise from necessity, and with an ill grace. We had rather be doing almost anything else. By degrees we are reconciled to our occupation. We are like horses in a *manège*,[1] or oxen or dogs taught to draw the plough, or be harnessed to a carriage....

In this Essay I have treated of nothing more than the inherent restiveness and indocility of man, which accompany him at least through all the earlier sections and divisions of his life. I have not treated.... the incentives and provocations which are administered to us by those wants which at all times beset us as living creatures, and by the unequal distribution of property generally in civil society....

For the same reason I have not taken notice of another species of irrationality, and which seems to answer more exactly to the Arabic notion of the *fomes peccati*, the black drop of blood at the bottom of the heart....

---

1   Riding school.

b. From Philippe Pinel, *A Treatise on Insanity*, trans. D.D. Davies
    (1801; Sheffield: Cadell and Davies, 1806), 4–16, 78–81

[Pinel (1745–1826) is associated with the emergence of humane psychiatry. This extract is interesting for its uneasy sensitivity to the social
and cultural contexts of insanity.]

1. Few subjects in medicine are so intimately connected with the
history and philosophy of the human mind as insanity. There are still
fewer, where there are so many errors to rectify, and so many prejudices to remove. Derangement of the understanding is generally considered as an effect of an organic lesion of the brain, consequently as
incurable; a supposition that is, in a great number of instances, contrary to anatomical fact. Public asylums for maniacs have been
regarded as places of confinement for such of its members as are
become dangerous to the peace of society. The managers of those
institutions, who are frequently men of little knowledge and less
humanity, have been permitted to exercise towards their innocent prisoners a most arbitrary system of cruelty and violence; while experience affords ample and daily proofs of the happier effects of a mild,
conciliating treatment, rendered effective by steady and dispassionate
firmness.... Thus, too generally, has the philosophy of this disease, by
which I mean the history of its symptoms, of its progress, of its varieties, and of its treatment, in and out of hospitals, been most strangely
neglected.... The particular histories, which we meet with in different
works, are chiefly remarkable for a few unconnected facts which they
detail. The important method of descriptive history has been too
much neglected. The great object of the physician and the author has
been almost uniformly to recommend a favourite remedy, as if the
treatment of every disease, without accurate knowledge of its symptoms, involved in it neither danger nor uncertainty.

2. The Asylum de Bicetre, which was confided to my care, during
the second and third years of the republic [1792–94], widened to a
vast extent the field of enquiry into this subject, which I had entered
upon at Paris, several years prior to my appointment. The storms of
the revolution, stirred up corresponding tempests in the passions of
men, and overwhelmed not a few in a total ruin of their birthright as
rational beings....

5. To believe that the different species of insanity depend on the
particular nature of its causes, and that it becomes periodical, continued, or melancholic, according as it may have originated from unfortunate love, domestic distress, fanaticism, superstition, or interesting
revolutions in the state of public affairs, would be, to fall into a very
great error.... Among the cases of periodical mania, which I have seen

and recorded in my journals, I find some which originated in a violent but unfortunate passion; others in an ungovernable ambition for fame, power or glory. Many succeeded to reverses of fortune; others were produced by devotional phrenzy; and others by an enthusiastic patriotism, unchastened by the sober and steady influence of solid judgment....

I cannot here avoid giving my most decided suffrage in favour of the moral qualities of maniacs. I have no where met, except in romances, with fonder husbands, more affectionate parents, more impassioned lovers, more pure and exalted patriots, than in the lunatic asylum, during their intervals of calmness and reason.

29. To say that the attempts, which have been made in England and France, to cure the insanity of devotees, have been generally ineffectual, is not precisely to assert its incurability. My plan would have been, could the liberties of the Bicetre have admitted of it, to separate this class of maniacs from the others; to apportion for their use a large piece of ground to till or work upon ... to remove from their sight every object appertaining to religion, every painting or book calculated to rouse its recollections; to order certain hours of the day to be devoted to philosophical reading, and to seize every opportunity of drawing apt comparisons between the distinguished acts of humanity and patriotism of the ancients, and the pious nullity and delirious extravagances of saints and anchorites;[1] to divert their minds from the peculiar objects of their hallucination, and to fix their interest upon pursuits of contrary influence and tendency.

c. From John Ferriar, *An Essay Towards a Theory of Apparitions* (London: Cadell and Davies, 1813), vi–vii, 15–19, 109–10, 137

[Ferriar (1761–1815) was a Manchester physician who, while explaining psychic phenomena empirically and naturalistically, stands on the edge of giving them a more philosophical credibility. Godwin drew on his account of traumatic hallucination during the Irish Rebellion (see p. 77).]

... [W]hen I consider the delight with which stories of apparitions are received by persons of all ages ... I cannot help feeling some degree of complacency, in offering to the makers and readers of such stories, a view of the subject, which may extend their enjoyment far beyond its former limits. It has given me pain to see the most fearful and ghastly commencements of a tale of horror reduced to mere common events,

---

1 People who have withdrawn from secular society to lead a prayer-oriented and ascetic life.

at the winding up of the book. I have looked also, with much compassion, on the pitiful instruments of *sliding panels, trap-doors, back stairs, wax-work figures* ... and other vulgar machinery, which authors of tender consciences have employed, to avoid the imputation of belief in supernatural occurrences. So hackneyed, so exhausted, had all artificial methods of terror become, that one original genius was compelled to convert a mail-coach, with its lighted lamps, into an apparition....

It is a well-known law of the human oeconomy, that the impressions produced on some of the external senses, especially on the eye, are more durable than the application of the impressing cause. The effect of looking at the sun, in producing the impression of a luminous globe, for some time after the eye has been withdrawn from the object, is familiar to every one.

This subject has been so thoroughly investigated by the late Dr. Darwin [Erasmus Darwin in *Zoonomia*], that I need only to refer the reader to his treatise on ocular spectra. In young persons, the effects resulting from this permanence of impression are extremely curious.... If I had been viewing any interesting object in the course of the day ... if I had occasion to go into a dark room, the whole scene was brought before my eyes, with a brilliancy equal to what it had possessed in daylight, and remained visible for several minutes. I have no doubt, that dismal and frightful images have been presented, in the same manner, to young persons, after scenes of domestic affliction, or public horror.

From this renewal of external impressions, also, many of the phaenomena of dreams admit an easy explanation.... Dr. R. Darwin seems to believe, that it is from habit only, and want of attention, that we do not see the remains of former impressions, or the *muscae volitantes*,[1] on all objects. Probably, this is an instance, in which the error of external sensation is corrected by experience, like the deceptions of perspective, which are undoubtedly strong in our childhood, and are only detected by repeated observation.

"After having looked," says Dr. Darwin, "long at the meridian sun, in making some of the preceding experiments, till the disk faded into a pale blue, I frequently observed a bright blue spectrum of the sun in other objects, all the next and the succeeding day, which constantly occurred when I attended to it. When I closed and covered my eyes, this appeared of a dull yellow; and at other times mixed with the colours of other objects on which it was thrown." [Ferriar provides accounts of atmospheric and paranormal phenomena such as the Brocken Spectre and second sight.] ...

---

1   "Floaters" that lead to distorted vision.

In medicine, we have fine names, at least, for every species of disease. The peculiar disorder, which I have endeavoured to elucidate, is termed generally HALLUCINATION.... But we may well be surprized to find, that impressions of this kind are registered, under the title of experimental philosophy....

[After providing several examples of hallucinations related to famous people, Ferriar turns to the Irish Insurrection.] My observations on this subject may be strengthened, by observing the great prevalence of spectral delusions, during the inter-regnum, in this country, after the civil war, in 1649. The melancholic tendency of the rigid puritans of that period; their occupancy of old family seats, formerly the residence of hospitality and good cheer, which in their hands became desolate and gloomy; and the dismal stories propagated by the discarded retainers to the ancient establishments, ecclesiastical and civil, contributed altogether to produce a national horror unknown in other periods of our history.

[Ferriar then provides eyewitness accounts of the apparitions seen on Portnedown bridge, which he explains naturalistically as optical illusions. He nevertheless concludes:] I have thus presented to the reader, those facts which have afforded, to my own mind, a satisfactory explanation of such relations of spectral appearances, as cannot be refused credit, without removing all the limits and supports of human testimony. To disqualify the senses, or the veracity of those who witness unusual appearances, is the utmost tyranny of prejudice. Yet, who, till within the last fifteen years, would have dared assert that stones fell from the clouds. Livy had regularly recorded such events, and was ridiculed for supplying those most curious facts, which must otherwise have been lost to natural history.

In like manner, I conceive that the unaffected accounts of spectral visions should engage the attention of the philosopher, as well as of the physician.

4. The Literature of Power

a. From Thomas De Quincey, *Letters to a Young Man Whose Education Has Been Neglected*, *The Collected Writings of Thomas De Quincey*, ed. David Masson, 14 vols. (1823; London: A. and C. Black, 1897), 10.46–50

[Thomas De Quincey (1785–1859) was best known as the author of *Confessions of an English Opium-Eater* (1822; rev. ed. 1856) and "Suspiria de Profundis" (1845), but was also a prolific literary critic and journalist. A later version of the distinction below appears in his essay "On Pope" (1847)].

... The word *literature* is a perpetual source of confusion, because it is used in two senses, and those senses liable to be confounded with each other. In a philosophical use of the word, Literature is the direct and adequate antithesis of Books of Knowledge. But, in a popular use, it is a mere term of convenience for expressing inclusively the total books of a language. In this latter sense, a dictionary, a grammar, a spelling-book, an almanac ... belong to the literature. But, in the philosophical sense ... even books of much higher pretensions must be excluded—as, for instance, books of voyages and travels, and generally all books in which the matter to be communicated is paramount to the manner or form of its communication.... It is difficult to construct the idea of "literature" with severe accuracy; for it is a fine art—the supreme fine art, and liable to the difficulties which attend such a subtle notion; in fact, a severe construction of the idea must be the *result* of a philosophical investigation into this subject, and cannot precede it. But, for ... our present purpose, let us throw the question into another form. I have said that the antithesis of Literature is Books of Knowledge. Now, what is that antithesis to *knowledge* which is here implicitly latent in the word literature? The vulgar antithesis is *pleasure*.... Books, we are told, propose to *instruct* or to *amuse*. Indeed! However, not to spend any words upon it, I suppose you will admit that this wretched antithesis will be of no service to us.... For, this miserable alternative being once admitted, observe what follows. In which class of books does the Paradise Lost stand? Among those which instruct, or those which *amuse*? Now, if a man answers among those which instruct, he lies; for there is no instruction in it, nor could be in any great poem.... But, if he says, "No; amongst those which amuse," then what a beast must he be to degrade, and in this way, what has done the most of any human work to raise and dignify human nature.... The true antithesis to knowledge, in this case, is not *pleasure*, but *power*. All that is literature seeks to communicate power; all that is not literature, to communicate knowledge. Now, if it be asked what is meant by communicating power, I, in my turn, would ask by what name a man would designate the case in which I should be made to feel vividly, and with a vital consciousness, emotions which ordinary life rarely or never supplies occasions for exciting, and which had previously lain unawakened, and hardly within the dawn of consciousness ... I say, when these inert and sleeping forms *are* organized, when these possibilities *are* actualized, is this conscious and living possession of mine *power*, or what is it?

... I presume that I may justly express the tendency of the Paradise Lost by saying that it communicates power; a pretension far above all communication of knowledge. Henceforth, therefore, I shall use the antithesis power and knowledge as the most philosophical expression for literature (that is Literae Humaniores) and anti-literature (that is, Litera didacticae, Paideia).

... For, let the knowledge be what it might, all knowledge is translateable, and translateable without one atom of loss. (10.46–50)

5. The Power of the Negative

[Unlike British social, medical, and psychiatric discourse, which pathologizes dissidence and sickness, the German Idealists attribute a philosophical value to it as "negativity" (Hegel) or the force of withdrawal and contraction (Schelling).]

a. From G.W.F. Hegel, *The Philosophy of Nature, Being Part Two of the Encyclopedia of the Philosophical Sciences* (1830), trans. A.V. Miller (Oxford: Clarendon, 1970), 428–39

[Best known for the *Phenomenology of Spirit* (1807), Hegel (1770–1831) published very little during his lifetime. Much of his work took the form of lectures, consisting of main points (also summarized in his published *Encyclopedia*), with elaborations that were only provided in the lectures, and that were known as *Zusätze* (printed here in a smaller font). There is thus no actual original text of the *Philosophy of Nature*. The text known by that name was first edited by K.L. Michelet in 1847 and is a composite text that puts together the detailed lecture notes left by Hegel himself and taken down by his students from 1805–30.]

[T]he individual organism can just as well not conform to its genus as preserve itself in it through its return into self. It finds itself in a state of *disease* when one of its systems or organs, *stimulated* into conflict with the inorganic power, establishes itself in isolation and persists in its particular activity against the activity of the whole.... Disease arises when the organism, as simply immediate, is separated from its inner sides—which are not factors, but whole, real sides. The cause of disease lies partly in the organism itself, like ageing, dying, and congenital defects; partly also in the susceptibility of the organism, in its simply immediate being, to external influences, so that one side is increased beyond the power of the inner resources of the organism. The organism is then in the opposed forms of *being* and *self*; and the *self* is precisely that for which the negative of itself *is*. A stone cannot become diseased, because it is destroyed in the negative of itself, is chemically decomposed and its form does not endure; because it is not the negative of itself which overlaps its opposite, as in illness and in self-feeling. Appetite, too, the feeling of a lack, is to its own self the negative, relates itself to itself as a negative, ... but with this difference, that in appetite this lack is something external, that is, the self is not turned against its structure (*Gestalt*) as such, whereas in disease the negative thing is the structure itself.

Disease, therefore, is a *disproportion between irritation and the capacity of the organism to respond.* Because the organism is an individual, it can be held fast in one of its external sides, can exceed its measure in a particular respect.... [For example] when the stomach is overloaded, the digestive apparatus functions as an isolated, independent activity, makes itself the centre, is no longer a moment of the whole but dominates it....

[Hegel describes different kinds of diseases, including "climatic" and "historical" diseases and finally *"diseases of the soul."* He then outlines three stages of disease—sensibility, irritability, and reproduction—following a contemporary physiological schema which acquires psychic resonances in his work.]

α) The first stage of disease [sensibility] is that it is *virtually* (*an sich*) present, but without any actual morbidity.

β) In the second stage [irritability] the disease becomes *for* the self; i.e. there is established in the self and in opposition to it as universal, a determinateness which makes its own self into a fixed self; in other words, the self of the organism becomes a fixed existence, a specific part of the whole. Up to this point, the systems of the organism had a selfless existence; but now, the actual beginning of disease consists in this, that the organism, being irritated beyond its capacity to respond, one particular part, a single system, gains a foothold in opposition to the self.... On the other hand, so long as the disease is peculiar to one particular system, and is confined within that system, it is easier to cure because only one organ is irritated or depressed. The system has only to be extricated from its entanglement with its non-organic nature, and kept within bounds....

γ) But the disease also spreads into the general life of the organism; for when one organ is infected, there is also an infection of the whole organism. The entire organism, therefore, is involved and its activity deranged because one wheel (*Rad*) in it has made itself the centre ... with the entire organism thus infected with a particularity, a *dual life* begins to be manifested. In opposition to the stable universal self, the whole organism becomes a *differentiating movement*....

Therapy: The medicine provokes the organism to put an end to the particular irritation in which the formal activity of the whole is fixed and to restore the fluidity of the particular organ or system within the whole. This is brought about by the medicine as an irritant, but one which is difficult to assimilate and overcome, so that the organism is confronted by something alien to it against which it is compelled to exert its strength....

The main point of view from which medicine must be considered is that it is an *indigestible* substance....

... The effect of introducing into the organism this poison, something simply inimical to it, is that this particularity in which the organism is fixed becomes for it something external; whereas the particularity, as disease, is still a property of the organism itself. Since, therefore, the medicine is the same particularity, although with this difference that it now brings the organism into conflict with its determinateness as with something external, the effect now is to stimulate the healthy energy of the body into an outward activity and to force it to rouse itself, to come out of its self-absorption and not merely to concentrate itself inwardly but to digest the external substance administered to it. For every disease (but especially acute illnesses) is a hypochondria of the organism, in which the latter disdains the outer world which sickens it, because restricted to itself, it possesses within its own self the negative of itself. But now the medicine excites the organism to digest it, and the organism is thus drawn back again into the general activity of assimilation; a result which is obtained precisely by administering to the organism a substance much more indigestible than its disease, to overcome which the organism must pull itself together. This results in the organism being divided against itself; ... the organism has been made dual within itself, namely, as vital force and diseased organism.... But if the organism, in virtue of its diseased state, is in the power of something other than itself, yet at the same time, as an animal magnetism, it also has a world beyond, free from its diseased state, through which the vital force can restore itself. That is, the organism can sleep within itself; for in *sleep*, the organism is alone with itself. Now while the organism is thus internally at variance with itself, its vital force endows it with an existence of its own.

b. From F.W.J. Schelling, *Ages of the World*, trans. Jason M. Wirth (1815; Albany: State U of New York P, 2000), 6–7, 107; 48–49

[Friedrich Schelling (1775–1854), German Idealist philosopher, was best known at the time for his *System of Transcendental Idealism* (1800) and his philosophy of nature. This extract and the one that follows are from the work of Schelling's middle period, which represents a darkening of his earlier idealism. Coleridge, who introduced Schelling to Britain, had read the *Freedom* essay (1809), and had heard of the *Ages of the World* project, which was not published in Schelling's lifetime, as he produced and discarded three unfinished versions, of which the 1815 version, published by his son in 1856, is the last.]

[The No that resists the Yes]

Love does not seek its own and therefore it cannot be that which has being with regard to itself.... It is in itself the antithesis of personality and therefore another force, moving toward personality, must first make it a ground. An equivalently eternal force of selfhood, of egoity, is required so that the being which is Love might exist as its own and might be for itself.

Therefore, two principles are already in what is necessary of God: the outpouring, outstretching, self-giving being, and an equivalently eternal force of selfhood, of retreat into self, of Being in itself....

Indeed, humans show a natural predilection for the affirmative just as much as they turn away from the negative. Everything that is outpouring and goes forth from itself is clear to them. They cannot grasp as straightforwardly that which closes itself off.... Most people would find nothing more natural than if everything in the world were to consist of pure gentleness and goodness, at which point they would soon become aware of the opposite. Something inhibiting, something conflicting, imposes itself everywhere: this Other is that which, so to speak, should not be and yet is, nay, must be. It is this No that resists the Yes, this darkening that resists the light, this obliquity that resists the straight, this left that resists the right, and however else one has attempted to express this eternal antithesis in images. But it is not easy to be able to verbalize it or conceive it at all scientifically....

Idealism, which really consists in the denial and nonacknowledgment of that negating primordial force, is the universal system of our times.... [But] Whoever does not acknowledge the priority of Realism wants evolution without the involution that preceded it. They want the bloom and the fruit that comes from it without the hard covering that enclosed it.

[The dark heart of history and personality]

No one will maintain that sickness is an actual or truly living life. Yet sickness is a life, albeit only a false life, a life that does not have being but that wants to elevate itself from not-Being to Being. Error is not a true, thus actual, knowledge but it is still not nothing. Or, indeed, it is nothing but a nothing that endeavours to be something. Evil is an inner lie and lacks all true Being. And yet evil *is* and it shows a terrible actuality, not as something that truly has being but as that which by nature has being in endeavouring to be....

If an organic being becomes sick, forces appear that previously lay concealed in it. Or if the copula of the unity dissolves altogether and if the life forces that were previously subjugated by something higher are deserted by the ruling spirit and can freely follow their own inclinations and manners of acting, then something terrible becomes manifest which we had no sense of during life and which was held down by the magic of life....

If we take into consideration the many terrible things in nature and the spiritual world and the great many other things that a benevolent hand seems to cover up from us, then we could not doubt that the Godhead sits enthroned over a world of terrors.

c. From F.W.J. Schelling, *Philosophical Investigations into the Essence of Human Freedom, Sämmtliche Werke*, ed. K.F.A. Schelling (1809; Stuttgart: J.G. Cotta, 1860), 7.346, 364; trans. Rajan

The individual member, such as the eye, is only possible in the whole of the organism; nevertheless it has a life for itself, indeed a kind of freedom, which it makes evident through the sickness of which it is capable.... The principle raised up from the ground of nature, by which man is separated from god, is the selfhood in him, which, however, through its unity with the ideal principle, becomes spirit. Selfhood, as such, is spirit, or man is spirit as a selfish, particular being (separated from God), which connection constitutes personality. Since, however, selfhood is spirit, it is at the same time raised from the creaturely into what is above the creaturely, it is will that glimpses itself in complete freedom....

Select Bibliography

Texts by Godwin

Caleb Williams. (1794). Ed. A.A. Markley and Gary Handwerk. Peterborough, ON: Broadview, 2000. [*CW*]

Collected Novels and Memoirs of William Godwin. Ed. Mark Philp. 8 vols. London: Pickering and Chatto, 1992. [*CNM*] [Vol. 5, *Mandeville*, ed. Pamela Clemit]

The Diary of William Godwin. Ed. Victoria Myers, David O'Shaughnessy, and Mark Philp. Oxford: Oxford Digital Library, 2010. http://godwindiary.bodleian.ox.ac.uk.

Enquiry Concerning Political Justice and Its Influence on Morals and Happiness. 3rd ed. (1798). Ed. F.E.L. Priestley. 3 vols. Toronto: U of Toronto P, 1946. [*PJ*]

"Fragment of a Romance." *New Monthly Magazine and Literary Journal* 37.1 (January 1833): 32–41.

History of the Commonwealth of England from Its Commencement to the Restoration of Charles the Second. 4 vols. London: Henry Colburn, 1824–28. [*HCE*]

The Lives of Edward and John Philips, Nephews and Pupils of Milton. London: Longman, Hurst, Rees, Orme, and Brown, 1815.

"Of History and Romance." *Educational and Literary Writings.* Ed. Pamela Clemit. *PPW* Vol. 5, 291–301. [*HR*]

Political and Philosophical Writings of William Godwin. Ed. Mark Philp. 5 vols. London: Pickering and Chatto, 1993. [*PPW*]

Thoughts on Man, His Nature, Productions, and Discoveries. London: Effingham Wilson, 1831.

On or Partly on *Mandeville*

Apap, Christopher. "Irresponsible Acts: The Transatlantic Dialogues of William Godwin and Charles Brockden Brown." *Transatlantic Sensations.* Ed. Jennifer Phegley, John Barton, and Kristin Huston. Aldershot: Ashgate, 2012. 23–40.

Campbell, Timothy. "The Business of War: William Godwin, Enmity, and Historical Representation." *English Literary History* 76.2 (2009): 343–69.

Farouk, Marion. "*Mandeville, A Tale of the Seventeenth Century*: Historical Novel or Psychological Study?" *Essays in Honour of William Gallacher.* Ed. Erika Lingner. Berlin: Humboldt U, 1966. 111–17.

Garside, P.D., J.E. Belanger, and S.A. Ragaz. "Publishing Papers" for *Mandeville*. In *British Fiction, 1800–1829: A Database of Production, Circulation, and Reception*. http://www.british-fiction.cf.ac.uk/. [*DBF*]

Granata, Silvia. "Poisonous Language: Mental Slavery and Self-Recognition in Godwin's *Mandeville*." *Confronto Letterario: Quaderni del Dipartimento di Lingue e Letterature Straniere Moderne dell'Università di Pavia* 26.51 [1] (2009): 81–102.

Handwerk, Gary. "History, Trauma, and the Limits of the Liberal Imagination." *Romanticism, History, and the Possibilities of Genre: Reforming Literature 1789–1837*. Ed. Tilottama Rajan and Julia Wright. Cambridge: Cambridge UP, 1998. 64–85.

Jarrells, Anthony. "Bloodless Revolution and the Form of the Novel." *NOVEL: A Forum on Fiction* 37.1 (2003–04): 24–44.

Leach, Nathaniel. "Mary Shelley and the Godwinian Gothic: *Matilda* and *Mandeville*." *Mary Shelley: Her Circle and Her Contemporaries*. Ed. L. Adam Mekler and Lucy Morrison. Newcastle upon Tyne: Cambridge Scholars P, 2010. 63–82.

Pollin, Burton R. "Godwin's *Mandeville* in Poems of Shelley." *Keats-Shelley Memorial Bulletin* 19 (1968): 33–40.

——. "William Godwin's 'Fragment of a Romance.'" *Comparative Literature* 16.1 (1964): 40–54.

Rajan, Tilottama. "Between General and Individual History: Godwin's Seventeenth-Century Texts." Special issue on Godwin, ed. Rowland Weston. *Nineteenth-Century Prose* 41.2/3 (Spring/Fall 2014): 111–60.

——. "The Disfiguration of Enlightenment: War, Trauma, and the Historical Novel in Godwin's *Mandeville*." *Godwinian Moments: From the Enlightenment to Romanticism*. Ed. Robert M. Maniquis and Victoria Myers. Toronto: U of Toronto P, 2011. 172–93.

Scheuermann, Mona. "The Study of Mind: The Later Novels of William Godwin." *Forum for Modern Language Studies* 19.1 (1983): 16–30.

Sherburn, George. "Godwin's Later Novels." *Studies in Romanticism* 1.2 (1962): 65–82.

Weston, Rowland. "William Godwin and the Puritan Legacy." *Nineteenth-Century Prose* 39.1–2 (2012): 411–42.

Selected Further Work on Godwin

Brewer, William D. *The Mental Anatomies of William Godwin and Mary Shelley*. Cranbury, NJ: Associated UP, 2001.

Brown, Ford K. *The Life of William Godwin*. London and Toronto: J.M. Dent, 1926.

Carlson, Julie. *England's First Family of Writers: Mary Wollstonecraft, William Godwin, Mary Shelley*. Baltimore: Johns Hopkins UP, 2007.

Clemit, Pamela. *The Godwinian Novel: The Rational Fictions of Godwin, Brockden Brown, Mary Shelley*. Oxford: Oxford UP, 1993.

Constable, Thomas. *Archibald Constable and His Literary Correspondents*. 3 vols. Edinburgh: Edmonston and Douglas, 1873. Vol. 2, 47–98.

Graham, Kenneth W. *William Godwin Reviewed: A Reception History 1783–1834*. New York: AMS P, 2001.

Kelly, Gary. *The English Jacobin Novel: 1780–1805*. Oxford: Oxford UP, 1976.

Locke, Don. *A Fantasy of Reason: The Life and Thought of William Godwin*. London: Routledge and Kegan Paul, 1980.

Marshall, Peter H. *William Godwin*. New Haven, CT: Yale UP, 1984.

McCann, Andrew. "William Godwin and the Pathological Public Sphere." *Prose Studies: History, Theory, Criticism* 18.3 (1995): 199–222.

McGeough, Jared. "'So Variable and Inconstant a System': Rereading the Anarchism of Godwin's *Political Justice*." *Studies in Romanticism* 52 (2013): 275–309.

Paul, Charles Kegan. *William Godwin: His Friends and His Contemporaries*. 2 vols. London: H.S. King, 1876.

Philp, Mark. *Godwin's Political Justice*. London: Duckworth, 1986.

Rajan, Tilottama. "Mary Shelley's *Mathilda*: Melancholy and the Political Economy of Romanticism." *Studies in the Novel* 26.2 (1994): 43–68.

——. *Romantic Narrative: Shelley, Hays, Godwin, Wollstonecraft*. Baltimore: Johns Hopkins UP, 2010.

——. "Uncertain Futures: History and Genealogy in William Godwin's *The Lives of Edward and John Philips, Nephews and Pupils of Milton*." *Milton Quarterly* 32:3 (1998): 75–86.

St. Clair, William. *The Godwins and the Shelleys: A Biography of a Family*. Baltimore: Johns Hopkins UP, 1989.

Tysdahl, B.J. *William Godwin as Novelist*. London: Athlone P, 1981.

Webb, Timothy. "Missing Robert Emmet: William Godwin's Irish Expedition." *Reinterpreting Emmet: Essays on the Life and Legacy of Robert Emmet*. Ed. Anne Dolan, Patrick M. Geoghegan, and Darryl Jones. Dublin: U College Dublin P, 2007.

Historical Background

Buck, Charles. *A Theological Dictionary, Containing Definitions of all Religious Terms* ... (1802). Rpt. Philadelphia: Joseph Woodward, 1826.

Dickinson, H.T. *British Radicalism and the French Revolution, 1789–1815*. Oxford: Blackwell, 1985.

Gardiner, Samuel Rawson (ed.). *The Constitutional Documents of the Puritan Revolution 1625–1660*. Oxford: Clarendon, 1889.

——. *The Fall of the Monarchy of Charles I*. 2 vols. London: Longmans, Green, 1882.

——. *History of the Commonwealth and Protectorate 1649–1656*. 4 vols. (1894–1901). Rpt. New York: AMS P, 1965.

Hill, Christopher. *Milton and the English Revolution*. London: Faber and Faber, 1979.

——. *The World Turned Upside Down: Radical Ideas During the English Revolution*. Harmondsworth: Penguin, 1972.

Woodhouse, A.S.P. (Ed.). *Puritanism and Liberty: Being the Army Debates (1647–49) from the Clarke Manuscripts with Supplementary Documents*. London: J.M. Dent, 1938.

From the Publisher

A name never says it all, but the word "Broadview" expresses a good deal of the philosophy behind our company. We are open to a broad range of academic approaches and political viewpoints. We pay attention to the broad impact book publishing and book printing has in the wider world; we began using recycled stock more than a decade ago, and for some years now we have used 100% recycled paper for most titles. Our publishing program is internationally oriented and broad-ranging. Our individual titles often appeal to a broad readership too; many are of interest as much to general readers as to academics and students.

Founded in 1985, Broadview remains a fully independent company owned by its shareholders—not an imprint or subsidiary of a larger multinational.

For the most accurate information on our books (including information on pricing, editions, and formats) please visit our website at www.broadviewpress.com. Our print books and ebooks are also available for sale on our site.

On the Broadview website we also offer several goods that are not books—among them the Broadview coffee mug, the Broadview beer stein (inscribed with a line from Geoffrey Chaucer's *Canterbury Tales*), the Broadview fridge magnets (your choice of philosophical or literary), and a range of T-shirts (made from combinations of hemp, bamboo, and/or high-quality pima cotton, with no child labor, sweatshop labor, or environmental degradation involved in their manufacture).

All these goods are available through the "merchandise" section of the Broadview website. When you buy Broadview goods you can support other goods too.

broadview press
www.broadviewpress.com